In the beginning, there was . . .

FIRE

Something was happening. Something powerful and inevitable. Unstoppable.

The plane was somewhere over the Ozarks; those looked like low, time-worn and rounded mountains below him, though in the moonless darkness it was impossible to be certain. Luke was sweating and cold. The whiskey had worn off, or at least worn thin.

Luke Munsen wasn't a man given to visions or premonitions; nonetheless he knew, impossibly, that the end of the world as he knew it was at hand.

Knew to look west-northwest out the window beside him, and watch the state of Kansas out beyond the horizon. Knew, five minutes later, to shield his eyes from blinding-glowing radiation as he saw the first flicker of light like a distant, tiny sun.

A nuclear explosion, turning three hundred square miles of Kansas wheat field into vapor and a deep, magma-lined pit.

Bantam Books by Alan Rodgers

BLOOD OF THE CHILDREN
FIRE

FIRE

Alan Rodgers

BANTAM BOOKS
NEW YORK • TORONTO • LONDON • SYDNEY • AUCKLAND

FIRE

A Bantam Book / September 1990

ISBN 0-553-28777-X

Published simultaneously in the United States and Canada

Bantam Books are published by Bantam Books, a division of Bantam
Doubleday Dell Publishing Group, Inc. Its trademark, consisting of
the words "Bantam Books" and the portrayal of a rooster, is
Registered in U.S. Patent and Trademark Office and in other
countries. Marca Registrada. Bantam Books, 666 Fifth Avenue, New
York, New York 10103.

PRINTED IN THE UNITED STATES OF AMERICA
RAD   0 9 8 7 6 5 4 3 2 1

For Lou

BOOK ONE

Three Days
at the
End of the World

Wednesday
July Thirteenth

Transmitted over the AP Wire
Tuesday, May First.

WASHINGTON (AP)—In a televised speech this evening, American President Paul Green swore publicly that the death of his wife would not go unavenged.

Soviet spokesmen, responding to the speech at the United Nations, expressed grave concerns. "We too mourn the death of Ada Green," said Ivan Illych, third assistant to the Soviet Ambassador to the United Nations, "but we cannot countenance threats, veiled or otherwise."

First Lady Ada Green died in a tragic series of accidents two weeks ago, while on a good will mission to the Soviet Union. Details of that death are still unclear, but unnamed sources report that she contracted food poisoning after eating a preserved fish in a Moscow restaurant.

According to reports, local doctors administered intravenous penicillin to treat the food poisoning. The First Lady had a severe allergy to penicillin, and the antibiotic sent her into shock, killing her in a matter of minutes.

Congressional reaction to the President's speech was remarkably similar to the reaction of the Soviets. House Speaker William Thergild, giving the televised Democratic response to the President's speech, expressed his sympathy for the President—and his reservations about the President's pledge.

"I honestly feel for the President," said Thergild. "All of us here in Congress do. He's been through a rough time—rough, hell. That man has been through a horrible and tragic time. But all the same, we can't have him bringing this nation to the brink of war for personal reasons. Can't. No matter how tragic his personal circumstances."

Other members of Congress, who asked not to be identified, were less charitable in their reactions.

"That man is out of his mind," said one New York City Congresswoman. "This is exactly the excuse he's been looking for since he took the oath of office. Do you know anything about that church of his? They're Armageddonists. They're looking for a way to bring on the end of the world. He's looking to create an Apocalypse. And this is the way to the beginning of the end."

Mountainville, Tennessee

Wednesday was the day that the President got on television and threatened to "nuke the Soviet Union into the Stone Age." Those were exactly the words he used; President Green wasn't anything if he wasn't plain spoken.

Nuking Russia into the Stone Age! Ron shuddered at the thought. So maybe they were Russians, so maybe they were on the other side of the world. They were still people. It wasn't like the President was threatening to send our soldiers to shoot at their soldiers—no, that'd be bad, but there were some kinds of bad that you had to cut a man a little slack on when he was President. That was the way Ron Hawkins saw it, anyway. Only it wasn't soldiers that the President was threatening to nuke. It was women and children and middle-aged men, and everybody else, ordinary people in cities and towns. Not that the President was saying it that way. He didn't have to; Ron knew it was true anyway. He read *Time*, and sometimes *Newsweek*; he'd read that article last year about How Our Missiles Are Targeted. It'd left him feeling kind of sick with himself, reading how if there was a nuclear war all of the first bombs would land in places where people lived.

Now the President was actually threatening to do it. Threatening to fire those missiles at real people on the other side of the world.

Lately Ron had begun to have serious regrets about voting for President Green in the last election. The man was too full of bluster. Or at least he'd got that way since he'd been elected. Full of himself, and looking for a fight. He'd seen men get that way when they were having trouble with their wives. *That* couldn't be Green's problem, anyway.

It didn't matter what his problem was—it wasn't right to have a man who let himself act that way running the country.

Not that there was a damn thing Ron could do about it. Except wait until the next election and vote for somebody else.

If there was a next election.

If there was anybody alive to vote for.

The only thing that could explain the President's behavior—some of it, anyway—was the way his wife had died when she was over there in Russia. Three months ago, on a good will trip. She'd come down with food poisoning or some such, an awful case of it. And some Russian doctor had screwed up, and before they'd been able to get an American MD in there to take a look at her the First Lady had died. After that the President—who'd always been what you might call an extremist—had gone clear over the edge.

Ron shook his head and bit his lip and went back to cleaning the third-floor men's room. He tried not to think about the end of the world, but dirty toilets were nothing you wanted to think about, not even while you were cleaning them.

And as he worked all Ron could see with his mind's eye was women and children screaming, suffering, burning as thermonuclear fires transformed them to light and dust.

He could still hear their screams ringing in his ears when Luke Munsen walked into the lavatory. Luke Munsen was one of the researchers here in the complex, a man with a Ph.D. in genetics or something like that. Ron had a hard time keeping the researchers' specialties straight; all of them were trained in the life sciences, and often as not two different degrees from different universities turned out to be more or less the same thing. And to make things even more confusing, a lot of them were doing work that didn't seem to have much to do with their college degrees.

"How do, Ron," Luke Munsen said.

"Fine, Luke. How about you? Working late?" Ron was on a first-name basis with most of the researchers, which, so far as he knew, made him unique among the custodial staff. But then, he was the only janitor in the institute with any real education. The researchers weren't especially full of themselves, the way, say, the doctors and administrators had been when he'd worked at the hospital—those people tended to assume that if you cleaned up after them you had to be some sort of a Cro-Magnon, or maybe even an Australopithecine. The Ph.D.s here were young and approachable and almost always looking for someone to bounce an idea off of, especially someone who wasn't likely to swipe it. Trouble was, most of the cleaning people here didn't take any interest in biochemistry. Not any more interest than you had to take to be polite.

"*Always* working late. You ought to know that by now. When was the last time you saw me out of here before eight o'clock?"

"Ha! When was the last time you got out of here by nine? I can't remember."

Luke was washing his hands. "Couldn't tell you. It all blurs together after a while. Sleep and work—sometimes I think I don't do anything else any more. Except eat, maybe. And even then I'm usually working while I'm at it—either that or sleeping, one."

Ron wondered exactly how a man could eat while he was sleeping—was it something like sleepwalking, maybe?—and then decided that he didn't really want to know.

"So," he asked, "how's the work going? You making any headway?"

Luke Munsen smiled, all glowy and enthusiastic like a four-year-old. "We're getting close—close, hell, we've done it. We've got a working bug. It *works!*" His eyes got brighter and brighter as he spoke. "Of course, there's still a lot left to do. Working with the new strain, fussing with it, making sure that it's going to keep doing the job, making sure that it won't do things we hadn't planned on. It could be years before we can actually put it to use. But we will be able to use it—I'm sure of that now."

Luke Munsen's project was an especially strange one—gene splicing applied to archaeology. He had a big grant from some museum in New York to develop a microbe that could reconstruct a fossil from the scattered bits and pieces of its DNA. The subject was weird enough that it gave Ron chills sometimes when they talked about it. Imagine it: turning a heap of old bones into an honest-to-God dinosaur. Imagine one of *those* getting loose in a lab. It wasn't something Ron wanted to clean up after.

"Luke—what happens if a bug like that gets loose? It sounds dangerous, especially when you think about it a bit. What happens if you remake a dinosaur and it gets loose?"

The researcher sighed, exasperated. "You too, Ron? I don't know how many times I've heard well-meaning people try to put a stop to our work just because they didn't understand it. Come *on*. You know the sort of precautions we take. That bacteria won't leave the lab here until we're sure that it can't live outside a petri dish. One of the first things we learned was how to cripple a strain. Believe me: we're *careful*. And besides—we don't want to make any living dinosaurs. We aren't trying to bring anything back to life. We want something that'll give us enough of a dinosaur to dissect."

Luke's face was beet-red; he was angry all out of proportion to the question, as though he'd had to answer it so many times that the thought of it infuriated him. It left Ron feeling kind of stupid, and uneasy, too—the last thing he needed was to have a researcher walking around angry at him. It wasn't like it could cost him his job, but enough hostility could make the job not worth keeping. And right now looking for a new job wasn't something Ron wanted to have to do. In another year he'd finally have his bachelor's degree, and then they could take the toilets and the floors and everything else and do whatever they wanted with them. Just not now. Not when he was so close.

"Sorry, Luke. I didn't mean anything . . . personal."

Luke Munsen blinked, and flushed again—with embarrassment this time—as though he'd suddenly realized that he'd got carried away. He was quiet for a long moment before he spoke.

"No—I'm the one who ought to apologize. You didn't earn

a response like that. You aren't some congressman dragging me up to testify because he thinks he can make himself more visible by crucifying me."

Ron didn't know what to say; all he wanted was to get out of the conversation gracefully. "Not me. I couldn't even get elected treasurer for the union local. Just asking a question. Didn't mean any harm."

"No—you didn't." He sighed. "Believe me, there isn't any danger. The bacteria aren't going anywhere."

"If you say it, then I believe it," Ron said. But the truth was that he didn't believe it at all.

Luke finished drying off his hands and tossed the towel into the waste bin. "You take it easy, Ron," he said, opening the lavatory door. "I've got to get back to business."

"Don't work too hard, Luke. You'll dig yourself an early grave." Luke didn't hear; he was already out the door and, from the sound of his footsteps, halfway down the hall.

Ron sighed and checked his watch. It read eight forty-five in the evening, which meant that it was time to make one final pass of the wastebaskets in the wing. It wouldn't take that long; he'd only have to check the offices where he knew the researchers kept late hours. Six, seven offices, the same number of labs, so spread out that Ron knew it would take more time to cover the distance between them than it would to empty the baskets.

He flushed the toilet he'd been cleaning, rinsed the brush in the clean water, and dropped it into the holder in his cart. He wondered if he should wheel the cart into its closet, just a couple of doors down the hall. It probably wouldn't cause any problem if he parked it in the corner here in the men's room, but that wasn't a thing he was supposed to do. Not that it had ever caused him any problem; the night supervisor tended to spend most of his time watching television. Ron rarely saw him except when he went to the lounge for his dinner break.

The hell with it, he thought, and wheeled the cart into the corner. If he put the damned thing away, he'd just have to wheel it back in here in another half an hour; there were three more toilets to clean. And the urinals, too.

He left the restroom, walked down the hall to the elevator, and rode down to the basement to get the big trash cart. Most of the offices and labs produced little enough trash that Ron could empty their wastebaskets into the garbage bag on his cleaning cart. Dr. Bonner's office (stress on the *Dr.*; Bonner was a European with strong ideas about the pecking order) Dr. Bonner's office, on the other hand, was one of those on the late run—and the man somehow managed all by himself to produce enough trash to fill a plastic garbage bag three times over.

Ron didn't look forward to visiting Bonner's office.

It wasn't just that the man was unfriendly. And he certainly was that; downright nasty, in fact. Bonner alone wasn't anything Ron would look forward to, but he wasn't anything to dread. Bonner wasn't the problem; it was his . . . project.

Ron wasn't quite sure what Bonner was trying to do, or why, but there was a *thing* in Bonner's laboratory. An animal, or maybe not an animal at all, a bestial nightmare of a creature with extra heads and limbs. And there was a light in its eye, a light that told Ron that it maybe had more brains in his head than Ron had in his own. Bonner kept the poor thing in a tiny cage right there in his laboratory, a cage not even big enough for the pathetic thing to stand up in. Just like it *was* nothing but some poor, dumb beast.

Which, maybe, was all that the thing was. Ron didn't have any proof that it was intelligent, just a deep twinge in his gut. But his heart didn't look at the thing like it was an animal, not for an instant. He'd never been able to go into Bonner's lab without feeling frightened and sick with himself from the guilt of not setting the creature loose.

He found the trash cart in its corner downstairs in the basement, and rolled it back to the elevator. When he got to Bonner's laboratory he parked it against the wall a few feet from the door.

He knocked on the door before he went inside. Bonner wasn't the sort of person you wanted to walk in on and surprise. He wasn't the sort of person you wanted to see at all, for that matter. Ron wasn't sure whether he was less eager to be in that room with the . . . *thing* while Bonner was there or while he wasn't. The creature was unsettling and physically repugnant, but there was something malignant about Bonner.

Ron waited three minutes after he knocked—which was more than was sensible, but not as long as he'd have liked to wait—but no one answered. So, finally, he took the big ring of keys off his belt and opened the door.

The creature was waiting for him inside, quiet and pensive as though it knew Ron was coming. Maybe it did; Ron almost always cleared out Bonner's trash this time of night.

The creature was a physical abomination, pure and simple. Three heads, and seven other knotlike protrusions coming up out of its shoulders—those looked like they were trying to be heads, too, but couldn't quite make the grade. Those heads were vaguely reptilian, and for all that there were so many of them only the one in the center looked to be alive. The heads had mouths like lion maws, and most of them had horns. Sometimes one, sometimes two; ten horns in all. More than anything else, the creature was like a massive, grey-pelted leopard. Not that much like one, maybe. Those lower legs, those feet, they were the clawed and padded feet of a bear. And it had hands, too—but more like the hands of a monkey than they were like a man's.

One of the slack-dead heads had a wide, grisly scar on its neck, just below its jaw. A scar from a wound that ought to have killed any creature, let alone one so horribly misformed.

Ron tried not to look the thing in the eye, but he couldn't stop himself. *What are you?* The question rose to the top of his mind all by itself.

The creature didn't answer, but its real head, the only one with eyes that ever opened, shifted, almost as though it had heard Ron ask.

It stared at Ron.

He shuddered, and he wondered—just as he did every night when he went to Bonner's laboratory—why he didn't find himself another job. Something simple and straightforward, something that didn't try to take away a piece of his heart. Something that would let him finish up those last few college classes, so he could have a real future.

Ron frowned. He was kidding himself, and he knew it. Almost every job wanted to carve out a piece of you, even cleaning jobs. Either it took that piece from you directly, by working you too hard or through conditions that went against your nature—or it took from you by circumstance, because of the people you had to work with.

The business with Bonner and the creature was some of both. Ron liked to tell himself that it was the only part of the job that caused him any grief, and all things considered it

wasn't much. When he wasn't in Bonner's office, he almost
believed it.

The worst part of Bonner's trash was all tied up and
waiting for him, four neatly packaged red plastic bags. Red
because the trash was contaminated waste, dangerous and
infected with God knew what. The contaminated stuff Ron had
to treat specially; it didn't go in the dumpster with everything
else. It went out to a small, sturdy concrete shack, where you
stacked the bags neatly and in the morning Adam Leitsky
burned them in the incinerator. Bonner had a couple of
wastepaper baskets, too, one under his desk and another a
couple of feet from the creature's cage, but the four red bags
were the part that Ron dreaded every night.

Sometimes Ron wondered what Bonner did that could
make four bags of contaminated waste every day. Wondered
what was inside those bags. Not that he was dumb enough to
try to find out. He hadn't been stupid enough to open up a red
bag when he worked at the hospital, where, by comparison,
things were safe. He sure wasn't going to develop unhealthy
curiosities here, where there were people chopping up genes
and turning them into microscopic horrors. Ron might be
thirty years old and still in school, but he *sure* wasn't stupid.

The creature began to make whining sounds as Ron
carried out the bags. He tried hard as he could to ignore the
thing.

He tried so hard not to see or hear the creature that his
eyes caught on Bonner's desk, and he saw that Bonner's
briefcase was still on it, half open. That meant that the man
was still in the building somewhere; he never left without that
briefcase. Ron didn't want to see Bonner—tonight he was even
less up to coping with him than he usually was. He grabbed
the last two red-plastic bags, heaved them up, and hauled
them out to the cart in the hall. That left only the two small
wastepaper baskets. He grabbed new plastic liners for the cans
and started to empty them.

He was in such a hurry that he somehow managed to
forget about the creature completely. He got the trash from
under Bonner's desk, stepped across the room, bent
over . . .

. . . and felt a *hand* touch his shoulder. He jumped six
inches off the floor and only barely managed to force back a
scream.

The hand stayed with him as he jumped, following the arc of his motion lightly, carefully. Like it was a butterfly resting on the cloth of his shirt.

The touch itself, the gentle pressure of fingerlike claws on the flesh of his back, they were only part of what scared Ron half out of his mind. There was something else there, too, something electric that ran through him from one end to the other and funneled itself toward his heart. A sensation so strange and soft that even as Ron felt it he wasn't sure it was real.

"*No!*"

Ron heard himself shout before he even knew what he was saying. Reflexively, he caught his balance and jerked himself away from the creature's cage. When he turned to look back he saw the creature's hand groping toward him slowly, easily, almost the way a lover's hand reaches out at night.

"No," he said. "*Stop.*"

And the creature did stop, and that unnerved Ron most of all, because it meant that the thing understood him. Which meant that the caged *thing* was human, or that it had a mind like a human's anyway.

The creature drew its hand back into its cage, and it stared at him, not angry or even sullen, but not pleasant, either. The thing was too grotesquely ugly ever to look pleasant.

(But couldn't a dog understand that much English, too? And dogs weren't human and they weren't especially intelligent.)

(No. Dogs learned like that when you taught them hard for years, or months, at least, and six weeks ago the *thing* had been a cub no bigger than an infant child, and now it was bigger than Ron, so big that it had to crouch inside its cage. No dog could learn *that* fast, not while it was growing.)

"What do you want from me?" Ron asked. The creature didn't answer. "Do you want me to let you out of there, so you can be free? Hell, I know how you feel. I wouldn't want to be locked inside Bonner's office, either. But I can't let you out of there. They'd just find you again in the time it took to scream bloody murder, and once they found you they'd fire me. And what good would that do either one of us?" The creature didn't move a muscle, not a hair. "What are you, anyway? What *are* you?"

The creature still didn't answer, but its hand started

toward him again, reaching through the bars of its cage, fingers probing the air between it and Ron—

"*No*. Don't do that. It's . . . weird. I don't like it."

A cough—no, a throat, clearing—from behind Ron. From the doorway.

Bonner. Oh God, it's Bonner.

"And what, pray tell, is that, Mr. Hawkins? What's '. . . weird'?"

Ron didn't know what to say; he wanted to curl up and hide someplace, anyplace. He tried to answer Bonner, but he didn't *have* an answer, and all that came out of his throat was a choking sound.

"The Beast isn't a pet, Mr. Hawkins. Not your pet. Not my pet. Not anyone's pet, not even the institute's. He isn't something to play with. I trust you'll remember that in the future?"

Ron nodded, because that was the only thing he could do. But Bonner didn't look like he was done with him, not by half. *Hell. Now I bet I'm going to lose my job* without *letting the poor thing out of its cage.*

"Do you have any idea, Mr. Hawkins, what kind of danger you're placing yourself in? What kind of danger your irresponsibility creates for everyone here in the institute? Let me tell you—"

Then, mercifully, the paging system crackled and hissed, and the voice of Ralph Hernandez, the night supervisor, came through the overhead speaker.

"*Attention, everybody. We got a bomb threat situation going on.*" Ralph wasn't real professional where it came to using the PA system. Not that it did him any harm. It wasn't something he did often, and none of the dozen people who'd be in the institute at this hour were likely to care much about his manner. "*This probably ain't going to amount to anything, but all the same I've got to ask you all to evacuate the buildings. If you can all meet me in the front parking lot so that we can get a head count against the sign-in log, it'll be much appreciated.*"

Bonner scowled and hissed. "I'll have you on your way now, Mr. Ron Hawkins. I've business to attend to before I leave the building, and no time in which to attend to it. I'm sure the same is true of yourself. I'll rely on your good sense to ensure that in the future you tend to your mops and brooms, and leave important business in more capable hands."

Bonner nodded sharply and turned away, like to say Ron ought to know he was dismissed. Ron couldn't decide whether he ought to feel insulted or relieved—but he turned and walked from the room anyway. By the time he was out the door it dawned on him that he was feeling both those things at the same time. Which was pretty damned strange.

Ron hadn't laid hands on another man in sixteen years, not since that night with Billy Wallace and Joey Harris at the all-night convenience store. After that night, and what followed after it, Ron had sworn off violence. There weren't many times he'd regretted it, either; life doesn't give a man that much call to go knocking other peoples' heads together. Herman Bonner, on the other hand . . . he was a man who needed taking down a peg. Ron pictured himself hauling off and slugging the little weasel, and the thought warmed him.

And remembered that he was a grown man, pushing past thirty, and that resolution or not there was no excuse for a grown man to resort to that kind of behavior. And sighed, kind of sad-like.

In the hall he realized that while he'd got the trash from both of Bonner's smaller baskets, he'd forgot to put a fresh liner in the second one. *To hell with him. To hell with his goddamn trash.* Of course, the lack of a liner wouldn't stop Bonner from using the wastebasket, and that would mean that tomorrow night Ron might have a mess on his hands—no. The thought of a mess tomorrow night was a lot less to cope with right then than the idea of having to go back into Bonner's office. Ron hung the plastic bag over the push-handle of the trash cart and headed toward the front parking lot.

Where Ralph Hernandez was waiting.

Ralph nodded when he saw Ron, and he checked his name off a list. And told him that he might as well take his dinner break now, since the building would be closed off for an hour at least.

That was a pain, since Ron generally brown-bagged his dinner, and the paper sack was in his locker in the lounge. Taking dinner now meant getting in his car and driving three or four miles before he found someplace to eat. Ralph was being cheap, making sure the lost time came out of Ron's pocket instead of the institute's, and for a moment the

pettiness of it annoyed Ron. *Where does Ralph get off,*
squeezing cheap over this kind of BS?

Ron was about to say as much when it occurred to him
that right at that moment the institute was the last place in the
world he wanted to be. The chance to get off the grounds was
a blessing.

He nodded at the supervisor and headed on without
saying a word.

Once he was clear of the security gate Ron fumbled
around at the dash until he managed to turn on the radio and
tune it to a news station.

It was time to make sure that the world wasn't going to
blow up before he had a chance to say good-bye to it.

He knew that if they were going to start shooting off
nuclear missiles it wouldn't make any difference whether he
was listening to hear it or not. It wouldn't, would it? He tried
to sort out the fear and tension that the idea stirred in his low
gut. An end like that might be a lot easier to take if he didn't
know it was coming—if he just ignored it death would be over
and done with before he even had a chance to regret it—

No. He wanted to know. If he was going to die like that,
turned to fire and dust in the time it took to blink, he wanted
to know about it. He wasn't sure why. Maybe it was because he
wanted to be able to make some kind of peace with the world,
or repent his sins so he could go to heaven. He didn't think so,
though. He had his regrets, but he made a habit of doing what
he could to make amends for them.

He wasn't one for church-going. And he hadn't had any
real faith in God since back when he was five—when he'd
heard two older kids talking about how there wasn't any Santa
Claus, and taken the revelation step-by-step through the
Easter Bunny, the Tooth Fairy, Batman, and God. Even
though he didn't have any real faith he tried to act Christian in
the best sense of the word, because it seemed like too
important a thing to take chances on.

No, he realized as the radio announcer read out baseball
scores for what seemed like every city in the nation, it wasn't
anything that deep or real or important. He wanted to know
about the end of the world for the same reason he always found
himself trying to step on a brake pedal that wasn't there when
he was a passenger in a car with a crazy driver: because there

was something in him that gave him a need to *try*, even when
it couldn't possibly make a damned bit of difference.

Ron was a mile away from the institute; the announcer
finally finished the sports and began to read through the
headlines.

Terrorists had bombed a bridge, not a hundred miles
away from Mountainville. Ron remembered hearing three
days ago that somebody had set off a bomb on a college campus
that was even closer. Most likely it was the same people.

A TV evangelist was announcing that he was going to run
for President, *again*.

Those crazy cross-and-dove people had put on another
protest in front of the UN, up in New York City. And this one
had turned into a riot, too.

And the Russians weren't backing down, not an inch.

The announcer finished reading through the headlines
and began to work his way through the details of the stories.
Ron listened impatiently through the terrorists and the evangelist and the cross-and-dove people, wondering if he was
going to be alive to wake up tomorrow. How could the radio let
all those other stories come first when President Green was
threatening to blow up the world?

*Don't they know? Aren't they listening to the news as they
read it?* They had to be. It was just too important *not* to listen
to. *Unless maybe they're as scared as I am, so scared that
they're putting off dealing with it as long as they can.* There
was something to that idea, Ron thought; it struck a chord. But
it didn't feel *right*, either. He shook his head, and sighed, and
waited, still driving toward town.

The man on the radio was just beginning to tell about the
Russians when Ron got to town, which was annoying. Ron had
half been planning to go into Denny's and get himself a decent
meal, maybe a chili burger or something, but if he did that it'd
mean not hearing what was going on, and Ron was feeling
more and more compelled to find out what was happening
right *then*, before the nuclear bombs could sneak up on him
and surprise him. So he turned into the Burger King, and went
through the drive-through.

Something by the restaurant caused an awful lot of static
on the radio, especially right near the lit-up plastic menu with
the speaker and microphone. Even when he turned up the
volume it was hard to hear. He ended up concentrating so hard

to hear that the girl inside the Burger King had to ask him three times what he would like to order tonight, because he was listening to how the Russians were saying they weren't going to take any more humiliation from the President ever again. He told her he wanted a Whopper and a Coke, and when she told him that they only had Pepsi he told her to just give him a soda. Actually he also used a couple of other words and his tone was more than a little surly, and when Ron heard himself he felt bad about it. Not that bad, though. He was too wrapped up in the news to feel much guilt.

Because he was listening to the beginning of the end of the world.

The worst of it was that the Russians were *right*. The President was pushing them around. Pushing them around about *bullshit*.

They'd caught an American trying to smuggle a hand-held nuclear bomb into the country, and they'd arrested him. They were going to put him on trial soon, the news said. At first they'd made wild claims about the man being an agent of the CIA or the NSC, but after a day or so they'd realized that that just wasn't so. The man was a crazy, a class-one lunatic who'd tried to enter the country on a tourist visa. Back home in Kansas, the man had been a member of one of those weird Protestant sects that made the John Birchers look like a left-wing reform movement.

The cross-dove-and-circle people, the same ones who were causing all the ruckus outside the UN.

The problem was that President Green was a member of that self-same crack-brain church. And the man the Russians caught had known the President for years, by all reports. He'd been an important part of the election campaign that'd got Green into office.

There was a lot of uneasy speculation about just exactly where and *how* the man had got his hands on a nuclear bomb. The security agencies were all denying that they knew anything about it. Ron expected they'd deny that sort of thing whether it was true or not, but even so he was inclined to believe them. They had better ways of getting things into the Soviet Union than tourist visas.

President Green wasn't denying a thing. Whenever anyone asked him whether he knew anything about the bomb, he ignored the question. But he was real firm on the demand that the Russians had to let the man go—let him go *now*, or else.

Congress wasn't real sympathetic. To say the least. Even the President's own Cabinet had come out against him—and an hour later the President had dismissed the lot of them. There wasn't much that anyone could do to stop any of it. The people in Congress were making a lot of noise, but what could they *do* about it? They could impeach the man, but that would take weeks, at least, maybe even months. It sure wasn't going to happen overnight.

It looked like it'd all be over before anyone could do anything to put a stop to him; President Green was threatening to blow the world to kingdom come, and the Official Soviet Spokesman was saying that the man with the bomb wasn't going anywhere but to trial, and from there to the gallows.

Ron took his dinner from the girl in the Burger King, parked the car in a spot a few feet away, and killed the engine. He turned off the headlights and turned the key back past the lock position so he could listen to the radio as he ate.

When the announcer finished reading the report, there was a tape of another man, giving an analysis of the situation. After him there was another, and another. Nothing that any of the analysts said was new. The things they had to say were interesting, and for a while Ron listened carefully—until they began to sound like parrots, repeating the same terrifying things over and over and over. . . . Before the last of them was done Ron turned off the radio, set his Whopper on the seat beside him, and sat there with his head against the steering wheel fretting quietly.

He was still sitting like that when the old woman tapped on his window. He didn't feel like talking to her—he wouldn't have wanted to talk to anyone just then—but he rolled the window down anyway, because it wasn't polite to ignore somebody when they were that close by.

"Have you heard the word, brother?" she asked him once the window was all the way down. Her eyes were all lit up and crazy-looking, and there was a tiny drop of spittle oozing from the left corner of her mouth.

"Uh . . . ?" Ron blinked. "Which word? Or about what, I guess."

She smiled at him, and Ron shuddered at the strangeness of that expression on a face so . . . worn. She was missing three teeth from the front of her mouth; two from the top and one from her lower jaw. And her blotchy, wrinkled skin was caked filthy with dirt.

"The *word*," she said. "*The word*." She reached down into one of the deep pockets of her overcoat and fished around until she found a tiny pamphlet, a little newsprint thing no bigger than Ron's hand. "Take this. It's important. You need it," she said, and she thrust it at him. Reached right in through the open window and shoved it to within an inch and a half of Ron's nose.

Her hand was so close to his nose that he could smell it, and he didn't want to think about where it smelled like it had been.

"What—?" Ron asked, but he knew what. Even though the pamphlet was too close to his eyes to focus on he recognized it; he'd found one just like it once, left on the seat of a bus. It was a comic book, sort of. Or maybe it was a religious diatribe in comic book form.

Two inches tall by four wide, printed on coarse white paper. And there in the upper left corner was that symbol: a cross with a circle that overlapped its top and right branches, and just above it, a tiny figure of a dove.

Those people again. Sometimes it seemed as though they were everywhere. Or as though their symbol was. Ron had even seen it on a few of those hardbound books in Herman Bonner's office.

He took the leaflet from the woman, and opened it, at least partly to get the scent of her hand away from his nose.

"Read it," she said. "You need to know."

He leafed through the pages, and as he did he felt an awful chill: the comic book was exactly what he'd thought it was. Not the same one he'd seen before, but something an awful lot like it.

And worse, too. It was all about the Book of Revelation, and about the Apocalypse.

"Two dollars," the woman said.

"What?" Ron shook his head—not to say no, but to clear it.

"Now you've got to give me two dollars. For the Word. To pay me, so that I can afford to spread it to others, too."

Ron almost closed the booklet and handed it back to her.

Bad enough that the woman was going around handing out tracts. Asking for money for them? It was too much.

Then it occurred to him that he actually wanted to read it. And what with the end of the world coming any moment now, what did money matter, anyway?

So he reached into his pocket, took out three one-dollar bills, and handed them to the woman. Before she could try to sell him anything else he rolled up his window, started the engine, and pulled out of the parking spot.

He thought about pulling over someplace, stopping to read the comic book, finish his burger. Glanced at his watch, read it by the light of a streetlight passing overhead. There wasn't time; he'd been away from the institute for more than an hour already, and even if there was a bomb scare going on, it was time to get back. Besides, the smell of that woman had pretty much killed his appetite—what little of it the radio report hadn't took care of.

He tossed the leaflet onto the dash, and forgot all about it.

When he got back to the institute the security guard was sitting in his booth looking bored. He had a television in there with him, and it was making a dumb racket. The man looked up from the screen, saw Ron, and pressed the switch that lifted the gate for him.

"Bomb scare over yet?" Ron asked. The guard frowned vacantly and shook his head. Ron was about to ask him what exactly was going on, but the guard was already watching the TV again, watching in such a video trance that Ron didn't think the guy would hear the question if he asked it.

So he took his foot off the brake and drove on to the parking lot, where half a dozen people were sitting around on the hoods of cars looking tired and impatient under the street lights. The professional staff had all headed home a while back, from the look of things; the only ones there were the two guys from maintenance, Ralph Hernandez, and the three other night-shift janitors. The situation was written all over their faces—the bomb scare was a bust, as dead and stupid as Ralph had said it would be when he got on the intercom. The bomb scare was a bust, and security wasn't taking any chances, security was going to search the whole institute, top to bottom, end to end, and Ron and Ralph and the rest of the night crew were going to have to spend the whole night sitting in the parking lot, staring at each other.

And there was not a damned thing to do but sit back and try to enjoy it.

Ron parked the car and cut the engine. It hung on knocking for thirty seconds after he turned off the ignition, and he promised himself for at least the thousandth time that he was going to break down and spend the money he needed to spend on that valve job.

When it was finally quiet he opened the car door and looked at the supervisor. "So, Ralph," he said, "why don't you let us call it a night and head out of here? We aren't going to be able to get anything else done tonight. You know that as well as I do."

Ralph shook his head. "Forget it."

Ron was going to ask him why—rib him, maybe, about being too cheap to let them go, even when there was nothing for anyone to do, but then Hernandez turned, and his face was shifted into the light, and Ron saw that the man's expression was tense and sour. Something was eating him, enough to put him in the sort of mood that Ron didn't want to have anything to do with. It was better, much better, to just let it go. Better to be bored than have the man take a leak on you.

The way the stray dog, the one Ron called Tom, was taking a leak against one of the shrubs near the corner of the institute's north building.

He nodded at the supervisor, to let him know that the matter was dropped, and sighed. Everyone was quiet, too quiet, as though they'd all asked the same question before, and maybe hadn't had the sense to let the matter go soon enough. Ron called the dog, more to break the tension than because he wanted to see the mangy thing.

"C'mere, Tom. Come on over here. That's a boy." For a stray, Tom was incredibly trusting. He didn't have a collar, but his brown coat was generally pretty clean—clean enough that sometimes Ron wondered whether the dog was a stray at all.

It took the dog a couple of minutes to walk across the closely trimmed lawn; Tom wasn't in any hurry. The dog only hurried when he caught sight of a rabbit or a squirrel, which wasn't all that often since he was too nearsighted to see anything more than a couple dozen yards away. When Tom *did* see that squirrel, though, then he'd run—run like Ron didn't know what. *Fast*. So fast that it was hard to believe it was the same dog.

Another thing that made it hard to believe that Tom was a stray was the fact that he never ate what he caught. The poor dog never even seemed to know what to do with a squirrel once he'd got ahold of it. Tom would just stand there, holding the thing down with one paw, and sooner or later the squirrel would realize it was still alive, and it'd take its nasty little claws or its tiny wicked-sharp teeth, and it'd start wreaking havoc with old Tom's foreleg. And the dog would yelp—almost scream—with surprise and terror, and he'd take off running like he thought the sky was falling.

Ron had seen it happen exactly like that, at least half a dozen times.

He turned in the car seat so that his legs hung out the door and his feet rested on the blacktop, watched the dog pace the last few yards toward him. Tom's tongue was hanging out, and he was panting, and he looked about as happy as a dog ever looks. He stopped a few inches from Ron's feet and sat down, panting, watching Ron expectantly.

"Heya, old boy. What's up with you, huh?" Ron stooped over and patted the dog on the head. "You hungry, boy?" Ron didn't have to wait for an answer; Tom was always hungry enough to eat your leftovers. Ron fished around on the passenger seat behind him until he found what was left of the Whopper he'd bought for dinner.

He tore the sandwich into bites he didn't think would choke the dog, and Tom took it from him eagerly. Eagerly, but not so eagerly that Ron was in any danger of losing a finger. When it was gone the dog sat up on his hindquarters and begged for more.

"Sorry, Tom. Ain't nothing else to give you." The dog didn't take that for an answer; he sat there, patient as a statue, panting and staring at Ron like a hungry orphan. Ron patted the dog's head and told him that he was a bum and a thief, but he couldn't manage to make himself say it in a tone that would make the dog ease off. Then he noticed the weathered stick on the blacktop not far from his feet. Bent down, picked up the stick, teased Tom with it a little; once Ron was sure he had the dog's attention he threw the stick hard as he could in the general direction of the north building. It flew out over the parking lot, and farther—it finally landed twenty yards into the lawn. Tom went chasing after it almost as hard as he chased after squirrels.

Ron had played this game with the stray before; the dog had some pretty strange ideas about playing fetch. Once Tom had the stick in his teeth he'd chew at it for a while, and eventually he'd carry it back to Ron. But he wouldn't give it to him. Instead, he'd taunt Ron with it, offer it to him and back away. Either that or show Ron he had it and carry it off in the opposite direction. Or lie on the ground and chew it like a bone, which was what he did this time.

That was fine by Ron.

Tom was still splayed out on the grass gnawing at the stick when Ben Hooper from Security came out of the north building. At first Ron was relieved to see him; if Hooper was coming out of the building, then most likely it meant that Security was finally through with the search, and that meant that they could finally get back to work. Not that Ron was all that eager to finish collecting the trash and start mopping the fifth floor, but it was a damn sight more interesting than sitting in the parking lot contemplating the lawn.

Then Hooper got a little closer, close enough to see his face clearly, and in the time it took to blink relief was gone and dread was in its place.

Hooper was scared. Pasty-faced, and sweating, and scared.

Oh shit.

"What's the good news, Ben?" Ralph Hernandez called out from his place on the fender of an old white Ford. Ralph was nearsighted—even with his contacts there was no way he could see Ben Hooper's face clearly from that distance. "We finally going to be able to get back to work?"

Hooper shook his head. "No good news at all. In fact, I'm going to have to ask you all to move your cars back to the far end of the parking lot. We got a live one in there right now. Lucky it didn't go off already—would have, too. Looks like there's something wrong with the clock they got wired to the damn thing. Got to call in the bomb squad from the county sheriff's department. Even clearing the Security people out of there."

Ralph's dark face went slack and pale. "Goddamn." He rubbed his eyes and looked around kind of queasy-like. "Christ all mighty." He coughed and swallowed. "You heard him, everybody. Better get a move on. . . . No. The hell with that. *Enough* of this shit. All of you might as well get the hell out of here. There's no way they're going to get this taken care of before the shift's through. And it isn't safe, anyway. Go on home. You left any loose ends, you try and be up early enough in the morning to give the morning shift a call and let them know what's what."

Thank God, Ron thought. Or thank Ralph anyway.

"I think that's just as well," Hooper said. "I don't know that anywhere on the grounds here is going to be safe if this damn thing goes off."

Ralph Hernandez nodded. He was already in his Buick; the engine was already running. Before Ron thought to say good night to him he was halfway across the parking lot, heading toward the gate at a speed that wasn't especially safe.

Ron waved to Hooper and started his own engine. For a moment he thought about the stray dog, Tom, who was still there on the institute lawn, wearing away at the stick like there wasn't anything special going on. Maybe, Ron thought, he should get the dog in the car and drive him off the institute grounds, or at least shoo him out the gate. But the stray was a stray, damn it. The dog was its own master. And besides, Security was always trying to shoo that dog off the grounds, and the damn thing never went in the direction they meant it to. Ron could end up spending an hour getting Tom the dog out the gate, and even then he wouldn't know for sure if the damn thing hadn't decided to hide in the bushes right beside the building where the bomb was, and he wouldn't know that it wouldn't just wander back in through under the barrier as soon as he was gone.

So Ron put the car into gear, and started toward the gate. He was the last one to get clear of it.

And went home, and slept—earlier than he usually got to bed. Sleeping wasn't any use; all night he dreamed of terrorists and bombs and nuclear explosions that woke him, and wore him, and sent him sliding back down toward miserable sleep.

Thursday
July Fourteenth

*(Radio Moscow shortwave broadcast
9.720 mHz.
01:00 UTC, Thursday, July 14.)*

. . . *our* Views *tonight on* News & Views *come from* Pravda *correspondent Gregor Samsa, who is concerned and upset over recent events in the United States. Gregor?*

Thanks, Anna. You are right: I am upset about the events in Washington these last few weeks. And frightened as well. And I know that I speak for the entire Soviet people when I say that I begin to grow angry and impatient with the constant bullying and humiliation we receive from the American President.

In recent weeks he has threatened us, belittled us, and insulted our nation beyond all reason. And for most of that time we have abided his abuse, for our collective heart was still heavy for the death of his wife in our land.

Now a madman has attempted to smuggle a nuclear device into our borders. By all appearances the criminal is the personal emissary of President Paul Green; certainly it is beyond doubt that they are close friends of long standing—and it is equally

25

apparent that no one else in the United States government was remotely involved in this attempted crime against all humanity.

Our grief over the death of Ada Green is still boundless, but we cannot allow ourselves to be cowed. The demands that Paul Green has made upon us are preposterous. We will not free the man who would have murdered so many millions of people. The nuclear criminal will be prosecuted. And in due course—after a fair, open, and public trial—he will be executed.

Mountainville, Tennessee

Ron prided himself on the fact that he was still in school.

He hadn't come from the sort of family where anyone expected to graduate from high school, let alone college; he'd dropped out a month and a half after he turned sixteen. Then he'd got himself into trouble a few times, but the law didn't get very serious with you when you weren't yet eighteen, and he'd only got himself into more trouble.

Then, the year he'd turned nineteen, Ron and two friends had got drunk out of their minds and gone shoplifting for beer in a convenience store at three a.m., and they'd been so drunk and so blatant that the clerk had seen them at it. And if that'd been all that had happened—if the clerk had been sensible and just shaken his head and called the law as soon as Ron and his friends were done—if that were all that had come of it he would have come out of it okay. Even if the cops had somehow traced them down and arrested them. Shoplifting could get you put in jail, but not in prison.

It didn't happen that way at all.

The clerk got tough with them, tough like he'd been ripped off a thousand times and finally had his chance to do something about it. He got a baseball bat out from somewhere, and stood in front of the door and locked it.

"You boys ain't going anyplace," the clerk said.

And Billy Wallace was too drunk to see exactly how mad the clerk was, and he'd gone at the clerk ready to grab the bat and good-naturedly whop him upside the head. But the clerk wasn't drunk, and he was *serious*, and he'd bashed Billy so hard and so fast that before Ron and Joey Harris even knew what they were doing they were jumping on the guy to keep him from pounding Billy into a bright-red pulp.

The clerk, of course, hadn't been any match for two guys, not even with him having a baseball bat. Especially since he was all caught up in pounding and pounding on Billy. But he hadn't given up without a fight, either, and before Ron and Joey got themselves and Billy out of that place the clerk was almost as bad a mess as Billy was.

Still, they did manage to get Billy out of there. They had to break down the door, and Ron didn't like to think about what they had to do to the clerk before he finally stopped coming at them. Breaking down the door set off half a million alarms, ones you could hear and ones that you couldn't, and they only got a mile in the pickup before every cop in that part of the city tried to pull them over at the same time.

Ron wasn't a minor any more, and the mess they'd made of the clerk had turned a little drunk-stupid shoplifting into a major felony. Ron had gone to jail, hard and fast and for a long time. Not just to jail, but to the state penitentiary.

Even that Ron could have learned to live with. Five years would have marked him, but it wouldn't have broken him.

What broke him was the six-foot-six-inch bodybuilder who spotted Ron on his third day in the prison. The man told him that he wanted Ron, wanted to know him the way the Bible uses the word. Ron hadn't wanted any part of *that*, and he'd said so. He hadn't taken any pains to be polite about the way he said it.

That night the bodybuilder somehow got himself into Ron's cell. And the man beat him. And beat him. And when he was done he raped Ron, but by then Ron wasn't awake to know about it any more.

He woke up in the prison hospital, with both his body and his spirit broken.

The prison chaplain, a Catholic priest, visited Ron in the hospital, and for some reason he decided to make a special case of him—to put a special effort into trying to talk a little sense into him. And because Ron was beaten and broken, for the first time since he'd been a small boy he actually paid attention to the good advice he was getting.

The priest gave Ron direction that he was still living by. And when he saw Ron straightening out, he'd helped him get the sort of lawyer that could get you out of any kind of trouble, and three months after he'd gone into the penitentiary he was free again, doing scut-work to keep himself fed and going to high school at night.

It'd been long and slow uphill since then. Slow but steady: in another year he'd graduate, and it'd all begin to come together.

He thought about Bonner, and bombs at the institute, and the nuclear missile that he could almost feel hanging somewhere up there in the sky above him. The way things were going, maybe all these years of sailing into the wind, trying to make something of himself—maybe they were all for nothing.

Ron was lying in bed already awake and thinking about wasted effort when the radio alarm kicked in and the morning news began to come through the speaker.

The news was even worse than he'd imagined . . . so unsettling that it made his own problems seem not very important at all. The President—the same man who'd worn that angelic smile through eighteen months of campaigning—the President had declared martial law. The Army, Navy, and the Air Force were all on some incredible kind of alert. Everyone was scared; up in New Jersey, in Newark, people were rioting in the streets.

The Speaker of the House had called Congress into session at midnight, and they'd *finally* got impeachment proceedings started. It was moving along, but there was no way it was going to happen quickly. Not quickly enough, anyway. And sometime during the night the President had ordered the Marines to arrest the Speaker and a dozen other senators and congressmen.

The Marines had ignored him.

That, Ron thought, might just be the worst thing of all. Crazy as the President obviously was, he was necessary. Or *some* President was necessary, anyway. Without him the country was paralyzed. Maybe the mail could still get delivered, but what would happen, Ron wondered, if the Russians decided to bomb *us* right now—would the people who had to fire the missiles listen to the President any more than the Marines had?

Ron felt himself shiver, even though the room was sweaty-warm. He didn't want to think about it. He didn't want to *live* in a world where you had to think about things like that.

Not that he had any choice. Except maybe the choice of killing himself before the bombs had a chance to kill him, and that wasn't any choice at all.

He shook his head and turned off the radio, before it could tell him anything else he wasn't awake enough to hear. The thing to do—the *only* thing to do—was to live through the day like it was any other day, and pray to God that things didn't get any worse than they already were.

He sat up in bed and rubbed his eyes with the heels of his hands.

A shower. It's time to take a shower. He always took a shower first thing in the morning; it was hard to wake up without one. A shower, and then a big cup of coffee, and then maybe something to eat. Or maybe not—sometimes Ron wasn't hungry in the morning, and cooking was more effort than Ron liked to go to when he wasn't hungry.

Half an hour later he was sitting in the kitchen, waiting for the coffee to percolate. It was eight o'clock, which meant that the morning shift had already been at work for most of an hour. It was time he finally broke down and called the morning supervisor, to let her know about the cleaning cart in the men's room and the trash dolly in the hall outside Bonner's office. He'd meant to be up early enough to have called them already, even though that meant being awake four hours before he usually got out of bed. But last night, when he'd reset the alarm, he'd seen 6:15 A.M. there on the glowing dial, and the thought of it had made him feel ill. He'd said the hell with it, and pressed the HOUR button one more time, and fallen back against his pillow.

Now it was late enough that the morning shift had probably already found the two carts, and seen everything from last night that hadn't gotten done. It wouldn't do a damn bit of good for him to call, but if he didn't do it the morning supervisor would bitch to Ralph Hernandez, and he'd have a lecture waiting for him when he got in at four o'clock. Or maybe he wouldn't; what with the bomb scare last night, there were certainly extenuating circumstances.

Still, I ought to call. The morning guy may not get into the bathroom until after lunch. Somebody could trip on that cart and break his neck.

He would call, Ron decided. Soon. After his coffee, probably.

The glass thimble on top of the percolator began to flicker brown, which meant that the coffee was ready—probably. Ron'd been using the same damned aluminum percolator for a year and a half now, and he still couldn't get it to make the same cup of coffee twice. He got out of the chair and poured himself a cup, opened the refrigerator, got out the cream, and lightened the coffee.

Coffee.

He'd feel alive again soon, he knew. No matter how bad this cup was. He'd been drinking so much coffee for so long that it'd become a negative option: he didn't feel awake at all until he'd had a cup or two, and when he didn't make himself coffee on Saturday morning he usually spent most of the day studying and dozing off.

He ought to call in.

Marge King was the morning supervisor. She was a severe woman, and Ron didn't like to have any more contact with her than he could avoid. That was at least a part of the reason he was putting off this call; Ron dreaded the idea of talking to Marge. Especially when the first thing she'd ask him would be why he hadn't called earlier. And then she'd berate him for leaving the cleaning cart in the bathroom in the first place—he should have parked it in the closet before he went to get the trash. If he didn't call, if he just let it go, maybe the morning guy would figure out what was going on, and maybe he'd find the carts when he needed them, and maybe there wouldn't be any trouble at all.

Ron sat down and stared into his coffee. Put in a couple of sugar cubes, stirred it.

Stared at the telephone, looked away.

Looked anyplace else at all; the walls, the kitchen window.

And that was when his eye caught on the little comic book the old woman had given him last night. He picked it up and opened it without even thinking how it was probably the last thing in the world he wanted to be reading. Before the fact settled through to him it was already too late—the leaflet was strange and seductive and frightening just the way a horror movie is. He couldn't have put it down any more than he could have walked out of *Dracula* before he had a chance to see the end.

The comic book told about the Apocalypse, which came at

the end of the world, and the *Rapture*, which was something
that came afterward. Ron had heard about the Apocalypse
more times than he wanted to think about, and the *Rapture*
sounded familiar, too, but he wasn't sure where he knew about
it from.

The pamphlet didn't help too much as far as making things
clearer went. It talked a lot about this *Rapture* a lot, but it
didn't go as far as saying exactly what it was—though it did
seem like maybe *Rapture* was something that involved people,
living and dead, going on up to heaven after the world had got
blown to pieces by nuclear bombs.

There was this dragon who was supposed to come down
out of the sky, and he was supposed to try to kill a baby that
was somehow like the Christ child, and trying to kill the baby's
mom, too. The booklet wasn't actually going as far as to call
him Christ—which seemed important somehow, but Ron was
damned if he could figure out why.

The dragon didn't quite manage to pull off killing the baby
or the mom, so instead it made the stars come down from the
sky, and that was the nuclear war that was the end of the
world—except it wasn't the end of the world.

So after the dragon blew up the world with bombs or stars
or whatever they were, it made this nasty, many-headed
Beast, just for spite or something like that.

The creature—the Beast. . . ? The picture in the comic
book looked unsettlingly like the thing in Bonner's office. Ron
had heard Bonner call the creature he'd made *Beast* more than
once. He couldn't, in fact, remember ever having heard the
man call his creature anything else.

The Beast was horrible and grotesque, and it had seven
heads, and part of it was like a leopard, and part of it was like
a lion, and its feet were like a bear's. And if you hurt it, no
matter how bad, no matter even if you burned off one of its
heads, it'd just grow back.

Ron thought of the wicked scar on the creature's third
neck, and he felt a deep, queasy-making chill run down the
back of his neck toward his gut. Was Bonner *trying* to make a
creature that would make people think it was the end of
the world? Why he should bother, Ron couldn't figure, since
the President was doing a pretty good job of making the end
of the world for real, and it was hard to imagine that anybody
needed convincing. Maybe the way that creature looked was

just a coincidence, but Ron couldn't see that. Bonner was too
careful, too punctilious, to do something like that by accident.
Even if the man had come out and said it right to his face, Ron
wouldn't have believed it. Not for a minute.

According to the comic book, that first Beast would create
a second Beast which would look a lot more like an ordinary
man, except that it would have horns coming out of its head.
Covered with hair, too—and the thing in the picture in the
comic book had a head like a ram's. Then this second Beast,
the one with the horns, was going to make everyone wear a
number on his forehead. Ron didn't like the sound of that at
all—he thought about seeing Billy Wallace get a tattoo needled
into his arm, back when they were both seventeen, and
thought about how even though Billy was drunk, the needling
had hurt him so bad he'd bit a hole clear though his lower lip.

Ron didn't want anyone tattooing anything into his forehead, no sir. Not him.

The comic book said that in real life these Beasts and
dragons would be things like the head of a church that the
comic book didn't like, or maybe they'd be the president of
Russia or whatever he was called. (Ron was never too clear on
that; the head guy in Moscow always seemed to have a
different title, or a different set of titles, depending on who he
was. Ron always kind of liked how Paul Harvey would call him
the Head Red—but that wasn't any *real* kind of title.) There
weren't people like that running any churches that Ron knew
of, certainly not any of them that were big enough for you to
think of them as being real. And Ron couldn't picture the head
of some church or even the Soviet Union having horns or
being all *that* evil. Sure, sometimes bad people got into
positions like that, but not generally *that* bad. Not in a big
country where the government and the people knew how to
cope with each other with any kind of decency. They said that
Stalin was evil, and that Nixon was, but both of them were a
long time back. The end of the world was going on right *now*,
nobody had to tell Ron that. And the closest thing to *evil* that
was part of running the world was President Green, and he
wasn't evil so much as he was bum-fuck crazy.

So where, Ron wondered, was this Beast that the comic
book was talking about? He thought about that for a minute
and decided that that Beast wasn't anywhere at all. He wasn't
even the poor thing in Bonner's laboratory—Ron had looked

the creature in the eye, and he *knew* it wasn't some kind of an antichrist. It wasn't that *bad*—it wasn't evil. Hell, it wasn't even bad at all, if you were asking Ron about it. There was a goodness about the creature, almost a saintliness.

The comic book went on to tell about another war, after all the bombs had fallen the first time, where all the good guys fought against all the bad guys, in a big battle outside a village called Armageddon, which was really supposed to be Jerusalem, only maybe it wasn't, because Armageddon was a real village in Israel, on the West Bank, and Ron had seen it on a map.

None of it rang true, and at the same time it did. The end of the world was the end of the world, and any way you wanted to tell it it was still the end. Maybe, Ron thought, you could kind of figure the way the world was now into the events that the comic book was telling about. Figure it like the way parents make up stories to convince a kid that a department-store Santa and another one outside asking for money don't mean that Christmas is a big fib.

You could figure it that way if you wanted—but you couldn't make it so.

The good guys, the comic book said, would win the battle outside Jerusalem—or Armageddon, or whatever it was—and when it was over all the bad guys would be thrown one at a time into a lake of fire. Then the good people would all go flying into the sky, flying to heaven like Superman, without any planes or helicopters or rockets or even wings. After that they could come back to earth any time they wanted, only the way the comic book made it sound you couldn't imagine them wanting to, because heaven, after all, was heaven.

The last page of the comic book—the inside back cover—was a list of things about What You Should Do To Prepare For The Apocalypse. Mostly it was things like giving money to the evangelist of your choice, and praying a lot, and trying to convert your neighbors to the Truth, and doing what you could to make sure that the unbelievers Got Theirs. Ron thought it was all kind of petty and small-hearted, even mean, but that could be because he was identifying more with the unbelievers than with the True Christians. In his book people were people, and what they believed and what they thought was precious had more to do with where they were born than with whether they were decent or not. Decent people acted decent, and they acted that way because they had backbone, and that was all there was to it. If there was a God, and he loved people more for their creed than for their decency, then Ron didn't think he wanted to go to heaven anyway.

Or, at least, that was the way he felt when he wasn't thinking about dying himself, and having to face whatever was waiting for him.

Ron looked at his watch; it read 9:17 a.m. The coffee in his mug was mostly gone, and the little bit at the bottom of the cup was icy cold. It was time, long since, to call in and talk to Marge King.

The hell with it, he thought. *I'm just not up to talking to her. Not now—maybe not ever*. It meant he'd have to suffer through a lecture from Ralph when he got in at four, but right then he thought that a lecture from Ralph couldn't possibly be worse than having to talk to Marge.

His stomach rumbled, partly from hungriness, partly from tension. He certainly *ought* to be hungry—he hadn't eaten since Burger King last night, and the stray had ended up eating most of that. He got up from the kitchen table and crossed the room to the refrigerator. There had to be *something* to eat inside it, or at least something to scrounge together. But there wasn't. Wasn't anything he had the stomach for, anyway. The cream for his coffee. A stick of margarine. A paper sack full of leftovers, but it'd been there for weeks, or longer—long enough that Ron couldn't quite remember what was inside it. A covered cast-aluminum pot, whose contents were as much a mystery as the bag's. A couple of oranges with mold spots on their sides.

It was time to go to the grocery. Time to clean out the refrigerator, too, but that was the sort of job Ron preferred not to cope with. He'd go to the store, and then, when he got back, maybe take care of the high spots in the refrigerator before he put the groceries away. Doing all of that would take at least a couple of hours, and Ron was hungry *now*. So he got himself dressed, got in the car, and drove to Denny's, which was what he'd meant to do the night before.

If Ron had called in to work before he'd left the apartment, he would have saved himself a nasty surprise. As it was, he didn't even know about the newspapers until he was halfway through breakfast.

Ron was sitting there in Denny's—dipping his toast into the yolk of his second egg and sipping at his coffee—when he looked up and saw that the woman in front of him was reading the *Herald*. He didn't like to make a habit of reading over other people's shoulders, which was rude, but before he even realized what he was doing he was reading the headlines and seeing the photo underneath them. The *Herald*'s always tended to do that to Ron—they were always so lurid and so overstated that it was hard *not* to read them. But even though he read them compulsively, at first they didn't even register. That was probably because he'd expected something about the President, or the Russians, or about the nuclear bombs—the same as the headlines had been yesterday.

> the beast from revelation
> alive in labs of mountain institute!

Underneath the headlines was a photo of the creature that Dr. Bonner had grown in his laboratory. The photo was blurry, and so big that it took up two thirds of the width of the page. Down below the picture was a smaller headline that told about the Russians' response to President Green. Off at the bottom corner of the page was the news about impeachment and President Green trying to get the Marines to arrest the Speaker of the House.

My God, Ron thought, *how the hell did they find out about the creature?* The institute was very careful about publicity, and careful about hiring people who were likely to get in touch with the newspapers. Genetic research was important stuff, but it was also something that got a lot of people awful upset. The wrong sort of press at the wrong time could cause the institute all kinds of trouble.

Trouble like that headline.

He tried to stop himself from reading any farther, because it *was* rude and he didn't like to do things he had to be ashamed of. And the type was so small that the story was hard to read anyway. But his heart was pounding and his ears were ringing, and he had to *know*, had to know right then and there. He strained his eyes until he could focus well enough to read, and read:

MOUNTAINVILLE—A failed bombing last night at
the Mountain Institute Genetic Research Facility has
led this paper to a fateful and unsettling discovery—a
discovery of facts which may have even more scope,
consequence, and bearing than those events currently underway in Washington and Moscow.

The discovery that the Beast of Revelation is
alive and breathing inside the institute's labora-
tories—not five miles from this office. Details as to
exactly how the Beast came into being and exactly
how it came into the institute's hands are not yet
clear. The Beast was discovered quite accidentally by
a police officer during the course of an investigation
into an attempted bombing at the institute. That
policeman, who has asked to remain unnamed, spotted the Beast during a follow-up search, and immediately called reporters from this

Then the woman holding the newspaper turned the page,
and there was no way for Ron to read any more without going
out and buying a copy for himself. He left the rest of his
breakfast on the table and went to pay the check.

When Ron got outside to the newspaper vending machine
he didn't end up buying the paper. He stood there for a minute
or two, staring at the paper through the machine's clear-plastic
window. Not reading it, just staring at the headline, staring at
the grainy black-and-white photo of Bonner's creature. And
wondering: *What in the hell is that newspaper trying to do,
incite the whole world to riot?* The Beast from Revelation was
one of those things that everyone *wanted* to get all upset
about. Decent people—basically decent people, anyway, people who honestly *meant* well—were going to start acting crazy
about that headline. About that photo. The same way they
started acting crazy when it came to subjects like abortion,
because there was something religious about it. Bombing
abortion clinics. And sometimes killing the people who
worked in them, because they wanted to protect some kind of
a right to life—only Ron always wanted to know about the right
to life of the people they were killing.

It was crazy. It was trouble. God knew what kind of a mob scene would be waiting outside the institute by the time Ron got to work. Maybe even bad enough that he wouldn't be able to get his car in the gate.

After he'd stood for a while there on the sidewalk outside the restaurant, Ron was so angry that he couldn't see paying for that paper, even if at this point it'd be a good thing for him to read it. So he walked out to the old car, and he got into it, and drove to the grocery. There wasn't any good reason to be buying groceries just then, Ron knew, because what good were groceries when you probably wouldn't be alive next week to eat them? He stopped the car at the traffic light, waited for it to turn green so he could turn left into the Winn Dixie parking lot. Closed his eyes for a moment as he waited, pressing the world away from him. The world was falling to pieces all around him, and Ron's gut knew, even if he couldn't have put it into words, that the only way to keep a grip on his life was to live like it was any other day, to anchor his sanity to the rhythm of ordinary life. Even if that rhythm was almost too quiet to hear in all the racket.

Ron spent the rest of the morning and most of the afternoon shopping, cleaning out the refrigerator, and getting the groceries put away. Around three o'clock he looked up and saw that it was long since time to go, and started getting ready for work.

In all that time he never turned on the radio or the television, and he never looked at anything like a newspaper. He didn't hear about the President making harsher and harsher threats, and didn't hear when the Soviets began making threats of their own. He never heard about all the reporters and foaming-at-the-teeth fundamentalists camped out outside the gates of the institute, not until he actually got there and had to spend twenty minutes honking the horn to get through the gate.

He was most of an hour late by then.

Inside Ralph was waiting for him, but not with a lecture or even a harsh glance. The man's expression, in fact, was relief. Some anxiety, maybe, but not anxiety directed at Ron. Before Ralph actually got around to saying anything, Ron caught a glimpse of the schedule on the wall behind the supervisor, and he saw what Ralph's mood was all about.

Ron was the only one besides Ralph who'd even bothered

to show up. Of the seven people who ought to be here tonight, four of them were red-lined on the chart, which meant that they'd called in. The other three were yellow-lined, which meant that they hadn't called and weren't in yet, either, even though it was getting on toward a quarter till five. Maybe they'd had as much trouble getting through the crowd as Ron had, but it didn't seem likely. Even with all those people making all that noise, Ron would have heard if there'd been another car behind him.

"Looks like you're it tonight, champ." Ralph almost smiled when he said it.

"Christ, Ralph, you expect me to handle the whole place by myself? Come *on*."

"No—I don't expect that. Just do what you can, all right? The trash. Police the floors. Anything that looks like a disaster. Don't kill yourself." Ralph sighed, but when the sigh came out it sounded more like a groan. "Do your best, okay?"

Out beyond the clogged feeder road that led into the institute, near the two-lane rural highway that ran beside the grounds, Tom the dog was having fun.

Tom wasn't a stray, exactly, even though Ron thought he was. But the farmer's boy who owned the dog had got old enough to be more interested in girls than dogs, and these last few years he left Tom mostly to his own devices.

Generally that wasn't a thing that Tom the dog appreciated. Dogs like company, and they like attention, and in that respect Tom wasn't at all exceptional. He spent a lot of time wandering the grounds of the institute, because there were people there, friendly people, and the guard at the booth wasn't usually paying enough attention to notice when a dog walked past him.

But today, today being out on his own was heaven for a dog. There were strange, sweaty, wild-eyed people all over the place. So many of them that there was no way to get through to the gate, much less get past it.

And three of those strange people had brought their cats with them.

That was the fun part.

Tom the dog didn't know from cats. They didn't *have* cats in these parts (folks in this particular neck of the woods having more taste than to own the things), and Tom had never seen one before. Still, cats are in a dog's blood. Cats are something to chase, and you didn't have to say that twice to Tom. Tom was discovering one of his basic, fundamental, biological drives, a drive that he'd never known existed. And exploring that drive was pure and clear holy joy itself for Tom.

Just now there was a cat lounging along the side of the highway, and Tom decided he was going to sneak up on it. Even though he'd been chasing this cat and the other two all afternoon, he hadn't yet been able to catch up with any of them. Tom was lucky as far as that went, even though he wasn't aware of and wouldn't have appreciated his luckiness. His heart *demanded* that he catch up with one of those cats, and, well, do something with it. If he had gotten one of them cornered, though, the thing likely would have taken out one of the dog's eyes with its claws. Or scratched his nose bloody, at least.

Tom didn't know that, and even if he had known it from experience he wouldn't have done a damn thing different, because chasing cats *was* in his blood, and he had to do it whether he wanted to or not. Ignorance, at least, let him find the joy of the chase. And that was a good thing. Or it was as far as Tom went, anyway.

Tom almost got the cat this time. The damned thing didn't even catch scent of the dog until Tom was five yards away from him. When it smelled him, and it turned and laid eyes on him, and it let out a screech like something from a pit in hell.

And the cat, a grey-and-black tiger-stripe, *ran*.

The cat was faster than Tom, and while it wasn't exactly smarter than he was, it was meaner and trickier by far. Five yards just now was the closest Tom had got to the cat all afternoon. That fact burned in Tom, and it hurt his canine pride—Tom was a dog who liked to *accomplish* what he set out to do, even when he wasn't sure exactly what that was.

So, as they ran alongside the two-lane highway, and the cat got steadily farther and farther away from him, Tom poured every gram, every tiny speck of his heart and soul and attention into chasing that tiger-stripe cat. If the world had exploded all around him at that moment, Tom would never have noticed the fact.

The cat, on the other hand, had begun to get pretty damned sick of being hounded. And while its body was running for all the cat was worth, its mind was someplace else altogether.

Scheming.

Thinking.

This dog, the cat decided, had to die. Though the cat was a mean-hearted little beast, it wasn't meanness alone that brought it to that conclusion—Tom had a good twenty pounds on the cat, and the cat knew it and was afraid for its life. Which isn't to say that the cat felt the least bit of regret or sympathy as it veered across the highway, straight across the path of the semi truck.

Cutting it so close that the cat itself only missed being crushed by the truck's right front tire by a matter of inches.

And Tom, just as the cat expected, didn't see the semi until its tires were already right there in front of him, and by then there was no way to stop himself or even slow down. All Tom could do was keep going, under the truck, missing the truck's left tires by the width of his tail.

Knocking his head on one of the axles, which was moving at seventy miles an hour, so fast that it burst the dog's skull and jerked it aside so hard that four bones in his neck shattered instantaneously.

It didn't end there, even though the dog was already dead. His carcass rolled over and over longwise under the truck, bouncing and banging and slamming against the pavement and the truck's jagged metal underbelly. Before the body came out the other end the dog's back bashed hard against the truck's bumper, and at an off angle, so instead of just falling on the asphalt and resting there, where it would have been pulped and pulverized by the traffic, the battered meat and bone that had been Tom the dog went flying, up from the bumper of the truck and out onto the highway's grassy shoulder.

Where, after an hour, the ants discovered and began to consume him. By dusk, when it grew cold enough that the ants lost their taste for dog meat, a pound and a half of his flesh was gone.

When Ron actually got out and into the main building and set to work, he found that the situation was even worse than he'd expected. The day crew had left things half finished all over the place, as though the whole lot of them had got up and walked out of the building at once. Worse than what they'd left were the things they hadn't even started—the floors, the toilets, the trash, none of it had been taken care of. And the mess wasn't the ordinary mess he would have expected after a day's neglect. The floors were thick with dust and grit, like the floors of an elementary school. Which probably meant that there'd been crowds of people moving through the halls earlier in the day. Reporters, likely. And police. Maybe even a few congressmen—Congressmen just loved to hassle the institute, and the news today was just the sort of thing they relished.

Every floor needed dust mopping and wet mopping and then probably dust mopping all over again. There wasn't time for that sort of work. If he'd been a dozen people there wouldn't have been that much time. And he wasn't twelve—only one.

So he started the workday where he'd left off the night before, with picking up the trash. The trash, especially the contaminated trash, was the one thing that *had* to be done, every day. The institute produced a lot of waste, and a lot of it was the sort of waste that could fester if you didn't look after it properly.

On his first run out to the concrete shack where he had to take the red-bag trash, he found Ralph Hernandez running the incinerator. The little shack was full and overflowing, and it was obviously necessary that someone take care of it, and soon, but it still surprised Ron to see Ralph there. It was the first time he'd seen the man doing honest work in all the time Ron had been with the institute.

Ralph didn't look too happy about it, either. He nodded at Ron when he saw him, but he didn't say a word, and the look on his face was so sour that Ron thought it best to just nod to the man and leave it at that. He headed back inside without either one of them saying a word.

Luke Munsen's laboratory was next, and when Ron got there it almost looked as though Luke was waiting for him. Luke was sitting at his desk with his briefcase open, fussing over paperwork. There was a bulging suitcase beside his desk. When he heard Ron he got up and met him at the door.

"Ron—I was hoping I'd see you before I got out of here. I owe you an apology. For last night, that is."

Ron blinked. So much had happened since he'd last seen

Luke that for a moment he didn't have any idea what the man was talking about. He remembered harshness, a little anger, but he couldn't remember the conversation they'd had well enough to be sure who'd been angry at who, or what about.

"Sure, I guess. I mean, don't worry—it's all right."

Luke shook his head. "No, it's not all right. I had no business talking to you that way. You asked a legitimate and intelligent question. Not only that, but you were a lot more right to ask it than I could have imagined."

Ron still wasn't quite sure what they were talking about, but that last bit was too provocative for him not to follow up on. "How's that?"

"The damned thing is *alive*."

And suddenly the air around them was thick as steam.

"How's that? What's alive, Luke?" Ron could guess the answer.

"This damned strain I've got—I'd thought I had the whole problem licked. And, well, I guess I did, too. But this is too much. The damned thing is—well, damn it, the thing is *alive*. So goddamned alive that I can't kill it."

Ron nodded. "I thought you said that wasn't supposed to happen."

Luke bit his lip. "I know I did." He sighed. "Look," Luke said, "here, look at this." He reached across his desk and took a thumb-thick stoppered test tube off a shelf. Inside was a trilobite fossil, strange and grey and shiny. Ron had seen pictures of trilobites before; he knew what they looked like. That's what Ron thought it was, anyway.

Until he saw the thing *move*.

"My God." For a long moment—the time it took to gasp—he was transfixed by the miraculousness of it: a *trilobite*, an ancient goddamned fossil . . . and it was alive. Then in the time it took to reel in the breath he'd gasped out the consequence of the thing sunk through to him. It was dangerous, as dangerous as the dinosaurs he'd dragged out of his imagination the night before.

Especially if the germs that somehow made it alive were catching.

"Exactly," Luke said. "We're trying to build a strain that'll give us good, inanimate models. *Dead* trilobites, not live ones. I've been trying to kill this damn thing all afternoon. Alcohol, formaldehyde, freezing it in liquid nitrogen. And it dies, too—for a good five minutes. That's about how long it takes the damned bacteria to turn the poisons inert. And twenty minutes after I froze it the trilobite got up and tried to crawl off my work table."

Ron could hear Luke running out of steam as he spoke. When he was done they just stood there for a moment, watching the trilobite try to crawl up out of the test tube. It never got very far; there was no way for its legs to find purchase on the smooth glass.

"It doesn't work on everything," Luke said. He reached across his desk again, took a cardboard box of fossils off the same box where he'd got the test tube. "Insects, plants, fish, no effect. You've seen what it does to the trilobite, but it doesn't have much effect on other arthropods." He shook the box. "No way of knowing yet what else it might work on, though. I sure didn't *design* it for trilobites."

Thick air—much thicker than steam, now. Thick like warm, sour coffee.

Luke nodded at the trilobite. "Burning should take care of it. If the temperatures are high enough, anyway. If it doesn't, well—don't think about that. Hey, what does it matter, anyway? Green's going to blow up the world tomorrow. You heard he gave the Russians a deadline? Tomorrow, noon. Eastern Standard Time. What does it matter that the trilobites are going to conquer the world if none of us are alive to worry about it?"

Ron thought about that. "Can't say I know. I don't suppose it *does* make a whole lot of difference."

Luke lifted his coffee cup from the desk, saw that it was empty, and crumpled it. Threw it into the trash can. "Damned if I know. Here we are at the end of the world and I'm flying off tonight to testify in front of a bunch of half-wit congressmen. And the worst of it is that it's beginning to look like they're right. What in the hell kind of life is this, Ron, huh? Tell me that—what in the hell kind of life *is* this?"

Ron shook his head. "I couldn't tell you. If you don't know, I sure don't.—What are you doing flying out tonight for, anyway? Have they got you testifying on Saturdays, now? Or are you going to spend the night in the air and still try to testify tomorrow?"

"No, it hasn't come to that. Not yet. Long as I'm going north I figured I'd visit a few friends who live in New York

City. I'll take the train down to Washington Monday morning. It only takes a couple of hours when it's running right."

Ron didn't think it was especially wise for anybody to be going to a place like New York under the current circumstances. But Luke was a grown man, and where he went was his own business. He certainly knew what was going on. And there were those who'd tell you that New York wasn't that dangerous a place, not if you knew your way around in it. No one would ever have been able to convince Ron Hawkins of that, but that didn't stop them from trying on occasion.

Ron nodded in the direction of the test tube where the trilobite was still trying to work its way free. "What're you going to do with that thing? You want me to haul it out to the incinerator and burn it?"

Luke blanched. "No. Thanks—really, thanks—but there's no way I'm going to let this thing out of my sight. Not until it's nothing but dust. Besides, your furnace isn't hot enough to make me comfortable about this thing. We've got a little oven around here someplace that can cook at a few thousand degrees—and if that isn't hot enough then we're all screwed, and it doesn't matter. Hell." He coughed. "Why am I talking this way? I'm going to talk to Congress Monday; I've got to *sound* responsible at least."

Ron shrugged, and reached over to empty the wastebasket. "I don't know. You got to get it off your chest someplace. Better here than there."

"Maybe so. Maybe so." Luke stole a glance at his watch. "Damn. I've got to get a move on. My flight is sooner than I'd like it to be, and there's still too much for me to do here before I can leave." He stood up, brushed his hands against themselves. Picked up the test tube and started toward the door. "I can get you to close up in here, can't I? Don't bother to lock the door—I'll be back in ten minutes."

"Sure. No problem." Ron felt a little confused and off balance—even when he was busy Luke didn't tend to make a habit of getting up and running off in the middle of a conversation—but sometimes, he thought, it was his job to feel ill at ease.

"Thanks. I'll let you know how it works out before I take off. I owe you that."

Ron nodded. He didn't feel especially that the man owed him anything, but it didn't seem sensible to argue. He reached under Luke's desk to empty the trash, and when he looked up again Luke was gone, left so quietly that he hadn't even made a sound.

The next laboratory was Phil Johnson's right down the hall, and it looked as though it had been visited by a cyclone from hell. Phil Johnson always was a slob, but that wasn't the whole problem—not even most of it. He had two assistants who cleaned up after him (necessarily so: Johnson didn't work with anything especially dangerous, but there wasn't any such thing as biologicals you could afford to be messy with). The mess itself wasn't pleasant to the eye, but the real problem was the trash—two or three cartsful of red-bag trash, drippy-looking stuff. The kind you couldn't pile too high in the trash wagon, because too many of those bags on top of each other would make the ones on the bottom burst. Ron didn't want infected trash bursting on him, not in a place where people spent their time cutting open germs and putting teeth inside them. Which meant that he had an hour's work ahead of him, piling red bags one layer thick in the cart, running back and forth to the incinerator. Ralph Hernandez, out there stoking the fire, was going to love him when he saw this.

Not that there was any choice; the stuff had to be burned.

Ralph wasn't anywhere to be seen when Ron got to the incinerator; he left the bags standing by the incinerator door and rolled the cart back inside for the next run. He had it parked in the hall outside Phil Johnson's lab and half refilled when he heard Luke calling him from the far end of the corridor.

"Ron," he shouted. His voice was elated—so full of relief that it made Ron uneasy. "The furnace worked fine. The damned bug is nothing but dust now." When he got close to Ron he reached into the breast pocket of the sports jacket he wore under his lab coat and took out the test tube that had held the trilobite. There was nothing inside it now but grey, dusty ash.

Ron looked at the glass vial, and he looked back up at Luke's too-cheerful face, and he said, "You're afraid, aren't you?" As soon as he heard himself ask the question he regretted it. It was the wrong thing to say; it was too pointed and too true and too real. Even if the damn thing *was* dangerous—*infectious*—the problem was Luke's. It was his to cope with and his to worry about. Ron didn't have any business making things any worse on the man than they already were.

Ron knew all that as he spoke, but still there was no way to stop himself. The damned thing worried *him*, too, worried him in a place that was so deep he didn't have any control over what it did.

Luke was staring at the floor, distracted and afraid and ashamed.

"You're worried," Ron said, "that that bug is going to resurrect itself all over again, even though it's nothing but a sift of ash."

There was a long still moment where neither one of them said a thing. When Luke finally looked up and spoke his face was red with embarrassment. "Yeah. I'm afraid. I'm scared out of my goddamned mind. I'm taking this thing with me when I go out of town so that I can keep an eye on it. What in the hell am I supposed to be, happy? I didn't ask for this thing to get out of hand. I didn't ask for this kind of trouble."

"I guess you didn't," Ron said. He was thinking that it was just the kind of can of worms Luke should have expected.

Luke tucked the test tube back into his breast pocket. "Yeah. Well. Look—I've got to get a move on. Plane leaves in an hour; I'm already pushing my luck as it is, as far as time goes."

Ron nodded and looked away; two bags of trash later he heard Luke's footsteps pacing away in the corridor, and looked up to see him heading toward the elevator, his briefcase in one hand, his suitcase in the other. By the time he had the cart loaded the elevator had come and Luke was gone. It was about then that the guilt began to sink in. What was he doing? Why was he saying things to make a man—a man who was clearly and truly his friend—so miserable? Even if he was right, even if Luke was being irresponsible with things almost as big and as dangerous as the nuclear missiles that the President kept threatening to fire off—even if he was right, was it really worth hurting a friend? It wasn't as though Luke wasn't concerned. Maybe he was working too hard to be easy about the situation, and maybe that easiness was something that scared the hell out of Ron, but it wasn't like Luke was ignoring the problem. If there was anything else Luke could have done, Ron couldn't imagine it.

Still. It was scary stuff, grave stuff that you had to take seriously, not try to laugh off. *Yeah*, Ron thought. *That's the way I feel about it. But what business do I have forcing that on my friends?*

And besides—maybe Luke's germs wouldn't work on anything but trilobites.

Maybe.

He frowned and shook his head and pushed the cart away from Phil Johnson's office, toward the freight elevator. There was too damned much to do for him to waste any more time ruminating than he already had.

Or so he told himself. It didn't stop him from brooding all the way down the elevator, out the service door, across the parking lot to the incinerator.

Which was roaring—the fire inside it was so hot and fierce that Ron could hear it from halfway across the parking lot. So loud that Ralph Hernandez didn't even hear him coming, even though the cart usually made a rattle loud enough to wake the dead. The supervisor didn't even notice when Ron parked the cart and started stacking bags of trash beside his feet.

"Be careful, Ralph. I'm stacking bags here down by your feet. If you try to take a step in that direction you're going to break—"

"What the fuck—" Ralph Hernandez, finally, realized that he had company, and the fact frightened him half out of his skin. "What the fuck are *you* doing here?"

"Whatever the fuck I'm supposed to be doing, I guess. Taking out the trash."

It was about then that Ron noticed the wild, guilty-scared look in Ralph's eyes. And noticed that the bags on the other side of Ralph weren't red, but translucent brown plastic—and filled, by the look of them, with files. The man wasn't out at the incinerator burning infected waste. And whatever it was that he was doing reeked worse than the waste shack behind them.

"You haven't got any goddamned business here. Get yourself the fuck away from me, and get yourself back to work. And *stay* the hell out of my way, understand me? I don't want to *see* you again tonight." As he spoke his voice went from crazy-scared to crazy-violent, threatening. Which struck Ron as one of the strangest moments in a week that was strange altogether; he'd known Ralph for years, and in all that time he'd never have described him as a threat.

Ron stooped down, took the last bag of trash out of his cart, set it by Ralph's feet. "Sure. I understand. Don't have to tell me twice." He turned and started rolling the cart back in the direction of the institute's main building.

"And if you saw something—if you know something you shouldn't—you keep it to yourself, you hear?"

"Sure, Ralph."

He probably ought to have wondered exactly what Ralph was up to. Certainly he ought to: the man's behavior was genuinely suspicious. It would have been good for Ron's health if he *had* wondered. But the man's hostility threw him off balance; it didn't even occur to Ron that he was in any danger. Not until it was already too late for him to do anything at all about it.

There were two other strange things that happened before that night came to an end for Ron. The first happened as he was filling his cart with the last of the mound of trash from Phil Johnson's office. (He hadn't quite decided what he was going to do with it if Ralph was still out at the incinerator; park the cart outside the loading dock, come back and take care of it later, maybe. Or maybe he'd go ahead and take it out anyway; he wasn't all that thrilled about letting Ralph intimidate him out of doing his job.)

Ron came out of Phil Johnson's office, dragging the last, heaviest bag with both hands, and as he came through the door he saw the door to Luke's lab peek open. He'd already seen Luke leave for the night. *Hell*, he thought, *maybe he forgot something and had to come back for it*. He wasn't up to seeing Luke again right then. He still felt too angry, and all at the same time too guilty about the anger, and he was sure that if he talked to the man he'd just say something that'd make the both of them feel worse. So he ducked back into Phil Johnson's lab, to avoid the conversation he didn't want to have.

The sound of a man stepping out of the lab, locking the door behind him.

Ron poked his head out the door a moment later, when he heard the sound of footsteps receding toward the elevator; more out of reflex than because he had any need to see the back of Luke's head—

And what he saw wasn't the back of Luke's head at all.

It was Herman Bonner—*Dr*. Herman Bonner—who had no imaginable business in Luke Munsen's office. The two didn't share projects, and they didn't care much for one another. In fact, Ron recalled, Luke didn't approve in the least of the way Bonner cared for the Bestial creature in his laboratory, and he'd said as much, in no uncertain terms, to the institute's administrators. And Bonner hated him for that. Hated him quite publicly.

Herman Bonner ought to have no business at all in Luke Munsen's office. And if he was poking around inside it at odd hours of the evening when he presumed he'd go unnoticed, then it meant that he was up to nastiness.

Ron knew that he was going to have to do something about it. There was no choice. Mixed as his feelings about Luke were at that moment, he couldn't in good conscience look the other way. Luke was his friend; if a creep like Bonner was prowling around among Luke's projects, Ron had to put a stop to it. Never mind the fact that the things Luke worked with were too dangerous to be tampered with by unfriendly hands.

It meant that Ron had to talk with the institute's administrators, as soon as possible. First thing in the morning.

Shit.

It was the first thing that had happened all night that genuinely threatened to leave Ron unemployed. Janitors were unimportant enough that they were hard to fire under ordinary circumstances—Ron had worked with enough lazy janitors to know that from experience—and the fact that Ron had showed up at all on a night like this would make him enough of a hero that he'd be just about impossible to fire for a month or two. Ralph Hernandez would have a hell of a time getting rid of him, even if Ralph was feeling crazy. And the harsh words with Luke weren't likely to do Ron any harm; Luke was a friend. But when Ron went to speak to administration—and he had to; if he was going to live with himself he didn't have any choice—the minute he went to the administrators he was putting himself in the middle of a very nasty fight among the professional staff. Which would leave Bonner with a powerful need to *get* him.

And, sooner or later, the man *would* get him, too. And when he did it'd cost Ron his job.

Shit.

When Bonner was clear of the hallway, Ron checked Luke's lab to see if whatever mischief Bonner had done was obvious or fixable. The doorknob didn't turn when he tried to open it; when he checked it he found that it was locked. Which meant that Bonner had a key to Luke's office. *Where in the Hell would he have got a key?* The sinking feeling in Ron's stomach grew strong enough to make him feel ill.

Ron took his keychain from his belt, opened the door.

The lights were off inside the lab; when Ron turned them on he didn't see anything unusual. Luke's desk, his chair; lab benches. Over there, by the left front leg of the desk, Luke's briefcase—probably left behind in his rush to get to the airport. Everything neat, spotless-clean. Whatever Bonner had done, he hadn't left behind a clue that Ron could detect.

So Ron turned off the light, closed and locked the door behind him. Tomorrow was too soon. He'd have to wait until Tuesday or Wednesday—whenever Luke got back from Washington—to talk to the people in administration; Luke deserved a chance to take a look around his office and see what harm had been done before the trouble started. *Or maybe he won't even want me to talk to them. That'd be a relief.*

The other peculiar thing that happened to Ron that Thursday night happened two hours later, when he was finally getting the last of the trash cleared away. It happened in Bonner's lab—Ron saved Bonner's office for last because he thought the man might still be lurking around someplace, and he wasn't sure he could cope with him, not after seeing what he'd seen.

Bonner's laboratory had always made him uneasy, but this time as he unlocked its door the sensation was particularly intense. Maybe the chill on the back of his neck was there because of what he'd seen Bonner doing earlier that evening.

Ron's gut told him otherwise. There was something in the room . . . singing. No, not singing; there was no sound. No noise at all; his ears heard only the dead silence of the building's empty hallways. It was an un-sound, and it wasn't singing at all, because instead of melody and harmony it had other, stranger, qualities. Analogous but not similar at all.

The beast, Ron thought. *The Beast*. It had to be Bonner's creature that he was . . . hearing.

Ron's fingers lost their grip on the doorknob, and the door eased open on its own. For just an instant—just an instant as his fingers reached up to turn on the overhead lamp—Ron thought that he could see the creature in spite of the room's darkness. Not that it glowed; the dark beyond the door was an ordinary, conventional absence of light. But for just that instant Ron thought he saw the creature plain and clear as day, watching him mournfully from across the room.

Perhaps it was a trick of Ron's mind. It must have been, in fact—there was no way Ron's eyes could see anything in a room that dark, not when they were so accustomed to the bright fluorescent light in the corridors.

But, of course, when his eyes finally finished blinking away the room's sudden brightness, the creature was exactly as he'd seen it in the darkness. And now, inside the room, the sound that wasn't sound or noise was clearer and more lyrical.

It was wrong.

Whatever was going on was wrong, and it was physically impossible, and Ron should have been scared. He should have been scared enough to turn around, bolt from that white-white room, slam the door behind him. Leave his cart behind him and run for his life.

He would have survived that night if he had.

He wasn't scared. It did not, in fact, even occur to him to be afraid. What he felt was . . . almost something sexual. No, he realized, not sexual. Sexuality was more burning, more demanding an arousal. Sensual. Like a cool breeze drifting along the sweat-damp skin of his neck on a hot day. Different from that, too: intimate and intense as though there had never been such a breeze or such a day ever before in his life.

Some small shade in his heart whispered that his life was almost over. He didn't ignore it—he couldn't have ignored a whisper that quietly intense—but he didn't mind it, either. It just didn't matter to him, in that one moment, whether or not he'd still be alive in half an hour. The moment was that powerful—that seductive and important. More important than his life.

That was what his heart told him then, anyway. If it had still beat to speak to him three hours later, it might have told him otherwise.

"What *are* you?" Ron heard himself ask, and he knew that he'd asked the question before, but he wasn't sure if he'd asked it out loud or in a dream. The Beast looked at him, and suddenly his heart *knew* something, but it didn't know the words to tell his mind exactly what it understood.

"You're . . . you're—" The other word was missing, and he had no clue where he should look to find it.

The Beast nodded at him, and he would have sworn that

it smiled, except there was no way that a mouth of that construction could smile recognizably.

"I've got to turn you loose," Ron said. "You shouldn't be in any cage. Not you."

As he spoke Ron looked at the cage, trying to figure out how he was going to get it open; there was a heavy steel bolt there where the bars met to form a door, and the bolt was secured with a padlock.

The light seemed to flicker in the Beast's eyes—no, there wasn't any light, nothing physical you could point at—the . . . *something* seemed to flicker in the Beast's eyes for a moment. Almost . . . indulgently? Tolerantly? Warmly, and with humor, and mercy, and ease; And in a way that told Ron that the idea was futile.

Then there was something in the music—not-music?—that was all around them, something understandable and almost real enough to be certain of. *You have to leave now,* it meant, it meant that clearly, even though there were no words to carry the meaning between them. *Run now, and in the moments that are left you will get far enough to survive.*

And Ron understood that, and the way that the understanding came to him made it impossible for him to doubt. Still, if he couldn't doubt, he could deny:

"That's silly," he said. He said the words out loud, even though he knew it wasn't necessary. "Don't be silly. You're important—more important than I'll ever be. I've got to get you out of here. The hell with my job and everything and anything else; God didn't make you to live in a cage. No sir. Not for another instant."

Already Ron was climbing on the bars, pulling on the cage door with all the strength in his arms and legs. Down there—the weld that bound the door-bolt secure—he could feel it beginning to stress. To give. If only he had more leverage, or stronger legs, or—or *more*—

Go now, the Beast told him. *You'll still be trapped in the blast, but if you run fast enough it might not kill you.*

"Blast? What blast? What are you—*talking* about?"

A vision, then, seen with his mind's eye—or perhaps he saw it with his memory: Luke Munsen's briefcase. On the floor of Luke's lab. After Luke had already left for the airport. After Bonner had skulked into the place, when he thought no one else would see.

A briefcase that couldn't be there, since Ron had *seen* Luke leave the building with his briefcase in hand.

The latch-weld suddenly burst loose; the force of the door flying free all at once sent Ron tumbling to the floor. And the Beast, in the instant that the two of them had left to live, reached down to help Ron to his feet. Their hands had only barely clasped when the bomb Bonner had planted brought the whole building to rubble in a hail of fire and dust.

Only Ron and the Beast were caught in the blast. Bonner and Ralph Hernandez were long gone from the scene; there were guards on the institute's grounds, but none of them close enough that the explosion could do injury.

It was twenty minutes to midnight on Thursday evening. Half an hour later the first hydrogen bomb fell, on a wheatfield in western Kansas.

Outside Mountainville, Tennessee

While Luke Munsen drove to the airport, President Paul Green got on the radio and declared that the country was in a state of "unlimited nuclear emergency." Luke kept his radio tuned to a rock-revival radio station—one that played old music from the 1960s—so he hadn't had to listen to too much of the noise and nonsense floating up from Washington these last few days. But this was *news;* big enough news that it meant that the civil defense network would be commandeering Luke's station within another half an hour. Big enough news that the station turned off the music and ran the President's speech live.

Luke gritted his teeth, tapped his fingers on the steering wheel, and sighed. What this probably meant most of all to him was that he ought to forget about the side trip to New York, and probably the main one to Washington, too.

Annoying.

Luke didn't like to concern himself with national or world affairs; his idea of maintaining a social conscience and perspective was to live his life fairly, to do his work well, and to mind his own business. He found government—on those occasions when he could not avoid coming into contact with it—tedious and annoying, and in general a waste of his time.

No, he decided. This was nothing but a lot of nonsense.

By Monday it'd all be over, and he'd have to fly to Washington and testify, and there wouldn't be any chance to stop by New York and make the visit he'd planned. He wasn't going to let these pompous idiots do that to him. No way. There wasn't anything real happening, not anything you had to worry about, and he was going to go on to the airport and not let it worry him. To hell with the elected idiots, and to hell with all their sound and fury.

When he got to the airport, of course, there was trouble with his flight. There was a lot of confusion, he gathered: apparently, even though the President was saying that the country was at war, the congress and the rest of the government were saying that the President was . . . well, mistaken. Right after the President had got off the radio, the Speaker of the House had got on and apologized for him to the world and to the Soviet Union in particular. The airlines were having trouble deciding what they were supposed to do. If the crisis was real, then they needed to keep the air clear of unnecessary traffic. If there wasn't any real crisis, then they needed to keep things as normal as possible, to help keep down the panic. Added to all of that was the fact that not many people were interested in being up in the air, what with the President talking about throwing nuclear bombs, and there were other people, too, who wanted desperately to fly to the places that they thought of as home—home being an important place to be at the end of the world.

Luke wasn't having any of it.

His regular flight was canceled—that airline had closed up shop for the duration. A few of the others were still running, but none of them had the simple hop down to Atlanta and then back up to New York. He went from one counter to the next, trying to find decent connections, and for a while he almost began to think that there wouldn't be any way to get up north after all. Never mind the simple flights; even the complicated ones had dried up. Maybe that was best. Maybe the fact that he was having trouble finding a flight was fate's way of telling him that he shouldn't be trying to go there in the first place.

Maybe.

The idea made him smile, but just the same he was about to say the hell with it and drive back to his apartment when the clerk at the Blue Mountain Airways counter where he was standing, looked up at him all amazed and delighted, and she said, "I did it! *There*, I did it!" And she'd managed to find him a flight to New York. And he had to take it, of course; after putting the woman to so much trouble, how could he not take it?

But now there was an awful foreboding in his low gut. There was something wrong here. Wrong with the whole world, whether he wanted to admit it to himself or not. And everything that happened from that point forward played to that foreboding. Starting with the connections themselves.

They were more complicated than airline connections had any right to be. No simple flight to Atlanta, or Raleigh-Durham, with a connecting flight to Kennedy. No such luck. There were three stops, altogether, and two separate planes. First a flight that ultimately went to St. Louis, with an interim stop in Memphis. Then another flight from St. Louis to La Guardia Airport in New York City, with a stopover in Indianapolis. It'd be nine in the morning before he got to New York, but he'd get there.

If everything went as it was supposed to.

If.

The thing to do, he told himself as he walked through the terminal toward a flight for which he was already late, was to turn around and get out of here and forget about all of this. To go home, and curl up in his basement with a big pile of blankets and a thick novel and a tall bottle of whiskey. And pray—he shouldn't forget to pray.

It would have been good for him if he had. But Luke Munsen was a man with considerable nerve. That nerve did not fail him—and by not failing it betrayed him. His feet went, one in front of the other, through the terminal hallways, through the waiting lounge outside the boarding gate. Past the check-in counter. Out, onto the boarding ramp. Onto the plane.

All that time his mind was blank as a sheet of clean paper.

He began to come back to his senses as the plane taxied to the runway, but by then the cabin was sealed and pressurized and it was already too late.

Much too late.

At least, he thought as he watched Mountainville's three dozen street lights recede from his tiny cabin window, the fear of nuclear death kept his mind off the thing in his breast pocket that could never be dead enough to suit him. That was a blessing, and thank God for it.

When the stewardess came by and asked him if he wanted a drink, he ordered a double whiskey, straight. She handed him two miniature bottles and a cup full of ice, and he handed the cup back to her and told her he didn't need the ice. Not now. He didn't want anything coming between him and his whiskey. She tossed the shiny-wet cubes back into their bin and set the cup on his tray.

Once she was gone he took a long, fiery pull of the whiskey and took a careful look around the plane.

There were only three other passengers aboard. All of them looked as scared as he felt, or maybe more scared. Luke took a second swallow of the whiskey, a third, and when he went to take his fourth he found that he'd already emptied the clear-plastic cup.

Damn. Two shots of whiskey and he couldn't feel it—not yet. He needed more. A lot more. Enough whiskey that he wouldn't have to worry. At least enough that worrying wouldn't concern him. With the plane so empty it wasn't too hard to get the stewardess's attention, anyway. He gave her a twenty-dollar bill, and had her leave him four more of the tiny bottles. By the time he got them all into his glass he was finally beginning to feel the effect of the first two.

Better. Easier. Or not better, exactly; the alcohol didn't make him feel good. It just made him feel less, and it was good to feel less of his circumstances at the moment.

He took a sip from the brimming glass and sighed. It wasn't until he'd had that sip that he realized that the stewardess was still standing in the aisle beside him. He looked up and saw that her hands were trembling, and that her eyes were tight and bloodshot and fearful-looking.

"I was waiting—I wanted to . . ." She pursed her lips and looked away; Luke half expected her to cry. "I just wanted to get your empties. Damn it all." She sniffled, and then suddenly her voice was a stewardess's, calm and serene and relaxed even though there was every reason to panic. "I'm sorry. Can I take those for you?"

Luke's head was spinning, partly from the whiskey, partly from confusion. "Yes—sure. Go ahead." He pulled his arms away from the tray where the bottles rested, to give her free access to the bottles. "Anything I can do to help?"

The question surprised her, threw her off balance; for just an instant she looked as though she'd reached the brink of her self-control. Was she going to scream—? No, already she was calming again, her face relaxing into a role it obviously found comfortable. "No," she said, "I'm fine. Everything's fine here."

"You're sure?"

She smiled. "Don't worry," she said. "Everything's going to be just fine." And she turned and walked away before he could say another word.

That conversation unnerved Luke maybe more than anything else had that night; maybe because the woman's voice so obviously told him that she was lying to him, and that probably she wasn't even admitting the lie to herself. She was like him, like a bad caricature of him, lying to himself, telling himself it was all going to work out. Being brave when that was probably the stupidest thing he could do.

He took a sip of the whiskey—a thin one, so that the cup would last—pulled the in-flight magazine from the pocket of the chair in front of him. And started reading. Reading was always good for keeping his mind from the world around him.

He was halfway through the magazine and almost done with the whiskey when he drifted off to sleep.

Washington

The Secret Service men kept telling Vice President Graham Perkins that there was nothing to worry about. The mob outside, they said, wanted the President's blood. None of the teeming mass out there had shown the least interest in Blair House, or in the Vice President. He was as forgotten now as he had been for the last eighteen months, and for once it was a blessing.

That was what they told him, anyway. Graham had trouble making himself believe it. He was certain, in his heart of hearts, that the bloodthirsty throng outside his window would kill him if only it knew to look for him.

It was a nightmare—a nightmare that stretched far into his past, and into the future as far as Graham Perkins could imagine.

For Graham the nightmare had started two years ago, all the way back at the Republican National Convention.

The convention where Paul Green had made Graham his running mate.

He'd been a natural choice; Graham was a good political balance for Paul Green. Where Green was a Midwesterner and a member of the party's right-wing fringe, Graham was from the East, from New England, in fact, and you weren't likely to find more centrist a Republican than Graham Perkins. He was so much a centrist, in fact, that there'd been those in Green's coalition who'd looked at Graham's Senate voting record and screamed at the top of their lungs that while he might *be* a Republican, he voted like a Democrat. And they'd wanted to know what business he had being on a ticket with Paul Green.

When he'd heard those people shouting, out there in the convention hall, he'd actually given two minutes' thought to the idea of turning down the nomination. Then it'd been a senseless idea; the people who were shouting were only the lunatic fringe of Green's coalition. They might be loud, and they might be unpleasant, but in the end they were too few in number to be genuinely important.

A hundred times since then Graham had wished he'd listened to his good sense there, in the steamy-sweaty Miami heat of that convention. He was certain now that his unconscious mind had been trying to speak to him, and he'd long since decided that he would listen to that part of him more carefully in the future. If he'd listened, things would never have come to this. It was even possible that without Graham on the ticket Green would never have been able to get elected—any Presidential ticket with the man's name on it was desperately in need of balancing. And there weren't many people who could have balanced him better than Graham had.

He almost did back out a week later, after all the loudness and excitement of Miami was over, and Graham and Paul Green had been able to take a day to get to know each other so that they'd be able to campaign together comfortably. Graham hadn't realized until that meeting exactly how unhinged Green was. The man tried to hide it. He even seemed to think he managed to succeed in keeping his crazier ideas to himself. He didn't. They were always there, flickering behind his small, pale eyes; caught on his tongue before they were spoken, but never caught before Graham saw them coming.

"So," Green had said, stirring a third spoon of sugar into

his cup of instant coffee, "what was it brought you into politics, Gram?" Paul Green had always pronounced his name that way—as though Graham were a measurement or a grandmother, and not himself. "What *brings* a man like you into this business?"

They were on the plane that the party's campaign committee had leased for the duration, flying cross-country from Virginia to San Diego. Once they got there, they'd have the rest of today and most of tomorrow to catch their breath and get to know each other. Then, tomorrow evening, the first big rally after the convention. They weren't quite alone on the plane, but they might as well have been. There were no reporters, and Green's closest aides were all asleep, trying to recover from the hecticness of the last few weeks—it hadn't been an easy ride into the convention for the Green campaign; Tom Cohen, from New York, had actually been a few delegates *ahead* of Green on the first ballot. The campaigning and politicking and infighting at the convention had been even more intense than it had during the primaries.

"Why politics. . . ?" The question caught Graham off balance—it had been years since he'd asked it of himself. Long enough, in fact, that he no longer had an answer for it. The truth was that political office had pretty well *happened* to him. He'd come back from Korea with a handful of medals, and there'd been a spot on the town council open, and before he'd even realized what was happening the town's mayor had him on the Republican slate. Fifteen years later he'd been a Senator. Still. It was the sort of question you had to have an answer for, or to be able to *make* an answer for, if you were a politician. Graham Perkins lied easily and naturally when the need arose; it wasn't a thing he was proud of, but he did it when he had to. "Government," he said, "is a place where I can make a difference. I think it's important to give your best to the world."

Green paused in the middle of setting his coffee on the table between them, and looked Graham in the eye long and deep and hard. After a moment he'd nodded, finished setting down his coffee, and sighed.

"I think I can understand that, Perkins," he said. "Hell—I can *see* that, if you know what I mean."

Graham *didn't* know what he meant, but he smiled anyway, as warmly as he could, and nodded in agreement.

Paul Green's grin was almost bashful. "I remember—I
remember . . ." he said. "When I was just a boy, I always said
to my Momma, I said, 'Momma, it's an evil world out there.
And somebody's got to do something about it. And Momma,
that somebody is gonna be me.' That's what I said. And my
Momma, she'd smile warm enough to light up the whole
room, 'cause I was her boy Paul. I'll tell you, Perkins—ain't no
woman can smile like my Momma could. All my life I been
watching, and I ain't never seen a one could do it. Not a
woman out there can hold a candle to *my* Momma." As he
spoke he took out a thick, vile-looking black cigar and lit the
thing. The smoke it gave off smelled, somehow, a little worse
than the cigar looked.

Graham coughed. "Do you really think the world is that
bad a place, Paul? Honestly, I'd be the last man in the world
to say that we lived in Eden . . . But *evil.* . . ? I don't
know."

Paul Green's tiny eyes seemed to grow even smaller. And
angry; the effect made Graham think of a rough New England
storm, welling up on the horizon. He sighed. "Perkins—how
can you say a thing like that? You're a bright man, and you're
not a bad man, I don't think. You've been living in this world
a good fifty years. Have your eyes been closed all that time?"

Green paused a long moment, waiting for an answer, but
Graham didn't know what to say. There was *invective* in
Green's voice, so much of it that he was half afraid Green was
going to put his hands around his neck and throttle him. He
frowned, and worked hard to keep the anger and the fear he
felt from showing on his face. "No, Paul. I wouldn't say my
eyes had been closed. But I can tell you: the world I live in
isn't an evil one. It may have its faults, but it isn't evil."

"You're *wrong*, Perkins. Bad-wrong. Have you ever read
your Bible? Have you noticed how much this nation—this
whole damned *world*—is like the cities of Sodom and Gomorrah? This world needs *cleansing*, Perkins. The kind of cleansing that only the fire of righteousness can bring!"

Cleansing by fire?

Green had cleared his throat, and flushed, as though he'd
said much more than he'd intended to. And then he'd changed
the subject completely, and steered conversation as far from
the subject as he could.

But Graham had heard what he'd said. Just as he heard

half a dozen more times over that day and the next, when Green had let himself slip. By the time their "getting to know each other" time was over, Graham was more than half convinced that the man was crazy enough to start a nuclear war.

Damn it, the idea was crazy—too crazy to believe. No one in his right mind wanted to blow up the world. And how could anyone who wasn't sane get as far through the political process as Green had? And Graham had already accepted the nomination. Sure, he could pull himself out of the race—but doing that would almost certainly put an end to his political career.

Looking back, Graham knew that had been what had really stopped him. Cowardice. Two thirds of his life, now, he'd been in politics, and he hadn't had the courage to leave that much of his life behind him.

The knowledge shamed him.

Outside his window the mob roared, surging in the street. It was Paul Green's blood that they wanted, and not Graham's; if he told himself so often enough and hard enough, Graham thought, he might actually begin to believe it.

Paul Green.

Green had been . . . well, stable wasn't a word that could really apply to a man like Paul Green. But it almost might; in the first fifteen months of his Presidency Green had proven himself capable and not nearly the lunatic Graham had feared he might be. And then, three months ago. . . .

When he thought about it Graham could almost find himself sympathizing with the man. His wife had gone off to the Soviet Union—ostensibly on a "good will" mission, though the fact of the matter was that the woman was using her position to travel as a VIP tourist—and she'd fallen ill. Some minor thing; food poisoning or some such.

Senseless—so senseless!

And the Soviet doctor who was treating her had made a terrible, terrible error, given her penicillin against the possibility of infection. Which would have been no problem at all, if not for the fact that the First Lady had been allergic to penicillin. Severely allergic; the reaction had killed her within twenty minutes.

Paul Green hadn't been the same man since. Bellicose, belligerent, constantly trying to provoke the Soviets into . . . into God knew what. And now this: sending a friend into the

USSR on a suicide mission. Sending him into the country as a tourist, carrying a portable nuclear device.

The Soviets had caught the man, of course. They weren't stupid; they took reasonable precautions. And what had Paul Green done? Had he acted ashamed for attempting something vile? No. Just the opposite. He'd demanded that they set his friend loose.

Now he was threatening to send the whole world to kingdom come if they didn't do as he asked. There wasn't much chance of that. Or so the Intelligence people had said this afternoon when they'd briefed Graham. The Pentagon had a firm hold over the people in the silos, and there was no way Paul Green was going to be allowed to call a first strike while impeachment proceedings were underway.

The man from Intelligence had seemed relatively certain on that critical point, but even so he hadn't managed to convince Graham—not beyond doubt, at any rate.

Somewhere out in the riot outside his window, a woman was screaming with rage.

Friday
July Fifteenth

Leigh Doyle was a would-be.

A would-be writer.

Oh, she made her living writing, all right. Made a good living, too; good enough to send her to Moscow for her vacation this year, just as it had sent her to Kenya last year and to Rio de Janeiro the year before. But the living she made came from writing the worst possible sort of trash for a supermarket tabloid, the National Interlocutor.

Leigh didn't harbor any illusions about the National Interlocutor. It was a rag, a godawful rag, and the work she did for it had no value whatsoever. None outside the wage that it paid her. Sure: she was one of the paper's best correspondents. She had a real knack for sifting through the news, sifting through the British and South American papers to find those unlikely stories that were the Interlocutor's grist. She had a knack for tracking down and following up those stories, too; she always managed to find fresh material and fresh angles that the other tabloids missed. Still, ephemera was ephemera, and Leigh didn't have a problem being honest with herself about the fact.

Just the same it pained her. Leigh had ambition

to be a poet or a novelist or maybe both. Despite that ambition she'd finished neither a single short story nor even a poem in the ten years since she'd left college. Whatever success she had as a writer of warped facts only added bitterness to her failure as a real writer.

A month ago it'd finally occurred to her that there was something childish about getting bitter at her own failure when the essence of that failure was the fact that she needed to sit down and get to work. What she needed to do, she'd decided, was take some time away from the Interlocutor, away from the world, and sit down and write. Vacation was the natural time to do it, but by then she'd already made plans for Moscow. Worse: she'd already made the kind of bargain-rate reservations that can't be canceled. And she'd already paid for them. That'd been a long, hard, moment—her career as a serious writer pitted inside her against the vacation to Moscow she'd been planning for years, the vacation that'd already cost two months' pay. And then it'd occurred to her that there wasn't any reason she couldn't have both. She had her laptop computer; more than once she'd used it to write up Interlocutor stories on planes or in hotel rooms, stories that she couldn't get over the phone. You couldn't get much farther away from the Interlocutor than Moscow, it seemed to Leigh. The paper's owner, Dan Keyes, was a crusty old Republican who liked to wander around the office lecturing anyone who'd sit still on the virtues of capitalism and the American way.

And certainly if she could write garbage while she traveled—certainly there wasn't any reason she couldn't write something serious on that little machine.

That was what she told herself. She hadn't even started anything on the long plane ride from New York. Hadn't written a word in the two days since she'd arrived. And here she was in a fashionable hard-currency restaurant called Tovarich, *struggling to find a story to write as she ate breakfast at the very*

table where the First Lady had come down with food
poisoning two months before.

There were stories all around her, she thought.
None of them were anything she could do justice to.

Over there, two tables away in the direction of
the door, was a Pakistani couple—or were they
Indian? For that matter, they could be Afghans. No,
they had to be Indian. She was berating him quietly,
talking to him sternly in low, harsh tones. No Moslem
wife could talk to her husband that way. Not if she
planned a long life. And the husband (were they
married? Leigh thought so, but there was no way to
be certain) the husband was this big barrel-chested
giant of a man, six-foot-four in his stocking feet if he
was an inch, and he looked as much like a small
animal cornered and under the lash as a man possibly could while he sat in a chair.

And over there—near the big window by the
door. Four men dining alone at small tables. Each of
them darker, more furtive, more suspicious than the
one beside him. Where am I, she asked herself, a
guest at a convention for spies?

That was a story, all right. But what did Leigh
know about spy novels? And anyway, spy novels
were just thrillers, or mysteries, or whatever they
were. They weren't poetry. No; their story wasn't the
story she wanted to tell.

Sitting beside the wall at the table to her right
was another man, a man nothing like the suspicious
ones in the front. He was alone, just as each of the
others were, but where the others seethed with dark
intentions and half-hidden motivations—this man
was sad looking. Lonely, even. Leigh felt for him; she
had an urge to speak to him, to try to drag him out
of whatever it was that put that soulful ache into his
eyes. . . . No. She mustn't do that, she realized
after only a moment. The thing that caused that
sadness in him was something darker and more
dangerous than anything inside the spies.

Spies? Whatever they were. It was the KGB in
this country, wasn't it? An organization like the CIA,
the FBI, and some dictator's secret police, all at once.

Those men had to be KGB agents, unless they really were spies from some other country. Which didn't seem likely; any spy as obvious as those men were would get himself arrested in short order.

The sad-looking man closed the book he'd been reading. Turned to Leigh and looked her in the eye. Had he seen her watching him? She was being obvious herself, she realized. Obviously what? She hoped that no one would mistake her for a spy.

She had to stop thinking like this. She was becoming paranoid as if she were a spy.

"Do you have the time?" the sad man asked. "I think my watch has stopped."

His accent was American. With the faintest drawl—the kind of accent you hear in the voices of people in southern Indiana.

Which was when it finally occurred to her: That's what I'd look like. If I were a spy and I didn't want to be obvious, I'd make myself seem like this man does. And I'd ask questions as innocent as that one. And I'd keep my eyes open, and I'd watch.

She looked at her watch, flustered. It read nine-thirty; for a moment Leigh couldn't remember whether or not she'd ever reset it to local time. She must have. It looked like nine-thirty in the morning outside. And she was eating breakfast, wasn't she?

"Half past nine," she said. "But I wouldn't set your watch on my say-so if I were you. I'm still not sure which day it is."

The man smiled, and when he did most of the sadness seemed to fall away from him. "Oh, it's Friday morning, all right. No question about that."

He was a story, Leigh decided. Just not any story she wanted to tell. Something down in her gut told Leigh that telling this man's story would be a powerful and unwelcome intrusion.

A waiter came by, refilled her coffee, refilled the man's. When he was gone the man reached out, extended his hand to Leigh. She hesitated only a moment before shaking hands with him.

"I'm Jack Hightower," he said. "Here on business from Cincinnati. Pleased to meet you."

"Likewise. Leigh Doyle. Here on vacation from White Plains. In Westchester, north of New York City."

The man cocked an eyebrow. "Vacation? Here and now? You are one brave lady."

Leigh smiled. "I like to think so."

The man pursed his lips. He looked worried—too worried to be a spy. "Did you manage to catch the news this morning?" And suddenly it occurred to Leigh that there was no way he could be a spy. No spy could ever look that worried. Not over a question that simple. "Is the President still talking like a lunatic?"

What? The President talking like a lunatic?

Leigh made her living reading and reworking news, but she didn't tend to concern herself overmuch with the kind of news you find in the headlines; the front page was the one part of the papers that didn't concern her directly. It was the one part of the paper she could afford to ignore, and she ignored it with a passion born of reading too much copy.

The only news she could ever remember having read for pleasure, in fact, was very old news indeed. A year ago she'd picked up a hardcover collection of Hemingway's dispatches from the Spanish civil war—back in the thirties. Beautiful stuff, Leigh thought. More like stories than they were like news reports. If all news were written like that she might even get a measure of satisfaction from her work. None of it was, of course. No one wrote like Hemingway. And no one in the papers even tried to.

Every once in a while her ignorance caught up with her in the worst possible way. Leigh had a sudden sinking feeling that this was just such a time.

The truth was, of course, that her situation was much worse than that. In fact, it was even worse than the warnings of her friends. People had kept telling her that this was no time when anyone in her right mind ought to be taking a vacation in Russia. She'd ignored them, of course. Most of her friends were Republicans. They always talked like that about the USSR.

"No," she said, "I didn't manage to catch the news. What's the latest you've heard?"

"I ran into someone from the Embassy on my way here," he said. His voice was very quiet. "The President's declared a state of unlimited nuclear emergency."

A phone rang somewhere not too far away. Somewhere over in the direction of the kitchen.

Unlimited nuclear emergency.

The man was planning to start a nuclear war. And here Leigh was, on the wrong side of the shooting gallery.

I should have gone to Australia this year. I knew it. Knew it.

That was when it finally began to occur to Leigh exactly what the story was she had to tell. Just a moment before the five KGB agents at the front of the restaurant got up and crossed the room and took her and the sad-eyed man into custody.

They took Leigh and the sad-faced man in a great, dark car that looked like a limousine from the nineteen-fifties. Two of the KGB men came with them, and all the while as they drove quickly through the twisted Moscow streets they kept their guns leveled at Leigh's heart. And at Jack Hightower's.

The guns didn't shake Leigh, because she did not see them. Not for more than a moment. She saw only the streets and structures that were the city of Moscow. And beyond the city she saw her world, balanced at the edge of war and self destruction.

And she thought of Hemingway.

How would he see this? she asked herself. What would Hemingway write if he were here and now, writing dispatches from the front lines of a war that was everywhere in the world all at once?

When she held herself still and quiet as she could, Leigh thought that she could hear his voice. Writing the story of the world she lived in; telling the tale of the city of Moscow poised at the edge of thermonuclear annihilation.

They took her and the sad-eyed man to a

barracks somewhere in a high, wide-windowed building. And left them there with a hundred other Americans. Others, too; Germans, British, French. She hardly noticed any of them; she went directly to the window, where she stood and watched and listened for hours.

Until it grew dark.

And then she looked around her, and saw that sometime during the day someone had brought the bags she'd left in her hotel room into the barracks that was their prison. She went to them, took her laptop computer from its case, and wrote the story that she'd heard all day.

It wasn't Hemingway, and Leigh knew that it wasn't, but all the same it was work she was proud of. And right there at the end of the world that was all that was necessary.

When she was done she saw that their jailers had supplied them with phones, and saw from the fact that most of them were in use that the phones were working.

And because the story that had told itself to her cried desperately to be told as soon as it possibly could, she called the office of the Interlocutor, *back in White Plains, and used her computer to send the story to them over the telephone wire.*

In transit by air over the South-Central United States

Luke woke briefly near Memphis, when the pilot spoke through the plane's intercom. There was trouble in Memphis, he said, and in St. Louis. The plane wouldn't land in either city; instead, it would continue on to Kansas City—this flight's ultimate destination. The airline would either find new connections for those passengers not bound for Kansas City, or put them up until connecting flights could be arranged.

The whole idea was too much for Luke to cope with, and he couldn't do anything about it anyway; he tucked his head deeper into the seat-back's padding and pushed himself down again toward sleep.

Before he was asleep he heard the plane's two steward-
esses gossiping in the aisle a few rows back from him. The first
said that the pilot had told her that there was rioting in the
Memphis and St. Louis airports, and that that was why they
couldn't land. The second asked her how she was going to get
home, and what she was going to do, and where she was going
to stay. There was a long gap—for a moment Luke thought
they'd stepped back out of earshot—and then the first asked
the second what it even mattered where they went, and if
there was going to be any home to go to in the morning
anyway.

Luke would have shuddered at the thought of riot-torn
airports, but the whiskey was too warm, and the sleep was too
comforting and seductive. Worrying over his immediate future
would have meant waking and clearing his head, and there was
no sense in that, none that he could see, so he closed off his
mind and hid from the trouble that pursued him—hid from it
in his dreams.

The next time he woke there was no way to hide.

The plane was somewhere over the Ozarks, he thought;
those looked like low, time-worn and rounded mountains
down below him, though in the moonless darkness it was
impossible to be certain. Luke was sweating, and cold. The
whiskey had worn off, or at least worn thin. His body hurt and
his head hurt and there was a demanding queasiness in his
stomach. All of that could be the effects of hangover and
tension. But those things wouldn't have woke him, not by
themselves. Luke was a heavy sleeper—he'd slept through
worse more than once in his life.

No, it was something else that had woke him. Something
like the foreboding he'd felt since the clerk at the Blue
Mountain Airways desk had found the flight for him . . . like
that foreboding, but much more immediate and intense.

Something was happening. Something powerful and inevitable. Unstoppable.

Luke Munsen wasn't a man given to visions or premonitions; the idea of such things, even in others, was preposterous
to him. Nonetheless he knew, impossibly, that the end of the
world as he knew it was at hand.

Knew to look west-northwest out the window beside him,
and watch the state of Kansas out beyond the horizon. Knew,
five minutes later, to shield his eyes from blinding-glowing

radiation as he saw the first flicker of light like a distant, tiny sun.

A nuclear explosion, turning three hundred square miles of Kansas wheatfield into vapor and a deep, magma-lined pit.

Washington

It was midnight when President Paul Green went to the situation room. In all the months since he'd taken office that room had never been empty at any hour of the day or night.

Tonight it was deserted, just like most of the rest of the White House. His staff was abandoning Paul Green, and he knew it. How could he not have known it? There was so much . . . *absence* all around him. They thought he was crazy. That was why they were all going away. Ignoring his orders when he could find someone to give orders to. Threatening to *impeach* him, for God's sake! Threatening, hell—they were actually *trying* to do it.

"I'm not crazy, damn it!" He shouted the words out loud, even though the room was empty and there was no one to hear what he had to say. "I'm *not*. There's a patriotic American trapped over there, trapped in the hands of those . . . those . . . *communists*. And they're going to kill him. All of you know damned well they're going to kill him. What am I supposed to do, just let them have him?"

As he spoke Green crossed the room, studying the blinking consoles and lighted terminals that he'd never really understood.

"This isn't my fault. It's not. Okay, maybe I *did* give him the bomb. It's still not my fault. The man is a private citizen. He acted on his own initiative. How was I supposed to know what he was going to do with a nuclear bomb? Yeah, so he told me what he was up to. Maybe he did tell me. I damned sure wouldn't have given him the thing if he hadn't. But how was I supposed to *know?*"

That was the console, over there. He was pretty sure. Usually there was a simple box with a red light, and all he had to do was put in his key and push a button.

Keys, actually. Two keys. One of them his, one of them for the Secretary of Defense. Green *had* that other key, along with his own. He'd taken it from the man when he'd called him into the Oval Office and fired him. Not that he'd wanted to give it up; Green had had to cuff him one upside the head to get the key from him.

No trouble at all sending off those missiles ordinarily. Green had even practiced it a couple of times, with the safeties on, of course. Trouble was, the black box had disappeared yesterday somehow, the same way a lot of other things had disappeared.

Well, let them take that stuff. They couldn't take away this room. It was too big to move, too delicate and vital to disable. And as long as Paul Green had this room, he held the fate of the world in his hands.

"I've known that man all my life. Went to church with him every Sunday. He's been like a brother to me. They've already killed my wife, damn them, and now they want to kill my oldest friend! I'm supposed to leave him to rot in some stinking Russian jail?"

That button, there. All lit up red and glowing. Of course that was the one. That was the one that'd allow him to set off the missiles without the box.

"I won't do it, you hear? Not for the whole goddamned world! *Are you listening?*"

No one was listening. The room in which Green stood was one of the three rooms in the world best shielded from electronic eavesdropping—perhaps, in fact, it was the best protected. It would have been hard to measure the difference.

And no one heard and no one saw when President Paul Green pressed the button that meant the beginning of the end of the world.

"Die," he said. And then he turned and left the console. Went back to his room. Tucked himself in bed and went back to sleep.

*In transit by air
over the Eastern United States*

It's the end of the world, Luke thought. He could still feel the atomic firelight warming his skin through the cabin window. *Right now, the bombs are dropping, and it's the end of the world.* He waited, pensive, for three long breaths, expecting his own fiery death to follow an instant behind the explosion. But he wasn't dead, he realized as the shock and sound of the explosion finally reached and rocked the plane, following behind the brilliance the way thunder follows lightning. The plane rocked and turned, but the pilot had it under control, and they weren't going to die. They weren't at ground zero, they weren't anywhere near it, and there wasn't another explosion. Not anywhere nearby, at least.

It's Kansas City that's gone, he thought. *It must be. What other city is there in that direction? Wichita? Why would anyone bomb Wichita?*

My God. Where are they going to land this plane?

Off in the west the thermonuclear light faded back down to a dim glow. Overhead the intercom hissed, and the pilot began to speak, then stopped. Luke could hear the faint sound of the pilot's cabin radio somewhere in that hiss, but it was too faint to make out whatever was being said.

Radiation sickness. I bet I'm going to die of radiation sickness. This high up, he was sure, the air wouldn't be dense enough to slow or still the rays. Or would it? Physics wasn't his field—far from it—and the physics he'd had as an undergraduate hadn't sat well with him. He'd listened as the instructors had spoken of things like time turned to mass, listened hard enough to answer the questions that confronted him on the tests. But really: what the physics people had to say was at least as preposterous as the nonsense that the psychics were always spouting—even if physics was true and real and empirical. Some parts of reality, if you asked Luke Munsen, were better left to specialists. Give him things that were alive and tangible, touchable and watchable. Even chromosomes, small as they were, had substance. In physics class even matter had seemed to turn unsolid.

Carefully, fearfully, he brought his fingers up to his face, probing to see if the radiation had peeled away the flesh it had touched. The skin was warm to the touch, and ever so slightly tender. Sunburned, almost. But it was whole, and it was firm.

The sensation of the plane beginning to lower itself in preparation for landing, and then the pilot's voice through the intercom: "We should be landing at Kansas City airport in another twenty minutes. No word yet from the tower in Kansas City as to the exact nature of the phenomenon off to the west a few moments ago—but then I'm sure we're all well enough informed to know what it was. If any of you are inclined to pray for the sake of our world, it might be wise to do so now."

Oh Christ. This is the last thing in the world I need to be listening to. He turned to look out the window, and watched as the fieriness in Kansas slowly faded down toward a glow. *Nuclear war,* he thought. There was a nuclear war going on, and here he was in a plane in the sky over the deepest heartland of targeted America—and he was alive. Alive. *Survivable nuclear war.* It was a catch phrase pasted together by some hawkish politician to justify an increase in the defense budget. It was *stupid.* But here he was, surviving.

Surviving for the moment, anyway.

Momma, save me from the crazy people running the world.

Twice more before they landed in Kansas City the plane's captain spoke through the intercom. Or maybe it was three times; Luke only paid enough attention to be certain that the man wasn't saying anything important.

When they reached Kansas City the landing itself went quickly and smoothly—too well, in fact, to be comfortable with. Four minutes after they'd first touched the ground, they were taxied and stopped and leaving the plane, walking out into an airport that was ominously empty.

The bomb had to fall somewhere around here. The whole damned city must be holed up underground someplace, hiding. Afraid that some fool is going to fire off another one. He looked out the boarding-area window and saw that the right side of the plane he'd just got off of was faded, bleached looking—bleached exactly the way years of sunlight will leach the color out of paint. *My God. If the blast did that to the plane, what did it do to me through the window?* The skin of his face was warmer, now—more than warm. Fiery, blistery. He reached up to touch it, ever so lightly, and felt tiny blister-pustules of sun poisoning. *I'm going to be okay,* Luke told himself. *It isn't anything worse than a sunburn. A bad sunburn. The sun is radiation, too, after all. Light is radiation. Radios are radiation. Radiation is normal, ordinary stuff.* That was what he told himself. He didn't believe it for an instant, not even the parts that were true.

There was one airline clerk at the counter just beyond the lounge, a scared-looking woman with washed-out skin and stringy-sweaty hair. She directed him to his "evacuation

flight," at a gate in another part of the airport. There was a
plane there bound for New York, she said, and it would be
leaving in a few minutes. She told him that if he went directly
there he'd have plenty of time to get to the gate before the
plane departed. She was right, too: even after he took a wrong
turn and spent five minutes lost in the airport's dry, carpeted
corridors, he managed to get to the right plane in time. Just
barely in time, but in time nonetheless.

If he hadn't made that wrong turn, in fact, there would
have been plenty of time. As it was he only had a moment at
the ticket desk, and then a rush through the boarding gate.

And when Luke saw Herman Bonner sitting at the
waiting lounge at the gate across from his—reading some
magazine as he waited for a flight that the sign above him said
was bound for western Kansas—when he saw vile Herman
Bonner in the Kansas City airport in the middle of a nuclear
war, there wasn't any way to find out what in the name of God
the man was doing there.

Which, perhaps, was just as well.

Washington

Paul Green woke at four in the morning, curious and
tingling as a child awake too early on Christmas morning. *Is it
really the end of the world? Is it really time for the Rapture?*
He had to know. He had to know *right then*.

Rapture.

Rapture was the real reason he'd given Bill Cartwright the
backpack nuke. It was a secret so big that Green would never
have said it out loud, but it was the truth. The world needed
the Rapture. And once he'd been in office long enough to
figure out how everything worked, he'd realized that there
were too many safeguards. There was no way he was going to
be able to start the end of the world with so many people
watching him. There were too many people standing between
the nation and nuclear war, too many people who'd *find* a way
to make peace, even if Paul Green did everything he could to
make a war inevitable.

That was over, now, though. All of those people were
away from him, gone of their own accord. The only problem
Paul Green saw right now was that he couldn't figure out how

he was going to find out about the Rapture. Ever since he'd been elected there'd been people around to tell him these things whenever he wanted to know them—mostly they were the same ones who kept trying to stop the Rapture. Now they were gone, and that was good, but there was no one to tell him what was happening. Sure, the Marines still had guards for him—extra guards—even though they weren't taking his orders. And there were the Secret Service people, from over at the Treasury Department. They didn't talk to him any more, but they still followed him around any time he even *thought* about going out in public. A few bottom-rung civil service types—secretaries, office assistants—had shown up for work yesterday. They weren't anywhere to be found at four in the morning, and even if they had been they didn't have the security clearance to tell him what he wanted to know. None of the people he'd be able to find had enough clearance.

The only ones he could still get to jump, in fact, were the press and broadcast people—and they didn't even work for him.

He could turn on the TV, turn to CNN. They kept themselves up on things pretty well. But he was *President*, for God's sake. It wasn't dignified for him to be getting his news off the television—not even *cable* TV. It wasn't *right*.

The Situation Room. Yes, that was the answer—there were a couple of screens in there that kept track of the status of everything, everything everywhere in the world.

Paul Green showered and dressed himself hurriedly, grinning with childlike excitement all the while. Such a day, such a day! Paul Green had dreamed all his life of the Rapture. Dreamed of ascending wingless into heaven. And now here the day was at last, the day when all of it was to come true.

When he finally got to the Situation Room, finally figured out which screen he had to read, his disappointment was tremendous. He'd pushed the button, all right. Only the people on the other end of the line hadn't listened to him. Almost none of them had, anyway. None of the submarine commanders, the people with the best missiles he had. None of the bombers. Small loss, there; the bombers weren't likely to get close enough to put their nukes anywhere that counted.

Silo missiles . . . nothing. Wait. No. Two of the techs down in the Eidner silos in west Kansas had launched their ICBMs.

And all of their missiles had malfunctioned.

One missile had lost track of itself in the instant after it'd launched, and the damned thing had turned most of two counties in Kansas into fire and dust. Two others had got themselves as far as the Arctic Ocean before their guidance systems had malfunctioned and sent them harmlessly down into the water.

Or maybe they hadn't malfunctioned at all. Maybe one of those high-handed fools at the Pentagon had purposely put a stop to his *Rapture*. Aborted those missiles intentionally.

Or maybe not. Maybe they *had* malfunctioned. It was certainly possible the other two had malfunctioned, wasn't it?

He should have expected it. It wasn't as if he hadn't been warned.

Someone from the NSC had briefed him about the problem the month after he'd taken office. The man had been a real technoid, almost impossible to understand. What he'd said broke down to this: no one was sure any more whether the missiles would even make it out of their silos. There was something the man said about computers, and the complexity of machines, and something he called beta testing. Paul Green didn't know computers from washing machines, but he could still get his hands around the concept. Nothing tricky worked the first time you tried it. Missiles had gotten especially complicated over the last twenty years. And with missiles the problem was worse than usual—kind of hard to figure out what went wrong when the thing that didn't work had already blown itself up. They were working on the problem, working on it real hard, but the problem was, the NSC man said, that they wouldn't really know whether they had the situation licked until they actually shot the things off with real live warheads.

Paul Green had looked that NSC man in the eye, and he'd felt himself smile a lot more hungrily than he'd ever meant to where anyone could see. And he'd said sure, why don't we shoot some of those missiles off? Just to test them out, like, of course.

And he'd thought to himself: Great. Test 'em out good and proper—nuke one of them Third World places, like maybe Lebanon or Iran, nuke it right down into the *Stone* Age.

The NSC man had said no, there were treaties the nation had signed. Treaties that prevented above-ground nuclear tests. And besides, there was no part of the country deserted

enough in large enough areas—if the missile went as far awry
as some of the experts thought it might, it was just conceivable
that it could destroy a town, or even a city.

Green thought, *Shit—who ever said anything about
firing off missiles aimed at this country?* He didn't say
anything. The secret he carried in his heart was too big for him
to share even a hint of it with some NSC man.

Now, though, there wasn't any need for secrecy. There
was no one left to keep the secret from.

Paul Green had asked that NSC man: what about all those
nukes that've been in the ground twenty, thirty years? What
about them—didn't they ever work in the first place? Anybody
ever test them?

Well, sir, the man said. They were tested, way back
when. And they *did* work. But it's been twenty years for most
of them. And even missiles get old. He made one of them
analogies: compared the missiles to a car left sitting in a garage
for twenty years. Green knew about that, all right. You
couldn't even leave a car sitting for six months, let alone
twenty years. Not if you wanted to go anywhere in it.

A cough, from outside the open door of the situation
room. The silence had been so deep and so thick that the
sound of another soul nearby startled Paul Green half out of his
wits. He only barely managed to keep himself from jumping,
and that was good—it wasn't dignified for a President to act
afraid.

"Sir." A man's voice; a young man's voice. It had to be one
of the Marines.

"I can't see you from here. Come on in and talk to me if
you're going to talk, don't just stand there. Don't like talking to
a man I can't look in the eye when I have to."

Green hadn't bothered to turn on the room's overhead
lights; there hadn't been much sense in it, what with all the
glowing consoles and blinking status lights. All the machines
were lit, and more than lit. But there wasn't light enough to
see a man's face—not properly. When the Marine stepped into
the half-dark room his features were so masked in chiaroscuro
and red reflected light that they looked . . . *satanic*.

"Sir, we've got to evacuate you to Camp David."

*Is he the Antichrist? Come here to pluck me from my
sanctum?*

"There's rioting outside, rioting so bad that there's no way to hold the people back much longer."

Herman says that the Antichrist will be coming soon. Why shouldn't he come first for me? After all, I'm President.

"Sir?" The Marine stepped forward, into stronger, yellower light, and Paul Green saw that he was only a Marine, nothing more, nothing hell-made or terrifying. "Are you well, sir?"

Green sighed. "Yes, son, I'm fine. Don't worry about this old tiger—plenty of fight still left in 'im. Now, what's this about Camp David?"

"We've got to evacuate you, sir. It's too dangerous for you to remain here any longer."

"Camp David, huh? Well. How about that."

"There's a helicopter waiting for you, sir. On the roof."

"The roof? What the deuce is it doing up there?"

The Marine frowned; the expression made him look even more boyish than he did already. *What're they doing,* Green wondered, *recruiting a boy that young into the Marines?*

"The grounds aren't secure any more. Sir. The mob has swarmed over the gates."

Green felt his heart give a little chill. *Heathens. Heathens coming for me, waiting for me on my own damned lawn.* "Time enough for me to go up and do a little packing?"

"If you have to, sir. Time is extremely critical just now. Sir."

There were things in his quarters that were personal, but all the things that were dearest to him Paul Green had long since sent home to Kansas. He'd seen this day coming from a long way off.

"That bad, huh? Damn. Okay, then, to hell with that. Let's get out of here."

The Marine led him to an armored elevator that Green had never even noticed before. Opened it up with three keys and a magnetic card, and took him to the roof where the dawn was already leaking greyly into the eastern sky. Overhead the helicopter slapped noisily at the air, keeping itself in the air a few feet above a White House roof that didn't look as though it could bear the thing's weight. The young Marine waved the helicopter down, toward the surface of the roof. Waved Green toward the machine's opening door . . .

And Paul Green saw a sight that froze him down into his

deepest, most secret heart—chilled and frightened him even more powerfully than the false sighting of the Beast had a few moments before.

As President Paul Green stepped toward the helicopter door, he got a view out over the edge of the White House roof, and for the first time he saw the rioters. No, they weren't rioters. They couldn't be rioters. A riot was a different thing completely, something with smaller scope, a thing with infinitely less raw *humanity*. This, Green thought, was . . . there wasn't a word for it. Green hadn't even had a concept for it until the moment he'd set eyes on it.

They want to kill me.

There were thousands of them—no, millions. As far as Green could see the streets were packed solid with writhing human flesh. And Green's eyes were still good, in spite of his age, good enough to pick out individual faces in the mass. There were honest, decent people out there—people he recognized, for God's sake.

And they wanted to kill him.

Paul Green was a politician; he'd spent his entire adult life working to earn the trust and love and dedication of these people.

And now they want to kill me. The realization wound its way around Paul Green's heart, and it killed a part of him.

Where is the Army? Where are the tanks? Someone has to stop these people.

A hand on his shoulder; the young Marine. The man had nerve, Green thought, laying hands on his President. But no, that wasn't fair. There was no way Green would have heard the soldier, what with the noise from the helicopter so close. And the Marine looked terrified, as though he realized the gravity of what he'd done.

"Okay," Green said, and then he realized that the man couldn't possibly hear him, and he nodded. A moment later they were in the helicopter, sailing out and away over the city.

They were five miles from the White House before the crowd down below thinned enough for Green to catch a glimpse of pavement.

"What happened to the Army, son? Don't they have some sort of a contingency plan for this kind of thing?"

"I wouldn't know about contingency plans, sir—I haven't got that kind of clearance. But the word is that most of the bases in the general area are under siege. Maybe as bad as the riot outside the White House."

"And there isn't anyone outside Camp David? Waiting for us?"

"No sir. Not in any great numbers, sir. Camp David's location isn't quite so public."

Out to the east the sun was beginning to rise. Green sighed. Camp David wasn't anyplace he needed to be. Out there he'd be even more isolated from his own people than he had been in the White House. It was time to set the next segment of the plan into motion—time to head out toward Kansas.

"Pilot?" Green spoke loudly, almost shouted, so that the man could hear him through his headphones. "Pilot, what base have you come from?"

The pilot turned, looked back toward him. "Andrews, sir."

Green felt himself smile. "Andrews, eh? Is Andrews Air Base still secure? Can you get me to Air Force One?"

"Yes sir, Mr. President. There's some serious trouble at the gates of the base, but no one's got inside yet."

In transit by air
over the Eastern United States

Luke Munsen fell asleep on the flight from Kansas City to New York. The flight was a nonstop—or maybe it was supposed to stop midway through, but couldn't; Luke wasn't too clear on that—and there was something wrong with the plane's ventilation system. Something that made the air inside the cabin warm and thick and stuffy, made Luke too sleepy to keep his eyes more than a slit open.

As he slept he had a dream.

He dreamed of the ashy trilobite that rested in the glass cylinder in his breast pocket. His dream began in the central lab, back at the institute, the laboratory with the smelting furnace, where he'd burned the little creature. At first, in the dream, he watched through his own eyes. Then somehow he was down in there in the hot and dark, and he realized that he was dreaming as the trilobite would have dreamed it. Maybe that should have frightened Luke; certainly he knew what was going to happen to the thing. To *him*, now. But he wasn't afraid, just mystified. Fascinated. The heat all around him was new and strange and powerful; the pain that it gave him was seductive and captivating as a lover. And the pain and the heat spiraled toward a more powerful intensity, until the crucible that held him began to glow.

He noticed, then, that his perspective was shifting again; that the deliciously powerful burning was fading from him. He was like a camera at the crucible's apex. The trilobite was down there below him, on the bottom of the crucible, and it glowed like the brightest ember of a fire. No, it wasn't a trilobite, not any more. It was . . . something mechanical. Sleek, fire-glowing cherry-red iron, complex and intricate as a design engineer's nightmare.

Something destructive . . .

It was a bomb. The thing was a bomb. A thermonuclear bomb.

How could Luke know that? He'd never *seen* a nuclear bomb.

Never mind, he thought. He knew.

And suddenly Luke realized that the crucible was no longer a crucible at all, it was a crimson-burning globe, strange and impossible as a surrealist's portrait of the world. As he watched the thing that had been the trilobite let loose and exploded in a plasma-cloud of atomic fire.

After a moment the mushroom receded, and the fire was just an ultra-bright pinprick on the face of the globe.

It's only one bomb, Luke thought. *An atomic bomb is bad, but the world can survive one nuclear bomb. It survived Hiroshima, didn't it? And Nagasaki?*

Then he noticed that there were tiny filaments of light spreading out from the explosion, like the strands of a fiery spider web.

And the sound of Luke's scream was so loud that it woke him from his sleep.

For a long moment after he woke Luke Munsen had no idea where he was or what he was doing there. He was in a high-backed chair with arm rests, dressed in thin-wool slacks and a tweed sportscoat. His shirt and his red-silk tie were sopping with the thick sweat that his dream had pulled out of him. It was day, and the air was cool and fresh the way city air is fresh on a slow day—crisp, clean, ever-so-faintly sour with yesterday's smog. He was in the cabin of a plane—yes, that was where he was, on the plane that went from Kansas City to La Guardia Airport in New York—he was in the cabin of the plane, only the plane was on the runway and the doors were wide open.

He was the only one in the plane. There was sound, harsh noises made faint by distance, somewhere out beyond the runway.

Luke shook his head, trying to clear it. Trying to make sense of his circumstances. What in the name of God was happening? Planes didn't land and leave their passengers sitting there, not in the world where Luke had always lived.

"Is anyone here? Where are we?"

There wasn't any answer. Not that he'd expected one. Luke knew from the *feel* of the plane that it was empty, but there was no way not to ask it.

He pulled himself out of the seat and stood for a moment in the aisle. He had to get out, figure out where he was. Had they landed in New York? If they had, he needed to find a phone, call Scott Lind—Scott had planned to meet him when he got off the plane, but it wasn't likely under the circumstances that Scott would even have tried to get to the airport, especially since Luke's original flight had been canceled. For that matter, Scott probably wouldn't be able to get here. The best thing, Luke thought, was to get a hotel room. If there was a hotel open and with a vacancy.

First I need to get myself cleaned up, at least halfway presentable—this filthy, I wouldn't even rent myself a hotel room.

And if he wasn't in New York, where the devil was he?

He took his suitcase from the overhead compartment, pulled out fresh clothes—shirt, socks, shorts, the navy suit he'd planned to testify in. It was the best he had with him; it would make him look respectable enough, hopefully, to get himself a room even with the situation as it was. Took the clothes to the plane's lavatory, where the tap—praise God!—was working.

Luke got a look out the plane's open door when he was on his way back to the seat to get his bags. The plane was in the middle of a runway, at least a quarter mile from a terminal that had seen a lot better days. The airport *was* La Guardia—over there, almost out of focus in the distance, was the Empire

State Building. At the far end of the runway in the other direction was Long Island Sound. There wasn't any sign of life anywhere in sight; no planes, no traffic on the highway off in the distance, no one on foot.

New York? Deserted? I can't cope with this. I need to curl up in my seat and go back to sleep.

He actually thought seriously about it for a few seconds. It was a crazy idea. Whatever was going on, it had to do with the President and the nuclear bomb and God knew what else. It wasn't safe here, out in the open. Even a hotel room wouldn't be safe, but at least it would be safer.

Luke Munsen should have stayed in that plane—he should have *known* not to leave. There were clues all around him, waiting for him to see them. The desertion all around. The fact that no one had bothered to wake him. The fact that the pilot hadn't docked the plane at the boarding gate. The Borough of Queens was so bristling with trouble that it was amazing that Luke Munsen survived even as long as he did.

He might never have died if he'd just curled himself back up inside his seat and slept out the rest of the day.

But Luke Munsen was rattled. All he could see was that he'd got himself into someplace dangerous, and that he had to get himself away, get to someplace safe and secure and . . . *sheltered.* The idea of it almost made Luke laugh—here he was, fearless Luke Growl-in-the-Faces-of-Fire-Breathing-Congressmen Munsen, burying his head in the dirt in the middle of a disaster. But what was he supposed to do, hike out to Scott's place on the Upper East Side, go on with his weekend tour of New York as though nothing had happened? Not likely. Chances were better than even that Scott wouldn't even be there when Luke got to Manhattan; the man had probably got his car out of the garage and got himself way the hell out of the city early last night, when the news had first begun to sound like real trouble.

I should have listened to that news. If I'd listened to the news and done what was sensible I'd be home now. Listening to the radio and trying to decide whether I wanted to try to get to the lab at a decent hour.

God. I wish.

The truth was, of course, that if he hadn't had a ten o'clock flight to make, Luke Munsen likely would have been in his lab the night before way into the small hours of the morning. And he would have died in the explosion that killed Ron Hawkins and the Beast.

He had no way of knowing that. He had, in fact, no way of knowing of the explosion.

Nor any way of knowing that his work had already begun to spread a plague.

So he set off across the broad, vacant runway, ignorant of his fate and far less afraid than he ought to have been.

In the near distance, just beyond the fence that set off the runway, he could see shabby houses, dingy apartment buildings. Cheap-built hotels that weren't cheap at all. Yes, this was La Guardia; Luke recognized the seedy, half-suburban architecture of this part of Queens.

It was an hour and a half before he saw another living soul. Forty-five minutes of that time he spent on the grounds of the airport, trying to get out.

The terminal buildings themselves were empty and locked up as tightly as they could be; locked far too well for Luke to get inside them. The runways were all fenced away from the streets outside. The fences were tall and topped with razor wire; the gates Luke could find were all chained and padlocked. Finally, in desperation, he looped his briefcase handle through the shoulder strap of his carry-on bag and climbed the fence in a spot where the razor wire had rusted through and fallen away. When he was nearly to the top of the fence the strap over his shoulder came loose and both his bags fell to the ground. He was about to go back for it when the palm of his left hand snagged in a jagged, rusty flaw in the chain link, and suddenly he needed something to be furious at, and the only thing he could think of was the bags that had dropped, and he said to hell with them, I don't need those goddamned clothes, those papers, anyway.

The truth was, of course, that he didn't. Luke Munsen didn't live long enough to need another change of clothes. He certainly didn't live long enough to need those papers.

Five minutes later he was on the far side of the fence, outside the airport. Heading toward the nearest of the hotels, which wasn't too hard since the hotels were the only buildings in this part of Queens that were more than a couple of stories tall.

The hotel was locked up as dead and dark as the terminal

had been. It took him another twenty minutes to find out that the three others he could spot were just as closed.

Where in the hell is New York hiding? Has the whole city run away from itself?

It just wasn't possible—New York was too big a place to evacuate overnight.

Everyone must be holed up in his apartment, hiding under the bed.

The way I ought to be.

He looked out onto the deserted highway that ran past the front of the closed hotel. *What am I going to do now? Hitchhike to Manhattan? Hitchhike—hell, there's no one on the road to give me a ride, even if people did pick up hitchhikers in this state.*

That was when he saw the bus. Far away, a pinprick in the western distance. A battered New York City bus, and even from here it looked to Luke as though the thing had driven all night through the fires of Hell.

the fires of Kansas

Literally: the thing was scarred by fire. Scarred by graffiti, and rocks. And when the bus got close enough for him to see it clearly Luke was certain that some of those words on the side of the bus weren't written in paint at all.

No. Those words, he thought, were written in blood.

bus to hell

I'm going to die if I get on that bus. I know it. I won't live three hours.

He was right about that, too—almost to the minute.

He didn't flag the bus down—he had enough self-control to keep himself from that—but he stepped out toward the curb, to watch it, and the driver stopped for him.

No, he thought, *I can't do this.* He tried to turn and run from the thing, but his legs ignored him. He wasn't in control of himself any more, not consciously. Something from deep in his id ruled him, some bit that lived in absolute terror of the emptiness in the streets. The bus was something horrible, his id knew that. But there were people inside it, at least, people that for all it knew were the last left alive in the world.

As the door opened the driver turned and smiled at Luke vacantly. The man's face was . . . wrong. *Vacant* wasn't the word to describe him; there *was* expression on the driver's face. Just not any expression Luke had ever seen on a human face in all his life. Like the expression he always expected to see on the face of an alien when he saw science fiction movies on television—only TV aliens were never *that* alien. Almost always when you saw those movies you got the impression that the costume designer was thinking about a dog or a horse or some bug, and not an alien at all.

Luke coughed. "I need to go to Manhattan," he said. "Does this bus go there?"

Luke waited for an answer with one foot on the bus's first step and the other still on the pavement. The driver didn't say a word—he just kept staring at Luke, strangely and quietly, his face painted and glowing with an expression that Luke could not understand.

A shout, from somewhere inside the bus: "Are you coming or ain't you? Get on the goddamn bus or get off of it. We ain't never going to get there, you keep us standing here in the middle of Queens."

Without even thinking about it, Luke stepped forward and up, and before he even knew what was happening the bus's door had slapped closed behind him, and the driver was slamming the transmission into gear, and they roared out and away so hard that the force of acceleration slammed him into a rail.

Oh my God—what have I done?

The bus was still accelerating.

For a moment he imagined that the bus somehow *was* bound for hell, imagined that he'd already died and reached some bizarre afterlife. *And if this bus is going to hell, does that make New York purgatory?* Even with circumstances as bad as they were, that thought nearly managed to drag a laugh out of him. *No. I'm not dead, and I'm not on a bus to hell. That's crazy thinking. Things are bad enough already; the last thing I need to do is go out of my mind.*

The man behind the steering wheel was definitely a New York City bus driver. He had on an MTA bus driver's uniform, and even though he was bone-thin and very tall it fit him perfectly. His jacket was filthy and torn in places, but unquestionably authentic. The man, Luke thought, was just in shock—that was why the strange expression, the filth, why he ignored Luke's question. Why, for that matter, the man was out here driving his bus today in the first place. That had to be it—the man was in shock and driving his bus aimlessly through the city.

Maybe, Luke thought, this was for the best, even if the driver was crazy. Sooner or later they'd have to end up someplace where the hotels were still open. It might take all day to end up in a place like that, but even if it did that had to be better than trying to walk to Manhattan. Which was the only other thing Luke could think of doing. He sighed, and relaxed a little; grabbed hold of the support pole near his left hand and climbed the last two steps to the floor of the bus.

Once he had his footing he reached into the back pocket of his slacks, digging for change to pay his fare. But when he finally had the money in his hand he saw that the fare box had been vandalized, and that there was no way to put the quarters into it.

"Should I give this to you," he asked the driver, "or—or what should I do with it?"

The driver ignored the question, just as he'd ignored the others Luke had asked.

Jesus. What am I doing?

This is crazy—just plain crazy. I've got to get off of this thing. He reached up and over, pulled the cord that made the STOP REQUESTED sign light up over the driver's head. "I'd like to get off, I think. If that's okay." The driver ignored Luke, and the sign, too. Worse than that, the man pressed even harder on the gas pedal, and the bus began to accelerate again.

I could yank him out of that seat, and stop this thing myself. The man was slight enough that Luke thought he could probably do it, even though he was pretty far out of shape himself. *I'd probably end up wrecking the damned bus—No. The only thing to do is sit this out and see where I end up. If nothing else, he's got to run out of gas sooner or later. Make myself comfortable and try to enjoy the ride.*

He put his money back into his pocket and took a look at the interior of the bus. It was a grim sight—grimmer, even, than the outside had been. There was the graffiti, of course, and the three seats that hung slack and broken from the wall. A two-foot gap in the floor near the well of the left-rear tire.

The sight that hurt worst of all was the people. The wreckage of the bus was nothing compared to them.

Luke had seen people like them before. They were

homeless, bag ladies, and derelicts. Junkies. Twenty, maybe thirty of them. There weren't many people like that in Tennessee, but Luke had seen them all the time during the three years he'd spent in New York getting his doctorate. Now that he was looking at them, Luke thought he could smell them, in spite of the air rushing through the bus's open windows.

Over there, five seats from where Luke stood, was a one-eyed woman who looked like she'd steeped for months in her own filth. Her socket was unpatched, open to the air; corruption oozed out of it and leaked down toward her nose. Two bulging plastic garbage bags lay on the floor near her feet, the contents of one of them spilling out, littering three feet in every direction.

A half-naked man clutching an empty bottle of Ripple had splayed himself across the floor and fallen unconscious. Crusty-dried vomit clung to the hair of his chest; his pants were half unzipped and stained badly with urine.

I don't belong here, damn it. I don't. I'm whole. I make a decent living. I'm doing something with my life.

There was an enormous woman sitting in two seats near the back door of the bus. She weighed four hundred pounds, to judge by the look of her, and her skin was as white and viscous-looking as the underbelly of a fish. Too much of that skin was showing; her clothes couldn't possibly cover all of it.

Don't think about it. If I think about this I'll go out of my mind.

Whiteman Air Force base,
Johnson County, Missouri

Damn those Russians, Paul Green thought. *Damn each and every one of them to the deepest pit in hell.*

How on earth was he supposed to have a war with the Soviet Union with those people throwing a revolution? It was exasperating. Infuriating.

Just now the plane was descending, getting ready to land and refuel at some damned Missouri Air Force base or another. It was good to be in the plane. Here in Air Force One Green was reconnected to the hub of the nation's defense apparatus again, for the first time in days. They still ignored his orders, but when he sat in this plane they could not keep him from hearing.

That's how he knew about the Russians, and about everybody else. The Soviets had tried to launch their nuclear arsenal as soon as they'd seen his two missiles heading at them over the Arctic Ocean, and their luck had been even worse than his own: not a one of their warheads had got more than a mile from its silo. Most of the missiles had exploded *inside* their silos, in fact; all of their missile bases had been destroyed, and destroyed with them were a third of the Red Army and most of the Soviet Air Force.

I should've expected it. They told me about this, too. The NSC man who'd briefed him last had gone into detail about the subject. The Russians didn't have good technical people, not in any numbers. Lots of good Ivory Tower-types, theory people. But no technicians. Not even on the lowest levels; they had to import their electronics from places like Singapore and (through third parties) South Korea. The Defense Department had a throttle on that—even the stuff coming out of Singapore—and they managed to keep the Russians from getting anything much more complicated than a video game machine. The Soviets still bought the stuff, and bought it in quantity. Those game machines were the best they could get, years ahead of anything they could produce themselves.

And, of course, the situation in the Red Army's missile silos was exactly what you'd expect, given the circumstances. There was complicated stuff inside a missile's guidance systems, and while they did manage to patch the things together, their maintenance people tended to do more harm than good. There was even one story that had managed to find its way into the Western press, about a technician (if you could call him that) who'd tried to clean rat droppings out of a missile's guidance system with a water hose.

In a fit of fury after the bombs had blown up in their faces, what was left of the Red Army had turned on the party apparatus and marched into Moscow. Even those divisions stationed in Eastern Europe were making their way back home—though it wasn't certain that they'd make it; a whole trainload of Soviet infantrymen had died in Poland, killed by a bomb that exploded as their train crossed the Vistula. Intelligence wasn't at all certain about that bomb; there was considerable suspicion that it hadn't been a bomb at all, but an antiaircraft rocket launched at the train by a renegade unit of the Polish Army.

As word of the nuclear explosions—and of the military uprising—spread through Moscow, the people had taken to the streets as well, whole mobs of them ripping party officials and soldiers—especially soldiers—limb from limb. There was word, unconfirmed, of similar uprisings in Kiev, Leningrad, Odessa, and Tbilisi.

Green's own government was in little better shape than the Russians'. Congress was in hiding—as it had been since he'd tried to have the Speaker of the House arrested—and the riots had most of Washington on fire. The military had its hands full keeping the mobs outside the gates of its bases.

Eight hours!

Eight hours, and every semblance of world order had disappeared. Most of Europe was still intact. Japan, too. But the superpowers were at their knees. At least for the moment. Word from Intelligence was that the leaders in Europe were going into hiding, too. They weren't taking any chances.

Air Force One touched down, its landing gear thumped and skidded three hard beats along the runway.

This wasn't the way it was supposed to be. How were they ever going to live out the prophecy if it kept going like this? How were they ever going to bring on the Rapture? How could they have a nuclear Apocalypse if there wasn't anybody else to fire missiles at them?

He had to talk to Herman about this.

Part of the prophecy was that the armies of Gog and Magog were supposed to do battle with the legions of the righteous. Gog and Magog were in Russia, that was clear as crystal. All you had to do was look on any old map from Bible times, and there Gog and Magog were, smack in the middle of the Soviet Union. *That* was Armageddon—the battle outside the gates of Jerusalem. How were they supposed to have Rapture without Armageddon—much less the nuclear Apocalypse?

The problems were getting tougher and tougher.

Praise God for foresight, Green thought. Months ago, when it first became apparent that there were forces in the government that would do anything they could to stop the Rapture, Green and his closest, secretest advisers (all of them were people from his church) had begun trying to place their

own people in command of the bases in the Midwest where the
nukes were kept. There weren't enough of his people in the
Air Force, or in the Army, to give Green real control of any of
the bases. But if he could get his people in command, Green
figured there were ways to *get* control of the bases. And his
people would have their orders. As soon as Green had ordered
the missiles out of their silos, his commanders would confine
the soldiers to their quarters, and bring in the armed militia
from the church. Once everyone was in place, the officers
would be dismissed, the enlisted men would be given the
option of becoming soldiers in the army of the righteous.

Their only real success so far had been at Eidner Air
Force Base, out in Cheyenne County, Kansas, where they'd
managed to put Bruce Thompsen in charge. He'd be enough,
if they played their cards right.

It was a dangerous plan, but it was working. Bruce
Thompsen had even managed to get a couple of his people
down into the missile silos. That had to be why those few
missiles had been launched, and no others. It was a real
accomplishment on Bruce's part, too: the men who worked
down in the silos were watched and screened very closely,
very carefully. And screened from the Pentagon, not just by
their base commanders.

Whiteman AFB, here, wasn't anyplace Green could feel
secure—no more than he could back at Andrews, in Washington. That didn't worry Green in any special way. He was
President, and because he was President there were some
things that no one in the country—military or otherwise—
could deny him. No matter how bad things were, no matter
what they felt about the things he was doing. His personal
safety. This plane. Air time on the television, during moments
of legitimate crisis. Oh, maybe they could've tried to stop
him—certainly the Army had guns enough to do whatever
they pleased. But the moment it raised a hand against him, the
Army would be by definition in a state of mutiny. What
American general could defy the Constitution and still live
with himself? Paul Green couldn't even imagine it; the sort of
man who was apt to become a career officer in the United
States' military was too steeped in the tradition of civilian
control to even see his own bias. Even the fact that the Chiefs
of Staff were ignoring his orders was unprecedented. No
matter how the events of the next few days unfolded, no

matter what the nation thought of their acts, the careers of the men responsible were at an end.

The plane taxied to a remote corner of the runway and came to a stop. Two minutes later Green saw the fuel truck coming toward them. Another ten minutes and the tanks would be full and he could get back in the air. Another hour—certainly not more than two—and they'd land at Eidner.

That was where he'd decided to go, as soon as he'd realized that it was Bruce Thompsen's men who'd launched the missiles. Herman would be there too, soon enough, and so would the others. And somehow they'd *find* a way to bring on the Rapture, no matter what it took.

PFC Bill Wallace was in a deep, cold sweat, in spite of the fact that the morning was the hottest in this part of Missouri yet this spring. There'd been rumors all over the barracks, all over the base, for weeks. Rumors about the President, and the Pentagon not listening to him. About nuclear war, and the fact that the generals were trying to stop it. The President, the rumors said, wanted a war for the war's own sake.

Bill shuddered, reached into the breast pocket of his uniform for a cigarette. Remembered that he was driving a fuel truck on the air base's runway, and swore at himself for nearly blowing himself and the truck to kingdom come.

Last night there'd been the explosion, far on the western horizon. Everyone who'd been awake had seen it, like a new sun rising from the wrong part of the compass, and that sun had burned long and bright enough to wake almost everyone before the sound and wind of the atomic explosion had reached the base—maybe a minute or so after the false sunrise.

Bill Wallace had been awake to see it all. He shouldn't have been. His duty-shifts had been in the day for a couple of weeks now. But he hadn't slept well these last few days; no one had. Three days ago General Simpson, the base's commander, had canceled all leaves and passes, closed and locked the base's gates. He hadn't stopped at that, either; he'd had every radio and television on the base collected and locked up for safe keeping, and that cut everyone off from the news. None of that had stopped the rumors about what was happening in the rest of the country. Crazy, self-contradictory rumors that had to come from people's nightmares. None of them were real enough to believe in.

The last certain thing that anyone had heard was that the President wanted to atom-bomb the Russians because they caught some friend of his trying to smuggle in a backpack nuke.

The man really wanted to put an end to the world. He was crazy, he had to be.

And now here he was, right here on this base, refueling Air Force One. You couldn't mistake that plane, sitting right there in the middle of the runway. Not that anyone was saying that was who it was.

And Bill Wallace was the one who had to refuel it.

It was a grave responsibility, and a terrifying one. And in a way, Bill thought, carrying it out was going to make him one of the most horrible war criminals in the world.

Maybe that was taking it too far.

Bill Wallace didn't have the world's largest sense of social responsibility. When he thought about global thermonuclear war, the thing that came to mind first was his own death. And still—and still—

This man was killing the whole goddamned world, killing it for no fucking reason Bill could see. And here he was, up to what evil Bill couldn't imagine, and all Bill Wallace could do was give fuel to the man's fire.

That thought made Bill feel sick with himself. Very sick. Which probably meant that he had a larger sense of responsibility for his world than he liked to admit. And he deserved to feel sick with himself, too, he thought: if he wasn't a part of a solution, he was a part of a crime.

Bill parked the truck a few yards from the plane's fuel intake, killed the engine. Two minutes later he had the hose out, the spigot clamped in. Turned the pumps on and let the tanks begin to fill. Which left nothing for him to do but wait the twenty minutes or so that the process took.

The tanks were halfway full when the escape door swung open over the plane's near wing. For a moment he was afraid that it meant some sort of trouble, that maybe someone was going nuts from having to cope with the ape-crazy President, and that Bill would suddenly have to get his gun out of the truck and rush to the defense of a man he thought a villain.

Then he heard the President's voice from inside the

plane—he'd heard it often enough on TV and radio to recognize it anywhere—heard the President saying something about fresh air being an improvement, even when it did smell like fresh kerosene.

Momma in heaven, Bill thought, *save us all from that crazy man*.

Another voice, farther inside the plane: "Yes sir, Mr. President." Probably, Bill thought, it was the pilot. Or even more likely, one of the plane's crew.

"You tell me something, son," the President said. "I want you to tell me something, and I want you to answer me honestly."

"Yes sir?"

"How come, when I pushed that button there in the situation room—and God damn it, I *know* it was the right button—how come when I pushed that button only three of our rockets got fired? And how was it that both of the ones that were headed toward where they were supposed to go just *happened* to fall into the ocean? Did you Air Force boys abort my missiles? *Did you do that to me?*"

My God, Bill Wallace thought, *the lunatic is* really *trying to do it. He really is trying to blow up the world*. He tried to swallow, reflexively, but his mouth was too dry and the contraction of his throat made him choke. Beside him, the fuel pump ka-chunked itself to a halt as the valves inside it realized the plane's tanks were full. *At least someone's trying to stop him. Maybe we'll all be alive tomorrow after all*.

The sound of the airman inside the plane gagging on his own tongue. "I wouldn't know, Mr. President, sir. I'm not cleared for that sort of information."

President Green cursed at the airman, and then Bill heard a banging sound that must have been the President pounding his fist on the plane's hard-plastic wall. And Bill thought: Wasn't President Green supposed to be some sort of a Bible beater? What was he doing cursing like a pimp? "Well then, son, you tell me, why don't you tell me: who the fuck do I got to talk to? Who the hell do I got to talk to around here to get a straight answer to a serious question?"

"Honest, sir—I haven't got the clearance for that kind of information. I've barely got enough need-to-know to get us around the hot spot out in Kansas."

"Well then, why don't you get yourself on that radio of

yours, and *find out* who the hell was responsible? And when you find out who it was, I want you to tell me his name and put him on the radio with me." A pause. "Don't just stand there—this is an order, son, from your President. Do you understand me?"

My God, Bill thought. *There isn't any hope. There really isn't. Somehow that man is going to get his hands around the right general's throat. It's going to happen—sooner or later, it's going to happen. And once he does, he's going to blow every last living one of us to kingdom come.* Through his mind's eye Bill Wallace saw the world that Green would leave behind him—a dead, dry, barren earth, scarred a hundred thousand times by glazed and glowing nuclear craters. And he hurt so bad inside at the sight of that world that all he wanted to do was curl up someplace and die, right then and there.

There wasn't time to curl up and die. There was a job in front of him to do. He reached over the plane's fuel tank, unfastened the clamp that held the hose in place. As he did, his left arm brushed against the cigarettes in his uniform pocket.

Cigarettes.

And matches.

The rich chemical smell of kerosene welled up through the intake valve.

Inside the plane, the President was shouting again. "Well, soldier? Do you have the man's name for me yet?"

And suddenly Bill Wallace realized that he was reaching into the pocket of his shirt. Taking out the matches. The cigarettes, too—if he was going to die he owed himself a last drag or two of smoke. Even if he had condemned himself.

What was he doing? This wasn't him. Bill Wallace didn't want to die. He wanted to finish this hitch and get himself *out* of the Air Force.

From the open door, above the wing of the plane: "Hey you—airman—what the hell do you think you're doing?" The man was in civilian clothes—Secret Service, most likely. Already he had his gun out. In less than a moment it'd be aimed at Bill.

Which meant that there wasn't time for cigarettes, or thinking, only for lighting the match, dropping it into the fuel intake, and—

Fire.

Fire everywhere, exploding, consuming, burning such fast, incredible pain, ruthless pain . . .

It was over for Bill before the explosion finished. He was the first to die by a second or two at least. The President and the eight inside the plane with him all were dead three minutes later; only the Secret Service man who'd tried to stop Bill Wallace survived the fire—the explosion threw his body much more than it engulfed him. The air base's fire trucks found him lying on the runway, and they did what they could for him, but it might have been kinder if they'd left him to die—the man spent his last twelve hours in a long quiet agony of burned away skin before his infections finally killed him.

The base's fire trucks were fast, and they did as best could be done, but even as soon as they reached the plane they weren't any use. The fire burned too hot, too bright. The chemicals and foams they had to fight it were too insignificant to choke a flame that raged so hot. Twenty minutes after Bill Wallace had dropped his match, the bodies of the President and the eight men with him were reduced to microcosmic dust, indistinguishable from the ash and fused metal that surrounded their remains.

Of all those who died in that fire, in fact, only Bill Wallace left enough of a corpse to gather up and bury. Three days after the fire, General Simpson, the base's commander, had those remains gathered up for burial in a quietly obscure corner of the base.

And he gave Bill Wallace a hero's funeral.

Queens Borough,
New York City

When Luke Munsen had finally resigned himself to the bus ride, he took a seat a few chairs up from the back door and made himself as comfortable as possible. That was a lot less comfortable than he'd have liked to have been; the woman in the seat behind him smelled powerfully of something that wasn't exactly urine, or sweat, or feces, but made him think of all three. There was some other scent mixed into her *melange,* too, but try as he did Luke couldn't place that smell. The mystery of it unsettled him most of all.

The bus's driver took them to a freeway of some sort.

Luke thought, at first, that he recognized it as the route that led from La Guardia to Kennedy airport, in the south part of Queens, but then they took a turn onto some other highway and for a too-long moment Luke was lost again.

He didn't get his bearings back until he saw graveyard all around him, and when he did he heard himself grunt involuntarily with fear.

The Interboro Parkway. He'd come this way by accident once, back when he was still in school. It led from the Grand Central Parkway out through this graveyard—a cemetery so large that it seemed to stretch to the horizon—and came to an end abruptly on the border between East New York and Bedford-Stuyvesant, a place so endless and so poor and so crowded that it made Luke feel cold and dead inside just to think about it. That day he'd come this way was years back, but the place had given Luke nightmares that still came to him sometimes. And that was in broad daylight, on a cold, clear winter day, in a year when there were jobs enough that no one was unemployed unless he wanted to be. It was a time when you could get lost in a place like Bed-Stuy and come out of it alive, and even unmolested. Especially if you moved quickly and kept your business to yourself.

But today. . . ? Luke shuddered. When times were hard Bed-Stuy was nowhere you wanted to be. Not by accident, not without a Sherman tank. If the rest of New York was hiding its head in the sand, Bed-Stuy would be out on the streets, tearing its already-ruined self to dust.

The highway was just as he remembered it, but worse. It wound its way from Queens to the worst part of Brooklyn through the graveyard in great, looping curves, gentle turns, but not so gentle as to allow anyone to drive safely at great speed. The bus's driver didn't have much concern for safety; he kept the gas pedal jammed down onto the floor. More than once Luke thought that the traction of their tires would betray them, that they'd all go skidding-sliding off into the cemetery. That might almost have been a good thing. The graveyard was quiet and eerie, almost beautiful in its way. The trees were dense and thick and full, the grass that covered the open ground was a deep, rich green. The stones themselves were old and ornate, elaborate and ancient looking. If he hadn't known that the driver was taking them down into hell, Luke might even have enjoyed the ride; the place reminded him of the make-believe haunted houses he'd seen in amusement parks.

As they drew closer to the highway's end, Luke began to see people off in the distance, turning over gravestones, setting fires. One man trying to destroy a mausoleum with a heavy iron pipe.

I've got to hide. To pretend I'm not here. The way I'm dressed, if any of those people see me they'll kill me. Every liberal bone in Luke's body wanted to believe that wasn't so. He wouldn't have raised a hand against a man because of the color of his skin—he *wouldn't*—but he was certain that the people in Bedford-Stuyvesant would kill him because of his. And if they didn't kill him because of his skin, they'd kill him because of the too-nice clothes he wore. He blushed at himself when he realized what he was thinking; there was definitely something bigoted about the whole chain of ideas. The people in Bed-Stuy were poor, hungry-hungry poor, and all but a few of them were black. But was he wrong? Would they kill him? God, he hoped that he was. He didn't want to die, even though he'd begun to see his fate written on the highway. Twice while he'd been in school he'd had to transfer from the Brighton-line shuttle to the A train, and that'd meant getting out of the subway and walking half a block along Fulton where it was at its worst. He'd seen the way the young men *watched* him, stared at him like he was a side of beef all ready to butcher and roast. And those had been good times. Even when the world was kind to them, the people in Bed-Stuy were poor and hungry enough to look at the rest of the world like they were cattle. And just now times were as far from being good as they'd been in Luke Munsen's life.

A few seats up and across the aisle there was a ragged man with a grizzly white beard who glared at Luke hungrily. Luke tried to ignore him, but it wasn't much use. Even when he couldn't see him, he knew the man was there.

A woman screamed somewhere far away, out among the headstones. Luke looked hard out his window, trying to spot her, but she was nowhere to be seen.

He was sweating.

His arm brushed against the glass vial in his breast pocket, and he took it out to check on the remains of the trilobite. It was still dead—still nothing more than the powdery grey ash it'd been since last night. In spite of his fear. In spite of the dream he'd had last night. Something in his heart was certain that the ash would resurrect itself any moment now—but that was obviously wrong. If the bug was going to resurrect itself, it would have at least started to change by now. The thing *had* to be dead—permanently dead.

He thought of the dream again. There was something prophetic in that dream, something certain—too certain to deny, even for a man who'd never taken such things seriously. He pictured the strongest part of the vision again: the image of the trilobite setting the whole world afire. If that was really so, if that really was something that was going to happen, then Luke was somehow going to be responsible for the destruction of the entire world. *Maybe I deserve to die*, he thought. The idea made him sad, but not completely afraid. Resigned. If he was the cause of some kind of a holocaust, his heart told him, then he *did* deserve to die.

The man with the grizzly white beard stared at Luke even more intently now. The vial, Luke thought, seemed to fascinate him. Luke had a sudden and senseless fear that the man would somehow scry out the vial's contents; he tucked it back into his breast pocket quickly, before the man could get any better a look at the thing.

It's over, he thought. *This, right here, right now—it's some kind of an ending*. He didn't understand the thought; if anyone had been inside his head to ask, he wouldn't have been able to tell where the idea had come from. Still, he didn't doubt it. He *knew*. The realization was that sudden, that sure—so real that he didn't even think to question it.

The bus rounded a final bend in the graveyard highway, and the road opened up into a fork. South and to the left was Penn Avenue, which led down into East New York. Fulton Street, the right-hand fork, ran eastward into the heart of Bedford-Stuyvesant. It didn't matter, Luke thought, which way the bus turned; either direction would lead them deeper down into hell.

But the driver didn't turn either way; he didn't even stop at the traffic light where the highway bled out into the fork. Instead, he kept the gas pedal pressed to the floor, and drove the bus straight into the tall brick tenement straight ahead of them, killing himself instantly, and smashing the bus into a strange tube of broken glass and twisted metal.

* * *

Luke woke twenty minutes later. There was a hand on his shoulder, and a voice in his ear, and his insides *hurt*—hurt bad as though someone had beaten him with a tire iron.

It was a boy's voice—twelve years old? Ten? Thirteen? Somewhere around there. "Mister, you got to wake up. You're alive—I know you are, you're talking in your sleep—and you got to wake up because it isn't safe for you to be here. There's people around here who'd skin you alive just to have a white man's hide hanging on their wall."

Luke tried to open his eyes, but it was a hard thing; the light made the pain in his gut more real, and opened up new pains in his head and neck.

"Come *on*, Mister. You can get up. I know you can."

Luke forced his eyes open, forced them to *stay* open this time. "I'm here," he said. "I'm okay." He was a long way from being okay, and he knew it.

"Okay, now, okay—can you sit up? If you can sit up I think you're going to be just fine. You ain't got nothing bloodied open, nothing twisted out of shape so as I can see it. If you can sit up, then it means that all your insides still hang together right. Go ahead, Mister—that's it, now. Try and sit up."

It *hurt* to move—hurt so bad that hurting wasn't the word for it. Luke Munsen didn't *have* a word for pain like that; he'd never lived that kind of pain before. *Please, God—let me die now, before I have to hurt any more. Please.*

There were other people from the bus lying on the ground, but none of them looked anywhere near as shaken as Luke felt. Behind him, the remains of the bus were afire, burning so hot that Luke could feel the warmth of the flame on his face even from here. Some of that warmth, he knew, came from the sunburn he'd got last night, when there should have been no way to get a sunburn. *There were more people than this on that bus. Are they all out of there already. . . ? Or are they still inside, burning to death?* He tried to get up off the ground, to get into the bus, to help get those people *out* of there. He tried but he could barely stand, much less get up and run.

"That's it, Mister. We're going to get you to a doctor now. My Daddy's got a car. He'll get you to a doctor, that's for sure. The big hospital toward downtown is still open today—I heard that from the men down at the fire department. Every other big building in the city closed up for the duration, and that hospital's still taking people in. Must be some brave kind of doctors in there, I'll tell you. If you can just get yourself as far as our building, my Daddy'll help you from there. Don't you worry, everything's going to work out just fine."

Luke tried to speak, but when he did the only sound that came out was a grunting noise, and the force of his breath hurt him so bad that he lost his balance, had to rest his hand on the boy's shoulder to find it again. When he tried to speak again, he held his voice to a whisper: "There were people on that bus—we have to do something. Help them. Save them."

The boy looked confused for a moment, as though the whole idea were strange and unreal to him. "Mister—look at that bus. Look at that fire. It's hot, *hot* hot. If there's anybody still inside there, he's already too dead for you or me to do him any good."

Luke's heart refused that at first; he heard himself stutter at the boy wordlessly in a low voice. He took a step toward the fire, another step, felt the heat of the fire move toward him in a shifted breeze, so hot that it dried his hair almost to the point of singeing.

The boy's hand, tugging at his sleeve.

"Mister, really, if anybody's still in there, there ain't anything either one of us can do for him."

Another gust of heat, and Luke felt himself dizzy—felt his knees buckle out from underneath him. The boy caught him before he could finish falling, and his thin, wiry arms pressed in the parts of Luke that were broken, and that brought the *hurt* back into him, and in the pain and in the daze there wasn't room for anything or anyone else. Not even room for Luke himself; when the boy led him away from the bus, he followed mindlessly, his mind blank and empty as the cloudless sky above him.

The walk was a short one—only half a block northwest along the street that bordered the cemetery—but for Luke it was an endless journey, each second split by agony into a thousand tiny, powerful shards. Each fragment of time so full of sensation that the sense of it was the sense of an hour.

There were young men (older men, too, but not so many of them) everywhere on the street, looting those stores whose windows weren't shuttered with metal. Not even the pro-

tected shops were completely safe; on the corner there were
six men, busy with crowbars, peeling away the store's steel
shutter one strip at a time.

Then, finally, the boy stopped, and led him to the
doorway of a tenement building whose first story was an
abandoned bodega. Led him into the building's entryway,
where for a terrified moment Luke thought that the boy was
going to lead him up the stairs.

Then he turned and let go of Luke's hand.

"You wait here, Mister. Me and my Daddy'll be down to
take you to the hospital in just a minute." The boy left, up the
stairs, without even waiting for Luke to answer.

*It'll be over, soon. The boy and his father will come down,
and they'll take me to the hospital, and they give me something
for pain. And fix me. I'll wake up in a few days, and all of this
stuff will be gone away.*

Luke leaned against the wall, breathed lightly, and made
himself as still as he could. When he was still, he could make
the pain . . . not go away, not exactly. But he could feel it
like it was somewhere else, almost like it was somebody else's
pain that he was borrowing for a moment. Almost all the pain
was in his gut—not just his gut; his whole abdomen, from low
pelvis to sternum. There was pain in his head, too, some sort
of a swollen knot. It didn't hurt anywhere near as bad as the
trouble lower down, but that had to be where the dizziness
came from.

The sound of the door opening. The boy. . . ? No, he'd
gone in the other direction. Up the stairway. Luke opened his
eyes, turned . . . and saw the filthy, greasy, glowering old
man, the one with the grizzly white beard who'd stared at
Luke on the bus. The man who'd seen the ash vial.

"You have something," the man said. His words were so
indistinct that they almost seemed to have melted together;
there was a spray of spittle from his lips as he spoke. "You have
something, and I want it."

He limped a little as he walked toward Luke; if the wreck
of the bus had harmed him in any other way, it didn't show
enough for Luke to see. The limp was slight enough, in fact,
that it could have been from an old injury.

"Give it to me."

"What do you mean? Give what to you?"

Without even thinking about it, Luke tried to clutch his

briefcase, and realized that he didn't have it any more. It was gone—left behind on the runway at La Guardia. Already he regretted losing it; there'd been important papers in that briefcase, some of them things that would be hard to replace. Things that he'd need Monday, when he testified for the Congressional committee.

What am I thinking? This man looks as though he's going to kill me, and I'm worrying about a Congress that may not even exist any more. And if it does exist, it won't be worrying about me on Monday.

But it *did* bother him. Not because of the hearings, or the trouble he'd have replacing the papers, or anything like that. It was more like . . . almost as though he was losing bits and pieces of himself. This far from home, it was almost like losing bits of his identity. First his bags, back when he was climbing the airport fence. Then losing control of his destination, when he got on the bus. And now this man wanted something more from him.

Luke knew what the man wanted. He wanted the one thing that Luke didn't dare to let go of, the one thing he had that was more precious than the self that he thought he was losing.

The vial.

"You know what I want," the man said. "I can see that all over your face. Give it to me now, and maybe I won't hurt you."

The man was close, now, close enough that Luke could smell him—bile, sweat, waste. The scent of something dead for a long time, and left exposed to the air. From here Luke could see tiny bugs—fleas, he thought—climbing around in the man's beard and through his hair.

"No," he said. "I won't give it to you. You can't have it." He pressed his hand against his breast pocket, to protect the vial—and felt nothing. An empty pocket. Before he even realized what he was doing, he said, "I don't even have it any more. If you want it, you'll have to go find it."

There was a crazy-wild look in the man's eyes. He shook his head, smiled wide enough to show that he was missing teeth. "You're lying to me."

"No. Not lying. I don't have it."

The man cursed, slammed his hands against Luke's shoulders, pounding the upper part of Luke's back hard into the wall. The man was stronger than he looked, stronger than ought to have been possible. "Where is it?" the man asked. "I saw you—on the bus you put it into your pocket." Hands, groping—patting Luke everywhere. "Where did you move it to? Where?"

"I don't *know* where it is."

Probing down into his groin, between his testicles—Luke tried to pull away, disgusted, and the man's fist slammed into his bruised, soft-swollen gut. That brought the *hurt* back more powerful than it had ever been. His body went limp everywhere, legs collapsing underneath him. All his muscles putty. Even the ones deep inside him; gases swirled around inside his intestines, moving of their own accord. His bladder emptied itself into his shorts. For a moment something deep inside him almost thought it was funny: *that* would keep the man's hands out of his privates. Then he caught another hint of the man's smell, and it wasn't funny at all any more. Filth wouldn't stop this man.

Nothing would.

The man cursed again, bent over, and lifted Luke's limp body up onto his shoulder; carried Luke out the door of the tenement, across the street, into the cemetery. As he walked the man's arm and shoulder dug deeper and deeper into Luke's abdomen, bringing him higher and brighter into an ecstasy of *hurt*. Luke kept expecting to pass out—how much pain could he feel, he wondered, before his mind slipped away into some dark corner of his self?—but he didn't black out, not until they were in the cemetery, and the man with the white beard let him drop, back-first, onto the ground.

When his head cleared, a few moments later, he was lying in the grass, mostly naked, and the man was tearing through his clothing one piece at a time. He tried to sit up, to tell the man to get away from him, but that wasn't any use. His body wasn't listening to him any more. And if it had been, the bearded man would only have ignored him.

From where he lay he could see a handful of tombstones, a scraggly tree and a handful of tall shrubs, and, over the shrubs, over the shoulder of the bearded man, the highest floors of the row of tenements that the boy had led him to. A woman with a Bible in her hand stood on the fire escape of the tallest building, and Luke could hear her shouting out at the world:

"Prepare yourselves," she said. Her voice was thunderously loud, it seemed to Luke—but at the same time it didn't seem as though she were shouting. "*Pre*pare yourselves! The end of all you've ever been is upon us, and the wrath of the Almighty awaits your sins!"

Not shouting at all—in fact, just the opposite. For all its thunder, her voice was gentle and soft and comforting.

"Listen, *listen* to the words in the Good Book: 'And there followed another angel, saying, Babylon is fallen, is fallen, that great city, because she made all nations drink of the wine of her fornication.'—You *look* in your hearts, children, and you *tell* me the true name of Babylon in our time! You *tell* me!"

Automatically, Luke felt the muscles of his throat trying to answer, in spite of the fact that he had no answer for her. The only sound his throat made was a faint grunt, or maybe a cough—partly because there were no words on his lips, partly because he didn't have the strength for speaking.

"That's right, children, that's right—Babylon is this city we all live in. And the end is at hand for all of us."

The bearded man had Luke's slacks off, now, and he was carefully ripping them to shreds, as though he expected to find some sort of a secret pocket hidden in among the seams.

"The time of *prophets* is coming, and it's already foretold here that you and I will be found wanting!—'And when they shall have finished their testimony, the beast that ascendeth out of the bottomless pit shall make war against them, and shall overcome them, and kill them. And their dead bodies *shall lie* in the street of the great city, which spiritually is called Sodom and Egypt, where also our Lord was crucified. And they of the people and kindreds and tongues and nations shall see their dead bodies three days and a half, and shall not suffer their dead bodies to be put in graves. And they that dwell upon the earth shall rejoice over them, and make merry, and shall send gifts to one another.'"

The woman charged on to some other idea altogether, but Luke's mind snagged on that last one. Back when he'd been in grade school, in catechism class, they'd studied the Book of Revelation. It had never made any sense to Luke, not even when the nun explained it all, but he remembered the passage the woman was reading. And she was leaving something out—about those prophets. The people weren't celebrating because the prophets were dead and left to rot away in

the streets. It was more like . . . like they were having
Christmas—or maybe it was celebrating Easter—because
three days later the prophets were going to rise up, come back
to life, and lead the people from their misery. Or something
like that, anyway; it'd been a long time since catechism class,
and Luke hadn't gone to mass in the years since high school.

Luke pictured prophets, ancient Biblical wise men, rising
up from the dead like trilobites in his lab. And he wondered:
would they be as hard to kill as the trilobite was? The whole
notion was pretty silly—silly enough that Luke started to laugh
without even thinking about the consequences, and brought
the *hurt* back on himself.

*Be still. I've got to be still, and live through this, and
maybe the crazy man will get tired of me and go away.*

The bearded man finished with Luke's slacks and let them
drop to the ground. There wasn't much left of those pants;
Luke wondered what he was going to do for clothes if he
managed to get himself free. Well, he was alive, at least—he
still had that much. So long as he was alive, did it really matter
whether or not he had clothes? It wasn't as though he'd freeze
to death without them. This time of year, even New York was
plenty warm enough, even in the middle of the night.

The man stooped, snatched Luke's suit coat up off the
grass. Started rifling the coat's pockets.

When he got to the breast pocket, the manic look in his
eyes turned wildly gleeful.

"You *dumbshit*," the man said. "You had it in that pocket
all along—but broken. I can feel it in there now, broken glass
and *powder*." He smiled so wide, so hard, that for a moment
Luke thought his face would split in two. Lifted his finger up
out of the pocket, to his lips, tasted the ash—

And screamed.

"You idiot! What kind of fucking junk is that? It ain't *no*
kind of junk—tastes like the ash from somebody's goddamn
cigarette! What fucking good are you? Tell me that—what
fucking use are you, carrying around an ashtray like it was a
vial of junk?"

*The man had thought that the trilobite's ashes were some
sort of a drug.* That *was* funny—or it would have been if Luke
weren't scared half out of his mind. The bearded man looked
murderously angry—and he was crazy enough, Luke thought,

that he wouldn't hesitate to kill. Not if that was what he wanted
to do.

"What is this shit—tell me that, huh? Why you carrying it
around like this? I bet you saw me coming. I bet you did.
Filled a goddamn crack vial with the stuff in your ashtray, just
to get me into this kind of trouble." The bearded man stooped
over Luke, his face not more than half a dozen inches from
Luke's own. "Tell me, God damn it—you planned this, didn't
you?"

Even if Luke had been able to speak, he wouldn't have
known what to say.

"Look at this shit," the bearded man said. He held the
jacket to Luke's face, so close that even though Luke's
breathing was faint, he could feel himself inhaling trilobite ash
through the open breast pocket. "You tell me what that is."

He didn't wait for an answer; instead he poured the ash
and glass into Luke's face, and smeared it into Luke's skin and
eyes with his rough-skinned hand. When he was done he
brought his fist down hard into Luke's nose; Luke felt his nose
break, felt shards of thin glass slide into the flesh of his cheeks.
"I'm going to kill you," the bearded man said. His fist came
down into Luke's face again and again, until the pounding was
only a strange jarring in the bone of Luke's skull, and then,
finally, no sensation at all.

After a long while, Luke felt the bearded man lift him up
onto his shoulder, and carry him away. He didn't see. He
couldn't have seen—his eyes had ruptured. A good while after
that he felt the heat and the impact when the bearded man
threw his broken body into the still-burning bus.

The fire there was much gentler, now. Low enough and
cool enough that it took most of twenty minutes for the heat to
cook Luke to death. That death would have been a long, slow
horror for Luke, but by the time it came for him he was long
beyond fear or pain.

Mountainville, Tennessee

The sun was coming up in Tennessee.

All night, smoke from the blazing fire at the Mountain
Institute had bathed the carcass of Tom the dog.

And much of that smoke had borne a peculiar and virulent

strain of altered bacteria—the strain that Luke Munsen had developed under contract to a natural history museum in New York. That bacteria infested everything in the general vicinity of the institute, now, and in Tom's remains they found something especially to their liking: they'd infected what was left of him, and set about doing exactly what they were designed and intended to do: recreating the original from the genetic evidence in the remains.

So Tom the dog woke from the dead at six in the morning, howling with the pain of being eaten alive.

It was the ants. It was the ants that were doing it. The same ants that had carried away his flesh the afternoon before—dissected and harvested him, bit by tiny bit—those same ants had woke promptly with the dawn, and continued their work directly.

Tom was alive again, now. Alive and being eaten alive.

Recreating Tom was, for the bacteria, simultaneously a more difficult task and a simpler one than the recreation of a trilobite had been. On the one hand, a dog is a creature infinitely more complex than a trilobite; on the other, there had been far more of Tom's remains for the bacteria to work with—there had been a great deal less work for it to do. Even given that after daybreak the ants were destroying Tom's flesh almost as quickly as the bacteria could rebuild it.

And the ants weren't taking away anything *that* vital, anyway. Mostly they were attracted to the bloody-open wound on Tom's left flank; the flesh they took was skin and muscle from his lower back and thigh. Nothing that a dog couldn't live without.

Even a dog that was already dead.

The real, critical damage to Tom was in his spine and skull—delicate, intricate bits of bone and membrane and ichor that the truck had shattered quite thoroughly. There were broken bones elsewhere, too, but they'd knit together long before his brain was anywhere near functional.

By five forty-five Tom's spine had been whole. The major portions of his skull had been recognizable not long after.

And now, at six his brain—which the truck's bumper had pulped and scrambled and pressed up into his sinuses—was functioning again, and Tom the dog woke thinking of evil, violent, vicious cats, who killed him with trucks, then brought him back to life with a pound of skin and muscle missing from his left hindquarter.

Tom woke, and he stood up on the three legs he had that could hold him, and he screamed with pain and shock and in indignation at his own existence. And because it was his instinct to run or to fight when there was trouble, and because there was nothing visible to challenge, Tom *ran*. That was certainly for the best, since the act of running shook free all but a few of the ants that infested him. And his upper leg began to heal over quite quickly.

The pain in Tom's leg began to ease when the dog was a couple of miles from the spot where he'd woke. A few minutes after that he realized that he wasn't certain why he was still running, and his run faded down toward a trot and finally a walk.

Tom was confused. There was something. . . . A truck. . . ? A car, maybe. . . ? A road. . . ?

The dog wasn't even altogether certain where he was; the long, hard run had taken him in a direction he'd never explored before. The whole world, it seemed to Tom, was strange and unsettling.

Then he remembered.

The smell of cat. It was a cat that had caused all of this. All the pain. All the confusion. The scent of cat was overlaid in Tom's brain with the scent of his own death.

Cat.

Tom wanted to kill him a cat, and Tom the dog had never killed anything in his whole life. The truth was that he wasn't even completely certain how to go about killing, though at the moment that absence of knowledge didn't seem to Tom to be terribly important.

Even if he had no idea how to go about accomplishing it, it was there and then, in that strange and alien knot of woods, that Tom the dog was imbued with his sense of mission. He was going to kill him a cat. He was going to kill him every damned cat in the world.

By noon he'd forgotten cats, and forgotten exactly what his mission was. But the sense of mission stayed with him, and the determination it gave him guided the dog as long as he lived.

* * *

Similar things were happening not far from where Tom the dog stood, in the ruin that had been the Mountain Institute. The bacterial strain that infected Tom festered and fermented in the corpses of the Beast and Ron Hawkins— where it found human flesh even more to its liking than dog meat. But their bodies were buried deep, under tons of rubble, and the weight of that rubble crushed the life from them even as the microbes worked to reconstruct the two.

The infection was spreading, too—through the wind that blew over the still-warm wreck of the institute. In the water that ran through the stream half a mile away. Everywhere that Tom the dog walked.

But the worst infection—the most powerful by far—was in Brooklyn, in New York City. In the ash that the weathered junkie had ground into Luke Munsen's face—and scattered into the soil of the graveyard around them. The ash was alive and teeming with the bacteria. *That* was the thing Luke had missed, the thing that his dream had tried to drive home to him: the trilobite wasn't impervious to fire. The consuming heat had, in fact, destroyed every microscopic trace that ever the trilobite had existed.

But the flame didn't sterilize the microbes.

Nothing could sterilize them.

Luke Munsen had brought a plague onto the face of the earth. And the plague was so powerful, so inevitable, that not even the fires of hell would drive it away.

BOOK TWO

Resurrection

Saturday
July Sixteenth

Leigh Doyle's dispatch
from Moscow,
as transmitted by modem
to the offices of the
National Interlocutor.

MOSCOW, WAITING FOR THE END

They rounded us up today—every American man, woman, and child they could find in the city of Moscow. Only excepted were those already inside the gates of the Embassy. The Soviets have treated us with civility and grace. Invading the United States Embassy would have been a violation of that civility, and no one here expects that of them.

They keep us in an Army barracks, but they do not keep us badly. There are telephones here, at least a dozen of them. No one has had trouble getting through to the States. Nor Europe. There have been two meals since first we were arrested. Both of them at least as good as the questionable fare served in Moscow hotels. The room where they keep us is big, well-lit, well ventilated; bunks line its northern wall.

Windows line the wall opposite.

I have spent these hours since my arrest watching Moscow through that window as I listen to my fellow detainees talk to one another behind me. Occasionally I look back to see them. For all that we are held prisoner and those out on the streets still walk free, the sight of them is grimmer. All of them out there are frightened, running; they walk as though the weight of the death of the world rested on their shoulders.

Perhaps it does. There are rumors here that nuclear war has begun. They are only rumors. The only hard and fast clue we have is the vague brightness on the east and south horizons. And the fact that this brightness has not dimmed as the day has worn toward evening.

Late in the afternoon I began to see something new about the furtive men and women who passed outside. Something more alarming than fear or dread: blood. Not one who passed after three looked untouched by violence. By four the sound of gunfire could be heard plainly in the distance. By five, when it drew dusky, I thought that I could see the edge of a riot spilling out into an alley not far from our barracks.

Moscow is waiting for the end of the world. It is not waiting quietly.

Leigh Doyle's dispatch
from Moscow,
as it appeared
(after editorial alteration)
in the National Interlocutor.

Exclusive to the National Interlocutor!

REDS RIOT OUTSIDE THE KREMLIN

Those Godless commies are at it again—trying to beat each other's brains out at the worst possible moment.

Incredibly, when our nukes took off for Moscow,

*red workers in Moscow took to the streets, where
they may well have thrown their no-good leaders out
onto their rears!*

    *Our own National Interlocutor reporter, Leigh
Doyle, was in Moscow just in time to see the commies
pull out their guns and start shooting their own
people dead.* "We could see a vague brightness on the
horizon," said Doyle, "as though a nuclear bomb had
exploded. And then there were mobs rioting in the
streets."

    *Leigh watched the riot from the window of the
building where the Russians are holding her prisoner. The commies arrested her, along with every
other American in Moscow, right about the time our
missiles first went up.*

(continued on page 46)

Washington

    Vice President Graham Perkins was an uneasy man.

    He was in a small, nondescript car, on the Beltway, and
he was afraid for his life. He had reason to be afraid; early that
morning the riot had found two congressmen and a Senator
hiding in an obscure hotel, and the mob had torn them limb
from limb. There'd been a camera crew on hand to record the
scene in gory, colorful detail.

    Graham had watched the tape three times now.

    There were three men in the car with him. Secret Service
men. They were taking him from Blair House, which had been
his home for the last eighteen months, to a place so hidden that
they wouldn't tell him where it was, or even mention it by
name. Blair House, they said, wasn't safe any more. Now that
Paul Green was dead, now that the people *knew* Paul Green
was dead, the mob was looking for Graham. They were taking
him to a place where he'd be safe until the nation calmed. A
place where the Speaker of the House would give him the oath
of office. Graham knew the Secret Service people were right to
be so careful, but still, he wasn't comfortable with the way
they'd taken possession of him. Wasn't comfortable with the
fact that the car they took him in wasn't a limousine, but a
weathered-looking Toyota with a sunroof. And most of all he

wasn't comfortable with the fact that they wouldn't tell him where they were going.

The car, at least, they had a sensible explanation for: a limousine would be much too conspicuous. If one of the mobs found them in the streets, it might well rip a limousine to shreds on principle. A car like this one, the driver had said, would be noticed by no one. Graham was inclined to agree.

It wasn't just the riots or the coarse Secret Service men that left Graham Perkins ill-at-ease. He'd been uneasy for two years now, since the summer when Paul Green had chosen him for a running mate. And with good reason.

Two days ago that crazy man had pressed a button, and before anyone had been able to stop him two counties in western Kansas had disappeared in a cloud of light and subatomic dust. And Graham knew that, as much as any one man could be, he was responsible for the fact that the lunatic had been in office in the first place. That responsibility, and the guilt that came with it weighed on Graham in the worst possible way.

Then, yesterday, Paul Green had died in some kind of an accident on Air Force One. The details weren't clear yet—the truth was that the whole situation looked pretty damned suspicious, even from this distance—and that meant that Graham was President. Or would be, once he took the oath of office. There were parts of Graham that thought he should feel—something. Happy? Excited? No; neither of those. A man had to die for him to become President. Graham could admit it to himself when he saw he'd been a coward, but there wasn't enough ghoul in him to be happy or excited at another man's funeral. He should feel some sort of a thrill, at least, he thought. What he felt was dread, ordinary, everyday, terror-struck dread. The nation was a wreck. The *world* was a wreck. Washington was still swarming with riots; last night both the White House and the Capitol had burned to the ground.

This wasn't a time when any sane man would want to be President. But now more than ever, the country needed the order and continuity—the sanity—that only the Presidency could give it. It was a matter of duty. Graham had done the nation a serious disservice two years ago, and he knew it, and his conscience demanded that he do what he could to amend the damage he'd done. Even if that meant risking his life—not just risking it; throwing his life away, like as not. Paul Green was already dead. So were the legislators that the mob had found this morning.

The Beltway took a deep, broad curve, crested a hill so steep that there was no way to see beyond it until they were on its far side—

—and the highway up ahead was blocked, clotted solid with cars and people. It made no sense—had the mobs gone suicidal? What were so many people doing here on the highway, where the traffic moved fast enough that it was hard for a car *not* to kill a man on foot? Someone—maybe one of the leaders of the riot—must have been in an accident. That had to be it. Or maybe they'd found another congressman.

Graham shuddered, tried to calm himself. He had to try to be inconspicuous—if he let himself be afraid it was certain that someone would recognize him. He had to hide his face. There—beside him on the seat. A newspaper. *Today's* newspaper. Irony, there; an almost surreal irony. The whole world was coming apart at the seams, and the newspapers were still coming out on time. More than on time—yesterday afternoon the *Post* had published an extra edition. The radio and television stations were all doing fine, too. And hadn't he heard today on the radio that the *National Interlocutor* had gone to a daily publication schedule for the duration of the crisis? The same way Nightline had got its start a few years ago, when the Iranians had taken the embassy hostage. Well, let the press make hay out of tragedy. Sooner or later, Graham thought, the riots would find their way to the papers and the stations. It was a matter of time—and not very likely all that much time, either.

The car was at the edge of the mob, now. Still moving, but moving slowly; no one was trying to stop traffic, but the crowd wasn't trying to get out of harm's way, either.

Someone was going to spot him, recognize him. He was sure of that. He buried his face deeper in the newspaper. Tried to read, in spite of the fact that it was impossible to concentrate. The front page was all full of the news he'd been living for two days; vanished counties in the state of Kansas, President Green dead in a fiery accident. The Soviet Union half destroyed by its own missiles, and crumbling politically. He opened the paper, partly to run from news he didn't think he could stand to read again. Flipped the page, and turned it again—there were strange headlines on page seven. Headlines

like something out of a bad novel. Or, for that matter, out of
the pages of the *National Interlocutor*.

A photograph that looked as though it were a still from a
low-budget film.

There were people all around them now, so close that as
the car passed their arms all but touched the Toyota's windows.
Why were they all here, on the highway? Twice Graham felt
himself beginning to look up, trying to see what the commotion was all about; he only barely managed to catch himself
before it was too late.

BIBLICAL NEMESIS CREATED IN GENETIC LABORATORY, the headline said. Yes, it *was* the sort of headline he'd have expected to
see if he'd picked up the *National Interlocutor* in a supermarket checkout line. It certainly didn't belong in the *Washington
Post*. Had the paper's editors lost their minds? The crisis was
bad enough that everyone was coming unhinged. Still, Graham expected better from the people at the *Post*. The photo
beside the story was . . . well, it made Graham feel ill to
look at it. Disgusting. A *creature* of some sort, covered with
grey, patchy fur. Several heads grew from its neck; only one of
them looked alive. There were peculiar growths on the face of
the living head—Graham thought they looked like misshapen,
misplaced teeth.

The sound of the crowd outside the car was softer,
now . . . or did it just seem that way? He wasn't sure. He felt
calmer, less threatened; almost as though the crowd were less
frightening a presence. It was the *thing* in the paper, he
thought. There was something absorbing about the strange
creature in the photograph. Captivating enough to pull his
mind away from the crowd. Soon they'd be past it, and he
could relax. To a degree, at least.

The article was from UPI, and it was very carefully
worded—full of "reported"s and "according to"s, very careful
to avoid stating anything as a fact. Apparently a newspaper
reporter down in Tennessee had actually seen the thing, and
photographed it. Police had been on the scene, and UPI had
direct quotes from them.

The Toyota wasn't moving any more.

Speculation was that someone had created the creature in
purposeful imitation of the creature from the Book of Revelation, but no one from the laboratory would speak on the
subject. Or wouldn't speak on the subject when there was still

a way to get in touch with them—two nights ago the building that housed the laboratory had been bombed, and now the whole place was closed indefinitely.

Something heavy thunked on the window not far from Graham's head.

Was the story real—or was it some sort of a hoax? It sounded as though it might have been real. And there was the photograph. It *could* have been faked. Graham had certainly seen more fantastic—and more realistic-looking—things in movie theaters. Certainly the *Post* wasn't trying to start a hoax itself; the way the story was couched made it all too clear that the editors found the story as incredible as any sensible reader would. Conceivably it was a practical joke on the part of a few Tennessee police and newsmen. Good sense said that it wasn't just possibly a joke, but likely one. He squinted at the grainy photograph . . . there was something about it. Something that nagged at him.

Graham knew what the nagging was, even if he didn't want to admit it. It was *real*. His intuition was sure of it. It was absurd, but he believed the story.

But if it *was* real, what did it mean? Was the creature actually the Beast from the Book of Revelation? Was it a sign that the beginning of the end of the world was at hand? Graham thought about the events of the last few days, and had to admit to himself that it was a real possibility. Still, it didn't ring true. It was almost as though . . . as though someone were trying to make the world believe that the events described in the Book of Revelation were about to take place.

"Keep your head down," the driver said quietly, casually, almost in a whisper. "Relax, keep reading the paper, and whatever you do, don't look up."

Graham's heart lurched.

There was a sidebar to the article—more a list of facts and figures set off in a box than a sidebar, really. A list from the NIH (amazing, Graham thought, that they were still functional enough to be handing out lists), of projects currently underway at Tennessee laboratory. He scanned the list, trying to spot the project that had produced the creature. None of them seemed very likely—but there was one project that caught Graham's attention: something funded by the Museum of Natural History, up in New York, for rebuilding prehistoric creatures from fossil traces of DNA. Fantastic stuff; it stirred Graham's imagination.

The car was beginning to move again, but ever so slowly now—barely even moving at all. Then, suddenly, it came to a dead stop again, and Graham realized that there was a terrible silence all around them.

Before he could stop himself, before he realized what he was doing, Graham stole a glance upward—and gave himself and his life away.

There were faces all around them, staring in at him. *Watching* him.

"It *is* him," someone shouted. "Get him—drag him out of there."

And everything went mad.

Someone tried to open his door, but it was locked, of course. Others were pounding on the glass, trying to break it.

"Don't worry, sir. This car is armored. The glass is specially reinforced."

It was true, Graham realized. Half a dozen people were pounding on the window beside him; one man had already got himself up on the trunk, and he was trying to kick in the rear windshield. But the glass held.

The driver began to force the car forward, gently, steadily, through the crowd. *He's going to kill somebody,* Graham thought. *More than one of them, if he doesn't stop.* He was about to tell the driver to stop when he realized how absurd the idea was—the mob outside meant to kill him. There wasn't any question in his mind about that. *Let the man do his job, if you want to get out of this alive,* he told himself. The idea of killing other people so that he could live himself left Graham sick with himself, but not sick enough that he wanted to give himself up to the mob.

He looked out his window, into the eyes and faces of the crowd; as he did he could feel the fear showing in his own eyes. That was dangerous, he thought; showing his fear would only excite them. There was nothing he could do about it; just then there was no way he could have hid the fact that he was scared, no matter how hard he'd tried. And he had to see their faces, had to see for himself what it was that drove the riot.

What he saw surprised him, and unsettled him even more deeply. There was hatred in the eyes of the people outside. And powerful lust for blood. Both those things he'd expected;

they were conditions necessary to bring ordinary people to riot. The thing that shocked him was the fear—absolute, stark terror hiding just behind the fury in their eyes. *They're even more frightened than I am,* he thought. *Of course they're frightened. It's the end of the world, and they think that I'm to blame for it.*

Something hard and dense hit bottom in Graham's gut. He looked away from the window, toward the floor, and covered his eyes. *And maybe they're right. Maybe I am to blame.* As soon as he'd thought it, he wanted to shout *No! I'm not to blame! It's not my fault! I didn't elect that man—you did!* Still: he didn't shout, he didn't even open his mouth, because he knew he'd had his place in bringing Paul Green to power.

The sound of hard-metal cylinders clanking together, inches away from Graham's ear—so sudden, so unexpected in a moment so tense that he nearly screamed in surprise. Clenched his teeth, to keep his quiet, to keep from completely losing his self-control. Turned his head, too fast, too hard, and saw that the Secret Service man beside him was holding a machine gun.

They *all* had machine guns.

Oh my God. Oh my God.

It was going to be a bloodbath. People—hundreds of people—were going to die horribly. Because of him. In front of him. Graham pictured them, bodies burst by machine-gun fire, bones and sweetbreads open to the air, blood all over everything oozing. Gushing.

A bloodbath.

Their blood would be on his hands, he realized. Literally. So much of it would get on everything.

The car was moving more quickly, now—grinding and thumping over the bodies of the people who'd been in front of them. Even with the car's windows closed, even with all the other noise, Graham could hear their screams as the weight of the car crushed the life from them. It wasn't clear up ahead, though. There were plenty more people to replace the ones that the Toyota's tires crushed.

How, he wondered, could he live with himself after this? How could he show himself in public?

He couldn't, he realized. Even if he got out of this alive—and he was going to, he was pretty sure of that—his career in politics was over. He couldn't live with this. He didn't *want* to live a life that could ever bring him to this ever again.

The man beside him unhooked the latches that held the Toyota's sunroof, began to stand.

My God. He's going to start shooting people. Wasn't it bad enough that they were crushing people wholesale under the car's tires? Bad enough they were killing people with the car, but there was no need, no call for gunfire.

"No," Graham said. "Don't do that."

The Secret Service man ignored him.

"God damn it, *stop*." Graham grabbed hold of the man's belt, tried to yank him back down into his seat. For all the difference it made he might as well have been trying to force a bronze soldier to sit; the Secret Service man was in much better shape than he was.

The sound of the machine gun was deafening. The man fired at the rioters all around them, but most of all he fired at the ones in front of the Toyota, and they picked up a little speed as that part of the crowd fell more easily under their tires.

Tiny spatters of blood began to land on the car's windows as the bullets sprayed out into the mob.

A scream welled up, somehow, from directly beneath Graham's feet.

No more killing, please, God. Just let me get out of here without killing anyone else.

The man who'd been standing through the sunroof ducked back into the car.

"The road is blocked up ahead," he said. "Looks like a big pile-up, maybe an accident that brought the mob here in the first place. We'll have to go around to the shoulder."

"Right."

The driver bore gently to the right; a moment later the man beside Graham was standing up through the sunroof again, blasting away at the crowd with his machine gun. The shooting seemed to Graham to go on forever, and while it was obvious that they were moving, if they made any progress Graham couldn't see it. Eventually he began to feel numb and out of phase with the horror around him. The only event that stood out in all of it was the one when the man with the gun came down to change ammunition clips.

Then, suddenly, it was almost clear up ahead of them. They were at the shoulder of the highway, which wasn't much of a shoulder at all—six, maybe seven feet of gravel, and then the land seemed to sheer away from them. Almost more a grass-covered cliff than it was a slope.

Off to what was now their left, beyond the wrecked cars, Graham could see that the highway was clear—wide open and empty of chaos. *A moment, now. Just another moment and we'll be free. Praise God.*

Then, just as they were getting around the smoldering Dodge that jutted furthest out into the shoulder, both of the Toyota's right tires lost their grip on the cliff-edge of the shoulder, and suddenly they weren't moving at all any more. The driver floored the accelerator, shifted into reverse, and floored it again, but it barely even caused the Toyota to budge.

We're going to die, Graham realized. There was a tiny, guilty part of him that was resigned to the fact—hat part of him almost welcomed dying. But the loudest thing in his heart was a desperate need to live, to let out the scream of horror that he kept sealed inside him.

In that moment, if Graham had had a gun in his hand, he'd have rolled down the window beside him and started firing out into the crowd.

And he would have enjoyed it.

The driver was cursing, trying and trying to rock the car into motion. It made no difference, and it was even making matters worse; each time the driver tried it, the car seemed to rock a little less than it had the time before. The man beside him was on a cellular telephone, calling for help that couldn't possibly reach them in time.

Up above, the man who'd sat beside Graham was still shooting out into the crowd, almost but not quite managing to keep them at bay. When he ducked back down into the car to refill his clip again, the mob surged forward—so many of them, so fast, so hard that just the weight of them was enough to tilt the Toyota so that it balanced on the cliff-edge.

A moment later the man beside Graham was standing, blasting away at the crowd again, but by then it was already too late. The mob could see what it had done. In spite of the gunfire they pressed the car further off balance. It didn't make any difference that they were dying; the ones behind huddled with the dead before them, shielding themselves and *pushing*.

The Toyota tipped, and tipped, lost balance and fell down the almost-sheer slope. It landed hard, upside down, crushing the head and torso of the man beside Graham.

His blood was everywhere, thick and wet and warm all over Graham, who hung by the waist from his seat belt. Blood in his hair, his face, soaking through his shirt and jacket, plastering them to his skin. Worst was the blood that kept seeping into his eyes. He tried to blink it away, but when he did the stuff dried so quickly that it glued his eyelids to themselves, and wiping away the blood with the backs of his hands only made things worse because there was gore on them, and something rough and gritty, too, and he had to pull his hands away because the gritty stuff *burned* the delicate skin of his eyelids, and scraped them like sandpaper. It left his eyes sealed shut completely, and Graham couldn't see at all.

A moment; two, and then the sound of the front doors opening. A breath after that and there was gunfire again—from the two men who'd been in the front, Graham assumed. The seat belt cut into Graham's waist terribly, but blinded as he was he didn't dare try to release it.

Not that it mattered. It was only a few moments later that the sound of machine guns went silent, and then the mob was yanking off his seat belt and dragging him out through the open driver's side door.

He forced his eyes open in spite of the burning and the tearing of dried blood.

And saw people, furious people, crowding all around him. Pounding on him. Someone had found a rope somewhere— no, not a rope, a thick, strong nylon cord. And someone tied a loop and a slip knot in the rope, and wrapped it around Graham's throat.

They dragged him back up the hill by that rope, strangling him with his own weight and with the friction of his clothes against the grass. Deep into the soft flesh of his neck as the cord dug, it didn't dig deep enough to black him out. Because the tightness of the cord pressed and crushed away his voice, he watched and listened in silent horror as they finished hauling him up the hill. Threw the loose end of the cord up into the air three times, until it caught on a spike that protruded from high up on a concrete pillar. And used that spike as though it were a pulley.

To hang him.

What kills a man quickly and mercifully when he's hung from a noose and scaffold isn't the choking and strangling of the rope. Even a heavy man suffocates from his own weight so slowly that his death is cruel and long and hard. No—compassionate headsmen make great effort to avoid that sort of execution. The thing that actually kills a hanged man is the snapping of his neck as he drops and then his fall stops sudden as the rope and the fine bones beneath his skull absorb the full impact of his descending bulk. It's a fast death, and a kind one, as executions go.

Graham Perkins was not a heavy man. Just the opposite, in fact—he was a spare man, and his bones were especially fine and thin. It would have needed a skillful executioner and a high scaffold to hang him properly. And the men and women who hanged him were not experienced, and even had they known of the need to use a scaffold, there was none available for them to use.

Which was why Graham Perkins died one of the most horrible deaths imaginable, dangling from a spike at the edge of the highway for three hours, struggling, eyes wide open. Screaming a scream that came from his throat as a faint hiss that no one could have heard four yards away.

After three hours, the exertion and the lack of air finally stole his mind away from him. The last half hour of his life, at least, was filled with gentle black oblivion.

Mountainville, Tennessee

Late that afternoon—about the time that the nation's Vice President was finally strangling to death at the edge of a highway—something collapsed in the deep basements of the ruin that had been the Mountain Institute. And when that basement gave way, the rubble that crushed the bodies of Ron Hawkins and the Beast sifted down into the void.

And left the corpses unburdened.

And the peculiar infection in their dead flesh set to finishing the task it had already begun: recreating life from the dead.

By midnight the work was half finished. And on Sunday morning Ron Hawkins woke from the dead in a dark hollow deep inside the ruin. And yawned and stretched as though he'd never died.

Brooklyn

Recreating Luke Munsen was a task at once simpler and more complex than the rebuilding of the dog, the creature, or Ron Hawkins. After the fire inside the bus had finally died away, his body had been set out on the grass inside the cemetery, and it had been left undisturbed. The infection had been deep inside him, even before he'd died, and because of that there were parts of Luke that had been rebuilt almost as quickly as they'd been destroyed.

The problem with remaking Luke was that he hadn't just died—he'd died and then his flesh had cooked long and slow inside the smoldering bus.

Most of him the microbes could rebuild from the DNA blueprint inside all his cells. If that were necessary. What it couldn't do, what it couldn't find anywhere in the blueprint or in Luke's corrupted flesh, was the chemical memory that had been Luke Munsen. His character. The *mind* that the fire had cooked away from his brain. Some of it was still there, of course; the fire didn't roast him thoroughly enough to destroy it all. Long stretches of memory and desire remained inside him, still intact. And the deepest, most important facts about Luke—the ones so essential to his nature that they permeated every iota of his being—those were indestructible.

Indestructible or not, the *Luke* inside Luke Munsen was violated by the fire, and violated more horribly than the weathered junkie who killed him could ever have violated his physical self.

And because his deepest self had been so violated by death, Luke Munsen was alive and whole physically long before he was able to wake from the dead. What he did instead of waking was dream—dream long and hard through the memories that still remained to him as his unconscious struggled desperately to reconstruct some semblance of itself.

And the thing he dreamed most clearly of all was the day of his grandmother's funeral.

He was sixteen that year. He remembered the day clearly, and in detail, in spite of the destruction of his mind, in spite of the fact that it was a day he'd rather have left behind him forever. His mother had cried and cried that day, but she'd cried most of all when there were people around to see her grief. And those times when she thought that there was no one to see her, her eyes had been dry and predatory.

Luke Munsen had loved his grandma, and the idea that she wasn't anything but food for the worms had made him deep and quietly sad. And seeing his mother turn Grandma's funeral into an opportunity for theater had made him ashamed for his mother and for himself.

Then the funeral service was over, and everyone was in black limousines, twenty of them, and they were riding across three counties to the cemetery where his grandpa was buried, and the now-open grave beside it, meant for her.

The ride took forever and a year, and all the way what Luke wanted was to be alone, to be alone and cry where he wouldn't have to be theater. He couldn't be alone because the only way out was to demand that the driver stop the car and let him off, and that would have been a scene worse than anything his mother could do, and he knew it. He never minded making scenes, not at that age, not if he had a mind to make them and thought he was right, but he loved his grandmother and he respected her, and he wasn't about to shame her, not even if she was already dead.

So he sat there as the limousine rolled across three counties, ashamed and grieving to himself, listening as his mother talked about his Grandma's will in a hungry tone she couldn't quite disguise. Luke's mother went on about all the time and care she'd lavished on Grandma these last few years, and he thought how maybe that was true, but even then, young as he was, he thought it was repugnant to want money because you'd given someone your time and love.

Then they were pulling through the gates of Grandma's cemetery, and he thought at first that it was an incredible relief because at least he could get far enough away from his mother that he wouldn't have to listen to her or see that look in her eye any more.

It wasn't better. It was worse, much worse. The limousine drove slowly for five minutes through what looked like bare fields of sickly, short-mown grass—no graves, no shrubs, almost no trees, just sun-scorched green-brown grass—and then it pulled to a stop beside three old trees that looked almost grotesque against the dead meadow.

The Hearse was parked in front of them. Fifty yards away there was a red and yellow tent pavilion planted in the field. Beside it was a folding mechanism made of canvas straps and aluminum poles, just the right size for Grandma's coffin.

Where are the graves? he thought as he got out the door of the limousine, faster than was polite but not fast enough to be rude. And then he saw them.

They were flat, all of them, all of the headstones were flat and set into the ground so that a lawn mower could pass over them without damaging its blade. No careful trimming, just mechanized eternal care.

It was cheesy cheap and petty in the worst possible way.

The priest who'd given the funeral service saw him standing there, looking lost and sick and appalled, and he must have thought Luke was confused because he stopped to speak to him.

"Her grave is over there," the priest said, pointing to the pavilion. His voice was gentle and quiet, with the smallest hint of an Irish brogue. Luke wanted to talk to him, because he needed to talk to someone, especially someone with a voice that gentle and that sane. He didn't dare. Not that day. He knew if he did he'd make so much noise, make such a scene that he'd be a disgrace. It was Grandma who was dead; it wasn't a time for Luke to be demanding attention. Not then.

So he nodded, and he thanked the priest, and he crossed the narrow gravel road and walked toward the pavilion.

And that walk was the worst horror, right then—worse, even, than twenty minutes later when they finally lowered Grandma into the ground. The graves were so close together that Luke could picture the dead holding hands without stretching as they rested, and the soil was set so badly above each grave that as he walked his feet could feel the outline of each coffin in the earth. And he knew that if he could ever bring himself to visit what was left of Grandma in this place, his heels would feel her coffin, too.

He didn't watch as they lowered Grandma into the ground. He tried to relax and let his eyes focus on the grass. He was numb enough by then that he could have watched if he'd decided to make himself, but he didn't want anything more to remember from that funeral than he had to. He heard the sound of the rope and pulley as it lowered her, and he heard the sound of dirt and other things spattering on the sleek black-painted wood of her casket.

As soon as he heard people moving away from the grave Luke turned and started to leave himself. Before he got three steps he felt his mother's hand on his forearm, stopping him, taking his attention. Luke looked up from the uneven ground and back at his mother, over his shoulder.

"You should know," Mom said. She pointed off to her left, at half a dozen unused graves with smooth, uncarved granite markers. Luke turned to look at them more closely. "Your grandmother bought those for the rest of the family, back when papa died. If you ever need them, they're in the family."

And Luke couldn't help himself any more; he didn't scream and he didn't shout, but he yanked his arm away from her and ran from there for all that he was worth. He didn't even run to the limousine—he went for the nearest open gate and left the cemetery on foot. Late in the afternoon he took a bus back to town, and when he got home he went to his room without saying a word. And no one said a word to him about it, not a single word.

Sunday
July Seventeenth

*From page 6 of the special
July 17 edition of the
National Interlocutor.*

MIRACLE MEAT!

*Shoppers in Mountainville, Tennessee, may
think twice before going to the grocery store anytime
soon—after all the pork in the local supermarket's
meat freezer sprouted strange, gooey hair and grew
into pigs!*

*It sounds incredible, but that's exactly what
happened, according to store-manager Amy Stout.
"All the pork in the case swelled up," says Stout,
"burst through the wrappings, and kept growing. We
weren't sure what was happening, but it looked like it
might be dangerous. We evacuated the store right
away, and then we called the sheriff's department."*

*Local deputies were busy elsewhere in Moun-
tainville. They didn't get to the store until late in the
evening. What they saw when they got to the Mountainville Market left them skeptical.*

*"I don't know anything about pork growing in
the meat case," says Mountainville Deputy Sheriff*

Louis Aronica. "When I got to the store there were half a dozen pigs rooting around in the vegetable bins. I don't know how they got there."

The pigs were later rounded up by the Mountainville Humane Society and taken to a local farm for safekeeping.

Brooklyn

So Luke Munsen woke from the dead lying on the ground in a New York City graveyard that seemed to stretch to the horizon, still remembering the dream of his grandmother's burial, but without any context in which to place that memory or the dozen others that he still had. And he woke knowing for certain only these three things about himself:

His name, and the name of the town where he'd been born.

The fact that he'd died long and slow and horrible, but so full of resignation that dying hadn't frightened him.

But the thing he knew most clearly of all when he woke from the dead was that he'd been responsible for the end of the world.

Mountainville, Tennessee

Ron Hawkins woke in the deep, uncertain dark, whole and alive and complete as he'd ever been. Woke as though waking from a long, deep sleep—and in the dark and in the fog of waking Ron had five long, confused minutes where he had no clue as to his whereabouts and no memory of the circumstances that had led to his death.

When he finally did begin to remember, his first assumption was that he hadn't died at all—that he'd been rescued somehow after the explosion, and that it was night and he was in some strange kind of a hospital. And he tried to settle himself down, to wait for a nurse or some such person to tell him where and why he was.

He didn't settle down for long. Only long enough, in fact, to realize that he couldn't be in a hospital, because he wasn't in a bed—not in anything even remotely like a bed. It was broken rock underneath his back—broken rock and damp concrete. It meant that he was still somehow in the wreckage of the institute, that he'd somehow survived the explosion.

The whole idea was bizarre. Someone must have investigated after the explosion, Ron thought, and when they did they should have found him. If that was so—and reasonably it had to be—then what was he doing here?

Well, whatever the reason is that I'm still here, I can't just stay here. I've got to get out.

That turned out to be more difficult than it sounded; when Ron tried to sit up his head hit rough, jagged rock. There was barely even room to move, much less sit. *Where in the hell am I? How did I end up in a place like this, and still live through it?* He reached back and up with his left arm, to see if there was room to move in that direction, but there wasn't—six inches from his head was solid rock.

Groped right and left; there was barely room to spread his fingers on either side.

Ron began to panic. He'd never been especially claustrophobic, but . . . Jesus. No—he wasn't feeling claustrophobic; a phobia is an irrational fear. Unreasonable. There was nothing unreasonable about being afraid—not here, not now.

I've been buried alive.

How deep was he? If there wasn't too much on top of him, he could probably push it aside, crawl up out of it. That was dangerous—it could just as likely collapse on him and crush him. Maybe it would come to that; maybe he'd have to try digging his way free. It had to be a last resort. There was still the direction in which his feet were pointed; he couldn't feel anything there. It wasn't a direction in which instinct would let him comfortably or easily move, but he didn't have a whole lot of choice.

It made him feel pretty stupid, too, squirming feet first along what amounted to a narrow shaft. At least there was room to move in that direction. Or there seemed to be, anyway. There was one bad moment when his right foot came up against something solid and unmovable, but then when he shifted to the left a little he found himself able to keep going. A moment or two after that Ron realized that his ankles were hanging free over some sort of a ledge; another moment, two, and he was pushing his chest out past the narrow space at the end of the shaft, moving out into a larger space. Much larger.

Maybe it was a chamber of some sort; it was hard to be sure in the darkness.

He had to go up, he decided. Not straight up—even if it was stable above him, which didn't seem likely, it'd be like climbing through a jungle gym in the dark. Dangerous. The thing to do was stay on his hands and knees, stay with the ground or the floor or whatever it was below him, and try to bear upward.

It would work. It would have to.

Twice as he crawled across the chamber his hands reached into something wet that wasn't water—something too thick, too slippery to be water.

The upward slant of the ground led him into another crawlway, this one a good deal wider than the one he'd awoke in. A couple of times he had to crawl or twist himself over debris that blocked his way, but mostly the path was pretty clear. And after a while, he spotted light up ahead of him. The light helped a lot; just knowing it was there made him move more quickly and with more confidence. He was out pretty quickly after that; less than an hour after he'd returned to life, Ron Hawkins was standing on his feet again, in the light and air, rejoining the world of the living.

His car was still parked in the far corner of the parking lot. The institute's main building was a wreck behind him. There wasn't a soul in sight—not even a guard, in the booth—and his car was still sitting there as though nothing at all had happened. If he got into it and drove home now, he wondered, what would happen? It was day out—look at the sun: it's midday, for God's sake—which meant that he'd been among the missing since late last night. Did they even realize that he'd been in the building? Did they think he was dead—?

That was when he noticed his uniform.

Which was soaked with blood. Dried blood, now, for the most part. More blood than Ron had ever seen in one place before. His blood, and he knew it. He wanted to tell himself that it couldn't be his blood, that he was fine, he felt fine, and how could it possibly be his blood? It had to be somebody else's.

His gut *knew* that it was his blood.

Knew it.

It couldn't be, he thought. Bleeding that much would kill

a man. And he was alive, wasn't he? He *was* alive. Ron didn't have the first doubt about that.

The blood must've come from someplace else—like that stuff he'd got on his hands as he'd crawled out of the rubble.

When he looked at his hands he saw that they were covered with some thin, oily fluid. God knew what it was, but it wasn't blood. He tried to wipe the stuff off, onto his slacks, but they were too crusty with scab-dried blood to absorb anything else.

I've got to clean myself. This is disgusting.

He found the spigot on the side of the administration building still working, and used it to clean himself as much as it was possible without a bar of soap. When he was done he walked out to his car and changed into the clothes he kept in the trunk for those nights when he felt like going out after work.

And felt human again, at least to a degree.

He stretched and sighed and opened up the car and sat on the front seat trying to figure out what he was supposed to do next. Going home was the obvious thing, but for no reason he could identify it didn't seem exactly *right*. Cleared his throat, in spite of the fact that there was nothing to clear from it.

Reached up above his head and took the shirt and slacks from the roof of the car, where he'd found them. And *looked* at them.

There were neat, regular tears along one side of the shirt, as though some massive set of claws had tried to poke through his ribs.

Or as though his ribs had broken and burst out through his chest, tearing his shirt.

No. It was a crazy idea. He felt fine.

He tossed the crusty clothes onto the seat beside him, put his hands on the steering wheel. Tried to *think*. Not that it was any use trying.

Without even thinking about it, Ron turned the ignition far enough to let the radio come on.

The little comic book was still on the dashboard, where he'd tossed it days ago. He leaned over the steering wheel, reached across the dash, picked the leaflet up. It was warm to the touch—warm enough that for half an instant the sensation spooked Ron—but that was because of the way the windshield trapped the sun, forced it down onto the dash. Nothing strange. Nothing to worry over.

There was something wrong with the radio. Instead of the news, the only sound it made was a long, monotone whine. It was off station, somehow, Ron assumed. He'd never understood how it was that radio stations wandered away from their frequencies like that, but he knew it happened. He reached down, twisted the dial . . . peculiar. The whine wasn't an off-station whine at all. It was a pure, clear tone, something someone was broadcasting on purpose. Like that high-pitched noise that the radio stations always sent out when they were doing the "This is a test. This is only a test," business—when they were testing the emergency broadcast network.

The emergency broadcast network?

Ron twisted the dial, searching for the sound of a human voice, or music, or *something*. Anything. Anything normal and ordinary at all. His hand moved so fast that he ended up skipping over half a dozen clear stations too quickly to hear what was on them. He made his hand steady, turned the dial back—and heard a man recite the station's call letters and say that it was half past noon on Sunday. A moment later a record started, something rich and complex and classical that Ron didn't recognize.

Well, it was ordinary radio, and that was a relief. Classical music wasn't anything you expected from an Emergency Broadcast station.

Wait: Sunday?

No. That wasn't possible. It was Friday—it had to be. It was Friday, because last night, before the explosion, he'd gone to work and it had been Thursday evening. Ron *knew* that. He hadn't been asleep any three days. Two days, whatever. He had enough of a sense of time to know what he'd lived through.

He glanced over at the blood-crusted clothes he'd woke in, and refused to even consider the possibilities that forced themselves at him.

Whether he wanted to consider the evidence or not, his gut was already beginning to understand what he didn't want to believe.

If he'd been dead for three days, there was no way his sense of time would be able to tell him that the time had passed. The same way a clock that's had its cord unplugged has no way of knowing that hours have gone by when it's plugged back in.

It's the end of the world. Just like in that comic book. It's the end of the world, and the dead are rising from their graves.

And I'm one of the resurrected.

No—it's got to be a mistake. The man on the radio made a mistake, that's all. It's Friday, and the man's tongue slipped as he spoke.

He opened the comic book, leafed through it, trying to get his mind away from the radio and the clothes, and half a dozen other things that he didn't even want to give name to.

The comic book.

Its crude drawings and ill-chosen words had something powerful about them, now, in a way that they hadn't when he'd read the book the other day. Like prophecy, somehow—like somehow the man who'd written the thing had seen what was coming.

No, that's wrong. It really is wrong.

The music stopped, and a news report came on the radio.

And as Ron listened to it, the whole world seemed to tumble down around his ears. It *was* Sunday. No question about that. Thursday evening—about the same time that the building had exploded around Ron and the Beast—the President had tried to fire off the nation's nuclear arsenal. Only a few missiles had actually been launched, and of those few all but one had been aborted and landed harmlessly in the ocean.

The one missile that hadn't fallen into the ocean hadn't gone where it was supposed to, either—it had fallen in Kansas, and now there was an enormous crater where there had been two whole counties. As the news had hit, people had started rioting in the streets.

Not just a few people, but millions of them.

Yesterday one of the mobs had found the Vice President, and they'd lynched him and left his body hanging along the side of a highway.

The army kept trying to get through and cut him down, so that the poor man could be given a decent burial. The soldiers hadn't been able to get close enough to reach him, not even with their tanks—well, maybe they could have with the tanks, if they'd really *tried*, but Ron got the feeling that it would have meant killing more people than anybody had the stomach for.

Whether they were a mob or not, the rioters were civilians, not soldiers, and it definitely sounded like the army didn't have the nerve for shooting down crowds of civilians who were only armed with sticks and rocks. Not over a corpse, anyway.

The news faded away—the man was still talking, actually, but Ron didn't have the heart to pay attention to any more of it—and Ron found himself reading his way through the comic book again. It wasn't right. Yeah, the world was ending, and a lot of the things that the comic book told about were happening. Some of the things that happened were so exactly the same that it was unnerving. Even so, the pattern behind the events was wrong. Almost as though someone important had read this same comic, and he was making the events that the comic book described take place . . . but all he could do was ape bits and pieces of the story. The bombs. The riots. The Beast-creature.

Ron turned to the page with the picture of the two Beasts on it. There was an eerie similarity between the first of them and the creature from Bonner's lab—a powerful similarity, as though the creature had modeled for the drawing. Maybe it had, in fact. But modeled badly. The *thing* on the page looked like an abomination against God—or it tried to; the artist didn't have the craft to make it truly an abomination—but the Beast from Bonner's lab, unnatural and unsightly as it was, wasn't any abomination against God. Even a casual eye knew that it held no evil.

Someone was behind this. Behind the comic book, the creature's appearance, the explosion. The riots. Someone had to be.

The whole idea was strange and paranoid. It wasn't any stranger than the fact that Ron was alive. Alive, and without a scratch on him.

Cold practicality sunk through the web of intuition and denial he'd wrapped himself in: how could he possibly have come through that explosion, come away from being buried in tons of debris, without so much as a stiff neck? Something was wrong. Unnatural wrong.

The second Beast on the page was a more . . . conventional-looking creature. And at the same time a more unsettling one. Unsettling because it almost looked like something sensible enough for evolution to have produced. Like something you'd find hidden in the deepest Andean jungle, or living quiet and unknown among the peaks of the Himalayas. It was shaped like a man, mostly, but it had a goat's head, with great spiral-curving horns. And it was covered with thin, pale-grey fur like the hair of a goat. The skull was enormous, ram-shaped yet large enough to hold the brain of a man.

And no goat had eyes like that. They were a man's eyes, or a woman's—human eyes. Evil-looking, sullen, and some-how familiar. Ron bit his lip, squinted, trying to place those eyes, trying to remember where he'd seen them before . . . and realized, and felt the bottom fall away from his gut.

They were Herman Bonner's eyes.

It was impossible, of course. What could Herman Bonner possibly have to do with the comic book? He was a biologist, an educated man—about as mean-hearted a man as Ron had ever met, nasty enough that Ron was willing to suspect him of anything.

The notion that he might have something to do with a comic book for religious fanatics stretched possibility beyond all reasonable bounds.

And still. They *were* Bonner's eyes.

It was a coincidence, Ron told himself. It had to be a coincidence. Or maybe the similarity wasn't as great as it seemed.

(There were connections. The creature. The creature from Bonner's lab. And those books on Bonner's shelves, books whose spines bore the same cross-dove-and-circle insignia that marked the cover of the comic book.)

There was something wrong with the whole damned world. Almost like a disease—a craziness disease. Ron had been alive a goodly while, and in all that time he'd never seen the world around him . . . *moving* like this.

(How could the creature from Bonner's lab possibly look so much like the thing from the comic book if Bonner hadn't made him look like that on purpose? Bonner could do that—designing living things was what a genetic engineer did.)

The world Ron had always lived in was a sensible place, a reasonable place. The things that were happening now seemed to have some guiding principle behind them—and there was nothing sensible about that.

And if there was someone behind all of it, that person had to be Herman Bonner. Or someone close to him.

No, he decided. That was crazy thinking. If he let himself start thinking like that, he'd go out of his mind—if he wasn't half out of it already.

Something strange—small hairs standing on end on the back of his neck, just below his ears. Almost as though an electric current had washed over the car. Ron looked up, trying to find some source for the sensation, trying to prove to himself that he wasn't having hallucinations. . . .

And saw the Beast.

Ron might never have recognized the creature if he'd only had his eyes to see it with. He didn't see it only with his eyes; when he looked up he saw the Beast with his heart and his gut and his back brain. And none of the deepest parts of him could ever fail to recognize it.

No matter how its appearance changed.

Not even now, when the creature was so incredibly altered. Altered so far that no camera could find the connection to what it had been just three days before.

For now the creature was the second Beast from the Book of Revelation.

When Ron could speak again, he said, "It's you, isn't it?" He asked the question even though he knew the answer. "How. . . ?"

The creature misunderstood the question, and instead of telling Ron how it was that its appearance had changed so dramatically, it planted a vision in his head. In the vision Ron could see himself, caught up again in the explosion that had killed him. Ron felt the hairs on the back of his neck grow even stiffer; felt a missing part of him brought home. His unconscious mind had neatly clipped away all memory of that last instant of his life—his recollection had ended just as the explosion's first roar had reached them. Now, seeing the moment again through the creature's eyes, it was almost as though he'd never forgotten.

It had happened too quickly for Ron to understand, but watching the scene as the creature watched it, the events all seemed lucid and self-evident. In the vision, Ron was looking into his own eyes—Ron was the Beast, his hairy arms wrapped around Ron, lifting him from the floor. All around them, the concrete walls of the building shattered into jagged artificial stones, and the floor under them went unsolid and unreal, and the air around them was made of fire and bursting dust. And there was something in that air. Something like an enraged swarm of insects, but smaller, far too microscopically tiny to see—but through the creature's eyes they were visible somehow. Not because his eye would resolve a thing that small, Ron thought. The tiny things were visible because they were portentous, and the creature saw most clearly of all the ominous things that surrounded him.

As the swarm swept over them, the building collapsed around and on top of them, and Ron watched his living body crushed and broken by a falling concrete strut. Saw his blood splatter and gush over the moving debris in which he lay. Saw his ribs burst up through his chest, saw them spear the bloody uniform shirt, like the sanguine claws of some impossibly gargantuan cat.

An instant of pain, and then the vision went infinitely dark. For a moment Ron thought that it meant that the vision had come to an end, but it hadn't. The deep dark went on for a time so long that Ron began to think it was as infinite as the dark itself—

Until finally he realized that he was surrounded by an unnatural glow.

A glow of just exactly the same hue as the swarm of microscopic portents.

Somewhere at the far periphery of his awareness was another light, of similar color and shape, and Ron knew that the light was his own body.

A catastrophe—a violent and terrible moving of the earth that surrounded them—and the glow began to grow brighter and brighter, until finally it seemed to light the darkness that surrounded him.

And the vision ended.

"That glow," Ron said, "the swarm. It's something from Luke Munsen's lab, isn't it? It's the reason we're alive now."

The creature nodded.

Ron felt numb and quiet—his mind went blank and empty. He should have had a thousand questions to ask. And God knew there were things to be done. He couldn't do any of those things; he felt too powerful a need to mourn himself. His mind was buried in a fog too deep for him to do anything but sit in the car, staring hard into the blistered plastic of his steering wheel as though it were a crystal that could tell him his future—or maybe tell him his past.

The creature waited for him quietly all that time. Half an hour of the wait the Beast spent standing, patient, barely moving. Then he made a little sound that wasn't quite a sigh, lifted his hindquarters up onto the hood of the car, and sat.

When Ron had sat that way for an hour, the shock finally began to fade. He yawned and rubbed his eyes and stretched. Craned his head out the window and said, "Are you hungry?" The creature shook his head no, and Ron realized that he wasn't hungry, either. He ought to have been hungry. He hadn't eaten in days, since late Friday afternoon—he ought to be famished, in fact. He wasn't hungry, or weak, or dizzy, or any of the things that he ought to have been from going without food for that long.

He got out of the car, walked a few paces to bring the circulation back into his legs. "What are you going to do, now? Where will you go?" Ron asked. "I can put you up for a while, if you want. There's room on the couch. It wouldn't be a problem."

The Beast shook his head again, and he pointed west, and Ron knew without knowing why that he meant a long journey. A powerfully long journey.

Ron looked down at the asphalt and thought about it for a moment—thought about the creature going away, going to some place *that* far away. It made him sad, and the sadness embarrassed him. There was something possessive about that kind of sadness; it meant he felt he was losing something that wasn't his to lose in the first place. And Ron knew: the creature was a precious thing. But it—not it; the creature was a him, not an it—but he wasn't anything precious that belonged to Ron, or even that could belong. So he stood there for a long time, staring at the ground, feeling sad and feeling worse and guilty for his sadness.

And all the while the creature sat there, patient as stone, not even watching Ron—not watching him exactly. Certainly not staring.

"Can you take me with you? Wherever you're going, can I go along?" The question came off his tongue before he had any idea what he was saying, but when he'd realized what he'd said he didn't feel a need to repeat it. Not even if it meant that he was trying to own something that couldn't be his. Not even if it meant leaving behind all the life he had.

The Beast looked at him—really looked at him—and suddenly Ron was certain that the creature had known all along that he would ask, known that they would travel together as long as he'd known that there was a journey to be made. He caught the tiniest glimpse of that journey as the creature foresaw it, and it was long, and it held terrible things—frightening things. They terrified Ron, but they didn't make him hesitate. And at the same time Ron saw the love he had for the creature that he couldn't admit to, and seen from that perspective it didn't seem so bad a thing. And he accepted it, even if he couldn't understand it.

"Well," he said. "Okay. You want to get in the car? You want me to drive, right?"

The creature shook his head again, and Ron realized that they'd be traveling on foot, and that struck him as crazy, just plain crazy. God made cars for traveling in, Ron was sure of it, and as soon as He'd done it distance walking had gone definitely and permanently out of style. If anyone had pressed him on the point he'd likely have admitted that his conviction was probably an exaggeration of the facts. But still.

On the other hand: the circumstances themselves were a lot stranger than the idea of walking off into the afternoon sun. If the creature thought they needed to walk, there wasn't any real reason not to.

"All right, then," he said. "We can walk. Why not. I need to get a few things—a couple changes of clothes, and like that. And my apartment's east of here, ten miles or so. It'll take us till midnight just to get back where we started if we walk it. How about if I run out there in the car and meet you back here? Then we can get started."

A sudden, unshakable sense of urgency—urgency that wasn't his own. A moment later, Ron heard the creature's strange voice, heard it without any sound in his ears at all: *You won't need them. They'd weigh you down, and there isn't time.*

"If there isn't time, then why don't you want to take the car?"

Ron waited a long time for the creature to respond, but there wasn't any answer, in his head or in his gut. So finally he shrugged and said, "Well—let's get started, if you're in such a hurry. No time like the present." Ron meant the words to be sardonic, but if the creature heard them that way it didn't show. He pushed himself from the hood of the car, stood, turned, and began walking from the parking lot. Almost like he'd been waiting for Ron to realize it was time to go.

Brooklyn

Luke Munsen woke to life amnesiac, and almost absent of his *self*, but he woke remembering enough to accept what had happened to him. No—*remembering* is too strong a word. The parts of his past that had brought him back to life—the bacteria, the beating, the ash crushed into his skin—all of those were like an uncertain dream. When, for a moment, he tried to remember them more clearly, the memory slipped completely away from him, and he began to think he'd woke into some surreal afterlife.

His hands had been folded over his chest, and there was a slip of dew-damp writing paper just beneath them. He was naked, or nearly so—someone had draped a sheet over his lower parts.

Trees, everywhere. Gnarled, green-green trees, lush and beautiful as anything he'd ever seen in a Japanese garden. It was grass underneath him; he could feel it pressed into the skin of his back.

Where. . . ?

Dead: yes, he remembered that. Luke Munsen was dead. Or had been dead? No, dead. Luke was dead, and this was heaven, or hell, or something—a grassy place full of beautiful trees. He sat up, trying to see, to take in the eternity he'd woke into. . . .

And saw a sea of graves that went on to the horizon.

Of course, he thought, *heaven is a place for the dead. Of course there are so many graves*. It was only sensible—wasn't a grave, after all, a dead man's home, the one thing in this world (or any other) that he had a right to call his own? If heaven was a good place then it'd have to have graves. He thought for a moment of the macabre, grassy plain where they'd buried his grandmother. He'd had a grandmother, he was certain of that, he remembered her burial clearly. Though when he tried to picture the woman herself his mind's eye showed him nothing. That cemetery had been a terrible place, an evil place, almost. A place for the mechanized care of the dead.

This graveyard was something different altogether—it was beautiful, even. You didn't have to be a living man to know that. This was a *home* for the dead, a place where you could have the sort of grave you wouldn't mind coming home to. Luke could picture that: coming out here on a cool, moist summer evening, stretching himself out over his grave, and watching the stars from it. The thought brought something warm and comfortable to his heart, a kind of satisfied, easy happiness that he'd rarely known when he'd been alive.

Death was a Good Thing, Luke decided. He had vague memories of a horrible death—or maybe they weren't memories at all, but vague traces from another dream—but even if he'd had to go through something that bad to get here, it was worth it.

He stood up and stretched, and the sheet fell away from him, and suddenly Luke felt as naked as he was. Which was strange, he thought—could nakedness even be a question in the afterlife? His mental picture of a man in heaven included a loose, flowing white robe. Luke wasn't sure that was realistic, or even practical; this afterlife included grass and soil enough to turn white cloth filthy. All the same, he took a good look at the bed sheet that lay at his feet, checking to make certain it wasn't a robe that the angels had left for him. It wasn't, of course—nothing but smooth, grass-stained cloth.

The paper that had been under his hands when he woke was damp, and when he'd sat up it'd clung to Luke's chest, pasted by sweat and morning condensation. And as he stooped to examine the sheet, it'd come loose and fluttered to the ground. Luke bent further, picked it up and read it.

This is Luke Munsen, it read, *to judge his name from the torn-up wallet we found not long after we found him. He was a stranger to us, but our son knew him for a few moments while he was still alive, and Andy says that Luke Munsen was a good man. May his soul rest in peace. —Mr. and Mrs. Robert Harrison.*

Even with as little real memory of the world as Luke had at that moment, it seemed a strange epitaph. Very strange. Not a *bad* epitaph, though; for all the peculiarity of the thing, reading it did something warm and soothing to Luke's heart.

He smiled and took a deep, yawning breath. The air was extraordinarily clean, just as he'd expected the air in heaven to be. It *was* heaven he'd awoke to, Luke decided. It had to be. Hell wasn't anything this nice. What was he doing here? He knew that he was responsible for the end of the world he'd been born in. Luke *knew* that—it was as indelible a part of his soul as anything ever could be. And if he was guilty of a crime that grave, he had no business being *here*. Something was very wrong; someone had made a horrible mistake. That had to be it.

Sooner or later, he decided, they'd have to realize what had gone wrong. And there was no sense at all in Luke bringing the mistake to their attention any sooner than was absolutely necessary. Let them figure it out for themselves.

He heard children's voices—or maybe they were the voices of adolescents—not far away at all, and suddenly Luke realized that he realized that he really was naked, naked and embarrassed. He grabbed the sheet, draped it over his shoulders as though it were a poncho. It wasn't clothing, not even remotely, but at least it was something.

What was that he was hearing? Cursing? They were cursing, whoever they were. Children cursing like good old boys who'd had a few brews too many. Luke was a long way from his religion, but even so he couldn't imagine cursing in heaven. This wasn't hell, it couldn't be hell, or even purgatory—it was much too wonderful a place. Too *decent* a place.

Which meant—which meant—

Luke didn't know what it meant. If it wasn't hell, and it wasn't heaven, and it wasn't purgatory, then all that was left was the world, and hadn't he destroyed that somehow?

Well, it had to be the world. Maybe it was still in the process of destruction. And if this was the world, then that meant that Luke was alive, either that or he was a shade. A ghost.—No, not a ghost; he was corporeal enough to have to worry about being naked, and why would a ghost have to worry about a thing like that?

Which meant he was alive. Had to be alive.

That couldn't be—he remembered dying, remembered it clearly even if he couldn't remember anything else.

Or thought he remembered it, anyway.

He wandered carefully in the direction that the voices

came from, stepping gently over other people's graves, staying close enough to the trunks of the trees to conceal himself.

He began to be able to see past the trees when the street was still a dozen yards away. The cursing voices had come from those teenage schoolgirls over there, what were there, half a dozen? Yes, half a dozen of them, maybe a couple more, giggling and telling stories full of curse words.

Schoolgirls from hell? Schoolgirls from hell in heaven? No, the whole notion was ridiculous. This wasn't any afterlife Luke could imagine. Couldn't be.

Well, then, if he was alive, what was he *doing* alive? Alive and completely unhurt, for that matter.

Something vague at the back of his conscious mind . . . something about germs?

A blank.

And then, suddenly, an image that seemed to come from nowhere: some strange insectlike creature on a dark sphere, the creature cherry-red as though it were afire. And suddenly the thing exploded, and in explosion there was light enough to see that the sphere was the earth, and the force of the blast split the world asunder.

Yes, that was it: a germ that was going to destroy the world—and that same germ was the reason Luke was now alive. *That* was it.

Someone screeched, off to the left of the schoolgirls, and the scream seemed to go on forever. Luke turned and saw that the scream came from a small boy sitting on the stoop of a tenement building. The boy was staring at him, looking him right in the eye, and his face looked unsettlingly familiar to Luke.

Screaming as though he'd seen a ghost. Maybe I am a ghost, and that's why he's screaming.

Luke worked his right arm up out from under the sheet and waved at the boy. "Hey," he said, "don't be afraid."

The girls had spotted him, now, too, but they didn't look afraid, so much—a little confused, but not afraid.

The boy's scream faded away, but he still looked scared half out of his mind. Luke stepped out, away from the trees. Toward the boy. "What's wrong? I'm not anything to be that scared of, am I?"

The boy just kept staring at him, transfixed, as Luke

walked toward him. He didn't say a word until Luke was almost close enough to touch.

"I'm not anything *that* bad, am I?" Luke asked.

And the boy said, "You were dead, horrible dead, and I saw you. I helped my Daddy carry you out to the graveyard. Your whole back side was charred away from the fire in that bus. You were *dead*, mister."

"I was?" Luke frowned. Thought hard, still trying to make sense of himself. "I was, wasn't I."

"Uh-huh."

The quiet went long and thick, but the boy did seem to calm down. "I'm sorry," Luke said, even though he wasn't sure why he was apologizing.

Then, suddenly, the boy's face went angry. "How come you had to go and get yourself killed like that? I brought my Daddy down, and we were going to help you, we were going to take you to the hospital, and when we got downstairs you weren't anyplace to be found. Then the next day we find what's left of you in that burned-out bus. You ain't got no *right* to go and get yourself killed that way."

"I don't?" Luke's memory was so shaky that he wasn't sure enough about anything to argue. Even so, it felt *wrong* to be blamed for his own misfortune. "I guess I don't," he said. "I already apologized, didn't I?"

The boy shook his head and made a small sound somewhere between a snort and a sigh. "Yeah. You said you was sorry."

The boy was staring off into the distance—staring at the graveyard, Luke saw when he followed the boy's line of sight. "It's a nice cemetery, isn't it?"

The boy blinked, and looked up at Luke. "Are you some kind of a holy man or something? My Momma's always talking about holy men, and always reading out loud from her Bible. I heard her talking the other day about holy men who wake up again after they're dead. Like Jesus Christ, or something." The boy took a good look around, to make sure no one else could hear them. The only people anywhere nearby were the schoolgirls, but they'd long since lost interest in Luke and the boy. "Are you Jesus, Mister?"

The question all but knocked Luke off his feet—partly because he knew that he wasn't, partly because he couldn't prove that he wasn't, not even to himself.

When Luke's heart had slowed enough to let him speak, he said, "No," and, "Well, no, I'm not . . . well, tell me, son, what's your name?"

"Andy Harrison. And your name's Luke Munsen, I know that because we found your wallet with your drivers' license picture in it, only there wasn't any money or any credit cards because whoever did that to you took it all. Even though your name is Luke Munsen, that still doesn't mean that you couldn't be Jesus Christ. Jesus did just like you did—he died on Friday, and then on Sunday he came back to let everybody know they was saved."

"Andy—" Luke started, and then his tongue stumbled all over itself, and he had to begin all over again. "Andy Harrison, I don't remember anything very clearly about what I was before I died. If you tell me long enough and hard enough that I was Jesus, I might even start to believe it, because I just can't be sure of anything. But I think that if I was someone as good and important as Jesus was—I think if I had been, I'd remember that. You understand what I mean?"

Andy just shook his head and stood and took Luke's hand. "C'mon," he said, "we got to go tell my Momma. She'll set you straight—Momma sets everybody straight."

Andy Harrison turned and led Luke up into the tenement building. On the third floor he stopped in front of the door to an apartment and motioned for Luke to wait. Then he burst inside, shouting, "Momma, Momma, I found Jesus," and Luke felt a sudden and powerful need to crawl under a rock and hide.

A woman—her voice was as familiar as the boy's had been, but Luke had no idea why—sighed and then she said, "Child, you've had Jesus with you since the day you were conceived. What kind of an epiphany have you brought yourself to now?"

Andy harrumphed. "*No*, Momma. Not I found him like 'I Found It.' I found him like . . . like . . . I found him like he's standing right outside our door."

"What? Andy, child, I declare—that imagination of yours. . . !"

The sound of cloth rustling, of a heavyset woman walking across the floor, toward Luke. The door swung open, and Luke felt ridiculous, standing in front of a strange woman dressed in nothing but a bed sheet, and there the woman was, her face painted by annoyance . . .

And she looked at Luke . . .

And seemed to recognize his face.

And Andy Harrison's mother screamed. Not a long scream, nor even a loud one. She was much too controlled a woman to lose herself for long; she covered her mouth with her hand to stop the sound.

She couldn't cover her bulging eyes, or the way her dark skin seemed to pale slightly.

"Dear God oh my dear God," she said. Her hand trembled as she lowered it from her face.

"No ma'am—honestly, I'm no one's Savior. I'm sorry your son's got that idea into his head. I've sure tried to convince him otherwise."

"No," she said, "not Jesus. Not Jesus."

She took Luke's hand and led him into her apartment, led him to the kitchen table and sat him down.

"I told you, Momma," Andy said. "I *told* you I found Jesus. He's the man I tried to help last Friday, the same man we had to carry away from the bus."

"Hush, child."

She looked at Luke carefully, staring into his eyes so hard that he began to wonder if there were some strange blemish on his cornea. She lifted her hand to his face, touched him, probing him so gently that it was almost a caress, but too purposeful. She lifted the curly-shaggy hair up away from his forehead, and touched there, too, and more forcefully.

"Not a single scar," she said, "There isn't a scar on this man."

"If I'm causing some kind of trouble," Luke said, "I can move on. I don't mean to be a disturbance."

The woman frowned and shook her head. " 'And after three days and a half the Spirit of life from God entered into them, and they stood upon their feet; and great fear fell upon them which saw them.' " She whispered the words, her voice all full of awe.

"But Momma," the boy said, "he wasn't dead any three days and a half—only two days and a half. Like Jesus, not like any old prophet. And he ain't all that scary, not once you get used to seeing him alive."

"Really, ma'am—please. I'm honestly not anybody that

special. I *feel* like I'm about as ordinary a man as I could possibly be."

She shook her head again. "No. Whatever you are, you're a miracle just because you're alive. I haven't ever heard about a miracle that was an everyday kind of thing."

"*See*, Momma? Jesus is miracles, and so is Mr. Luke Munsen. I told you he was Jesus." Andy smiled a self-satisfied smile. "Say, Mr. Luke Munsen Jesus, you want your wallet? We was going to give it to the police and tell them what happened to you, only the police haven't stopped hiding yet."

"Please. Don't call me Jesus. I'm not God. I don't want to be God."

"Okay. You want me to get your wallet or not?"

Luke blinked, trying to shake away the confusion. "Uh . . . yes. Sure, I'd like to see it."

The boy got up from the table, almost ran from the room. A moment later he was running back, his face so full of *fun* that it threw Luke off-balance. He spread the wallet out across the table and looked gravely at Luke.

"It was like this when my Daddy found it," he said. "Somebody really bad must have got hold of you."

Luke examined the wallet. There was nothing in it but a driver's license, a bank card, and a couple of grocery store check-cashing cards. Not enough to tell him much about himself. He looked carefully at the photo on the license, trying to get used to the sight of his own face. It *was* his face, all right, and he recognized it, but even that recognition was . . . uncertain. If the boy had looked up at him at that very moment and told Luke that it wasn't his face at all, Luke would have believed him.

There was a signature underneath the photo—a clear, crisp, easy signature, *Luke Munsen*—and even though Luke knew it was his name and knew that it had to be his signing, he didn't recognize it. The letters weren't even remotely familiar, and the whole effect of the signature was somehow alien.

Luke pushed the wallet away, sighed. Looked around, looked to see anything but the wallet and its evidence of his own alienated identity. Saw the sheet still draped around his shoulders, held tight at the center of his chest with his left hand. And for at least the dozenth time in the last half hour Luke Munsen was embarrassed at his own nakedness. Or near-nakedness.

"I need to get myself some clothes," he said. "There isn't any money here, but I know I have money someplace. I'd remember being broke—it'd be a tough thing to forget. Not that it does me a whole lot of good when I can't get at it."

The woman sighed. "It doesn't matter whether you have any money or not. There isn't anyplace open for you to spend it." She shook her head, pushed her chair away from the table, stood. "Let me get you some of Robert's clothes. Would you like to use our shower?"

Luke flushed, embarrassed; he hadn't meant to be asking for anything, but suddenly he realized that it must have sounded as though he were. He didn't want to be a beggar, or a sponge, but the truth was that he needed any help he could get—he wasn't in a position to be proud. He was lost, and naked, and filthy, and he wasn't even sure who the hell he was—not positive, anyway. "Yeah—if I could, I'd appreciate it. I . . . uh . . . I don't really feel too comfortable about taking from you, though. Is there anything I can do to . . . earn the favor?"

The woman scowled. "Don't be silly. The hand of God has touched you. I don't know why, I don't know how, but I know it has. It's an honor to have you in our home."

"Maybe so, ma'am—"

"My name is Barbara. Barbara Harrison."

"Maybe so, Barbara. Just the same I'd be happier if I didn't get too deeply in your debt."

"You'll find a way, I'm sure," she said. And turned and walked from the room.

A moment later she was coming back, her arms full of clothes and a clean towel. She led him to the apartment's bathroom, and told him that he shouldn't take his time since the hot water didn't tend to hold out very long, and handed him the bundle of clean clothes. And then she left him there, the bathroom door still open for him to close, and Luke feeling stupid and awkward and a lot like a mooch. What could he do? He couldn't do anything, except the obvious, and he knew it. He closed the door and set the towel and clothes on the edge of the bathroom sink. Let the towel fall to the ground, and took a good look around him.

The bathroom was spotless, tidy and scrubbed clean right down to the deepest crack in its tile. But it was the bathroom of a tenement apartment; it was a hundred years old, at least, never renovated, and its construction was unsound. No one had ever intended the pitted porcelain sink to last a hundred years—nor were the crazed tiles that covered the walls, nor the tub with its long, deep copper-rust-green water stains, nor the chipped pull-chain toilet, meant to do service for a century. Barbara Harrison kept her home *clean*, and she kept it as well as anyone could possibly imagine, but no matter how well she kept it the place was still old, and marked by time.

Luke Munsen couldn't possibly have put words to that thought. He'd lost too much of his *self* and his experience of the world. He did still have his prejudices, his unconscious assumptions about the nature of the world, even had the ability to do those things he could previously have done without bothering to think about them, but he didn't have enough of his own *experience* of things to analyze and sort an idea that complex. Still, if Luke couldn't have explained the apartment's oldness, he felt it—*knew* it with his gut even if he couldn't have told another soul what he knew.

And as he turned the water taps to find a comfortable temperature, found it, and turned the knob that forced water up through the shower head, he thought about *oldness*. Thought about growing old and being old as the tenement building. Imagined his body somehow untouched by age, just as it'd somehow been unscarred after a death by fire. Thought about his *self* being that old, older than a self was ever meant to become. Maybe, he thought (and he thought this too without the words to convey it), his self would be somehow like the contents of this room: still functioning, somehow, against good sense and all probability, but desperate to fade into dysfunction and disuse. Crying out to be retired and abandoned. What if he got so old that being alive became a chore—an unhappy chore—but there wasn't any way for him to die?

What if he honestly wanted and needed to die, but couldn't die?

The idea made Luke sad. So sad that it still haunted him when he finished washing and turned off the tap. It even distracted him a long while after that.

He took the towel from the pile on the edge of the sink and dried himself; dressed himself in the blue denim slacks and flannel shirt that Barbara Harrison had loaned him. Rolled the cuffs of the shirt sleeves and the pants legs, both of which

were too long for him. Brushed his hair with the hair pick
beside the sink. Opened the bathroom door and stepped back
out into the apartment.

There was a man at the kitchen table, now, too, along with
Barbara and Andy Harrison. The man was clearly Andy's
father; the resemblance between them was too striking not to
notice. He was tall—tall enough that his height was obvious
even when he sat—and darker-skinned than his son or wife,
and there were bits of grey in his short velvety black hair.
When he saw Luke the surprise showed on his face—surprise,
and a little bit of fear, Luke thought. He didn't scream the way
Andy and Barbara Harrison both had when they'd first set eyes
on him; he didn't make any sound, in fact, not even so much
as a grunt. Luke decided that the man's wife had warned him
about Luke. Either that or he had a very quiet nature.

He stood as Luke walked into the room, and reached out
to shake his hand. "I'm Robert Harrison," he said. "I'm very
pleased to meet you."

His voice was quiet, and so reverent that it made Luke
more self-conscious than he already was. He took the man's
hand, and shook it, because there wasn't an awful lot else he
could do under the circumstances. "I . . . well, thank you, I
guess. I'm—pleased to meet you, too."

And suddenly the whole situation was too much for Luke
to cope with. He had to get *out* of that room, had to get away
from the Harrisons, no matter how kind they were, no matter
how well meaning. If he stayed in that room five more minutes
he might start believing the things that were so visible in their
eyes. And he didn't think he could abide his own company if he
began to think such things about himself.

"Can I get you a cup of coffee," Barbara Harrison asked,
"or maybe a soda? I'll bet you're awfully hungry, in fact—I
don't imagine you've had a chance to eat yet today."

"No—no, I'm all right. Not hungry at all, in fact." It was
an honest answer; he *hadn't* eaten yet that day—hadn't, in fact,
eaten since dinner Thursday night, though he couldn't have
named a time if he'd had to. He didn't feel any need for food.
"But I could use a little fresh air. Would it hurt you if I stepped
away for just a few moments, took a short walk around the
block?"

Robert Harrison frowned, almost guiltily; his wife's lower
lip pursed with disappointment. "Why, of course it wouldn't,"

she said. "Sometimes a body needs to be alone. Certainly we can understand that."

Which pushed Luke's need to get away almost out into the open, and made him feel still more like a heel. He made himself smile and thank her for her hospitality, and he promised that he'd be back in just a few minutes, even though he knew he wouldn't.

He wouldn't be back, he knew, because he was afraid. And because he didn't think he was strong enough to hold onto himself against the tide of the family's conviction. Not now, anyway—maybe later he'd be able to resist it, when he'd had more time to relearn himself.

"You be careful, Mr. Luke Munsen Jesus," Andy Harrison said. "Don't you go getting yourself killed again."

"Andy—!"

"I will, Andy. You be careful, too."

And Luke left.

Outside, the air was still clean and cool and summer-rich. If Luke had remembered the things he'd known about New York, remembered the powerful, dank filthiness of New York in summer, he'd have understood why the freshness of the air seemed so strange and wonderful to him. He didn't have the things he knew about New York, though. Didn't have them or a hundred thousand other things any more. And all he could do with the air was enjoy it.

And enjoy the mild early afternoon sun, and enjoy the clear, sheer blueness of the sky, and the greenness of the cemetery that stretched out in front of him as far as he could see. He let himself wander out toward the cemetery, and was halfway across the street when he realized that he wasn't wearing shoes, and that he needed them, because the sun-cooked pavement was burning his feet.

The only place to get shoes, of course, was from the Harrisons. Which meant heading back into the tenement, back into their apartment, and taking more from them that he had no way to repay.

No, Luke thought, *to heck with that. I owe more than I want to already. I can get by barefoot.*

He finished crossing the street, began to wander in among the grave sites. The grass was cool and soothing to his feet, especially so after the burning heat of the pavement. The lacing of shade and sun through the leaves fascinated the skin of Luke's face. A cool breeze drifted across his neck, and it smelled of grass and pine and oak, and for a moment Luke almost began to believe again that he was in heaven. He stopped himself, because just then tying himself back into reality seemed more important than the possibility of paradise.

This place was drawing him back into that confusion.

Wonderful as the cemetery was, it wasn't good for him to be here. If he was going to be alive, he had to press himself back into coping with life and the world. This was too beautiful and too distracting—a part of the world so wonderful and unreal that it drew him into fantasy. The best thing he could do was get himself away from it.

He turned and began to head away, back out toward the street . . .

And then he saw the girl.

No, she wasn't a girl, she was a woman. Her skin was clear and smooth, like a young girl's, and her eyes were bright and round as though time hadn't had the chance to wear them. The set of her neck and the line of her bust were full the way a woman's get as she reaches the complete maturity of middle age. Luke couldn't have explained that distinction and the line of reasoning that led to it any more than he could have explained the others, but he saw it all the same.

The woman was nude, but she didn't seem self-conscious of her nakedness. Not even when she looked up and saw Luke watching her.

Something passed on her face. Recognition, maybe—yes, recognition. And for half an instant all Luke could think was *Oh no, not another one, not another one who saw me while I was dead and now I'm alive, and now she's going to scream, oh God please don't let her scream*.

She didn't scream, and Luke realized that it wasn't that she recognized him but that she recognized something *in* him.

And—

And—

And she walked toward him across the moist soft grass, and came to him and took his hand. And led him off deeper into the cemetery.

He couldn't do this. He couldn't let her do this to him. What he needed was to be alone, to be alone where he could sort himself out of the confusion. He needed to stop *now*
now

and pull his hand away from her. If he didn't he might lose himself forever. There was something in his blood, pushing him, pressing him. *Desire*. Need that called him more demandingly than pastoral beauty of the graveyard. Need more siren than the quiet faith of the Harrisons.

And when Luke tried to stop, he couldn't.

Already he could feel the rhythm of her body too close to his seeping into his *self*, muting it—changing it—

Luke's heart lurched, and the alien press of the woman's presence turned to fear and rejection, and the rhythm that held him broke just long enough to let him pull free. And he stopped dead in his tracks, sudden and jolting *stopped*, and he pulled his hand away even though her grip didn't want to let him go.

"I can't," he said, "please."

She reached for him, her hand extending quiet and insistent out toward his.

"No," he said. "Stop that." He pulled away, stepped backward. "I'm confused half out of my mind right now—I need to be alone. Need to get used to myself. Wherever you're going to take me right now, it's got to be the worst possible thing in the world. I *can't* go with you—if I did I might never find my way back."

She smiled at him knowingly and stepped toward him, still reaching for his hand. Luke tried to step farther away, but when he did his left shoulder pressed into the trunk of a tree, and he lost his balance but the tree was there and there was no way for him to fall, and she just kept moving toward him, her naked body pressing against him as she took his hand and pulled it toward her, and the soft warmth of her fingers was so . . . so . . .

And her breasts shaping themselves against his ribs, through the flannel of Robert Harrison's shirt . . .

And the light faint smell of her, the gentle scent of her skin so close to him . . .

And his body was responding—*God* it was responding.
no, please God no

Luke almost lost himself, then. Almost but not quite.

He put his free hand on her shoulder, and gently, firmly eased her away from him. And because he'd already said *no* as many ways as he knew how, he asked her a question, any question, just the first question that wandered through his mind.

"Who are you?" he asked. And because that seemed to give her pause, he said, "Why do you . . . What do you need from me?"

And Luke saw something big and powerful as all of creation rise up to the surface of the woman's soul.

And burst.

All at once the woman's body went slack, as though she'd somehow been made from rope that now had come untied. Her hand fell away from his; Luke had to reach out and catch her to keep her from falling too hard into the grass.

desire—God she was beautiful. beautiful. so perfect that even now her presence made a warm fog swirl all around luke. he wanted *her, and knew he didn't dare to have her*

He eased her down to the ground, where she sat staring vacantly at the bark of the tree behind Luke. He stepped away and watched her, almost afraid that she'd somehow fall over onto her side and hurt herself. She didn't, though—she just kept sitting there staring at the tree, or maybe something beyond it.

After a while Luke stooped down to look her in the eye, and he said, "Are you okay?" and there was something strange there in her eye, something familiar . . . or not familiar; something alien but recognizable. "Who *are* you?" he asked her again, even though he knew he shouldn't, knew that it was cruel—and it *was* mean, because as soon as he'd asked it she began to cry, and that made him feel like a real louse.

Everything that was sensuous seemed to go out of her when she cried; instead of being sultry and desirable her nakedness became . . . vulnerable. Vulnerable and sexless as an infant's naked body. He looked at her breasts—guiltily; his eyes had avoided them since he'd first noticed her—and saw them as round lobes of soft flesh not much different from the flesh of her upper arms.

And something inside Luke relaxed, and went easy, and suddenly she was just another confused person, confused as he was, and Luke felt a bond to her.

confused as he was

He leaned back against the tree and let himself slide down toward the ground, sat in among the tree's thick roots staring into the cemetery facing half away from her.

Not even the cemetery seemed threatening to him, now; Luke couldn't have said why, but for the moment, at least, he didn't think it had the power to draw his self away.

The woman cried for five minutes, and then she was quiet, but just as sad.

"Can I help?" Luke asked. "Is there anything I can do?"

She looked . . . not at him, not exactly, but toward him and down, at the grass near Luke's waist.

"No," she said. It was the first he'd heard her speak, and her voice surprised him—partly because he'd begun to wonder whether she could speak at all, partly because even in the single word Luke could hear something rich and melodious in her voice. Something beautiful. Luke kept waiting, expecting her to say something else, but she didn't.

"Are you okay?" He asked her, even though he knew she was as okay as she was going to be. Asked because he felt a growing tension that he didn't understand, and words were the only way he knew to break it.

The woman nodded, absently—more absorbed than distracted. Then she seemed to come into focus; she looked around deliberately, as though trying to make sense of where she was. And when she looked Luke in the eye he almost thought for a moment that she was someone else completely. As though something—a demon, or maybe some less sinister spirit—had possessed her. It wasn't so, of course. Even as confused as Luke was, he could parse that much of reality from fantasy. And when he looked at her more closely he knew that it wasn't any essential change he saw, only . . . an awakening. Or something like one.

"Where is this place?" she asked. "It doesn't seem familiar."

"It's a cemetery in Brooklyn," Luke said. "Northeast Brooklyn—Bedford-Stuyvesant, I think. I'm a little vague on the specifics."

The woman raised an eyebrow, looked at Luke uncertainly. "Are you certain? It's changed a lot since the last time I was here. If this is the place I think it is."

Luke shrugged. "I think—I think this place has been this way a long time. At least as long as I've been alive." He sighed. "I don't know that that's saying much."

She nodded, understandingly; Luke wasn't sure what it was she understood. He looked away from her, off at the sea of graves in front of him. Her nakedness was beginning to distract him again.

"Are you cold?" he asked, even though the temperature of the day around them was too perfect for anyone to be cool, or warm, or anything but comfortable. "You can have my shirt if you need it." Big as the shirt was on Luke, it'd cover the woman almost as well as a dress. He had it half unbuttoned before she even had a chance to respond.

She looked down at her breasts for a moment, almost puzzled, as though the concept of nakedness was almost an alien thing. Then all at once her face was full of stress and recognition, and she reddened with embarrassment. So ashamed that she looked away from him as she reached out to take the shirt from him.

Luke handed it to her, and she stood up to put it on. Buttoned it, all the way up to the very top button at the collar. When she was done she reached out to take his hand. And she said, "Come with me. Please."

Luke wasn't afraid any more. Wary, maybe. He had a sense of himself, but not an unshakable sense. When he saw her hand reach out for him he hesitated. He might even have said no, but he heard the need in her voice, and it wasn't sexual—just plain human empty loneliness. He didn't have it in him to refuse that kind of need; it wasn't threatening, and anyway he felt too damn much of it himself to deny it in anyone else.

She led him a long way through the cemetery, to a quiet place where Luke could hear the sound of a stream burbling—though when he looked to find the water he saw no sign of it. God knew what that meant. Twice along the way to that place they crossed service roads; tiny, badly paved things that made Luke think of someplace deep in the backwoods. One time they even had to pass through a tall archway that told them they'd moved from one cemetery to another, though for all Luke could see it made no difference.

She hardly spoke at all along the way—the only time she did speak was when they passed an eerie monument sculpted in the form of a withered, bone-thin little girl. The woman stopped and frowned when she saw that, and she said, "Yes, this is that place." Said it so softly that even in the hush that surrounded them Luke only barely heard her.

When they reached the woman's destination she lay

herself down on the reclining slope of a grassy knoll, and after a while Luke lay down beside her. And a long while after that they both drifted off to sleep.

He woke when the moon was high overhead. It was a full moon, more than light enough to see by, and there were people laughing hard somewhere far off in the distance. The woman was sitting up, leaning over him. Looking into his eyes.

"Make me warm," she said. There wasn't any mistaking her meaning.

Luke . . . Luke wasn't inclined. She attracted him. There wasn't any question of that. But the desire he'd felt for her had faded away hours back. Perhaps that was because he felt too much for her, too much sympathy and pain—he'd long since guessed at the nature of the bond that was between them.

Or maybe the absence of desire was just because of the doughy fog that followed him up from sleep.

Maybe. It wasn't a thing he could be certain of, not even while he felt it.

He responded anyway, because of the bond he felt for her—even though it didn't seem right, or even good. Maybe he shouldn't have done it. But how could he not have? She needed him, honestly needed him, and Luke wasn't made of anything cold enough to let him ignore a need like that.

Whether it was the right thing or not, it worked out well enough. And better than that. Luke reached up, and kissed her, and after a moment his heart followed him into the kiss . . . and after that the night was a perfect-warm moonlit blur.

Monday
July Eighteenth

Transcript of a conversation between
Herman Bonner and our agent.
Recorded the evening of 7/18.

H.B.:   *I've failed, Tim.*

Agent: *Failed, Dr. Bonner? I don't understand.*

H.B.:   *Yes, failed. Roll up your window. The*
            wind . . . bothers me. I need a President.
            We need a President. Paul Green was crit-
            ical to our plans—

A.:   *I did my best with him, Dr. Bonner. Fol-*
            lowed your instructions to the letter. And it
            went just like you said. I put the . . .
            preserved . . . appendix into the nutrient
            bath with the germ culture you gave me,
            and just like you said, it grew. And kept
            growing until it was the President, whole
            and untouched as though he'd never died.
            Absolutely incredible, even if. . . . How
            did you get ahold of his appendix, anyway?

H.B.:   *I took it from his desk. (Laughs.) Paul was*
            such a sentimentalist. After the operation

                   he had it sealed in alcohol and used it as a paperweight.

A.:   Ugh.

H.B.:   *I had little hope of resurrecting Paul. I do not count the mindless, vegetal thing we grew as my failure. I suspected that there was too little of his self to resurrect preserved in the refuse of that operation. It was necessary to make the attempt, but neither of us can be faulted for the result.*

A.:   *Then how did you fail?*

H.B.:   *I failed just now. At Arlington. While you waited for me in this car.*

A.:   *I still don't understand. What were you trying to do there at the cemetery?*

H.B.:   *I was trying to find a President to replace the one we've lost, of course. Last night I sprinkled the graves of seven great men with the bacteria that would recreate them from their remains. And today I returned, and. . . .*

          (Five minutes of silence on the tape, here.)

A.:   *(Tentatively.) What happened when you went back to the cemetery?*

H.B.:   *I freed them from their graves. They owed me their lives, damn them! But of the four who woke with their minds intact, none would abide my will. Not even one.*

A.:   Oh.

          (There is no small measure of fear in our agent's voice at this point, but Bonner does not seem to hear it. This is especially peculiar in light of the fact that Bonner seems to have a sixth sense about these things; every other agent we have planted in his camp has disappeared, thoroughly and untraceably.)

H.B.:   *Now, while I think of it. There is something we must discuss.*

A.:   *What's that, Dr. Bonner?*

H.B.:   *(Hesitates.) I know that I can trust you, Tim. Know, in fact, that there is no one else*

I can trust as I can trust you—not even
Reverend George. You alone have faith
enough never to doubt me. What I am to
say to you now you must share with no one,
not even the Reverend. Do you understand
me?

A.: Sure, Dr. Bonner. If you say so, I won't tell
another living soul.

H.B.: Good. You understand, don't you, Tim,
that in order to save this world we must
destroy it—totally and utterly? You understand that only a world that no longer exists
is utterly free from evil?

A.: (A pause. The fear is showing through the
agent's voice again.) Never actually thought
of it in exactly those terms. Now that you
mention it, though, it does make an awful
lot of sense. Still—how could we do a thing
like that? We only have a couple dozen
missiles, and even those aren't working just
now. Not nearly enough to blow up the
world.

H.B.: They'll be enough. You're going to help me.

A.: (Confused.) Me? Gosh, Dr. Bonner, I don't
know anything about blowing up the world
with a couple-dozen nukes. I'm only a
computer technician. Until you helped me
find Jesus I was just a tech for the Air
Force. I had good clearances, because I
used to do maintenance down in the silos,
but—

H.B.: Yes. Exactly. I have a plan. Listen closely:
this earth is made of geologic plates—plates
that are, in comparison to the size of the
planet, relatively thin. And these thin
plates float atop a vast sea of molten rock.
No?

A.: Why, sure. It's the kind of fact you pick up
if you listen close in junior high.

H.B.: And these plates are unstable, are they not?

A.: I seem to recall something along those lines.

Guess I wasn't listening that close, back in school.

H.B.: *What I need from you are the exact locations of the world's most unstable spots— the twenty spots which, if they all were simultaneously struck with atomic explosions, would send the world's crust falling in against itself. We must bathe this world in its own molten fire. And cleanse it.*

(There is something unsettling about Herman Bonner's voice as he speaks these words. He does not sound entirely human.)

A.: *Oh Jesus.*

H.B.: *What?*

A.: *Nothing, Dr. Bonner. Just a little confused. How am I supposed to get ahold of this information? I'm really not a geologist. Just a computer tech.*

H.B.: *Your clearances give you access to all sorts of information in the Air Force's computer network, don't they? Surely you can find what you need to know.*

A.: *(A long pause.) I guess they do.*

H.B.: *Good. Begin the moment we return to Lake-of-Fire. Work as quickly as you can.*

A.: *Yes sir. Oh, damn—a detour. We're going to have to get off the Beltway. Hope the access road will get us where we're going. Well, it's not like we've got any choice— they've got it blocked off with tanks. Dr. Bonner, can I ask you a question?*

H.B.: *Certainly.*

A.: *You—you're not really just a person, are you? I mean . . . you aren't human, are you?*

H.B.: *(Pleased.) No, Tim. I'm not. (Grunts.) What is that—there on the side of the road?*

A.: *You mean that man crawling around on his hands and knees?*

H.B.: *Yes, that man. Stop the car. Pull up alongside him.*

A large Post-It note covers the bottom of the final page of the transcript. It reads as follows:

> *General, we have to stop this man. Stop him now. I know that we don't want to get involved in fighting here on American soil. I know that there's no one to give us orders, and that we have no standing orders to cover situations like this. We don't have a lifetime to sit around contemplating the moral and ethical questions: this guy is crazy. And he's serious. And there's a reasonable chance that this scheme of his—the one that involves bombing along the Pacific ring of fire and the Mid-Atlantic ridge—there's a chance that it just might work. I sure don't want to be around to find out the hard way. Send in a couple of divisions now. Take these people out, put the whole lot of them under arrest before it's too late.*

Below this, written in a finer, more careful hand:

> *We have noted your suggestions, and expect to decide whether or not to act on them in the near future.*

Whiteman Air Force Base,
Johnson County, Missouri

Bill Wallace woke just in time to avoid being late for his own funeral.

What woke him, as it happened, was the trundle, rock, and push of pallbearers' shoulders ever-so-slightly out of sync as they carried his casket from the base chapel to Bill's open grave. It was another few groggy moments after that before he got enough of his wits about him to realize that he wasn't in some sort of a dark room, nor waking in the dark part of the night. There was time, in fact, for his bearers to set the coffin into its sling and the base chaplain to get well into Bill's eulogy before Bill tried to roll onto his side.

He knew something was distinctly *wrong* when his head and shoulder pounded into the casket's wooden lid. Knew, even if it was too dark to see; even the smallest bunk in the most crowded Air Force barracks had more room in it than that. Still, it wasn't a thing to panic over. He was disoriented, and for the life of him he couldn't remember where he was, but life in the Air Force was like that sometimes: it woke a man up in tight spots that he couldn't quite remember getting into in the first place.

Which was about when he heard exactly what the chaplain was saying, somewhere not far away at all. Heard his own name, being taken in the past tense. Three times in the same sentence.

He remembered: slowly, uncertain, like the memory of a bad movie he'd seen months before. Remembered murdering his own President, knowingly and with malice aforethought. Which had to be about the biggest sin a soldier could commit, even if he did think he was doing it for the good of the world.

And began to remember that he'd died while committing that murder.

That was when Bill Wallace panicked.

Panicked big time.

Screamed loud and long and hard enough to wake the dead; squirmed and writhed and pushed every which way, trying to find the way out of whatever the hell kind of a hole he was in—

Not a hole. Not a box. Not a room.

A coffin.

And started pounding on the lid above him. Shouting. Demanding that someone let him out. Screeching like a teenage girl at a horror movie. Not that it did any good; some fool had gone and nailed the damned thing shut. It was a good twenty minutes of scratch and pry and thunder inside that box, hammers working loud and ungentle to free him, before Bill Wallace saw the light of day in his new life. By then his throat burned and tasted bloody, like the raw steak he'd eaten once on a dare.

Brooklyn

It was morning, and Luke woke alone with his shirt still beside him on the grass where the dead woman had thrown it the night before. Where was she? He looked around, saw no sign of her. There wasn't any sense in looking for her; he knew in his gut that she wasn't anywhere nearby. He didn't need any physical evidence to be certain of it. For half a breath Luke almost began to suspect that she'd been a dream—a succubus, maybe, created by his imagination.

That was just more nonsense. She'd been real, real as the grass burns their lovemaking had cut into the skin of his back.

He picked up the shirt, shook the loose bits of dry grass from it. Put it on, buttoned it. Found the denim slacks where they lay crumpled on the far side of him, and put them on.

Wherever she was, he decided, he'd see her again soon. Decided? No, not decided. It was something that was going to happen whether he wanted it to or not. Whether he planned to find her or not, he'd see her. He knew that it was going to happen as surely as he knew his way out of the cemetery, even though he'd only been through it once before, even though the walk to this place had been so full of distraction that he barely remembered it.

Luke was beginning to *know* things like that, and it didn't occur to him that it might be anything strange. He didn't remember enough of his past to see the idea as he would have just a few days before—see it as something absurd. Embarrassingly silly. The truth was, of course, that he wasn't just beginning to *know* things—Luke had always had little intuitions, and sometimes he'd even had prophetic dreams. And he'd ignored them, dismissed them exactly because they embarrassed him.

When he left the quiet knoll he had no sense of where he was going, nor any sense that he moved purposefully. Even so, he walked almost directly to the part of the cemetery that faced the tenement building where the Harrisons lived, and walked there by a route far more direct than the one by which the woman had led him to the knoll the afternoon before.

Which is not to say that the sense that guided Luke was omniscient, or even reliable. If it had only given him the tiniest alert, if he'd even begun to look down as he walked into that clearing, Luke would have seen the wound in the earth where the grave was—there's something spectacularly ominous about an open grave.

Even more so a grave so old as that.

His sense of things wasn't strong enough, certainly, to shake Luke from his distraction—which is why he stumbled at the edge of the woman's open grave and all but fell into her rotted, empty casket.

Even as he slipped down toward it Luke knew that it was the grave of the woman he'd first seen yesterday. It had to be. The broken dirt was exactly that old, dried the way it would be exposed to sun and air for most of a full day. And more . . . there was the sense of her about this place, the sense of a body tied for years and years to a piece of ground.

Luke only barely managed to catch himself, to keep himself from falling by wrapping his arms around the only thing available.

Which was the woman's headstone.

It was a tall, high monument stone—almost more a monolith than a monument. It was cut from soft white marble, her name set into the stone with fat brass capitals made from brass or bronze or some such material that had begun to green with corrosion. Streaks of that green stained the white stone; it almost seemed the mark of some impossibly alien coppery blood.

Christine Gibson

The letters down below that were carved into the stone— they were smaller, almost unnoticeable because of the size of the woman's name.

1814–1891
In Warm and Eternal Memory

Luke used his grip on the monument to lift himself up away from the edge of the open grave. It was shallower than any grave ought to have been—not more than a couple of feet deep, to Luke's eye. Even if he had trouble remembering things like the fact that graves are by tradition six feet deep, good sense said they needed to be deeper than this one.

Maybe the ground above it had worn away over the years. That made at least a little sense. The monument at the head of the grave would have likely settled down into the soil at about the same rate as the erosion. The soil around the grave was pushed up and out, as though it hadn't been dug away, but lifted aside. Lifted by the lid of the casket.

Lifted aside when the woman rose up out of her grave.

Luke imagined himself waking that way—waking in a coffin closed dark and buried in the ground. The idea of it was enough to make him shudder . . . Luke wasn't especially claustrophobic, but even so he could understand the fear of small places. Especially places as small as a coffin.

There was a litter of faded-rotted silk scrap mixed with the bits and pieces of pine straw and dry humus around the grave's edge. Some of that silk, Luke saw, had once been an elegant evening dress. Near the foot of the grave were the cracked and dried remains of a pair of patent-leather shoes.

He still hadn't looked down into that grave. He was afraid to, for no reason he could put a name to. But just as he knew to be afraid, he knew that to let that fear rule him would be much worse that anything he might be afraid of. Luke steeled himself, looked down into the grave—

And saw her.

Saw the woman with whom he'd spent the night before.

Her eyes were open; she was awake and alive. And she was as naked as she'd been when he'd first seen her. And more modest: her hands were folded over her breasts, as they must have been the day she'd been buried.

She blinked when she saw Luke looking at her.

And smiled.

In his mind's eye Luke saw the fiery red insectlike thing again, saw its brightness build in intensity until the thing exploded.

That explosion was his doing, somehow, and Luke knew it. And he was just as sure that sight below him was a result of the explosion.

"Hey mister." The voice of a young boy—Andy Harrison's voice. "Mr. Luke Munsen Jesus—where you been? I've been looking for you everywhere!"

Luke looked up from the grave, shook his head, trying to clear it. The boy couldn't possibly see Christine Gibson from where he stood. Which was good, Luke guessed. Or was it? Luke was too confused to make sense of anything.

"Where. . . ?" Luke coughed. "No place. Just around here."

It *was* Andy Harrison; Luke saw the boy coming through a part in the shrubbery off to his left.

"It figures," Andy said. "You want to find a dead man, you go look in the graveyard. I should have expected it."

"Uh," Luke said. Partly it was a wince; partly a result of an absence of words.

Andy stood at the edge of the clearing. From there, Luke thought, he'd be able to see that it was open. It wasn't likely he'd be able to see down into it. "Have you been raising the dead again, Mr. Jesus? You ought to leave these cemeteries alone, you know. They're real pretty just the way they are. You go raising all those dead people up out of their coffins, this place'll have more craters than the moon does. I saw the moon on TV—it ain't a handsome place. It'd be a shame to have a view like that out our front window. It's the only good view we got, after all. The back windows don't look out on anything but the airshaft." He held out a pair of sandals. "Here, put these on. They're my Daddy's, but if you adjust the straps they should fit you all right. Can't have you going around barefoot like this, can we?"

Luke groaned. "I'm not Jesus, damn it."

He crossed the clearing, took the shoes from the boy. Slipped his feet into them, bent down and fussed with the straps until they seemed comfortable. All that while frowning at himself; he'd said the words a lot more forcefully than he'd meant to. Almost harshly. Before he spoke again he paused and made himself calm down—not that it did much good. "I just spent the whole night performing sinful acts with a woman I'd never seen two days ago. God's son would never commit a mortal sin, would he?"

Andy frowned. "Heck," he said, "that isn't any surprise. Jesus loves people—my Momma says that all the time. Why should a Luke Munsen Jesus be any different?"

Luke was all but speechless; he was appalled at himself for saying what he had to a boy as young as Andy, and even more appalled by the boy's answer. When he could finally speak he said, "Andy—honest. I'm not Jesus. Really, I'm not. Please don't call me that . . . it almost makes me feel like I'm pretending to be something that I'm not."

The boy just shrugged. Shook his head.

"Come on," he said. "We got to get going." Something deep and loud rumbled far off in the distance. "You hear that? If we hurry up and run, maybe we can make it."

He grabbed Luke's hand, and before Luke knew what was going on, the boy was leading him out of the cemetery at a dead run.

"Make what? Where are you going?"

"To the subway. They finally got it running again."

Subway? The image of a train roaring through a tunnel, and Luke was in the tunnel, too close to something that big, that fast, that loud—

"Hey—don't slow down. You've got to run if we're going to get there before the train leaves the station." Suddenly they were out of the cover of graveyard trees, bolting across the street without even pausing to check for traffic—not that it mattered; there wasn't a car anywhere in sight.

Luke was far out of breath, and confused, and a little afraid. "Why—?" he asked, or tried to—mostly the question got lost in his gasping for breath.

"Why what? Come on, *run*. We're going into the city. Don't you remember?"

Luke didn't remember anything of the sort, of course. And his memory of the events since he'd first reawoke the morning before was careful and clear. He tried to say so, but it was hard to find the wind to speak.

Out onto a short block, under a monolith of overhead train tracks—when he saw it he almost thought the boy was going to make him bolt up the four flights of stairs to that train's platform, but he didn't, they just kept running under the dark corroded steel girders, out into a large, ugly plaza, again without bothering to check for traffic. And this time they should have been wary of cars; there weren't many of them, but the half dozen that were moving through the plaza were moving at speeds that pavement that rutted couldn't support. Twice, as they ran cars came perilously close to running them down. They weren't hit, though; God knew how they got so lucky, but they did. Finally they were on the plaza's far side, darting down a stairway that led into the ground—

—dim incandescent light, the reek of urine, and . . . something else, something dead and fermented—

—they ran through a vast underground corridor with concrete floors and filthy tile walls and iron bars caging everywhere. It was a wonder of some sort, Luke thought, a spectacle of the kind that the whole world would remember. It had to be. Or . . . or maybe it just seemed that way, maybe if he remembered more of himself it wouldn't be so spectacular.

The sound of roaring, exactly the sound of roaring in his vision a few moments before, but louder and more real.

Fifty yards along the concrete floor, and then they were at a bank of turnstiles, filthy corroded painted-iron things that stood between them and the stairway that led down to the train. Andy paused and fished a pair of strange, two-color coins from his pocket, put them into two of the turnstiles, and motioned Luke through. Then they were running again, down the stairway to the train platform.

The train was just coming to a stop when they got there. After a moment doors opened all along the side of the train that faced them, and they stepped into a car that was all but empty, took seats not far from the door.

When the doors had closed and the train was moving again, Andy sighed and looked up at Luke. "Usually you can't hear a train when it's that far away," he said. "Not even a beat-up, noisy one like this. It's so quiet these last few days—since everything got so crazy. This train must have been two, maybe three stops away when we first heard it. That's quite a distance."

Luke nodded, even though he didn't understand enough of the context to make sense of what the boy was saying. Besides, it was loud in the train, and louder because the windows were open, and it was hard even to be sure of what the boy had said. "Are you going to tell me where we're going? And even better, tell me why?"

Andy frowned. "Don't you remember—we talked about it last night. Going to take you into the city, get you some money. Get you some clothes that fit you right. And then you can take me out to lunch for giving you a hand."

Luke blinked. "I didn't talk to you last night—I haven't seen you since yesterday afternoon."

The boy looked pained and thoughtful for a moment, and then, suddenly, his expression brightened. "Yeah, that's right. But I was going to talk to you about it, only I couldn't find you. I sure *meant* to tell you. Not my fault you had to go sneaking off into the cemetery to do dirty stuff."

Luke thought about that. "I guess it isn't. Still, it would have been nice to get a little warning."

Andy was digging into one of his pockets again. "You forgot your wallet again yesterday, back at our place," he said, and handed the wallet to Luke. "You always leave important stuff behind like that?"

"Um," Luke said. He took the wallet, opened it, saw the picture of himself that it wasn't comfortable seeing, and closed it again. The question made him uncomfortable, too—even more uncomfortable than the picture had. Maybe that was a clue to something from his past, he thought; maybe he did tend to misplace important things. It was possible. But it didn't *feel* right. No, he decided; it wasn't right. The discomfort was some other thing . . . something . . . he didn't know. There was something important he was leaving behind, leaving more and more of it every moment, and it wasn't just his past.

Something. Something obvious, something he knew about—he was sure that he knew if he could only just . . . just . . . something. Something he knew about that he couldn't put his finger on.

"Don't you ever answer a question when somebody asks it, Mr. Jesus?" The boy looked put out and upset, but Luke suspected it was more in fun than real offense. He wasn't sure. "Momma says that about Jesus—she says it all the time. 'Andy,' she says, 'God works in strange and mysterious ways. He doesn't always answer what you ask him. You remember that, child.' Momma sometimes talks a little crazy, but that always seemed kind of sensible to me."

Luke started to answer, but then he realized that his voice couldn't carry over the thundering sound the train made as it moved through this part of the tunnel. The boy's voice carried, but it was shrill, or at least higher in pitch than Luke's was. Besides, Luke didn't have an answer for the question; when he thought about it he realized it wasn't the sort of question you were supposed to be able to answer. So he shrugged, and smiled, and pointed at the window and pointed at his throat, hoping that the boy would understand that it was too loud for Luke to talk. Andy seemed to; he nodded when Luke pointed.

Luke stood and looked out the window, trying to get a look at the tunnel they moved through. It wasn't much use; most of the light out there came from the windows of the train—it might have been light enough to see by if he were out in the tunnel, but it certainly wasn't light enough to see out by. His eyes were used to the brightness of the light inside the car, and they couldn't focus on the vague light that shone through the window. Well, maybe he could see out there a little bit—or maybe not. It was only a glimpse or two, and always whatever he saw was gone so quickly that Luke wasn't certain that he'd seen it. A wild nest of wires, covered with soot—though it could have, just barely *could* have been some wildly enormous spider. A girder, covered with layers of dust as thick as mold, or maybe it *was* covered with mold. A dirty pipe that looked as though it had once been bright red. Or was that a handrail in an abandoned station? Luke wasn't sure. Twice it grew bright as they pulled through white-tiled stations without slowing, and Luke began to wonder if they ever would stop.

Then the train pulled into a third station, and Luke heard the screech of the brakes engaging suddenly, felt himself almost pulled off balance by his own inertia. He sat back down as they slowed, and turned to Andy. When the train was stopped, and relatively quiet, he asked, "How far are we going? How long will it take?"

Andy cocked an eyebrow, thought about it. "We're going a good distance. It'll take most of an hour, if the train doesn't get stuck."

Stuck? Luke felt claustrophobia closing in on him again. "Does that happen often? Do the trains break down in the tunnels?"

The boy held out his hand, made an uncertain, waving motion with it. "Mostly it only happens when you're in a hurry. Like at rush hours, when all those commuters are trying to get to work. Except for the times that the train breaks down because it doesn't think you can take it that day."

Luke shuddered. "Great," he said, though he didn't think it was great at all.

The train doors closed, and then they were moving again and the noise was so loud that there wasn't any sense trying to talk. Luke looked around, trying to figure out how he was going to keep himself from going stir-crazy . . . an hour was a long time to keep his mind occupied on nothing at all. He could read the ads that ran in a long continuous strip along the space between the ceiling and the walls of the subway car. More than half of them were written in Spanish, though; he understood just enough of the language to recognize it and wonder what the signs said. And the walls were covered with graffiti—most of that was inscribed in strange marks that might have been letters or even words, but might just as well have been hieroglyphics from some civilization he couldn't remember.

It wasn't the sort of thing he'd choose to spend an hour puzzling over—but it wasn't as though there was much else to do. By the time they reached the stop where Andy had them change trains—its sign read WEST 4—by the time they changed trains Luke had managed to decipher ANTON LIKES ESTRELLA, JOHN McC. EATS DICK (which made him wince for Richard), and the fact that a female celebrity named Chita wanted all pregnant women to get themselves tested for some sort of a disease.

The ride on the second train was short by comparison; it only stopped twice—at 34 STREET and 42 STREET—before they got off at 47–50 STREETS ROCKEFELLER CENTER. That train was clean, too, or relatively clean, full of bright plastic colors and shiny steel. And quiet. And it was *air conditioned!* Luke had completely forgotten the idea of air conditioning before he stepped into that train. It was a wonderful thing, the way it turned the fetid air of the subway tunnels crisp and almost fresh. Especially after the thick, gusting-in-through-the-windows stuff he'd had to breathe for so long in the first train. It was such a strange and dramatic difference, so . . . fascinating that it distracted Luke so much that the boy almost didn't manage to get him out at their stop before the train closed its doors and started moving again.

But he did manage to get Luke out of the train, into a place so full of so many people that an hour before Luke wouldn't have been able to imagine so many of them all in one place. And police officers, too—it almost seemed that there were more police officers around than there were people without uniforms.

"Is it always like this," Luke asked, "so many policemen all around?"

The boy didn't answer right away—he was too busy looking around him. Probably, Luke thought, he was trying to figure out which way they should go. They were standing on the subway platform, and the quiet train was pulling away from them. There was dirt everywhere, on everything, fine grainy brown-grey dirt that made Luke think more of filth than it made him think of soil.

The policemen made him nervous—even if they did all look clean and well-groomed and basically friendly. They made him nervous because every damned one of them had a gun hanging from his belt, and even if Luke didn't remember a lot of things he knew what the fuck a gun was. Guns were things meant for turning people's heads to jellied pulp on the sides of walls. And there were so damn many people in this place that it seemed certain to Luke that any gunshot that missed its mark would necessarily find another, unintended target. This wasn't any place for guns. It surely wasn't a place for so many of them. "Is it?" Luke asked again. "Are there always so many of them?"

After a while Andy finished scanning the train platform and shrugged. "Not usually," he said. "Most often there are one or two police at this station. But this is the part of the City where all the rich tourists are, and with all the trouble the last few days, and the fact that anything that happens right around here has a good chance of being on the news, they probably want to make sure that nothing happens. And with all these police it probably won't."

Luke nodded, but he didn't feel as reassured as he'd've liked to be. He'd have been a lot more comfortable if the police could have got by without their firearms.

Andy started up the nearest stairway. "This way," he said. "I think there's a bank machine in this part of the tunnels. Any of them ought to take your card."

"Right," Luke said. Said it even though he didn't have much idea what the boy was talking about.

Andy led him up off the platform, through a caged-in area and out through a hinged gate, then along a confusing series of corridors, some parts of which were lined with tile, like the subway tunnel, and other parts of which were lined with shops.

A few of those shops were broken open and wrecked inside, as though looters had attacked them.

Finally they turned into a tiny shop that wasn't a shop at all, just a little glassed-in cubbyhole with a pair of strange-looking machines in it. Andy stepped aside and looked at Luke expectantly, as though waiting for him to do something.

"Well," the boy said, "go ahead. Don't just stand there."

Luke felt himself frowning. "Go ahead and do what?"

Andy let out a groan that was partly a frustrated growl. "Go ahead and stick your card in the machine and get yourself some money."

Luke blinked; it was beginning to sound familiar, but it still seemed amazing. "Really? That's all I have to do—stick a card in and the machine'll give me money?"

The boy's face was beginning to look concerned. He looked over at the machine hesitantly. "No, that's *not* all you have to do. You got to put your card in the machine, and then you got to punch in your special secret number, and then you just kind of answer the questions that it asks you so that you get what you want." He glared up at Luke. "You *do* know your special secret number, don't you?"

Luke thought about it—no number came to mind. "Not off hand." He took his wallet from his pocket, looked at the cards inside it, trying to remember any sort of a clue at all. It wasn't any use.

The boy let loose with a string of swear words that would have made his mother blanch. "How're you going to get yourself any money if you can't remember your secret number?" he asked and cursed some more. "How we going to eat lunch in this part of the city with what I've got in my pocket? I'll tell you—I'll tell you. Some Jesus you turned out to be." He cursed once more, more quietly.

Luke stared into the video-screen face of the strange machine. It *was* familiar. Vaguely familiar, anyway. He could almost see himself . . . walking up to it, putting his card into the slot. Tapping—yes, tapping four numbers on the membrane key pad. Pictured it so clearly he could almost see which numbers his fingers touched . . . numbers . . . but then the vision receded, and the harder he tried to bring it back the farther away it seemed to get.

"Damn," he said, and blushed because he'd cursed in front of a child, even though the child had cursed in front of him. "It isn't any use," he said. "I can't remember."

"You're sure?"

Luke nodded.

The boy kicked at the wall—not very hard, but hard enough for his sneaker to leave a dirt scuff. "All right," he said, "I got enough to get us a soda, anyhow. C'mon—might as well go on."

Back through more tile corridors and hallways lined with shops—no, not back; this was a different route altogether. The shops here were brighter, the floors cleaner. *Almost like a mall*, he thought, and wondered what a mall was.

They finally ended up in a peculiar place with a lavender neon sign that read McDonald's Café—a place that Luke found strange and amazing for reasons he didn't understand. It was bright and clean and almost elegant, in a way, and alien and familiar all at once. Andy motioned for Luke to sit in one of the booths that were covered with a velvetlike cloth, and left Luke waiting for a good five minutes while he bought sodas for them at the counter.

The restaurant was crowded—even more crowded than Luke would have expected from the crowds in the corridors. None of the tables were free, and most of them were full. Twice while Luke waited people came out from the counter where they sold food and asked if he'd mind if they shared his table; he felt a little guilty when he told them he was waiting for a friend to join him. Part of that guilt came from the way they looked at him when he said it—looked at him as though he were lying, and ought to be ashamed of himself. When the boy came back and sat down across from him, Luke was glad to see him, and grateful that he wouldn't have to see that look in anyone's eye again for a while.

"I got you a Coke," Andy said. "That okay?"

"Sure," he said. "I guess. Should I know what a Coke is?"

The boy rolled his eyes upward, opened the white paper bag that he'd set on the table when he sat down. Pulled out two tall white-and-yellow wax-paper cups with clear-plastic lids. "Yeah," he said, "you ought to know. Here. You'll remember when you taste it, I bet. Coca-Cola is special stuff."

Luke took the cup, lifted up the lid, began to lift it to drink—

"No," the boy said. "Not like that. That isn't the way you drink a Coke at McDonald's." He reached across the table, took the cup back. Pressed the lid back down until it snapped firm. Lifted a straw from the table where a pair of them rested beside the bag—Luke hadn't even noticed them before—and pressed one end of the straw through a cross-slit in the top of the cup. "There," he said. "Now drink it through the straw."

Luke looked up at the boy, raised an eyebrow.

"Go ahead. You've got to suck on a straw to drink through it, in case you don't remember."

"I know," Luke said, even though the truth was that he hadn't been certain. He lifted the cup, drank through the straw . . . and felt sweet thick water burst fizz all over his tongue, inside his mouth. Biting, burning ever so slightly; felt surprise paint itself all over his face, and heard the boy laughing outrageously across the table from him. For a moment he almost thought that there might be something wrong with it, that maybe the boy had played some sort of a trick on him. No; after just a second or two the fizzing stopped, and there was air in his mouth along with the fluid, and it was just sweet and strange and even a little subtle, not unsettling at all. He swallowed, which was a little awkward, since the gas and the fluid didn't want to go down the same way, and some of it went down into his lungs—

And he tried not to cough, because he knew if he did the soda that wasn't completely swallowed would go spraying everywhere, in every possible direction, and even if Luke didn't remember a lot of things he knew it wasn't polite to cough what you were drinking all over everybody and everything in a restaurant—

And across from him Andy was laughing even harder, laughing so hard that he looked like he was having trouble breathing, too—

And it finally sunk through to Luke himself how ridiculous he must look, and when he started to laugh all his control went away, and at least he'd managed to get most of it down, which meant that when he burst out choking and coughing and laughing all that came from his lungs was a fine, fine spray—not even a spray but a mist that hung in the air and drifted and sparkled tiny stars of reflected fluorescent light when Luke opened his eyes to see it.

My God, he thought, and didn't know why *that mist my God that mist* . . . and he was terrified and afraid and responsible—responsible for God knew what and God knew why but oh God he'd done it now and he was still coughing like a dying diesel, whatever that was. And made himself stop for fear of doing something even worse.

Andy was still laughing, but not so hard, and he was watching Luke, and he said, "You're awful funny, you know that Jesus?"

And Luke was too afraid of whatever he'd done to even mind being called Jesus again, not even though it was in public. Whatever he'd done was so bad that any moment now people were going to start dying, Andy included, and with that hanging over Luke's head nothing else seemed especially important.

The end was coming any moment now. It was just a matter of time. A breath; two breaths. Three. And the world was still there, and everyone in the room was still alive and *breathing* for God's sake.

Breathing.

"Hey," Andy said, "let me see that wallet of yours. I got an idea."

Luke reached into the back pocket of his jeans, took out the wallet and handed it to the boy, all without surfacing from his funk.

Andy opened the wallet, looked at it deliberately for a long while. And then suddenly his expression brightened. "Yeah—that's the ticket. I think I got it." He pulled himself up out of his seat. "You wait here, okay, Jesus? I'll be right back."

Luke nodded absently. He wanted to say something, wanted to stop the boy because he thought he wouldn't ever see him again. The weight of . . . responsibility—of *culpability*—was too much on him to let Luke move, or even speak. He tried to get himself to ask the boy to wait, anyway, but Andy was gone before Luke's lips even began to move.

And Luke was alone in a crowded room, waiting for the destruction he was certain he'd begun. He took another sip from the soda, more carefully this time. It was more familiar, now, like something he'd experienced a hundred thousand times that was only beginning to come back to him.

Nothing was happening. Whatever act it was that Luke had committed, its consequences were hiding. Waiting.

Or maybe there weren't any consequences at all. Maybe . . . maybe he hadn't done anything he had to feel responsible for.

Time wandered past him, around him. People went by, entering and leaving the restaurant. None of them *looked* as though he were about to die, or even suffer the consequences of some dire act.

Maybe nothing *would* happen. Luke's gut told him that he'd done something . . . something ultimate, something of such consequence that no one in the room would ever recover from it. But it was hard not to believe his eyes. The people in the restaurant were fine; even happy, or as happy as they could be with the world they lived in turned on its end. And when he looked at them individually, his gut told him no fearful things about their fate. Just the opposite, in fact: good things waited for these people.

I'm just shaken up, he thought. *Confused and shaken up. I ought to be, under the circumstances. There's nothing wrong here.*

Took a deep breath, let it loose.

Sure there isn't. And knew there was, but began to relax anyway. Whatever was wrong there was nothing he could do about it now. Which, as it happened, was true, at least to a degree.

A hand on his shoulder—and a smell just a breath behind it. A reek even worse than the smell of urine in the subway tunnel; more powerful and more intimate than any smell that drifted up from a concrete surface could ever be. And more *alive*, too. Alive the way smelling salts are almost alive, and warm and real and near as a lover is in the hottest part of the summer. And putrid, too, and fermented.

What in the name of God? And Luke turned and saw the old woman. *She* was where the smell came from. There was a crazy light in her rheumy eyes, and the line of drool that wandered down her chin and down her neck was dried crusty along its edges. She held a dirt-scuffed plastic shopping bag in her free hand.

"You," she said. "Yes, you're the one. I've come a long way to find you."

The smell was too much for Luke. He probably should have been curious, or should have felt bad for her, at least. He didn't. All he could think to do was try to get away from the woman before some magical power of contagion began to make him like her. He eased away from her on the seat, and her hand fell limply to her side. He'd've stood and put even more distance between himself and that woman, but she blocked his way; there was no way for him to leave his seat unless she moved aside.

"To find me?" Luke asked. It was more a stall than a question, really, but as he heard himself ask it he realized that he was eager to hear the answer. Did she know something about him—about who he was? Had she known him? He didn't think so. He didn't think he could have forgotten a woman like that.

Over the woman's shoulder, Luke could see a man who looked like the restaurant's manager coming toward them.

"Yes, to find you. You're the other one—the other one who needs to hear the word."

She stooped and reached into the shopping bag. Took out a small pamphlet and held it out to Luke. Before he realized what he was doing he'd taken it from her.

"Read it," she said. "You need to know."

The manager was right behind her, now. "We can't have you soliciting here in the store, ma'am," he said.

And the woman shuffled off, without even taking the time to answer the manager, or to explain herself to Luke. He watched her leave, and then turned to the manager, hoping for something like an explanation. The man only shrugged, confused as Luke was, and went back to his work.

Two minutes later, his wallet fell onto the table in front of him with a loud *thunk* that nearly frightened Luke half out of his wits. He looked up and saw Andy grinning at him.

"I did it," the boy said, "I did it. Take a look inside."

Luke picked up the wallet, opened it; inside were crisp green slips of sturdy-looking paper with the number 20 written in every corner. Ten or so of them. "That's money, isn't it?"

Andy let out an exasperated groan. "Yeah, that's money. You, mister, you're rich—you know that?"

Luke didn't remember being rich. He said as much. And said, "How'd you do that? I thought you needed some kind of a number."

"Well—maybe not rich. But you got more money in that account than anybody *I* know ever seen." He grinned even wider. "I figured your special secret number out. It wasn't that hard." He handed Luke a folded slip of sweat-damp white paper; Luke unfolded it and saw inside a four-digit number that the boy had scrawled.

"How did you manage that?"

"Your driver's license, there. It's only got two numbers on it that you'd use often enough to know them by heart: your address and your zip code. I tried them both, then tried them backward. It turned out to be your address, last number first, first number last."

"Huh," Luke said. "I'll be. What do you know."

"I know I'm hungry, that's what I know. And there's someplace over in Rockefeller Center where I've always wanted to eat. And you can take me there. Then we can go get you some decent clothes . . . and then, well, we'll see."

"Okay," Luke said. "If that's what you want, why not."

North-Central Tennessee

The creature set a hard pace for Ron, and a long and steady one. It was a peculiar route they took; west-northwest, to Ron's sense of things, and they walked all but as straight as a bird would travel. So straight, in fact, that they ignored all but a couple of the roads and trails they came upon. Still, their way was surprisingly clear; the going was as easy as though they were traveling along a trail or walking along the shoulder of a highway.

The thing that surprised Ron most, though, was the fact that he was able to keep up with the creature in the first place. And for so long—they walked all afternoon, through the night, and when the sun rose they were still going. He kept expecting to get tired, or hungry, or maybe to drop with sudden exhaustion. He didn't, though. When the sun rose Ron felt as good and as fresh as he had when they'd started off the afternoon before.

More then once as they went Ron got a deep, unsettling feeling in his gut—an absolute certainty that they were being followed. They'd walk out into a quiet dusty expanse of ground, where their tread made no noise, and behind him Ron would hear the sound of . . . not the sound of footsteps, exactly, but the sound of something moving. And he'd turn too quickly for whatever it was to hide, so quickly that his neck hurt from the motion, and try to see whatever it was behind him.

There'd be nothing. No one would be anywhere in sight. No one but the creature, and Ron himself.

They paused about an hour after dawn near the top of a hill, where the creature checked his bearings against the sky and against the terrain below them. That's what Ron thought he was doing, anyway; the creature didn't say and Ron had no way of being certain on his own.

"Why . . ." Ron thought about his question, rephrased it. "Why did the explosion change you so much? How did you end up looking . . . so different?"

The creature looked up, away from the broad, gentle valley below them. Looked at Ron. And for what must have been the hundredth time Ron felt the small hairs on the back of his neck stand on end. Not from fear, or from any of fear's close cousins; more from—something like awe. Something like the awe he felt in church sometimes when he was very young, when he'd look up and see the so-real wooden Christ staring down at him, his carved face full of pain and suffering and compassion and love. Even then Ron had known the story of Jesus dying horribly on the cross so that he could Atone For Our Sins. And he'd look up and see the Christ in such awful and everlasting pain like that, and all he'd be able to feel was gratitude and love and mystery and awe, and he'd think, *I love you too, Jesus, I love you too.*

Yes, he thought. That was exactly what he felt when the Beast looked at him.

The creature almost seemed to see that as Ron felt it, and when he did he looked away—almost embarrassed. Almost as though it were a thing he ought never to let himself hear. And then he put his hand on Ron's shoulder, and lifted Ron's fingers to his goatlike face with his free hand . . .

And Ron was small, so very tiny, in a room so stark and bright and white—it was Bonner's laboratory, Bonner's laboratory seen from some impossible and alien perspective. The creature's perspective.

The Beast's perspective.

Ron was the Beast, and he was in Bonner's lab, and he was so tiny that the poor creature couldn't have been more than a day old, or two days, maybe, and he was strapped down too tight to even squirm, strapped to something that Ron knew was an operating table, even if the creature hadn't, then.

And Herman Bonner had a scalpel in his hand. And the blade was coming down toward him.

"*No,*" Ron shouted. "Please—enough, enough. Don't show me any more."

And the vision stopped.

"My God," he said. "He did that to you with a knife." How much surgery would it have taken to make a creature born to look as the Beast did now—impossible, but so natural and obvious that his uniqueness seemed more an oversight of evolution than an aberration—how much surgery would it have taken to make a creature that looked so *right* into a thing as unnatural and alien as he had been?

Only two afterbits of the vision were still rolling toward him—gently, as though the creature had tried to stop them, but couldn't. The first was a sense of repetition, as though the same horror had taken place over and over again. And the second was the ghost of pain. Incredible, vivid pain, from a great distance.

"And he didn't use an anesthetic."

The Beast looked at him uncertainly, as though he were uncertain what exactly an anesthetic was, and then he nodded.

Ron felt himself shudder.

"Someone needs to lock that man away, lock him up and not ever let him loose." And Ron was thinking worse things; he wanted to do to the man more hurt than he'd just seen— *felt*—done to the creature.

The Beast must have seen that in Ron's heart the same way he saw all those other things, because his half-animal face suddenly went sad and grim, and he shook his head. Whatever Bonner's sins were, Ron would only bring evil on himself by trying to set things even.

It was true, too, and Ron knew it. "Yeah," he said. "You're right. Even so it'd do my heart good to see him run over by a truck."

The creature didn't seem to approve of that, either, but he didn't make a point of showing Ron what he felt.

There was something else, too—the creature's reversion to his natural form. That was obvious, Ron thought: he remembered the strange bacteria Luke Munsen had been working on. The bacteria that wasn't supposed to have any effect on people, wasn't supposed to bring anything back to life—and did, anyway. Somehow it had got loose in the explosion at the lab, and that was why he was alive now when he should be dead. He wasn't a scientist, but he'd gone through basic college biology last year. He knew what DNA was. He knew what Luke was working with. He didn't understand the bacteria, but he understood enough of what it was supposed to do to realize what had happened to the creature. Every creature carries a blueprint of itself inside its cells, inside its genes, and Luke's microbes were meant to weed out that blueprint and rebuild from it. And that rebuilding had recreated the Beast in the form he was born to have.

Mechanical noise from somewhere not too far away. Slapping, sputtering noise. Like a machine gun. Or a helicopter. Ron looked up and out, toward the noise, and saw that it *was* a helicopter.

A helicopter in the middle of nowhere, at an ungodly hour of the morning.

And it was coming straight toward them.

"What the—?"

Ron looked over at the creature, and saw an expression on his face that almost looked . . . impatient. Certainly the look wasn't a look of surprise. Had the creature known the thing was coming?

Well, Ron thought, he seemed to know when a lot of things were coming.

"What is it?" he asked. "Why is it here?"

The creature didn't answer.

The thing was closer, now—close enough for Ron to see the symbol painted on the helicopter's side.

He recognized that symbol. It was the same symbol that had been on the comic book the old woman had given him. The same symbol that those crazy fundamentalists used when they bought air time on television.

On the spine of those books in Herman Bonner's office.

A cross, bright white against the green-black of the rest of the helicopter. Off-center and high on the upward arm of the cross was a delicate circle—a halo, almost. And through the circle a dove was flying.

Peculiar stuff.

When they used that symbol on television, the background was always stark black, and the TV screen somehow managed to produce a color for the cross that to Ron's eye looked brilliant—whiter, somehow, than white.

The helicopter was closer now, much closer, and it wasn't slowing down. Two hundred yards? One hundred? Maybe even closer than that.

And weren't those crazy circle-dove-and-cross people the same church that the President belonged to? Had belonged to, Ron corrected himself, remembering the report he'd heard yesterday on the car radio—the report about the President getting himself killed in a plane wreck. Ron wasn't certain about the word *church*, either; was it appropriate to call something a church when most of the flock attended via the television sets in their living rooms? Whether they were a church or not, they were big. Big and everywhere. Once or twice Ron had even heard that they owned a lot of stock in some of the country's largest corporations. He hadn't taken those rumors very seriously . . . but still, it was possible. It wasn't hard to see that they took in a lot of money from their television ministry. That kind of money could buy all sorts of things.

Like helicopters.

Ron kept wanting to think that it was some kind of a mistake, that the helicopter was out here in the middle of nowhere flying toward them . . . just by coincidence. But if that was so then why was it coming at them so directly? It didn't seem likely to Ron that they were just intent on being neighborly enough to say hello.

And if they were here because of Ron and the creature, then how in the hell had they found them—so far from where they'd been last night? So far from anywhere at all. How, for that matter, had they even known the two of them were alive?

It was too strange for Ron. Too improbable. Everything was these last few days.

The helicopter was much too close, now, and still coming at them. A second, three seconds, ten seconds away. Ron pictured himself skewered on the helicopter's skids, or maybe even hacked into chunks of warm bloody meat by its rotor, and found himself possessed of an overwhelming compulsion to run for his life. Until the Beast set his arm on Ron's shoulder again, and suddenly he knew that everything was going to be all right, that all he had to do was stand steady and unafraid, and the powerful machine would go by them without doing any harm.

Something was charging up the hill toward them, Ron saw in the corner of his eye. Or maybe it was charging toward the helicopter. Ron stood steady, calm; the creature's touch made it easy to be easy about the world. He looked down and saw . . . Tom the dog? What was the dog doing here? And Ron would have sworn that the dog's expression looked self-righteous and protective, even though he'd have sworn a moment before that a dog's expression couldn't convey that much.

Ron remembered then: the sense that something had

been following them. That explained the dog, easily, but what about the helicopter?

It didn't matter what the explanation was; the helicopter was too close now for Ron to care about anything like that. It was all but on top of them. Close enough, if he reached up and out, to touch the foremost tip of its right landing skid. It had slowed, too, to the point where it was barely even moving.

And the dog crested the hill and lunged, insanely, at the painted steel flank of the helicopter.

Ron's eye followed the arc of the dog's leap, saw the poor thing smash himself, and his eye couldn't bear to look at that too closely; it continued along the same arc, past the cross-and-circle emblem, toward the open door of the helicopter—

Where he saw the video camera. Focused on him—no, focused on the creature.

And suddenly he remembered the way the Mountainville paper had reacted when they'd first got word of the creature. And he knew that however the people in the helicopter had found them, they were here to turn Ron and the creature into a spectacle. Or worse than that, they meant to start a witch hunt.

"Oh Christ," he said, mostly under his breath. Not loud enough for any microphone to hear under the helicopter's racket, anyway. Then, louder, "Go away. We don't need any trouble." When he heard himself he knew that he hadn't spoken loud enough for anyone else to hear him. He was about to start shouting at them, maybe even try climbing up into the helicopter and take that camera from them, when he felt the creature's touch on his arm, and he knew that if he did it would only make things worse than they already were. Likely, he realized, it was exactly what they wanted—good footage of an irate madman attacking the television screen.

A moment, two moments. The dog was crumpled in a heap, whimpering in pain. And Ron realized that the dog needed comfort, that he probably wasn't seriously hurt, but he needed attention, and that need was more important than anything the cameramen or the helicopter might do. And the creature was already moving toward Tom, and Ron began to do the same. Out of the corner of his eye he saw one of the cameramen shrug his shoulders; before he got close enough to pat the dog's head, the helicopter was moving out and away from them, as though it had lost interest entirely.

They didn't want pictures of the Evil Creature comforting a hurt dog, Ron thought. It would spoil their theater.

Tom the dog wasn't that bad hurt at all, though his pride seemed to be severely bruised. The creature was stroking the coarse fur of the dog's back already, and Tom began to pant sheepishly. Ron bent down and kneaded the loose fur just behind his ears, and after a moment of that the dog began to look as though he'd never been hurt at all.

Ron grinned and shook his head. The dog, he was convinced, was a ham—maybe even more of a showman than the cross-dove-and-circle types who were tracking after them with television cameras. That was just as well; the dog was obviously on their side (if side was the appropriate word) and the other side seemed to have it all over Ron and the creature as far as showmanship went. They needed whatever help they could get.

Thought about that for a moment, and realized that it was more than a little paranoid. All the people in the helicopter had done was take some pictures of them; there wasn't any call to go and draw sides. Certainly not yet. Maybe the fundamentalist types didn't mean any harm.

Not that Ron believed it for a moment. Still, getting confrontational too soon would only make matters worse.

"You okay, boy?" he asked the dog. "What are you doing following us so far? What's got into you?"

Tom looked up at Ron soulfully, but he didn't answer the question. Not that Ron had expected him to.

The creature stood, moved away from them. When he was five yards away he stopped and waited purposely, as though he meant that they needed to get going again.

Ron looked back down at the dog. "Think you can walk, huh, Tom? You might as well walk with us instead of skulking along behind."

The dog was still looking up at him earnestly; he didn't move a muscle when Ron asked the question. So Ron got up, and began to act as though he were going to leave without him, and the dog certainly understood that—he was on his feet and following before Ron was three paces away. He walked without a limp, too, which made Ron suspect that attacking the helicopter had caused the dog less harm than it'd seemed at first.

The walk wasn't anywhere near so long this time. Not

more than a couple of miles, in fact—out across the valley that had been below them, over the far hill, and into a small town.

As they descended toward it Ron caught sight of the helicopter again, on top of another hill that lay to the west of them. It was far enough away that he couldn't see the people inside it. He didn't have to be able to see them to be certain that they were watching. He touched the creature's shoulder and pointed to show him, but the creature wasn't concerned. Not any more concerned than the dog would have been.

And that wasn't a fair comparison, and Ron knew it: Tom was a decent dog, and a good one, but he didn't have the sense . . . well, the truth was, he didn't have the sense God gave a dog. The creature, on the other hand—Ron suspected that the creature just might have more of a mind than he had himself. The idea was sobering, but it didn't threaten him especially. There was too much *good* about the creature for Ron to find him a threat. Even if the creature was smart, even if he was smarter than Ron was . . . there was something *innocent* about him. Something that hadn't been marked by the world, in spite of anything Herman Bonner might have done to him.

Ron thought there was, anyway. It didn't escape him that a certain amount of the assumption came from his ego's need to reassert itself. After all: innocence gave the creature naiveté, and in Ron's own opinion he himself was anything but naive.

"They're trouble, you know," he told the Beast. "Those people over there mean us nothing but harm. You especially— if they mean me wrong it's only because I'm with you."

because I'm with you

Ron heard his own words echo in his ear, and knew that the creature was asking if he was afraid—asking if he felt a need to get himself out of harm's way.

"No," he said. "I'm not afraid. Not afraid enough to be scared away, anyhow. But I am worried for you. Why are you walking right into the middle of trouble? There isn't any need for it."

The creature didn't give any answer, except to shake his head and look away.

The town was a small one, almost too small to call a town. It looked prosperous; the two-dozen houses and the three or four stores were old enough to be weathered, but if any of them were in bad repair, Ron couldn't see it.

They were still fifty yards from the edge of town when the old man spotted them.

He was sun-worn and leathery skinned, and he looked old only the way a man who's worked all his life with his hands can look old, but there was nothing frail or unhealthy about him. He wore denim overalls and under them a faded flannel shirt, and a grimy baseball cap with an advertisement for a motor oil distributor.

At first he didn't seem to react to them in any special way. About the way Ron would expect anyone to react, seeing strangers come into town on foot, and at an hour that was too early for sensible folk to be awake, let alone traveling. He looked at Ron warily, set a careful eye on the dog . . .

And then he saw the Beast.

And then he reacted. God did he react.

He looked, for a long moment, like the impotent victim in a bad horror film—terrified out of his mind, in danger of death from a heart attack as much or more than he was from whatever peril he'd laid eyes on. And he screamed, of course—long and loud and hard enough that by the time he was done there wasn't much chance that anyone in the town was still asleep. And then his scream drifted off and away, into the hills, and the bug-eyed terror receded from his face. And he began to . . . to *see* the creature, not just to see the alienness of his physical body but to *see* him the way Ron had first seen him just before the explosion that had killed them both.

And he took off the baseball cap, and fell to his knees, and begged the creature for forgiveness.

And the Beast walked up to him, and shook his head, and held out his hand to help the old man to his feet.

The old man took the creature's hand with a look of such immense gratitude that it embarrassed Ron to see it. "I'm sorry," he said. "I'm so sorry. Can you ever forgive me for not knowing you when I saw you?"

The creature looked at both of them, and they both knew that there wasn't anything to forgive.

"It's an honest mistake," Ron told the man. "Anyone could make it. Besides . . . he isn't anyone you ought to know. It wasn't God who put him on this earth. I don't think so, anyway."

The old man shook his head nervously at Ron. "But he is—can't you see that? He *is*."

"No. Honest. He's something special—special isn't even the right word—but I'm pretty sure that all the special about him isn't anything his maker intended. I think I can tell you that for a fact."

The old man just kept shaking his head, telling Ron how wrong he was.

There were more people out on the street, now; two or three dozen of them, at least. Most of them were staring— some terrified, some agape. But there wasn't a one of them, not a single damned one in the whole town, that didn't clearly know the creature for an omen. Each one of them, Ron thought, likely saw him as an omen of a different future. There was no way you could set eyes on the Beast without knowing that his existence meant something powerful and important about the future of the world.

The old man was holding his cap down by his hip, now. "The two of you look as though you've been traveling all night," he said, and then he noticed the dog. "Three of you, that is. Sorry. Can I take you down to the café here and buy you a little breakfast?"

Even after walking all that way—and most of it in the dark, at that—Ron still wasn't especially hungry. He hadn't eaten and hadn't been hungry, either, in all the time since he'd found himself woke back to life yesterday morning. It was a peculiar thing, and more than a little unsettling. Still: even if he didn't feel a need for food, there was something . . . something sensually appealing about the idea of a good meal. He looked over at the creature, and when he nodded Ron told the man they'd be much obliged.

The café, well, the café was almost more a diner than it was a café, except that instead of being housed inside some silvery trailer that wasn't going anywhere it was in an old cement-block building that looked as though it might once have been home to a garage. There couldn't have been more than a couple of dozen tables inside it, and small tables at that, but even so most of the town somehow managed to follow them inside. By then there wasn't a one of them who hadn't realized that the creature was something special and important and good, and they were all hushed quiet and reverent as though they'd somehow found themselves in church.

"There isn't any call to be so quiet," Ron said. "Neither one of us is going to think bad about you if you talk." And someone laughed at that kind of involuntarily, and then there was a sort of general chuckle that passed around and through the room. It wasn't long after that before the room began to sound like a celebration. A powerful celebration—kind of the sound Ron would have expected on Christmas day in the living room of a family with two dozen children.

The waitress brought them coffee, and she was about to hand them menus when Ron ordered for both the creature and himself: eggs and potatoes and toast and bacon and a couple of fat glasses of orange juice from the squeezer he saw up by the counter. Breakfast the way it ought to be, at least according to Ron. Even Tom the dog got food: a couple of minutes after the waitress had taken their order the cook came out of the kitchen with a thick long ham bone; the dog, who'd parked himself dutifully beside the creature, took the bone greedily, as though it were his due.

A small boy with a bad limp walked up to the creature while they were waiting for their food, and asked the Beast to cure him.

"I busted my leg right well last summer," he said, "and the bone never grew back together like the doctor down to county hospital said it would. You can heal me, can't you? I can tell you can. Nobody got to show me twice."

The creature looked at the boy, and Ron hurt for him having a boy need him like that when there was nothing he could do. He could feel the creature's pain, he thought—but maybe that was just Ron confusing his own hurt with the Beast's.

"Sure would be nice to be able to go hiking down by the crick again," the boy said.

"Son," Ron said quietly—too quietly for anyone but Ron and the creature and the boy to hear—"son, the creature isn't Christ. There's nothing he can do that'll cure you."

The boy looked at Ron, and looked nervously back at the creature, and for just a moment his eyes looked angry and resentful. That didn't last very long; part of the . . . whatever it was about the creature was a thing that calmed and soothed. Ron had a hard time imagining himself doing things he wouldn't be proud of in front of the creature.

"He's awful special, I just know he is. Don't even have to

look at him to know that. If there's anything or anyone in this world that can fix my leg, I know it's him."

"I—" Ron choked on his words, and lost them. He looked at the creature, but his animal face was unreadable. Then two things happened, both at once: a woman came from the far side of the room, calling, "Jerry!"—

And the creature reached out for the boy, and he hugged him, plain and simple hugged him, and there wasn't anything that looked like cure in the hug, but there was love, and sympathy, and gentleness. And then the woman was there with them, and she was crying, whether from hurt or from frustration Ron couldn't say, but she was saying "I'm so sorry," with a deep drawl, and the creature pulled her into his hug and they just stood there like that for the longest time. After a while she sniffed and took her son by the hand and said that she thought she should leave them to their breakfast, and she went away, the boy limping beside her. Ron almost expected to hear her scold the boy, but she didn't.

Then the waitress came out of the kitchen with their food, and when the creature saw what was on his plate he didn't seem to have much stomach for it. He picked a little at the toast and the potatoes, and he drank the juice, but he left the eggs and bacon alone. He didn't make any special show of distaste, though, and Ron ate his own breakfast with a great deal of pleasure.

When he was finished eating and sipping at his coffee, the old man at the table beside them—the one who'd invited them to breakfast—offered Ron a cigarette, and he took it and thanked the man, and that cigarette and that cup of coffee were just about the best Ron had ever had in his whole life. As he smoked and sipped he and the old man talked quietly about nothing at all.

Whiteman Air Force Base,
Johnson County, Missouri

The base commander, General Simpson, wasn't happy to see him. Not even remotely.

He gave Bill time to clean himself of the scent of embalming fluid and get himself a uniform, and then the commander sat him down in his big office with its furniture that was nice enough that it might have been civilian.

And he frowned. And went back to the paperwork on his desk, leaving Bill with nothing to do but sit there upright in his wooden chair and stare at the wall. For most of half an hour, or maybe longer. It was still hard for Bill to say about time; being dead all that while had left him disoriented.

However long it was, it was *long*. Longer than an airman can wait comfortably. Which is pretty darned long, when you consider that to Bill's way of thinking most of what the whole darned Air Force does most of the time is wait for there to be somebody who needs shooting at or shooting down or to have a bomb dropped on him. And most of the time there's nobody around who fits that particular description, so most of what the Air Force does to earn its keep is standing around and looking tough and waiting. Bill thought. Of course, he also thought he was pretty good at sitting around and waiting himself, and even if he was waiting now pretty successfully, he wasn't very comfortable about it.

"Son," the general said, finally—pushing aside the papers on his desk, folding his hands. Frowning again, like an uncle who was disappointed in his favorite nephew. "Son, I don't rightly know what you're doing alive right now. I don't know how it is that you're healthy and whole when two days ago we had to pour what was left of you into that coffin. I do know one thing: you'd've done all of us a big favor if you'd managed to keep yourself dead."

He paused, as though he wanted to hear what Bill had to say for himself. Which he didn't have a thing to say, of course.

"Yes sir." Which wasn't precisely—or even remotely—anything like what Bill had to say about the subject. He wasn't one to address a general otherwise.

"You know, when you were dead, you were a hero. Not a hero like we could tell anybody about it. Or even admit it to ourselves out loud—officially you had to be a criminal. After all, you were responsible—deliberately responsible, and we knew it—for the murder of President Paul Green of these United States.

"We also knew that you did us all a favor. More than a favor: you gave your life to save the world from a holocaust. So long as you were dead, we could all live with those contradictions; vilify you at the same time we very quietly buried you with your own flag, which is a fitting thing at a hero's funeral."

Bill could feel himself blushing. Partly because he was touched and honored; partly because he was ashamed and embarrassed. Also because he wasn't quite sure what it was that the general was about to drop on him, but he knew that whatever it was it didn't sound as though it were likely to be altogether pleasant.

"But you *are* alive, and if God knows why or how, He isn't telling. And because you're alive we've got to *do* something with you. The obvious thing is to let you stand trial for murder. We can't, of course. The Air Force and the country owe you something for what you've done; and putting you on trial would give the Air Force an even larger black eye than the one you've already given it. We can't very well just leave you here, either—if word got out. . . ." The general coughed. Pushed a thin manila file-folder across his desk, toward Bill. "These are your duty papers, son. In your own way, you turned out to be an easier problem to solve than I might have expected. As soon as the brass in Washington got word about your unlikely resurrection, they had plans for you. Apparently you aren't the only . . . phenomenon of this type that's out there right at the moment. And just as you might guess, it's a phenomenon they find themselves quite concerned over. To put it a little more bluntly: they're doing research, and you've been drafted as a guinea pig. Go ahead. Take a look at your papers."

"Yes sir." Bill reached tentatively forward, took the folder gingerly from its place on the general's desk. Opened it. And saw that a man with another name was being reassigned to a research project.

In the demilitarized zone.

In South Korea.

Bill was amazed, unsure of how he ought to react, even half in doubt as to whether the general had given him the right folder. He stared dumbfounded at the paper in front of him for a time that was long enough that the general probably took it as a sign of disrespect. Which wasn't by any stretch a thing that he'd intended.

"Yes, Private. We've changed your name. And we're sending you to Korea. That's where the Pentagon is having the research done: the political situation here in the States at the moment—well, let's be frank. *Unstable* is a mild word for it. The Brass doesn't want to take the chance of civilian government stumbling into this project. So they're putting it in a place where we don't *have* any civilian government. And if you don't like having your name taken away, my apologies. There's no room in this Air Force for PFC Bill Wallace any more; your name is Ted Roe for the duration. And if you have any sense you'll use it for the rest of your life."

Bill wasn't altogether certain that he'd be able to answer to somebody else's name—he'd spent too many years answering to his own already to get used to another. He said as much to the general, who scowled and slapped his hand down hard on the wooden surface of his desk.

"Take a good look at that name, Private. No, not Private: you're *Corporal* Roe, now. And your middle name is William. You're Theodore William Roe, and if need be you can tell people you answer to your middle name. And that's the long and the short of it. When you leave this office you are to go directly to the airfield. Because you are now a highly classified property of the Air Force, between here and there you are to hold your head low, so as to avoid being recognized, and you will speak to no one. You will board your plane—it will be the only plane on the runway—and once aboard you are to speak to no one until you reach your destination, where appropriate personnel will be waiting to escort you. The only exception to any of this will be that you may speak once en route, but only to the extent that is absolutely necessary to avoid attracting undue attention to yourself. Are you clear on this?"

Bill was clear, all right. Though he wasn't especially enthusiastic. "Yes sir."

"In that case, Corporal Roe, you're dismissed." He stood up, reached across his desk to shake Bill's hand. "It's been my pleasure to be your commanding officer."

North-Central Tennessee

All told, they spent a little more than an hour in the roadside café. As Ron sipped at his coffee the people of town began to come up to them and ask them questions; not that he or the creature had any of the answers. Some of them asked about their future, or about the future of the world, and more than one asked them if God was still alive and if he loved the world. Ron was certain that he was and that he did, but not nearly sure enough to say so from the position of authority that they saw him in.

The creature didn't take it well at all. Not that he treated the townsfolk badly, or acted anything but a saint. But the fact that they *needed* and there was nothing he could do for them wore hard on him; Ron didn't need any special vision to see that. They'd ask their questions and he'd touch their arms or hold them, and eventually they'd go away not knowing a damn thing they didn't know before, or at least nothing they wouldn't have known if they'd given it a little thought. They'd be happier, at least, anyway. After a while Beast began to cry—not pointedly histrionically sobbing or heaving or anything like that, just tears seeping kind of gently from his eyes in a way that didn't seem to affect his behavior or his dignity especially.

When the last of them had come and gone, the creature stood to leave, and Ron went to pay the check. Before he could even lift it from the table the old man had picked it up himself, and he refused to let Ron have it. He'd invited them, after all, the old man said. So Ron let it be, and the old man paid for them.

Almost everyone who'd been in the restaurant followed them as they walked to the far edge of town. For a while Ron began to wonder if they'd all be coming with them, but when they'd passed the last house the creature turned back and *looked* at them, and suddenly there wasn't any doubt in anyone's heart, not even Ron's, that the three of them had to travel on alone.

Over the heads of the townspeople Ron could see that the helicopter was still on the far hill, watching them. *Trouble*, he thought. What did those people want with them? Were they going to keep following them?

As he watched, the helicopter took off and began to move toward them.

It was only a moment before it was passing low overhead; as it passed Ron saw a video camera mounted on its side swivel to watch him. And then it just kept going, northward, over the horizon.

New York City

Luke and Andy ate in a place that called itself a café, too. But the place where they ate was a much more expensive one—even if the food was not one whit better—and there was no one volunteering to pick up the check for them. Not that it mattered; Luke had plenty of money. By Andy's lights, or anyone else's, damn near. All his life Luke had worked, and worked hard; he'd never spent money as quickly as he'd made it. Even young as Luke had been when he'd died, he'd left two full years' income in the bank.

Not that Luke understood what he had. All he knew was that the money he had in his pocket was plenty as far as the prices on the menu were concerned.

They ate in the restaurant that called itself the Bistro Café, a strange place with floor-to-ceiling windows that faced out onto a concrete grotto of some kind; from where they sat and ate it almost seemed like a giant aquarium, filed with air. That's what Andy said, anyway: he told Luke that it reminded him of the Brooklyn aquarium, out at Coney Island—only instead of watching a bunch of fish swim around, you got to watch people shopping at the tables they had set up, or watch them staring at the fountain that spattered water all along the far wall. In winter, the boy said, the whole place outside there was a great big ice-skating rink.

Toward the end of the meal the boy disappeared for a long while—he had to go off in search of a men's room, finding which, apparently, was no small matter—and Luke was left alone at the table for most of twenty minutes. When half the wait had passed, Luke remembered the pamphlet that the strange, vile-smelling old woman had given him, and because there was nothing else to do he took it from the pocket where he'd put it and began to read.

It was strange stuff; fascinating and vile all at the same time. A comic book about the end of the world, and at the same time not a comic book and not about the end of the world at all. It was identical, in fact, to the comic book that the same old woman had given to Ron Hawkins several days before and thousands of miles away. Even as off balance as Luke was, he could see the . . . derangedness of the pamphlet's author. Of course, he had an advantage that the comic book's intended audience could not have had: he'd already died, and lived through it, and he knew that death wasn't something he had to live in fear of. He thought about that a little more, and decided that it was exactly true: the comic book was playing on the fear of death in its readers. Took the idea one step farther . . . and almost began to wonder if all religion was playing on the fear of death. Maybe it was, in fact. And yet . . . there was something wrong in that thought, too. There was a deep feeling about God in Luke's gut, a reverence, and he didn't think that reverence had anything at all to do with death, or with being afraid of it.

"What you reading?" Andy asked him, plopping himself back down into his seat.

"Uh?" Luke blinked, pulled himself up out of his fugue. "Comic book. Something someone gave me while I was waiting for you back at McDonald's." He tossed it to the boy.

The boy opened the pamphlet, flipped a few pages. "I've seen these before," he said. "Those cross-and-circle people are always handing them out. Or trying to sell them to you." Handed it back to Luke as though it were nothing at all. "So," he said, "let's go get you some clothes. You can't wear my Daddy's shirt forever—not just that one, anyways. You're going to start to smell like a derelict if we don't get you something to change into soon."

Luke thought of the way that the old woman smelled, and shuddered. He didn't want to smell like that—didn't want people thinking about him the things that the smell made him think of the old woman. He picked up the check, stood. "Do I take this up to the counter?"

Andy looked around. "Yeah, looks like it. Don't forget to leave a tip."

"Tip. . . ? Oh, yeah—a tip." Luke took out his wallet, opened it.

"Figure twice the tax."

"Right," Luke said, as though he'd known it all along, even though he hadn't. He took two bills from his wallet, dropped them on the table; walked across the room and paid the woman who stood behind the register.

Andy led him up to street level, to a shop that looked and *felt* too expensive. It wasn't, though; the money in his wallet bought him shirts and slacks and underclothes, and when he'd paid for it all there was still plenty left over.

"What now?" he asked the boy. They were standing outside the door of the clothes shop; the plastic shopping bag under Luke's left arm was bulging and almost uncomfortably heavy.

"I don't know. You want to do a little window shopping, maybe?" Andy started walking north along Fifth Avenue; Luke followed him.

All around them were shops filled with fur coats and jewelry and chocolates too expensive to eat. "You want to buy a window? Is this really the place to buy it?" Even if they could find a shop that sold window glass, he thought, if they bought it here they'd pay three times what it was worth.

Andy sighed; exasperated. "Not shop *for* windows. Shop at them—window shop. Like wandering up and down the street, looking in the windows at things you want to buy but can't afford. And sometimes wondering why people who have money spend it on things like they have in some of these places."

"Uh." Luke looked out toward the far end of the street; there were tall, full trees up ahead. The Avenue seemed to lead into a park a few blocks from where they stood. "Does that mean we can't buy anything?"

Andy shrugged. "You can if you want. Shouldn't, probably. Spending money sort of goes against the spirit of window shopping."

Luke thought about it for a while; it didn't make a whole lot of sense. Was the boy joking with him again? Maybe. And maybe not. He sure *looked* serious. He always looked serious. Luke decided that he'd play along, or play it straight, anyway; it was a good response to a joke, and if Andy wasn't joking, then maybe window shopping was something he could learn to enjoy.

They went four blocks before the boy actually paused anywhere long enough to get a good look inside any of the store windows. The shop that finally did catch his eye wasn't one of the expensive-looking ones; just the opposite, in fact. The place was worn and tacky-looking. It had a big, dirty five-color plastic sign that read UPPER MIDTOWN CAMERAS and below that $ave! Be$t Price$ on Fifth Avenue! The store's two windows were crowded floor to ceiling with cheap computers, adding machines, radios, tape recorders, typewriters . . .

even cameras, but not many of those. There were little hand-written signs all over the place, describing the merchandise—all of them said *sale!*, but not a one of them had a price on it.

Off to the left there were televisions, three of them all playing to the same station—what? There, on the screens, what. . . ? Luke recognized the face of that man . . . from somewhere. And that, that—*creature* beside him. . . ! Luke didn't know why, but the sight of the thing, even just seeing it there on the screen . . . gooseflesh, all over his back, his neck, his upper arms. Luke *knew* that man. And something in his gut was certain that it knew the creature, even though the truth was that he'd never seen anything like it before. They were standing on top of a hill surrounded by forest, and the man looked angry and belligerent—furious, in fact. Looking at the man's expression, Luke was glad that he was nowhere near him.

A piece of the image on each screen cut away, and suddenly there was a man dressed in dark robes in the screens' lower corner, speaking to him like a newscaster. The man looked nothing like a newscaster.

Andy was watching the screens now, too, from over Luke's shoulder. "What's he saying?"

The boy looked up at him indignantly. "How am I supposed to know what he's saying—I can't hear through that glass any better than you can. Do I look like I can read lips?"

Luke felt himself blush. "Sorry. I guess you don't."

"Well, I can, but that's beside the point. He's saying something about . . . about some kind of a beast, and a revelation . . . 'voice of Armageddon'—I don't know. Weird stuff. I think he's saying that the Beast from Revelation has showed up on earth. You know—666, tattoos, everybody has to have his own credit card, all that stuff. It looks like he's saying something about a radio station, too. And he wants everyone to send them all the money that they got."

"Really?"

"Well—not exactly. He does want people to send him money, though. As much as they can possibly afford, and then maybe some more, too."

The man Luke thought he recognized was looking right into the camera, now, and shaking his fist at it. Luke thought he might attack the screen, but then suddenly the *creature* put his arm on the man's shoulder, and before anything else could happen the image on the screen changed completely, and they were watching the man and the creature walking into a small town. The people of the town seemed . . . terrified when they first set eyes on the creature, but after just a moment in its presence the creature seemed somehow to enchant them. Worn, tired-hearted people seemed almost to glow under the spell of that enchantment; one gnarled old woman, Luke would have sworn, seemed to grow younger as she looked at the goatlike thing.

And as each of the people in the town fell under the enchantment, numbers would appear on his forehead:

666

They weren't real numbers; Luke could tell that just by looking at the screen. The numbers were something that someone in a television studio had superimposed over the faces of the townspeople. Even still, they chilled Luke's heart.

"The man says that the creature there is the Beast from Revelation. He says it's the next sign that we're living through the end of the world."

Luke stared, agape.

"Do you believe him?"

Luke shook his head. "What?"

"Do you really believe that that thing's the Beast from Revelation? Do you really think we're all going to die?"

"Uh—" Luke didn't know what to say. "I don't know. Maybe. Do you?"

"Nah." Andy kicked the ground with the toe of his sneaker. "My Momma knows all about God and all of those things. She taught me pretty good. And she always told me, 'Don't you never trust nobody who wants to sell you God. God don't charge admission—God loves you for free, or He don't love you at all.' And God loves wicked people, too, so it don't make any difference at all."

"What has that got to do with the Beast? I can see the thing with my own eyes. Even if the man just wants money, it doesn't seem to me that he's necessarily wrong about the facts."

The boy shrugged. "Maybe," he said. "Maybe so. My Momma's been talking about the end of the world a lot lately, too. But this guy—I don't make a habit of believing what anybody has to say when what they really want is my money."

The scene on the television screens changed again: they were walking away from the town, now, and the camera was zooming in on the creature and the man Luke thought he recognized.

"What's he saying now? What are they doing?"

The boy stared hard at the screen. "Holy shit," he said. "Holy shit."

He looked up at the street sign on the corner, grabbed Luke's hand and dragged him away. Running. Around the corner and down a long, tall, canyonlike block.

"What? Why?"

"They're crazy. *Crazy.*" Jogged to one side to avoid a thick-wet pile of dog droppings. "They're taking over ABC. The television network. He's telling everybody who's watching to go to the ABC building and help take it over!"

ABC? Television network? It sounded familiar, but not familiar enough to make sense of. Taking it over how?

"I don't get it. What did the man say?"

The boy cursed again. "He said that they were 'commandeering the ABC television network in the name of God for the duration of this earth.' And that the network would 'henceforth be known as the Voice of Armageddon.' The man's saying that because the Beast is here, they can do whatever they think they have to. Something like that, anyway—hard to follow all that, just reading lips. Can you understand *that?*"

He couldn't, of course. Not that Luke's pride would let him say so.

He began to understand when they got to the end of the block, though; what he saw there was almost self-explanatory. Buses. Buses everywhere, so many of them parked in front of the dark-stone building with the black *abc* sign that there was no room for traffic to get by around them. Thirty, forty, maybe even fifty busses. And people carrying protest signs, and television cameras—none of those said *abc;* instead they all had a strange monogram with a cross and a circle and a dove.

And there were people with guns, too. The cameras stayed away from those people. In fact, the cameras were very careful to avoid the real violence—the shooting. The bodies heaped in the building's courtyard. The man near the door who was gouging out the eyes of a security guard with the handle of his placard.

"Oh my God," Luke said. The sound of breaking glass

somewhere high up above, and a moment later there were bodies flying down onto the pavement, spattering unrecognizable a few yards away from the corpses of the security guards.

And suddenly he was afraid for his own life. And for the boy's.

Luke put his arm around Andy, backed the two of them away from the carnage, crossed the street, all the while not even looking at whatever they were backing toward. Eyes transfixed by the violence and the death and the spectacle. Far across the way the cameras were focused on a screaming mob of fundamentalists who played to the camera, charging toward a part of the building where there were no doors or any real fighting. Backing away, charging again.

Then someone came out the door of the building, and he shouted, "It's done! We've got those heathens all cleaned out of here," and the mob cheered and the cheer broke off all of a sudden as the door of the nearest bus opened and a man came out of it.

A man in black robes.

The same man Luke had seen on the television a few moments before.

"We've got to get out of here," Luke said.

Murder. They were killing people for no good reason at all, and now the man was smiling self-righteously for the cameras. Luke had lost a lot of himself, but he sure as God knew that murder was a crime—not just a crime but the worst possible sort of crime. Not that there was a whole lot Luke or the boy by themselves could do about it—except get themselves killed, maybe. Luke had already lost enough of himself, just dying once; he wasn't eager to lose any more.

The sound of sirens, coming toward them. *Police, finally.* How could they get through all this traffic? Luke heard the sirens turn, and start moving toward him. He turned to look around the corner and saw dozens of blue-and-white police cruisers moving too fast toward him—

—saw with the corner of his eye that the ONE WAY sign on the post beside him was pointing in the other direction, that the police cars with their flashing lights and bleating sirens were moving the wrong way on a one-way street. Not that it mattered; there wasn't any traffic getting by the crowd of buses any more.

And the cameras swiveled to watch as the mob surged out

onto the Avenue to overwhelm the police. All but two of the
cameras, anyway; those two focused on the man in black as he
marched triumphantly into the building.

The sound of screeching brakes and gunfire, coming from
the Avenue, and Luke looked up and saw a policeman wielding
nothing but a nightstick get his head blown off by a fundamentalist's machine gun, and Luke's body suddenly unfroze itself,
and he grabbed the boy's arm and ran back the same way
they'd come—

And one last thing happened as he turned to run: his eyes
passed over the bus that the man in black had emerged from.
Luke saw another face there, staring out at him wide-eyed and
horrified.

Luke *knew* that face. Knew it, and knew it was trouble in
the worst possible way.

He tried to put a name to the face, and failed. Then
something strange happened: a name welled up from somewhere deep inside him, from a place that he knew wasn't
memory.

Herman Bonner.

And something else, even more cryptic and unsettling,
from the same place:

Herman Bonner wants to kill the world.

By the time Luke heard that he was halfway down the
block, running for his life and for the boy's. Running was the
only thing he could do, he told himself. The whole idea that a
man wanted to kill the world was silly. How could a man want
to kill the world, and even if he could want to, how would he
actually do it? He couldn't, of course. Luke told himself that at
least half a dozen times, even said it half out loud, under his
breath so quiet that he hoped the boy might not hear him.

And besides: if the man was actually capable of such a
thing, there was nothing Luke could do to stop him. And it
wasn't his responsibility, anyway.

Luke told himself all those things. He didn't believe them
for a moment.

Washington

Monday evening the plague came down to Washington
from New York on the Amtrak Metroliner.

At nine o'clock the man who brought it down—he'd been sitting three seats away from Luke Munsen when Luke coughed out the soda that'd got itself into his lungs—at nine o'clock on the Washington Beltway the man who carried the infection tossed the butt of his cigarette out the window of his Buick.

And the butt fell to the ground not thirty yards from where Graham Perkins's body still hung.

The Vice President's body was a hard case. Hard enough that all by itself it had closed off half of the Beltway.

Sunday afternoon the governor of Maryland had called out the National Guard to clear the streets, and especially to clear the highways. For the most part, the Guard had accomplished what it had set out to do; most of the riots had lost their steam by Sunday. But the mob that'd lynched Graham Perkins still surrounded him, and that mob was still angry enough that it wasn't about to let him go. Worse, the mob was still growing. Perkins's bodyguards had killed or maimed several hundred people before the mob had finally managed to do them in, and each man killed had ten friends who wanted to avenge him.

And Monday morning, when the Guard had got around to trying to clear off the Beltway, they found a mob more stubborn that the rest, one that didn't listen when someone got on the bullhorn and told them to go home. It took the guard four hours just to clear off half the highway, and when that was done the commander sighed, exasperated, and told his men to split what they had in half and route all the traffic through on the eastbound arm of the highway.

The mob wasn't going anywhere, he said, and it wasn't worth killing civilians over. Eventually, they'd have to calm down and go home.

That was when, finally, a corporal had noticed the Vice President hanging from the lamppost.

Within half an hour the real army had shown up and taken over. Not that they'd done things a bit differently; even a vice-presidential corpse wasn't worth killing people over—no more than a highway was.

At eight o'clock on Monday night, when the infected man had tossed his cigarette butt out onto the pavement, the army and the mob were still facing each other, stalemated. Half an hour later the wind shifted, and about the same time a car's tires had hit the butt *just so*, and sent the thing popping up into the air, shaking loose tiny bits of microscopic life—

And ninety seconds later the infection was spreading through the crowd, and within three minutes it was in Graham Perkins's corpse. And it began rebuilding him.

Not that it was any use.

Oh, it managed to put him back together, all right. His corpse was nowhere near as badly mangled as Luke Munsen's, or even Ron Hawkins's.

But the corpse of Graham Perkins still hung from the nylon noose that'd killed him. And as the microbes began to bring him back to life and back to consciousness, the noose began to strangle him again.

Now and again the wind would shift Graham Perkins, or someone passing would jostle him, and sometimes the movement would ease him back blissfully down toward death. And sometimes it wouldn't.

Three times as he eased up again toward life Graham prayed to God to let him die, and die for good. His prayers went unanswered.

Brooklyn

Because of the riot, the boy steered Ron through an entirely different subway route on their return to Brooklyn. Or mostly different, anyway—somewhere down in south Manhattan they switched to the train that ran near to the gate of the cemetery, the A train. This time the transfer was more complicated—it meant walking through a confusing set of tunnels, some of which were badly lit, and some of which seemed to have lost their lighting altogether. The boy, thank God, knew his way even in the dark, and none of the three strange men who lurked in the dark parts of the tunnels seemed inclined to threaten them.

This time the A train they rode in was as quiet and as clean as the F train they'd taken on the last leg of the trip into the city. Or nearly as clean, anyway. It was air-conditioned, too, which was an enormous relief after the stifling heat in the dark tunnels.

When they were on the train and sitting, the boy looked

at the bag under Luke's arm. "So," he asked, "where you going to go?"

Luke blinked. He hadn't even considered the question; the truth was that it hadn't even occurred to him to consider it. "Go. . . ?"

"Yeah, go. You can't just keep going back to that grave-yard, you know. It ain't right. You aren't dead any more. Cemeteries aren't a fit place for living people to stay."

Luke pictured the cemetery; there was a powerful appeal in that image. More than he was comfortable admitting to.

"Maybe you're right. But where in the hell am I *supposed* to go?"

The boy spent a long moment staring out the dark window across from them. He shrugged. "A hotel, maybe? You could stay with us if you wanted to, but it's kind of tight already." He chewed on his lip. "Hotel wouldn't work, either. Just about all hotels these days want you to have a credit card to check you in, even if you plan on spending cash. And if you had any, whoever killed you must have took 'em."

Luke shook his head. "And I've already used enough of your hospitality. Maybe the cemetery is the best place. For now, anyway. Sooner or later I've got to try and find my way back to my life—whatever the hell that means. At least I've got the address on my driver's license."

Andy lifted an eyebrow at him; the expression looked pretty silly on his twelve-year-old face. "Really, you don't want to go back to that cemetery. It ain't good for you." He paused. "Hey—I got an idea. I got a hide-out—don't go there too much any more. It's still a good place. A good apartment in an old condemned building that the junkies and the bag people never figured out how to get into. You can stay there. There ain't no furniture, but it's still got to be better than sleeping on top of other people's coffins."

Luke wasn't sure that it would be, but all the same he said "Why not?"

So that's what they did when they finally got off the subway: Andy led Luke back through Bedford-Stuyvesant, past the boy's own tenement, to a building three blocks farther down. It was the only structure still standing on that particular block; vacant lots littered with rubble bordered it on every side.

"It's even got a shower that works," Andy said as he led

Luke around the far side of the tenement. "The water isn't hot, but it's water, anyway. I was here the day the man from the city came to shut the water off. Man spent three hours looking for the valve that'd do it, and he never did find the thing." The boy stopped beside a boarded-over basement window, bent down, as though he meant to examine it.

No—he didn't just examine it. He slipped his fingers under the base of the plywood . . . and lifted it, exactly as though he were opening a window.

"I used to know old Mr. Stevens, who had the basement apartment here before he died. Used to visit him sometimes. And I used to see him open this window all the time—it was all he had for a window on this side of his apartment, and the landlord never got around to replacing it after the glass got busted." The boy squatted down, slipped through the opening. "After Mr. Stevens died, and the city closed the building up, they probably thought this window was already boarded up. But it wasn't. It was just a board doing duty as a window."

He was staring up at Luke from inside the building, now. "So," he said, "are you coming, or aren't you?"

"Guess I must be," he said. "Here, take this." Handed the boy the bag of new clothes; slipped down in through the open window.

Inside the building was powerfully dark—so dark that for a long moment Luke was afraid to move for fear of stumbling.

"You coming or not?" The boy's voice, from the far end of the room. Or Luke thought it was a room, anyway; he couldn't see well enough to be sure.

"Give me a minute," Luke said. "Let my eyes get used to this." By the time he said it, of course, he could see . . . well, not see, really, but his eyes could make out enough of the chiaroscuro to tell that the floor was bare and smooth. And that Andy stood in a doorway fifteen feet away, waiting for him.

"Well, hurry up. Don't want to spend all day just walking up a few stairs."

"All right, all right."

The stairways weren't quite as dark as the basement had been; there was a skylight high overhead, and more light came through the open doors of the apartments. They'd walked up four full flights of the stairs when Luke asked the boy why they were going all the way to the top of the tenement.

"You could probably use one of the other apartments," Andy said, "but I don't think you'd want to. Bunch of sloppy people lived in those places—they left their garbage all over the place when they moved out."

"Ugh."

"This way—in the front on the right." The boy was already in the apartment before Luke cleared the last of the stairs. "I haven't been here since I was ten, but it hasn't changed any."

The apartment was a little dusty, but otherwise it was clean, and the wide windows that faced the cemetery lit it very well. There wasn't any furniture, but there was an old army blanket in the corner by the left window.

"There was a broom around here someplace, wasn't there? Yeah—I left that thing in the kitchen. Here it is. Get this place at least halfway decent for you."

"Oh, you don't have to do that—" The boy was already doing it, and quickly, too; sweeping in broad swift strokes that stirred the dust almost as much as moved it. It took him three minutes to get most of the dust out into the hallway; when he was done he took the army blanket out into the hall and shook the dust from it.

"Why don't you make yourself comfortable," he said. "I got to go back home, let my Momma know that I'm all right. I'll come back for you in a couple of hours and we can get you some dinner."

"Yeah—sure. I could use a little bit to catch my breath."

Andy tossed the blanket back into its corner and ran off down the stairs; he was gone before Luke even had a chance to get used to the idea that he was leaving. Luke sighed.

The boy rattled him—definitely rattled him. He wasn't sure whether that was the fault of the boy's rambunctious nature, or whether it might just be part of the way the world still seemed strange to Luke. Not that it made any real difference; Luke liked the boy, and he enjoyed his company, even if Andy did leave him feeling out of phase with the world.

Luke sighed again, and looked around the apartment. There wasn't much to see, of course; white walls made of chipped plaster. Tall, wide windows that let in the sun. The blanket, on the floor in the corner; the broom leaning against the doorjamb. In the kitchen there were empty cabinets hanging open and a rusted old hulk of a refrigerator that looked as though it might attack Luke if he tried to open it.

And there—on the opposite side of the door from the broom—the bag of clothes Luke had bought. Andy must have set them there; Luke had forgot to take the bag back from the boy once he'd climbed down into the building. That was the thing that needed doing; it was the whole reason for the trip in to Manhattan today. Luke needed to wash up and get into some clothes that were meant to fit him.

The tub was nested with cobwebs and worse things, but cold water from the shower head rinsed all that away well enough. There wasn't any soap, nor anything like a clean washcloth, and as it ran the water got so cold that Luke had to hurry out of it. All the same, it was a shower, and it left him cleaner even if it didn't leave him clean. When he was done he stood in the bathroom for a few minutes, letting the warm mild early-summer air dry him slowly, and then he went back to the apartment's living room, opened the shopping bag, and dressed himself. The clothes he'd bought weren't all that different from the ones he'd borrowed; blue jeans, flannel shirts. Good black-canvas running shoes.

Then he sat down on the floor, and he stayed there for a long while, staring out the window at the sky and the cemetery that stretched to the horizon. Eventually he realized that even though he wasn't especially tired, his heart needed sleep; so he reached over and got the army blanket, bunched it up into a pillow, curled up on the floor and drifted away into the warm afternoon sun.

At noon, when the mild summer sun was high overhead, Christine Gibson began to feel the rosy glow of a sunburn on her face and her breasts. And feeling it she knew that she could no longer lie resting in her open grave, but had to rise and leave. And find the life that waited for her.

She sat up, opened her eyes. Blinked away the sun and the stray wisps of her hair that wanted to go everywhere. Out beyond the clearing, beyond the trees at its far end, the world outside the cemetery was waiting for her to discover its metamorphosis.

Metamorphosis? Yes, Christine thought: that was the word that she wanted. She wasn't sure yet how long she'd been . . . away. It had been a long time. So long that the weather had rounded the edges of her headstone, taken long strides toward washing her name from its surface. Time like that would metamorphose the world, she thought. The questions were how far, and into what, and whether the world where she was was a world where she could live.

She stood, stepped out of her shallow grave. Started out across the clearing. It didn't matter whether this was a place where she could live or not; Christine was alive and she was here and no one had given her a say in the matter. Except maybe suicide. Suicide was always a choice, even if it wasn't a good one. Or it would be a choice if she could find a tool to commit it with. She tried to imagine . . . and couldn't. It wasn't even an option; she didn't have it in herself to take her own life. She shuddered. Bad enough she'd had to die once—and the way she'd died! Dying again wasn't a thing that appealed to her.

Christine frowned, squinted as she stepped out from a knot of trees and the sun fell directly into her eyes again. She opened them after a moment, looking down to avoid the brightness . . . and saw her naked breast lit by the sun, exposed for anyone to see. She felt her cheeks flush with embarrassment. It was too much; she had to find clothes, and find them quickly. Almost, she began to wish that she'd taken the shirt that the man had loaned her—*Luke Munsen.* That was his name, and she knew it though she'd never been told and he'd never said it aloud. When she'd woke so early this morning—before it was even dawn—she hadn't felt right about taking the shirt. She'd taken something from him last night, something that he hadn't meant to give. And that taking weighed on Christine's heart like an anchor. She couldn't bear to take anything else from him after she'd done that.

Which still left her on the thin strip of land between the cemetery and the street, naked and embarrassed. Unable to go forward and expose her nakedness any further to the light of day. Unable to go back, because it could leave her naked forever. And she might have stayed there forever, stuck permanently between progress and retreat. If it hadn't been for the bag lady.

Christine didn't think of her as a bag lady. In her time there had been no such thing—not by any such name, at least. There'd been beggar-women. Even beggar-women as old as time, as this one was. And often they'd smelled as foul as this woman did. But the woman dressed in layers and layers of fine clothes turned to rags, carrying three great sacks filled what were so obviously all her mortal possessions—she was a new thing to Christine. Fascinating at the same moment she was disgusting.

The bag lady rounded a corner and spotted Christine; crossed the street and walked toward her as Christine stood paralyzed there at the edge of the cemetery.

"I've brought the word," the old woman said, puffing and out of breath from hurrying and from the weight of her load. "I've brought the word to you."

Word? Christine couldn't begin to imagine what she meant by that. Which word? And how?

The old woman was stooped over, now, fishing down through her great sacks of filth and ephemera. "Here," she said. Stood, held out a leaflet. "This is it. This is the word I've brought you."

I'm supposed to take that from her, Christine thought. *That's what she wants, isn't it?* Yes, it was. Christine was still powerfully confused from her resurrection, but she wasn't stupid.

There was no reason for Christine not to take that leaflet. None that she could even begin to imagine. Still she hesitated; began to raise her hand to take the leaflet—and stopped.

That was just as well, because in that instant the beggar-woman hesitated, too. And changed herself completely.

"No," the old woman said. "It isn't the word you need to hear. There's no need for you to hear the word—not this one nor any other. No reason. It's something else you need." And she held out her hand, and Christine took it without thinking. And the beggar lady led her away into the afternoon.

They'd gone three blocks before Christine realized that she'd forgot about her nakedness. And for just an instant she felt the embarrassment coming over her again. Only for an instant: somehow the presence of the beggar-woman who did not beg made it hard to care whether she was dressed or clothed.

"Where are we going?" Christine asked. She felt no more concern for the answer to the question than she felt for the sensation of the sun on her bare thighs.

"Soon," the woman said, "soon."

Which wasn't an answer, precisely. And wasn't the absence of an answer, either.

They were blocks from the cemetery, now—on a road paved with crumbling cobblestones, lined with broken brownstones and lots vacant of anything but garbage and debris. The old woman turned and led Christine out across one of those lots. There were sharp things on the ground, there—broken glass and rusted nails and other shards of sharp, corroded metal. Christine felt them as she walked, felt their edges rasp against the skin of her bare feet, but they didn't cause her any pain, nor did even the sharpest knife of glass break the skin of her soles.

Strange. Was there some unknowable magic surrounding the old woman? Magic that sheltered Christine too? It was a hard thing to accept. For all that the miracle of life had recovered her from death, Christine wasn't inclined to believe in miracles or sorcery. No, Christine decided. It was just dumb luck that kept her feet from harm.

They were halfway to the street on the far end of the waste when the old woman suddenly stopped. "Here," she said, "this is the place. Help me."

And she bent down and started digging through the rubble. At first Christine thought she was seeking out new clutter to add to her sacks, and wondered how she could possibly help, since she couldn't begin to tell what the old woman might value in that rubbish. No; she wasn't adding anything to her bags. She was digging away the rubble, digging down toward something buried down below. That, at least, was something she could understand. Christine stooped, began lifting the loose bricks and trash, tossing them aside.

After just a few minutes the cellar door appeared. A few more and it was cleared enough to open.

A cellar door that led into the foundation of a building that had long since been demolished.

The old woman pulled away the broken, rusted padlock. Lifted open the door.

And began to climb down the stone steps that led into the cellar.

Christine watched her, frightened that the old woman would stumble on a broken step or fall into a nest of rabid vermin. Not that any such thing happened.

"Come on," the old woman said. "You need to come down here too. There isn't much point to this if you don't."

Christine set her teeth. Braced herself against a fear of

rats. And followed the old woman down into the dark. By the
time she set foot on the bottom step it was clear that the
basement was neither as dank nor as dark as Christine had
imagined it: the floor beneath her feet was powder-dry with
dust, and the light that streamed in through the open door was
more than enough to illuminate this part of the cellar.

The old woman was over there, by the wall—sifting
through great mounds of junk. Christine followed her, waited
to be told what help the woman wanted from her. She said
nothing for the longest while, and Christine began to feel
uneasy that the old woman had forgot about her completely.

"Can I help you with that?" Christine asked when she saw
the woman begin to lift the great cracked vase that was near as
large as she was.

"No," she answered. "This is the last of it." And set the
vase down on the basement floor, effortless as though it were
an empty sack. Slid the brass-hinged wooden trunk out of the
corner where it had sat beneath the vase. Unhooked its
latches, thumbed open its lock, and lifted its wide clamshell
lid. "This was her hope chest," the old woman said.

Whose hope chest? Christine wanted to ask—but didn't
ask, for no reason she could name.

"Don't bother asking who," the old woman said. "She left
here long ago, lived a long life, and died continents away from
this place. Her story isn't yours." The old woman lifted out a
wrinkled white-cotton dress; held it up in front of Christine,
measuring the size. "It'll fit you well, I think. Go ahead—take
it. Put it on. Do you hesitate because you fear she'll soon
return to claim her hope? Don't worry there. She's buried far
from here, and anyway her hopes changed a thousand times
after she left these behind."

Was that the reason for her reluctance? Christine wasn't
sure. She was still too confused, too unsure of all the things
that give a body reason to be alive. Anyway, she took the dress,
pulled it over her head. She needed clothes, and damn the
place they came from.

"These shoes," the woman said, "Such fine shoes. Her
mother spent enough for them to feed the family for a month."
And threw them on the floor, not far from Christine's feet. She
rummaged in among the linens and the gown for several
moments, but nothing else came forth. When she finally stood
upright again—carefully wiping her hands on the filthy hem of

her skirt—Christine was already dressed and shod. She closed the chest, sat on top of it.

Christine stared at her dumbly, uncertain what the woman would do next.

"Sit, sit," she said, pointing Christine at a filthy parlor chair on the far side of the room. "Bring the chair over here and sit. We need to talk."

"Talk?"

"Yes, talk. There are things you need to say. No, not there—bring the chair here, into the light. Where I can see you."

I need to say? "What do you mean?"

The old woman frowned. "You already know."

Christine didn't. Really didn't. She shook her head. "No," she told the woman. "I don't have anything to say."

A sigh.

"You do, though. Sit quiet, sit tight, and listen to yourself for a while. You'll hear."

And they did exactly that—both of them sat quiet as church mice for a good five minutes. Christine heard nothing. Then, finally, the old woman spoke.

"What do you want from life? What did you want, when you were alive before?"

"I—" but there was no answer for that question, either, because Christine could find no desire in her heart. "I'm not sure. I'd like to be happy, I think."

"Yes," the woman said. The answer didn't seem to please her. For a moment she seemed distant, distracted—as though she were concentrating on something far, far away. "Last night. . . . Last night, why did. . . ?" She paused, waiting for Christine to answer. But the question was so vague that she could find no way to approach it. "You weren't alone last night."

Christine felt her cheeks flush again; she felt violated, as though the woman had intruded on something that was none of her concern.

"No," she said. "I wasn't." And didn't say another word.

Maybe the old woman could see that she was angry; certainly she hesitated a long while before she said anything else. After a while she did ask the next question:

"You didn't love him, did you? How could you?—you hardly knew that man."

"No," she said, "I didn't." And it surprised Christine twice when she said that. First because it was a question that didn't deserve the dignity of an answer. Second—and infinitely more unsettling—because when she heard herself say those words she knew that they were a lie.

"Then why. . . ?"

Christine frowned, ignoring the intuition she wasn't ready to cope with yet. "Old habits die hard," she said. "I needed someone close. I needed the warmth."

The old woman shook her head. "You're lying to me. It doesn't matter: you know what you need to know." She lifted up the larger of her great sacks, sifted through it. Took out three one-dollar bills and set the sack down again. Held the bills out to Christine. "Take these," she said. "They're all I have, but you need them more than I do."

Before she understood what she was doing, Christine had the money in her hand. "I can't take—"

"You can. You will. This isn't any fortune. The money is worth so little now, much less than when last you were alive." She nodded toward the open cellar door. "Walk the city. Learn to know the world again. If you see a man selling flowers on a street corner, buy yourself a rose."

Christine looked down at the money in her hands. The bills were nothing like greenbacks, but still there was no mistaking what they were.

"One last thing," the old woman said, "before we go." She was stooped again, fishing deep down into her smaller bag. Christine caught a glimpse down into it over the woman's shoulder, and for just a moment she thought that she could see the infinities of heaven inside it. That had to be an illusion. Then the woman stood quite suddenly, and she held out her hand.

In that hand she held a pendant, a silvery chain that was brighter and more silvery than silver could ever be. And from the chain there hung a stone like like an opal, and more brilliant. A stone that shimmered and shone with the fiery light of a star.

"Wear this near your heart," the woman told her. "One day soon it will mean your life—and much, much more than that."

Christine took the pendant; she was too transfixed and ensorcled by its beauty to even begin to refuse it. After a moment she lifted the chain over her head, set it around her neck. And tucked it under her blouse, because she was afraid that if anyone else saw that gem they'd covet it, and try to take it from her.

When she looked up again, not ten seconds later, the old woman was gone.

Late that afternoon, when Christine found herself again at the edge of the cemetery that she'd risen from, she walked quickly and deliberately into it. And tossed the rose she'd bought herself with the old woman's money into her own open grave.

Luke woke a lifetime later in an apartment that was almost entirely dark, and he woke feeling . . . *wholer* than he had in all the hours since his rebirth. Andy was kneeling beside him, holding a candle, and he was saying, "C'mon, Mr. Luke Munsen, c'mon and wake up now." As he spoke he shook Luke's shoulder not too gently with his free hand.

Luke sat up—slowly, afraid he'd jostle the candle—and rubbed his eyes. They were gritty and irritated from the dust that the boy hadn't cleaned too thoroughly off the floor and the blanket.

"I brought my Momma and my Daddy with me," he said. "I hope that's okay. They wanted to see you. And we brought you some dinner."

"Uh," Luke said. He could see the Harrisons over their son's shoulder; they stood reverently with their hands folded in front of them. "Great. Good to see you people again. Sorry I can't be much of a host."

Barbara Harrison smiled meekly; her husband shook his head as if to say the surroundings weren't important.

"Go ahead and sit down, if that'll make you more comfortable; there aren't any chairs, but if you don't mind the floor, you're welcome to it."

"That's very gracious of you," the woman said, and both she and her husband sat almost as if they'd been commanded to.

Luke frowned. "And it's gracious of you to say so, but really—I'm the one who's in debt to you. There isn't any need for you to act so uncomfortable."

Robert Harrison coughed, in a way that seemed very pointed.

"The dead out there are rising from their graves," Andy said. "Did you do that while you were sleeping? Are you really Jesus, Mr. Luke Munsen? Or at least some kind of a Saint, anyhow?"

Luke shook his head, trying to clear it. "What? Dead people rising?"

"Climbing right up out of their graves. Go take a look out the window if you want, and see for yourself. They're a lot like you were when I first saw you yesterday—real confused. Even more shook up than you were, in fact."

Luke stood, crossed the room. Leaned out the window and looked . . .

"Just like I said—" the boy's voice, from just behind Luke's elbow, startled Luke half out of his wits "—you got that gorgeous cemetery so full of craters that it looks worse than the moon. Honest, Luke Munsen, why'd you have to go and do a thing like that?"

"Andy—!" Barbara Harrison said in a scolding tone, "Don't you speak that way to Mr. Munsen."

In the bright-blue light that shone from the street lamps Luke could see people wandering around the graveyard, and in the street that ran beside it. Ordinary, healthy people, by the look of them. As the boy had said, they looked shaken and disheveled. And they were naked too, all but half a dozen of them.

The boy's parents were standing beside them now too. "Has God spoken to you," Robert Harrison asked, "or is He only acting through you?"

Luke flushed; the question embarrassed him. And it frightened him too, for reasons that he didn't understand. "I—No. God isn't talking to me. He really isn't. And I don't think that I'm His instrument, at least not any more than anyone else is."

The man nodded gravely.

"Please," Luke said, "don't think this of me. I'm really no one special."

"Aw, come on," Andy said, and he shoved Luke's elbow good-naturedly. "You show up Friday, half dead and needing a doctor, and inside of ten minutes you go and get yourself killed. Then you manage to get yourself resurrected by Sunday morning, and by Monday night half the dead people in New York are alive again. Now you're trying to tell us that there's nothing special about you?"

"I—I'm not God," Luke said, "and I don't want to pretend to be. Wouldn't I know that sort of thing? And wouldn't it be some horrible kind of a sin to lie about it if it wasn't so?"

The boy shrugged. "Okay, then. You're a saint. Saints don't always know about it when they're saints. In fact, I imagine that the best ones wouldn't ever know. Being humble is part of being saintly. It only stands to reason."

Luke shook his head; there weren't any words left in his cannon. "I honestly don't think you're right."

The sound of footsteps coming up the stairs.

"Oh," Barbara Harrison said, "that'll be the Johnsons. Or maybe it's the Jenks family. They all wanted to meet you; they were supposed to drop by about now."

Andy looked up at Luke; there was guilty mischief in his eye. "I think you may be having quite a bit of company tonight," he said. "There were an awful lot of people who wanted to see you."

Part of Luke was almost tempted to run and hide somewhere—the part of him that was afraid he was becoming some kind of an animal in a zoo. It was a silly fear, and he knew it. No one had him locked up. If he got up and left right now, running or not, no one would try to capture him. It wasn't even likely that they'd follow him.

"It is the Jenkses," Andy whispered up at him as a man, a woman, and three small children walked into the room. Two of them—the man and one of the young girls—held candles. "They're okay."

Mrs. Jenks looked at Luke suspectingly at first, as though she wondered if he was some evil creature who'd somehow deceived the Harrisons. That suspicion lasted only a moment; as she looked at Luke she seemed to see something that he couldn't even see in himself. And she crossed the room, her whole family just a step behind her. "I'm Stella Jenks," she said. "Is it true what Barbara says? Are you the one who brought the miracle?"

Luke felt a powerful urge to crawl under a rock and hide. "I don't know," he said. "I think—I think that maybe it touched me, anyway. I don't remember very well, but they tell me that I died. And now I'm alive again." Luke looked away. "The boy and his father know better than I do. They're the ones who carried my corpse out to the cemetery."

She was staring at him, trying to read him very carefully. "My child," she said, "my little boy, here. Two weeks ago the doctor told me that he's got a cancer, one of the cancers that they can't do nothing about. Will you lay your hands on my boy and heal him for me?"

"Mrs. Jenks—"

"Stella."

"Stella, I'm not a healer. Honest I'm not. I don't know how to work miracles, even if a miracle did happen to me. If you want me to hold your child, I'll hold him for you. But I wouldn't know how to heal him any better than your doctor does. Hell—not even that well. At least your doctor can give him something for the pain."

She frowned. "Maybe," she said, "maybe some kinds of miracles are catching. Haven't you looked outside? Haven't you seen that cemetery?"

"I've seen it," Luke said. He let out a long, hard sigh. "I've seen it. Okay, I'll hold your boy. I don't imagine I can hurt him, anyway." He knelt down to look the boy in the eye. "What's your name, huh, son?"

"Larry."

He couldn't have been more than four years old. And he was sick, sick *bad*—Luke could tell that just from the way the child's skin hung so loosely over the bones of his face. From his eyes so yellow that even in the dim candlelight Luke could see the tinge. Seeing him hurt Luke so badly that the only thing to do was put his arms around the boy and hug him, and when he did Luke felt himself begin to cry. "You get better, you hear me, Larry? You get better."

Felt the boy's head nod against his shoulder.

Pulled back a moment, to look the boy in the eye again. "You promise me. Huh? I want you to promise me that you'll get well."

The boy nodded again; his expression was solemn. "I do. I will—I promise." Larry wiped away a wet spot on his cheek where one of Luke's tears had fallen.

"I'm counting on you," Luke told the boy. And after that Luke needed to be alone for a while. So he got up, and went to the back of the apartment, and shut himself up in the bathroom in the absolute dark. And waited the time that it took for his gut to stop hurting.

When he came out again there were more people in the living room—more of them than Luke could count at a quick glance. Enough that there was trouble moving from one end of the room to the other. They all seemed to watch him, he thought—but not stare at him. They were more polite than that; they watched him from the corners of their eyes as they talked to one another.

He found Andy Harrison by the left window in the front of the apartment—pretty much exactly where he'd been the last time Luke had seen him. "Are there more like that?" Luke asked him. He spoke quietly as he could, afraid that someone else might hear him. "That little kid—he *needed* so bad. And his mother thought what he needed was me. Maybe the boy thought that too; I don't know. But . . . God. I can't cope with that, Andy. I can't." Andy was looking at him cold and hard, poker-faced. Luke wanted to stop talking, wanted to shut up and go away, but the boy's silence was so icy that Luke found himself throwing more words into the fire, trying to warm the air. "That little boy was dying, and he was coming to me for help, and there wasn't a damn thing I could do for him, not a damn thing. If I have to go through that again . . . I don't know. Alive or not, I think I'll just curl up and die."

Andy just stood there, staring angrily at the wall, not looking at Luke at all. After a while he shook his head. "You got a lot of nerve, you know that, Mr. Luke Munsen." He was looking at Luke now, and growing angrier as he spoke. "Being a miracle is a responsibility. You say you're not Jesus—okay, you're not Jesus. You say you aren't some kind of a saint, like my Momma thinks, then you're not a saint, either. You're still special—something awful special happened to you. Something miraculous. How can you be like that? If Larry Jenks and his mom think that maybe it'll help him to see you, how can you begrudge them that? Are you so afraid of seeing the mean parts of the world that you won't do what you can to make a difference? How can you be that low?"

"I—no. *No.*"

"No what? You want to try to tell me that it isn't so?"

Luke started to raise his voice, caught himself, stopped before he'd said a word. The problem was that denying what the boy had said was exactly what he wanted to do. And . . .

and much as he wanted to deny it, he knew that there was at least a measure of truth in the accusation.

A large measure of truth, most likely. But the boy was just a *boy*, damn it. What did a boy—maybe he was twelve, maybe he was thirteen—know about life? What business did he have lecturing Luke about responsibility?

What did it matter how old he was? He was right, and Luke knew it.

"Yeah. I guess that's what I was going to do." Sighed. "And I would have been wrong. Don't beat me up about it, okay? Let me think. I need to think."

Andy Harrison huffed. "Yeah—I know what you're going to do. You're going to sit around stewing in it until you can find yourself a bunch of good reasons for acting like a dog. You go ahead. I seen it before. I know about reasons: they don't make anything right. They just make it easier to live with being wrong."

"Yeah. Well." Luke was looking out the window, watching the cemetery. It was quiet out there now, empty and deserted. The graveyard almost seemed to call out to him, as though it wanted him to rest inside its bosom. "Okay, then. What in the hell do you want me to do? Pretend I'm something that I'm not? Mumble silly words and tremble my hands over their heads? You think that's any better?"

"No—but if they want you to care, if they want your attention, is that so much to ask?" He shook his head. "You owe that to them, if you ask me. God put you here for a reason."

There was a grizzled, unwashed old man standing beside them now, listening. Watching—waiting for a pause in the conversation. Luke turned to him guiltily. A man who looked familiar somehow that Luke couldn't quite identify.

"You cured that Jenks boy," the man said. "Can you cure me too? I got no disease—not anything but getting old. I'm going to die soon. My bones say that; I can hear them. I bet you can hear them too, if you listen. Can you help me—please? I don't want to die, Mister. Please don't let me die."

I didn't cure that boy! Luke thought. He held his tongue. He glanced across the room, looking for Larry Jenks, to reassure himself—

And saw the boy playing tug of war with his oldest sister. Even from here Luke could see the change in him. His eyes were bright, pure white and healthy; his skin was smooth and clear the way a child's skin should be. And for all that an hour before he'd looked too weak to carry his own weight now he was winning the contest with a girl who had to be at least twice his age.

Luke reached out and put his arms around the old man, and held him and held him. And loved him, and to hell with the fact that the man's clothes felt oily, that he smelled like old shoes mislaid in a brewery.

And the man hugged him too, and he said, "Oh thank you Mister, thank you—God loves us all, he loves us, doesn't he?"

And Luke smiled and patted the man's back and he thought *Yes, I think he does.*

After that there were others, standing, waiting just outside arm's reach. He took each of them in his arms as they came to him. Only a few of them seemed to have any disabling illness, but each of them seemed to have . . . something compelling in his eyes. A need, maybe. Or maybe it was only a desire.

They want me to love them. Luke couldn't have said for the life of him where the thought had come from. But he knew it was so as soon as he heard it inside his skull, and he knew that Andy Harrison was right.

They drifted away and into their own conversations and lives when they'd got what they needed from him. When the last of them was gone, Luke looked up and saw the woman—the woman from the cemetery. She seemed less dazed now, and . . . there was something strong about her, as though . . . Luke wasn't sure. She walked through the door and stood against the wall beside it, as quietly and unsettlingly in awe of him as every other person in the room. Not quite the same awe that all the others in the room were full of; somehow it was almost intimate and personal. She was dressed, now—in a wrinkled grey-cotton sundress. She wore the dress well, in spite of the wrinkles; she managed, in fact, to make the dress look beautiful.

Luke looked the boy in the eye. "Did you tell her to come here too? Do you know her? How—?"

The boy looked at the woman, then looked back up at Luke—looked at both of them hard and careful. "I haven't ever seen her before. I can tell, though. There's something . . .

some kind of a connection between the two of you. Isn't there?
Something important."

"I—" Luke felt himself growing afraid again, without understanding why. "I don't know. I know her, yes, but . . .
that isn't what you mean, is it?"

The boy shook his head. "No, that isn't what I mean. It's
like—look at her. Look at you. I didn't have to tell her where
to go to find you. Even if I knew her to tell her, it wouldn't
have made any difference. She's going to know where you are,
no matter where you go. Can't you tell that, just seeing her?"

Luke looked at the woman long and careful as he could
without staring at her, but hard as he tried he couldn't see
what the boy had. He saw something, all right, but whatever
it was he saw wasn't as sayable as that. Something powerful,
something frightening. Nothing he could put a name to.

"I'm not sure," he said, and there was something more he
meant to say, but the words evaporated away before he could
say them, and before he realized what he was doing Luke was
crossing the room toward her. That was rude, a small voice
inside him said. Rude to the boy. It wasn't right to walk away
in the middle of a conversation. Luke only barely heard that
voice.

He was beside the woman, now. Not looking at her, not
exactly, but not looking away from her either. She seemed to
watch the floor as though it were a bonfire that might consume
her; for just an instant she glanced up at him shyly, but before
her eyes even had a chance to focus she looked away again.

"I've missed you," she said. That sounded strange to
Luke; it hadn't been a full day since he'd last seen her. And her
voice—had he ever heard her voice before? Had she spoke in
all of last night? He couldn't remember. Her voice was
beautiful, he decided; rich and melodious and elegant; it had
the slightest trace of an exotic accent.

He smiled. "It hasn't been that long," he said. "A little
while before sunrise, maybe? I think I remember dawn
creeping out around the edges of the sky."

"A day? Only a day, really?" She was looking out the
window, now, focusing on something off beyond the street
lights. "So much has happened. Too much. This world . . . I
don't know it. There were times when I thought that only you
were real."

Luke flinched. "Don't say that. Please. I'm hearing too many things like that tonight."

She smiled, nodded; she even almost seemed to understand the problem. "It happened to you too, didn't it? You were . . . not alive before too, weren't you?"

He nodded.

The fingers of her right hand teased the cloth belt of her sundress. "I think I knew that from the moment I first set eyes on you, even in all that awful confusion. It's like a bond somehow. I feel it when I see those others out there, all those ones who are still confused. It's much stronger when I look at you."

"What is it—what do you think it is? What makes that feeling?"

She shrugged. "Maybe we all knew each other in heaven, and don't remember any more. Is there a special tributary of the Lethe for people who return to the living?" She smiled when she said it, and Luke knew that she'd told a joke, even though he'd missed the punch line. "I don't know. Maybe it is . . . something like that. It has to be, doesn't it?"

"I guess it does," Luke said, and then the both of them were quiet for a long while. "Who were you—back before? Who are you? Did I know you, maybe, or know of you?"

She shook her head. "No. I'd remember if we'd met. And all of that life is behind me now. Let it rest."

"I don't remember very well—a lot of things I don't remember at all. I think it might be because of the way I died. Andy Harrison told me about that."

"You said my name," the boy hollered from across the room. "I heard that."

Luke turned, looked up at him. "You did, huh? Didn't know I'd spoke about you loud enough for you to hear."

"I heard. What you saying about me, Mr. Luke Munsen?"

Luke smiled. "Horrible things, you can be sure of that."

"I bet. I bet." The boy turned away, fell back into heated conversation with his father.

"He's a good kid," Luke said. "A little unsettling, but good. He's the first living soul I saw after . . ." And the words fell away again, as though he'd never had them. *After what?* God knew what; Luke didn't.

After he was alive again.

"Yes," she said, as though she understood more than he'd said. "That's important, isn't it?"

As soon as she'd asked the question, Luke realized that it *was* important. "I think it might be. God only knows what that means."

She nodded; so gravely that it almost seemed silly. And before he could stop himself Luke was laughing—not quite out loud, but it shook his expression and shook his shoulders even though he tried to stop them. After just an instant she was laughing too, and then there wasn't any need for Luke to hold it back. The two of them doubled over laughing so hard that the room was watching Luke again. And Luke didn't even care.

Tuesday
July Nineteenth

Broadcast over the ABC
television network on
the afternoon of July 18.

(Theme music.)
Stay tuned for a special live bulletin from ABC
news.
(Twenty-seven seconds of silence.)
This ABC News special bulletin is coming to you
live from the headquarters of ABC itself, in New
York City. Violent protesters, as yet unidentified,
have attacked this building and are at this very
moment heading toward the studio from which this
broadcast emanates. Their intentions are still uncer-
tain, but we have heard gunfire, and we are no
longer able to reach the security personnel on the
building's ground floor.
The protest started about twenty-five minutes
ago, and at first it was raucous but fairly conven-
tional. Fifteen minutes ago this office received frantic
calls, when our security personnel first sighted ma-
chine guns among the crowd. New York City police
were called at that time, but we are unable to tell

*whether or not they have responded, since the phone
lines to the security desk died almost immediately.*

What?

Dear God, they're in the hall.

The newscaster stares away from the camera for
fourteen seconds, terrified, until finally we hear the
sound of a door shattering. We hear the sound of a
machine gun—

No!

—and the newscaster screams before the channel goes dead.

From the Good News Hour,
*broadcast on the Voice of
Armageddon Television Network,
7:00 a.m. Eastern Standard Time,
Tuesday, July 19.*

Bust-shot of anchorman; behind him is a map of
the Soviet Union. Superimposed over the map are a
red hammer and sickle and the words GOG AND
MAGOG.

*The forces of evil continue to gather strength in
the nations of Gog and Magog, which still insist on
referring to themselves as the Union of Soviet Social-
ist Republics. Armies are massing in the South and
Central Asian portions of that fearful nation.*

A window opens up in the upper-right corner of
the screen—inside it is grainy video footage of a riot
in Red Square.

*Those few of the righteous who live captive
within the confines of the evil empire have taken to
the streets in an attempt to bring down their evil
leaders. So far their efforts have only succeeded in
shifting the power among the heathens.*

*Meanwhile, at the gates of the fair city of Jeru-
salem, Arab surrogates for the evil empire continue
their relentless attack on the forces of the righteous.
This report by our Good News Hour reporter Carl
Tappan, live from the city of Jerusalem. . . .*

Footage of jet aircraft taking off from a desert

runway; as the jets fade into the distance cut to a dead battlefield—smoking hulls of Soviet tanks in the foreground. Off in the distance we see a long, steady series of explosions.

Can you tell us, Carl, exactly how it is that the infidels are already within fifteen miles of Jerusalem? How is it that Israel has fallen so far and so quickly?

A new voice—this one is thick with a drawl that sounds like Kentucky, or maybe southern Indiana.

David, the Israelis were caught off balance by the direction the attack came from. Their border with Jordan is a long one, and for better than twenty years it's been peaceful. They didn't expect the Jordanians to attack—and as a matter of fact, they didn't. Even if they had, the Jordanian army isn't large enough to pose much of a threat to the state of Israel. Who could have expected the Syrians and Iraqis—who've long been bitter enemies—to mount a joint attack? And even more unexpectedly, to mount it not by way of the Golan Heights, but by first attacking the Jordanians? The fact is, David, that no one here even considered for a moment the idea that there might someday be Syrian soldiers crossing over the Jordan River. They managed to make that crossing less than three hours after they blitzed over the Syrian border with Jordan, and managed to catch the Israeli Army so badly unprepared that most of the West Bank was lost before the Israelis could rally back. The Syrians and Iraqis aren't gaining much more ground right at the moment, but the fighting here isn't over by any stretch of the imagination. There's some fear, in fact, that the Saudis or possibly even some of the gulf states may reinforce the Arabs. Colonel Qaddafi, in Libya, has already offered them his help—though so far his offer has been ignored. Right now the fighting is so intense and the outcome is so unsure that any new forces on either side could tip the balance completely.

The scene shifts again, to a small town in the rural south. Clearly visible in the foreground is a microphone marked with the letters *abc*.

Thanks, Carl. Now to Dean Grant in Tylerville, Tennessee, for this report.

David, strange things are happening down here in the South. Frightening things, that seem to indicate that we are indeed on the threshold of apocalypse. There's a cemetery here in Tylerville where people are rising up out of their graves even as I speak. Crippled children are healing spontaneously. And the whole town is waiting for translation expectantly—absolutely and unshakably certain that it'll come any moment.

And David, I think they may be right. Billy Wilson, here, is one of the ones who lived through this miracle.

The camera pans again, to focus on a brown-haired, freckled boy. He may be nine years old; he may be ten.

I was an awful mess, the boy says. He bends down, rolls up the left leg of his blue jeans. There is nothing in any way remarkable about his leg. *My leg was all knurled up and twisted around inside. He put his arms around me and now I can run just like I was any boy. Even been swimming a couple times. I tell you, boy, it's something.*

Who's that, Billy? Who put his arms around you?

I can't tell you. Kind of like a creature, kind of like an animal and kind of like a man. With a weird face like a goat's, and hair all over him, and he stood up and walked just like a man would. He was kind of like Jesus, all . . . holy like that. He told us he wasn't any Jesus, and how can you not believe somebody like that when he tells you something? I can't, tell you that. Jesus or not, he was somebody special. He put miracles on all the people here, on me, on everybody sick in this town. Even did that for the dead ones in the cemetery: when he was gone a few hours they started rising right up out of their graves. Resurrection! Boy, it's something.

Superimposed over the boy's forehead, now, are the numbers 666.

We cut momentarily to a clip of a manlike,

goatlike creature. When we return the boy is looking at a photograph.

Is that the one who healed you, Billy—the Beast from Revelation? The Antichrist?

That's his photo, all right. I wouldn't never have called him that.

Return to studio.

Thanks, Dean. There's frightening news for all of us: not only has the Antichrist come to earth, but decent, innocent people are falling under his spell. These are perilous times in which we live, aren't they, my friends?

Perilous times indeed.

And these phenomena aren't confined to one town alone—similar dark miracles have taken place throughout Tennessee and Kentucky, and in the Northeast as well. The dead are rising in the morgues of New York City, and in more than one of that city's cemeteries—graveyards so large that in many states they'd constitute whole counties by themselves. The dead are even coming to life in Philadelphia, Boston, and the nation's erstwhile capital, Washington . . . though the phenomenon isn't as common there as it is in New York or the mid-South.

In Oregon today the lower house of the state legislature passed a secession bill; if it passes in the state senate and is signed by the governor, Oregon would become the first state to secede from the Union since the Civil War. Federal authorities—those few still available—are refusing to comment on the measure.

*In transit by air
over the Sea of Japan*

Bill Wallace—he was still Bill Wallace in his own book, no matter what it was the Air Force decided to call him—spent most of the hours-and-hours-long flight to South Korea in a fugue, a half-state that wasn't quite sleep and wasn't quite wakefulness, either. He wasn't tired, not especially. But there wasn't much else to do; nothing to read. Nothing to watch but endless miles and miles of ocean and clear sky. Nothing to listen to but the steady thrumb of jet engines outside the plane's cabin. No one to talk to, even if he hadn't been under orders to keep to himself; he was utterly and totally alone in the plane's passenger compartment. There was a two-man crew up in the cockpit, but neither of them had seen fit to ask him the time of day. Most likely, Bill thought, they were under orders not to talk to him, just as he was under orders not to talk to them.

Bill Wallace had never been especially susceptible to loneliness. Keeping to himself was a thing that came pretty naturally to him. Still, this was extreme; another day or two of this and he'd have a pretty clear idea of exactly what isolation was.

He sighed, yawned. Lifted his hands to his face and rubbed his eyes. Maybe it wouldn't be as bad as all that. Certainly if he were going to be a guinea pig the people who experimented with him would have to talk to him. Wouldn't they? He hoped they would. And if they wouldn't talk to him, then maybe at least they'd have a few good books he could read? Or a TV, anyhow. Something. Anything that didn't amount to staring at the walls around him. Bill had had enough of that already.

More than enough.

So much, in fact, that he'd even begun to get bored with marveling over the miracle that allowed him to be alive when he'd already died. It was the only thing he'd had to think about on the trip out from Missouri, but even as incredible and wonderful as it was—literally, absolutely, and positively amazing—it wasn't enough to sustain a trip this long all by itself.

Nothing was.

So Bill set himself back into his memories, and nibbled at the edges of those things that still . . . well, not haunted him. Bill wasn't the type of guy who carried around things that haunted him. But there were things that didn't go away; small aches like the pain in his left forearm that on winter mornings would take him back to the day he'd busted it, in a game of sand-lot football the year he was fifteen.

That football game was the least of the things Bill thought of at times like this. There were other things, memories that had a much larger claim on him. Things that very nearly *did* haunt him.

Like that night when he and Ron Hawkins and Joey Harris had tried to lift a couple of sixes of beer out of the 7-Eleven on Ridgedale Road back home in Mountainville, and ended up being attacked by a deranged store clerk wielding a baseball bat. Well, maybe not deranged; maybe the man was just at wits' end from people shoplifting in his store so much. Whether he was deranged or unbalanced or just plain hep up, he'd beat Bill to within an inch of his life.

The ache from the broken arm was nothing beside the aches and pains the clerk's baseball bat had made for Bill. Those aches and pains were morning things, and things that came to him in damp weather. They were nothing next to the guilt that found him at moments like this one. There'd been four people in that store that night: Bill, Ron, Joey, and the clerk. And of the four of them only Bill had managed to keep himself out of jail. Ron and Joey had gone away to the state penitentiary—sent there on the clerk's testimony, and on the evidence of the store's video camera. Even the clerk had spent a little time in the county jail for assault; the same camera that had put Ron and Joey away had recorded the things he'd done to Bill in considerable detail.

The camera had caught Bill too; and all he'd done was try to lift a couple of sixes of beer. And try to take a baseball bat out of the hands of a man who was crazy enough to use it. Which wasn't to say that he wouldn't have done a lot worse if he'd had the opportunity. If it'd been Ron there, or Joey, Bill would have been all over the clerk's ass. How could he not have? It was the right thing to do. Down in his gut he still couldn't understand how or why it was that Ron and Joey had had to go to jail for doing something that was right. Sure: Bill's lawyer had explained it to him, back when he was still in the hospital—explained how when you're doing something against the law and somebody gets hurt, it's all your fault. Like you'd gone in meaning to kill somebody, almost, even if you hadn't. Bill didn't get it. All he knew was that the way things turned out, Ron Hawkins and Joey Harris had gone to jail, and Bill had come out of it with a clean enough record to get him into the Air Force. For all he knew, they were still in there too; in all the years since then he hadn't had the heart to check up on

either of them. Which was, maybe, the thing that made him
feel most guilty of all.

He tried not to think about the look on Ron Hawkins's
face, the last time he'd seen him. Which was in court, when
they'd hauled Bill in to testify at Ron's trial. Right at the end
of that trial that'd only lasted, what, three hours? Maybe not
even that long. Maybe a little longer, but not by much, for
sure. The judge had hit his wood hammer on his high desk up
there in the front center of the courtroom, and he'd said that
Ron was guilty with this belligerent and meanhearted look on
his face. Guilty of armed robbery, and of assault with intent to
kill. Which made even the prosecutor look a little surprised,
and kind of pleased. And then that judge had said that Ron was
going away for fifteen years to life.

And Ron had looked—well, Bill had seen a look almost
exactly like that once before. When he was twelve, and him
and his mom took the dog to the vet, and the vet put this
rubber glove on his hand, and put a little KY jelly on it. And
proceeded to explore the dog's bohunkus with his fat-long
middle finger. Bill had expected the dog to try to squirm or get
away or something, but Bill and his mom had their hands on
the dog's shoulders, and the thing had known it didn't dare try
to go anywhere. It got this look on its face: wide-eyed, and
violated, and offended, and . . . betrayed. Bill thought that
the other part of the look on the dog's face was betrayal, but
even to this day he wasn't certain.

Anyway, that was the look on Ron Hawkins's face, the last
time Bill had seen him: violation and offense. Betrayal. The
understanding and certainty that he was thoroughly and
utterly doomed to slide down into the deepest hell there is on
earth. His eyes had bugged out, just like the dog's, and his
mouth had fallen slack and open. And he'd turned to look at
the public defender who'd done him so little good. . . .

Bill didn't want to think about that look any more. Not
that he had any choice; at that moment in his existence there
was nothing else for him but the memory of Ron Hawkins
falling down toward hell.

So he just relaxed and learned to live with it for that last
hour before the plane finally found its way down in between
the shoulders of the mountains there at the edge of the Korean
DMZ. And after he'd lived with it for a bit, Bill Wallace

decided that maybe there were a few things that haunted him. Sometimes, anyway. When the world got too quiet.

Well, he thought: the answer was to keep the world from getting quiet.

Right. He was being sent off to be a junior assistant guinea pig, and he was under orders to keep his mouth literally, totally, and completely shut. And somehow he was supposed to keep things from getting too quiet. Fat chance.

And then the plane fell down through a curtain of clouds that looked as though it never parted, sailed down between mountains that seemed too sheer and too close together to ever allow a plane to land, and in a moment it had landed anyway, on a runway nestled impossibly between the hills.

For a while things were anything but quiet.

The crew got out without saying word one to Bill, which was kind of what he'd expected. At least they had the courtesy to leave the door open for him.

That wasn't the interesting part, of course. The interesting part came a few moments later, when he climbed the stairway down out of the plane. And saw the man who'd come to meet him. Who was dressed in a sweater and a tie and a lab coat. Wearing a badge that said he was a civilian research assistant.

And Bill Wallace (or Roe or whoever he was, now) recognized that man.

He'd known him most of his life, in fact.

Because the man who waited for him in the jeep was Joey Harris.

Brooklyn

The crowd finally finished filtering away a little after midnight, and Luke and the woman were alone again. She stood waiting for him, leaning against the kitchen wall, when he came back from saying good-bye to the Harrisons.

"Will you love me?" she asked him, smiling.

Luke nearly choked on his own tongue; he wasn't ready for the idea, much less the question.

"I . . . I don't know." He looked for anything at all say, just to keep from having to answer her. "Have we known each other long enough for that?"

Her smile went wistful, patient. "I think we have. The circumstances allow for changes in the ordinary rules."

Luke looked at his feet; he could see in the candlelight that his new shoes were already scuffed. "You haven't even told me your name," he said. There was something more there; the words hurt as he said them.

"I'm Christine," she said. "But you knew that, didn't you? And you're Luke. Luke Munsen."

He *had* known—known since he'd read her headstone when he'd almost fallen headfirst into her grave. That wasn't the point—or, at least, it wasn't the point as Luke had intended it.

"I guess—I don't know. I think it's too soon for me to say. Can we ease off a little? This is making me uncomfortable."

She nodded, just as patiently as she'd responded to everything else. "Would you like to come with me? I'm going to take a walk."

Luke rubbed his chin with the back of his hand, coughed. "Sure," he said. And blew out all but one of the candles, and used that one to guide them from the building.

They walked a long distance and back again that night, talking hardly at all, and what little was said was trivial; a comment about a strange façade; maybe a warning when the potholes in the sidewalk looked too dangerous. Once Christine remarked on the strange color of the moon.

Washington

It wasn't until two a.m., when he woke from death for the sixth time, that Graham Perkins realized where he was.

It was so obvious that it amazed him that he hadn't figured it out until then.

Graham Perkins was in Hell.

A very special Hell, he decided as he tried desperately to drag air in through his disfigured throat. A Hell for those who can be held accountable for the deaths of millions.

The realization gave him a measure of comfort—the first he'd felt since he'd come back to life five hours before. If he was in a Hell where he'd die a thousand times for each of the deaths on his conscience, then there was justice in that. Rightness. And hope too; if he suffered hard enough and long enough, might not his own suffering atone for the suffering of others? It was possible, just barely possible.

Graham tried to calm himself, to bear his torment with dignity. *Grace*. Grace as in God's grace. Was it a bad thing to think of God, here in the deepest pit in Hell? Graham wasn't sure. His faith had never been strong enough—he realized that now. He'd never studied God's word carefully enough— never read the Bible, rarely gone to church. If he'd even listened to religious broadcasts—the sort of thing Paul Green was so involved in—if he'd even bothered to watch a few revival shows he'd know the things he needed to now.

Maybe Paul Green had been right.

Maybe God was a thing a man needed to devote his life to. *I love you, God*, he thought. It was as much a plea for mercy as it was a sentiment. More so, perhaps. *I should pray*.

Yes.

He started with the Lord's Prayer, and wound his way through every one of the half-dozen prayers he knew. He was beginning his third Hail Mary when the wind shifted his weight, and he began to die again.

Grace failed him then. Hard as he tried to preserve his dignity—the dignity of prayer—his body only grew more desperate, and before he could stop himself he was struggling, arms and legs flailing wildly as he hung from the noose. Hands clawing at the high-test nylon cord that held him. And all he could think was *I've failed you, God, I've failed I've failed I'm sorry*.

Not that it made a damned bit of difference.

*South Korea
at the Edge
of the Demilitarized Zone*

Bill Wallace's first impression of the DMZ was no impression at all. The runway where he'd landed was like the runways at home—long, thin tracks of concrete or asphalt or some such, running parallel with strips of grass. When the jeep began to move he got a glimpse of the base, and it was an Air Force base, and it looked like any other base that'd been built in the forties or fifties. The land it was built on was all at right angles to itself—steep hills that turned to mountains if you stood back a few feet and looked up—which made it pretty distinct from Whiteman, back in Missouri. That was true enough. On the other hand, Bill had been to the Air Force Academy, out in Colorado (not as a cadet, but he'd been to the place all the same), and it was enough like this place that if he hadn't known where he was he could have mistaken the one for the other.

Well, okay: maybe not. The land here was different; greener and more alive. Wetter. The pines that grew on the sheer hillsides were more lush and closer together than the trees tended to be around the Academy. And even though the dirt was brown and sandy and leached, it was nowhere near as sterile as the dirt in Colorado.

Joey Harris hadn't said a word to him when he'd seen him.

Oh, his eyes had bugged out a little. And there'd been this expression on his face: partly recognition and being generally glad to see him after a lot of years. Partly shock, and surprise. And partly fear, as though he'd set eyes on a ghost—as though he'd heard that Bill had died, and how.

All the same he hadn't said a word. Which meant that he was under the same orders that Bill was, not to speak with him and not to attract any attention in public.

Bill was definitely ready for this state of affairs to come to an end. He wasn't sure how much more he could take of being shunned, even if he was under orders that amounted to it.

Joey took the jeep left around a corner; right, right, and then left again up a street so sheer it might have been a cliff. This base *was* like the Academy, Bill thought. The street plan was every bit as senseless and confusing. Four hundred yards without a turn, and then the buildings dropped away and they were moving along a loopy, curving road that bisected an enormous field marked by pocks and odd debris, shell-shocked from the war. Half a mile and the road straightened out again, and they were moving through undeveloped land along the base of a hill that was nearly large enough to call a mountain. And just when Bill thought they were going to drive out into the wilds forever, the alien brush and the dense pine-woods opened out on the left, to reveal a lone, squat, cinder-block building. Perched at the base of the hill like some unnatural blemish on the earth. Surrounded by its own electrified security fence, with its own security booth—and the booth was manned by two airmen, each of whom had a machine gun in hand. Which might not have been an awful lot of security, if

you didn't consider that it was on an air base in the middle of
the DMZ, and surrounded by so many soldiers and airmen
that Bill had a hard time imagining them all in one place.

The nearer of the two recognized Joey; hit a switch that
caused the motorized gate to swing open. Nodded them
through.

"We can talk now, I guess," Joey said. "If we aren't secure
here, there isn't anyplace for three thousand miles in any
direction where we would be. How the fuck are you, Billy? I
thought you'd—" He coughed. "—well, I thought you'd
bought it. You sure don't *look* like somebody who'd got himself
killed in a kerosene explosion. Was that an exaggeration? Or
was it somebody else who killed the President—somebody
with your name?"

Bill felt his jaw clench, his stomach churn. He wanted to
talk, all right. He didn't want to talk about this. "No. That was
me. What do you think I'm doing here?"

Joey shrugged. "Beats the hell out of me. All I know is
that you're the third classified . . . 'package' we've got in
today. Very classified. All three of them people, all of them
being rushed around and treated like they were some entirely
new form of radioactive material. The dazed black man from
New York. The boy from Tennessee. And now you. You don't
have to talk about it if you don't want; the Major'll brief me
soon enough. Just hasn't been time yet."

Bill grunted. "I'd better not," he said. "Orders."

Joey nodded. "No problem." He parked the jeep not far
from the windowless building's only door. Climbed out, waved
his hand to tell Bill he should follow.

"Last I saw you," Bill said, pulling himself from the jeep,
hurrying to catch up, "you looked as though you were going
away for a long while. What are you doing here? How did you
ever end up in a place like this?"

He grinned. "Yeah. I would've, too." He stopped a
moment; hesitated before starting toward the door again.
"After they sent Ron away I finally broke down and called my
grandpa, asked him to get me a decent lawyer. Grandpa's got
that kind of money. And he said he'd do it for me too—so long
as I got back in school and stayed there till I graduated college.
And then he fixed it with the judge so that I had to keep that
promise and stay in school, or I would go to jail. And fixed it
so that when I finished it'd all come off my record." He laughed

a little, which partly sounded hollow and partly sounded real. "Still not sure whether I should hate him for running five years of my life or thank him for running it well." He looked away, off toward the east, where it was almost possible to see the Sea of Japan through the scrub. "Both, I guess."

Bill followed the line of his sight, trying to figure out what it was he was looking at. Saw nothing but pine trees and hills rising up around them in every direction. And smelled the salt-wet scent of the sea.

That meant they were somewhere near the coast. Which didn't tell Bill much, since he'd never been stationed in Korea, and knew next to nothing about the place. He wasn't even certain he could see it on a map.

"I guess."

"Yeah. We'd better head in, huh?" Stepped toward the door; set his hand on a science-fiction–looking silver-green plastic panel. Which must have been a lock of some kind, because a moment after he'd touched it the door beside it clacked open.

It never ceased to amaze Billy, the sort of high-tech tomfoolery that the Air Force would spend money on. He'd spent a lot of time over the years wishing that they'd spent a little more of it on paying airmen a living wage.

Inside the building—it was a bunker, almost—was even more sterile and white than the outside had been.

Directly in front of them was a stairway that lead down. Into the heart of the mountain.

Joey led him down the stairs. Through a couple of doors, and then down again, two more flights. Into a foyer where another airman—security insignia on his arm—waited. This one recognized Joey too. He still made him put his palm on a screwy silver-green plate like the one upstairs. After a moment something beeped near the plate, and Joey led Bill past the guard without waiting for the airman to say he should.

Through a set of double doors, and suddenly the atmosphere was very different. The same walls, the same architecture: institutional. But where the rest of the building's interior was painted in a harsh shade of blue-white, here the tone was warmer. Easier on the eye. As was the lighting. The only source of light was the strip of fluorescent lamps overhead, but in this hall someone had taken the time to install the sort of fluorescent tube that gives off light that's easy on the eyes. For a moment—just a moment, mind—Bill almost began to suspect that he'd stumbled into one of those few places in the Air Force where people actually take pains to make the circumstances pleasant. And then it began to sink through to him: there was a reason why they'd gone to that kind of trouble.

The same damned reason why they were buried under thirty feet of dirt and rock and mountain and security.

Because whoever it was who was in command of this operation spent *a lot* of time here.

Lived here, more likely than not. Buried deep underground at the edge of a war just waiting to start all over again. Hidden so far from the sun that it might as well be the Antarctic.

And no one had to tell Bill that he was going to be buried down here for a while too. He could see that coming already.

It wasn't a thing that appealed to him. Not by a long stretch.

"This way," Joey said, turning a bend in the hall. They'd gone what, twenty yards already? Thirty? Far enough that Bill couldn't imagine that they were still underneath the cinderblock building they'd come in through. He had a momentary vision that they were in an endless maze of tunnels; a catacombs hidden in an exotic place, built especially by and for the United States Air Force. The idea chilled him, which maybe it shouldn't have, being as he was a *part* of that self-same Air Force. He shrugged inwardly. Probably there was something in that reaction that he ought to pay attention to. He didn't have the stomach for it; Bill had had enough of contemplating already that day.

Joey was a good half-dozen steps ahead of him, now, turning again—this time to rap, lightly, on an office door. And open it without waiting for an answer. Beyond him, Bill could see that the hall they were in went on for a hell of a long way. Maybe they *were* in some sort of a catacombs, he thought—and then rejected the idea again, because it wasn't something he wanted to think about.

Because Bill was still a good way behind Joey, he heard the woman's voice from inside the office before he set eyes on her. "Ah! Joseph. You're back," she said. *Joseph?* She had to be talking to Joey. In spite of the fact that Bill had never in his born life heard anybody call Joey Joseph. The woman's voice was low and smooth, and it wasn't young. She had the kind of no-accent you hear in people from Iowa or Pennsylvania. "You've got the next of them . . . with you?" A small stress, there, on the word *them*. So faint a stress that Bill was almost uncertain that he'd heard it.

Joey had stopped square in the middle of the doorway, and he still stood there. Bill wasn't sure exactly why he had, but as long as Joey did there was no way Bill could see the woman without peering over Joey's shoulder. Which he sure didn't want to do right at the moment—that was no way to go about meeting whoever it was Joey reported to.

"Sure do, Major. The one from Missouri. Turned out to be somebody I went to high school with."

And suddenly, listening to Joey's voice that'd lost so much of its regional flavor—so much of its *Joey*ness—Bill was wishing that he'd got around to telling Joey about the fact that the Air Force had decided to change his name. If Joey called him by his own name while his papers had him listed under another. . . . It'd be awkward at least. And if he did: would this woman-major know who he was exactly—know what Bill had done on that airfield four days ago? Maybe she would. And maybe not; the general back at Whiteman might not have felt there was an absolute need to pass it on.

Which was not to say that there was a damned thing Bill could do about it at this point.

"Well, show him in, Joseph. Don't just stand there."

"Oh," Joey said. He stepped forward and aside. "Sorry. Come on in, Billy."

And stepped into the room, to see a woman with iron grey hair sitting at a steel desk—the kind of olive-green government-issue desk Billy had seen at least a thousand times since he'd joined the Air Force. His first glance told him that there was nothing outstanding about her; that she might as well have been any other woman who was still in her prime but leaning hard into late middle age.

And then he began to see it.

The firmness of the lines on her wide, sharp-featured face. The—he didn't know what to call it. *Presence* was the word that came to mind, but even as he thought it he knew that it wasn't exactly the right name for the thing. When she looked at Bill, he knew that he was being seen for what he was and what he could have been and what he might have been. And most of all for what he'd done.

And on top of that she was an officer, and not just an officer but a major. Bill wanted to go find an enormous rock someplace, crawl under it and hide for whatever time he had left on earth. Not that that was among his options. He had to introduce and present himself, no matter how awkward that was going to be with Joey there in the room—

And hesitated too long, and she beat him to it, which was very bad form.

"So, Corporal Roe. How was your trip from Missoura?" Which was exactly how she said the name of the state, as though it ended with an *a* instead of an *i*.

"Very quiet, ma'am. And a little dull. But it wasn't—"

"Roe?" Joey was looking at both of them a little cross-eyed. "Who's Corporal Roe? Major Carver, this is Billy Wal—"

"Hush, Joseph. The man in this room with us is Corporal Theodore William Roe. And if you know him by another name, you can keep that to yourself."

Washington

General Curtis Young stood not thirty yards away from Graham at the moment he began to panic and die again. The General's nerves were badly on edge—not so much from what was happening as from what wasn't. Standing on a highway, waiting, threatening, with machine gun and canon aimed at the eyes of civilians . . . it wasn't work for a soldier. It wasn't even work he'd wish on policemen, for that matter. For the tenth time in less than a day he wished he'd taken the post in Holland that the Pentagon had offered him two years ago. Europe was still sane—or sane by comparison to this, anyway. The governments over there were still lying low, or the people at the heads of them were, anyway. At least they were still governments. Half the cities in the US had lost their police forces, and not many of those had yet managed to find them again. The fact that Maryland was organized enough to call out its National Guard almost seemed like a miracle. And Congress—Congress was even more of a joke than it ordinarily was. The last Senator anyone had seen was the one who'd got himself pummeled to death by a mob on television Saturday.

The worst thing that had happened to anyone over in

Europe was when the two American airmen had got themselves roughed up on leave in Paris.

Definitely, Young thought. He definitely ought to have
taken the post in Holland. He shook his head, lifted his
binoculars to take another look at the mob.

"Sir?"

It was the lieutenant—the one who was writing the day's
report. Young recognized the man's voice.

"Yes, Lieutenant?"

"The report, sir—it's ready for your signature."

The mob was quiet, tired-looking. Well, Young thought,
it was about time they got tired. Even if these folks had lost a
lot of family when they killed the Vice President, how in the
hell were they supposed to maintain a riot for days on end?
There wasn't any sense in it. It was time for them all to pack it
in, go home, and go to bed. And in the morning they could
begin putting the nation back together.

"Anything in there I need to read, Lieutenant?"

"Not especially, sir."

A sound—someone shouting on the far side of the barricade. In the direction of the Vice President's body. Young
turned, adjusted the view of his binoculars, focused them.

Another shout—this one clear and distinct, understandable.

"He's alive!"

Young didn't want to believe that it was what he'd heard.
But it had been. It was too clear to question.

Finished focusing the binoculars.

"Oh my dear sweet God," Young said. "Oh my dear sweet
God."

As he watched the Vice President's corpse seemed to
come to life all at once; the man's arms flailed wildly, reaching
for the cord that he hung from. *How can he possibly be alive
after all this time?* Young could see through the binoculars that
the cord had crushed the man's throat; there was no way he
could possibly be breathing, no way blood could possibly reach
his brain.

There were men below him, panicked, beating the Vice
President with two-by-fours. They looked . . . more surprised and frightened than vicious. As though they were
beating the man more from fear of him than because they
wanted to kill him.

Young set the binoculars on the portable table beside him. The Vice President was struggling so wildly that Young could see the motion even without the binoculars. "He's alive, Lieutenant. Wake the men who're off duty. Get them ready for trouble. We're going to have to go in and get that man." He lifted the bullhorn from where it lay beside the binoculars.

"Isn't that . . . a little premature, sir? Shouldn't we get authorization before we start shooting? Sir?"

Young heard the media people, out behind his men, catch sight of the Vice President and begin to wake up.

"Take the field glasses, Lieutenant—look for yourself. The man's *alive*. There isn't time for authorization. Not if we want to keep him alive."

"Yes, sir. I can see without them."

The lieutenant hurried off; Young heard him shouting orders before he'd even decided what he was going to say over the bullhorn.

"You there—you with the clubs. Move away from the Vice President. Move away from the man and let him be, and no one else will get hurt."

They ignored him, of course; Young had expected it. No matter what they were doing they deserved fair warning. More than deserved it: giving it to them was necessary. Bad enough Young was going to have a civilian bloodbath on his hands. He didn't want it on his conscience—or on his record—that he hadn't tried to minimize the trouble.

"Kill him!" someone shouted. And then there was a gunshot from somewhere in the mob—the sound of a cheap revolver, Young thought. Christ—it was worse than he'd realized. He hadn't thought that there were any firearms in the crowd.

The bullet missed the Vice President, if that was where it'd been aimed. The three with the two-by-fours were still there, beating on the man, and they were drawing a crowd, now. There wasn't any time to lose; Young had to send people in for the Vice President *now*.

"Lieutenant," he shouted, "send them in. Get that man *out* of there."

And the men went in, with their steel helmets and their rifles and their flak jackets.

And the whole world went out of its mind.

As the cameras watched.

South Korea

Bill saw the boy for the first time that evening at dinner.

He was an ordinary child. Happy and healthy; blond and blue-eyed and freckled. Charming the way a child can be without giving it any special effort—or even meaning to be.

None of that, of course, was what caught Bill's eye.

The thing that caught his eye was the way the boy glowed like a cloud lit up with heat-lightning when Bill first set eyes on him, looking across the room as Major Carver led him in.

Bill blinked, surprised; did a double take, because that was the kind of thing he expected to see when his eyes were playing tricks on him. And sure enough, when he looked at the boy again—looked him in the eye good and slow and careful— he was nothing but a boy. With blond hair. And blue eyes. And freckles.

He's touched, Bill thought. And wondered where the thought could have come from, because he sure didn't know anything about being touched or anything like that. Fact was, he couldn't even have said what the phrase meant. Let alone have thought it.

Touched, said the voice inside his head that was his own voice but couldn't possibly be him. Said it all insistent like Bill ought to *know* what it meant.

Well, he didn't know. And it was dinnertime, and he was hungry, and by damn Bill was going to eat. Maybe not all that hungry, actually. But Bill Wallace was a man who liked his dinner.

So he sat at the table, and he smiled politely when Joey—or Joseph or whoever the hell he was now—introduced him to the boy and to Major Janet Carver's other two assistants. One of those two was a civilian, like Joey; the other was a naval lieutenant who still looked a little wet behind the ears. Almost like he'd just managed to get himself out of Annapolis in the last couple of weeks. (Bill had never had an awful lot of respect for junior officers, even if they were officers. Sure, an airman had to follow their orders. And he had to treat 'em like they were somebody special. But no one ever told Bill that he had to believe in a lieutenant who was ten years younger than he was.)

All of which was pretty darned peculiar, when you got right down to it. Here they were, officers, enlisted men, civilians. Even a child. And they were all sitting at the same table for dinner, like it was some kind of a family meal or something.

Weird.

When he'd sat through all the introducing he could possibly take, a corporal came in wheeling a meal cart. Handed out plates and glasses and trays, set a tall pitcher of iced tea in the center of the table. And took the one empty seat for himself. When he was done Joey introduced him as their supply clerk, which in English probably meant that he was the Major's private secretary.

And for a long time they were all kind of quiet, what with eating and all.

Major Carver—Major *Janet* Carver—had turned out to be some kind of an MD-type doctor, along with her being a major and all. Which made her rate pretty highly in Bill's book. It was almost like she had rank twice over. First thing she'd done after Joey had taken him to her was show him to her doctor's office and give him a real physical. Pretty damned thorough one too—the kind of physical that always left Bill feeling kind of embarrassed. So to speak. Even when it was a man-doctor giving it to him. Anyway, while he was in there getting his self all probed and looked at and explored, Major Carver told him a little bit about what she did for the Air Force. Which was research. And about what he was doing there—most of which he could have guessed at. Except for the part about there being other people who'd come back to life, just like Bill had.

Maybe there'd been a hint of that in that stuff Joey said about packages that were actually people. Maybe. If it was anything it wasn't much more than a clue. Major Carver came right out and said it: miracles were happening all over the east half of the country. People coming back to life when there hadn't been enough of them left to give a proper burial. Cripples getting right up and walking, graceful as you please. Sick people sitting up in their hospital beds and acting like there'd been nothing wrong with them in the first place.

And the Air Force wanted to know about it. Air Force, hell: the whole damned Pentagon wanted to know. And they were going to find out too, by studying Bill and the two other people who'd been brought here.

Bill had to admit that it pleased him to be such a center of attention. He wasn't sure how much he liked being classified. Which was the other thing Major Carver had said—all three of them had been classified top secret or some such. Which wasn't at all as though they'd given Bill a jumped-up security clearance. More like they'd made him into one. Which meant that, as of now, he couldn't go out and take a pee in the woods without an armed escort. And he could completely forget about talking to anyone outside the research project.

Which he could expect to go on for months. Years, maybe.

That was the part he didn't like especially.

Though it wasn't like there was a damn thing he could do about it.

Someone at the far end of the table coughed; Bill looked up, automatically, to see—

The boy was glowing again. Glowing, damn it, *glowing*.

Blink.

And not glowing at all. Not doing anything but being a boy.

He's touched, Bill heard himself thinking. *He's touched, and you can see it because it's touched you too*.

Which didn't make a damn bit more sense than the words Bill'd heard in his head before. He frowned, shook his head. Bill was seeing things. Hearing things. Under the circumstances it was kind of understandable, and that was all there was to it. The thing to do was ignore it; sooner or later his head would clear and the world would go back to normal.

So he looked at his food. Set himself back to the task of putting it down—which was getting to be a considerable task, since Bill was beginning to lose his appetite. And that was a shame too, when you considered that dinner was some kind of a beef stew on top of egg noodles, and was a high cut above your everyday Air Force chow.

The beef was a little on the rare side. Rare stew beef? That was kind of screwy, wasn't it? Yeah, it was. Oh well; it wasn't bad. Just the opposite. Exotic and peculiar and kind of nice.

Hadn't that first bite of stew been crumbly and well-done, cooked half to death the way stew usually was? It had. Bill remembered it clearly enough. Even if he had been a little distracted when he'd dug in, the memory of taste and texture was still clear.

The bite after that one was right on the edge of being raw.

What was wrong with the cooks here? Well, they were in Korea. Maybe they had a Korean cook working down in an Air Force kitchen someplace in this maze. Bill had never ate any Korean food, but he'd had take-out Chinese, and that had certainly been an alien experience. Hadn't been raw, though. Kind of what you might call lightly boiled—and definitely cooked through, no matter how alien it was.

Listen to what I'm thinking, Bill thought. And this time it was no question but he was thinking for himself. *If anyone was listening to me he'd've thought I was one of them red-neck racist types like you find up in the hills*.

By this point Bill was finding himself pretty agitated. Partly for obvious reasons, partly for ones he couldn't quite put his finger on. He took him a good look at his half-cooked stew, pushed the bowl away, looked up and around the dead-quiet table—

And there that boy was again, glowing brightly-as-you-please.

And, being agitated and all hep up about the raw stew, Bill had his mouth open before he could manage to put a stop to himself.

"You cut that out," he said to the boy. "What're you doing taking a shine that way?"

The words fell onto the quiet table like rocks falling down out of a sack of gravel.

The boy looked up from his dinner—*his* stew didn't look half-cooked, Bill noticed—and smiled at him cockeyed like he didn't quite know what he was talking about. He'd stopped glowing again by this point, of course. Now that everybody at the whole darned table was staring at the both of them.

"Cut what out, Mr. Corporal Roe? What kind of shine you mean?"

Bill sighed. Embarrassed. He could feel hot pressure in his cheeks like they were turning red. "Nothing. Not nothing. Just a little off my feed from flying across that ocean, I guess."

None of them were eating any more; everyone at the whole damned table was staring at him. And not just like he was crazy, either. Though there was some of that. Mostly they were staring at him transfixed, like . . . like he was something in one of their experiments. Which, Bill reminded himself, he was. Up till that moment Bill had felt a lot more like an airman who'd pulled himself weird duty than he'd felt like a rat in some scientist's laboratory.

Major Carver coughed. " 'Taking a shine,' Corporal Roe?"

Bill frowned. Blushed. There wasn't any sense in discussing it. Or, maybe more to the point, there was a lot of sense in *not* discussing it. Bill didn't want to get himself dissected like some laboratory rat on account of him being crazy enough to see things.

Not that the Major-doctor woman was about to let it go.

"Did you see something, Corporal Roe? Do you think you're hallucinating?"

Bill wasn't completely uneducated; he had his high school. Couldn't have got into the Air Force without it. He knew about "hallucinating"—it was seeing things, like what happened to those dumb kids who took that LSD acid stuff, or ate some of those magical mushrooms. He'd almost got involved with that nonsense himself, back when he was in high school.

Bill sure didn't want to get himself busted out of the Air Force on some drug charge.

"No ma'am. Not hallucinating. Just my eyes acting a little weird, kind of."

"What, exactly, did you see, Corporal?"

Bill looked away. Looked at his stew, because it was in front of him and it was something he could stare at. There wasn't any getting away from a question that direct. Not without insubordination. Or lying. And he knew that this wasn't any kind of situation where he ought to be telling any lies.

"Well, ma'am. It was kind of like I looked at the young fellow there, just out of the corner of my eye. And when I looked at him, just for this little moment, it was like he was glowing."

The silence was so thick that Bill could have heard dandruff falling on his shoulder. And it went on forever.

"It could have been a trick of the light, I guess," Bill said. "You all got some kind of screwy light bulbs in this room, maybe?" Which was maybe a good question to ask, and Bill knew it, because he knew that someone had taken the trouble to install some kind of easy-on-the-eyes light bulbs in here, just as they had in the hall.

More silence.

"No, Corporal. There isn't any way that the light here could cause you to hallucinate."

And more silence still. And Bill was beginning to feel like he was under a microscope, and everyone was still staring at him. And his ears were ringing, and his hands were beginning to shake. And he pulled his bowl of stew back toward him and dug back into it, even though he wasn't hungry any more and the stuff was pretty darned gross. Because if he didn't do something, anything, right there and right then, Bill thought he'd go out of his mind. . . .

The first bite went plop right into his mouth without Bill even looking at it.

And that was a serious mistake.

Because the gravy-covered cube of beef in Bill's mouth was raw.

Raw. And warm. And bloody and quivery as living flesh.

And Bill forgot all about the fact that the spotlight was already pointed at him. And he screamed, and spat that hunk of meat right back into the bowl he'd taken it from. Where it bled and pulsed, just as though it *were* alive.

That caused a real stir. It took the attention off of Bill and the fact that he was seeing things real thoroughly. Not quite as thoroughly as when, a few moments later, everyone noticed that their own dinners had turned just as raw as Bill's.

Washington

It wasn't as simple as it should have been, of course. The crowd—which just a few moments before had been quiet and tired—was wide awake before the first soldier crossed the barricade. The mob might have been a bunch of untrained civilians, but all the same it fought well and hard—partly because they were furious, partly because none of Young's men had the heart or stomach for killing unarmed civilians.

The worst of it was that the mob *wasn't* unarmed. Every one of them had a rock or a two-by-four or a carving knife, and there were more guns, half a dozen of them, at least. Two

256 *Alan Rodgers*

soldiers were shot point-blank in the face, where neither their helmets nor their flak jackets could do them any good.

After that the men seemed to remember how to shoot, and the sound of their machine guns filled the highway.

And the bloodbath started.

A line of stray machine-gun slugs hit the lamppost above the Vice President's head; one of them cut through the cord that held him. No one saw that in the confusion. Not even the ones with the two-by-fours who'd been beating him a few moments before.

And the Vice President, confused and unnerved and gasping for air, crawled down the embankment, off the highway, away from the riot.

And no one noticed.

Not until the fighting was done, and bodies covered the pavement, and someone thought to identify the dead.

South Korea

What with all the commotion, no one ever did get around to asking Bill about the glow again. Which was just fine with him.

Major Carver had taken one good look at her bleeding stew, and she'd said something or other about biologicals and infection, and she'd told her corporal to quarantine them off right away. A moment or two later Bill had heard her mutter something to the effect that she didn't expect it to do any good if they were dealing with something that virulent—was that the word she'd used?—and she said it quiet enough to give Bill the feeling that she hadn't intended anyone to hear it.

Then she'd turned to the Navy lieutenant, and said, "Lieutenant Reynolds, Mr. Smith." A nod to her other civilian assistant. "I want you to take one of these bowls to your lab, and I don't want you to leave until you've isolated the agent responsible for this reaction. I'm serious. If you find yourself falling asleep on your feet, Corporal Conrad here will bring you a cot. Regardless, you're not to leave—if you're awake I want you working. Do you understand me?"

The lieutenant said, "Yes ma'am." The look on his face was the look you expect from an airman who's just been told that he's got to sweep a runway by himself with a push broom. Smith didn't look much more enthusiastic.

And the Major had turned to Joey. "Gather up Mr. Rodriguez, the police officer from New York, and bring him to my lab. Take Corporal Roe with you, in case you need help. I'll bring young Mr. Williams with me myself. There's work to do—a whole night's worth of work to do—but I want our subjects where I can keep an eye on them." The major paused, huffed. "Don't just stand there with your mouth open, Joseph. Get *on* with it."

Joey closed his mouth. Shrugged. "Yes ma'am. If that's what you want." Kind of sarcastic-like—or maybe not sarcastic, exactly, but right there on the edge of it. Which probably would have got Bill busted down to private all over again, for insubordination. It was a mild reaction from a civilian who was being asked to put in overtime without being given any choice.

Three minutes later they were in that long white corridor again, walking a lot slower than Bill was comfortable walking these days. Especially when he was under orders. There wasn't much to do about it; Joey was the one who knew where they were going. If Bill went on ahead of him he'd be sure to end up in the wrong place.

"Don't you think we ought to get a move on? The Major sounded in some kind of a hurry, I'll tell you."

Joey let out a long breath; slowed almost to a stop to think about the question.

"She gets that way sometimes. I don't see that there's anything to be done about it."

Which struck Bill pretty strangely, even if he wasn't quite certain what it meant. "How's that?" he asked. He hadn't seen an awful lot of Major Janet Carver. What he had seen of her had impressed Bill rather highly.

"I don't get it," Bill said. "What're you talking about?"

A silence that went on for longer than it ought to have, and Joey had this weird look on his face, like he was about to say something. For a minute Bill thought Joey was actually going to answer the question; but then his expression changed again, as though he'd thought better of it. "Never mind," Joey said. And after that he didn't say another word until he opened the door to the policeman's room.

When they got there, Bill saw that there was one thing about Joey that hadn't changed: he still got all slick and sweaty when he was nervous. And it *was* nervousness that had him in such a sweat, too. Bill could see it in his eyes, the lines on his forehead and around his mouth. All over his face. At first Bill thought that maybe it was because of the conversation they hadn't quite had, just a few moments before. No: look at the way Joey hesitated, not wanting to open the door. What on God's earth was in there, to make him shake like that?

"You going to be okay, Joey?"

And Joey snapped. "Don't call me that, damn it!" His voice was shrill. Or as shrill as a baritone ever gets. Just shy of hysterical. "My name is *Joseph*. Or Joe, if you have to. I'm not seventeen years old any more, and no one, no one, calls me Joey."

It gave Bill more than a bit of pause. He was about to say something sarcastic, something biting—and then he stopped himself. It wouldn't do for him to get into a tizzy, too; not if Joey was about to slip a cog. "Sure, Joe." The word tasted strange on his lips. "Joseph. Whatever you want. What's in that room? What's got you all hep up?"

And Joey or Joseph or whoever the hell he was stopped dead in his tracks. Stopped moving, stopped trembling, everything. Let out a small sound that sounded as rattled as every other thing else about him. Turned, looked Bill in the eye.

"There's a man in here," he said. "A policeman who got his head blown off in a riot in New York City. And he's alive."

That didn't sound all that frightening to Bill; he'd been dead himself not even two days ago. It wasn't worth interrupting over.

"There was a picture of him, right when it happened: the TV cameras, from ABC. Live on the networks. Right before the crazies took over the place. One minute he's a cop, armed with nothing but a night stick. Trying to stop a riot when the rioters are armed with machine guns. The next minute there's blood and bone and brain-meat flying everywhere, and the cameras are getting all of it, taking it in and sending it out into the air."

Joe took in a breath. Let it out slow.

"I was watching the satellite feed when it happened. ABC, just a couple of minutes before it went down. I saw it, damn it—I might as well have been there. And three hours later someone notices that something is *breathing* inside a body bag." Bill saw Joe clench his jaw. Reach forward, set his hand on the doorknob, turn it. Press the door just far enough open that Bill could tell the room inside was pitch black. "I saw him, damn it. I *saw* how he died."

Joe finished opening the door. Reached in and turned on the light. Stopped again.

"There's something else, too," he said. And waited for Bill to ask him what he meant.

There was something here—something wrong. The way Joey was acting, that was it. None of the things he was talking about—none of the things he'd told Bill about—seemed like anything that ought to make anybody tremble before he went into a room. Let alone Joey, who took it real easy when he heard how Bill used to be alive. "Yeah? What's that, Joe? What else?"

And Joey stepped back, toward Bill—to one side and away from the door. Kept his arm extended, holding the door open.

"See for yourself."

And Bill saw the man.

At first there was nothing special about him at all. A dark, kinky-haired, sallow-skinned Hispanic. Puerto Rican, from the look of him; or maybe he was a pale Negro. Staring off into space absently. Prone abed but wide-eyed and awake. His face was slack, vacant; at first Bill thought that was the face of a man at the far end of exhaustion.

And then he got a second look.

And saw that the void behind the man's eyes was deeper and more impenetrable than tiredness or contemplation.

Saw that there was nothing behind those eyes at all.

"Trouble is," Joe was saying, "That man isn't really alive at all. Gives me the creeps in the worst possible way."

Dead, vacant eyes.

"No," Joe said, "that isn't saying it right. I could live with the creeps. Being around the walking zombie makes me sick with myself, right down to the core."

Sick with himself: that was exactly what Bill was feeling. Dead down inside, like the fever he had when he was twelve that made him so tired that he wanted to let go of the world and slip away and die.

" 'Walking zombie'? He can actually walk?"

"Not very well. There's just about enough of him left that

if you take him by the arm and drag him, he'll follow you. Not very well; sometimes he just stops, and there's nothing you can do to get him going again."

Bill stood, still as stone, staring. There was nothing else *he* could do. "Have I got this right? We've got to share a room with this thing for the rest of the night? And maybe longer?"

"That's right."

Bill shuddered. "Okay, then. Might as well get to it." He crossed the last few steps to the man's bedside, pulled away the sheets, took the man's upper arm. Tried to pull him upward, or maybe get him to sit himself up. It wasn't much use; the body was enough like putty that when he lifted the arm that arm itself was the only thing that moved.

"We've got to lift him out of bed ourselves," Joe said. "Once he's on his feet you can get him to walk. He won't get there on his own."

"Oh," Bill said. This job was going to get unpleasant. There was an odor in the air, here, close to the man who wasn't entirely alive. A smell like—like filth, and worse than that. The smell that skin gets when it chafes against itself too much for too long. Sick, sweet, sour. Decay.

Joe crossed the room, went to the far side on the man's bed. Bent and took his arm. "We both need to lift at the same time. *Now*," he said, and they heaved that man, all jellylike mass of him, to a sitting position. Where Bill held his back steady while Joe pulled his legs around so that they hung over his edge of the bed. "Come around, and help me get him to his feet." Bill did, and a moment later they were leading the dead man from the room—Bill holding his left arm, Joe holding his right. It was a little tricky getting out the door, what with three abreast like that, but they managed.

Washington

All Graham could think as he crawled down the embankment was *God loves me, God loves me and He forgives me. In spite of all I've done*. Already the constriction in his throat was beginning to ease; he could feel blood pulsing up through the fat veins of his neck. Even his larynx—which just a few moments before had felt as though it'd been crushed permanently and hopelessly out of shape—even his larynx seemed to be reforming itself.

There was gunfire all around him, and blood. Old blood, scabrous and brown, and fresh stuff, too, that made his trembling hands and knees feel as though they'd slide out from under him. People screaming in pain as they died violent deaths.

I'm still in Hell, he thought. *God has freed me, but I'm still in Hell. I've got to crawl up, out of here. Crawl my way free of here and find God. God wants me and needs me—why else would he set me free? God's waiting for me, somewhere not far away at all.*

The only path that led away from the place, of course, wasn't a path up out of Hell at all.

Just the opposite. It led down, down the embankment and through the gaping ruin of a chain link fence.

That fact should have told Graham Perkins something. He should have known what he was doing, even as addled as he was. Should have known that he wasn't escaping from Hell, but crawling down into another, deeper and more subtle ring of the inferno.

Whether he ought to have known or not, he didn't. When he was free of the broken fence he edged along the sidewalk, certain that sooner or later he'd find heaven, or purgatory, at least. He kept crawling for a whole block and a half, wearing his hands and knees raw and red with his own blood.

And then the limousine spotted him.

The driver braked suddenly as soon as he began to pass Graham—suddenly enough to add the sound of screaming rubber to the chaos on the Beltway. A moment later the back door eased open, and a man stepped out.

A smiling man—and after Graham had taken a moment to absorb the smile, he realized that he recognized him.

From the White House. It was one of the men from Paul Green's "kitchen cabinet"—though no one ever actually used that term. There weren't many who knew about the dozen or so people who had special access to the Oval Office; certainly Green himself had taken pains to keep their comings and goings unnoticed. It was one of the few things Green actually *had* been discrete about. Likely that was because all of his cronies were deeply involved in the fundamentalist sect that the President had been a part of.

Graham even knew this one by name—they'd been introduced at a cocktail party a few weeks after Green's inauguration.

Herman Bonner.

What was **Herman Bonner** doing here, in Hell? Herman was a Christian, just **as Paul** Green had been. It didn't make any sense. Unless—

Unless maybe . . . unless maybe he was here to save Graham.

I'm redeemed, Graham thought as he took Herman Bonner's hand.

And that was the moment that Graham Perkins lost his soul.

South Korea

Someone brought a tray of dead things around eight. At nine they brought a corpse.

Long about midnight the dead-eyed man started to drool.

That was plain and simple too much for Bill Wallace, and he said so out loud as he got up and walked away from the corner of the room where he and the boy had been told to sit and watch the dead man.

The major cocked an eyebrow when she saw him there staring over her shoulder, but then she got a glance at the way that *thing* was drooling like that, and she said, "All right, then Corporal. I take it you want to help us here?"

Which was a sincere relief. "Yes, ma'am. Anything I can do to be of service."

She frowned. Took a good long look around the lab. "Do you see the table over there? The glass dishes set out on it? Yes, you do. Get yourself a pad and pen out of the cabinet" she pointed "near the door. Second drawer. Make yourself a list of the contents of each dish. It won't be hard; they're all labeled. I want you to check the contents of each dish every half hour, and note any changes that you see. If there are no changes, I want you to make a note of that, too."

Bill took a long, hard look at the table. It wasn't your regular sort of Air Force work she was asking for, but it didn't sound too complicated.

"Got that?"

The dishes on the table were where Joey and the Major had put those giblets that the quarantine-suit people had wheeled in half an hour back. Well, that was a relief; for just a moment Bill had been afraid he'd have to go into the adjoining lab and keep an eye on that corpse they'd brought in on the stretcher. Bill'd noticed how Joey had to go in and check on it every little bit or so.

"Yes ma'am. No trouble 'tall."

Two minutes later Bill was standing beside the lab table, making his list. The work wasn't that tough, Bill decided. And this was all there was to being a scientist? Bill pictured himself as some kind of a Dr. Frankenstein, decked out in a white lab coat and Coke-bottle glasses and one of them pointy little mustaches. Grinned. Maybe there was something to this business of getting yourself enough college to do desk work. A damn sight easier than runway sweeping.

The dishes were all labeled, just as the Major had said they'd be. Labeled twice, in fact: once with a common animal name that Bill didn't have any trouble understanding, once in Latin that Bill couldn't make sense of and could only barely recognize for what it was. *The heck with that*, he thought, scribbling on his pad; as long as he took down something understandable, there wasn't any need to copy down those jumbled-up foreign letters.

The first dish was marked CHICKEN, and there wasn't much mistaking it. Looked like a drumstick sitting in that glass dish. Fresh out of your grocer's freezer. Well, not exactly like that. But pretty darned close. There was dark, fresh blood seeping out around the open knuckle. And the skin on the drumstick there looked fuller, like Bill imagined the skin of a live chicken would look underneath the feathers. Not that he'd ever seen a live chicken, let alone a live chicken without its feathers. Mountainville, where Bill grew up, might've been a small place in the middle of nowhere, but it wasn't any farm-town, and Bill wasn't any farm boy.

The contents of the next dish were pretty familiar-looking—two cubes of the stew beef from dinner. Still covered with gooey-looking gravy, still leaking blood. It didn't look as though it'd changed at all since dinnertime. Which surprised Bill pretty thoroughly; it'd only taken twenty minutes for that stuff to uncook itself. Surely it would have changed more than that in the hours since then.

Well, it hadn't, and he wasn't going to be able to figure out why himself. He scribbled on his pad: cow—*looks the same as it did at dinner*. Which didn't sound any too scientific, but the Major would just have to understand about that, since Bill wasn't any scientist.

The next dish was PIG, and it was a different matter altogether. CHICKEN and COW had both looked . . . well, butchered. Looking at them you could still see nice clean edges where somebody had took a knife to the meat. The PIG stuff was different—it didn't look at all like something you'd see at the butcher's counter. Not at all. More like some kind of a bleeding, stringy-red slime-mold you'd expect to see growing at the bottom of a vat. Very disgusting. How did you go about describing a thing like that on one line of paper? Bill wasn't sure. So he put down *large mess* on the line beside PIG. And hoped he'd be able to explain to the Major later on, when she asked about it.

Beside PIG was CAT, and it was even more disgusting than PIG was. It wasn't just dead—it was *dead* dead. And whole, too, where all the other dishes had just been hunks of meat. CAT looked like he'd spent a good six years soaking in formaldehyde—and it *was* formaldehyde; Bill knew the smell of it well enough to recognize it anywhere—it looked like it'd spent a good six years pickled in that stuff. There was a long slit down the center of the thing's belly, like someone way back when had cut it open to take a look inside. CAT, Bill wrote, *very dead*.

Disgusting as CAT was, MONKEY did worse things to Bill's stomach. Not that he looked worse—nothing could have looked much worse than CAT did—but he looked just about as bad, and the fact that he looked like a tiny caricature of a human being made it pretty hard to take. With the skin of his chest slitted open and hanging loose that way, he almost *did* look like a man, a tiny little bare-chested fellow with his suit jacket hanging open. *How long have you been sitting in that vat of formaldehyde, huh, little guy?* For half a moment, looking into its cute little wide dead eyes, Bill was half afraid that it was going to answer. It didn't answer, though—it just kept staring dead-eyed at Bill, like it was the world's best poker player.

MONKEY: *as dead as* CAT. *Maybe deader*.

Then here was the dish marked DOG, only Bill didn't see

any dog in it all. Just this oversize drumstick, which Bill (who wasn't any butcher, truth to tell) would have took for a turkey leg if it weren't for the label. CAT and MONKEY were clearly laboratory animals, dissection stuff like the frog they made Bill chop to bits back in junior high. But dog, here—dog looked a lot like CHICKEN did. Which is to say that dog haunch looked like it'd come out of somebody's refrigerator, same as the drumstick did. These Oriental types here in Korea, they were dog eaters, weren't they? Bill thought he remembered hearing a couple of airmen come back from here, telling horror stories about it. *Ugh*. He wasn't too sure how much more of this he could take. Not that it mattered whether he could take it or not; he was an airman and the Major had told him this was what he had to do and he had to do it. No two ways about it. So he looked real close at that haunch of DOG, and he saw how the open bloody wound end was just like the PIG, lots of little fibrous tentacles growing up out of the meat. And he wrote that down.

It got a little easier after DOG, which was a good thing. A plate with a dried up dead ROACH on it, and even if it was a little gross Bill'd sure seen worse. CARP wasn't anything but a fish fillet. Two plates full of shriveled up stuff marked BRINE SHRIMP and PLANARIAN WORM. A FROG and a LIZARD, both of which looked like things that had got themselves mooshed out on the road. A busted-open CLAM, which Bill looked at and tried to figure out what he was supposed to be able to say from looking at it. Two hunks of meat, marked HORSE and SHEEP, that looked like they were fresh in the butcher's case. A dead SPIDER. MOUSE and RAT, both of them clean and lily white like lab animals. Little blots of blood on their backs where someone had taken the trouble to sever their spines. And a headless RABBIT that was probably from a lab, too.

When he'd made his notes on the last of them, Bill turned away from the lab table and let out a long breath. The big round-face clock there on the wall by the door said that it was twenty after twelve, which meant that he had a good twenty minutes before he had to make another round and start over with CHICKEN. Twenty minutes. Time enough to have a cigarette. If he had any, which he didn't, since he hadn't had a chance to get by a commissary in a lifetime or so.

"Joey," he said, about a second and a half before he

remembered that he wasn't supposed to call him that any more, "you got a couple smokes I can bum?"

Joe was sitting in front of a computer terminal just then, pounding away on its keys. "Quit three years ago," he said. Without bothering to look away from the computer screen. "Sorry."

Damn.

"You're welcome to one of mine, Corporal Roe. There in my purse, on the chair. Help yourself."

Which brought the Major up a couple more points in Bill's book. It wasn't often when he'd been offered a cigarette by an officer.

"Thank you, ma'am. Much appreciated."

There they were, just like she'd said: a gold-and-red pack of Winston 100s sticking out of that little side pocket on her handbag. Beside the cigarettes were three packs of matches; Bill took a cigarette and one of the matchbooks, started to light up—

"You'd best step outside to smoke it; God knows what the combination of smoke and formaldehyde would do to your lungs." There wasn't even a hint of reproof in her voice—just a little concern.

"Yes ma'am. Thanks again."

It was a plain relief getting out of that room, with all its smell and presence of death. Already he was beginning to wonder if maybe there wasn't some way to get out of having to look at all that dead . . . *stuff*. The thought of looking in on that disgusting mass of PIG again did a lot to make sweeping runways look appealing. Maybe being a scientist wasn't all that much fun after all. There was an idea: maybe he could volunteer to do something else, something a little more in the line of work airmen ordinarily did. Maybe he could volunteer to tidy up that runway he'd come into this base on, for instance.

Ha—fat chance of that. The major wasn't likely to appreciate the suggestion; the whole reason he was down here inside this mountain was because he was too classified an object to allow to be seen in the light of day.

Someone was shouting, somewhere in some vague and distant tunnel; the sound of it was barely recognizable from where Bill stood. And was that noise the clatter of a machine gun going off? It was. Best to tell the Major about it. He looked around for an ashtray to put the cigarette into. Saw none and quashed the butt on the tile floor. Wincing as he did it—Bill had cleaned enough floors in his time in the Air Force to know how much trouble it was to get rid of a cigarette scar. Opened the door to the lab, went inside.

"Major Carver, ma'am—"

"Not now, William. This is a critical moment, and I'm very busy. I need you to check up on your dishes right away."

"But Major—"

"The dishes, William. *Now.*"

It was an order, plain and simple. Stated in a tone of voice that ought not to be ignored. So Bill said "Yes ma'am," and he got his pad from where he'd left it by the Major's purse. And he went back to the table to check on his charges.

Which were even more disgusting now than they had been before.

CHICKEN hadn't changed all that much; it was maybe a little more raw-looking around the edges. COW hadn't changed at all. PIG, on the other hand—PIG was another story altogether. If Bill hadn't've *known* it was a piece of meat, if he hadn't seen it before when there was still the chance to recognize it, he'd never have figured out what it was. It looked like some kind of an amoeboid mass from a science fiction horror movie, all crazy strands of bloody fibrous ook heading off in every direction. Pulsing. And growing almost visibly; not long ago it'd been a tiny hunk, no bigger than a half dollar, and now it took up a full fourth of the plate it sat on. *I probably ought to tell the major about this, too. I bet she still isn't in any mood to listen.*

Bill glanced across the room; the Major was at that computer terminal now, typing away even more furiously than Joe had been a little bit before. Nope. There wasn't any sense interrupting her. Not if Bill didn't want to get his head took off. He shook his head, went back to work.

CAT hadn't changed a bit; he still looked like something that should have long since been put to rest. But MONKEY— MONKEY was a sight that gave Bill a wicked case of gooseflesh. There was a thin slick of fresh blood of the open flesh of his chest, and the tiny little veins there were *pulsing.* The loose chest skin that'd looked so much like a dinner jacket just a little while back had begun to fuse itself back onto the rib cage. And the glassy eyes that had been so dead were darker—not yet alive but neither entirely dead.

The haunch of DOG was growing, too. There was a great, fibrous mass—like the mass of PIG—growing out to meet its nonexistent hip. And it wasn't just growing, it was alive—as Bill watched the leg twitched at the knee.

He made his notes, moved on. ROACH, CARP, PLANARIAN WORMS, BRINE SHRIMP, FROG, CLAM, SHEEP, SPIDER, MOUSE, RAT, RABBIT—none of them had changed in any way that Bill could see. HORSE was a little redder than it had been, but not that much redder; it hadn't changed even as much as CHICKEN.

The strangest thing—the thing that sent Bill running over toward the Major and her computer terminal, and to hell with how she felt about being interrupted—the strangest thing was LIZARD.

Which wasn't in its plate any more.

LIZARD had got up and walked away; it was halfway across the table, prowling furtively. Looking at ROACH with a light in its eye that struck Bill as being distinctly hungry.

"What *is* it, William? What's so important that you insist on interrupting me?" Major Carver wasn't pleased with Bill at all. Not in the least.

"It's the lizard, ma'am. It's got up and walked away." Boy, did that sound stupid; Bill was beginning to feel like a character in a bad TV show.

"What lizard, William? What kind of a lizard are you talking about?"

Bill coughed. "The lizard that you asked me to watch, Major, ma'am. I don't know that I can tell you exactly what kind of a lizard it was—I know you had that plate labeled there in Latin and all, but those foreign words don't make much sense to me."

And Bill could see on her face how the idea finally reached home inside her: curious and then unbelieving and then surprised and finally panicked. Which was a pretty strange expression to see on the face of an officer, and Bill would've said so to anyone who cared to ask.

"Where is it, Corporal? Are you absolutely certain that you didn't brush it off the plate yourself?" She was already up out of her seat there by the computer terminal and running halfway across the room.

"No chance of that, ma'am. And even if I had knocked it

off the plate, there's no way I would could have moved it all the way over there by the roach without knowing that I'd done it. And moving it wouldn't have made a dead, dried out lizard alive enough to nibble on that bug like that."

She was standing over the ROACH plate now, staring wide-eyed at the lizard. Wide-eyed and afraid.

"No, Corporal. I don't suppose it would have."

The sound of shooting was closer now. Close enough to hear right through the laboratory's closed door. And wasn't that a larger explosion? A fragmentation grenade, maybe? It was. The Major didn't seem to hear it at all. Bill stole a glance over at Joe, who was hunched over the lab table at the far end of the room. And just as oblivious to the sound out in the halls.

"Ma'am . . . ?"

The Major didn't answer him right away; the look on her face said that she was too wrapped up in thinking about the lizard to notice much of anything else.

So, louder this time: "Ma'am . . . ?"

"What now, Corporal? Has another of your pets decided to get up and walk away?"

"They don't ordinarily conduct live ammunition exercises down here in these tunnels, do they?"

The Major scowled. "Of course they don't. Why should you ask such a question?"

The woman Major was definitely getting furious with Bill, and he knew it. Wasn't there some saying about people who had to give bad news, and that you ought not to get rough with them? Somebody, Bill thought, ought to tell it to the Major. Just so long as it didn't have to be him.

"Because there's people shooting off some automatic weapons out there in your hallway." There it went again—another grenade? And closer, too. "Or not far from your hall, anyhow."

That one only took an instant to sink through. Probably because of the sound effects.

"Sweet Jesus," and she was off again, running across the room. Heading for the wall phone this time, which wasn't much use since she couldn't seem to get through to anyone on it. After a moment she hung up the phone and came back to the table. Stood there awhile surveying the various dishes. (PIG was even larger, Bill noticed. And wasn't that dim light in MONKEY's eyes a little brighter?) "We haven't got much time," she said. "It's the North Koreans out there in the halls. Has to be. God knows what they'll do when they find us."

Bill frowned. "North Koreans, ma'am? What on earth are they doing over here?"

The Major sighed, shook her head. "They've been looking for an excuse to invade the South for thirty years. And with the trouble at home, they're probably assuming that we're in no shape to respond to them." Her face was angry; her hands knotted up in tight little fists. "They're wrong, of course. The Army—the Marines and the Air Force—all of them are keyed up and ready for a fight. The North Koreans may be able to overrun us here in the DMZ, but we'll be in Pyongyang before the week is over." She sighed again. Smiled, just a little. "Meanwhile we've got to get our notes off to Washington. The computer link is up, even if the phones are out. Give me your notes, William. Joseph, do you have anything to add that isn't on the computer already?"

"It's all in there, Major Carver."

"Good. If they come for us before I'm done, don't try to fight them. We're researchers, not infantry. Much more valuable alive than dead. Even alive in enemy hands."

When the North Koreans kicked the door open five minutes later—just as the Major was finishing—they didn't bother asking for surrender.

Two of them burst in, all but simultaneously. And in a moment all five of them were dead: Bill, Joey, Major Carver, the boy, and the drooling policeman.

Brooklyn

It was long after dawn when they got back. Whatever sleep Luke may have lost he didn't miss; he felt as rested when they were done as he had after his nap the afternoon before.

Andy was waiting for them on the stoop outside the abandoned building when they got to it. "Where you been?" he asked, mock-belligerent. "I been waiting around for you all morning."

"Went for a walk," Luke said. "Waiting? I didn't know I was supposed to be here."

"Well, of course you were. I was going to show you around the City today. Museums, that kind of stuff. All tourists are supposed to go see museums when they come to New York."

"Huh. I'm a tourist?"

"You aren't from around here, are you? I think we would have heard about it if there was anybody like you around this city. If you aren't from around here, then you're a tourist."

Luke blinked. "Well. I guess I am, then."

Andy looked up at Christine Gibson. "You can come, too, if you want. I bet you'd like the museum, too."

"I . . . I'd love to," she said. There was something in the sound of her voice, Luke thought, that seemed like a shadow of something she didn't want to say. He didn't know what it could be.

So the boy led them back down into the subway, and out into New York, which in the course of a single evening had lost every iota of the sanity it had spent days regaining. Andy couldn't have known it, of course, but the last place in the world he should have taken them was back into New York.

They took yet another route this time—all the way on the A train to COLUMBUS CIRCLE, then a dozen steps across the platform to the K local. Two stops more and they were coming up across the street from the Museum of Natural History.

They were too early to go inside when they got there, so Andy suggested that Luke could take them all out to breakfast at "one of those yumpie places over on Columbus." Luke was just a little apprehensive at the suggestion, though he didn't care much one way or the other about the money. The word *yumpie*—well, it made him nervous. It sounded familiar, but he had no exact recollection of exactly what a yumpie was. Was it some obscure, Middle Eastern creature—like a camel, perhaps? The idea of eating strange game for breakfast didn't appeal to Luke. Well, it didn't matter. He wasn't feeling especially hungry anyway, though he would have enjoyed a meal. If the food the restaurant served didn't appeal to him, he'd just have coffee.

Coffee Luke remembered, and clearly. Coffee was important.

When they got to the restaurant, its menu was pretty conventional. A little on the fancy side, maybe, but certainly not exotic. There wasn't a single yumpie dish on it. Or none that Luke recognized as yumpie, anyway; though Andy's Eggs

Benedict were covered with a strange, yellowish sauce that looked as though it could have been made from a yumpie purée. Luke ordered eggs and toast for himself, to stay on the safe side. He noticed that Christine did the same.

Andy talked all through the meal—talked even while he was eating, whether there was food in his mouth or not. Mostly he told cruel, funny stories about other children in the school he attended, and in spite of himself Luke found himself laughing at them.

They were almost ready to pay the bill and head on to the museum when Luke heard the sound of gunfire, and the enormous plate-glass window shattered into a hundred thousand pieces that covered them and their table and everything nearby.

Christine and the boy both screamed; Luke probably would have screamed himself if he hadn't been too confused and afraid to think of it. There was more shooting as Andy dragged all three of them down toward the floor; it shattered the rest of the restaurant's windows. And plastered the maître d' to the far wall, where the blood leaking out through the hole in his chest turned the white shirt of his tuxedo slick crimson.

Andy yanked a table onto its side, and the three of them huddled behind it. "We've got to get out of here," he said. "But where in the hell are we going to go? Where's that machine gun?" He peeked over the top edge of the table, ducked down again more quickly than Luke's eyes could have focused. "Holy shit," he said. "You got to see this!"

Another hail of bullets; one of them hit the table in front of them—and burst through, tearing a hole the size of Luke's fist in the thick wood. And the bullet *kept* going, too—into the plaster of the wall behind them. Luke felt it pull at his hair as it burst past him. Sharp bits of splintered wood bit into the soft skin of his cheek.

Andy's dark skin seemed to pale. "This table ain't going to do us a damn bit of good," he said. "We got to get over there, into the corner, by that brick wall." It was the one place along the restaurant's front that hadn't been floor-to-ceiling glass. "Stay low, and go as fast as you can, before those police start shooting again. I didn't even know that the police in this city *owned* machine guns. They own 'em, all right. Just don't know how to use 'em."

And he bolted out from behind the table, across the room. Luke took off a few steps behind him—

And nearly tripped over the corpse of a woman with a bullet through her neck when he looked out onto the street and saw a vicious-looking reptile the size of a three-story house, eating a man in a policeman's uniform.

Tyrannosaurus rex, Luke thought. He had no idea where the words could have come from. Were they a name, maybe— a name for the reptile? It seemed likely.

The policeman screamed as the reptile bit off his arm and spat it out; more bullets, going in every direction—most of them aimed at the dinosaur, few finding their mark. Even the ones that did hit home didn't seem to make much of a difference.

"Don't just stand there, Luke Munsen—you want to get yourself killed?"

Bullets, spattering holes in the plasterboard wall behind Luke; and suddenly he was running again. Three beats and he was huddled beside the boy, hiding in the small shelter that the section of brick wall afforded. Luke hadn't even caught his breath before Christine was huddled with them.

"How about that, huh?" Andy said, "A dinosaur on Columbus Avenue. Pretty cool, huh?"

"Um," Luke said. He was having trouble appreciating the novelty; he was still afraid for his life.

"He's winning, too. It don't seem to make any difference at all, no matter how much they shoot him. Look at that— those cops are going to be dinner!"

And what happens, Luke wondered, *When it gets done with them? Will it come over here and make a meal of us?*

Behind them, Luke heard someone groan, heard the sound of movement. He looked back and saw the maître d', impossibly, lower himself from the wall the bullets had pasted him to, and begin to crawl back toward the kitchen.

"That's a tyrannosaurus," Andy said. "I seen one of them in one of the books at school. Man, they are *bad*."

The dinosaur screamed loud enough to rattle the brick wall as machine gun bullets dug into its head, bursting its left eye. Bloody, rheumy pulp rained down everywhere.

"Meanest dinosaur ever made. It could kill anything alive. Did, too—they were always hungry."

Suddenly the creature was turning tail and running away,

south down Columbus Avenue, screaming all the while. The
police—those of them that were still alive and whole—
followed as best as they could, but before they'd covered thirty
paces the dinosaur was four blocks away.

"We need to get ourselves away from here," Andy said.
"The streets aren't safe—none of them. No telling which way
that thing will go next. Need to get ourselves behind some
serious rock walls, like down in the subway, or . . ." He
looked across the street, and the back side of the Museum of
Natural History. There was a gaping hole on one side of the
building, a little larger than the tyrannosaurus. Pretty obviously, it was where the dinosaur had come from. "Perfect,"
Andy said. "That's perfect."

"You want to hide in there? Come *on*—what if there's
another one inside it? You're out of your mind."

"If there was another one, we'd have heard it already. You
heard the kind of noise that thing makes. Don't be a weenie,
Mr. Luke Munsen."

And the boy bolted out of the restaurant, into the street.
Through the small park between the sidewalk and the museum's back wall. And in through the hole in the museum's wall.

"Oh, *Christ*." Luke wasn't eager to go out onto that street,
much less into the museum and whatever trouble waited
inside it. But he couldn't just leave Andy to whatever fate
waited for him inside that place; not if he wanted to be able to
live with himself. He turned to Christine. "I've got to go in
there and get him out of that place. You may want to wait
here . . ."

"No," she said. "I'll come with you. I'm not afraid."

There were a dozen bodies out on the street; all but two
or three of them uniformed. At least a couple looked as though
they might still be alive, and Luke would have felt an
obligation to do what he could for them if Andy Harrison
hadn't set off into a place that put him in even greater need of
help. There was still shooting in the distance, but none of it
seemed to be coming toward them.

"Well," he said, "let's go." And took Christine's hand,
crossed the street and the park at a dead run. They stopped
when they reached the ruptured wall, and Luke hesitated for
most of a minute before he led them in.

It was dark inside, and ominous looking; the only light
came from an emergency lantern high up in the room's corner.

A storage room, from the look of things, Luke thought; there were orderly stacks of crates everywhere reaching nearly to the room's high ceiling, many of them covered by dusty tarps. At the far end of the room was another rupture like the one Luke stood in front of.

There was no sign of the boy anywhere in view.

"Are you afraid?" Christine asked him. There was no malice in the question, and certainly no fear of her own. There was a little sympathy, and that embarrassed Luke. He didn't like the idea that he was afraid where anyone else could see it, but the truth was that he was scared half out of his wits.

"No," he said, "of course I'm not afraid. What's to be afraid of?"

"Nothing is, I suppose. If you say so." She smirked as she said it, and that only embarrassed Luke more. He climbed up into the rupture in the wall, and she followed, just a moment behind.

When they got to the far end of the room, into the broad corridor that led from it, they could see two more broken passageways marking the tyrannosaur's path. "He's probably down there someplace. That kid is crazy. Crazy. What on God's earth is he trying to do—find more dinosaurs? He's going to get all of us killed. *Again.*" He cupped his hands around his mouth, shouted: *"Andy?"*

There wasn't any answer.

Christine frowned. "I think we'd better hurry."

"Yeah."

And they ran, down one corridor and then the next, and three others after that, following the trail of wreckage the dinosaur had left in its wake. It wasn't a hard trail to follow; anything but. Three times they heard sounds of violence in the rooms off the corridors, and Luke called out Andy's name, but there wasn't any more answer than there had been the first time he shouted. Other rooms echoed with quieter, more ominous sounds. Luke kept his quiet when he heard them. They weren't likely anything to do with Andy Harrison; Luke couldn't imagine Andy in trouble and not making a racket.

They'd covered at least three hundred yards when they came to the last broken doorway. Beside it was a great brass plaque that read REPTILE ROOM; it was bent and hanging at an odd angle.

Luke hesitated again before he went inside. He knew

there was something inside that he didn't want to see—knew it without any evidence or reason.

And he was right.

Not that there was anything he could do *besides* go inside; he had an obligation to the boy, and certainly to the boy's mother. He couldn't just leave him there.

It was even darker inside the Reptile Room than it was in the corridors. The only light inside it came from the hallway, and from the hall at the far end of the room. If the room had ever had the sort of emergency lighting that most of the rest of the building did, something had destroyed it. The tyrannosaurus, maybe.

Or maybe something else altogether.

After Luke's eyes had spent a moment adjusting, it was more than enough light to see by.

"Pretty cool, huh?" Andy's voice—twenty yards away? Thirty? It didn't matter exactly how far. What mattered was that they'd found him.

Don't look, Luke told himself. *There isn't any reason to look. Whatever it is he's talking about, I don't want to see it. All I need to do is walk across this room, grab his hand, and drag that boy out of here—kicking and screaming or not.*

There wasn't any way to avoid looking, of course—not if he didn't want to break his neck.

And he saw—

—saw in the dim light dinosaur bones, whole skeletons with ropy-veined flesh growing on them like some terrible fungus. And wholer, half-formed things he didn't want to put a name to. Blood, everywhere, oozing from the things. Flesh dripping away where it lost its hold on bone.

Something shifted off in the corner to his left. Luke heard it moving slowly, unevenly, saw only the least hint of shifting chiaroscuro as it went. A shadow much too big to be the boy's. Even from that vague seeing he knew that whatever the thing was, it was carnivorous. Carnivorous and hungry and becoming more alive with every second that passed.

He shuddered. He still hadn't figured out exactly where Andy Harrison was. He had to find him and get all three of them the hell *out* of there.

"He's over there," Christine said. She pointed ahead and a little to the left; Luke looked in the direction she pointed and saw a shape that could have been a boy. It *was* Andy—he turned when he heard Christine speak, and turning moved him into the light. Not far enough to see clearly, but far enough to recognize.

"Yeah," he said—said quietly, almost in a stage whisper. "I'm over here. C'mon over, and be quiet, too—it's feeding. Don't want to scare it off."

Feeding? *What* was feeding? Luke wanted out of that room more than he could have imagined was possible. He crossed the dozen yards between himself and the boy more quickly than was safe, given that he couldn't see the floor well enough to have much idea what he might step on or trip over. Twice his feet nearly went sliding out from under him when one or the other of them managed to find its way into something thick and viscous. When he was a couple of feet away his ankle caught on a thick, fleshy bone; if Christine hadn't caught his arm he'd have gone flailing head over heels into the jumbled mass of God-knew-what on his the right.

"Look at that, huh," Andy said. He was staring off at the back left corner of the room, the same corner where Luke had seen the hint of something moving a few moments before. "Don't get to see nothing like that at the Bronx Zoo, do you?"

The angle of light was different from here; where before the thing in the corner had been grey shadow in the blackness, here it was . . . not clear, exactly. But plainly visible.

"It's a pterodactyl," Andy said. "Seen one of them in a book, too. Flying dinosaur."

The thing stood upright on two feet, like a man, but otherwise it was nothing like a man—its head was long and sharp, crested with a leathery grey peak. And where a man would have had arms the pterodactyl had wings like a bat's, with sharp-fingered claws at the center of their forward edges.

And it was eating—gnawing and grinding at the bloody-fleshy bones of the half-formed things around it.

Luke put his arm on Andy's shoulder. "We need to get out of here," he said. "Let's go."

"Aw, relax," Andy said. "I want to see what it does with the bones when it's done with them."

"Let's *go*, I said." Luke's voice was louder and angrier than he meant it to be; mean and noisy enough that it embarrassed him. "This place is *dangerous*. If we don't get out of here soon, we won't get out at all."

And two things happened at once:

The first was Andy Harrison, saying, "Mr. Luke Munsen, sometimes I'd *swear* you were a weenie—"

The second was the pterodactyl, looking up at the sound of Luke's voice, and seeing them, and screeching. And bolting after them, as though live game were infinitely preferable to the taste of half-dead meat.

"Oh fuck," Andy said. "Now look what you've done." And he took off, running for his life toward the door at the far end of the room.

Luke and Christine were only a moment behind him.

"That thing is *fast*," Andy said. They were in another corridor, long and better lit than the Reptile Room had been. "But we got one thing going for us: flying things don't get on too well indoors. You ever seen a pigeon got itself inside? It's a sad sight."

If Luke had ever seen such a thing, he had no memory of it. He didn't say so; he was too busy running to spare any breath on speech. How the boy could be so long-winded and still keep a pace Luke could barely match was beyond him.

Andy looked back, over his shoulder. "It's catching up with us," he said. "We ought to turn off somewhere—flying like that, the thing'll probably overshoot when we do."

And, without giving any more warning, that's exactly what he did—turned and slammed open a glass door marked with the words EGYPTIAN ROOM. Burst through and just kept going. Luke and Christine almost missed the turn themselves; the flying monster shot by, squawking with annoyance.

It didn't gain them much, of course; they'd barely made another thirty yards before Luke heard the sound of the glass door bursting to shards behind them.

In front of them, a glass-enclosed exhibit with a sarcophagus—and beside it, inside the glass, was a man clothed only in strips of crumbling yellow linen. He looked confused and terrified; he pounded desperately on the glass that walled him in, trying to break free. It didn't do him any good.

"Look at that," Andy said, "the Living Mummy. I read about him in the comic books."

Comic books? Mummies? Luke wasn't especially clear on either one. All the same he recognized in the man behind the glass the same confusion he'd felt himself when he'd come back to life three days before. He wanted to stop and try to help the man out of his prison, but there wasn't any time—not if he wanted to live. Besides, that case was made of something strong and thick, and it was bolted shut; he wasn't sure he'd be able to get it open, even if he tried.

The ceiling was low, here, and the aisles were narrow—which meant that there was no way for the pterodactyl to fly. And it kept bashing into things, too, which slowed it down even more. The dinosaur's troubles weren't much of an advantage; already Luke was getting tired; he didn't know how much longer he'd be able to keep going. And the pterodactyl didn't look the least bit winded.

Behind them the dinosaur caught sight of the man trapped in glass, and decided he might make an easier meal. The living mummy screamed in mortal terror at the sight of the thing, but when it tried to attack him, it didn't have any more luck getting into the enclosure than the man had getting free from it.

Andy ducked behind a partition, slowed down, stopped. "That'll give us a couple of minutes," he said, "but we got to think this through. Running away from this thing just ain't going to make it." He looked around, frowning. Then he saw the painted-steel door marked EMERGENCY EXIT   DO NOT OPEN   ALARM WILL SOUND, and his eyes brightened. "I got it," he said, "got it. Oh, man, this is great, just wait till you see this."

The door was on the other side of the room, narrow-wise, surrounded by a large collection of papyrus scrolls. The boy bolted across and waved to Luke and Christine, trying to get them to follow him. Luke glanced around the corner, saw that the pterodactyl was still trying to break through the reinforced glass, and still not having much result. So he went ahead and crossed the room, to see what the boy was getting at. When he was halfway there, he looked back and saw Christine shrug and follow.

"It's like this," Andy said. "You got to hold the door for me while I check inside here. Sometimes when you go into one of these you can't get out again. Okay?"

Luke reread the alarm warning on the door, shook his head, and said he would. Andy pushed on the swing-bar, and a shrill siren began to sound—loud enough that it hurt Luke's ears to hear it. He winced as he held the door open for the boy. What was he doing in there, anyway? Why didn't they all just get themselves out of there, while the pterodactyl was still distracted? It didn't make any sense. He looked in, trying to figure out what Andy was up to. The door led into a stairwell; Andy had gone up above him somewhere. Whatever he was doing, it was lost on Luke.

"It's going to work," Andy said, coming down the stairs. "Going to work just fine. These doors are plenty strong enough, and they open the right way. Both of you wait right here. Be ready to run—upstairs and through the open door on the next floor."

And he went out, into the center aisle of the Egyptian Room, picked up something that looked like a bronze vase. And shouted: "Hey, you! Hey stupid monster!" Threw the vase, hitting the pterodactyl square in the head. "Why don't you chase after somebody who can run, huh? What's the matter, don't like to work for your dinner?"

And took off like a bolt of lighting when the dinosaur came after him.

"Go," he said to Luke and Christine. "Go on, upstairs. Hurry!"

And they went, in spite of the fact that Luke felt like he was abandoning the boy in a bad spot, and Christine probably did too. The door barely even had a chance to swing shut behind them before Andy slammed through. It didn't even have that much chance to close before the pterodactyl bashed into it.

"Get *out* that door," he shouted to Luke. He was taking the stairs three at a time; down below him the dinosaur was struggling to press through the steel door frame. "Get out my *way!*"

"You're out of your mind," Luke said. He moved anyway. When Andy was on the second-floor landing he stooped and picked up the old brick he'd used to prop open the door, and threw it at the pterodactyl, hitting it squarely just above the eyes. Hit it hard, too—which wasn't hard enough to do the monster any harm; instead of flinching it screamed, enraged, and finished pressing itself through the doorway.

Andy laughed.

"Got you now, sucker."

Behind the monster, the door that led from the first-floor landing swung closed.

Andy stepped back, into the second-floor hallway, and pulled the stairwell door shut behind him.

Andy was still laughing; he got ahold of himself long enough to smile smugly. "Couldn't just leave him there in Egypt, trying to eat the Living Mummy like that," he said. "He might have got through eventually. And if it had that much trouble eating its way through a little bit of Plexiglas, there's no way it's going to get through a reinforced-steel fire door. No way."

The sound of the monster slamming against the stairwell door; the door and its frame shook a little, but not enough that it worried Luke.

"Fine," he said, "just fine. Now let's get ourselves out of this place. Get back to Bedford-Stuyvesant, maybe, where it's safer. I'm not cut out for this tourist stuff. All right?"

Andy frowned. "You're just no fun at all sometimes, you know that, Mr. Luke Munsen?" He shook his head. "Yeah, okay. Let's get going." Up ahead was a red-glowing EXIT sign, above a floor that looked as though it opened onto another stairwell. When they got to it the door swung open silently, as though its catch had been permanently disengaged.

And inside, staring out the window on the landing of the floor above them, was a policeman. He was facing away from them, but even from the angle at which they stood Luke could see that he carried a machine gun of the same make that the police fighting the tyrannosaur had.

Guns like that were dangerous—if you asked Luke, more dangerous than pterodactyls, maybe even more than tyrannosaurs. He started to back away quietly, easy as he could, afraid he'd startle the man—

"Hey," Andy said, "look at that. It's another cop with an Uzi—"

And the man jumped half out of his skin, and turned, and before anyone even realized what was happening the policeman was firing his gun reflexively.

Ten seconds later Luke Munsen and Christine Gibson and Andy Harrison were lying all but dead in the dim, tiled corridor, and the policeman was running toward another part of the museum, for fear that someone would learn what he'd done.

It only took Luke Munsen a few seconds to die in the clinical sense. One of the half-dozen bullets that'd hit him had ruptured the major artery that linked his heart and his lungs; blood rushed out through it into his chest cavity so quickly and copiously that his heart lost the will to beat almost before it felt the shock of the bullet's impact. And the moment that his heart stopped, Luke Munsen was dead.

Dead or not, his brain lived on a few moments longer.

And as he lay dead on the hallway floor, Luke Munsen had a vision. It began as his brain starved from the absence of oxygen, and when, an hour later, the microbes that had remade him once remade him for a second time, the dream continued with no interruption or transition that he could detect.

And his death and his life merged seamlessly into one another.

In the dream, Luke was alive again for the first time, and he was in love. Or thought he was in love; he was fourteen, and tripping all over himself, and he felt something that made him flush noticeably every time he got near that girl. If anyone had actually sat him down and asked him what exactly it was he wanted from her, he would have been uncertain of an answer. All the same, he would have told that someone he was in love—or might have told him that, if he were able to get far enough past his shyness to even apply words to the subject.

The point of the dream wasn't love, or blooming erotic need, or the confusion of attraction and true bonding. The point was the way the confusion in his heart and in his blood made the spiderweb look, that morning in late fall.

Luke was in junior high, and he was walking to school the shortest way, only it wasn't really the fastest because it led a mile and a half along sandy-dusty paths through brambles and thin woods, and it was hard to make anything like a decent pace when the ground sifted out from under your feet as you walked. That morning when he'd woke, there'd been thick fog everywhere, grey-blue-white outside his window, so thick and bright that it occluded the view completely.

His mother was awake; he could hear her in the kitchen banging pots very pointedly. Since he'd decided he was in love, Luke's mother made him even more uncomfortable than she usually did. She'd always asked questions about him and girls, and right then those questions seemed even more of an intrusion than they usually did.

The fog outside made Luke feel strange and magical, almost as though he'd found himself on some kind of an enchanted alien planet. If he had to talk to his mother that magic would dissipate as quickly and as thoroughly as the fog itself.

So he took his shower quickly, and dressed and grabbed his books, and left without breakfast or good-bye.

And that was how he came to be on the path to school half an hour earlier than he ought to have been, when the fog was still settling out to fat diamonds of dew on everything, and before anyone else had tracked through and turned the sparkling beads into an ordinary slickness of water.

It was also why he saw the spider web. No spider web that big and intricate and silvery could have survived the passage of a dozen children; someone would have destroyed it with a rock or a stick or a tight-packed clot of dirt. If there was destruction like that in Luke, though, that morning it was drawn up into him so far that he'd never have found it if he'd known to look.

He saw the web when he turned that fifth bend in the path. And in the peculiar bent of his mind that week, that morning, the spider web shining silver dew in the morning sun was the most incredible and beautiful thing the world could possibly have offered him. He stepped off the path, closer to it—afraid to touch the web for fear he'd harm it, afraid not to touch it because it was too beautiful a thing not to take into his hands and savor.

And then he saw the spider.

And seeing that thing turned the entire experience on its ear.

The spider wasn't just ugly and menacing, the way all spiders are.

It was *malign*.

Small, impossibly small for a creature that had built that large and perfect web. And it didn't even look like a spider—it was tiny and crablike, black as pitch except for a bead of blood-red on its carapace.

And as he looked at it, the thing turned toward him and stretched its maw hungrily at him—almost the way a dog bears its fangs at a thing it wants to kill.

And Luke ran, ran the whole half-mile to the school yard,

and when he got there he went to the deserted place along the back side of the boys' gym, and sat on the concrete stoop of the back door that no one ever used. And spent the half an hour he had to himself shivering with a fear he didn't understand.

That was the first part of the dream: a memory, vivid as though he'd relived it.

The second part was harder and meaner and less real.

. More immediate, too: in the dream he was himself and it was the present, and the only confusion he had was over what he was doing in the place where he was.

Which was an enormous room, a room the size of four city blocks. It was crowded with seats, arranged like a theater's rows. And all of those seats were filled with sweating, shouting bodies.

The shouting was all in unison and in time; if it hadn't been so raucous and so loud he might have thought of it as chanting. Far away, in the center of the front of the room, was an elevated podium; as Luke watched a man stepped up to it, and he began to speak into the microphone.

Luke recognized that man. For a long while he couldn't place the memory—where had he seen him before? When? And then it came to him: the bus. Luke had been standing on a side street in Manhattan, watching the carnage at the ABC building. Terrified. Guns everywhere, going off in directions no one intended. And that man had stepped out of a bus, and he'd seen Luke, and he'd turned white as a sheet.

An echo in Luke's head:

Herman Bonner.

Herman Bonner wants to kill the world.

Yes, Herman Bonner—that was who it was. Who *was* he—besides just a name? Luke had known that man, once; known him more intimately than was comfortable. The more he thought about it, the more certain he became.

Herman Bonner was talking, now, speaking cryptically with an accent that was unplacably alien. Strange, senseless talk—something about . . . *Rapture,* and something else about an Apocalypse to come. What was all of this? And why would anyone want to kill the whole world? Luke shook his head, trying to clear it.

There was only one way to find out what it was all about, he decided. The way to find out was to ask.

He stepped out, into the aisle, and shouted, so that the man would hear him so far away.

"Herman! Herman Bonner!" And the man stopped dead in the middle of his speech.

The crowd went silent, too.

And he looked afraid.

"Why do you want to destroy the world, Herman? I don't understand."

And Herman Bonner went white as a sheet, and his jaw hung slack for a long moment. And finally he said into the microphone, "This is a heathen—an infidel. Kill him if you can. Be certain that he does not escape us."

And suddenly there were angry bodies everywhere rising out of their seats, coming toward Luke, and before anything else could happen the dream went black, blacker than night.

And there were words.

West. West toward Kansas, and beyond the lake of fire.

And Luke woke. And waking, he knew what he had to do.

BOOK THREE

The Voice
of
Armageddon

as the first of them klonked onto Bill's head he knew from the
feel of it that the tiles were made out of styrofoam or cardboard
glupped-up stuff like that. Didn't weigh anything to talk about.
thirteen, Bill thought, *I don't really mean king a look at one of*

Wednesday
July Twentieth

From the Good News Hour,
*broadcast on The Voice of
Armageddon Television Network,
7:00 a.m., Wednesday, July 20.*

> *This morning, unfortunately, my Good News
Hour friends, the news is not as Good as we'd like it
to be. The truth is, in fact, that it's not good at all.
Sinister things are happening in this world you and I
share, and it is perhaps time for all good Christians
to be putting the affairs of this life in order. If those
words sound discouraging, take heart: It's a better
life that waits for you on the far side of the Rapture.*
> Cut to a tape of Vice President Graham Perkins,
recuperating in a hospital room.
> *Not all the news is bad, my friends: The Vice
President of this nation has been found, alive and
well, and he's now safely in the arms of good,
God-fearing Christians. As you all know, this nation
has been without a leader for most of a week now,
since our beloved President Paul Green died in a
tragic aviation accident. Mr. Perkins suffered grave
abuse for several days at the hands of left-wing
terrorists, but with the help of the forces of righ-*

*teousness he managed to escape from their hands.
The Vice President is recovering from his injuries
quite rapidly, and is expected to be well enough to
take the oath of Presidential Office early this afternoon.*

*That historic ceremony will be televised live
from the revival center here in Lake-of-Fire, Kansas.
At the moment it's scheduled for two o'clock, but that
may change, depending on Mr. Perkins's condition.*

*And in Washington this morning, more violence:
two low-level members of Congress held a news
conference to assert their supposed claim to the
Presidency and Vice Presidency of the United States.*

Footage of a mob attacking a podium; if one
looks closely it's possible to see that the rioters all
wear arm bands emblazoned with a cross, a circle,
and a dove.

*The two pretenders were quickly and spontane-
ously put in their place by an angry crowd of
righteous Americans.*

*In the sodomistic State of California, where the
ongoing crisis has as yet had no direct effect, business has ground to a halt. People aren't showing up
for work—or very few of them are.*

Where is everybody, you ask?

*Well, the truth is, no one's sure. At first it was
suspected that the people had evacuated the cities, as
they had in most of the Northeast and Midwest. That
doesn't seem to be the case—rural areas aren't being
overrun; desert resorts aren't reporting much more
business than they do during the height of the tourist
season. And in cities like Los Angeles consumption of
power and water are at ordinary levels.*

So where is everybody?

Cut to a shot of a bearded man with bloodshot
eyes and greasy, stringy, shoulder-length brown hair.
In the foreground is a microphone bearing a circle of
cardboard marked with the symbol of a cross, a
circle, and a dove. If one looks closely it's possible to
see that the side of the microphone still bears the
embossed-plastic *abc* logo.

Where is everybody? the man asks. *Where the*

{BLEEP} do you think *everybody* is? It's the end of the world. They're all out getting high, getting laid—partying. It's all one big orgy out here, man. What do you geeks think about that, *huh?*

Return to studio.

Shades of Sodom and Gomorrah, eh, my Good News Hour Friends?

We'll be right back with more Good News after this message from the Reverend George.

BBC shortwave broadcast
15.070 mHz.
13:00 UTC, Wednesday, July 20.

This is London calling.

The nuclear disturbance in the atmosphere has cleared enough today that we're beginning to receive scattered reports from the United States on the amateur bands, and the news we're receiving is nothing short of incredible. Literally, as it happens: the reports are more than a bit hard to believe.

We have badly confirmed stories, to begin with, of dead persons reanimated—stories that would be discounted completely if not for the fact that there are so many of them.

Religious fanatics—apparently zealots of the same stripe as the nation's late president—are on the move throughout the States. A group that calls itself "The Voice of Armageddon" has commandeered the ABC radio and television network, at gunpoint. And earlier today, when the American Speaker of the House and President Pro-Tempore of the Senate held a news conference to announce that they were reorganizing the nation's government, an angry mob, apparently made up of people from the same organization, tore the two quite literally limb from limb. In the process, several reporters attending the conference were also killed. Reporter Jim Burns, who covered the event for the BBC, is now in critical condition in a Washington-area hospital.

It's rumored that these radicals will be announcing a provisional government of their own some time late today, which may explain the recent incident in Washington. We do have confirmed reports that they've managed to get control of at least a portion of the US nuclear arsenal.

The American military is still keeping a low profile, as it has throughout the crisis. The Pentagon has a deep-seated tradition of bowing to civilian authority, and with no such authority available to defer to, it's been unable to act—or unwilling to do so. And what of American forces in Europe and Far East? Here in Britain and on the continent they're keeping an even lower profile than they are in their own country; all American soldiers have been confined to their bases since last Friday, when two young men on an overnight pass were found by an angry crowd, doused with gasoline, and burned alive.

In Asia, it's another story altogether. Late Monday evening the communist dictatorship in North Korea launched an attack on the South, intending to take advantage of the confusion. The Americans stationed there and their South Korean allies have been fighting tooth and nail to repulse the invaders; other Asian nations, afraid that they, too, will be attacked, are treating their American bases with considerable reverence.

The Canadians still aren't having much luck with their attempts to close off their border with the United States. The Canadian government admitted today that while they've managed to keep the border crossings shut in the more developed parts of Ontario and Quebec, refugees are still getting through from the US in great numbers—in the west, principally, but in eastern Quebec and the Maritime provinces as well. The rumor in Ottawa is that the border will reopen officially in a day or two if tensions continue to ease.

In other news, the French Premiere spoke in public today, without incident—which marks the first public appearance of a head of state in the EEC since the current global crisis began.

Currency markets reopened in Bonn, London,

*and Tokyo today, to light trading. Officials in New
York hinted that that city's financial markets may
reopen before the end of the week.*

*There is, as yet, no verifiable news from the
Soviet Union. All reporters and foreign personnel
are still being held in "protective custody" at the
Hotel Intourist; they have been allowed to use the
telephones, but only to make monitored calls to their
embassies and nations of origin. All foreign embassies are similarly quarantined.*

*At the United Nations today Secretary General
William San Juan called on the United States to
provide increased security personnel for UN headquarters in Manhattan. New York City officials were
quick to point out that in spite of all the disorder in
the city, the UN and the area surrounding it has been
relatively quiet. Former New York mayor Edward
Koch added that he didn't think the UN was important enough to draw much attention during a real
crisis. The American State Department, which has
been answering its telephones since Monday, refused
to comment—*

Lake-of-Fire, Kansas

The Reverend George Stein turned off the monitor
abruptly. He'd heard enough, and more than enough; there
wasn't anything substantial in the BBC report that hadn't been
in the network news from CBS and NBC. None of it was
pleasant to hear. It needed paying attention to, anyway; and
he'd gone to no small trouble to be able to listen to it. Radio
signals didn't travel well here so close to the Lake of Fire that
the missile had created. Just the opposite, in fact. If they
hadn't managed to get control over that satellite, had it picking
up signals and beaming them down, there'd be no way to
receive any news at all, bar the telephone.

George Stein was sick of the news. He was sick of the
news and uneasy and since last night a lot more than that; since
last night he'd begun to be afraid. Not terrified. Not scared out
of his wits. Honestly, plainly worried and afraid. Something
was wrong, dead wrong. Things were happening that Herman

Bonner had never told him to expect. And even Herman himself had seemed surprised at them.

And just a week ago things had been so . . . controlled. Controlled and orderly and down to the smallest detail happening exactly as Herman had said they would.

Except for Paul's death. Paul's death was the one event that had seemed to surprise Herman.

Still: Herman was a genius. There wasn't any question of that. Still wasn't—not even now, though, things were happening that put a deep unease on Herman's face. The way that creature—Herman's ersatz Beast—was walking cross-country straight toward them—and at such a pace! Nothing could keep a pace like that for days on end, without sleep or rest to speak of. It wasn't possible. Nothing made of flesh could do it. And yet the Beast was doing it, and so was the man with him. It wasn't hard to track their progress; Herman had planted a homing device in the core of the Beast's thigh bone when the thing had still been in its infancy. That was how they'd found it days ago, when they'd wanted footage of the Beast for television.

There were things about that creature that had bothered George Stein right from the start. The effect it seemed to have on people in its immediate vicinity, for one. Herman had told him to expect that, it was true. Not like that, though. Not so strong. That town . . . the whole damned town. Acting like children would the first time they'd set eyes on Santa Claus. It was enough to shake at the core of George Stein's faith. How could a thing that had that effect on people be evil? How could he call it evil?

Well, it wasn't evil. Or at least there was no reason to think it was evil. Not necessarily, anyway. It was just some poor dumb beast that Herman had grown in his lab to help them get the upper hand on the end of the world.

Herman had told him about that years ago. The end of the world—Armageddon, the Apocalypse, the Rapture, all those things in their turn—were coming. And soon. Anyone with half a lick of sense in his head knew that; certainly no one had needed to tell George Stein. Or Paul Green. Paul and George had been especially close in those days, back when Herman had come into the church. They'd been together that Sunday afternoon, drinking coffee after church in the quiet room behind the chapel.

And Herman had said, the forces of the Beast are out there. Planning. Waiting. Setting snares large enough to trap the world.

There wasn't any debating that. It was patently and obviously true.

We need to do planning of our own, Herman had said.

And Paul had said, of course we need to. We do that. Why else do we spread the word?

Herman had frowned. Yes. It's good. Yet it's not enough.

George had felt his left eyebrow arch with skepticism.

And Herman had nodded. Yes, yes—listen to me. A thing that's done to you is beyond your control. Can any good Christian afford that? Can we allow the world to run amok? No. To carry the day of the Apocalypse we must own it. To own it we must make it before it is created upon us.

A beat. Two beats, three; and the brilliance of it had sunk through to George. Paul Green's face, across the table, was almost aglow.

The Battle of Armageddon was like any other war, George realized. It would belong to those with the initiative to fight it. To wait here passive and quiet in Kansas would be to sign away all title to this world and the next.

It had gone on from there for the better part of twenty years. This last week the moment of realization had come to them . . . and now—

Now something was wrong. Herman's plans, Herman's so-perfect plans that never faltered—the plans were beginning to show flaws.

Paul was dead in a freak accident.

This strange creature was coming for them.

That man in New York—the one who'd sent Herman's hackles on end when they were taking over the network—who was he? And how had he managed to get into the revival hall last night to ask Herman that cryptic question—in front of the entire flock? Fifteen thousand people, when you counted all of those who'd been watching over the church's closed-circuit relay. And before anyone could set hands on him, he'd disappeared. It almost seemed unnatural. Almost, hell—it *was* unnatural. George Stein had seen enough unnaturalness in his life to recognize it when he came across it.

Then there was that poor man Herman had managed to turn up in Washington—the Vice President, Graham Perkins.

He'd somehow managed to live through an experience that no man should have to survive, and he needed serious psychiatric help. He certainly didn't need to be taking on the responsibility of the presidency. But here they were, about to use the man to assert a claim to legitimacy when they set up the provisional government. *George* was about to use him. He was feeling pretty sick with himself about that.

And there were hints everywhere that his own organization—his organization and Herman's—was doing things . . . that George didn't approve of. Evil, violent things that he couldn't possibly abide. There was no one in the entire organization who could authorize things like that—no one but Herman.

George shuddered.

And worst of all, George realized, was the fact that he was beginning to lose faith.

How could they incite so many people to riot against that poor, dumb, and *innocent* beast? There was evil there, and George knew that he was at the heart of it. Or so close to the heart that the distinction wasn't worth making.

Maybe it was time to ease up and back away. Maybe they were wrong—maybe they'd been wrong all along. He'd said as much to Herman not two hours ago, at breakfast. Herman hadn't taken the suggestion any too well. Well, to hell with him, then. George was the one in charge, here, not Herman Bonner.

He glanced at his watch. Fifteen more minutes and he'd be on the air. It was time to touch up his makeup, straighten his tie; there was no way he could go in front of the camera looking this disheveled.

He stood, noticed himself in the mirror—

And felt ill looking at himself. How could he let himself be involved in business like this—much less stand at the center of it?

What he ought to do was go out there in front of the camera and take this whole business apart once and for all. On the air, live, admit to some of the horrible things he'd done. Even if there were a couple dozen nuclear missiles here on the base they'd renamed Lake-of-Fire, none of it would last long once it'd been exposed to the light of day.

Six minutes; it was time to head out to the studio. He was just turning to leave when he heard the knock.

"Hello? Come on in; it isn't locked."

"Good morning, George." Herman again, with his strange, unplaceable accent.

"Morning, Herman. What can I do for you? Only got a minute—I've got to get out there and get to work."

"Forgive me, George," he said, reaching into the breast pocket of his beige-corduroy jacket. He didn't sound even remotely apologetic. "I've worked too long, too hard toward this. I can't allow you to undo all my efforts now."

"What in heaven's name are you talking about, Herman? I've got to go. I'm on live in—"

Herman was taking a gun out of his breast pocket. A sleek black pistol with a silencer.

"No," he said, "you're not going on. And certainly not live." Smiled like a hungry snake. "Good-bye, George."

And George Stein died.

Northwestern Kentucky
approaching the free bridge
at Old Shawneetown

Mostly as they walked Ron wasn't thinking at all. Not that he was numb or tired or even just losing interest; more it was as though the rhythm and the pace of the walk were a song that absorbed all of him. On the few occasions when he did drift far enough away from the song to think, he was amazed. Three days, three solid days of walking, with only a single stop back in Tylerville, Tennessee—and even then they'd only stopped for an hour or three. No food since that one meal. And he wasn't tired, and he wasn't hungry, and he actually felt better than he had in his entire life.

It was a time so good that it made Ron a little uneasy; a part of him expected something horrible to happen, afraid that his life needed to set itself in balance by bringing evil on him.

That part of him was right, of course. Horrible things lay in wait for him, and for the creature. The fact that they waited for him had nothing at all to do with balance, but they waited for him nonetheless.

They crested a high, round ridge, and down before them was the Ohio River. It had to be the Ohio; it wasn't nearly wide enough to be the Mississippi, and it was much too substantial to be the Cumberland, let alone the Tradewater. Half a mile to the west was a bridge—the Shawneetown bridge, he thought by the look of it, though there was no way to be sure at this distance. He'd been over that bridge twice, years ago, and he felt that he ought to be able to recognize it without having to use a score card. The trouble with traveling by car was that you never really got a *look* at the things around you. Not the way he had on this trip. Walking, he was beginning to think, had a lot to recommend it.

A week ago, it'd been years since he'd walked more than a mile at a time. And now he was ready to go out and preach to the converted. The world, he thought, puts a man in strange places sometimes.

The dog had wandered away an hour or two before dawn. It wasn't the first time he'd disappeared, but it was the longest so far. Well, Ron thought, Tom the dog would find them again when he was ready to. He had before; he would again.

They walked down the slope and sideways toward the highway that led onto the bridge. It would be strange to walk on paved ground again. They hadn't been avoiding highways— not exactly—but their route hadn't paid a whole lot of attention to highways or to trails of any kind. A few times—almost by chance, it seemed to Ron, though the creature hadn't made a point of explaining it—a few times their route had followed along the shoulder of a road for a mile or two, and those times they'd been in rural areas, where there was little traffic. Some traffic, even so; more than once they'd nearly been run over by motorists too wrapped up in gaping at the creature to pay attention to their steering wheels.

There wasn't any traffic to speak of right now. Once, when they were still three dozen yards from the highway, a semi truck roared by. If the driver saw them Ron didn't have any clue of it.

They were halfway across the bridge when trouble came for them.

It came, again, in the form of a helicopter. This one was a military helicopter, armed with machine guns and rockets and God knew what else. And instead of wanting to watch them, it wanted to kill them.

It flew up over the ridge on the far side of the river, and in the time it took to cough it had plunged down toward them, and then it was etching lines of bullets into the soft tarry pavement on the bridge's surface.

It turned in the air for just an instant before it started shooting, and as it did Ron saw the army insignia and serial number painted on its side. And just above those, drawn more crudely and in a slightly different shade of white, was the same insignia he'd seen painted on the helicopter that had video-taped them in that town in Tennessee.

A cross. A circle. And a dove.

Ron didn't have any sense about these things; he just stood there, staring, eyes wide and mouth agape. If the gunner's aim had been even a little better Ron Hawkins would have died a second time.

The creature's instincts were better; when the helicopter had passed them Ron saw him step out from behind a heavy iron girder. He pointed off into the distance behind Ron, where the helicopter was banking and turning around, and suddenly Ron was consumed by a powerful need to run that hadn't come from his own heart.

"Jesus," he said.

And they ran.

Up ahead on the left, just beyond the far end of the bridge, were a pair of squat one-room concrete huts; they looked to Ron like maintenance huts for the bridge. Beyond those, away from the road, was thick broad-leaf forest.

If they could get into that the helicopter wouldn't be able to see them well enough for the gunners to take aim.

There was a reasonable chance they wouldn't live long enough to try hiding. Already the helicopter was close enough to fire at them.

Closer, bullets exploding into the tar all around them—

And Ron felt a bullet crease the fleshy part of his shoulder. It didn't dig deep enough to break him, or even to throw him off his stride, but there was wet blood everywhere all over the right side of his shirt, and God it hurt hurt hurt. He didn't let it stop him; he was afraid that if he did he'd only make a better target of himself. In front of him he could see three great crimson swatches of opened flesh nestled in the grey hair of the creature's back.

He ought to be dead, with wounds like that.

The creature wasn't dead. He wasn't even slowing down, no more than Ron was—and Ron had a lot less reason.

And Ron wanted to stop, even though he wasn't letting himself. He wanted to curl up around the gouge in his shoulder and die.

And that's exactly what would happen if I did. Whoever it is in that helicopter would kill me. I'd die again forever this time. I know that. Know it know it know it—

And felt another bullet shatter the low ribs on the left of his back. The impact of it threw him off his feet, sent him flying breast-first into the warm-soft-rough of the black tar pavement of the bridge. Rubbing, abrading open the skin of his face; his shirt spared his chest some of that, until it tore away and left him open. He would have died, then, lay there waiting for the gunship to finish turning him into wet meat—but that was the moment that the helicopter passed overhead, overshooting them, and there was no way they could swivel their guns around fast enough.

The creature was above him, now, not running for his own life but lifting Ron onto his bloody shoulder, and Ron wanted to say *No leave me here don't worry about me let me die just take care of your own life,* but the bullet had done something to his ribcage that made talking impossible. Or too painful to think about, anyway. And anyhow it sounded like something a dying cowboy would say to John Wayne in a bad western. Bad enough Ron had to be dying; he didn't want to die sounding like an idiot.

"I can run," he said. Whispered, actually, and even as a whisper the words weren't especially intelligible. "You don't have to carry me." It wasn't true, of course. He didn't even have the strength to move his head away from the bloody pit in the creature's back that leaked sticky red out into his eyes. His pride wouldn't let him resign himself to being a burden.

The sound of the helicopter turning, coming back toward them again. The sound of machine guns—

—Ron craned his neck, trying to see where they were, whether they had a chance of getting to the shack before the guns could kill them, and saw an antipersonnel rocket blow out of one of the helicopter's cannons, and it came so close to them that its burning-warm sulfur breath stung his eyes. It didn't hit them, though; it shot over and by them, exploding into the bridge's surface thirty yards behind them.

And they were off the bridge, only twenty feet from the concrete shack, and behind them the bridge swayed and began to shatter. Smoke and dust and flame from that rocket and the next obscured everything, and that was a blessing since the machine guns could hardly aim at targets they couldn't see.

Ron felt the creature reach the wall of the shack and slump against it with exhaustion. It was safe here—for a moment, two. Until the helicopter came back around it wouldn't be able to shoot at them, so long as the wall shielded them. By then they could be inside, on the other side of the wall—

Right.

How long would it take before they landed the helicopter, got out, walked around, and shot them point-blank?

No time at all.

They weren't safe here, not by a long stretch. They had to get into the woods, where the green canopy of leaves could hide them. Had to get there quickly.

The creature knew that; already they were moving again, off into the woods. A steady pace; walking, not running. Running wasn't necessary—it was only ten paces before they were under the cover of leaves . . .

Ron came back to when the Beast set him down in a bed of dry leaves. Or maybe it wasn't coming to. Maybe he'd never been unconscious. It was a close thing, and kind of vague. The wound in his back must have been even worse than he'd realized to leave him so dizzy with the loss of blood. He clenched his teeth, braced himself for pain as he tried to sit—and sat. The pain was less than he expected. He shook his head, lurched, stood. *That* hurt. But not unbearably.

The creature was staring away from him. Ron turned to follow the direction of his gaze and saw that he was watching the concrete shack and the still-crumbling bridge behind it. There were more helicopters, now; Ron could see two of them out over the river. He heard another pass directly overhead. There was no way to see that one; the green mat of leaves above them was too thick. The creature glanced at Ron, and Ron felt his anxiety wash over him. They had to go. Had to keep going. It wasn't safe here, not safe enough to keep still.

"Use words," Ron said. "It gives me the creeps when you make me feel things like that."

It unsettles you either way.

That was true enough. Hearing a voice inside his skull that wasn't his own was a terrifying thing. And even more it left him feeling violated; no matter how he felt about the creature, no matter how special he was, hearing that voice made Ron want to push away from him.

Still.

It wasn't sensible, trying to talk by parsing out images and sensations, not with people trying to kill them.

"Use them anyway, would you? I'd like to be able to feel like I really felt the things I feel," he said.

The creature shrugged. *We need to go.* He nodded toward the river, where the helicopters were still moving toward them. *They'll be here soon. Soldiers? Out of the helicopters. On foot. Searching for us under the trees. You can walk?* The last was half a question and half a statement, almost as though he knew that Ron was feeling better, but wasn't sure Ron knew it.

Ron nodded. He *was* feeling better. That was a strange thing, only a few minutes after a bullet had broken the thin bones in his ribcage. He reached around to probe the wound with his fingers . . . and felt the skin already grown over mottled flesh and broken bone. It ached fierce to touch, but all the same it was touchable. The wound was healing faster than any wound had right to heal.

He looked at the creature. "It's the same as when we died, isn't it? Something remakes us when we're hurt. And probably why we could walk hard for three days with barely any rest or food. Do you think?"

The creature only shrugged again and started walking away, deeper into the woods. Ron followed him, confused.

They hadn't gone a hundred yards before Ron heard the sound of boots crushing through the leaves behind them. *We should run,* he thought. The creature wasn't running, and Ron was sure that he'd heard the sound. It was too loud not to hear. Still walking, he turned his head back to see if he could spot them, and he did; they were at the edge of the forest, by the concrete shack, looking at the ground for sign of a trail. None of the men were in uniform, though they carried military ordnance. They all did wear black armbands that looked as though they might be marked, but at this distance he couldn't see well enough to be sure. It didn't look as though they'd spotted Ron or the creature yet—likely that was because it was too bright there at the edge to see far into the thick-dark woods—but soon enough they would, Ron thought.

"We need to hurry," Ron said, quietly as he could. "Hurry or hide."

The creature shook his head. *No. It isn't time. Soon enough it will be.*

"What do you mean? Time for what?"

The creature didn't answer; he kept walking, carefully, steadily up the long low rise away from the river.

A hundred yards beyond the crest of the rise the forest fell away into cornfields. Before they stepped out into the light the creature hesitated for a good three minutes. He looked worried, Ron thought—more worried than Ron had ever seen him before.

It isn't certain here, he told Ron, finally. *The way through the fields . . . is long. Three miles? They could kill us here. They may.*

Ron frowned. There was something that didn't make sense—something. . . ? The bullets. The lab back in Tennessee. They'd both died once before, and nearly died again just a few moments ago. And now Ron felt—didn't feel fine, or even well, exactly. Well enough to cope. And maybe better. What was to fear in dying?

If we die they will take us. And the one who guides them, he knows—he will know?—he will make us dead forever.

He watches time. He finds strange things.

None of that made the first bit of sense to Ron. Watching time? *Finding* things? "Is that how they found us—in Tylerville, and then out here on the bridge?"

No. The creature set his hand on his right thigh, and with his mind's eye Ron suddenly was seeing inside the thigh's flesh, deeper down into the hard round bone at its center. It was that grisly scene again, where Bonner was operating on the infant creature, searing, consuming pain because there was no anesthesia, and Bonner had the thigh wide open and he was drilling into the bone. Then the drilling stopped, and he reached over to the instrument table, picked up a tiny piece of intricately complex metal and plastic. Ron felt him drop it into the drilled hole, and begin to sew the flesh back together around it. . . .

Ron shuddered, trying to shake off the memory of the creature's pain. "A tracking device? A transmitter inside you?"

The idea of it made Ron almost as queasy as the image of surgery.

The creature nodded. *I can feel it sometimes. The bone has grown closed around it, sealed it in.*

"It's hopeless, then. No matter how we run, they'll find us."

No. Not hopeless. But hard things wait, and cruel ones. We need to go. To hurry, now.

The sound of another helicopter, somewhere south of them.

And they started into the long corridors of green that seemed to lead off into the horizon, the creature leading at a dead run.

Stay low. If we're careful, they may not see us. The Beast hunched over and bore to the right, so that the high leaves on the cornstalks hid him. Well, not hid him. His shoulders were too wide to be shaded by even the longest leaves. Still, they made him less apparent from the air, Ron could tell. He stooped and tried to run the same way, without much success; he kept stumbling over the dirt that piled at the bases of the cornstalks, and over the stalks themselves.

The sound of the helicopter's engine shifted, and suddenly rushed toward them. The creature threw himself flat and lay still against the corn—so suddenly that Ron only barely managed to stop short of running over him. But he did stop, and as soon as he had he crouched down to hide.

The helicopter paused when it was directly above them.

Had it seen them? Would the men inside start shooting again? If they did there wasn't much chance that Ron or the creature might survive it. Lying here in the dirt, they made easy targets. Or maybe they'd send men down for them on a rope. That would be a slower death. Ron was sure he'd end up murdered all the same.

A voice, amplified electronically, came from above: *"We know where you are. Surrender peacefully and we can all avoid further bloodshed."*

Ron felt his heart sink down toward his gut. He didn't want to die. He didn't know why they were trying to get him and the creature to give themselves up, but he was sure that it didn't mean that their intentions were any less malevolent.

The creature was watching him—staring at him with

tense, almost fearful eyes. *Bluffing. They don't see us*. He
glanced up at the helicopter. *Don't speak. Be very still*.

Ron was sweating, now. Nervous sweat, from tension. He
didn't know how much longer he could be absolutely still
without going out of his mind.

The helicopter wasn't going anywhere.

In front of him he saw the Beast beginning to ease away on
his hands and knees. His shoulder passed so close to the
cornstalks that Ron would have sworn they'd touched. If they
did there was no sign of it in the plants. Was he supposed to
follow? He didn't think he could move that carefully, no matter
how he tried. If he didn't try he'd be left here, sitting alone
under the guns—

The creature turned his head ever so slowly, ever so
gently, and looked Ron in the eye. *No*, he told Ron. *Stay still.
No matter what happens now, be still until I call you*.

And Ron closed his eyes and shivered with the tension of
pent-up fear. His body wanted to *run*, or scream, or die, or
something. Anything at all except keep still. He set himself,
forced himself not to panic. And kept still, even when the
sweat began to trickle down his forehead and into his still-
closed eyes. Working its way between his eyelids, burning-
stinging. He tried to blink it away, but that wasn't much use;
mostly it only spread the sweat around and drew it deeper into
his eyes. What he needed to do was blot it away with the
sleeve of his torn shirt. He didn't think he dared to move that
much. Not now. Not yet.

There. It was gone—for now. He opened his eyes—

The creature was gone.

Ron felt very, very alone.

He tried to find some sign of the Beast, ahead or off among
the other rows. . . . Was that him, there? Yes, it was,
running diagonally across the field thirty yards away, almost as
though he was *trying* to get the attention of the people in the
helicopter—

And he had it, too. The gunship was moving away to
follow him, guns bursting and tearing away the corn.

Now. Run straight, and as quickly as you can. A pause.
No matter what you see, keep running.

And Ron took off, running with every bit of effort he had
to give. If anyone in the helicopter saw him, they ignored him.
When he looked to his left he could see that the creature was

running, too—and he was moving farther and farther away
from Ron.

They were going to kill him. There was no way to avoid
that. Why was the creature doing this? Did he want to die?
Maybe he was trying to sacrifice himself, so that at least Ron
would survive? It was possible. The idea depressed Ron, made
him feel sick with himself. He ought to be the one to die, if
anybody had to. If that was what was going to happen . . .
why? They'd been in a bad spot, with the helicopter hovering
over them, trying to bluff them into making better targets of
themselves. At least they weren't being shot at. If they'd just
waited, maybe the helicopter would have gone away to search
a different part of the field. And now—Ron didn't want to see
the creature die. He didn't think he could live with himself if
that happened.

Maybe, he thought, he should try to distract them. Draw
them to himself.

Even if he did try it, he thought, it probably wouldn't
work. It had to be the creature that had drawn them. Ron
couldn't imagine anyone thinking he was interesting enough
that they'd go to so much trouble to kill him. Sure; if he was in
the way, they'd kill him. And likely they'd want him after
they'd killed the creature—because of the connection between
them. By himself he wasn't worth their effort, and he knew it.
Whether they'd seen him or not, they weren't likely to bother
with him until they had the creature.

Besides—the creature had told him to run, and to keep
running, no matter what. God knew he had his reasons, even
if Ron didn't understand them.

They were going to get the creature. Ron glanced across
the field and saw the helicopter only half a dozen yards behind
the Beast, and as he watched he saw a bullet shatter one of the
creature's great ramlike horns. He was covered with blood,
and it was hard to tell but it looked as though his right arm had
been mutilated by gunfire. There were gaping holes in his
back, too, and maybe his legs, but those were hard to see
because they were drenched with the blood that was running
down from his upper body.

How could he still be alive with wounds like those—much
less move? How could he *run*—run faster than Ron could even
think about running?

Then there was one final burst of gunfire, and the creature

took the whole round square in the center of his spine. It tore a hole in his back and out through his chest—a hole the size of Ron's fist, maybe larger. Ron could see through it even at this distance.

And suddenly the question of how the Beast could take so much abuse and still run was moot. Because he pitched over face-first into the dirt. And he didn't move at all.

Ron just kept running, as though his life depended on it—and the likely truth was that it did. Partly he ran because he was afraid, and partly he ran because the Beast had asked him to when he was still alive. And most of all he ran because his mind went grey and there wasn't any other thing he could think to do.

South Korea
at the Edge of the DMZ

Bill Wallace woke from the dead for the second time needing to go to the bathroom in the worst possible way.

He made such a rush for the door marked LAVATORY, in fact, that he didn't even notice the holes in his uniform, nor the crusted bloodstains that covered it.

Nor did he notice the chaos in the laboratory all around him; the pressure in his bowels was too desperate for him to notice any of the dozen things that ought to have seized his attention. And when he finally got into that lavatory, finally got his bloodstained pants down around his ankles—it only got worse. Much, much worse. The cramps! As though there were something alive inside him, and it was clawing its way toward freedom through his low gut.

Which was when he remembered dinner. Remembered eating half a bowl of stew. The other half of which had come to life right there as it'd floated in the gravy.

Dear Lord—Dear Lord in Heaven, I'm going to give birth to a cow.

For a moment he almost imagined it was so. Until he looked down at his belly and saw that it wasn't especially misshapen or distended, saw that there was no room inside him for a cow or a bull or even a calf. And thank God for that.

The cramps were still there, still pressing and hurting inside him even if there wasn't any possibility of Bill giving

birth. And they stayed with him. Pushing, lurching, pain
working its way down and around inside Bill. Five minutes
when he ought to have been screaming in agony, only he
couldn't scream, because his jaw was clenched tight to hold in
the pain, and if he let go of it for even a moment Bill knew that
he'd come loose at the seams. . . .

Until finally it started to make its way free from him.

Which was even more painful. A sensation so intense, in
fact, that Bill blacked out under its intensity.

And came to, not long later. Right as rain and feeling so
well that at first he Bill suspected that he'd dreamed the
sensation of giving birth—

Which was when he got up from the throne and saw the
four perfect cubes of living beef. Floating in the toilet water.
And flushed them away out of disgust before it occurred to him
that this was exactly the kind of thing that the Major wanted to
know about. Well, to Hell with that; there wasn't time for
research if they were getting themselves overrun by communists. Bill fastened his bloodstained trousers, buckled his belt
that had gone stiff as his blood had dried on it.

Outside, in the lab, that boy was glowing again. He was
the only one besides Bill who was awake and alive, though the
Major was moaning in gentle agony off against one wall—she
was alive but nowhere near awake yet. And Joe, off against the
wall opposite, had too much complexion for a real corpse. And
then there was the dead policeman, who lay on the ground
near his chair, still wide-eyed and drooling. There were
bloodstains all over his torn hospital smock, but Bill could see
that the wounds underneath them were healed over. Still, the
dead policeman didn't really count as being alive again, since
he hadn't really been completely alive in the first place.

"Hey!" the boy shouted. "You stop that! You stop that
now." At first Bill thought he was shouting at him, but when he
turned he saw the boy glowing and shaking his hand that had
one finger bleeding, little droplets of the red stuff spattering
on the walls and ceiling. The boy had his back to Bill—he was
over by that table where Bill had had to check out all the
different dead things, back before the commies showed up and
killed them all. What had he got his finger caught in? What
was he shouting about?

And then Bill saw.

Saw that the boy was playing with MONKEY. Who wasn't

too dead any more. Matter of fact, old MONKEY wasn't dead at
all. Not even remotely.

He was sitting on the lab table holding his dish above his
head as though he were about to throw it at the boy. Making
screeching noises that sounded even more threatening. Blood
from the boy's finger all over his lips.

"You put that down, now," the boy said. "It isn't nice to
throw your dishes around. You might break something. Or
hurt somebody." Bill was right behind the boy, now; before
either the kid or the MONKEY realized what was going on Bill
had reached right over the boy's head, grabbed the dish out of
the MONKEY's hands. Which made the little beast screech so
loud that Bill nearly jumped out of his own skin to hear it.

"There you go," he said, and he set the dish on the far end
of the table, far out of the MONKEY's reach. Out of it for the
moment, anyway; there wasn't nothing to stop the MONKEY
from scurrying across the table top and picking the darned
thing up again.

"You didn't have to do that, Corporal Roe," the boy said.
"He would have put it down. I know he would."

"Huh. You know he was going to bite you like that? And
if you did, how come you let him get his mouth near your
finger?"

The boy frowned, but he didn't say anything.

MONKEY had backed a little ways away from them, toward
the back side of the table, and now he was grooming himself.
And grooming his, er, his. Privates.

The boy was still glowing. How could he glow like that
and not know about it? How could he glow like that, and
everybody else acted like they couldn't see it?

"C'mon, son," he said. "We need to give MONKEY over
there a little privacy." He put his arm on the boy's back, led
him toward the far end of the table. "What's your name, son?
I know you told me a while back, but my memory is a little
strange these days."

"My name is Jerry Williams, Mr. Corporal Roe. How
come MONKEY is playing with his ying-yang like that? He's
going to pull it clear off if he doesn't stop, isn't he?"

Bill blushed.

Coughed.

"He's just trying to straighten it out, Jerry. You don't
worry yourself over it, huh?" He looked around for anything

that was interesting enough to get the boy's eyes off of MONKEY.

And saw PIG. And DOG. And noticed LIZARD crawling around on the ceiling.

"He's getting all red," Jerry said.

"Say, Jerry! Will you look at that? Look at that plate there, the one marked PIG. Look at how big that stuff's got, huh. D'you see it before those commies came in and blew us all away?"

And the boy did turn, thank God. Just barely in time to keep from having to see that MONKEY erupt.

"Sure didn't. What is that gross stuff?"

"I ain't too sure. When it started out it weren't nothing but a pork chop."

MONKEY was licking his fingers.

PIG was a great sprawling mass of stringy flesh that sprawled out and all over the table; so large, now, that the mass of it could have filled a basin.

"Really? That weren't nothing but a pork chop?"

"Nuh-uh. Not one bit more when it started out. Give it another day or so and the damned thing'll be a full-grown pig."

This last was obvious from the condition of DOG. Which had grown from a skinless, hairless, oversized drumstick of a haunch—grown into something that was very nearly a dog. Oh, it wasn't whole yet. And the hair that covered the mutt's skin wasn't much more than down. Nonetheless it was recognizably a dog. Half-formed forelegs. Hollow, eyeless skull—Bill looked into those eyes and he could see the blood-red plasm inside growing to form a brain, glands, God knew what else.

"Dog wasn't nothing but a back leg last night," Bill said.

"Huh," Jerry said. "That's pretty cool, all right. Hey—you want to go take a look at that dead guy they wheeled in here last night? I bet he looks really neat. Aw, come on—can we?"

Bill shrugged, relented. At least it'd keep the boy from getting another look at MONKEY.

Jerry ran ahead into the adjoining lab, pulled the sheet off the corpse with the same enthusiasm most kids used for unwrapping presents under the Christmas tree.

The corpse wasn't a corpse any more. It certainly wasn't any "dead guy," because it hadn't ever been a guy in the first place.

She was a woman, an oriental woman with long jet-black

hair and eyes that were even darker. Open, living eyes—off balance and confused, but powerfully alive.

"She's beautiful, ain't she?" Jerry asked. And she *was* beautiful. Just about the prettiest woman Bill had ever set eyes on, in fact.

And she was glowing, just like the boy.

"What is this?" Bill asked. "First you go and get yourself all lit up like a light bulb. Now her too. Tell me damn it—and stop acting like you don't know what I'm talking about!"

The woman stared at Bill numb and dumb.

The boy shrugged. "I don't know, Mr. Corporal Roe. How come *you're* all glowy like that?"

And Bill looked at his hands, and saw that they were glowing. And looked at his reflection in the polished-steel cabinet and saw that his image bore no sign of the strange light.

Nor did the boy's.

Nor did the woman's.

Bill frowned, and shook his head. "Damned if I know," he said, and maybe that wasn't something you ought to say in front of a small boy, but it didn't really matter because he said it under his breath so low that it was nothing but a mumble even to Bill's own ears.

"What's that, Mr. Corporal? What'd you say about how come we're glowing?"

"No," Bill said. "I don't know." Coughed. "I don't know how come."

The Major was groaning again out in the other lab.

MONKEY screeched.

The mass of mostly-formed flesh that was DOG howled mournfully.

Joe didn't make a sound. God knew what it was that was keeping him so dead.

And that was when the first of the bombs hit ground above them.

And the walls and the floors shook like it was an earth-quake, and the lights flickered, and ceiling tiles popped out of joint and came clattering down toward them; when Bill saw the biggest of the things head down toward Jerry's head he jumped, caught the boy in a flying dive that sent both of them pounding into the floor. Where the damned ceiling tiles fell on the both of them, anyway. Not that it mattered much; as soon as the first of them klonked onto Bill's head he knew from the feel of it that the tiles were made out of styrofoam or cardboard puffed-up-stiff like that. Didn't weigh anything to talk about.

Great, Bill thought. *Now I'm really making a fool out of myself*. Or that was what he thought until he saw the fissure.

Up there in the rock, above the metal grid that had held the ceiling tiles. In all the hours since Joe had brought him down here, it was the first sign Bill had seen that showed him that they really were in something that might as well be a cave. Might as well be, hell—this place *was* a cave. Though from the look of the rock up there it was a man-made cave, cut into the rock that was the mountain with chisels and jackhammers and explosives.

And the fissure in the rock up there was getting wider, and longer, and the whole damned mountain was about to fall in on them.

Bill looked at the oriental woman. Looked at the boy. He looked scared half out of his mind, but the woman was still too dazed from the newness of her resurrection to react much to the explosion. Bill had to get them out of there—but how in the hell was he going to move a woman who was dead to the world? And what about the others, halfway between life and death out there in the other lab?

A slab of stone the size of a kitchen table split loose from the fissure and smashed into the floor.

Its near edge wasn't more that ten inches from Bill's feet.

There wasn't time.

No time at all.

He had to get himself and the boy the hell out of that place while he still could. And if it meant leaving behind people who couldn't begin to fend for themselves, then that was what it meant.

He stood, took off out of that laboratory at a run. Dragging the boy by the wrist.

It wasn't until they'd made their way to the surface, not until Bill and the boy were catching their breath there on the side of the ravaged mountain, that Bill saw the Oriental woman and the dead policeman come up out of the ground. Following them.

And it wasn't until they were just a few feet away that Bill realized that coming out here into the open was a horrible mistake. Because that was when the artillery shell hit ground not thirty yards from them. Most of the force of the blast blew out away from Bill and the boy and the two zombies, but even still the rain of dirt and rocks was all over them. In Bill's eyes, his hair; one rock the size of an egg hit him hard in the place where his neck met his left shoulder.

He had to find cover. It wasn't safe out here. Not with those flares of rocket exhaust out there on the horizon. Not with the sound of more explosions so close. Even if that one room down below had been about to give way, it was still safer down there than it was here.

Which wasn't to say that Bill was planning to go back underground.

Because there wasn't any way to get there any more.

Because the missile that had sprayed them with rock and dirt had landed square on the concrete hut that led down into the warren.

And blocked off the way down into the tunnels.

Another rocket hit ground ninety yards up-mountain.

Where in the hell are we going to go?

There was nothing anywhere in sight that looked like it would hold up to a few hours' worth of shelling. Nothing but pine woods and countryside that was already beginning to look like the surface of the moon.

The air was cool and dry, but Bill's skin was beginning to soak with sweat that turned to mud as it dampened the dirt that covered him.

I've got to think.

The shelling was coming from that direction, over there. South, wasn't it? Yes, it was: Bill remembered catching sight of the DMZ as his plane had landed, and that was in the other direction. Which meant that it was friendly fire. American rockets. Or South Korean, one. The smartest thing to do would be to get back over to that side of the fighting. But how in the hell to get there? From where he sat leaning against the boulder halfway up this mountain, he could see that the shells were falling all over the place between here and there. A few went out beyond them, to the north. Not many; they were just about at the extreme edge of the rockets' range.

There it was: that was what they had to do. Head north, toward the DMZ, and get themselves out of firing range.

Which meant heading straight into the hands of the North Koreans. Who'd already killed them once.

Bill thought about the machine gun round that had torn through his belly last night, when the North Koreans broke into the lab and killed the lot of them. And then he thought about what it'd feel like to be turned into a heap of blood and broken meat by an American rocket shell.

And stood.

"C'mon," he said to the boy. "We've got to get out of here."

And headed north along the side of the mountain. Toward the DMZ.

The zombies didn't have to be told which way to go; they followed on their own.

Gallatin County, Illinois

It took Ron better than a quarter of an hour to run the three miles to the far edge of the field. By the time he got there he was exhausted, and he was beginning to come back to himself, too. And almost wishing that he could crawl back into a small dead shell.

The creature was dead.

Permanently dead. If those people had their hands on his corpse, then there wasn't any hope for him. The Beast had told Ron that.

It was hopeless.

For four days since he'd first come back to life, everything about Ron had orbited around the creature. Without him. . . ? Ron didn't know. He could go back to Tennessee and try to rebuild the life he'd had before. He could. Not that it'd be easy. The institute was gone, which meant that he didn't have a job. He could find another job like that one in the space of a week, of course. . . . *No.* That possibility was nothing but empty. And besides, the creature had had about him a consuming sense of mission, and Ron had felt a powerful commitment to that mission, even if he hadn't understood what it was.

What he ought to do, he decided, was try to fulfill that mission. He owed it to the creature's memory. But how to fulfill? They'd been traveling west, and a little to the north. And whatever they were headed toward had to do with the people who used the cross and the circle and the dove as their emblem.

He needed to think about it.

Ron was still thirty feet from the edge where the field gave way again to forest when the dog came running across the field toward him.

He was panting, and he looked about as happy as any dog ever did. Ron stooped to pet the dog when he was beside him.

"Heya, boy. Where've you been, huh? And how'd you get over on this side of the river with that bridge blown out behind us? Did you cross over here before we did?"

The dog didn't give any answer, though for some reason Ron had half expected him to. It was that way a lot with dogs, he decided; you end up talking to them so much that you expect them to be able to hold up their end of a conversation.

"He's dead, boy. Bad news, huh? I saw them kill him. Pretty horrible stuff."

The dog stood there, still panting, basking in attention.

"So what are we supposed to do now? You got any ideas?"

No response.

"Sometimes, dog. Sometimes you're no help at all."

Ron heard the sound of helicopter engines again in the distance. God knew what they were up to, but whatever it was it meant that it was time to get out of plain sight.

"Come on, boy. Let's get into that woods. Probably no harm in relaxing a little once we're there."

The forest here was thicker, deeper-feeling than the woods between the bridge and the cornfield. Ron found a big, broad rock in a place where the sun streamed down among the trees, and he sat down to think. When he was comfortable the dog decided it was a good idea too, and he curled up beside Ron, closed his eyes and drifted off toward sleep.

What he had to do, he decided, was find those cross-and-circle people. Find where they *lived*. Where was he going to find them? And what was he going to do once he found them? Ron shook his head. Sighed.

The helicopters were getting close again. Hadn't they done enough already? God. They were going to come looking for him, now, too. Murderers. They were murderers, and they meant to kill him.

If he just sat here, taking in the sun, it wouldn't take them more than half an hour to find him. An hour at the outside.

And so what if they did? He was feeling fatalistic, Ron realized. A big part of him didn't care enough about being alive to struggle for his life. Let them take him, and do whatever they wanted to him.

Why not?

The depression got even worse when he realized that he didn't have an answer for the question.

A helicopter was passing directly overhead; Ron looked up in time to catch a glimpse of it through the opening in the trees.

Beside him, Tom the dog woke up enough to whine fearfully. And then suddenly he stood and looked around, his ears and rump trembling with tension. And he bolted out into the forest.

He didn't look as though he were running away from anything so much as he seemed to be running toward something. Ron forgot about his funk long enough to go chasing after the dog.

It wasn't easy; a dog is a lot more suited to running over uneven terrain than a man is. It wasn't that hard, either. Even though the dog was moving harder and faster than Ron was, Ron managed a good pace himself—the injuries he'd taken at the bridge were all but gone.

Strange. Strange and unsettling. Ron should have known to expect it, of course. Just not so quickly. . . !

The dog reached the top of a low hill and turned back to look at Ron expectantly. Barked, twice—Ron wished there was a way to silence him; if he didn't stop, Ron was sure, he'd draw the soldiers to them. Tom waited until Ron was nearly at the summit of the hill before he started running again, not straight downhill but hard to the left and down. *That's crazy*, Ron thought. *Dogs don't wait around to make sure you don't lose track of them. They come and go as they please, and to hell with whether or not anybody else can follow.*

It was exactly what the dog had done. And it was a good thing, too; the route he took was complex enough that there was no way Ron would have been able to follow it by guess.

He chased after that damned dog for the better part of another half a mile before they came out into the tiny, thick-dark hollow with the stream.

The creature was there.

He was there, and he was alive and unscratched as he'd

been when they'd started across the bridge from Kentucky. And he was waiting for them.

"I saw you *die*," Ron said. It was the only thing left in him. The grief was leaking out of his heart, and he had nothing to replace it with. Nothing but a hollow feeling.

Tom the dog was prancing around the creature's feet, wagging his tail furiously. The creature shook his head.

No. You saw . . . a ghost? An illusion? No. You saw the desire in their hearts. The soldiers' hearts. Made visible; I helped them see what they wanted to see. He sighed. *They know their mistake now. They're searching again.*

Ron couldn't make much sense of that, but he got the idea behind it, anyway.

"You could have told me." He kicked at one of the smooth round stones embedded in the dark soil by his feet; it came loose and rolled down into the stream.

The creature frowned, and shook his head ever so slightly. *There was no time.*

Another of the helicopters went by overhead.

We need to go.

Ron felt his shoulders sag. He didn't have the heart for running; he didn't have it in him to do anything but sit down and be confused.

That wasn't an option, of course. There wasn't time for confusion, unless he wanted to get all three of them killed. He looked around, kicked at another stone. It didn't budge.

"We can't just keep running," he said. "They can catch up with us faster than we can run. And there isn't any way to hide, either, as long as they can track you."

The creature nodded. *Still. We must run.* And he turned away, and ran.

The dog was only a couple steps behind him. Ron shook his head and took off after them.

The three of them ran due west through that woods for the better part of an hour. Helicopters followed them all the while, more than a little uncertainly—probably, Ron thought, that was a function of using a radio to track a moving target that couldn't be seen. The helicopters always seemed to know more or less where they were, but never to know exactly; often they'd fire their guns or rockets, but they were always yards away from actually hitting the creature—and never even that close to hitting Ron or the dog.

They'd been running for forty-five minutes when Ron stopped hearing the helicopters.

That was trouble. It meant that they were actually thinking, setting some kind of a trap. Or that was what Ron guessed it meant.

And he was right.

Ambush stepped out at them from behind a mossy boulder ten minutes after Ron last heard a helicopter. Ambush was a man who wore denim overalls over a t-shirt stained by motor oil. A black armband bound his right bicep, and on the armband there was a patch embroidered with the symbol of the cross and the dove and the circle. He stepped out from behind the boulder when they were only three yards from him, and point-blank he started firing.

He would have got them, too.

He would have got them if Ron hadn't been so edgy and nervous that as soon as he caught sight of the man stepping out from behind the rock he dived forward, into the creature's back, dragging him to the ground.

And the creature, falling, rifle exploding just above his head, had slammed into the man's knee, and all three of them had gone down, and the man kept shooting but it didn't make much difference since he was firing into the air.

Their ambusher hadn't lived long after that, because Tom the dog was all over him, and before Ron or the creature could do anything to stop him he'd ripped out the man's throat.

The sound of men in boots running toward them, from half a dozen different directions. Ron got to his feet, and saw that the creature was already standing, pulling the dog away from the man's corpse. *Run*, he told him, as Ron stooped to take the man's rifle. And then, *No—leave it. It will only bring trouble.* And Ron let it drop and ran even if he did think it was crazy to be unarmed when there were people shooting at him. There wasn't time to argue the point.

"Which way?" He could see more of the un-uniformed soldiers, now; the closest couldn't be more than sixty yards away. That one started shooting at them, wildly, as though he were unable to aim properly while he ran. The creature finally managed to drag Tom away from the dead man, and he took off running, carrying the dog, in the same direction they'd been moving before the ambush.

Ron followed him.

Not far now. There's something ahead . . . that can stop them.

"Stop them? What can stop them? What are we heading into?"

I don't know that. I only know that it can happen.

Twenty yards ahead—thirty?—Ron could see a thick wall of green where the forest came to an end; the weeds and bushes were too thick to tell from this distance what was on the other side of them.

More shooting at their backs—a lot more. So much that it didn't matter that none of the people behind them could run and aim at the same time. Leaves and dirt burst up from the ground near their feet as bullets hit the soil. . . .

And then Ron and the creature were bursting through the wall of green at the forest's edge, and they were safe, he knew, he knew—

And then Ron saw where he was.

The soldiers weren't shooting, or even running. Not any more.

There was a red-and-yellow banner strung high between two tall pines, not a dozen yards away.

SOUTHERN ILLINOIS
BAPTIST YOUTH CAMP

And there were a thousand-thousand children picnicking in that broad, grassy clearing. None of them more than twelve years old. Twenty or thirty adults—camp counselors, Ron thought. Rough-wood cottages spread out around a pond off in the distance.

"Oh my God," Ron said. "Oh my dear God."

They'd led the gunmen into a crowd of children.

"Creature," Ron said, "creature, we have to turn back. Have to. We can't let them follow us here. Those people are murderers; they won't hesitate to start shooting here, even if it means killing children."

The creature turned and looked at Ron, horrified, but it was already too late—the children were crowding around them, drawn to the Beast the same way the people in Tylerville had been. So many of them crowding so close that there was barely any way to move, let alone run back into the woods and get themselves killed. And *kept* crowding; by the time the two-dozen soldiers had made it out into the cleared field, every child and adult at the picnic was pressed into the crowd, trying to touch the creature.

One soldier—he looked as though he might be their leader—cupped his hands and shouted. "All of you, move away from these two. We're here to arrest them in the name of God and the United States of America."

The children ignored him. To be fair, it was only barely possible to hear what he'd said over the din of a million happy campers.

"This is an order! Move away immediately, or face consequences! This pair is a dire threat to the security of the nation and the future of the world. Your lives are forfeit if you do not follow instructions!"

Someone at the far edge of the crowd threw a gooey wad of chocolate picnic cake at the man; it struck him just above his left eye.

And the man reeled, more out of surprise than because the cake did him any harm, and as he reeled his arm twitched, and two rounds from his machine gun burst out into the crowd.

And the bloodbath started.

Maybe—just maybe—the firing of those two rounds was an accident. All the same, as soon as he'd fired them and the first three children died, his men were firing too.

The truth was, of course, that they had to fire. Where any ordinary crowd would have bolted and stampeded away at the sound of gunfire and the sight of bloody-gory death, the children surged forward, into the sights of the guns. *Does the creature do that to them—do they love him enough to die for him after only seeing him for a few moments?* Ron looked in his own heart, and realized that he'd have done the same thing. Hell, was doing the same thing; even now he was trying to get at the soldiers, to put himself in front of the guns. Partly he tried to do that out of concern for the children, of course. He didn't want them dying to protect him.

He looked over at the creature, three yards away in the crowd, and saw him wild-eyed and panicked, trying even harder than Ron tried to put himself in front of the guns. He wasn't making any more progress than Ron was. The dog had fallen out of the creature's arms, somehow; Ron hoped that it wasn't getting trampled in the crush.

If the soldiers hadn't fired their guns and kept shooting, they'd have been overwhelmed in a moment. As it was they nearly were anyway; only the press of falling bodies kept the mob of children from surging forward and pulling the guns from their hands. The bodies of children piled at the soldiers' feet and piled higher, until finally they began to form a barricade.

It went on that way for a good three minutes before Ron saw the first of the dead children rise. The boy was at the very bottom of the heap, but at the edge of it, too, so he didn't have to struggle too hard to unbury himself. The soldier in front of him—the one in charge, who had chocolate smeared all over his forehead and matted in his hair—watched dumbstruck as the child freed himself and rushed toward him. So dumbstruck that the boy had the gun out of his hands before the man got his senses back.

Luke Munsen's bacteria—the stuff that resurrected us. It's here, already. Spreading faster than we're walking cross-country.

The soldiers didn't cope too well after that. There were children—angry, violent children—all over them, ripping the guns out of their hands, dragging them down to the ground and keeping them there. Beating them, once they were pinned. Ron saw one boy jump feet-first onto the face of a soldier; the man's nose broke, and instantly there was blood everywhere, and when the boy stepped away Ron saw the man's left eye hanging out of its socket and his jaw gaping wide and slack at an angle that meant the bone inside was completely shattered. He tried to scream, but with his jaw such a mess all the sound he could make was a nerve-wracking gurgle.

"Throw them in the lake!" someone shouted. And Ron saw the man with his eye out of place hoisted up on the shoulders of a dozen children. He looked around and saw the others lifted, too, and the crowd started melting away toward the pond at the far end of the clearing. All of them—all of them that were alive enough to walk—were trying to help carry away the disarmed soldiers.

When the last of them filtered away Ron and the creature

were left standing alone in a bloody field scattered with the half-alive bodies of wounded children.

None of them seemed especially interested in the creature any more.

"I don't understand," Ron said. "How can they . . . just wander away from you like that? Five minutes ago it looked like they wanted to build a church around you. And now they've all wandered off, and there isn't one of them looking back."

The creature didn't answer that; he only shook his head and turned west. The expression on his face was grim and defeated and hopeless. Guilty.

Nine hours, he told Ron. *We have nine hours before more of them come to hunt us.*

Lake-of-Fire, Kansas

George Stein woke from the dead in chains.

He woke clutching his chest, trying to close over a wound to his heart that had killed him.

And what his hand found when it reached into the wound was no wound at all; the skin over his sternum was as smooth and unbroken as it had been the day he was born, and the breastbone itself firm and strong and unhurt. For a moment, before he felt the chain bolted to his ankle, he almost thought he was waking from a bad dream.

It wasn't a dream, of course. None of it had been a dream. If he'd had any doubt after he realized that he was chained by the leg to an army cot, it evaporated when he saw where he was.

In one of the rooms that made up Herman Bonner's quarters.

It only took him another moment after that to remember the strange reports from New York and from the mid-South. Stories about dead people coming back to life. Herman had hinted that he knew what caused them—he hadn't come out and said it, but he'd made it pretty clear to George that one of the men in his laboratory had been working on a strain of bacteria that might have that effect, and that the germs might have got loose in the blast Herman had staged to free his ersatz Beast.

George had suspected something else, listening to Herman—something that Herman *hadn't* hinted at, but that was right there between the lines when George stopped to think about it. Herman had *known* about that bacteria. He'd known it would get loose when he set off his bomb. And he'd known what kind of havoc it would create when it started to spread. Maybe he hadn't known *exactly* what it would do, but he'd had a damn good idea of the consequences. And that infection was here, now, right here inside the gates of the base. Those strange microbes were inside George, else he wouldn't be alive and healthy now.

Herman Bonner was up to something. Something bad enough that he'd never let George see more than a hint of it, and likely hadn't let Paul Green see any more than that. And whatever he intended was dear enough to him that he'd murdered a man he'd known for years.

George shook off the chill in his heart and sat up on the edge of the bed. The chain was long enough to let him sit up, long enough even to let him stand up and walk half a dozen paces. Herman was nothing if he wasn't generous with his friends.

Three of the rooms Herman had taken for himself had broad, tall floor-to-ceiling windows over the runway that faced out toward the Lake of Fire. The view was spectacular; and more than that. Thrilling, the way only something dangerous could be. Oh, the man with the Geiger counter—that Air Force technician Herman had taken under his wing when everyone else on this base had been . . . *seen* to—Herman's tech had insisted that at this distance there wasn't any danger from the radiation. Whether that was true or not, it defied good sense. How could a molten hole in the earth the size of two counties *not* be a danger? If it gave off light enough to brighten so much of the sky at night, how could it not be giving off radiation, too? Three evenings ago he'd visited Herman in this very room, and the only light they'd needed was the glow from the Lake of Fire. It had been dim light, true, and eerie, but it had been more than enough to see by. Well, it *was* giving off radiation, the technician had said. The five-headed missile that had landed fifty miles from where they stood had struck some kind of a nuclear research facility on the far end of the base. No one was sure exactly what sort of a facility it had been—it was classified so thoroughly that no one on this end of the base had known the first thing about it. But whatever it was was serious; there had been some kind of an apocalyptic meltdown, much worse than he'd have expected from an ordinary commercial nuclear plant. Still, the man had said. They were twenty-five miles from the crater the explosion had created, and twenty more miles from the Lake of Fire that burned at the crater's heart. There might be a little visible light, but whatever hard radiation could reach them from forty-five miles away wasn't anything they had to worry about.

Might as well fret that the lake would burn a hole straight through to China, and that the heathens there would invade them through it. And he'd laughed.

George hadn't thought it was funny; he'd glanced across this room, to Herman, and seen that he wasn't laughing, either.

It was late afternoon, now, and dim; the sky outside was thick with storm-clouds. Off in the distance the Lake of Fire was almost like a sunset in the wrong direction—but wider. No setting sun ever consumed so much of the horizon. He stood, walked as far as his chain-tether would allow him, so that he could glory in the beauty that the lake painted on the sky—

And as he moved forward he saw the plane.

It was in the foreground, right there on the landing field outside the building. Until he'd stood it'd been obscured by the bottom edge of the window's view.

"Dear God," he said. And didn't even notice that he'd taken the Lord's name in vain.

Out on the runway was a dark green plane—it looked enough like an airliner that George thought it might be a transport, but he didn't know enough to be certain—and strapped piggyback to the top of it was a nuclear missile. The missile was nearly as long, end to end, as the plane itself.

He heard the door to the room swing open behind him, but didn't turn to see who it might be. Who else could it be but Herman?

"Remarkable, isn't it, George?" Herman's voice, all right.

George didn't have an answer for him; he was still too appalled to speak.

"Our technician tells me that all of the rockets were too close to the blast that created the Lake of Fire. Not close enough to explode, but close enough that the electronics that guide them were destroyed. Hence the need to deliver them . . . a bit more directly, shall we say?" He smiled. "We considered removing the warheads and using the troop transports as makeshift bombers. Certainly that would be preferable to sending good, God-fearing men on suicide missions. Unfortunately, it happens that disassembling the missiles disarms the warheads completely—and quite irreversibly. Even as it is, detonating them is no small matter. They're designed quite carefully not to detonate in any way other than the one originally intended."

George swallowed.

"This is crazy, Herman. You're going to get that plane to fly halfway around the world without stopping to refuel it? And if you do stop it, no one in his right mind will let it into the air again." George didn't know what sort of range planes like the troop transport had, but he couldn't imagine it flying all the way into the Soviet Union with all the extra drag the missile would add. "And anyway, what's the point of bombing the Soviets now? They're too busy fighting among themselves to be a threat to anyone else."

Herman smiled. For a long while he didn't say a word, and when he finally did speak George thought he'd changed the subject. "They've finally mobilized the National Guard in New York," he said. "Even with all their . . . *peculiar* difficulties, they should be able to take the network headquarters from us in a day or two. Another thirty-six hours after that, and the ABC people can use the hardware in that building to take the Voice of Armageddon from us—or at the least to force it off the air."

Herman was still smiling strangely. His smile had always been a thing that made George uncomfortable, but this was different somehow. It brought George not just the familiar mild discomfort, but dread. Herman Bonner had plans, and down deep in his gut George was certain that there was evil in those plans. He even began to wonder how he could possibly have known the man for so many years and not known that evil for what it was.

"The answer, of course, is to destroy the building. The Voice of Armageddon can function well enough without it, no matter how susceptible it may be to the equipment in that building." Herman turned and stared wistfully out the window, in the direction of the Lake of Fire. "We don't have access to that sort of ordinance." He was beginning to chuckle in a way George found even more unsettling than the smile. "So what do we have access to?"

He wheeled around to look George in the eye, his expression demanding an answer. And George answered him, even though the only sound that would come from his throat was a whisper.

"Missiles. Atomic bombs. Dear God in heaven you're going to destroy New York."

Herman clapped his hands, exuberant. "Marvelous, George. Marvelous. You've always been a quick study; I've always prided myself on you because of it."

George blinked, shook his head; there were hints of something in that last statement that he didn't want to think about. Whatever it meant or didn't mean wasn't especially important when it stood beside the nuclear destruction of the nation's largest city.

"Herman—Herman, listen to me. There isn't any need for this. There isn't any call for it. Have you lost your mind? This isn't war against an evil empire. It isn't forestalling Armageddon, or even taking its reins. It's murder. The murder of millions and millions of innocents."

Herman shook his head, just a little sadly. "No, George. Not murder—cleansing. Cleansing of the vile city that is Sodom to our time." There was no passion in his voice as he spoke; George suspected that not even Herman Bonner believed a word he said. "You've softened, George. You've lost your vision. I saw that in you yesterday; it's why I saw a need to dispose of you—and to keep you disposed."

He's lost his mind, George thought. *Lost his mind completely. . . . Unless it's me that's changing.* And realized that just maybe it was so. He felt a guilty chill at the possibility that he could have stood in a room like this one and reasoningly considered the destruction of the city of New York. He tried to imagine himself conspiring with Herman to set loose a nuclear holocaust on his own nation—and found that it was easier than he wanted to admit even to himself. How different had it been, after all, when he and Herman and Paul Green had sat down to plan the destruction of the Soviet Union so many years ago?

I've got a lot to atone for.

The telephone rang in the next room; Herman disappeared to answer it. He reentered George's room a few moments later, beet-red and eyes bulging with anger.

"They've escaped me," he said. And left, shutting the door behind him without another word of explanation.

South Korea
at the Edge of the DMZ

It took them most of half an hour to get around the mountain, and during that time half a dozen rockets hit close enough to send them to the ground for cover. Their luck wasn't all bad, though; when they finally did get around the turn of the mountain the land was scarred but still, and the sound of rockets was just an echo in the distance.

We don't have to go all the way into the DMZ, Bill thought. *We're out of range here. There isn't any sense going any farther*.

It was an enormous relief.

There was a thin, clear spring flowing along the mountainside not a dozen yards from where Bill stood when it occurred to him that they could stop running. He looked at the boy and told him that they might as well clean themselves up and reconnoiter a little. And walked to the spring and fell to his knees and rinsed the muddy grit from his face and hands in water so cold and so pure that he could almost taste it through his skin.

When he was done he sank back onto his rump and let out a long slow sigh. There was still shelling off in the distance someplace. Well, maybe not that far in the distance. Right here the world was clean and lush and beautiful, and for the life of him Bill couldn't begin to imagine anything that could be important enough to get killed over. Much less to kill. The boy was wading in the spring that wasn't any deeper that the tops of his feet, chasing after water bugs or tadpoles or some such. Even the zombies seemed more alive here, somehow. The woman—God she was beautiful—her especially. She still hadn't said a word, but her eyes . . . they were more nearly alive now. Not just staring off into space mindlessly. She was watching Jimmy, watching Bill, too. Was she coming out of her funk? Yes, Bill thought. She was. Another hour, maybe two, and the shock of rebirth would have faded enough for her to realize where she was. Bill realized that he was looking forward to that moment, and the realization surprised him. Though it shouldn't have. Of course he was looking forward to it. She *was* beautiful; even if there had been nothing else to draw him to her, her beauty alone would have done it.

And there was something else that drew them together. Something that Bill had seen three times now, but still didn't understand:

The glow.

The glow that Bill, the woman, and the boy all shared.

Bill smiled, basking in the sight of her. And the question rose up out of him before he stopped to think that there was no way she'd be ready to understand it yet.

"Who are you?" he asked her. And saw from the change on her face that she either understood or almost did, saw her begin to try to answer—

And that was when the first shell managed to reach this side of the mountain. And sent an avalanche of dust and stones and larger, slower things rolling down toward them.

"Christ," Bill said. They had to get going again. The big rocks, the boulders rolling down from high on the mountain, weren't going to come close enough to be a problem. The next rocket would come closer. Maybe too close. They had to keep moving if they were going to stay out of range. He stood; nodded to the boy, the woman. "Okay," he said, "let's get back at it."

There was no way Bill could have known for certain that they were heading straight toward the North Korean lines. After all, he wasn't any psychic; he didn't know the future. If he'd thought just a little farther ahead, he could have guessed it. After all, Allied lines were behind them. That was obviously where the shelling was coming from. And it only stood to reason that they were trying to hit something. Which had to be the North Koreans. Bill couldn't have known that the NKs had fallen back to their fortified positions on the far side of the DMZ, but he could have guessed that, too: it was the only reasonable place for them to retreat to.

To be fair to Bill, he wasn't the only one who didn't realize how far the NKs had retreated. If the Americans and South Koreans to the south had known, they wouldn't have bothered shelling territory the enemy had already given up.

Bill didn't think far enough ahead to realize any of those

things. Maybe he might have if he'd paid a little more attention, back in basic training. They hadn't taught him a whole lot back then about strategy or logistics, but they'd taught him some. Which was more than he'd learned in the years since, years that he'd spent mostly marking time. Fueling planes; working cleanup details. Grunt work that you didn't have to think about to do.

Instead of heading sideways, toward the sea or the high mountains and away from the fighting, Bill Wallace led the four of them straight into the hands of the enemy.

That took a while.

What came first—before Bill and the boy Jimmy and the two dead people fell ultimately and disastrously into the grip of the North Koreans—what came first was the awful business in the DMZ. And worse things at the edge of it.

Carnage. Utter and awful and powerful carnage.

The near edge of the DMZ lay only a couple hundred yards beyond the base of the mountain, and there were two striking things there by the bunkers and the barbed wire and the barricades. Least of them was the amazing forest—dense and thick and untouched as a virgin jungle—that lay just beyond the line. Bill had heard tell of that forest, from airmen returned after duty in Korea. Wild things lived in it, things that man had long since hounded out of the rest of Asia. Big cats. Bears. Wild dogs so feral you couldn't tell them from wolves. One guy, back at Whiteman, told Bill about standing watch on the line at six in the morning, and right there not ten feet from him in the dawn light was a full-grown deer no bigger than a rocking horse nibbling at the fine leaves on the low branches of a tree.

For all that, for all the wonder of it, the forest just didn't seem too important compared with the carnage at the near edge of it.

Carnage? No, that was too mild a word. There wasn't a word that Bill could think of that could begin to make the sight real.

And the smell—the smell came to them before the sight, before they passed through the stand of pine that hid that part of the line from their view. Sour/sweet, like a hair burning, rancid wax—and some other smell that brought Bill back to the coffin he'd woke in just days before.

He saw the bodies when they were still in among the pines. So many, so close that in places they covered the ground like a carpet. American uniforms, South Korean, North Korean. Thousands, thousands—more than the eye could begin to count. Most of them piled up on both sides of the barricades, but not all of them. A few scattered, farther back. And there, near the spot where the barricades had been bulldozed to make way for supply trucks: bodies lined up neatly in front of the wall of a barracks, and an even string of bloodstains and bullet holes on the wall. As though the fifty Americans and South Koreans there had been lined up and executed by a firing squad. Which could only have happened if they'd surrendered.

By the time they reached the first of the bodies, the smell was so intense that it gave the boy a case of the dry heaves. The shelling was getting close again, but Bill stopped, waited; put his arms around the boy's shoulders to help him through it. Which didn't seem to help much, but Bill hoped that it was something. After a while, when the boy was closer to still than he was to convulsing, Bill said, "C'mon, Jerry. It won't be any better until we get past it." He looked up, saw that the oriental woman looked kind of green at the gills, too. Nodded to her. "You too." And she seemed to understand. The policeman's eyes were as dead as they'd been the first time Bill saw him.

Then they were moving again, picking their way through a sea of corpses toward the road the invaders had cut through the barricade. Bill did his best not to see them, even if he did have to look down to keep from stepping and stumbling on the dead. When he tried hard, hard as he could, he could just barely manage to look down at the sight of endless death without telling his heart exactly what it was his eyes had taken in. Once the boy did stumble, but Bill caught his arm, stopped him from landing down among the corpses. Which was a victory of sorts, a small triumph over the infinitude of death and destruction.

The last half-dozen yards were the worst. The bodies were piled especially high and thick there. Pressed and bunched together, from the look of them, by the same bulldozer that had broken down the barricade and cleared a trail through the forest. Too close together to walk around them; so close that there was no way to get by without walking over the bodies, stepping gingerly on a carpet of putrefying flesh. More than one of those corpses was crushed, pulped to the point where it was hard to be absolutely certain that it'd once been human.

It was too much. Too much. Bill almost turned back, headed into the shelling and the sound of gunfire in the distance. Would have done it, too, but he had a duty to the boy—had it because the boy was a boy and Bill was a full-grown man—and heading back into the shelling was sure death, and Bill knew it. And not just death: getting hit by one of those shells would give them the dead policeman's fate. Whatever it was that had brought them back to life would bring them back again. Even if there was nothing but a mindless mass of flesh to restore.

There were only three yards left to go when the boy froze up. Stopped dead in his tracks with one foot on a dead captain's face and another in the groin of an enlisted man. He didn't scream, he didn't shout. When Bill turned back to see him he wasn't sweating or trembling or crying; his face wasn't a mask of fear or disgust. The only thing in his eyes was a sort of dead-eyed shock—and that was just maybe the worst possible thing, because it made the boy look so much like the vegetal policeman. . . .

Who hadn't changed at all. For all the difference in the policeman's face, they could have been in Oz, walking through the field of poppies. Bill stole a glance back at the woman, expecting her to be the same, or nearly so—but she wasn't. She stood behind the cop, and her face was a sweat-slick mask of disgust and self-loathing, and seeing her so beautiful, so deep in agony, Bill almost lost what little determination and self-control he had left to him, only barely managed to keep himself from turning tail and running into the sound of blasting death on the far side of the mountain.

But he didn't. At the very heart of things, he couldn't. For all that he'd have denied it any day that anyone cared to ask him, at his deepest root Bill had too much backbone in his soul to fold under pressure when others depended on him. And instead of turning tail and surrendering to death, Bill reached over, lifted the boy in his arms. And carried him the last ten feet to the bulldozed trail that led into the forest.

The woman and the dead policeman followed, only a couple steps behind them.

It went quickly after that; Bill felt only a moment or two pass in the time it took to follow the trail into the forest through the shattered barricade. The last of the corpses wasn't more than a dozen yards beyond it. A little father and he let out the breath he didn't realize he'd been holding back. Set the boy back on his feet. Turned to the woman to be certain that she hadn't lost her mind.

"Are you okay?" he asked her, though he didn't really expect an answer. He got one that surprised him.

The woman nodded. "I will be," she said. She said it in English, spoke with an accent so American that to Bill's ear it sounded like no accent at all. She lifted her hand to her forehead, wiped away the sweat that was trying to run into her eyes.

"You're sure?"

She hesitated, nodded again. "Yes."

The boy was trembling, now—which Bill supposed was for the best, since it wasn't like being froze up with shock. Bill stooped, took a good long look into his eyes. There were tears in them, now, big fat wet ones that rolled wide down the boy's cheeks. "How about you? You going to make it, Jerry-boy?"

"Nothing wrong with me, Corporal Bill." Which was a lie, plain and simple. Bill reckoned as how it was a brave lie, and he didn't challenge it.

"Think you're up to walking?"

"Uh-huh."

So Bill patted him on the back, and told the boy that he was a trooper straight out of hell, and they started off again down that path. Which was actually more of a dirt road, when you got right down to it.

He led them about a half mile, far enough to get clear of the stink of death, before he headed off the trail, into the woods. A couple minutes' walk, there—far enough to keep them from being spotted from the road—and he found a clearing where there was time and room to sit and rest and lick the wounds inside their hearts. And he had them sit, and they rested there on the grass in the warm afternoon sun for half an hour, listening to the sound of rocket shells in the distance.

I-70
Not Far From
Zanesville, Ohio

Luke and Christine were in Ohio already when Andy pressed the back seat of the car out of joint and poked his head out of the trunk.

"So," he said, "when are we going to stop for lunch? I am seriously hungry."

The racket and the sound of the boy's voice were sudden enough that Luke swerved out of his lane and very nearly ran up onto the median. When he had the car under control again he shook his head and glanced back at the boy sternly. "What are you doing here?" he asked. Not that he needed an answer. "You stowed away in there? Dear God, your mother must be hysterical. We need to get to a pay phone, call her. Let her know you're all right."

Andy sighed theatrically; Christine, in the front seat beside Luke, looked as though she were trying to choke off a fit of hysterical laughter. "Momma *knows*," he said. "You think I'd just take off without telling her?"

"What?"

"You heard me. Are we going to get some lunch or not?" The boy's voice was definitely impatient. Stubborn, too.

This is ridiculous. A small boy stows himself away in the trunk of my car, announces his presence once we've gone too far to turn around and take him home. And then he starts making demands. If I had any good sense I'd ignore him. He wasn't ignoring him. Over there on the left was a small green sign that said GAS—FOOD—LODGING and after all, wouldn't it be nice to get off the road for a bit. A cup of coffee, some lunch—yes, he thought, it'd be nice. Besides, it'd give him a chance to decide what to do with the boy before they got any farther from his home.

"So?"

Luke turned on his blinker. "Okay, okay—let's get some lunch. And while we eat you can tell me what you're doing here."

Andy harrumphed and finished crawling up out of the trunk. Once he was clear he reassembled the back seat and made himself comfortable.

As he pulled off the interstate, Luke tried to figure out how the boy had managed to stow himself away in the trunk, and why. The last time he'd seen Andy was . . . he'd been there in the crowd that had said good-bye to Luke and Christine, hadn't he? Or had he? So many faces all crowded around; it was hard to be sure of anything. He'd definitely seen him a few minutes before that, when his mother had decided that she had to call out the entire neighborhood to see them off. And there hadn't been a moment after that when either he or Christine hadn't been right there in the car. . . .

No wonder she was laughing. She'd known the boy was in the trunk all along—she'd just been waiting for him to show himself.

Luke shook his head; he felt more than a little stupid. He turned to Andy. "How do you feel about Denny's?"

Turned back, to watch the road, and saw through the rear-view mirror when Andy raised an eyebrow. "Who's Denny?"

"Denny's is a coffee shop. A whole chain of them, kind of like McDonald's—only with waitresses. And a bigger menu. They have them all over the country."

"Not in Brooklyn they don't. It sounds okay, long as you think it's an okay place to eat. And anyhow, when'd you start remembering so much? Just two days ago I had to tell you what a McDonald's was. Now you sound like an authority on the subject."

"I—" Suddenly, and for no reason he wanted to name, Luke felt his gut press hard against itself. He didn't want to cope with that question. Didn't want to think about it. "Yesterday, I guess. After the museum."

After the dream.

"Well! Doesn't that just go to show you? Getting yourself killed in a place full of monsters is good for something."

Luke didn't respond—he didn't want to encourage the boy to drag them into anything like that again, even if it did seem as though he might have a point.

Instead, he tried to sort out the events since he'd woke in that museum. Luke had woke from the dead for the second time there in the Museum of Natural History—woke up clear-headed and remembering things about himself that he'd thought lost forever. Human things: the apartment where he'd lived for the last seven years. The way his father smiled when they all sat down for dinner on a holiday. His first big date, back in high school. Work was still a fuzzy thing, and so were all sorts of small details—the banister in the museum's stair-well had seemed an incredible and intricate device. He remembered college clearly, and graduate school, too—though if he'd learned a thing in either place he had no clue of it. But he woke that afternoon without the feeling that he was about to walk into the sort of commonplace trouble that toddlers learn to avoid, and there'd been few moments since his first resurrection that Luke hadn't felt that peculiar dread hanging over him.

Christine and the boy had both begun to stir by the time Luke was sitting up. He looked around, remembering where he was as the last bits of his strange dream faded away from him. He tried to focus on that dream; it was only moments away from him in time, but it was already fading away from him in the familiar way that all dreams do. There was a comfort, there, even if it was another loss—if only because it *was* so familiar.

One thing was with him, clear and unquestionable and demanding. The need to go. To move on—westward. There was an image attached to the need, too: the image of a vast lake made of flame and magma.

"Hey," Andy said. He looked groggy, as though his eyes couldn't quite yet focus on the world around them. "That was fun. You want to do it again?"

Luke groaned and shook his head. "No," he said, "don't even think about it. We've got to get you back home to your folks, and then I've got to head on. There isn't time for me to stay here any more—there's something I need to do."

The groggy look in Andy's eyes went away very suddenly. "Oh yeah? What's that? You want some company?"

Christine was looking at Luke uneasily. Had she had a dream like Luke's? Or was she afraid that he meant to leave her behind? There wasn't any need for that, Luke thought—if she wanted to come along with him, certainly she was welcome. Andy was another matter altogether. He was young enough that he needed looking after, and besides, Luke couldn't really take him away from his parents. And even if he could have, he wouldn't have wanted to. He was a good kid. But he was a lightning rod for trouble. Luke didn't know what it was his dream was sending him toward, but he knew in his gut that it would be dangerous—dangerous enough that he couldn't expose the boy to it in good conscience, let alone allow him to run headlong into the worst of whatever waited for them, dragging Luke and Christine with him.

"No," he said. "You've got to stay here with your folks."

Andy started to protest, but Luke shook his head and frowned, and that had quieted him. And Luke had actually believed that that had been the last of it. Looking back, he decided, he should have known better.

Luke stood up, brushed the dust from his slacks. Noticed the bullet hole in his shirt, crusted with dried blood. Shrugged because there was nothing he could do about it.

"So," the boy said, "how you going to get where you're going? Airports are all still shut down, you know. Trains, too—not even the buses in the Port Authority are running."

Luke turned, looked down at the boy. Shrugged. "I hadn't thought that far, to tell you the truth."

"You want to buy a car? My Uncle Tim's got an old junker he's been trying to sell for months. I bet he'd give you a real good price."

They were going downstairs, now; just ahead was a painted steel door that looked as though it led out of the building.

"You think the car'll hold up to cross-country driving?"

"Sure. It may be a junker, but it's a great old junker. Uncle Tim's handy with a wrench—kept it up real good."

What am I doing—buying a used car from a twelve-year-old boy. It's ridiculous. And stupid.

"Come on, I'll show it to you once we get back home. Maybe Uncle Tim'll even loan it to you if you promise to bring it back. He ain't been doing anything with it lately but moving it from one side of the block to the other so they can sweep the streets."

Luke had ended up buying the car—Andy's uncle had only wanted a few hundred dollars for it, and there was enough in Luke's account that even a few hundred dollars didn't make much of a dent. Even so, Luke wasn't sure he was getting much of a bargain; the car looked as though it might not have the three thousand miles of life in it that he needed. Well, he'd thought, regardless: this is what's available. And he'd bought the car. Three hours later he'd gathered up the clothes he'd bought two days before, and he and Christine were getting in the car and heading off as the crowd waved to them.

He and Christine had never even discussed whether or

not she was coming, and she never asked why he felt the need
to go. There were a few moments when he hadn't been certain
whether she meant to come or not, and he meant to ask her if
she wanted to but there wasn't time and they weren't alone and
the question was just too damned awkward anyway. And in the
end, when he was ready to leave, she'd been in the car,
waiting for him. And even if he hadn't understood why he'd
been glad she was there.

Now it turned out that Andy had stowed away with them,
too. It wasn't even remotely a thing he was glad of. He was
worried for the boy, and worried about him. What he had to
do, he decided, was . . . what, drive him all the way back to
New York? There wasn't time for that. There'd been too much
urgency about his dream. He could try to send the boy back to
his folks. Or try to, most likely with no result; even if he'd
known of a handy airport or bus station where he could take
the boy to send him back, the buses and the planes were still
out of service.

It was a problem. Enough of a problem that Luke was still
working it over and over in his mind when he pulled into a
parking spot in front of the restaurant and turned off the old
car's ignition.

When they were inside sitting in a wide booth, waiting to
place their orders, Andy had looked up from the menu (he had
it turned to the page with the ice-cream sundaes) and he'd
said, "So, where're we going?" And he'd grinned eagerly,
mischievously.

"We" aren't going anywhere, Luke had wanted to say.
That wasn't the thing to say—or it wasn't anything he wanted
to say before he'd actually decided what he was going to do.
And besides, he didn't have an answer to where *he* was
going. So far something deep in his gut had guided him at
every turn. First through that confusing webwork of wide,
crowded highways that surrounded New York; now for hundreds of miles along Interstate 70. There was a map of some
kind in the glove box, but there hadn't yet been any need to
consult it.

Whatever it was guided him purposely—Luke was certain
of that. He hadn't driven this part of the country since he'd
been in college, and even with the memory that had come
back to him his recollection of driving this area was very dim.
He did remember enough geography to know that he was

heading toward Kansas from New York about as directly as was possible.

"Hey, Luke Munsen—why don't you wake up and tell me where we're going?"

"I'm not honestly sure. All I know is that I've got to get there."

Andy giggled and rolled his eyes up toward the ceiling. "What kind of an answer is that? I tell you, Luke Munsen, you're pretty darned strange sometimes."

Luke felt himself smile in spite of himself. "I guess I am."

There was one other alternative—an alternative he hadn't even considered. He could just leave the boy behind, let him find his own way back to Brooklyn. *Right. Abandon a twelve-year-old boy in the middle of nowhere.* Luke felt a guilty inward shudder for even letting himself think about the idea. No matter what they were heading into, it was better than letting the poor kid try to shift for himself five hundred miles from home.

"How're you going to get anyplace if you don't know where you're going? I don't know about you sometimes, Mr. Luke Munsen."

Luke looked up and saw their waitress standing at the edge of the booth where they sat, waiting to take their order. She was a relief, in a way, since she gave him a good excuse to duck out of the conversation. And at the same time he found himself a little embarrassed at the idea that she might have overheard them.

"We're having a little trouble with the meat this week," she said. "You might want to order fish. Or cheese."

Luke looked at the woman carefully, tried to figure out what she meant by *trouble.* There wasn't any clue in her expression.

"That's okay. I want a banana split." Andy said. "With extra whip cream and chocolate. And an extra large Coca-Cola, too."

The waitress turned to Luke, raised an eyebrow as if to ask whether he thought it was wise to let the boy order that much dessert without a meal beforehand. Luke shrugged; it didn't seem to him that a banana split and a soft drink could do much harm to a child who'd already lived through death. He ordered a cup of coffee and a grilled cheese sandwich for himself, and Christine asked for a sandwich of some kind or another—the names on the menu were all silly enough that it was hard to tell what some of the sandwiches were without reading the descriptions.

When the waitress was gone Luke looked out the window beside him, at the parking lot, and tapped his fingers softly on the wood-grain Formica of the tabletop. He didn't know what he was heading toward, didn't know what would happen when he reached it, but there was a deep feeling in his gut—a certainty, almost—that it would be very bad. And since the boy had appeared that foreboding had become even worse—darker and more certain.

He turned, looked the boy in the eye. "What am I going to do with you?"

Andy rolled his eyes again. "Whatever you want to do, I guess."

Luke frowned, shook his head just slightly without really meaning to. "No, I'm serious. This is too dangerous. It's not right for you to be with us. And there isn't time to take you all the way back home. Do you have any relatives in this part of the country? Anyone we can leave you with? And if you don't, what in the heck are we supposed to do with you—drop you off at an airport and let you wait until the planes start running again?"

Andy sighed. "Haven't you figured it out yet? I'm *supposed* to be here."

"Oh, come on. Supposed to what? That's nonsense." Luke lifted his right hand to his face, tried to rub some of the tension out of the small muscles just above his eyes. "Be real, Andy—"

Christine coughed. "He is, Luke."

It wasn't the first thing she'd said since they'd left New York. Not quite. It was the first time that she'd actually said anything substantial.

"He *is* supposed to be here. Wasn't he in your dream?"

Luke felt uneasy, unsettled, as though the world were pressing in on him. He could see the waitress coming from across the room with his coffee, and he knew that as soon as she got there the question would fall into the space between moments and he wouldn't have to answer it. And that sounded like a good thing—a very good thing. But it wasn't right.

"No. He wasn't."

"He was in mine. There's something important that he has to do."

And then the waitress set his coffee on the table, and asked them if there was anything else she could get them, and by the time they'd all said that there wasn't, the unease had faded away.

"Yeah," Andy said, "you see? Even she says so. I'm *supposed* to be here. You think my Momma would have let me come along if I wasn't?"

Luke sighed. "I don't know." He poured cream into his coffee, watched it swirl up in cloudlike billows. There was almost a pattern to them, he thought—almost . . . a vision? No, a vision would be clearer, more knowable. This was the back of his mind trying to talk to him, to prod him with a memory or an insight. And failing. "I don't know."

"Well. If you don't know, then how come you're still talking about leaving me stranded at some airport? How about that, huh?"

Christine laughed.

"Let me think, will you? I can't think with you leaning on me like this. Maybe you do have a point. Maybe. I still don't want you getting yourself killed when I'm responsible for you."

"Already happened once. Didn't do me any harm."

"It's not like that, Andy. You ought to know that if you know so much else. Whatever we're heading toward, it isn't like getting hit by a couple of bullets from the gun of a high-strung policeman. It's dead like there isn't a trace of you left."

"Yeah. I know." Andy said those words. The look on his face said that the idea had never occurred to him.

"Nobody *has* to die," Christine said. "It isn't hopeless."

"No. Not hopeless."

"That's good." The boy sounded genuinely relieved. "What do you think is taking her so long with that banana split?"

Luke blinked, tried to follow the connection, decided that there wasn't one. Andy had a real gift for *non sequitur.* "All that extra chocolate sauce you asked for, I bet. Wouldn't be surprised if they had to send out for more. Or maybe your banana came to life and tried to crawl out of the kitchen."

Andy harrumphed.

Movement outside the window caught Luke's eye; he turned to focus on it and saw a squirrel running across the restaurant's lawn. Not just running, the way a squirrel darts from one place to another—not just running but fleeing, hard and fast and terrified, as though there was something behind the poor creature that wanted to steal its life away.

There was nothing behind it.

Luke turned away, unsettled and confused for no reason he could name. Looked back at Andy across the table from him. "All right. If you want to come with us, I won't stop you. If you run off and try to get yourself killed like you did at the museum, you're on your own. Understand?"

It was a bluff, and Luke knew it; to judge from the look on the boy's face, he did too.

"Sure," he said. "I understand. Hey—here she comes. There's the ice cream. 'Bout time, too, huh?"

Lake-of-Fire, Kansas

Graham Perkins felt happy and comfortable. Better than he had in years, in fact, and that was no small thing—there'd been some of the best moments of his life in those years.

It was cheating, of course, to feel so good. They'd given him drugs to help him feel better. Less hysterical. Sedatives? Mood elevators? Both, Graham thought. Maybe other things, too. It was a Good Thing, even if he did have to get it from a syringe. The world needed him. Herman had told him so, and Graham believed it. Other people told him, too. Christian Counselors? That was what Graham thought they called themselves. And there was more than that. *Graham* knew that he was needed. Knew it just as he knew that there was God's work to be done, because God had seen fit to free him from hell.

And make him President, too. Not two hours ago Herman had led him in the oath of office while the cameras watched and sent his image all over the country. All over the world, via satellite. The Voice of Armageddon Network had affiliates all around the globe, just like ABC used to.

There was God's work sitting right here in front of him, on this table. A long speech that he was supposed to give in a few minutes, on television. Well, not that long. It'd run about five minutes, he thought, to judge from the length of it. Not that long at all, except that it felt long because he was having trouble concentrating. He forced himself to focus on the words, to read them when his eyes didn't want to read.

My friends, it started, *my fellow Christians across this country and around this planet, the time has come for grim decisions*.

There was something in those words that almost made Graham uneasy. When he started to think about why they might do that, the drugs washed over him like a tide, and then he was having trouble concentrating again, but the world sure was a wonderful place.

Grim decisions indeed. We find ourselves besieged by the armies of evil—of Gog and Magog; of Sodom and Gomorrah. And the time has come when we must strike out against them with the fire of righteousness. And that is a grave decision indeed.

The words weren't making a whole lot of sense. Not mostly. But senseless or not they were scaring him silly. How could he be scared of something he didn't even understand? It was just plain stupid. He took another tablet from the bottle that his favorite Christian Counselor had given him, and started to feel better almost immediately.

There was a solution, now that he thought about it. And the more it floated around in his head, the happier the idea made him feel. The idea went like this: if the words were that scary, there wasn't any reason he had to pay attention to them. He could just read them to the camera, without paying any attention to them. Like back in grade school with the pledge of allegiance—nobody ever thought about that when they said it.

He practiced that for a while, there in the white room with the table. By the time they came to take him to the studio, he had it down real good.

*Inside the Korean
Demilitarized Zone*

They didn't talk very much. Bill figured that that was because none of them had anything to say—or maybe if any of them did he didn't have the presence of mind to say it. After twenty minutes Bill fell asleep there in the small meadow washed in sun, and as he slept the sound of shelling in the near distance was music, almost. Like a lullaby whose meter and melody were as uncertain as their lives.

For all that his dreams were sweet and easy—romantic dreams but not erotic. About a letter he was writing to the woman he loved, only the letter had no words and when he tried to picture his love's face, to remember her name, he could find neither. Then, when he'd dreamed for half an hour, the shelling stopped. And what should have turned his easy, pretty dreams to something even more pleasant did just the opposite: and his dream turned to a nightmare, where something powerful and endless chased Bill as he searched desperately for some grail that he could not name.

And woke to the sound of a small, frightened voice whispering in his ear.

". . . in the woods, Corporal Bill. There's people in the woods, and they got guns. And they're walking real quiet, like they was hunters."

It was Jerry's voice. He had his hand on Bill's shoulder, and he was shaking him ever so gently. Waking him up.

"Who? What?" He whispered, quiet as the boy. Which—groggy as Bill was—he might not have thought to do if the sensation of being hunted hadn't followed him up from sleep.

"Soldiers."

Bill forced his eyes to focus. Slow and silent craned his neck to look out toward the source of the sound of footsteps. And saw them.

A dozen of them. Soldiers in uniform, moving through the forest as quietly as they could. Which wasn't all that quiet, what with that many of them all wearing heavy boots, walking through the pine straw and twigs and fallen leaves on the forest floor.

They weren't American. Bill could tell that from a glance. It took another long moment to be certain that they weren't South Koreans; the only North Korean uniforms he'd seen before were the ones on those few enemy dead back by the barricade.

"Damn," he said. Said it very, very quiet. There wasn't a thing they could do if they were spotted—not with twelve of them, all armed. And Bill and the boy and the two zombies all caught out in the open without as much as a pocketknife among them. He whispered in the boy's ear: "Lie quiet. If we're lucky maybe they'll think we're dead. Or maybe they won't see us at all."

There was a chance it'd work. A good chance. Bill's clothes and the boy's both were marked with bullet holes and scabrous bloodstains.

The boy nodded, and went still as stone. Before he closed his eyes Bill stole a sidelong glance at the woman and the dead policeman. She was asleep—looked that way, anyhow—and the policeman did a pretty good job of passing for a corpse, even if his eyes were open. Bill let his eyes fall shut—

It didn't work, of course. Half a minute—maybe not even that long—after he closed his eyes the soldiers were shouting in some language that Bill didn't understand that had to be Korean. Directly after that Bill could hear the lot of them tromping heavy-footed into the clearing. Talking to each other with voices that seethed hostility. One of them—Bill thought, judging from the way he barked at the others, that it was the one in charge, but it was hard to be sure of that with his eyes closed and all—one of them walked right up to Bill. Hauled back his leg and kicked him *hard* in the gut, like he was testing to see if Bill was alive, trying to provoke a reflex reaction. Bill took the force of it limp and quiet, not even letting himself so much as grunt. Which made it hurt even more than it would have anyhow. Worse than getting shot to death, because at least when somebody shot you you got to die. And one of the nice things about being dead was that once you were there you didn't have to feel a thing.

The NKs were laughing.

Had he reacted? Did they know he was alive? Oh God, Bill thought. Say it wasn't so.

The touch of a bayonet on his temple. Maybe he'd fooled them and maybe he hadn't, but the NKs weren't going to take any chances. They were going to blow his brains out, just to be certain—

Bill braced himself. Thought about how death wasn't really that unpleasant—

Thought about the dead policeman zombie. How the man had got his brains blown out, just like this, and now he wasn't nothing but a vegetable with legs—

No.

Bill reached up, quick as he could, moved the bayonet away from his head. . . .

And the NKs laughed and laughed and laughed.

"Get up," said the man who once again had his rifle pointed at Bill's head. Even from just those two words Bill could hear how thick the man's accent was—so thick that Bill wondered if he actually understood the words he was saying.

Well, whether the NK understood what he was saying or whether he was just aping a phrase he'd learned by rote, there wasn't any question about what he wanted Bill to do. Bill looked at the barrel of his gun, which stared down at his nose from a distance that couldn't have been more than a couple inches. There wasn't much question what the man would do if Bill didn't do what he wanted. *Boom*, and there Bill'd be, six hours, a day, two days from now. Opening his eyes to a world he didn't recognize; mindless as the dead policeman.

So carefully, slowly so as not to get the NK excited, Bill got to his feet. Put his hands in the air, because he'd never had to surrender before and that was what people always did in the movies when they had to give themselves up.

Were those lieutenant's bars on the uniform of the man who still had his gun pointed at Bill's face? He thought they were. He wasn't sure; the man's uniform wasn't much like the uniform of an American lieutenant.

There were other soldiers hitting the boy, the woman, the cop with the butts of their rifles. Shouting orders a little less comprehensible than the one the NK lieutenant had shouted at Bill. The woman and the boy both got the message quickly enough, but the policeman didn't respond at all until one of them grabbed hold of his collar and hauled him to his feet.

Even then all the cop did was stand in the position the NK lifted him to—kind of funny, Bill thought. Almost like he was made out of silly putty.

The NK lieutenant barked another incomprehensible order, pointed at a tree on the near edge of the clearing, and the soldiers used their bayonets to herd the four of them into a line. Then he moved along that line, looking carefully into the eyes of each of them. When he got to the woman he leered, took her chin in his hand, and said something to her in a voice so full of brutal lust that Bill didn't have to understand it to be offended. His free hand, now, so rough touching her breast—

She spat in his face, cursed at him in Korean that was as fluent as her English; without even giving it a moment's

thought, Bill lurched toward the man, intent on ripping out
the soft flesh of his vile throat with his bare hands—

And suddenly there was a bayonet in his belly sliding
through his skin into his gut, or maybe there were two or three
of them, and Bill thought for sure that he was going to die
again. No; none of the blades were following through. The
wound was deep, but it wasn't deep enough to kill. Which was
a shame, because it hurt bad enough that Bill wanted to
die. . . .

When his knees started to sag out from under him,
someone grabbed Bill's collar, pulled him back up to his feet.
Then for a long time the world was a black place that held
nothing but Bill and his closed eyes and the bright pain down
below his ribs. But the brightness faded after a while. Or grew
dim. And Bill opened his eyes again and the four of them still
stood at the edge of the clearing, but now there was only one
NK standing there with his rifle trained on them. The rest
were at the clearing's far edge, talking quietly at each other in
heated tones.

The one who was guarding them wasn't watching any too
carefully; his attention seemed more focused on his friends
than it was on his charges. Not that Bill was in any condition
to take advantage of the fact.

Still. He turned toward the woman. Her jumpsuit wasn't
torn, wasn't any more disheveled than it had been when they'd
been captured. "You're . . . okay?"

She nodded.

"What did he say to you?"

She frowned. Shook her head. "You don't want to know."

Bill thought about that. Realized that he probably didn't.

"And you?" she asked. "Can you walk?" She nodded
toward the far side of the clearing. The hardness melted from
her eyes as the subject changed, and what was there now was
nothing but concern. Concern for Bill that made him feel shy
and warm inside, and to hell with the pain in his gut. "They're
going to march us north. Can you walk? For miles?"

Bill gritted his teeth. Carefully brought his fingers to his
abdomen, probed at the edges of the wounds. And found to his
surprise that they were far less tender than he'd expected—he
was healing even more quickly than he had before. "It won't be
a problem," he said. "I'll be fine."

That was when the NK lieutenant came back and started

barking orders. Which weren't any more comprehensible than anything he'd said before, but after a moment his grunts were prodding Bill and the other three with their bayonets, and there wasn't much question about what they wanted. They were marching them out toward the dirt road. And once they got there, they'd head north, toward the NK lines.

They hadn't gone three miles when the NK lieutenant broke his leg.

It was the stupidest thing, the way it happened. About twenty minutes after the shelling had started up again—nothing heading in their direction, but wherever it was going was close enough to make a godawful racket. They'd just gone round a big bend where the road swerved to avoid a mountain, when one of those shells hit ground a damn sight closer than any of the rest had. And the lieutenant, still walking, looks over his shoulder to get a fix on exactly where the hell it hit dirt. Doesn't spot it right away, and keeps walking—and then whump, down he goes like a sack of potatoes. It was a real sight; Bill only barely managed to keep himself from laughing. The lieutenant barked again—real shrill this time, like he was in some genuine pain—and everyone stopped, and Bill got a good look at exactly what the hell had happened: the idiot had tripped over a long, thick root. A root that the bulldozer hadn't torn loose, but just pressed flat—and not even all that flat. Damn thing stretched across the road like a trip wire thick around as a man's wrist.

Which was when Bill saw the NK lieutenant's leg. Which wasn't just busted, but broke so bad that the bone stuck out of his shin white like a candy cane when you suck all the red stripes off it. Except that there was still a lot of red, red blood, but it was oozing down out of the wound and through the center of the bone where it was broke.

Quite a sight. Awful grisly, too.

The lieutenant was howling, now, screaming bloody murder as he caught sight of the bone and the torn flesh poking out of the leg of his trousers.

How in the hell had he managed to get a break like that, just tripping over some stupid root? Bill couldn't imagine, but there it was in front of him, no denying it had happened, and there wasn't anything else in the lieutenant's general vicinity but the root and the road and one hell of a lot of dust. Bill shrugged, inwardly; the man had a talent for self destruction, he guessed.

What in the hell were they going to do about it? That leg needed splinting and taping. And quick. And if the lieutenant was going to go anywhere he was going to need a stretcher. And somebody to carry it. Well, Bill thought, it wasn't his problem. All he had to do was sit back and enjoy it—

And that was the moment that the cavalry finally decided to come over the hill.

Well, not over the hill, strictly speaking. It came round the bend in the dirt road, and it wasn't cavalry in the traditional sense of the word, but a division's worth of tanks, and infantry right there with them. It was a relief, plain and simple: one little turn in the road and suddenly he wasn't a prisoner any more and he wasn't stuck between lines any more and—

And the NK lieutenant, his eyes all wide and crazy with pain, was shouting orders. And he was picking up his AK-47 from where he'd dropped it on the road. And he was turning around and shooting at an oncoming division of tanks, like he seriously believed he had a chance of taking it out by himself—

And then the rest of the NKs were shooting, too—

And all Bill had time to think before the Americans opened fire, all he could think before he died for the third time was *shit*—

Outside Chester, Illinois

Hours, Ron thought. *Hours and hours*. He'd been running for so long that his sense of time was twisted in on itself and all but lost.

It had been morning when they'd left behind the scene of the massacre at the summer camp, and now it was dusk. And all that time he and the creature and the dog had run. As quickly as they could—or maybe it was as quickly as Ron could. The creature ran always a few paces ahead of him, and more than once Ron had seen him look back at him nervously. He didn't actually go so far as to tell Ron to hurry—he knew Ron was doing his best—but he was worried about the time they were making, Ron could see that. Well, Ron *was* running

as fast as he could—his body could probably move a little faster
if it had to, but every time he tried to speed up . . . after a
few yards he felt the world fading away around him, felt
himself blacking out because his lungs couldn't possibly draw
in enough air to cope with running that fast for any length of
time. Even as it was he could feel himself on the edge of
dizziness.

They were in a half-suburban area—mostly undeveloped
woods, but built-up enough that there was always a house in
one direction or another that you could see through the trees.
They turned, to avoid a hill, and suddenly the trees thinned
and Ron could see a river up ahead, big and wide and
muddy-looking. And a bridge—for a moment Ron almost
thought they'd been running for hours just to loop back around
on their own trail. Until he saw the river below the arching
towers of the bridge. And realized that wide as the other river
had been, this one was powerfully wider. Wide as an inland
sea.

*The Mississippi. My God—the Mississippi. How long
have we been running? And how fast? We've crossed the state
of Illinois—crossed it at the narrow tip, sure, but crossed it all
the same.*

There were more than a dozen helicopters swarming
above the bridge. Maybe more. Three or four others hovering
above the river's near bank.

Too late. The words came from the creature. *Too late.* He
slowed to a walk, stopped.

Three helicopters broke away from the ones above the
bridge and moved toward them.

And the creature just stood there, looking defeated.
Waiting for them to take him away, or kill him, or do
God-knew-what it was they intended.

"*No,*" Ron said. "You can't just give up. You'll get yourself
killed. Get both of us killed."

*There isn't any hope. Black, horrible things wait for both
of us.*

"Like hell they do. Nothing's happened till it's happened.
I won't *let* you give up." The helicopters were getting close;
Ron looked around, looked for cover. There was plenty of it, of
course—the trees were thin enough right above them that he
and the creature could easily be seen from the air, but there
were places they could hide only a few yards away. Which

wouldn't get them safe for long, of course. Not as long as they could be tracked by radio. What they needed, Ron decided, was a forest dense enough to block the radio transmitting from inside the creature's leg.

Not that there was any such thing.

It was an idea, anyway. At least he was still thinking.

He put his arm on the creature's back, pressed hard enough to get him moving again. The wounds were all but healed, now. "Come on. Let's get out of sight." And the creature followed him, even if he was still filling the atmosphere around them with despair.

Radio. Radio. How to hide from radio? Then he remembered what happened to the AM receiver in his car every time he drove under a concrete overpass. *We need to hide . . . under something massive. Like the bridge over there, or somebody's basement or—Christ, I don't know.* He wasn't even sure that a basement would be enough to hide them from the radio. And if it wasn't, and they were found, there wouldn't be any hope of running. They'd be cornered. And even if they could hide, they couldn't hide forever.

They were on the side of the hill, now, under the cover of a tall pine. Overhead the first of the helicopters roared by low enough that the wind of its passing made the tree's trunk sway.

The dog cowered and whined at the sound of it.

A dozen yards farther up the hill was a brick split-level house. It had to have a basement, Ron thought. Or he hoped it would. The only choices he could see were running and going up to the house and asking the people who lived in it for sanctuary. They'd help the creature. Everyone they'd come across had wanted to help the creature. Everyone but the people who were trying to kill them, anyway. And running was hopeless in broad daylight with the creature dispirited.

Ron looked at the creature, pointed toward the house. "They'll help us," he said. And started uphill, running from tree to tree for cover.

He was only halfway there when he stumbled over the iron manhole cover and fell face-first into the pine straw that covered the ground.

That's what he thought it was at first: a manhole cover. And what was a manhole cover doing out on a hill in the middle of nowhere? Even under the circumstances it was a curious enough thing that he took a moment to examine it as he picked himself up. And, of course, it wasn't a manhole covering at all.

How could it have been?

It wasn't a manhole covering, but the surface cap of a bomb shelter.

That was clear from the words stenciled in raised iron:

THORNDYKE MFG.

AIR-RAID

WARREN

Just below the words was the round three-part fallout shelter symbol.

The creature was a few feet in front of him, looking back as he waited for Ron to get to his feet.

"Give me a hand with this, huh?—I think we've found our sanctuary."

Another helicopter passed by above them. It seemed to pause for just an instant, and Ron had a momentary surge in his low gut when he thought the thing was going to hover up there and start shooting at them. Then it roared forward again; after a few seconds it was only another noise in the distance.

What. . . ? The creature stood beside him, now, looking down at Ron as he tried to pry the plate out of the iron circle it rested in. There was a handhold on the edge meant just for that purpose, but years of dirt and debris were settled into it, made it hard to get a good grip on the metal.

"It's a bomb shelter," Ron said. "The walls inside it ought to be thick enough that they won't be able to track that thing in your leg. These things are always made of thick, reinforced concrete, lined with lead. Radio waves can't get through it."

Finally, the metal lid began to give. Slowly at first; it was *heavy*, and the sediment around the edge held it tightly in place. When he had it an inch out of the hole Ron slid his left hand under the crack, so that he could use both arms to lift, and as he did his right hand nearly lost its grip—he only barely managed to keep enough of a hold on the thing to keep from smashing his fingers. "Are you going to help me with this or not?"

And the creature stooped and lifted the iron lid out of the ground as effortlessly as Ron would have picked up a dinner plate.

"Christ. If it was that easy for you, why didn't you lend me a hand sooner?"

The creature didn't answer.

Where the lid had been now was a metal-lined shaft with a steel ladder that ran down along one side. And the shaft was made of lead, not iron—it wasn't corroded, the way the iron lid had been, and it was soft enough that the lid had left deep scratches in it. Fifteen feet deep, or maybe twenty; it was hard to see, what with the sky getting dusky and light falling at an angle across the hill. "We've got to climb down in there. You coming?"

The creature nodded.

"Good. I'm going to go down. As soon as there's room, you follow me—put the lid back on once you're inside; if they come by this way on foot we don't want it too obvious where we've gone."

Ron lowered himself into the shaft, started to climb down the ladder. And saw Tom the dog staring at him cow-eyed and already looking abandoned.

There was no way they were going to get that dog down the shaft. No practical way.

"Christ."

The dog could shift for himself, couldn't he? It was the creature they were looking for, and maybe Ron, too. If the people who were chasing them even remembered that there'd been a dog with them, odds were they wouldn't recognize him.

"It'll be all right, Tom, boy. We won't be down here forever."

The dog snorted.

"Well, be that way. We'll be back anyway. And don't hang out right here waiting for us, huh? You might draw their attention to the place."

The dog stared, poker-faced.

"The hell with you, then. No time to argue with you." And he started down again.

He was only a couple of rungs from the bottom when he heard the creature climb in above him. Stepped off the last rung, onto the concrete floor at the base of the shaft, turned and saw a door that reminded him of a bank vault—massive and lead and instead of a doorknob it had a wheel like a steering wheel eighteen inches across. He put his hands on the wheel, braced himself, and threw all his weight into turning the thing; at first he only barely managed to budge it, but then finally it began to move and after a few inches it spun easily.

He looked up just in time to see the creature lower the iron lid onto the top of the shaft, and then suddenly it was terrifyingly dark. He forced himself not to think about the darkness, turned the vault-wheel around and around until finally the door swung inward.

There was no more light inside the bomb shelter than there was inside the shaft. Ron wasn't sure whether he'd expected that there would be, or even whether he should have expected it. No one had been here for years, maybe even for decades; if anyone had left a light burning surely the bulb would have gone out by now. If they were lucky there'd be electricity—though he'd never heard of a battery that could hold its strength for years without maintenance, he guessed that there had to be such a thing, and if there was then a person who could afford to build a fallout shelter in his backyard could hardly afford not to have it. He stepped forward—behind and above him he could hear the creature descending—groped along the inside of the doorway for a light switch.

Found one, turned it—

And wished immediately that he hadn't.

The walls of the shelter were lined with shelves, and the contents of those shelves had destroyed themselves. Five shelves of cans whose contents had rusted through and bled out onto the boards that held them in a mess of rust and goo turned to something like cement. The sacks of flour and cereal were worse—consumed completely by mealy bugs that were everywhere now, dead and dried, long since starved to death when they'd consumed everything there was to consume. Most of all the bugs' corpses were piled in the gutted sacks, but they peppered the floor pretty thoroughly, too, and the piles of clothes on the shelves on the far wall showed signs that the mealy bugs had tried to eat them, too. And failed, mostly. Though not before they'd done enough damage to leave the clothes useless.

Dead things all around him. Scores and scores and scores of dead things.

The bacteria. My God, the bacteria. Would the bacteria even have an effect on insects? It had worked on the trilobite in Luke Munsen's office, sure, and that was something like an insect. On the other hand, from what Ron knew of the reproductive habits of insects, he suspected that if the bacteria was going to resurrect them then the world would already have been buried in flies and mosquitoes, and a plague of roaches could only be a day or two away. It couldn't be. But say—just say that it could. If the starved bugs in the shelter started coming back to life . . . what would they eat? What was there to eat? Nothing. They'd already consumed all that they could inside that room. The only difference now was that Ron and the creature were there, and God only knew if mealy bugs could become hungry enough to acquire a taste for flesh.

"We've got to—" Ron said, and he backed away "—got to get out of here. I don't think it's safe." He was so unnerved that it was hard to get the breath to speak, and the words came out in a whisper. And that was a good thing as it turned out, since that was exactly the moment when he heard the sound of heavy boots treading on the metal plate above their heads.

And he froze—both of them froze. Ron held his breath for a long moment then slowly, gently so as not to make a sound, he let it out.

We've got to go in there. Go in and close the vault shut behind us. They can't figure out where we've got to yet, but as long as we're here in the shaft they can use that radio to track us. Sooner or later they'll look in here.

He waited two minutes, until he was sure that the soldiers weren't too close by, looked up at the creature and pointed into the shelter. Stepped forward carefully, careful not to make a sound. A moment later the creature was in the tiny room beside him, and Ron eased the door closed and swung its bolt home behind them.

Once it was shut he figured it was safe to talk quietly.

"We've got to get across that bridge, don't we? That's why we're here, right? And it's also why there are so many of them above it, isn't it?"

The creature nodded. *If we can get there we'll be safe from them. I can't tell you why. Or how. I can't see it clearly.*

"Then we'll have to do it, somehow or another. It'll be better once it's been dark for a while. Harder for them if they can't see to shoot at us."

The creature shook his head. *It isn't possible any more. That much I do know. Black things wait now. Horrible ones.*

"It doesn't matter whether it's possible or not. We can't just walk out there and let them have us, and we can't just curl up inside here and play dead. If you have as much foresight as you seem to, you ought to know that. The only time things are really hopeless is when you decide to give up hope."

The creature shrugged. *That isn't what I see.*

He didn't offer any further argument.

Tom the dog didn't hang out by the shaft and mope. He might have been a dog, but he had more sense than that. On the other hand, he didn't just wander off and attend to his own business, either. There were soldiers all around, hard-eyed, hard-hearted, wicked people wandering everywhere in the woods. From the moment he set eyes on the first of them he knew that they were somehow a part of his *mission*.

He wasn't sure, at first, exactly what it was he was supposed to do about them. Something, though. Something. It wouldn't do to let them get away. So Tom followed the first pair he happened on, shadowed them quietly and unnoticed as only a half-feral dog can track.

Whatever it was they were after, Tom thought, they weren't going to get it on his watch. No sir.

He watched those men for most of an hour, waiting to see what it was they were up to.

Which was No Good, of course. Tom the dog didn't doubt that for an instant. And then, finally, he saw it: saw the thing he'd known was there to watch for. The men were climbing the hill, the one that Ron Hawkins and the special creature had crawled down inside of, the hill with the split-level house on top of it. They were climbing the hill toward the house, walking right over the metal thing that covered the hole. Only this time, instead of walking right past it, one of the hard-eyed men stopped and looked right down at it.

And seemed to recognize it.

He called to his companion, pointed at the metal thing.

Tom the dog wasn't stupid. Not him.

He knew what they were about to do. They were going to pick up that funny metal thing, just like Ron and the creature had, and they were going to crawl right down inside and get his people.

Get them, and do horrible things to them, with guns. The

thought of it made him furious, angry and defensive and selflessly courageous the way a bitch is when something threatens her pups—even though Tom wasn't ever going to be any mother and neither Ron nor the creature was a young dog.

And Tom went tearing out of the underbrush, lunged for the throat of the nearest soldier. And damn near got it, too—the man only barely managed to shove Tom away from him before the dog's teeth dug into the soft flesh of his throat, but he did manage, he shoved Tom away, threw him right on top of the weird metal thing and then the man and the other one, too, both of them had their guns out and they were shooting and shooting Tom, and Tom was dying right on top of the metal thing, blood all over the place.

Well, dying wasn't that bad, Tom decided. It'd happened to him before, and it hadn't caused him all *that* much trouble.

When they were done, and Tom lay there half-dead on the metal thing with the blood still leaking out of him, neither of the men seemed to have much taste for examining the metal thing any more. And that was fine with Tom the dog, even if he did hurt like all kinds of hell.

After a while Ron cleared himself a spot on the floor—swept aside the tiny corpses of the mealybugs so that he could sit on the floor without feeling them crushed underneath him. The creature was less careful when he sat down. Which made Ron's stomach a little queasy; there was nothing between the creature's rear end and the dead insects but hair and his hide.

They sat that way for hours, waiting for the soldiers to lower their guard, waiting for the darkest part of night. After a long while Ron fell asleep for the first time in days—the first sleep he'd had since Sunday morning, when he'd crawled out of the ruin that had been the institute. He dreamed foul dreams of an endless army of bugs, consuming the flesh from his bones while he was still alive and screaming. When the dream woke him—heart slamming around inside his chest, sweat soaking his clothes and dripping on the floor—when he woke and looked around the mealybugs were still as dead as they ever had been, and the creature was staring listlessly at the floor.

"How long have I been asleep?" he asked; the words come out rough with the sleep in his throat.

The creature looked up away from the floor, looked at Ron. His eyes looked dead and glassy. *Hours*.

"It's time to go, then. Are you ready?"

The creature nodded.

"Okay, then: as soon as we get outside, we run for everything we're worth, straight toward the bridge. If we move quickly enough they'll have trouble tracking us. Shouldn't be able to see us too well in the dark, either—not well enough to get a bead on a moving target. When we get to the bridge, we just keep running. It'll be lit, most likely, and they'll be able to shoot at us. With a little luck they won't get a good look at us until we get there. We made it across that other bridge this morning, didn't we? In broad daylight, too. We can make it across this one."

We can try.

Ron stood, opened the vault door. "You'll have to go first, to lift the lid up there. Don't wait for me when you get outside—it'll only make you a better target. I'll catch up." He stepped back from the door, so that the creature could get past him. A moment later he was shutting off the light in the fallout shelter and swinging the door shut behind him. Turning and turning the bolt until it swung home. Climbing up the ladder through the shaft that the creature was already clear of, out toward the starry night sky.

By the time he was on his feet and running, the creature was already a dozen yards away, running toward the bridge with the dog beside him trotting with an awful limp, and two of the helicopters had broken away from the ones over the bridge. Shooting at the creature, even though he was still far out of range and impossible to see—guns already blazing spots of blue-white fire in the night. Ron heard the bullets wreaking havoc in the forest all around him, but not a single one of them came anywhere near the creature. Let them waste their bullets, Ron thought. Let them empty their guns out now, and maybe by the time he and the creature were on the bridge, the soldiers would be too busy reloading to kill them.

The bridge was a quarter of a mile away. That was Ron's best guess of the distance, anyway. Most of the distance was downhill, too, which made running easier and faster. They'd end up coming up to it from the left, without even setting foot on the highway that led to it, if they kept going the way they were. That was just as well—the highway was pretty well-lit. If they had to run on that for any distance they'd be in trouble, since they wouldn't even have the bridge's struts and cables to hide them.

The helicopters flew past them, fifty, maybe sixty yards off to the left. A few moments later they were coming around again, firing into the woods on their right.

It's going to work out fine. No matter what the creature thinks, it's going to work out fine. In a little bit we'll be on the bridge, and then all we have to do is get across it. Still running, Ron took a good look out at the bridge. It was long, and peaked—its center pushed high up above the water so that ships could pass under it. The really striking thing was its length—the river looked to be half a mile wide or wider here, and the bridge extended in onto the land for another quarter of a mile on either side of the water. No matter how hard they ran, no matter how fast, they were going to be targets for a long time.

Which meant, maybe, that the creature was right. That the whole situation was hopeless.

Ron felt a little of the life sag out of him. He kept running anyway. He had to; if he stopped for even a moment, he thought, he might not be able to get started again.

The helicopters came a little closer on their third pass— close enough that Ron heard the rush of air as a bullet passed too close to his head—but that was as close to the mark as any of them got.

Up ahead, the creature and the dog were climbing up onto the bridge approach, moving out into the bridge where there was light and all those helicopters with their spotlamps up above were swarming like wasps. The creature hesitated, looked back to make certain that Ron was behind him—

"Go on," Ron shouted. "They'll kill you if you just stand there!"

And right away he wished that he hadn't said it so harshly, because there'd been something in the creature's eyes. It was almost, Ron thought, as though he'd been saying good-bye.

There wasn't time to think about that, or to think about what it meant. He had to keep running. They both had to keep running—all three of them did, though the dog didn't seem the least bit winded. That was the only hope—if it was any hope at all. And running was getting hard, too. Ron's lungs ached from the ragged pressure of his breath; his arms and legs, starved for oxygen, had begun to numb. Soon, he thought, he'd begin to feel dizzy.

He climbed up over the embankment at the edge of the bridge, lifted himself onto the roadway. Pushed his legs against the pavement, *ran*. It was easier going here—even if it was more dangerous, the bridge's smooth surface was easier to run on. Not that he could possibly outrun the bullets that were showering down all around him, now.

A mile. God in heaven, an entire mile of this. From this perspective, the peak at the bridge's center looked insurmountable; it almost seemed to rise up into heaven. *Don't think about it. Just run. If I think about it I might not be able to keep going, and if I stop he'll come back for me and both of us will die.*

With all the helicopters they had up there over the bridge, Ron had expected the run to be a constant hail of gunfire. It wasn't; the gunships came through one at a time, slowly, moving steadily. And there were long pauses between the time when one would pass over them and when the next would begin shooting. Which made sense, of course: if they moved too close together they could end up shooting each other down. It wouldn't save himself or the creature, Ron thought, but it was something.

Sooner or later, he knew, one of those bullets would hit him. More than one, likely. He'd covered fifty yards of bridge already, and not a one of them had hit him yet. That was luck, wonderful luck, but he couldn't expect it to hold out. Better luck yet, the creature, up ahead of him, was still unhurt, and the people with the guns were aiming at him more than Ron.

But the luck did hold out. Ron got all the way to the bridge's central crest before the first bullet struck home— struck the creature in the left arm, just above the elbow, tearing the flesh into something like ground meat and sending blood everywhere. In a way, though, even that wound was a blessing; the force of it sent the creature reeling off to the right, and exactly where he would have been a dense burst of gunfire dug a six-inch-deep gouge in the bridge's surface. And even if it sent the creature reeling, it didn't stop him. He caught himself, pulled himself back into balance, and kept running—all without losing a beat or losing his pace.

We're going to make it. We're really going to make it. The idiots in those helicopters don't know how to aim. That was probably it exactly, he thought. Whether any of those people knew how to use a gun or not, they'd never used anything like those guns before—let alone used them to shoot from a moving gunship.

We really are going to make it.

The creature was still running, not slowing down at all, in spite of his wound. All three of them—Ron, the creature, and the dog—were moving quicker, in fact, now that they were going downhill. *Another half a mile, just another half a mile, and we can duck off into the scrub on the other side, and to hell with whether they can track us or not. It just won't matter.* Which was maybe a little overoptimistic, but it helped him run so he thought it anyway.

They were only a hundred yards from the far edge of the bridge when one of the helicopter pilots figured out what the problem was. And changed tactics so radically and thoroughly that neither Ron nor the dog nor the creature had a chance.

Ron began to realize something was wrong when he heard the shooting stop. He looked up, over his shoulder, and saw a helicopter carefully—ever-so-slowly, ever-so-carefully—lower itself between the bridge's cables and begin descending toward him.

No, not toward him. It eased right over him, without even hesitating. Ron looked up as it passed, and saw that there weren't more than five feet of clearance on either side. It was crazy. Crazy. If the pilot wasn't careful—if he didn't really know what he was doing—they'd move a little too far to one side, or a breeze would catch them, and the rotors would hit one of those cables and the helicopter would go down hard and maybe take the bridge with it, too.

It was going to work. He knew that in his gut. Maybe it'd end up killing the helicopter and crew, but all the same it'd work.

When they were three yards behind the creature—not more than a dozen feet in front of Ron—they started firing. At that distance, with those guns, it might as well have been point-blank. The creature tried to make himself a more difficult target—dodged right and left, stopped suddenly so they'd overshoot—but it wasn't much use. Ninety seconds after they'd started shooting at him from so close, the creature was a great bloody mass of raw flesh falling to the pavement, and the helicopter had slowed to a crawl, hovering not more than a couple feet from the bridge's surface, and they were still pouring bullets into his corpse.

Tom the dog lunged at the helicopter, attacking its skids and clawing long, bright-metal scratches in the gunship's paint. The scratching made a wicked fingernails-on-the-blackboard sound so loud that Ron could hear over the rotors and the shooting. It didn't make a whole lot of difference to the helicopter's pilot. Or the gunner.

Ron Hawkins screamed with rage, and he was right behind the helicopter, now, ducking aside to keep from being chopped to death by the rear rotor, and in his rage he reached down and grabbed the helicopter's near landing skid—

And with the strength that came to him in rage and fear and concern, the same strength that lets a mother lift an automobile off her dying child—

He lifted the near side of the helicopter.

Throwing it off balance. Sending one of the overhead rotors into one of the massive cables that suspended the bridge; disabling it completely, but not before the force of sideways lift pulled the helicopter out between the cable it'd hit and the next.

And the helicopter went out, over the river, and plummeted down into it like a stone.

With Tom the dog still attached to the skids by his biting mouth.

He had a moment. Just a moment. Time to lift the creature's corpse up onto his shoulder, carry him away—

Helicopters, all of them by the sound of it, moving close—

God. God in heaven so much blood so much shredded meat and skin Ron felt ill from the sight and touch and smell and over there his leg, the Beast's leg barely even connected to itself—

Wait. Over there by the leg. A tiny scrap of metal there beside the fragments of shattered bone.

The radio transmitter.

If they could get away from here, they'd be free.

If there was really much chance of that—Ron looked up, over his shoulder and he braced himself to lift the creature's corpse, looked because it sounded as though all the helicopters

were about to descend on him at the same time and start
shooting—

And damned near, that was exactly what they did.

A complete and total lack of coordination.

One of the helicopters lowered itself right into the rotor of
another, and all holy hell went loose; the rotors shattered and
went hurling off into the dark—but not before they ruptured
the fuel tanks on the upper gunship, and suddenly the
kerosene that had been inside the tanks was afire, and then it
was exploding. Before the first helicopter could finish plummeting into the river the second was a spectacular ball of
flame, and the explosion, like some fiery contagion, rocked the
swarming gunships, sent them reeling into each other and set
them afire.

Ron lifted the creature's carcass onto his shoulder and ran,
before he could be caught up in the burning and fiery
convulsing going in every direction.

The creature was *heavy*. Heavier than Ron would have
imagined, even knowing his size; it was hard to move at any
speed at all, carrying him. Ron did his best, but the truth was
that even though his body went through the motions of
running, he could have walked faster. Which was a bad thing,
since some of the helicopters were plummeting onto the
roadway too close behind him, and debris was flying everywhere and he could feel bits of fiery metal digging into the skin
of his back. He needed shelter, needed to get the hell out of
the way and needed to get there now. Needed to find a place
to hide and wait while the creature's body rebuilt itself. Not
that there was a building anywhere close enough. Over there,
down below the bridge where it ran over the riverbank.
Railroad tracks—a whole damned railroad yard—and a freight
train sitting idle with its boxcars wide open. It wasn't the best
place in the world, but it'd do.

He hurried as much as he could off the bridge, doubled
back to the railroad yard. Barely managed to keep from
stumbling as he crossed over a dozen sets of tracks, running
toward a car with the words PACIFIC AND SOUTHWESTERN RAILROAD
stenciled in wide pale letters on its side. Lifted the creature's
body up onto the bed of the car through the half-open sliding
door. Climbed inside himself, and dragged the corpse farther
into the railroad car, but not out of the light that shone through
the doorway.

And looked at the damage. Really *looked* at it for the first time. It was a grisly sight, blood everywhere—not just on the corpse, but all over Ron, too, so much that it made his clothes heavy, wet, and slick—fragments of bone spearing out through pulpy rags of torn skin and shredded flesh. And worst of all, that leg. There hadn't been time to feel ill while he'd been carrying the creature away from the bridge, but now—he felt his stomach churning again, trying to force up food when he hadn't eaten.

Most of the creature's body—his skull not excepted—was pulped and mutilated, but still more or less in place. But his leg, his left leg was torn clean through halfway up the thigh; all that held the lower part to his body was a wrist-thick rope of meat and skin along what had been the outside of the thigh. Maybe, Ron thought, he should press the two ends back together. That didn't seem wise. Just to begin with, they wouldn't fit properly—there was a good four inches of meat and bone missing between them. They weren't meant to fit together, not directly, and God knew what kind of harm he could end up doing by trying to graft them together. That big vein over there, for instance. Ron didn't even see what it was supposed to attach to on the lower part of the leg.

No, he decided. Whatever it was that had resurrected himself and the creature back at the institute—the same thing that had resurrected the children at that camp—whatever that was, it knew what it was doing. Knew? Whatever. Anyway, it was best not to interfere. Ron sat down facing the doorway, rested his back against the wall.

After a while Tom the dog, soaked and filthy but not much the worse for wear, jumped up into the boxcar, snorted, and found himself a warm corner to curl up in.

A long while later Ron fell asleep again.

Lake-of-Fire, Kansas

Herman was cursing in a language that George Stein had never heard before.

George had never figured out exactly where Herman Bonner had come from, why he'd come to the United States, or even why he was as driven as he was. Hearing him curse unintelligibly got George thinking about all those questions all over again. Not that this was the time to ask. George Stein was at Herman Bonner's mercy, and he knew it. There were people here in the Lake-of-Fire complex who owed their allegiance more to George Stein than they did to Herman, but there was no one but Herman who knew George was alive. He could scream at the top of his lungs and hope that someone might hear him, but it wouldn't do any good. Herman had taken pains to have his suite of rooms soundproofed when they took the base over. At the time it had seemed a little strange to George, but it certainly wasn't anything he was going to make a fuss about. Back then there hadn't been any point; he'd trusted Herman.

Herman was cursing because of what they'd both just seen on the closed-circuit television—the closed-circuit feed from the video camera on the helicopter. Herman had come up here to watch it with George—God knew why he wanted George to see it with him, but he did—and together they'd watched that poor fool and that pathetic, innocent Beast get themselves torn to ribbons as they tried to cross the Mississippi.

They'd managed to kill the Beast, all right. Only it hadn't worked out exactly the way Herman had planned. Before they could kill his companion and retrieve the corpses the poor fool—the one Herman kept calling a floor-sweeping imbecile—the poor fool managed, alone and unarmed, to destroy an entire battle squadron of helicopter gunships. And walk away, unscratched. From the way Herman was cursing, George suspected that there weren't any more helicopters to replace the ones he'd just lost. Not military ones, at least.

The richest part of the whole scene was that they'd been able to watch it even after the last of the helicopters had plummeted into the river. The first wreck—of the helicopter that had mutilated the Beast with gunfire—had somehow managed to snap the camera clean off the side of the gunship. It had fallen onto the pavement intact and still broadcasting. And shown them all holy hell flying loose as the gunships burst against one another.

After just a little while the scene had grown ominously still.

George was still watching the screen. It was still, and quiet, and watching it gave him good reason not to pay attention to Herman's cursing. Well, maybe not good reason.

Reason, anyway. It didn't show much, now that the fireworks were over. A railroad yard, dim and deserted; one train in the foreground, but it was dark enough that it might have been abandoned there. In the distance, the river—so wide, so vast that even as background it consumed half the screen.

Still and serene as a painting.

Beautiful, in a way.

Herman's fury was reaching new peaks; he was staring at the video screen now, too, and he was beginning to look as though he might assault it. George almost grinned at the idea, in spite of his unease—the image of Herman trying to destroy a television with his bare fists was a comical one.

That was motion, there on the screen, wasn't it? It was too dark in that spot for the camera to convey the image clearly. Hard for George to be certain what he was seeing, if he was seeing anything at all. He leaned closer on the edge of the bed Herman had chained him to, trying to see more clearly . . . Herman saw him doing it. Grunted suspiciously. And stooped to stare right into the picture tube. He'll blind himself that way, George thought, and then thought, well, then, that's fine. When he realized what he was thinking, he wasn't proud of it. It was a vindictive sentiment as much as it was a desire to deprive Herman of a measure of his capacity to work harm. George Stein didn't want to have to think of himself as a vindictive man, even though he knew there were vindictive elements inside him.

"What's that?" Herman asked. His voice was frayed at its edges, and there was more than a little about it that sounded unhinged to George. "What have you seen? Tell me, damn it!"

George shrugged. "Hard to say. Thought I saw something move."

Herman turned to face him, looked hard into his eyes. "You saw something. I know you did. It won't go well for you if you try to hide it. You know, George. You know, I've always wanted to hurt you—really *hurt* you. You'd hurt so well, I think." George felt himself blushing—felt strange and embarrassed, almost as though he'd been propositioned. How could he have known a man so many years, and not known this about him? He suppressed a shudder; it didn't seem wise to let it show. There was something sick about that man. Powerfully sick, and even evil.

"It's there on the screen right now, Herman. Look for

yourself. A figure—a man, maybe?—running through the railroad yard."

Herman turned, looked, still only a handful of inches away from the screen. And spat onto the carpeted floor beside the set. "It's him. The janitor. Carrying my Beast. Can't you see that from there? Are you blind? Or were you lying to me?"

"Lying to you, Herman? Lying to you about what?"

"*You know.*" He didn't say those words loudly, or with any threat in his voice. He said them in a voice and in a tone that George had always imagined the prophets using—maybe even Christ himself. Herman sighed. Stood, stepped away from the television set. Walked over toward the window, and stood as close to it as he'd been to the picture tube. He stood that way, still as a statue, for the longest time. Staring out into the dark.

The plane is out there, George Stein thought. *The one that the fools have strapped the missile to. The one Herman told me they're going to drop on New York City.*

"The plane is fueling now," Herman said. "Soon it will leave us forever." He lifted his hand to his lips, coughed. "In the morning, I think. Some little time before dawn."

George didn't want to think about the plane, or about the bomb strapped to it. All those millions of people who lived in New York would die. Die horribly. It wasn't George's doing, and there was nothing he could do to stop it, but he bore a share of the blame for the destruction that was to come. Or thought he did.

There wasn't any avoiding the subject, though. He stood, walked as far toward the window as his chain would let him. Lights were on, out over the runway. Smoky clouds of warm vapor were billowing out from the fuel tank, into the cool morning air. The transport, and the missile bound to it. Loops, loops, and loops of grey-metal cable tied them together; in places the cable was bolted into place. The arrangement looked secure, if it did look strange. He couldn't picture the missile coming apart from the plane by accident in midair.

Couldn't picture it coming free on purpose, either. Where would it go? Rolling off the wing?

"Herman," George asked, "how is your pilot going to deliver that thing? How's he going to get away once he's done it?" George already had a suspicion as to what the answer was, and it made him feel even more sick with himself than he did already.

Herman snorted. "Really, George. The question doesn't become you. . . . We have a volunteer, of course. What did you think? Do you want me to say it aloud? Well then, I'll say it: we have a volunteer. A kamikaze pilot, all our own. He'll fly his plane to exactly the right place, and then he'll press his switch. And die gloriously to kill the infidels and pagans."

George wasn't sure how he was to respond, or even if he should respond at all. "Yes."

The image on the television screen was still again, now. The young man who'd carried the Beast had disappeared into a railroad car just as Herman had walked away from the set. And now what? Something was going to happen, any moment now. Something dramatic and important. George knew it with his gut—he could feel it like a spring turned tight and about to snap.

Herman seemed to sense it, too; he wheeled around suddenly to face George. Looked him in the eye, and hissed. "What? What is it now?"

George blinked, shrugged. Tried to stay calm, in spite of the fact that he felt . . . spooked. Almost exactly the way he'd feel if he'd found himself in an abandoned building in the darkest part of night, hearing sounds with no source he could imagine. "What's what, Herman? You've got me at a loss."

Herman made a noise that was almost a snarl; he was still staring into George's eyes. He didn't blink.

That was when he saw it, saw the thing so critical and important. A small thing, really. Small enough that if he hadn't seen it it would've had no importance at all.

The television screen.

The train on the television screen was moving. Moving north, toward St. Louis.

"Tell me," Herman said. He was prowling around the room, now. Looking closely at every little thing, inspecting every detail.

"I still don't understand, Herman. Tell you what?" George tried to keep his voice as innocent as he could, but he wasn't sure it was innocent enough.

Until the train had started to move, all the camera had shown of it was three cars. There'd been no clue as to which direction it might move in. If the train could get clear of the camera's field of vision before Herman got a look at it, he'd have no way of knowing where it had gone. And that would be a very good thing. The Voice of Armageddon network had an important regional hub in St. Louis; the city was a lot more important to the VOA than it ever had been to ABC. Herman had all sorts of people at his disposal in St. Louis. If he knew that that was where the train was headed, he'd have a real opportunity to try to kill them again.

All George had to do to keep that from happening was not look directly at the screen. Wear a poker face, to keep from giving Herman any clue of what was about to happen.

Herman turned again, suddenly, maniacally. For a moment George thought he was about to stoop and focus directly at the screen, but then he saw that it wasn't the screen that had his attention, but the window. He was looking to make certain that there was nothing wrong with his missile.

Through the periphery of his vision, George could now see that the car the young man had climbed into—the Pacific-Southwestern car—was the last before the caboose. The train was moving awfully fast. In a moment it'd be off the screen entirely.

And then Herman was striding across the room, furious, his face filled with a thousand violent things George could see waiting for him. When he got to George, he lifted him by the lapels and shook him, shouted unintelligibly into his face. When the shout was done he calmed a little. "Tell me what it is you've seen, damn you! Tell me!"

And turned away for just an instant, trembling with frustration.

Turned toward the television.

The instant was enough to show him the train's last car moving out of the camera's field of vision.

Thursday
July Twenty-First

It is past midnight in this part of Chicago. The stockyards and slaughterhouses—enormous places that ordinarily work day and night to fatten, kill, and pack the meat for most of the nation—are utterly empty of the sound of man and woman.

There is a reason for this.

Though no one is there to hear it, the din from the stockyards is deafening.

Early today someone noticed something strange in a

meat-packing plant. Something frightening. And before the day was out the phenomenon had spread to every packing house in the city.

Two hours ago it reached the slaughterhouses. By then there was no one to see it; even the night watchmen had fled in fear.

The worst of it is that what they all ran from was only the beginning of the process. They ran from the sight of hams and pork butts growing wild bloody beards of flesh like alien mold. Ran from the seeping pig-blood on the floors that grew and grew deeper no matter how it was cleaned; blood that transformed the water used to clean it, just as Christ transformed his water into wine. Ran most of all from the sound of whole fresh carcasses wheezing headlessly with pain. Even the tenders and slaughterers and butchers of cattle took flight, afraid that whatever infected the pigs would soon contaminate the steers.

And now it is long after midnight, and the butts and the hams and the carcasses are no more; now there are only swine grown whole from the wreckage of their bodies.

They are hungry, these pigs. For millennia they and their forebears have been bred only to eat. They know nothing but the need for food.

The first to wake turn on the still-growing remains of their fellows, but this lasts only so long, and anyway the taste of swineflesh is oddly unsatisfying to a pig. They root around inside the packing houses, searching for anything that will fill their gullets.

There is nothing, of course.

One of them finds an old broom. Its wood, its straw, neither are to the pig's liking—but they are something, anyway. Something to chew with teeth that could easily crush bone, something to press down into the yearning stomach . . . and as he eats another, larger pig comes round the corner. And sees the food that was the broom and charges, intent on taking it for himself.

And the smaller pig screams in fear and challenge and indignation.

Screams mightily.

The sound of that scream is startling; it sends pigs all

throughout the packinghouse running when there is nowhere
to run—

Running into walls. And lockers. And doors.

The two that hit the front door of the packinghouse are too
much for it. Heavy wood shatters, bursts flying splinters in
every direction.

And then the pigs are free.

Two dozen of them from that packing house? Three?
Certainly no more. What others there might have been rest
inside the bellies of their brothers. Tomorrow their remains
will be excrement, worn from the trip through the gullet but
not digested. And they will grow.

That is tomorrow. Tonight there are three dozen pigs free
on the street, and they are hungry. They root at the weeds that
grow from the cracks in the sidewalk, which are insubstantial.
Sniff at the wood of telephone poles, but the wood is polluted
with tar, and therefore unappealing. Three of them find the
remains of yesterday's newspaper; they make short work of it.

Then one of them catches scent of the stockyard, where
there are cattle and so much food to fatten them. And charges
off to hunt, like the wild boar who was his ancestor. The other
pigs, seeing him run, follow. What follows can only be described as restrained chaos. The stockyards are fenced and
walled with sturdy stuff; built strong to withstand the press and
lurch of frightened bulls. The pigs, of course, do not know this.
They charge, screaming blood-hungry the need in their bellies, ram their heads against the high, strong pen-walls. Pen-
walls that are cast from poured concrete reinforced with steel.
Even the weight of a mature boar has no affect on it. But the
strength of the walls effects the pigs: their screams of hungry
challenge turn to wails of agony as skulls and snouts and jaws
pulp against man-made rock.

And then the sound of screaming and the smell of blood is
everywhere in the streets, spreading like an infection among
the slaughterhouses and the stockyards and the packing
houses. Everywhere the animals stampede, pounding into the
walls and the fences and the pens that hold them. And
everywhere that a wall or a door or a cage is weak, animals are
free. Pigs, most of them. Only the cattle in the stockyards are
alive, and few of those walls give.

An hour, and these pigs have spread themselves everywhere in the city.

Two hours, and the first herd of them finds the patrons of an all-night diner.

And the pigs eat those patrons—five men, three women, plus the waitress and the cook.

Eat them alive.

Later, the pigs will find others. Many others. They will be eaten too.

That is the start of the terror in Chicago. Tomorrow the pigs will wake in Moscow; two days later they will wake in Beijing. Men will kill them whenever they appear, but when they do the pigs will only rise again, hungry, murderous, and strong.

South of St. Louis, Missouri

It was the creature's death scream that woke him.

The sound of it pulled him up out of sleep all at once, gasping and terrified and wide awake, and he opened his eyes and saw fresh blood spilling out all over the floor of the car rolling toward the back end of the train. The wide artery in the creature's legs spurting out its last few spurts, and the creature was dying all over again from the loss of blood that began as soon as his heart started beating.

Over in his corner, Tom the dog whimpered in sympathetic pain.

They were moving. Sometime while he'd been asleep they'd started moving, and that hadn't even begun to wake him. Which meant that he'd been sleeping more deeply than he would have thought possible—he hadn't felt that tired. Hadn't felt tired at all, in fact. His body needed sleep, he realized, even if it didn't demand it.

He crawled over toward the creature. Except for the leg . . . well, it would have been an exaggeration to say that the rest of him was healed. He was still black and blue and twisted out of shape and while the skin had grown over his wounds it was hairless, and there were places where it was thin enough to see through. Re-knit—maybe that was the word. His body had begun to re-knit itself.

Especially the leg.

That leg . . . Ron winced at the sight of it. It *was* growing back together. Half the flesh that had been ripped away was regrown. And the bone was growing back, too. But the gap was still wide enough that Ron could have put his fist through it. And that fat artery there—he still couldn't see what it was supposed to connect to. It was less ragged than it had been, but it was still wide open; blood leaked from it steadily.

Ron still didn't want to interfere. He didn't know anything about bodies or doctoring. Chances were that if he did anything it'd cause more harm than good. If he didn't do anything, the creature would bleed to death again as soon as his heart started beating. Ron bit his lip. Hesitated. And carefully as he could he pressed the lower leg up toward the stump. It didn't fit, of course—but it left less of the creature exposed.

On I-70 in Illinois
Approaching the Junction with I-55

Two things happened to Luke at once, right about the time he passed the sign that said ST. LOUIS 36.

The first was that his certainty abandoned him—abandoned him completely and absolutely. All the way from New York he'd known beyond any doubt exactly and precisely where he had to turn, where he was going. Seen the turns and curves in the highway with his mind's eye hours before he was anywhere near them. And now, very suddenly, he was lost. Oh, sure: not lost completely. He was on Interstate 70 in Illinois, and the sign said that he was less than forty miles from St. Louis. And there was the map in the glove compartment if he needed it. But he no longer had any sense of *going* somewhere.

Maybe, he thought, it was time to pull over and wait. Maybe that was what his gut was telling him. Andy and Christine both were dozing. If he pulled over and rested his eyes for a while they wouldn't even have to know about it. And he hadn't had any sleep since he'd started driving, back in New York. Maybe he did need some rest.

He told himself these things, but he didn't believe them for an instant. Something was wrong, and Luke knew it.

He looked down at the gas gauge, saw that it read less than a quarter of a tank. It *would* be a good idea to stop for gas.

That, at least, was true. It wasn't exactly necessary, not yet, but it would be soon.

He was arguing it back and forth with himself when the other thing happened to him, and one that was a lot worse than just the loss of purpose.

It was a vision, a vision of pure and complete horror, absolute and total destruction. And for the longest moment he didn't even realize that it was a vision. It was that strong, that real—all but indistinguishable from the truth.

It started as a glow, up ahead of him on the highway. A powerful and blinding glow in the shape of a low dome that gradually bulged and turned in on itself. And finally grew upward and straight, a wide column, and billowed into a mushroom cloud.

An atom bomb.

A memory—of a film back in grade school. Grey, scarred footage projected onto the pull-down screen at the front of the classroom, the one that doubled as a map of the world when the teacher flipped it around and let them see the back side. A film projector in the half-dark aisle beside Luke's desk, going sprok-sprok-sprok like a dying metronome not quite in time.

A film of Hiroshima, in Japan, where they dropped the atom bomb back in World War II, and there on the classroom wall had been a mushroom cloud exactly the mate of this one. After a while the film cut away from the mushroom cloud, and it showed them other things, more intimate ones. Small children with oozing sores and swellings that looked impossible. Amputees. Shadows of terrified men and women, etched into the walls of buildings by the atomic light, and the voice on the film told him that those shadows were the only traces of the dead that remained.

And an explosion just like that was waiting for Luke. He knew it with an absolute and unshakable conviction. Somewhere up ahead, somewhere soon. Or maybe it waited for them in this very spot.

The only hope, he knew, was to keep going. To keep going and never slow down, not even for an instant.

So he did exactly that drove and drove hard and fast, and didn't hesitate or pause for anything. Not even later on, crossing the Mississippi River bridge into St. Louis, when the helicopter passed over them twice, and then shadowed them from above for the longest while.

On the Outskirts of St. Louis

Ron tried to sleep again after the creature died for the second time that night, but he didn't have much luck. Instead of sleeping, he sat for most of an hour staring out the door as countryside rolled by too dark to focus on.

He didn't even notice, at first, when the creature started bleeding again. Partly that was because it started so gradually—to begin with the bleeding was slow and slight, welling up out of the mutilated leg instead of gushing as dramatically as it had before. He might not have noticed at all if the creature hadn't started making gentle writhing movements, and he might even have failed to notice the movement—it was that slight—if it hadn't been for the sound.

Small, mewling sounds. The kind of sound he'd have expected from a small animal that had been abused to within an inch of its life. Maybe the sound of a dog mewling because it was about to die.

Tom was still over in his corner, wide-eyed and fearful.

He crawled back over toward the creature, to see if there was anything he could do, and saw him clutching at his chest. And his face—a mask of incredible agony, even though he wasn't yet conscious. Ron looked down at the creature's leg. It was growing back together, but it was growing all wrong. At a weird angle. That'd take care of itself, he thought, but there was still a big gouge covered with something that looked like bloody mucous membrane. And the fat artery was right there pointing out of the gouge instead of growing in to make its connections; it looked almost like the business end of a garden hose.

As Ron watched a pulse of blood welled up out of the artery. The bleeding stopped, and Ron thought he heard a sucking sound, but it was hard to be certain with all the noise of the train's motion. And then blood was coming out again. Bubbling out, literally—there were glassy, beady bubbles in the blood.

And that was when Ron understood.

Understood why the creature was mewling in pain. Understood why no matter what Ron did now the creature was

about to die again. And understood why the creature's vision
the evening before had been so bleak and hopeless.

Ron didn't know anything about medicine. Honestly
didn't. He'd heard horror stories about junkies who shoot air
into their veins, and about divers who come up from the deep
too quickly and get the bends. He knew that was one of the
most horrible ways that anyone could possibly die.

And the creature's veins and arteries had to be all but
filled with air by now. If the wide-open vein wasn't enough by
itself to let air leak into him, every time his heart started
beating—every time he began to come back to life—his heart
drew air right up into him. Ron took off his shirt, tied it around
the creature's leg to make a tourniquet. If Ron could stop any
more air from getting in, eventually the creature's blood would
absorb the air that was already inside him. Or Ron hoped it
would. He wasn't sure, and anyway it wouldn't be absorbed all
at once; likely it'd kill him a dozen more times—whenever a
bubble reached his heart, his brain, even his kidneys—before
it was gone.

No wonder the creature had been so dispirited and afraid.
It wasn't just his own death that he'd seen looming in front of
him. It had been—would be—horrible, excruciating death
over and over again.

They were rolling into St. Louis, now; over there Ron
could see the arch, lit up and beautiful. The train would
probably stop here—St. Louis was a major railroad city, wasn't
it? He thought about that for a moment. The train was moving,
and that was good, but it was moving north where the creature
had been guiding them west. When they stopped it'd be best
if they got off of the train and found a more sedentary hiding
place until the creature was recovered.

The sound of a helicopter overhead. Ron's heart surged
with fear to hear it, but when he craned his head toward the
door to get a glance at it he saw that it wasn't a military
helicopter, but one of the smallish ones used for commercial
purposes. He sighed, felt his heart slow, felt his shoulders
relax. Soon they'd be pulling into the railroad yard, and Ron
could get himself and the creature both away from this
damned place. That would be a very good thing.

Even as he thought it the train began to speed up
dramatically, and as a bubble reached the creature's brain, and
he began to convulse and die for the third time in less than a

day, Ron watched the train roar past the railroad yard and just
keep going.

Lake-of-Fire, Kansas

George was never quite certain how he managed to
survive Herman Bonner's attentions that night. There were
things Herman did to him that should have killed him, he
thought. And there was worse, too—worse than the abuse
and the beatings. Worse than that half hour when Herman
strapped him to the bed, turned off the lights, and carved
shallow patterns in his skin with a blade so sharp that it almost
seemed to whisper as it touched his flesh. No: the worst was
just before Herman Bonner left the room at two or maybe
three in the morning, when he was straddled over George and
pounding on his skull with something that might have been
a pipe. And suddenly Herman lurched, and groaned, and
whispered something passionate that George couldn't understand. . . .

And when it was done George thought he knew how a
woman feels when she's brutalized and raped. The horror of it
left him numb and dead inside; unable to sleep but too still
inside to really be awake. After an hour or two the pain in his
body was gone, and he could feel from an incredible distance
that the microbes that had brought him back to life and made
him physically whole again. The wounds in his heart weren't a
thing that anything but time could heal, and they were deep
enough that they wouldn't ever heal completely.

He was still staring mindlessly at the window at five in the
morning, when Herman came back, wearing pajamas and
slippers and smiling an easy, self-indulgent smile.

"It's morning, George. Glorious morning. So much is
happening! In a moment the missile-plane will rise up into the
heavens. And that train—even as I speak that train is coming
into St. Louis. Soon we'll have those two in our hands, to
dispose of forever!"

He sighed, contented—almost blissful.

"Come, George—come to the window. You have to see."

George was too dead inside to respond, even if it'd been
a thing he'd been inclined to respond to.

"Ah. Your chains. How can you possibly come to the

window when your chains won't let you move that far? Here. Allow me to—" he reached into a pocket, fished out a set of keys. Stooped, and unlocked the shackle that bound George's leg. Took his hand, pulled him up from the bed, led him half-forcibly to the window. George was too numb to resist. "Allow me to assist you."

The plane was taxiing on the runway, building velocity toward flight.

"Sodom and Gomorrah shall perish," Herman said. "Glorious, isn't it, George? Glorious."

George heard himself grunt—not just grunt; there were words, trapped in his throat. Something he was trying to say. Whatever it was, he didn't have a hint of it. The words came from a part of him hidden too deep for him to know. The two of them stood watching as the plane reared up and raised itself into the sky. And kept watching for a long time after.

They'd been standing there for the better part of an hour when Herman left him standing by the window, turned on the television. "We have people at the railroad yard, waiting for the train to arrive. And one of the network's helicopters watching to be certain that it does. Come—stand beside me. You must see this for yourself."

George heard those words, just as he'd heard all the others. He had no more will or desire to respond to them than he had to respond to anything else. Eventually Herman came to him again, and took his hand, led him to the bed where he could watch the screen.

The image of a train, moving through an industrial park at the edge of a city. Day just beginning to break. George recognized that train from somewhere . . . but where? PACIFIC-SOUTHWESTERN. Yes, that was it. From last night. This was the train, the car, where the young man and the Beast had taken refuge. Herman had found it, and he was having it followed.

Then the camera swept across the industrial park; in a moment they were moving with the helicopter over a vast river—the Mississippi? George wasn't sure, everything was too vague. It had to be the Mississippi, didn't it? Or did it even matter?

"It's better," Herman said, "that we don't follow them too closely. It might make them wary."

Up ahead were bridges, three of them, at least. It was

hard to be certain from this angle, but there might have been a fourth. The helicopter rose, so as to give itself enough altitude to clear them, and their view improved. George could see traffic moving across the bridges. Not much traffic—it was too early for there to be much traffic—but there was some.

And Herman Bonner gasped. Stood up from the bed where he sat beside George, and disappeared into the other room. He left the door ajar behind him; after just an instant George could hear him speaking over the phone. "That car—" he said "—an old Dodge, crossing the I-70 bridge. Have it followed. *Closely*. I must see."

And then he was back in the room, closing the door behind him. After just a moment the image on the screen shifted again, to show an old car crossing one of the bridges. George almost felt himself recognize the driver, but then the sensation slipped away from him. Maybe he had seen the man before, but it couldn't have been more than once.

"I knew," Herman said. "I knew." He was hunched over, watching the screen carefully as the car finished crossing the bridge and bore right, to stay with I-70, the signs said. "It is him—that Munsen man. He's coming for us, just as I knew he would. We will have him too, I think."

The phone was ringing in the other room; Herman left to answer it. This time he closed the door behind him completely, but even so George could hear him. These rooms were soundproofed from the rest of the building, not from each other.

"What do you mean the train isn't stopping where you expected it to?" A pause. "What do you mean our people aren't certain whether or not it will stop in St. Louis at all?" Another pause; this one much longer. And then Herman sighed, and George could hear in that sigh a powerful, barely-contained rage. "We must have them," he said. "We must destroy them. All of them. Divert the plane from its journey toward New York. Do it immediately. Have the pilot detonate his missile over St. Louis. . . . Don't argue with me! Do this now!"

George heard all of it very clearly. Partly because he was standing just behind the door, waiting for Herman to return. And when Herman did, just a moment later, George Stein strangled him to death.

St. Louis, Missouri

All through St. Louis, Luke Munsen worried over the needle of his gas gauge. Somewhere in the thirty miles before the river it had plummeted down from a quarter of a tank, toward empty. It was time to stop and get gas, time to stop and get gas this very instant, if they didn't want to get stuck on the shoulder of the Interstate.

He bit his lip.

The urgency that had taken hold of him told him that he didn't dare stop, not yet. On the other hand, if he got stuck out here they wouldn't be able to move at all any more. Maybe. That was thinking ahead, and the urgency in his gut was too demanding to allow for foresight.

The need to move finally relented, just a little, as they crossed the Missouri River into a suburb call St. Charles. It was a good thing that it did, too; as Luke pulled the car off the interstate, around the cloverleaf, and into the gas station, the car began to cough with the need for fuel. Maybe, he thought as he eased the car to a stop and turned off the engine, the urgency had relaxed exactly because it was the last possible moment. The idea was a little too unsettling for Luke to accept, but even if he couldn't accept it, he couldn't dismiss it, either.

Christine and Andy were both beginning to wake. She yawned, covering her mouth, lifted her hands to her eyes to rub away the sleep; the boy opened the door beside him and stepped out to stretch his legs.

Luke got out and set the pump to fill their gas tank.

"We going to eat breakfast soon? I'm hungry. Growing boy's got to eat, you know."

"Not yet," Luke told him. "No time. We've still got a way to go before we can relax again."

The boy grunted. "Now what do you mean by that, Mr. Luke Munsen? What's such a big hurry?"

Luke frowned, shook his head. "Damned if I know. But it's real enough. This is a bad time to stop. Wouldn't even have stopped for gas if it hadn't been absolutely necessary."

The boy shook his head and smiled ruefully. And then, after just a moment, the smile disappeared, and Andy's eyes

seemed to glaze over. Strange, Luke thought. Not all that
strange—more likely than anything else it meant that he
wasn't getting enough sleep. Luke wasn't a parent, and he
didn't know much about kids, but he did know that they
needed their sleep. Which was just as well—the more Andy
slept, the less likely he was to drag all of them into trouble.

Luke turned to watch the pump's meter. The tank would
be full, soon. Already it had taken in as much gas as it had the
last time he'd filled it—there. The pump-valve disengaged;
the tank was full, or nearly full. He grabbed the pump handle,
squeezed the grip to top off the tank. He let the valve
disengage three more times; decided that he was wasting time
he didn't have. Put the pump handle back into its socket, put
the cap back onto the gas tank, and went to pay.

When he got back to the car, Andy Harrison was gone.

Lake-of-Fire, Kansas

Killing Herman Bonner didn't work.

Not even for a moment.

George Stein hadn't expected it to—hadn't expected it to
leave Herman dead for long. Even as shaken and numb as he
was, he wasn't stupid: if that bacteria, the stuff that kept
reviving him and putting his body together when Herman took
it apart, if that stuff had infected him, it had infected Herman,
too. George could kill him, but he couldn't kill him for long.

Still. Still. It would leave him dead for a time. And more
important was the act of murder itself. George Stein was a
religious man, and a good man, he liked to think. And he knew
that intimate murder was perhaps the vilest sin one man could
commit against another. And he knew that few things in his life
had soothed his soul the way that murder did. It should be a
foul thing, he knew—squeezing and squeezing Herman's thin,
wiry neck, feeling his thumbs press deep into the man's
arteries and windpipes. Watching the skin of Herman Bonner's
face redden deeper and deeper, shift finally toward a blackish
ocher. His eyes bulged out spasmodically—but not *just* involuntarily. Herman's bulging eyes, his contorted features—they
were a mask of terror, not just involuntary movement.

And it was good, because Herman Bonner had hurt
him, and violated him in ways that George Stein had never

imagined that he could be violated. Until he felt Herman go slack and dead, and George Stein began to come back to his senses, and as soon as he did he was ashamed of himself.

He had a lot to atone for. And, it seemed, every day there was more.

That was when he remembered St. Louis.

Dear God, he thought, *Herman's sent them out to destroy that city. I've got to stop them, stop them—*

He looked down at Herman, and saw him still and cooling, discolored, tongue protruding. He was dead, no question. George let his hands relax, stood to walk into the other room, where he'd call *somebody* and get that damnable thing stopped. . . .

He didn't get very far. Before he was even fully erect Herman was all over him, alive because he'd never died, he wasn't human, he wasn't something you could kill—and he was *furious.* . . .

And strong. Stronger than any man his size could possibly be. Before George Stein even knew what was happening Herman Bonner was picking him up and throwing him across the room, and he was flying through the air until his neck and the back of his head smacked all his weight into the opposite wall, breaking his neck.

It was a long time after that before George Stein was alive again.

Inside the Korean
Demilitarized Zone

Bill didn't die, the way it turned out. Not precisely. Nor, precisely, did he survive. Two of the three bullets that tore into his abdomen burst and destroyed vital sweetbreads. Those wounds by themselves would have killed him over the course of hours, if it weren't for the microbes thriving in his blood; as it was, they were no real threat.

It was the third bullet that brought Bill to the borderland between life and death, and held him there for hours. It struck him in the stomach as the force of the first two threw Bill toward the ground—struck, because of the incline of his fall, at an angle. An angle that sent it through Bill's center, instead of toward his spine. And instead of lodging in the hard muscle of his back, as the first two bullets had, this third round sunk itself down into the cavity that held his heart.

And that was the first thing that killed Bill: a heart attack, brought on by bruise and laceration of his heart. Not that Bill knew the first thing about it; by the time the heart attack killed him, he was already insensate, deep in shock.

The second thing that set out to destroy Bill was the acid in his stomach. Which that same third bullet had set loose into his middle abdomen. Where it began to digest his insides, just as though they were food.

Again, it wasn't any damage the microbes couldn't have undone. By the time his heart was ready to attempt to restart itself, five minutes after the heart attack, the peritonitis had done its damage, and the repair had barely begun. And as the blood began to surge through the great arteries in his abdomen, the one nearest his stomach—weak and corrupt from self-digestion—burst. And sent blood gushing all through the space between Bill's sweetbreads.

And Bill died again, instantly.

Still: in its way the burst artery was a blessing. The blood that flowed from it was more than enough to absorb the stomach acid, and even as Bill died an ounce of it was clotting around the bullet hole in his stomach. If it hadn't been for the bullet beside his heart Bill would have begun to recover immediately.

The bullet *was* lodged beside Bill's heart. And when, twenty minutes later, his body tried to restart itself again, that bullet killed him all over again. And killed him for the stupidest reason: Bill's heart was more than strong enough to throb with a gumdrop-sized knot of lead crouched beside it.

It wasn't the presence of the bullet, in and of itself, that killed Bill for the third time in less than half an hour: what killed him was a tiny nick in the bullet's skin. A nick that scratched at the membrane of his heart, tearing it with every beat. Again and again, ever so slightly. Until, after a little less than two dozen beats, the scraping became too much and Bill's heart seized up for the third time.

And the process of rebirth started all over again.

It went on like that, with Bill living and dying and living and dying, for most of three hours.

Never in all that time did Bill's brain starve completely for lack of oxygen; the intermittent beating of his heart was just enough to hold him just above the edge of brain death.

And lying for hours in that place that wasn't life and wasn't death, Bill Wallace began to dream.

Just as Luke Munsen and Christine Gibson had dreamed not long before.

And just as the life that sustained him wasn't entirely life—just as Luke's and Christine's dreams had not entirely been dreams—the visions that came to Bill were something other than mere seeings.

At the very beginning of the dream, Bill was alone in a dim room that was lit by nothing but the candle on the desk in front of him. He sat at that desk, writing a letter with a fine-tip ball-point pen on unruled white paper.

His first awareness was that he'd been writing for a long time. So long, in fact, that he had no memory of ever having started.

He did know what he was writing: a letter to his long-lost love.

Which was a peculiar thing indeed, since he hadn't had a steady girl since he'd been nineteen. And while she'd been a swell girl, he hadn't loved her then and knew that he didn't love her now.

> *It's strange here,* he wrote, *and no fun at all. But if everything goes right I'll be home soon, and then. . . . Please remember always that I love you very, very much. And miss you more than I know words to say.*

And then the dream fell out from under him, and the desk and the letter and the girl he loved but didn't know were all gone, just as though they'd never been.

From the moment the new dream began, Bill knew that he wasn't alone inside it.

Here, looking at him quiet and expectantly, was the beautiful Asian woman. Her hair the color of the onyx his grandma gave him when he turned eighteen. Skin that seemed the color of gold when you mixed it with copper, but wasn't that exactly, because nobody really had skin that looked like metal. Her lips so thin, so fine; and her eyes almost the same blue-black color of her hair, but brighter.

Why was she here? This was Bill's dream, not hers. And when Bill looked at her he knew that she was no dream-phantom; the people in his dreams were never so exact nor so mysterious as the woman who sat there on that grassy hill beside him.

The boy, Jerry Williams, was playing on the summit of the hill beside theirs. And somewhere invisible in the distance was another presence that Bill thought he recognized—though where he recognized it from he couldn't say.

The black-eyed woman was smiling at him.

"Who are you?" she asked him. "Why do I know you?"

Bill blinked. Frowned.

"You followed me," he said. "From down in the tunnels. You remember, don't you? We were all together. You and me and the boy and that dead man. We walked a couple of miles together. Out around that mountain. Into the DMZ."

Now it was her turn to frown. "No," she said. "Of course I remember that. How could I forget the explosions? That man. That same man who killed me. The bodies. . . !" She looked away. "No. I've known you longer than that."

Bill shrugged. "News to me. First I saw of you was in the laboratory, there—just when you was beginning to wake up."

Her lips pursed; she looked uneasy. "Who are you, then? Have I seen you . . . in the news maybe? On television? In the papers?"

Bill thought about that: it was possible. Just barely. He hadn't been around to see it himself, but it was pretty likely that he'd made the papers as the man who'd killed the President. It wasn't anything he wanted to talk about if he could avoid it. "Could be. I might've been in the papers round about a week ago. Any idea," he hesitated, because the question he was about to ask was one that struck him as indelicate, "any idea how long you been dead?"

It was indelicate, too. Had to be, to judge by the way it made her expression so distant. Made her warm black eyes look cool and still as lake water in the starlight.

"No," she said, finally. "It's summer now. I died in early spring. When the trees first began to green with soft small leaves."

And for the longest time she didn't say another word. Didn't make a sound, in fact, until Bill got tired of the emptiness in the air and spoke up himself.

"You got any idea where we are?" he asked her. "Any idea what we're supposed to be doing here?"

The woman shook her head. God she was beautiful.

"Maybe we should get up. Walk around a little. See if there's anything else here besides us and the boy and the hills and the grass."

She hesitated again before she answered. "If you'd like."

They were down in the low between their hill and the boy's when Bill's foot twisted out from underneath him and sent him stumbling into her. For a moment he thought he was going to end up throwing both of them into the grass—but the black-eyed woman was amazingly strong; she caught him up in her arms and before he could understand what was going on she was holding Bill gently as he'd try to hold a child.

Gently as he'd hold a lover.

Her arms were wrapped around him. One reached between his neck and right shoulder. The other supported him from the ribs below his left arm. Her hands met, one above the other, at the center of his spine.

His arm was around her waist; Bill could feel the firm soft skin of her waist through her silk blouse.

There was a dance like this, he thought. And wondered if he'd pulled that dance up out of memory, into his dream. Bill wasn't enough of a dancer to be able to name it, but he'd seen it before, in movies.

"You're stronger than I'd realized," he said.

She laughed. "This is a dream," she said. "A dreamer is always as strong as he lets himself believe."

Bill wasn't any too sure what she meant by that. It didn't matter, much; his head was too full of the sight of her looking so beautiful down into his eyes. He wanted to reach up and kiss her, and—and do whatever felt natural after that. He held back because he didn't know if that was what she wanted, and he wanted her so bad that he didn't know that he could take it if she told him to stop.

And then all of the sudden it didn't matter, because she lowered her face and kissed his lips ever so light, so dry like a feather that the electric power of it sent a chill that washed all through him.

So wonderful, so basic and necessary and needful that Bill wondered how he'd managed to go through an entire life without ever living though that kiss before.

And two things happened, the one right after the other:

The boy screamed, up on the hill before them.

And night fell sudden as a curtain over the sky that had been blue and bright as noon.

"What?" Bill felt the word rise up out of his throat involuntarily. Suddenly he was standing, looking up a hill that was far taller than it had been only a moment ago. The woman he loved was beside him—

No. That couldn't be her. Could it?

She turned to him. Nodded. And he saw her face. And saw that it was her, the same oriental woman he loved who followed him up out of the tunnels below the Korean DMZ.

She was wearing a full suit of armor.

Armor like a knight's armor, at least in spirit. In detail it was modern and sleek; black-painted steel and high-impact plastic from a technophile's dream.

She raised her sword above her head, and lightning struck it, and it glowed. And she told him to follow her up into hell.

That presence again. The same dark, invisible presence he'd felt when this portion of the dream first started.

The presence that he recognized.

Just out of sight in every direction; silent but just on the verge of speaking.

Bill focused himself as he followed his one true love, tried to peel the confused half-memories away from one another, tried to figure out just how it was he recognized that presence—

Did it have anything to do with the reason the boy was screaming, why night had fallen so suddenly all around them? He didn't *think* so—

And that was when he recognized it.

Recognized him.

The dead policeman. The presence was the dead policeman.

And it wasn't the threat; the dead policeman's aura was like a love that protected them from the cold and harshness of the night.

They were almost at the crest of the hill. A step; another. One more and they saw over the rise, saw the boy. . . .

Oh dear God. Bill saw the boy. Saw the thing that menaced him. And horrible as that thing was Bill knew that it was real, because it was too terrible to be anything his own imagination could have made. He knew his limits; knew his faults and his propensities. Nothing Bill would ever imagine would look like that. Never—not even if he lived for a million years.

It had ten heads, each of them fully formed and alive. Reptilian heads, every one viler and hungrier-looking than the one beside it. And from the topmost center of each head there was a horn like the horn of a rhinoceros. Mouths like lions' maws. More than anything else, the creature reminded Bill of a massive, grey-pelted leopard. Those lower legs, those feet, they were the feet of a bear. And it had hands, too—but they were more like the hands of a monkey than they were like a man's.

One of those hands held the boy high in the air by the neck of his t-shirt; dangled him above the hungry sets of jaws as though he were some tasty bit of food—

"The Beast!" his lover shouted. "We have to kill it while we still can!"

And she charged the foul, foul thing, leading with her sword—

And the Beast from Revelation laughed. All ten heads rising toward the moon, baring their throats to the edge of her blade as though it were only inconsequential danger. And his love charged close, drew back her sword to cut—

Before her blade could begin its forward arc the Abomination grabbed her by the wrist of her sword arm, and lifted her, and Bill heard the sound of shattering bone.

And he leapt at the thing himself, armed with nothing but his bare hands, armored by nothing but a t-shirt and denim slacks. He dove for its waist which would have been an underbelly if the damned thing hadn't been erect on its hind legs—trying to push it to the ground where the woman and the boy would have the leverage of their feet to defend themselves. Bill might just as well have been trying to tackle a tree or a concrete lamppost, for all the difference he made; the Abomination wasn't even shaken, and the impact was so bad it'd like to break Bill's neck, and in an instant there were jaws as large and strong as a bear trap clamped into his scalp, trying to crush his skull—

And just as sudden as day had turned to night, Bill was falling to the ground and was the boy and was the woman who he loved, and where the Abomination had been rock and metal against his body there was nothing at all but the ground rushing up to meet him.

There was something else above him now; and Bill looked up to see it.

"Get away, Herman. You haven't got any business here. Not now, and not ever in a place like this." And there in the air where Beast had been was an oval portal like a door into another world, and the Beast was drifting away, evaporating into wisps of vapor thinner than fog.

Bill looked up, into the portal—and found himself staring eye-to-eye with the President he'd murdered.

He shook his head, trying to clear it. "I killed you," Bill said. "What are you doing here? Have you come back to haunt me or something?"

There was a twinkle in the man's eye that wasn't like anything in any picture of President Paul Green that Bill had ever got a look at. It looked unnatural on him—kind of like Boris Badinov from the Bullwinkle cartoons dressed up in a Santa Claus suit. Bill thought that maybe it wouldn't have seemed quite that way if he hadn't seen so many pictures of the guy acting like a raving lunatic.

"No," the President said. "I wouldn't hurt you." And he looked genuinely wounded. Not like a put-on at all, but like Bill's question really had hurt him. Still, Bill was suspicious of the man. Even if he was dead, and dead for good by all accounts. Even if he had saved them from the Abomination from the Book of Revelation. Even if he was acting like some kind of a fairy godfather.

"Then why're you here?"

The President sighed. Patiently.

The boy was on his feet, examining the place where the portal into some other world met the air in this one. "He's here to save us from that *thing*," Jerry said. In a tone of voice that suggested it was a matter of indisputable fact. "Aren't you, Mr. President?"

"No. Herman couldn't have done you any real harm. Not here. No matter how real he seemed, he's got less claim here than he does on the land of the living."

Made no sense at all to Bill. Not one bit.

Jerry harrumphed.

The woman stood. Her clothes were silk now—nothing but fine, dark cloth. She looked Paul Green carefully in the eye, scrutinizing him.

"Then why are you here?" she asked. Her tone of voice

was pleasanter than Bill's had been, but it still wasn't exactly friendly.

"Because there's someplace you must be. All four of you who're with me now. And that place is far, far away from here, and you've little time to get there."

"Is that so?" Bill asked. "Well, I'll tell *you* something, Mister—"

The President held up his hand, to silence Bill. And damned if Bill didn't shut up.

"There isn't time," he said, "to argue. You must wake now. And find a plane. And fly it east, to Kansas. To the Lake of Fire, in Cheyenne County, in the west part of the state."

Behind him, now, was a woman who looked older than time. A dirty woman, dressed in rags. She glowered at the President impatiently. He turned to her, said "Yes, I know, I'm leaving now." Turned back to Bill and the woman and the boy. Smiled, nodded, and vanished into thin air and his portal with him.

For a moment it was day again in that hilly, grassy place—and then they were waking. On the bed of a truck that moved along a dirt road faster than anything ought ever to have moved.

The Major was there. Major Carver. And the boy, and the Oriental woman, and the dead policeman—those three lying on the dirty flatbed along with Bill. Joey and the Major's other assistant, the lieutenant fresh from Annapolis. The only one missing was the private or corporal or whatever he was—the Major's gofer. Chances were, Bill thought, that he was out chasing after something now.

The Oriental woman lay beside Bill, holding his hand.

He looked over at her, saw her watching him, and there was a question in her eyes that Bill couldn't answer, because all he had was a question of his own.

"Corporal Roe," the Major said. She cleared her throat. "Do you always talk in your sleep, Corporal Roe?"

What? Bill blinked, tried to clear his head. "Pardon me, Major? Talk in my sleep?"

"That's what I asked you."

"No ma'am. Not so far as I know. Can't say I'm ever awake to hear it, though."

"And you, young woman? And you, child?" She nodded at the Oriental woman. At the boy.

"No," she said. She sat up to face the Major, let go of Bill's hand.

The boy shook his head.

The Major sighed, and her sigh sounded exactly like the President's sigh.

"It doesn't matter. Much as I wish it could, what I saw here the last two hours can't have had anything to do with talking in sleep."

"What's that, Major Carver, ma'am? What'd you see?" It was the boy who asked the question. Bill wasn't any too sure that he wanted to hear the answer to it.

"I saw you healed," she said. "I'd expected that. You, young man, had a fractured skull; I all but saw it mending." She pointed at the woman. "Two bullets smashed your spine. The third one broke your neck." Pointed at Bill. "Seizures. At least two dozen of them, and every one stopped your heart." She waved her hand to encompass the three of them. "And all through that, dead and alive, the three of you were talking. Talking to each other. And responding." She looked at Bill. "I checked your pulse, damn you. And there wasn't any. You weren't even breathing, but you drew a breath to answer her."

She paused as if she expected one or another of them to say something. None of them did.

"Then, not five minutes ago, Officer Rodriguez over there started speaking. Officer Rodriguez, whose pupils don't even dilate in the dark. Speaking in a voice I couldn't help but recognize. And I think you know what he said."

Bill looked away from the Major. He felt violated; as though he'd found someone eavesdropping on something so private that it was almost sacred.

"What do you want from us?" The Oriental woman asked her. "Why did you listen?"

Bill looked up in time to see the Major scowl. "What did you expect me to do, sew my ears shut? Don't be impertinent, Ms. Park."

"What do you want from us?" Her tone was plainly hostile, now.

The Major stood, furious. Her fist clenched.

"What in the Hell do you think I'm going to do? Where do you think we're going?" She stamped her left foot, and Bill felt the thunder of it on the flatbed through his rump and thighs.

"I'm putting you on a plane. All four of you. And sending you to Kansas."

She didn't bother telling any of them about the tiny tracer bugs she'd planted underneath the skin of their arms.

St. Charles, Missouri

Again! The boy had gone and disappeared again. And he'd chosen the worst possible moment to do it, too. Damn, damn, damn, damn, *damn!* Luke should have known—shouldn't have let that boy out of his sight, not even for an instant. Shouldn't even have let him travel with them. Should have found a nice, suburban neighborhood to drop him off in, someplace quiet and safe, and let him find his own way home.

There wasn't time to go searching for him. Wasn't the first damned moment to spare. But for all the promises Luke had made to himself when the boy had first turned up, for all that he'd promised himself that if the boy made trouble for himself, he'd leave him to it—in spite of all of that Luke didn't even consider leaving without him.

Christine was still sitting in the car, half awake, eyes not quite open.

"Did you see which way he went?"

"Uh—? Who went? Andy, you mean?"

"Yeah. He's disappeared." Luke looked around, tried to spot the boy. Maybe it wasn't as bad as all that; maybe he'd only gone to the men's room. No, there he was—out in that field. Sixty yards away already, and still heading out.

"Christ." This was going to take more time than they had. Long enough that he couldn't just leave the car here and go chasing after the boy; he couldn't leave the Dodge blocking the pumps for as long as it'd take to bring Andy back. Luke got into the driver's seat, started the car, moved it to the edge of the gas station's lot. "You want to wait here—watch the car—or. . . ?"

"No," Christine said. "I'd better come with you."

Whatever the hell *that* meant.

"All right—if that's what you want. We've got to hurry. Are you awake enough to run?"

"I'll manage."

Andy was wandering away from the interstate, into a field

of tall, dry grass beside the state road that the gas station was on. In the distance there were railroad tracks—elevated tracks on a bulwark of earth.

Andy was making a beeline for the train that was stalled on those tracks. Getting farther and farther away from them, even though it didn't look as though he were running.

And there was no time at all for chasing after him. Not a single moment to spare. Luke knew it with his gut, knew it with a deep conviction. And he was right.

He took off running across that field with Christine beside him, running for all he was worth and stumbling over stones and ruts because the grass was too tall and too thick and he was in too much of a hurry to pay attention to where he was going.

Andy was climbing up onto the mound of earth now. Climbing up onto the train tracks and over them. Disappearing from sight.

That was when Luke stumbled into the worst rut in the entire field, a deep, narrow rut dug by rainwater from the palisade off to the left of the field. A rut just wide enough for his foot to stumble into, but too narrow to let it out, and Luke went down, slammed face-first into the grass and the stones and the hard dirt. Christine stopped and reached down to help him up, and Luke got to his feet right away, of course. But it was hard running so shaken up and with his ankle screaming at him the way it was, and even though he ran on it he ran slowly.

Out, across the field. Up onto the railroad mound, and over the tracks. Paused to try to sight the boy—and almost missed him altogether, because he was only a dozen yards away. Standing beside an empty freight car, looking in through the open door.

"C'mon, Mister Luke Munsen," he said. "C'mon over here and see this—you got to *see*."

"See what? Andy Harrison, you little pain in the—" Luke stopped himself "—We've got to get out of here. Got to get back on the road right now, right *now*—" He was marching along the edge of the tracks, between the train and the sheer drop on the other side of it. He was going to grab the boy, grab him and lift him up on his shoulder like a sack of potatoes, and he was going to *haul* him back to the car, and get all three of them the hell *out* of there—

When he got to the door of the freight car, he stopped, stopped dead in his tracks as stunned and in awe as Andy was.

"It's him," Christine said. She was climbing into the car, and her face was a mask of pain and concern. "It's the one from my dream. He's the one the dreams came from, I think."

She walked to that incredible . . . thing, that incredible creature that lay writhing in agony on the floor of the freight car, and she stooped to touch his face, to caress it with love that tried to drain away a little of the pain but couldn't take any of it and maybe Luke thought he ought to be jealous but it just wasn't possible, it just wasn't in him to feel it because he loved that creature at least as much as Christine did and maybe more.

"Luke Munsen? What are you doing here?"

And Luke looked up and saw Ron Hawkins, sitting on the far side of the car beside a filthy dog he almost remembered, and even if it was strange and impossible for him to be here, *God* it was good to see him, see him and remember him, he was a friend and the fact that he was there gave Luke a connection to his still-vague past and God that was a good thing.

"Same damn thing you're doing here, I bet." And remembered the urgency. "We've got to get out of here," he said. "Is he well enough to move? We've got a car not far from here. Got to hurry—there's no time at all."

"Hurry where? From what? There's no way he—" Ron nodded toward the creature "—can just get up and walk away from here, you know. Something's wrong with him, seriously wrong."

"Then we'll have to carry him, that's all. I'm not sure what's going to happen—but . . . I had a dream, maybe an hour ago. A dream? No, not a dream. I was awake, and driving; there's no way you could call it a dream. A vision, maybe?" Luke frowned. "I've been having a lot of dreams like that one, lately. We got to get *away* from here."

Christine looked up at him, away from the creature. "What did you see?"

Luke hesitated a long moment before he answered; he was afraid to say. And cursed himself for spending time they didn't have. "An explosion. An explosion like the film of Hiroshima and Nagasaki that they showed us back in grade school."

Andy was the one who broke the silence that followed.

"Oh shit," he said. "Are we going to get out of here, or what? Come on somebody. Let's carry the big fella out of here."

Ron shuffled over toward the creature, and together he and Christine slid the creature across the floor of the boxcar. Luke and Andy took his shoulders and lifted him out—

By then, of course, it was already too late. The fact was that it had been too late for them to get far enough away from the moment Andy had first set out across the field.

They had the creature halfway out when Luke lost his footing on the steep incline that led down from the train tracks, and he went tumbling ass-first down the stony dry dirt embankment, and Andy and the half-dead creature were only an instant behind since there was no way the boy could support the creature's weight by himself—

And all three of them inside, Ron, Christine, and the dog Tom all came rushing down to help—

And that was the moment that the man in the plane triggered his nuclear warhead over the Mississippi River near Cahokia, just south of East St. Louis, and everything for miles and miles and miles around disappeared in a mushroom cloud of death and fire and subatomic vapor and pain.

Disappeared forever, without leaving behind a trace.

Friday
July Twenty-Second

Transmitted by satellite link
Friday, July 22.

JERUSALEM (REUTERS)—*Israeli forces today pushed the joint Syrian-Iraqi army back across the Jordanian border, and launched a counter attack on Damascus through the Golan Heights. The Israelis claim to already be within 10 miles of the Syrian capital.*

There are also unconfirmed reports that they have cut off lines of supply to the Iraqis and Syrians still fighting near the Jordan River. Israeli officials refused to comment on these reports. One official, who refused to be named, branded them "rumors—unfounded speculation."

Egyptian representatives to the emergency meeting of the Arab League, now taking place in Tunis, condemned the Syrian-Iraqi attack as "criminal aggression." Jordanian King Hassan, attending in person, called for the universal condemnation of Syria, Iraq, and Libya, which he accuses of having supplied Syria with material support. The League as a whole has not yet taken a position on the conflict.

BOOK FOUR

Global Thermonuclear War

Saturday
July Twenty-Third

Transcript of a
conversation between
Herman Bonner and
our agent. Recorded
the morning of 7/23.

H.B.:   *You're on time as always, Tim. I appreciate*
that.

A.:   *Of course I am, Dr. Bonner. What did you*
need from me?

H.B.:   *Several things. Several things. First, though,*
I wanted to check the progress of your missile
program. How is it coming? Will you have
them ready soon?

A.:   *Later this morning, if everything stays on*
time. No reason why it shouldn't. (Pause.)
Which reminds me of something I keep mean-
ing to ask you.

H.B.:   *Yes. . . ?*

A.:   *Well . . . we've never talked about this, so*
I'm not real sure. All these weird things that
keep happening all over the country, all over

> the world. . . . Like all those weird things
> in the newspaper about that animal that's like
> the Beast from Revelation. Like all those
> people who die and come back everywhere.
> Like how the newspapers always seem to
> read these things just the right way. Are we
> involved in that somehow? It almost seems
> like we have to be.

H.B.: Of course we are, Tim. Why do you ask?

A.: I thought so. It's just that I've been wondering. . . .

H.B.: (Impatient.) Wondering what? Speak directly—there's no time for this.

A.: Wondering how come we've got to do all this
if what we really need to do is blow up the
world. To make it clean. I mean—why don't
we just go ahead and drop those bombs, and
to heck with all this stuff? Does it really
make any difference?

H.B.: Ah. That's what you're getting at. I should
have known. Yes, Tim—yes. It does make a
difference. All the difference there can be.
The fate of the world was written a long time
ago, written by a hand far mightier than
yours or mine. If we are to have any hope of
accomplishing our ends, we must produce
that fate as nearly as possible. Otherwise we
are doomed to fail.

A Post-It note mounted in the center of the page obscures
what lies below. It reads as follows:

> When are we going stop this man, General?
> We're left with almost no time at all. And we've
> already lost St. Louis. I gather that our man is
> actually arming these bombs? Why, for God's sake?
> If the Air Force isn't up to the job, I'll march into this
> base and strangle him and Bonner with my bare
> hands. I don't care if they've got the man who's
> legally our President with them. We need to put this
> to an end.

Below this, written in a finer, more careful hand:

> *Show a little patience, Ben. We're working on it.*
> *Our man is in fear for his life. If he sabotaged*
> *Bonner, the man would kill him. And have someone*
> *else do the work. At least he's feeding us information,*
> *and thank God for that.*

Lake-of-Fire, Kansas

By Saturday afternoon, George Stein had begun to pray that God would let him die. Die forever and for real and permanently. His heart *needed* an ending; the scars that Herman Bonner had left on his soul over the last two days were too deep to ever heal. His shame twisted him too hard, too far; there was no way he could ever grow easy with himself again. George Stein didn't just want to die—he wanted more. He wanted the death that atheists see waiting for them: pure and sweet oblivion.

A total and final end for body and soul.

It was a vile thing to pray for. George Stein prayed for it all the same.

Not that it mattered. If God heard his prayers, he didn't heed them. Three times since the sun had come up this morning he'd felt the life bleed away from him through broken arteries, and each time he'd woke only a short while later in coagulating pools of his own blood. And looked up, reborn, to see Herman Bonner leering at him.

Herman kept him chained much more carefully now. George had spent most of the day chained to that filthy, blood-crusted bed, each leg, each wrist bound individually. Then, half an hour ago Herman had kicked him till he woke, taken his chains from the bedposts, and carried him to the front of the room. George would have tried to fight him off if he'd had the strength, but he didn't have it—he was so weak, in fact, that he hadn't even had the spirit to try to fight.

"I want you to see this, George," Herman said. And he hoisted George up toward the ceiling, and looped the chains that bound his wrists into a wide, heavy-gauge, white-painted hook—a hook George hadn't noticed before, and whose original purpose he couldn't imagine. Herman left him dangling like a side of beef in a meat locker. "It's the culmination of everything we've worked on together for years. It's important that you see."

George grunted. He didn't want to see whatever it was Herman Bonner wanted to show him, and anyway there wasn't strength enough in his neck to lift his head to look out the window.

Maybe Herman understood that, or maybe he was just impatient. Regardless, it wasn't a sight he was about to let George avoid; he put his hand under George's chin, pressed his head back and up until it was wedged between his arms and George could see. . . .

George had thought himself beyond pain and feeling. Thought that there was nothing left to do but die, and that there was nothing more Herman could do, to him or otherwise, that could stir him. Until he saw what Herman Bonner was doing, and the bottom fell out from under his stomach all over again.

The landing field outside the window was filled with transport planes—twenty of them, at least. And each of the planes had a missile attached to it, or in process of being attached.

Dear God.

It was the end of the world Herman was planning. And there wasn't a damned thing George Stein could do about it.

"Apocalypse, George. *The Apocalypse.*" Herman ran his fingers through his hair, preening. Let out a long, satisfied sound that was somewhere between a groan and a sigh. "Enough to destroy a score of the world's largest cities, and if all of them detonate at once—perhaps! perhaps!—the damage to the world's tectonic structure will start that *final* cataclysm!" His eyes were filled with something—lust? No, not lust. Lust was a purer and more human thing. "So soon . . . it's been so long, and now so *soon*. . . ."

George tried to speak, but at first all that came from his throat was the sound of moving phlegm. When he tried again, his voice was faint and unsteady, but the words came out, at least. "Why, Herman? Why would you want to destroy the world God made?"

The . . . *desire* in Herman's eyes brightened, and after a moment he began to laugh. "It really isn't in you, is it, George? If you can ask the question, how could you ever understand the answer?" And he lashed out, suddenly, with his fist, pounding George's diaphragm so hard that he felt the pressure squeeze his heart.

It was quiet for a long time after that; George wanted to speak, wanted to respond, but there was no way he could with the wind knocked so far out of him. It came back slowly. Too slowly, in thin ragged breaths that weren't enough to let him speak. And when he finally could speak, the words were a pale whisper.

"God loves you, Herman," George said. "He loves us all. He'll still forgive you if you only let him."

And Herman laughed and laughed and laughed.

And that was faith, damn it, it was the most important thing in George Stein's life—the most important thing there ever could be, if you asked George.

No matter how important faith was to George Stein, Herman Bonner's laugh made him ashamed of it and of his words. That shame was the worst sacrilege George could imagine.

Death would be better. Much better. It *was* something to pray for.

Herman smiled at him, hungrily. "You want to die, don't you, George? You'd like me to strap you to one of my rockets—to let the cleansing nuclear fire erase you from this world forever." He moved close, so close that George could feel and smell his warm, fetid breath. So intimate that it made George want to feel ill, but he hurt so bad already that it was hard to tell if it added anything. "Yes. You do want that, don't you, George? It's too bad. It's the one foul thing I can't give you. I *want* you here with me—want you here to see my final solution for this world. You've been so much a part of it . . . it would be a poor thing to lose you now. A poor thing indeed."

Herman was . . . touching him. Intimately, painfully.

"They're dead, you know. The ones who were coming for me. Reduced to subatomic dust in my wondrous explosion. There's nothing, now. No one. To interfere, or threaten or—stop my plans. Of all those who could oppose me, George, only you are left alive. And you're no threat to me." Again, the ravenous smile. "You're my darling, George. My pet."

And George was afraid and ashamed and he wanted death

with a need almost as strong as the need in Herman Bonner's eyes. "Stop, Herman. Please. Stop."

Herman didn't stop. Instead he did something so physically excruciating that George nearly blacked out. "George— do you know that I lied to you, George? I did. It pains me to admit it, but I did lie. There is still one threat left. An entire army of a threat. Three divisions of conventional soldiers and airmen, sent here from other bases in the Midwest. Camped not twenty miles from here, just beyond the Nebraska border. They've been there for two days, now."

Three divisions? If the real army was here three divisions strong then it was all over. Wasn't it? It was, unless Herman had something more up his sleeve.

"They don't worry me, darling. Do you know why?"

George Stein might have answered if it hadn't been for the pain. Pain so intense that he could barely hear through it, let alone speak.

"Exactly because they *have* been there for two days. Something in the Pentagon has gotten stuck, George. Jammed so thoroughly that no one there can act—only watch. Watch as they wait for me to bring on the end. Not that I'm relying on them to be such fools, you understand. Not for a moment. I've called our own people in from all over the nation. We'll have more than enough to match them, man for man."

And then the agony was too much, and George blacked out, and though that should have given him some relief, what it gave him instead was an hour of nightmares.

Cheyenne County, Kansas

They were a million miles from nowhere on a dirt road in Kansas when the tires finally began to go. Ron had listened to Luke Munsen worry about those tires for at least five hundred miles. He kept wondering why Luke didn't just pull into a gas station and get them replaced. Ron had even come out and said it to him directly, once: "Why don't we pull over and have somebody take a look at them? I've got my credit cards, if money's a problem."

Luke hadn't quite ignored him. His answer wasn't anything that Ron could parse, though: "There isn't time," he'd said. Said it so quietly that Ron'd had to listen hard to hear him. "They'll hold out long enough. They'll have to."

Loud, harsh sounds were coming from the tires. Especially the left rear—the tire all but directly under Ron's seat. Luke was driving too damned fast for these dirt roads. That was part of it, at least.

The car didn't have a spare. If he didn't slow down soon the tires would blow, and then they'd be slowed down permanently. Slowed to a walk.

Andy Harrison and Tom the dog were getting out of hand again; there wasn't room in this car for that boy and that dog and Ron's peace and quiet, too. Ron wasn't sure there was room enough in the whole world.

Christine, up in the front seat, smiled ruefully and sighed, as though she were thinking exactly the same thing. The creature seemed to grin in his sleep, which had grown a lot less fitful over the last hour or two. Luke Munsen didn't seem to notice—the boy, the dog, the creature, or anything else.

Luke had been like that, all urgent and bothered, ever since that bag lady had woke the lot of them, back on the edge of the ruin of St. Louis. She'd woke them like some fairy godmother in a fable Ron had long since forgotten, using her grungy cane like a wand to touch each of them gently, just above the eyes.

"Wake up," she said again and again as she woke them, "time to wake and face the world. There isn't time to be a layabout!"

The bag lady. The same one who'd handed him the comic book in the parking lot of the Burger King a week and a half—and a couple of lifetimes—before. Ron was the first she woke, and he watched rheumy-eyed and confused as she moved among them. It was as strange a sight as any he could think of seeing: a strange, mottled, filthy old woman who was somehow at the same time some kind of an angel. Ron Hawkins didn't understand it, and he didn't for a moment pretend to himself that he did.

She came to the creature last of all, and she hesitated beside him. "You," she said. "You're the special one. The one who's hurting so." Her voice was sad, almost defeated. "There's nothing I can do to help you. Nothing I can do to ease your sleep." And she bent down to kiss him on the forehead. Stood, sniffled, and turned to head away.

It was Luke who tried to get her to stop; he had more of his wits about him than anyone else.

"Hey," Luke called, "wait. Who are you?" He stood and tried to follow the woman, but he was still too groggy; he stumbled over his own feet. "Why are you here? Why did you hand me that comic book, back in New York?"

The woman didn't answer him. Not really. She turned back for a moment, looked at them, shook her head with an expression that might have been sadness mixed with faint reproach. "You need to go west. Much farther west—to the Lake of Fire, and on beyond it." Coughed, long and hard, as though she were bringing up a lot of mucus. "You're safe, for now at least. They think you're dead." Sighed. "None of them really know very much about the size of an atomic blast."

Then she turned again, and continued away from them across the scorched grass, toward the bluff covered with withered trees. Ron watched her, dumbstruck, until she disappeared from sight at the top of the bluff; in the corner of his eye he could see Luke watching her, too.

When she was gone Ron turned and looked at Luke. "She gave you one of those comic books too?" Luke was still staring up at the top of the bluff, even though the old woman was no longer anywhere in sight.

"Uh." Luke blinked. Turned toward Ron. "Yeah. She did. You too? One of those strange little comic books from the people who took over the network?"

Ron nodded.

A long, quiet space. "I wonder how in the hell she gets around. Can't imagine her driving, and there hasn't been time for her to have walked here from New York City."

Ron shrugged.

The young, dark-skinned boy was on his feet now, standing in front of them. "So, Mister Luke Munsen," he said, "we going to get on the road like the lady said, or aren't we?"

"Andy. . . !" Luke sounded more than a little annoyed. Exasperated might have been a better word. He seemed to catch himself, and when he spoke again his calm seemed forced. "Yeah. You're right. We ought to get going." He looked around, counting heads. "There's room in the car—just barely, but there's room. If it's still in one piece, that is."

Andy was staring at Ron. "Who're you?" he asked. "You were that guy up there with the creature, weren't you? I saw you on TV."

Ron didn't know what to say, exactly; the question threw him off balance and embarrassed him a little—not that he could think of any reason why it should embarrass him. "I'm Ron Hawkins, and that was me inside the train. Why—?"

Andy cut him off, which was just as well, since Ron didn't have any idea what the rest of the question was supposed to be: "I'm Andy Harrison, and I'm here to keep an eye on Mister Luke Munsen and his lady-friend here, Christine. How come you didn't catch up with us sooner? It sure took you long enough."

"What?" Ron found himself getting even more confused. "Catch up with you? I don't think we could have caught up with anybody if we'd tried. We walked here from Tennessee."

The boy shook his head; he looked skeptical. "Don't try to tell me that you walked here from anyplace. I saw you there inside that train car, traveling like some bum in a hobo movie. You can't fool me that easy." He eyed Ron impatiently. "You going to tell me or not—how come you took so long getting up with us?"

Ron sighed. Coughed. He was beginning to get it, he thought. The point was that there wasn't any point. The answer was that there wasn't any answer. "Okay then," he said, "I guess I'm not going to tell you. And if I'm not, I might as well be up front about it, right?"

Luke seemed to be enjoying himself; Ron got the feeling that his friend had been through this before.

The boy looked just a little off balance himself. Or maybe *deflated* was a better word. "I guess so," he said. And spotted Tom the dog. "Hey, what's your dog's name, huh, Mr. Ron? He looks like a real cool dog."

"Tom. Come on over here, huh, Tom? Somebody wants to meet you." The dog stood, with some considerable effort, and walked toward them unevenly. "You know how to introduce yourself to a dog, don't you, Andy?"

The boy glared at him with eyes that could have turned water into stone. "Of course I do. What do think I am, stupid?" Frowned. "How about you tell me how *you*'d go about it, though? Just for comparison purposes."

Ron grinned. "Like this:" he said, and held his hand out

toward the dog, "so that he can sniff the back of your hand, get to know who you are." The dog was licking Ron's fingers. "If he's okay about that, you can pat him on the head and get to know him a little better."

"Huh. How about that." And then, "Cut that out," when the dog started licking his arm halfway up the elbow.

Luke slapped Ron's shoulder, not too hard. "Come on. Let's go get the car. Then we can drive it back here."

Ron nodded. He followed his friend up the embankment at an angle that took them to the near end of the train.

It was good to hear voices again—real, honest-to-God voices speaking in English that he could hear with his ears. It wasn't something he'd realized he'd missed.

When he got near the top of the embankment he saw that the train lay out of kilter in its tracks—derailed, but not fallen over. A few paces ahead of him Luke was saying "Dear God," and for half an instant Ron thought he was swearing at the damage to the train. Then Ron caught a glimpse of the city of St. Louis, over the embankment and across the Missouri River, and as soon as he saw it he knew that whatever was wrong with the train didn't amount to anything at all.

Fire.

Fire across the river that stretched from one edge of the horizon to the other, leaping, bursting towers of flame that spun off into fiery twisters and dust devils that spread the damage like a plague.

"Sweet Jesus."

Ron stepped forward, caught a glimpse of the far side of the train with the corner of his eye. Saw the brown paint that had covered the railroad cars was now scorched—burned and blister-peeling in fist-size flakes.

"We'd better get to it," Luke said. "No telling how long it'll be before it spreads across the Missouri."

And then they were off, trotting across the field that lay before them, toward an old gas station. Into a weathered Dodge in its parking lot. The car's paint was blistered all along its rear—which had faced into the blast—but otherwise it looked whole to Ron. Luke took a good look at the thing and seemed to come to the same conclusion.

Five minutes later they'd all crammed themselves into the Dodge, and Luke was wheeling the car up onto I-70.

And they were all heading west, toward Kansas.

Near Flagler, Colorado

Leigh Doyle got lost on the road from Denver to Cheyenne County.

It was an incredible thing, damn near: there wasn't road enough to get lost on out here. And the President's directions had been so clear. "Take Interstate 80 East from Denver, across the state and into Kansas. Get off at Kanorado, just over the Kansas border. Take the county road north, on up through St. Francis, and past it three miles until you see a dirt road open up on your right. Old Road. The name is written large on a wooden sign; you won't be able to miss it. Follow that road until you come to the edge of the Lake of Fire. When you get there, park the rental car and wait. After a while, you'll know what you have to do.

"It sounds like an awful trip, I know—driving from Denver to Kansas. There's a little airport not thirty miles from where you're going, but you won't be able to find a plane that'll take you there. It's too close to the . . . to the site of the explosion. Even getting to Denver will be difficult. And anyway, the drive won't be that bad. Two hundred fifty miles of wide, empty freeway—you ought to be able to cover it in an afternoon."

That was all the time it would have taken, too, if she hadn't stopped to get herself a soda in Flagler. Such a little town—it ought not to have been possible to get lost in it. The grocery where she'd stopped had been just out of sight of I-70, and when she got out she hadn't been sure whether the way back was left or right. She guessed wrong, of course. Even that wouldn't have been a problem if she hadn't been so caught up in thinking about the wild goose chase she was on that she'd driven twenty miles before she realized what she'd done.

It was a wild goose chase, too.

Had to be.

The call that started it had come two days ago, while Leigh was sleeping late in a clean soft bed in a tourist hotel in Helsinki. Yesterday someone in Moscow had finally decided to deport her, along with the rest of the Westerners in that barracks-cum-prison. They'd been disorganized about it, and the plane had taken forever getting off the ground, and then after it finally landed the Finns spent three hours deciding whether they were going to let any of them into the country. Which they did, finally, when the American ambassador came down and vouched for all of them. She hadn't got to the hotel until late, and when she did she slept the sleep of the dead. It'd been the first good sleep she'd had in a week, what with the lousy quality of the bed in the Russian hotel, and then the nasty little mattresses in the barracks.

When the call came, at seven, she'd been so deep asleep that she'd almost ignored it. But whoever it was was persistent, and after the seventh ring Leigh had reached over and lifted the receiver off its cradle and mumbled into it something that wasn't quite a word.

"Hello? Miss Leigh Doyle? This is Paul Green, the President of the United States. I need to speak to you."

That'd woke her up, real fast. "What? Who?" *Why me? What would the President want with me?* "How can I help you, Mr. President?"

Mind you, now: Leigh Doyle had sworn that she was going to start reading the newspaper headlines. At least for the duration of the crisis. Avoiding them had got her into trouble that was above and beyond what she wanted to live with. All the same she hadn't seen a newspaper since she'd got into the country; there had been no time for that last night.

She had no way of knowing that the President she was talking to had died—died forever—more than a week before.

She had no way of knowing that a ghost had called her on the phone.

"There is a mission, Miss Doyle, that I need you to undertake for me. A peculiar mission, but a vital one nonetheless. And it is a mission that only you can accomplish."

Leigh caught sight of herself in the mirror, looked away. Rubbed the sleep from her eyes.

"I don't understand, Mr. President. What kind of a mission? And why me?" What was she saying? This was the *President* she was talking to. She recognized his voice. A body couldn't go around saying *no* to her own President. Just couldn't. "I mean, of course I'll do whatever you need me to do, but. . . ."

"Good," he said. "I knew I could count on you, Leigh." How could he know a thing like that, Leigh wondered. It seemed like an impertinent question, and anyway there wasn't time to ask it, because the President barely even paused before he said, "I need you to take a plane to Denver, Colorado. The earliest flight you can find. A nonstop, if you can find one. When you land go directly to the rent-a-car desk, get yourself a car, and drive out to Cheyenne County, Kansas." Then he'd started giving her the directions. When he'd finished, the phone had gone dead almost immediately.

A busy man, our President, Leigh had thought, and she'd showered and she'd dressed and gone down for breakfast.

Where there'd been a copy of the *International Herald Tribune* waiting at her table. And right there, on page one, was the story about the Memorial Service in Washington.

The Memorial Service for President Paul Green—the very man she'd talked to, not twenty minutes before.

She'd scanned the story quickly, followed the jump to the middle of the paper, where the back story told her that Green had died the week before in an airplane wreck, that the fire that followed had been so intense that no one had been able to produce a body for the funeral.

By the time she finished the story, Leigh had pretty well decided that she was going out of her mind. There were other bizarre stories, too—stories of dead people rising up out of their coffins. The kind of stories she'd have picked up on immediately for the *Interlocutor*. Stories that she'd never have expected to find in a paper like the *International Herald Tribune.* They were filled with so many specifics, so many infinitesimal facts, and so little hyperbole that it seemed as though they had to be true. For a moment Leigh almost thought that the phone call from the dead President must have had something to do with those stories—but then she read through it all again, and noticed that there was one thing that all the reports of resurrection had in common: a cadaver. And it was pretty plain, rereading the story of the President's death, that the accident that had killed him had left behind no corpse.

She paid her check with a credit card, got up and left the hotel coffee shop. Most of her meal still lay uneaten on her plate.

She walked deliberately to the hotel lobby, where the desk clerk stood patiently waiting for the end of his shift.

The telephone switchboard was directly behind him.

"I had a phone call this morning," she said, "didn't I? At

about seven a.m. It would have been long distance. From overseas."

He raised an eyebrow. "You are in room. . . ?"

"It's—" she fished through her purse, found her key "—239."

He glanced at the switchboard. "No, madam. You've had no calls. The morning has been very quiet, and I would have remembered connecting an overseas call." He coughed. "There were twenty minutes this morning—yes, around seven—when the phone in 239 was off hook. No call was made. I thought perhaps you had jostled the receiver in your sleep. I was about to send the bellman up to let you know when you set it back into its cradle."

Leigh could feel how the skin of her face was flush with embarrassment. "That isn't possible. How would you know if I just picked up the phone?"

"Our switchboard, madam. A small red light goes on when you lift your phone. When you make you connection the color of the light becomes green."

I didn't imagine that call. I know I didn't.

"Perhaps . . . it's possible you were dreaming. Could you have lifted the handset in you sleep? I have seen it happen before. Our guests dream vividly at times."

He thinks I'm out of my mind. And the embarrassment that colored Leigh's cheeks turned to anger. It wasn't any dream. She knew when she was dreaming, damn it. She said "No," and she turned and walked away angrily before the clerk could say another word.

Leigh had gone back to her room, and there she'd sat staring nervously at the wall for most of twenty minutes. How could a dream give directions that detailed? There they were, on the hotel-supplied telephone note pad, where she'd scribbled them as the President spoke.

Was she going out of her mind?

Finally she'd decided that it didn't matter. If the President of the United States needed her badly enough to telephone her from the far side of eternity, then it must be that he needed her for something important. And if she was crazy she was crazy, and there was nothing to be done about it, and what did it hurt to spend the last few days of her vacation in the West? It hurt nothing at all, of course.

And Leigh had packed her bags, checked out of the hotel,

and got a cab to the airport. By noon she'd be on an airplane flying over the Atlantic.

Cheyenne County, Kansas

That was where they were now: deep in Kansas. Almost to the far edge of it, if Ron's guess was right; he'd seen so many miles and miles of flat, dry, monotonous farmland roll by that he was certain the state couldn't possibly go much longer. Maybe that was wishful thinking. Ron was pretty sure it wasn't; Luke Munsen had a feverish look in his eye—eager, desperate, and fearful—and Ron suspected it meant that whatever it was that guided him was becoming . . . immanent.

Whatever that meant.

Off to the right now, in the distance, was the Lake of Fire Luke had been mumbling about since they'd set off. A pretty spectacular sight. All the same, he avoided looking at it; he wasn't sure, but he thought he remembered hearing that radiation was dangerous to the eyes. Ron decided he'd be happier once they were clear of it.

The noise from the left rear tire was getting even worse. Ron leaned forward, tapped Luke's shoulder. "Say, Luke," he said, "don't you think you ought to slow down a little, maybe? That tire isn't going to hold out much longer."

And exactly at that moment, exactly on cue and before Luke could respond, the tire blew. Spectacularly, exploding like a shotgun all at once as its overheated, overpressed air burst out and tatters of decayed rubber flew out in every direction, and the force of it and the fact that there was nothing but the rim to support the axle sent them veering off to the right. Luke, to his credit, was braced for it; he managed to keep the steering wheel more-or-less under control.

Until the stress got to the point where it was too much for the three remaining tires, and two more of them blew out from under the car all but simultaneously. After that it didn't matter whether Luke had the steering wheel under control or not; there was nothing left to steer, and the car was skidding on its frame across the packed dry clay that was the road's surface.

A moment later it was over, and they'd managed to come to a halt without the car turning over. How they got that lucky Ron was never sure.

.   And Luke, in the front seat, was cursing a blue streak.

"Damn, damn, damn, damn, *damn*." He punctuated each *damn* with his fist on the steering wheel. Ron winced for him, to watch it.

"Hey," Andy said, "that was fun. You want to do it again?" Beside him, the dog had regained his footing on the front seat-back; his mouth was wide open and panting.

Christine turned back and looked at the boy; shook her head and frowned. Ron saw her mouth *Not now*. Which, all things considered, seemed to Ron to be pretty good advice.

Luke threw his door open, got out to take a look at the car. Which was pointless, of course; they didn't have one spare, let alone three. Even if they'd had them it likely wouldn't have solved the problem—Ron was pretty sure the car's suspension would be shot after the way it'd dug into the clay.

"Look at that, hey, Tom-dog? Right over there. Out in the middle of Nowhere, Kansas, and we managed to have a wreck in front of the only cemetery for a million miles in any direction. Just like home, huh?"

Luke was out in front of the Dodge, now, cursing a blue streak. Ron glanced over at the boy, a little uneasy that Luke was talking like that in front of him. If Andy was hearing it, Ron couldn't see any sign of it. Well, he thought, likely the boy'd heard worse in school. Still, Luke shouldn't talk like that in front of a child—it set a bad example. Whatever it was that had lodged so inside him, Ron decided, had to be fierce. It wasn't like Luke to be so ill-considered.

Luke came back around the side of the car, looked inside long and slow, almost as though he were surveying them one at a time. "There isn't time for this," he said. "There's no time at all." He looked at Christine, frowned. Bit his lip. "Can you wait here? Watch the creature, and the boy?" He nodded toward the creature. "We can't just leave him here alone. He's too important. Somehow. Don't ask me how." Sighed. He looked ashamed of himself, Ron thought; the realization made him sad.

Ron could see Christine in the rear-view mirror, looking worried. She smiled anyway, and she said, "If that's what you need, I'll do it."

And Luke nodded, and thanked her. Looked at Ron and nodded again. "Come on, then," he said, and Ron realized that Luke wanted him to get out of the car and hike off into the distance with him, and found himself a little annoyed because it wasn't a thing he'd volunteered for, or even been asked to do. Didn't even know what it was they were going to do when they got wherever they were going. He had a commitment that had brought him here, it was true, but that commitment was to the creature, not to some inscrutable vision festering between Luke Munsen's ears.

Which, in the end, was probably more or less the same thing. Luke and the creature were both drawn by the same force—near as Ron could tell, at least. If Luke needed him, it was likely an important thing. And if the man was rude about how he asked for what he needed, it still wasn't worth arguing with him about it.

Ron shook his head, opened the door beside him, got out of the car and stood. Luke was already half a dozen yards down the road, heading toward the setting sun, into God-knew-what. Ron followed, but he didn't hurry to catch up.

Cope, Colorado

When Leigh Doyle realized that she'd gone twenty miles in the wrong direction, she'd pulled the car over onto the shoulder of the road, opened the glove compartment, and took a good look at the map that the rent-a-car company had given her. Fished through her purse until she found the directions she'd jotted down after her conversation with President Green. Compared them with the map.

She was on a state road that would, in another five miles, take her to US Highway 36. Which ran east and west. In one direction toward Denver; in the other toward Kansas . . . and the first Kansas town it ran through was St. Francis. Ha! The President's directions would take her, penultimately, right through St. Francis. There wasn't any need to backtrack. All she had to do was make a right on 36, and she'd be set.

She closed the glove box, left the map sitting on the passenger seat. Put the car in gear and started off again, feeling like she'd made a real triumph over the cussedness of the world.

Everything went just fine, too, until she got to Cope,

Colorado, and found that the bridge over the dry Arikaree River had collapsed the night before.

When she got to the place where Highway 36 fell away into the empty bed of the Arikaree, Leigh Doyle got out of the rent-a-car. Breathed in the warm-dry East Colorado air that was so alien to her Westchester County lungs. And let the breath sift out in a sigh that wasn't so much exasperation as it was weariness. Jet lag mixed with the unsettling suspicion that she'd lost her mind. Suspicion, hell—just now it seemed pretty damned likely that she'd taken leave of her senses. And that was Leigh's own estimation; she was afraid to guess what anyone else would think of her if they knew she'd flown halfway around the world at the request of a man who no longer existed.

She walked past the barricades, up to the edge of the broken bridge. And saw that the river was dry; and not very deep. Twenty minutes and she'd be able to climb down the near bank, cross the sandy-powdery bed, and scramble up the bank opposite. Even in her high-heeled shoes.

There was no way the car was going to get across. Sure, she could get it down there—and maybe it'd even be intact when she reached the river bed. Even if it was, there wasn't any way it was going to get back up again. Not in either direction.

The only thing to do was head back, all the way back to the interstate. Damn. Leigh didn't care at all for retracing her steps. She went back to the car, ducked in, took out her map. . . .

Well.

Maybe it was possible.

Possible not to have to go all the way back; there was another way around the bridge. It meant going back along the road that had taken her to 36, and turning left at the road she'd jogged by on the way up here. Taking that road for a mile or two until she got to state road 59—which would let her out onto US 36 again, not ten yards away from the far side of the bridge.

Well, why not?

And Leigh started off. Positive and satisfied and feeling triumphant again. She was going to get where she was going, and she was going to use her own good sense to get there, and to hell with the broken down bridge and the dry river and being out in the middle of a nowhere that she'd never seen before.

And she kept feeling that way, long after she missed the turn at SR 59 without even noticing. In fact, it didn't even occur to Leigh that she'd got herself into a mess until five miles after the pavement on the road she traveled had given out.

Dirt roads didn't bother her; in their way they were prosaic. What stopped Leigh and her car dead in their tracks was when the road gave out completely, and suddenly she was driving through a fallow field thick with grass so tall it blocked her windshield.

*In Transit by Air
over the Western Rockies*

For Bill Wallace, the flight home from Korea wasn't as lonely as the flight out had been.

Lonely or otherwise, though, it was every bit as unpleasant.

First there was the dead policeman, alive and unalive and lurking in the background haunting them, like some ghost made out of flesh and blood. And then the boy: innocent and plainspoken; charming. After a few hours his charm and his innocence became things that grated on Bill. If anyone had asked him why that was, Bill couldn't have answered the question. Maybe the boy was annoyingly syrupy. And maybe the problem was that Bill was in a bad mood. Which he was.

He was in a wicked mood, in fact. And that mood didn't have a thing to do with the boy or the undead cop or being stuck for most of a day inside a transport plane.

What it did have to do with was the Oriental woman. Her, and Bill himself.

Bill wasn't sure what he was supposed to feel about that woman. Besides attracted to her, that was—being attracted to a woman who looked like that was something that came as natural to Bill as breathing did. He'd been attracted to her from the very first moment he'd seen her, in fact, back when she was still as vacant and stunned-looking as the dead policeman. That wasn't the trouble: the trouble was the dream he'd had.

The dream they'd both had.

About how he loved her, and how he'd always loved her, and how she was the one true lover of his soul.

The one true lover of his soul.

Even the words were scary, because they weren't his words—Bill wouldn't ever use words like that. Not on his own. "The one true lover of his soul"—? Phooey. Crap. BS. What kind of man went around thinking words like that? Bill was pretty sure that he didn't ever want to find out. What was Bill supposed to do, feeling like that about a woman he didn't hardly even know? And she didn't look any more comfortable about the situation than Bill felt. Bill would walk by her on his way to get a cup of coffee, say, or going to the can. And he'd pass that beautiful woman who was his and who wasn't, and he'd want to lean over and kiss her real gentle on her forehead, just like he always did. Only he never had, and probably never would, and each time he only barely managed to stop himself before he made a fool of himself.

Confusing. Just like it was confusing when half the time she looked like she wanted him to hold her, and half the time she looked like she was going to haul off and slug him if he tried it. The whole situation made Bill feel like he wanted to crawl out of his skin and hide some place. Not that there was anyplace inside a transport plane that a body could hide, with or without his skin.

Bill yawned, tried to pretend that he didn't feel like he did. Looked out the window. Where were they, now? Over land, which meant they were well on their way. Mountainous land; dry, sharp hills pointed skyward toward them like a sea of knives. Had to be the Rockies. Where was it they were going? Kansas? Kansas was pretty far west. If they were lucky, they'd be there soon. And Bill could get out of this damn plane and get himself some privacy. Sort out all the nonsense running around inside his head.

He turned away from the window. Yawned again. Caught sight of the dead policeman, who was drooling again. Damn it, why didn't somebody clean him up? How could they let him soil himself that way? His line of thinking got about that far before Bill remembered that there wasn't any "they" aboard this plane. Just Bill and the woman and the boy and the cop.

And, up in the cockpit, two pilots and a navigator. Of all those people, Bill was the only one you could say had a responsibility to look after the dead policeman. He was an enlisted man, after all. And if there was anybody who ought to be seeing after scut work, it was an enlisted man. The folk up front were officers, and anyhow they were busy. The boy and the woman were civilians. Or maybe the woman wasn't; but if she belonged to any kind of outfit, it likely wasn't the US Air Force.

All of which came down to the fact that Bill needed to get out of his seat and clean the cop. He unbuckled his seat belt, got up, walked back, got himself a couple paper towels from the john. Wet them in the sink so they'd clean the crusty-dry part of the drool off the cop's chin. Went back to the cabin and spent the better part of five minutes cleaning solidified spittle off the policeman's face.

They passed into a cloud bank just a little bit before Bill finished; by the time he was done the cabin was dusk-dark. Dark enough that he was half afraid he'd stumble over his own feet and break his neck when he went back toward the john to stuff the towels into the waste bin. Maybe he ought to go up front, Bill thought. Get one of those pilot-types to turn the lights up.

Yeah.

He dumped the paper towels, started back toward the cockpit—and the plane hit turbulence. And the floor started moving around underneath Bill's feet. The heck with the lights and talking to the crew; it was time to get himself sat down. Time to put his seat belt *on*. Be glad that they were still in the air, and not plowing into some mountain in the middle of nowhere.

Then suddenly they were falling, and instead of jumping around underneath his feet, the floor wasn't anywhere that Bill could find.

Oh shit.

And he knew that he was in some kind of trouble.

I'm going to break my effing neck, he thought. Any instant now his head would hit the ceiling, and his skull would bust wide open. Splat. Brains all over the place like shit in a pig-pen. And in an hour or a day or a week Bill would come back to life a vegetable drooling brain-dead deadman like the cop.

Oh boy.

And he kept waiting to hit. The roof. The ceiling. The

floor. Walls, anything. He didn't hit any of them, because the
damned plane was still falling, which meant that Real Soon
Now they all *would* be hitting one of those damned mountains—

Which was when the law of gravity came back into effect.
And Bill went down, hard, break-your-bones hard. Not toward
the floor because he wasn't over the floor any more. What Bill
came down into, in fact, were the arms of the—of the woman.
The oriental woman who he loved and didn't know and if he
knew her name damned if he could remember it.

Real embarrassing. Bill would like to broke his back on
the armrest of her seat if she hadn't caught him. God she was
strong. Arms like a wrestler's, even if they did look like a
woman's arms. What kind of a woman was she? Her strength
confused Bill, and left him a little ill-at-ease. He hadn't ever
met a woman who looked like a woman and smelled like a
woman and who was strong as an ox. Wasn't at all sure he liked
the idea.

She was looking into his eyes real intense now. Like she
wanted to tear his clothes off and have her way with him.
Which made Bill even more uncomfortable, for no reason that
he understood. Surprised the hell out of him, too. Who ever
heard of a man who wouldn't jump at the chance to have his
clothes took off by a woman who looked like this one did? Bill
hadn't, that was for sure. And here he was, being exactly that
kind of man he'd never heard of.

"Uh," he said. "Thanks for the save. Guess I owe you
one."

And as he spoke that something in her eyes changed
again. Just like it had all those times before, but more so. And
instead of looking hungry for him, she looked disgusted. Real
sudden-like, as though it'd just come over her what exactly it
was she was thinking. And she hissed, and she pushed him off
of her, out into the aisle. Where Bill landed ungently on his
rear.

"You," she said. "Stay away from me. Keep your hands to
yourself."

Which left Bill at least as confused as the nonsense
running around inside his own head. He shook his head—
more to clear it than to tell her *no*. "Hold on a minute," he
said. "The only hands that did anything in the last five minutes
are yours. You think I *meant* for this damn plane to send me

flying into you? You can guess again about that, I'll tell you. And it wasn't *me* looking all cow-eyes into *your* face, no ma'am—"

There were other things he was going to say, too, but Bill never got the chance. About the time that woman heard the words *cow-eyes* she was rising up out of her seat like a raging bull. Before Bill even knew what was going on she was all over him, pounding his head into the floor again and again and shouting at him, only there wasn't any way to tell what it was she was saying because of the sound of his own brains pounding on the rug. There was a measure of déjà vu in the sensation, only it wasn't déjà vu because it hadn't happened before, Bill only thought it was going to, back when he was all up in the air because the plane was falling.

She paused a moment, grabbed him by the collar. "You *will not* speak to me this way. Do you understand?"

And Bill was going to answer her, he really was. Only before he could talk she hit him again, even harder this time, the heel of her hand *crack*ing into the place where his nose met his upper lip. And then there was blood all over the place, his blood coming out through his nose that was maybe broken. For a while that went on forever all he could do was lie on the floor of the plane gasping for air. With the woman straddled over him nothing but a presence weighing on his chest. Not even noticing the fact that she'd stopped hitting him.

Then, finally, the panic for air ebbed. And Bill opened his eyes, and saw her staring at him with her mouth hung wide in horror and denial.

"I've hurt you," she said. Said it in a voice Bill would have used to tell a friend that his mother died.

"Sure did," he said. "You got a tissue or something? Or maybe could you let me up to get a paper towel from the can?"

She pursed her lips. "I'll get it." And she was gone, and Bill could sit up again.

The boy had woke from his nap; he was staring at Bill now. "You okay, Corporal Bill? She wrassles pretty good, don't she?"

"Uh," Bill said. "I guess she does."

Then she was back again, kneeling just above Bill, dabbing at his face with a damp paper towel.

"I'm sorry," she said. And from the look on her face Bill thought that there were other things she wanted to say, too. Things she wanted to say that she couldn't find the words for.

"It's all right," Bill told her. "I love you too." Mostly he was being sarcastic when he said that, but the woman didn't take it that way. For just a moment she looked shocked, violated by the suggestion.

And then she nodded.

"Yes," the woman said. "It is unwise to hide from such a thing. Isn't it?"

Took Bill half a minute to figure out what she meant by that. And when he finally did he wasn't one bit less confused.

Lake-of-Fire

It was dusk when George Stein woke again.

Outside, on the runway, a ground crew was fueling the first of the transport planes; nuclear missiles had been strapped and bolted onto the tops of all but the last three of them.

And there was nothing, not a single damned thing, that George or anyone else could or would do to stop them.

Not a thing.

Was Herman in the room? George couldn't see him. His line of sight was limited by the angle at which he hung from the chains; if Herman were behind him, sitting or standing quietly, there'd be no way he could know for certain. If Herman wasn't there, it was strange—he'd been with George continuously for two days, now. Or been there, at least, every moment that George was awake and alive. He craned his head back and to the side, to get a better view, and saw that the room was empty.

Knowing that Herman was nowhere nearby took a weight off George. He was feeling better, now—and not just because of Herman Bonner's absence. His body was recovering, remaking itself. And if he still wished that he were dead, he felt an obligation to the world. And that obligation gave him reason to live.

Herman had said it, not long before George blacked out. George was the only one left. The only one who knew what Herman was doing, and knew to try to stop him. But how? The chains weren't about to melt away of their own accord. Or crumble away from the hook that suspended him, and send George falling to the ground. He looked up at that hook. It was long, and sharp, and curved wickedly inward; even if he could manage to get himself rocking back and forth there was no way he'd be able to swing far enough forward to free himself. Could he try to grab hold of the chains, and climb them like a rope, hand over hand? He wasn't sure. The chains had cut off the circulation to his hands—they felt cold and dead, too numb to lift anything at all, much less George's entire weight.

He looked around, trying to see if there was anything nearby that would help, but there wasn't. Herman had taken care to shove the couch away from him, and neither the television nor the chairs were close enough to be of any use.

No. The only thing to do was to try to climb the chains. George set his teeth, forced the fingers of his right hand to uncurl. And began to try to free himself.

Cheyenne County

The creature began to wake only a moment before Christine heard the first scream from the graveyard.

Andy and the dog were playing in that graveyard.

Christine Gibson gasped, and turned to look to see what had happened to the child, and saw him standing between two tombstones in the dusklight, looking dumbfounded and a little afraid. The dog beside him, braced and barking at the air.

"You heard that?" he asked her. "It wasn't me. I swear it wasn't." Looked around, as though making certain that there was no one else nearby who might overhear him. "Came from down there. Down there in the ground."

And that was when Christine realized what she'd heard.

And shivered, shivered right down to the deepest place inside her.

"No," she said, too quietly for the boy to hear. And if anyone had been there to ask her what it was she'd denied, she'd have been unable to answer.

She turned to look into the back seat, where the creature still weak and beaten lay with his eyes half open. His body was fine, now, she thought. He'd suffered so, died painfully again and again for so many hours that his spirit was all but gone.

He doesn't have the heart to be alive any more, she thought. And she knew it was true, and knowing made her very, very sad.

That didn't matter. She couldn't let it matter. She put her hand on his wrist, and looked into those beautiful, tired eyes. "They need you," she said. "I know who you are. What you are. I dreamed that I saw you . . . so many times before we found you on that train. You can tell them—things that I couldn't make them understand, even if they heard me."

She remembered. Waking in the dark, in the close-press of wood and rotted velvet that was her coffin. Unable to move, to breathe, to think—

For her, at least, the grave had been so shallow. She felt cold and afraid inside when she thought of what it would have been like to be trapped under six heavy feet of earth. . . .

"Help them understand that it's all right, that they're alive and fine and that nothing will happen to them, just as long as they stay calm. All they have to do is press their way out, press out and dig up through the soil. And soon enough they'll be free."

It wasn't true, of course. There wasn't any way to be free of that deep a grave soon enough. But the screams from the graveyard were spreading from one to another like an infection. If they panicked it'd be worse, much worse. She knew because for just a moment before the soil above her had finally opened away into daylight, she'd felt that panic. And she couldn't bear to hear it coming from the throats of others.

She was out of the car, now, outside and on her feet and opening the door beside the creature. Taking his hand, helping him out of the backseat—with only half his cooperation—leading him to the graveyard.

"Make them calm," she said. She could hear panic in her own voice as she spoke. "Please make them calm."

The creature nodded, looking down at the dry grassy soil. Uneven ground, where Christine could pick out the shapes of coffins where the dirt had settled around them.

And he knelt, set his hands on the ground. Still and quiet for so long that the boy and the dog both stood still to watch and Christine almost began to lose heart, lose hope—

Then the screams began to quiet. Slowly. And all at once they faded, and the only sound was a small child buried somewhere in the earth and crying.

"We need to help them out," she said. Looked around, fretting. So many graves.

The boy groaned. "How we going to do that?" he asked.

"We haven't got any shovel. I can tell you there ain't one in that trunk. What you want to do, scrape them all open with our fingernails?"

She didn't have an answer.

"All of those people in the graveyard back in Brooklyn got out pretty good on their own. Probably easier to push your way out of the dirt than it is to dig your way into it." Scratched his head. "Course, none of them started screaming, either. What do you think started that here? Pretty strange, if you're asking me."

She wasn't sure what to say or think; she could feel the panic easing, but it was still in her blood.

"You okay? You don't look so good, you know." He waited for her to respond, but before she could find the words the boy was talking again, about another subject entirely. "Maybe it's him that set them off." He nodded toward the creature again. "All sick like he was, and hurting so. Kind of like how when one person starts pushing in the subway all the rest of them get crazy, too? You know what I mean?"

Christine didn't know. The fact was that all the experience she had of subways had come in the last week—they were something that had happened to the world in the time that she'd been gone from it. She found them strange, and incredible, and more than a little frightening. If the boy wanted to use them to prove his point, it'd end up lost on her. Christine didn't say any of that; she wasn't comfortable admitting her ignorance. Instead, she nodded.

"That's exactly what it is, I bet you." He walked over to where the creature still knelt on the ground. Set his hand on the creature's shoulder in a way that was somehow almost fatherly—Christine had calmed enough that the sight was almost comical. The creature looked up from the ground, into the boy's eyes. "You've got to calm yourself," Andy said. "Make yourself stop hurting. You're scaring people—almost like they can feel it, too. Huh?"

Yes. The creature nodded.

A few feet away—not far from where the creature knelt—the soil was stirring as the first of the graveyard's dead began to rise up out of the earth.

Outside the Gates
of Lake-of-Fire

"I need a cigarette," Ron said. "*Damn it* do I need a cigarette."

Luke didn't pay him any mind. He was too busy staring at the tall, tall chain-link fence—the one with three feet of razor wire on top of it. Trying, Ron guessed, to figure out how they were going to get over it.

Ron didn't like it one bit.

Come on, he thought. There had to be some sort of an alarm on that fence. No matter how high it was—no matter what kind of meanness they put on top of it—this far in the middle of nowhere no fence could be secure without someone standing guard in front of it. Unless it had one hell of an alarm system. Forget spies and saboteurs—they'd have teenagers sneaking around here on weekend nights, cutting the chain-link with tin snips and necking beside the silos.

And if there *was* an alarm, it wasn't likely they'd get a hundred yards inside the base before there were soldiers—or whatever they were—all over them.

And what was the point of that?

No point at all. No point that Ron could see.

There Luke was, staring at the hyperthyroid chain-link fence, transfixed as though it were the Oracle at Delphi. Half a dozen times since they'd started away from the wreck of the old Dodge, Ron had spoken to him. And near as he could tell Luke hadn't heard a word he'd said, not even once.

So now what? Any moment now Luke was going to come up with a stupid and dangerous idea for getting past that fence. Something that'd get them into shit deep enough for swimming in. And Ron would have to follow him. He'd come far enough along already that he had an obligation to see this through to its . . . conclusion? End? Whatever was coming. Ron wasn't in the grip of a vision the way Luke so obviously was. His gut still knew that they were heading toward something with finality. Death, or maybe real rebirth. It *was* best to stay with Luke, and be what use he could. Important things were on the verge of happening. If he had a contribution to make, Ron thought, he wanted to make it.

"We have to climb it, I think," Luke said. "The wires ought to be over there, in the ground a few inches on the other side. Which means that we can't dig under it without disturbing them. And if we had wire cutters—which we don't—we'd set them off when we went through. But if we climb up to the top, and jump down, the jump can carry us clear."

Luke waited for him to answer, but Ron didn't say a word.

"So? What do you think?"

Ron cursed. "I think you're out of your mind. What do you expect me to think?" Looked away; looked up and across at the fence. "What about the razor wire up there?"

Luke shrugged. "Just be careful of it. Push it aside. Isn't sharp in every direction."

Right.

There had to be a better way to get inside. An old gate, maybe—chained shut and unwatched. A neglected spot where the fence had fallen of its own accord. Something—anything. Before he could say anything Luke was already halfway up, moving fast and determined toward the crown of razor wire, and when Ron told him to wait up and give the whole business a little more thought, Luke just ignored him.

"Come on, Luke. This is crazy. Wait up."

He was up toward the top of the fence now, carefully widening a gap in the wire.

"You're going to break your neck, jumping down from there."

"So? Are you coming or not?"

Not, Ron thought. But he braced himself and started up the fence anyway. It wasn't a time for taking a stand over no issue at all. Besides, he wasn't really afraid of getting hurt trying to climb over a fence. Worse things had happened to him over the last week. His real objection, as much as he had one, was to getting himself hurt for no good reason.

He was halfway up when Luke Munsen lifted himself up over the razor wire and jumped; Ron saw the cuff of his slacks catch in the nest of sharpened wire, and for a moment Luke was falling askew toward the ground, heading toward a hard fall on one leg, and something was going to break, and—

No, Luke landed rolling, hard and grunting but not disastrously. He grabbed his knee and rocked back and forth, hugging it for the longest while. It wasn't disjointed and there wasn't any blood, and in a moment, Ron knew, he'd be well enough to walk. Had to be.

Ron wasn't that lucky.

Oh, he got to the top well enough. But that wire—it

frightened him. Intimidated him. So where he should have
kept calm and made himself the master of it, he shied from it,
tried to press it away from him with the tips of his fingers.

It was a serious mistake.

Ron pulled the gap wide with his left hand, heaved
himself up and onto the rail at the top of the fence—

And the wire slipped.

Slipped just a bit. That bit was enough; one of the
thin-sharp razors molded into the wire slid into the soft flesh of
his thumb and split it wide, wet-bloody and burning painful as
it dug a gouge out of his thumbnail from the underside.

And Ron swore. And pulled his hand away, instinctively,
to lift it to his mouth to suck the blood from the wound—
except it never got that far. Because as soon as he let go of the
wire it sprang back, returning to its original position—and
where it wanted to be was where Ron's shoulder was now.
Razors dug through his shirt and into the meat of his upper
arm, shredding flesh and skin, and the wire was cutting and
wrapping and digging all around him, folding him into a bird's
nest of knife-sharp metal.

And Ron didn't think; he jumped.

That was his second mistake.

What he should have done was calm down in spite of that
pain and the fact that his own blood was leaking out all around
him. Calm down, and carefully but firmly take hold of the
razor wire and press it away from him. And, once it was under
control, hold it down with the sole of one shoe while he
jumped.

He didn't think. He panicked, jumped straight into the
thick of the razor-wire snare that surrounded him.

Later, he decided that he'd been lucky. It could easily
have been a lot worse than it was.

The wire didn't tear the skin off his face and chest, even
though there was every reason that it should have. And it
didn't manage to cut his throat and tear his neck open, even
though it ought by rights to have done that, too. It did leave
him a cut-bloody mess from head to toe, and one long loop of
wire wrapped around his left leg as he jumped and turned his
outward leap to an arc that slammed him bloody-face-first into
the fence. As he hit the fence the wire loosened, sprang free,
and released him—leaving him free to fall head-first to the
ground eight or nine feet below.

He was lucky there, too, when it got right down to it. The fall only knocked him senseless—it didn't split open his brain-case, crush his neck, or any of the other more interesting things that it could have done. And when he'd finished falling and his body lay still and face-down on the grassy Kansas soil, Luke Munsen came and helped him back to his feet.

"Can you move?" Luke asked. "Can you run? You've hit the trip-wire. If they've got people watching their security equipment, they'll be here any moment."

"Uh." Luke was holding out his hand. Ron reached up, took it, tried to sit up, but the throb and the swirl inside his head were too much. His stomach clenched, dry-heaved; his body went slack and sank back toward the ground.

Then Luke was pulling him up, lifting him to his feet anyway, and Ron's knees managed to lock instead of buckling, so suddenly he was standing in spite of himself.

Luke levered himself under Luke's arm, set his own arm across Ron's back. "We've got to try to get away from here," he said. "Come on. You can try to walk, can't you?"

And Ron could, he could try at least, and they started off. All but stumbling, at first—Ron with his knees locked and tottering from one leg to the other and over again, almost as though he were walking on stilts. He kept going, and as he went his balance and his sense began to come back to him. By the time they'd covered thirty yards he was walking under his own steam, and Luke gradually eased away and let him support himself.

"You set the pace," Luke said. "We need to run, if you can. Move as quickly as your legs will let you."

"Yeah." The dizziness was clearing the way a fog clears as the sun warms morning air—fading gradually, but even as slow as it was it was a faster recovery than he had any right to expect. Soon, Ron thought, he'd be able to run. "I'll be okay in a minute."

And it was true: two minutes later they were moving at a quick trot, and the spot where they'd climbed the fence was out of sight in the woods, and somewhere back there and off to their left Ron could hear the sound of men moving through the woods, shouting.

"Let's hope that none of them is much of a tracker," Luke said. Ron grunted to answer him. How far did they have to go? he wondered. Wondered where Luke was leading them—not

for the first time. And wondered whether there'd be as much
cover along the way as there was now—a woods in the middle
of Kansas when they'd seen nothing but grainfields for hundreds of miles was a real blessing. How much of a blessing like
that could they expect? And why was the base here wooded in
the first place? That one, at least, had an answer he could
guess. The trees were here to keep prying eyes from having a
clear view of the base. They'd been planted—and watered,
too, most likely—by the Air Force.

They came to a trail that led through the woods, but Luke
ignored it. Avoided it—actually turned them away, to the left,
and led them into a thicker part of the woods at an off angle to
the trail.

Three hundred yards; four hundred. Ron could still feel a
little of the daze from his fall. Only a little of it, and even that
was fading quickly. "Where are we going? How much farther?"

Luke ignored that question.

To be fair, there was good reason for him to ignore it.

Because that was the moment that the woods faded out
around them, and opened out into the concrete runway.

A runway crowded with a score of airplanes.

Big, substantial planes—military planes, to judge by their
markings and by their drab green paint, but shaped more like
airliners than like combat planes. Transports? Ron thought
that was the word for them.

The striking thing wasn't whether or not they were
transports, or their markings, or even the planes' color.

The striking thing was the fact that there was a missile
strapped to the top of each of them. Great, long missiles—each
very nearly the length of the plane that bore it. Too large,
certainly, to fit inside the plane.

No one had to tell Ron what those missiles were, or what
they were for.

Like . . . like pregnant birds, Ron thought, and almost
laughed to himself at the idea, in spite of its absurdity. And
wrongness, too—no pregnant bird could carry its womb above
its spine. It would defy the architecture of vertebrate anatomy.
He'd seen something like those planes before—photographs of
the Space Shuttle in *Newsweek*, bolted on top of a 747 being
flown cross-country. That much he understood; you strapped
one vehicle on top of another when you couldn't get the first to

fly. When you wanted to put it someplace, but couldn't get it to go there under its own steam.

And they weren't just relocating those missiles. They could do *that* with a truck—the things weren't so wide like a Space Shuttle that you couldn't get them onto a highway. It had to be that the missiles weren't working for one reason or another, and someone wanted to use them anyway. Who? Someone never meant to have his hands on such engines of destruction—else they'd be used as they were designed to be. The people who were supposed to be entrusted with such things would know how to work them as they were supposed to work, and how to fix them when it became necessary.

Thick black electric cables ran out from the forward doors of the jets, up into the missiles' warheads. When Ron looked closely, he could see the bolts that would hold them fixed in place against the wind. Those were there to ignite the bombs, Ron thought. They had to be. These planes weren't bombers— they were kamikaze planes. On a far more destructive scale than that of the original kamikazes.

Atomic bombs. Someone wants to destroy the world.

That was an exaggeration, certainly. Twenty atomic warheads couldn't destroy the world by themselves.

Could they?

There wasn't any way for Ron to answer that question. He wasn't sure he wanted to know, anyway.

Without realizing what he was doing, Ron had wandered out onto the runway. He walked among the planes impossibly jury-rigged and sewn together.

This is why we're here, Ron thought. *This is what drew Luke to this place. We've got to stop these things, before they can get off the ground.*

He turned to Luke, to tell him that he understood.

The man was nowhere in sight.

Off in the distance there was an endless-looking caravan of cars and pickup trucks and vans pouring in through one of the gates of the base. Ron thought he could see men in uniform in the backs of the pickups. At this distance it was hard to be certain exactly how they were dressed.

Near St. Francis, Kansas

It took Leigh Doyle hours to get to St. Francis from the overgrown field. Two hours? Three? After a while she lost track of time. One road became another and another, and there were no street signs. Maybe there had been once. If there had then someone had moved them. Maybe teenagers out on a drunken ride. Maybe a scrap-metal collector adding to his hoard.

She found St. Francis, finally, by accident—when the rutted dirt road she drove on gave out behind a convenience store. Where she decided that it was time to give up her pride and get some directions. Pulled her rent-a-car around to the front of the store, to the parking lot—and saw through the dusk the glow of the Lake of Fire. The glow that consumed the entire eastern horizon. Leigh parked, got out of the car . . . and found herself transfixed by the aurora, unable to do anything but stand and stare.

"It's beautiful, isn't it?" Who? Oh. The clerk. Standing behind the counter, inside the store. Talking to her through the glass doors that hung open to admit the warm, dry summer air.

"Um." She blinked, trying to clear her head. "It's wonderful," she said. "That's where the bombs fell, isn't it?"

"Sure is. What a night! You should have been here. Or maybe you shouldn't have."

She looked at the man—or was he a boy? He looked very young. Cocked an eyebrow at him. Found herself drawn to glance back at the bright horizon; resisted the pull. "Tell me," she said. "I've been away . . . since it happened. Away from the country."

The boy (man? young man?) smiled. He had a handsome smile; easy, relaxed, hiding nothing. "What's to tell? *Boom!* in the middle of the night, and light so big that everybody with his eyes open for thirty miles around goes blind, and the noise so loud that went on so long. And I get up out of bed expecting to see the Angel Gabriel here to tell us it's the end of the world. After a while the light that's bright as day fades down to dusk, and in the morning everything facing east is bleached like from a dozen summers. And there's a gouge in the ground," he nodded toward the Lake of Fire, "big as the Great Salt Lake. It isn't full of water; it's full of fire."

Leigh tried to imagine herself there at the edge of a

nuclear holocaust, waiting for the second coming. And pressed that image away from her heart.

"Lots of us around here were sick for a while, after the blast. Lately I've been getting better. And some of those who lost their sight can see again."

Leigh thought of the stories she'd read in the papers on the plane from Finland. Stories of resurrection and miraculous healing happening all over the world. Thought of the telephone call that had come from a man who'd left behind nothing on this earth to resurrect. Maybe, she thought, the Angel Gabriel *was* coming for them—coming to announce the end of the world. She bit her lip. It was a crazy idea. Leigh knew that the world was a more rational place than that, even if she did write for the *National Interlocutor*. And especially so; working with material that bordered on fantasy made Leigh uneasy about her grip on the world. Because of that uneasiness, she overcompensated, and cast a skeptical eye on things that give most people pause.

She cleared her throat. "I need directions," she said. "To St. Francis, Kansas. Can you point me there?"

The young man smiled again. "I could, I guess. There isn't really any need. 'Cause you're already here—this is St. Francis."

Leigh blushed. "Oh."

"Anybody in particular I can point you toward? You here to visit?"

"Ah—no. Passing through. You could steer me toward the county road—the one that runs along the South Fork Republican River."

The young man pointed east. "Take 36 here a hundred yards. It'll be your second left. You sure you know where you're going? The county road is only barely passable; comes close enough to the Lake of Fire that you could toss a penny into it from your window. You'd have to toss it pretty hard, but you could do it."

"I know," she said, "I know." And then she was thanking the man; getting in her car. Waving good-bye, starting the engine, leaving. Ten minutes later she made that final right turn, onto OLD ROAD, a grassy, dirty thing that very nearly wasn't a road at all. Half a mile more and there was no farther she could go, because the road fell away over a bluff that overlooked the Lake of Fire. And just as the President had asked her, Leigh Doyle shut off the engine of her car, rolled down the window, and waited for the obvious to come to her.

Cheyenne County

That monster was one cool guy. Better than any old Frankenstein, or Dracula—even cooler than the living mummy they got to see in the museum back in New York.

Or, at least, that's what Andy Harrison thought. Look at him there, Andy thought: standing in the middle of a graveyard, whispering down into the ground. Oh, sure, he wasn't making any sound. Whispering was the word for it all the same—it wasn't like he spoke any words or anything, but you could hear his voice in your head if you listened real hard. Hear it even if he meant you not to. And Andy could hear it even now, when he was trying to talk to the people coming to life down inside the graves—when that old monster wasn't trying to let himself be heard by anyone on this side of the dirt. It wasn't easy, but Andy *could* hear it when he tried.

Be calm, the creature said. He was staring hard down at that grave where they'd heard the little kid crying just a little while ago. *Press yourself up through the soil. It isn't hard.*

They listened to him, too. Already there were two dozen people who'd crawled up out of the graves because the monster had told them how. Mostly they were sitting on the ground or on their tombstones, staring off into space and looking dazed and confused. Andy wondered if there was anything the monster could do about that. It seemed an awful shame to him—people getting to be alive all over again, and even though they were alive they were dead to the world. Andy kind of suspected that there wasn't anything the monster could do about it. The kind of confusion that was all over those faces wasn't anything that was the matter with a person's body—it came from shock, from adjusting to important things that had suddenly changed. Andy had seen it before; it was the kind of thing you saw a lot of out in Bedford-Stuyvesant. Especially on the faces of junkies and crack-heads. There wasn't anything anybody could do about that kind of shock but get used to the world all over again.

Except for the shock, though, most of them looked pretty normal. Or healthy, anyhow. It was hard to think about people as being normal when they were filthy with dirt from head to toe, and so pale and pink-skinned as though they'd never-ever been out in the sun. (Which, of course, they hadn't—at least not since they'd got to be alive again.)

The thing that made them look strangest of all was the way they were dressed.

Or not dressed, when you got right down to it.

Which was to say that for the most part they were naked.

Oh, most of them had clothes—some clothes, at least. Fancy stuff, like you'd wear for a wedding, or to go to church or to the theater.

The kind of fancy clothes people get buried in. (Which made Andy think: *Hey, what are those undertakers trying to do—turn heaven into some kind of an opera?* And he got a good chuckle out of that, even if it did make Christine look at him pretty funny.) Fancy coffin clothes, only they'd all gone to rot, and they were falling off of all of them—all except that man over there, who'd got himself buried in a polyester leisure suit. Andy made a note to himself about that: when the time came for him to get himself buried—if it ever did come, what with death turning so transient lately—when his time came, he'd make sure they buried him in something plastic. No way *he* was going to come back to this earth buck naked. Not Andy Harrison, no sir.

Andy scratched his head, tried to figure if there was anything he could do about the problem. Realized that there wasn't, because they were in the middle of nowhere, and Luke was the only one who'd brought any clothes, and his were all used and seriously sweaty. Shrugged, and turned his attention to something else.

Which, as it turned out, was the dog.

That dog was pretty all right, Andy had decided. Tom was his name, wasn't it? Yeah, Tom—though to Andy's way of thinking, all dogs were named dog, first name, middle, last. Tom the dog was staring at Andy. Which meant, Andy guessed, that the dog had finally got bored with watching holes in the ground dig themselves.

Well, then, heck. If the dog could stare at him, Andy could stare back at the dog. Which he did: stared at the dog wide-eyed and intense, and tensed up his body like he was about to pounce.

"Dog," he said, pretending like he was some kind of a

snarling cat, or maybe just an angry squirrel. "*Dog*—I'm gonna getcha!"

That set Tom the dog off real good.

Real good. The dog barked loud and high, half in challenge and half in fear. And took off running toward Andy about as fast as Andy had *ever* seen a dog run. Not to say that Andy had seen that many dogs, growing up in Bed-Stuy and all. Andy turned and ran from him, dodging between the gravestones and changing direction just enough to throw the dog off. And when, in spite of his ducking and dodging, the dog was almost right behind him, Andy stopped dead in his tracks, turned around, lunged toward the dog. Shouted "Boo!" and the dog shrieked in terror—shrieked, yelped, and took off in the opposite direction.

Andy laughed and laughed and laughed—doubled over laughing and finally lost his balance completely. Fell onto the ground with its broken dirt and holes that had mostly filled back up with dirt as the dead people crawled out of them. Still rolling with laughter and now the dog was on top of him, licking his face, and rolled into one of those half-open graves, trying to get away from the dog's too-long slimy tongue. Which left him covered with dirt that caked up where the dog's licking had wet his face.

Looked up, and saw the monster staring down at him.

A look on his face. . . . A puzzled look, Andy thought it was. Like he was stretching inside, trying to think in a way that he didn't usually think.

Andy stood. Brushed away some of the graveyard dirt that covered him. Looked around, and every grave that he could see was a pit of sifted earth, and behind that a headstone. Which meant that the monster was done—he'd done it. Actually gone and woke the dead. Or at least every one of them that he could find.

The monster was still staring at him—his strange, alien face all scrunched-up and intent.

Ron . . . Hawkins? Ron Hawkins? Made a sound that was like a sigh, but wasn't a sigh at all. *The one who traveled with me.*

A pause. The monster was waiting for an answer, Andy thought. As though he didn't really know what a name was, and wanted Andy to let him know if he'd got the concept right.

"Yeah," Andy said. "That's his name. He told me."

Where has he gone? Has something happened to him? He isn't nearby.

Andy frowned. "He went off with Luke Munsen, a long while back. When you were still sick—but not too much before you woke up." He pointed. "Went that way. Don't know how far. Didn't say. Though maybe it couldn't have been all that long a way. Luke took off at such a pace that there wasn't any way he could go too far before they both ran out of steam."

The monster shook his head; he looked grim.

No. Not far. I know where they've gone.

When the last of the dead had risen from his grave, the creature turned to Christine and she heard his voice inside her head again.

It's time, he said. *We need to go.*

She didn't know exactly what he meant. She could guess; they'd been traveling purposely for days—moving steadily toward something only Luke had been able to see. It didn't surprise her that the creature could see it too. It made sense that the creature was drawn to whatever it was; Christine had enough sight to know when others had true vision. She'd seen it in Luke from the moment she'd first set eyes on him. Seen it in spite of the fact that Luke was unable to see it himself.

And she could see vision in the creature. Great, powerful, consuming vision.

Andy Harrison and the dog were standing just behind the creature, and beyond them was a small army of men and women only just reawakened to the world.

"Are you sure?" she asked. Asked it not so much because she had any doubt as because she was afraid.

The creature nodded, and Christine turned to the car, to try to remember if there was anything she needed that was still inside it—but there wasn't, of course. She'd brought nothing with her, at least partly because she owned nothing in this life.

I don't want to go with them, she thought. *There's something wrong here, something dangerous and wrong and inevitable. Something's going to happen.*

And she thought of her grave again, dark and warm and suffocating like a womb that had turned itself into a prison. And wanted to scream, but stopped herself because life was frightening enough without admitting fear out loud. "Where. . . ?" she asked the creature, but she knew as she asked where they were going.

An ending, the creature told her. *An ending for the world.* He shrugged. *Or perhaps a rebirth.*

Christine bit her lower lip.

And suddenly the boy was running toward her, laughing. Grabbing her hand. The dog, three steps behind him, barking and wagging his tail.

"Come *on*," Andy said. "You can't miss this! It's important. Probably going to be fun, too."

And before she knew what she'd done, she'd let him pull her a dozen paces down the road. And then it was too late to turn back or even hesitate a moment longer.

The dirt road went on for miles: long, flat, dry miles of land that seemed empty of everything. No trees. No houses, let alone buildings of any other sort. Nothing but fields of high green grass that might have been wheat and might have been something similar; never any sign of a soul besides themselves. In the distance, consuming the horizon, was a lake of fire. Mostly Christine kept her eyes away from that; it gave her deep chills to even think of it.

All the while no one said a word—not the creature, who had no voice for the ears to hear, nor the legion of those no longer dead but neither yet entirely alive. Certainly not Christine, afraid as she was because her heart was certain that she'd reopened her own coffin—and certain that soon it would close again around her, and leave her trapped forever.

Maybe the boy spoke. If he did there was no way to know it; Andy and the dog were always somewhere in the near distance, sometimes in front of them, sometimes behind, playing a game that looked a lot like tag. If he ever said anything to the dog or to anyone else, he was never near enough for Christine to hear it.

The quiet and the lonesome emptiness were what made it strangest of all when Christine saw the bag lady standing, watching them from the field on their right—standing in the open not far away at all, and no one but Christine seemed to notice her.

The same woman who'd woke them from their stupor, back at the edge of the destroyed city.

The same woman who'd found her the dress that she still wore. And given her the pendant that hung hidden from her neck. (Even now she could feel its stone warm against her breast.)

Very strange. Strange even in a week filled with resurrection and impossibility.

Christine paused, and stood there on the road staring back at the woman, and no one noticed that, either; first the creature and then the half-alive who followed him stepped around her, moved by, and kept going as though she were invisible or unreal.

The old woman was staring at her.

"Who are you?" Christine asked the question without realizing that she'd spoken—and asked it quietly enough that there was no way the woman could have heard it.

Whatever the distance was between them, the old woman smiled at her coy and knowing, as though she'd heard the question and didn't mean to answer. And continued to stand there, on a small rise in a gold-green wheatfield. Waiting, Christine thought—waiting for what? She knew the answer to that question, just as she'd known the answer to all the questions she'd asked that day.

Waiting for me to come to her. But why? What did the woman want from her?

Christine didn't want the answer to that question. It was buried in her past, in the life she'd lived and died so long ago, and the thing she wanted most of all in this life was to leave that life behind.

The old woman wouldn't allow that, Christine thought. Or couldn't, maybe—maybe that was a better word.

There wasn't any avoiding it, or any sense in trying to avoid what was coming. So Christine crossed the road, strode across the field through its wheat like a shallow sea, waist-high and powdery. Until she stood only a few feet from the old woman, looking up at her because she stood on the rise.

"Let it be," Christine said. "All of that is dead and buried. Let it sleep with all the other things that died when I did."

The old woman smiled. As she did the wind shifted—it was a breeze, really, not a wind at all—and Christine caught the scent of her again. A foul scent; filth and decay and fermentation. And death—ever so faintly. The smell that Christine had woke to in her coffin. "The dead have risen," the old woman said, "and you among them."

"No," Christine said. "I left that life behind me, in my grave."

Even as she said the words she knew there was no way to defend them.

Lake-of-Fire

It was a good five minutes before Luke even noticed that Ron wasn't behind him any more. By then he was already walking through the service door, unchallenged because the man who ought to have been there to stop him was off in the wrong part of the woods with every other guard who was on duty, hunting for him and Ron in a place where neither one of them was.

Luke pushed through the spring-hinge door behind the loading bay, and once he was inside he turned to hold it open for Ron—and that was when he saw he was alone.

It didn't matter. He couldn't let it matter. Ron was necessary here, somehow. Luke knew that.

He frowned.

Luke didn't know that part—he didn't know any of the *hows* or the *whys*.

Whether Ron was necessary or not, there wasn't time to turn back and search for him. The situation was too urgent to turn back, even for a moment. And besides, Ron wasn't a boy; he could take care of himself. Or take care of himself, at least, as well as the circumstances would allow.

Luke still didn't know where he was going. Didn't know why he was going there. He only knew from step to step where he needed to be next, and knew that whatever it was that directed him hadn't lied to him yet. Not for a moment.

And it was urgent—it burned at him, pressed him to hurry—

Toward what?

Wait. There, right there in the hallway, standing in front of him and not standing there, too. An image, like a ghost or a memory that called itself. The image of a man, who he'd known for a long, long time.

He'd seen that man, in New York, when the fundamentalists had stormed the network building. Seen him in that strange dream, too—the dream he'd had the second time he'd died.

Herman Bonner.

That was the man's name.

There were words that went with the image, too:

Herman Bonner wants to kill the world.

In New York, when Bonner had seen Luke, he'd looked as though *he'd* been the one seeing the ghost. Looked . . . *afraid* of Luke.

Luke felt a chill he didn't understand. He kept going anyway, and after a moment the vision faded.

He had to kill that man.

Kill? Was that even possible? The only people he'd seen honestly die—and stay dead—since he'd first woke in Bedford-Stuyvesant were the people in St. Louis, where the bomb had fallen. He wasn't even absolutely sure about them; he hadn't seen them die, and there weren't any bodies to examine. But he couldn't imagine that anything could resurrect men and women who'd been reduced to light and subatomic dust.

No, killing him wouldn't be possible. Luke Munsen didn't have an atom bomb, and anyway even if he'd had one he didn't have the heart for murder. But what do you do with a man who wants to sterilize every bit of life on the face of the world—a man who might well be able to accomplish the task?

Bury him under a mountain, maybe?

It was a silly idea. But there was something, something he had to do. And maybe whatever it was he had to do, maybe it wouldn't be enough by itself to stop the man. Luke knew with an absolute faith that whatever he'd do was necessary. Not sufficient, maybe, not by itself. Necessary, all the same.

Here, on the left. A stairwell. In, through the fire door. Up.

Up until there wasn't anyplace else to go—five flights of stairs, concrete steps with textured steel reinforcing plates set into their edges.

Out through another fire door, into a hallway.

Toward the end of the hall. A door—heavy, made of wood by the look of it. Luke knew before he touched it that the door was locked and bolted; knew that turning the handle wasn't any use. He also knew that heavy as it was the door was made of flawed wood—knew, impossibly, that there was a fault in the woodgrain that ran from just below the lower bolt, on the right side of the door, up to the top-center.

Luke stepped back six paces. Ran toward the door, leading with his shoulder. And hit it square, all his weight and momentum slamming dead into the weakest spot in the wood-fault—

And the door burst, and shattered around him.

And there, sitting stunned in front of a computer console, was Herman Bonner.

Cursing. Getting up out of his seat. Coming toward Luke furious and angry, and if there was fear in his eyes Luke couldn't see it.

No—not fear. Murder.

Herman Bonner's eyes were warm and hungry with bloodlust.

And suddenly Luke realized that the thing that had guided him was gone—all his conviction, all certainty evaporated. He was alone and he was fighting for his life and he didn't know why or how or what he should do.

Herman Bonner leaped at him, laid into him with a flying tackle that sent them both flying back out into the hall where they landed with Luke's back pounding hard into the smooth, hard tile, and the air gasped out of him and Bonner was on top of him and pounding Luke's face with his fists, and it finally occurred to Luke that he had to fight back if he was going to get away, and he threw up his hands to protect his face.

And that helped, some; anyway it made a couple of punches go flying off in the wrong direction. Luke grabbed one of the man's wrists as he pulled back to strike again. Grabbed the other—with a little more effort, since Bonner knew to expect it—used the arms like levers to try to throw the man off of him.

Which wasn't any use. Herman Bonner wasn't going anywhere—not unless he wanted to go there himself. And even if Luke had his hands by the wrists, he wasn't strong enough to control them. Strong enough to keep the man from striking him, maybe.

Barely.

And maybe not.

Certainly not strong enough to keep Herman Bonner's hands from pressing steadily toward his throat. Toward his neck. Down in toward the soft skin and flesh and the delicate conduits of air and blood that carried Luke Munsen's life.

And slowly, firmly, gently, Herman Bonner strangled Luke to death.

As he died, Luke heard the sound of gunfire in the distance.

Ron Hawkins wasn't alone on the runway.

It took him a while to realize that. There were planes— big, hulking, empty planes—everywhere, and at first their presence masked away the three men at the far end of the field with their fuel truck and its hoses.

And after he got used to the idea it was even more striking: how could a single truck fuel all these planes? Well, it could, he guessed. Of course it could. One at a time, slowly, steadily. Of course a single truck could fuel an army of planes. If it had a year to fuel them! Why on God's earth would they use just one truck? And the answer to that was obvious, too, when he thought about it. They were only using one truck because they only had one truck; if the base had others they'd somehow been destroyed, or maybe abused beyond their ability to function. That sounded likely. A real army depends as much on its mechanics as on its soldiers, and Ron couldn't imagine that any of the fundamentalist irregulars who'd tried to kill himself and the creature—couldn't imagine that any of them would make much of a mechanic.

For that matter, how had they gotten these planes rigged together—how had they managed to get the missiles piggy-backed to them? Did these people seriously expect them to function?

Maybe they did.

Ron thought of the blast in St. Louis that had knocked all of them unconscious—even though they'd been miles and miles from its center. Yes, the missiles were functional all right, even if they did look like something from a Rube Goldberg cartoon. Ron paused, turned. Looked carefully at the jet beside him.

It was an enormous plane, even larger close up than it had been from a distance. At least a part of that bigness was the fact that Ron had never seen an airliner from this angle before—every plane he'd ever entered he'd got into by going through a steel-and-canvas-covered walkway—those accordionlike things that ground crews always somehow managed to attach to airliners. *A house,* Ron thought. The plane was the size of a house. And the missile on top of it? Nearly as long as the plane itself, so large that it took five heavy steel straps— each of them as wide as Ron's chest was broad—to hold it in place. Each strap wrapped clear around both the plane and the missile, and bolts bound it home every foot or so.

Up near the cockpit a thick nest of wires ran from the forward door to the missile's warhead.

These people had one man, at least, who could make these things work—even if he didn't seem to know how to make them work as they'd been intended to.

Which, when it got right down to it, might as well be irrelevant. How the things were rigged together was only important if knowing could help Ron to disable them. He thought about that for a minute. Thought about how he could possibly do anything to disable two dozen planes, by himself, and without a knife or a gun. Let alone anything that was really suited to destroying aircraft, like a small tank, or even a bazooka.

He could try to start a fire. The airlines were always warning you not to smoke when you were on the ground in a plane. God only knew what would happen if the missiles caught fire; if even one of those warheads reached critical mass, Ron thought, it'd start a chain reaction that'd destroy half the Midwest.

Or maybe it wouldn't. What did Ron know about nuclear weapons? Not a damn thing. He had most of a BA from Mountainville State's School of Business, and years of experience as a janitor. Neither one of those things told him anything at all about physics or mechanics or engineering. He was working toward a business degree, not one in the sciences.

Still: there was another weak spot. One that was just as obvious and a lot less likely to bring on catastrophe.

The wires.

Right there, out in the open. Bolted to the steel fuselage of the plane. Secured against the wind, but not secure from vandalism.

Ron took a running jump toward the wires. Managed, just barely, to get a secure grip. And climbed hand over hand toward the nuclear warhead.

Cheyenne County

" 'Mother of harlots,' " the old woman said, " 'and abominations of the earth.' "

And Christine looked away, and winced. Tried to hide from her memory, but it wasn't any use. She didn't want to be ashamed of her life. Her other life. She'd sworn long ago that she'd never allow anything or anyone to make the path she'd had to choose a source of humiliation. And the fact that her past disgraced her hurt all the more because of that vow.

"Yes," she said. "I birthed him."

And said nothing at all for a long time after.

They were walking again, now. Away from the road at an off angle—not following any marked path, but the line that they traveled was so direct that Christine suspected that the old woman was leading them someplace.

The old woman was quiet for a long time, too.

For all that Christine had been the madam of the house, and for all that her house did its business brisk and well, it had been years since she'd been with a man herself. She had grown old, and was long past desirability. And she was easy with the fact. When she'd realized that she carried a child, she'd known that it couldn't be any ordinary child.

There was no way she could have known exactly how extraordinary it was.

At first she had suspected that the growth and blooming inside her abdomen was a disease—a cancer perhaps. Cancer of the womb. Maybe some disease even more horrible. Even if she'd never had a child herself, she knew pregnancy; over the years she'd nursed more than one woman through childbirth. And as the months passed she became more and more certain that it was a child inside her—until, finally, on that morning when the house was totally and utterly deserted, she felt the onset of labor.

"You were the only one who saw him born," the old woman said, finally. "You gave birth to him alone, without warning—and at a moment when your . . . home was empty. And once you'd given birth to him, he murdered you."

Christine shuddered. Images of the scene forced themselves back on her. Her own blood everywhere as she screamed at the top of her lungs—screamed and screamed and screamed, but there was no one to hear her. And the child . . . infant, soft, and vulnerable as any newborn she'd ever seen. And at the same time not vulnerable at all—not even remotely.

"He's at the root of it," the old woman said. "Source and fountainhead of the evil that surrounds us."

"I know. I've known that since the moment I awoke."

She'd opened her eyes when she felt the child push free from her, and seen—a babe. And something else, too: something vile and powerful and inhuman, thirsting with the need for death.

She'd tried to tell herself it was only the agony of birthing that made her mind's eye see the foul *thing* where nothing but her child ought to have been. She'd seen women have visions and hallucinations, and she knew that pain could cause them. Even visions as foul as this one that seemed to overlay the head of bloodthirsty reptiles over the face of her own infant son.

Then the infant had sat up and wiped the blood from its eyes—moving purposeful, agile, and direct as any adult—sat up, wiped the blood from its eyes. Looked at her, and seen what she'd seen in him. Leaned forward, reached into the birth canal from which he'd just emerged. And used his tiny fingers to tear open one of the great arteries inside her. Christine had felt the blood rush out of her all at once; three moments later the breath and life had faded out of her, and she'd died.

The old woman shook her head. "He killed you because you could never mistake him for anything but what he is. And because there is vulnerability for him in the connection between you."

Christine thought of the infant. Thought of the man whose image she now saw, sometimes, in her dreams. She couldn't begin to imagine any way that she could be a threat to such a man. "I can't believe that," she said.

The old woman shrugged. "Nevertheless, it's true. You're right to know that if you confronted him alone he'd only murder you again. Still: you are his greatest weakness in this world. Any scheme to put an end to him requires you."

The road was out of sight now. The horizon was nothing but wheatfields in every direction but one—behind them and off to the left was the Lake of Fire, glowing brilliantly in an early evening lit otherwise only by the moon.

"Where are we going? What is it you want me to do?"

The old woman turned, looked at her. There was light enough for Christine to see her smile.

"Soon enough," she said. "Soon enough you'll see."

Lake-of-Fire

Luke was hanging from the ceiling when he came to.

Beside him was a man he almost didn't recognize—it took him a long moment to realize that the haggard, beaten man dangling from the hook beside him was the same one he'd seen sermonize on television so many times.

It took him another long breath to realize that this was a man he'd have expected to be one of his captors, instead of a fellow prisoner.

He was awake and alive, but when Luke looked at him carefully he could see signs of deep and grievous abuse; the man looked as though he'd been tortured to death again and again.

Luke winced at that thought when he realized that it was more than likely exactly true.

And wondered what Herman Bonner had planned for him.

"He's gone, now, I think," the man said, "gone from this suite of rooms, I mean. He was in an awful hurry to truss you up. Kept saying something about the sound of gunfire. This room is soundproofed—no way to hear shooting when you're in here, even if it was right out in the hall. You hear anything like that?"

Luke's eyes were blurry; he squeezed them shut, opened them again, cleared them a little.

"Yeah," he said, "I think I might have. Hard to say for sure."

"I'm George Stein," he said. "I was trying to get out of here, before Herman brought you in. How are you? Up to trying to escape?"

Luke grunted. "Luke Munsen. Yeah, I'm okay—give me a minute."

Dragged in a deep breath; another. Luke felt his head

begin to clear. His sense of whatever it was he had to do next was still gone.

Which meant that he had to think for himself. And maybe that was a blessing. *All right then*, he thought: *I've got to get out of here*. Before Herman Bonner could begin doing to him the things he'd done to the TV minister.

And he had to do what he could to stop that man from destroying the world. Which was a little more obvious, even if there wasn't any obvious way to set into the task.

And he had to try to find Ron Hawkins.

The last place he remembered seeing Ron was back at the airfield.

The airfield that he could see from the window in front of him—

And sure enough, there Ron was, crawling around on top of one of the pregnant jets, yanking wires and cables out of the missile's warhead. On the runway not far from him were half a dozen men with machine guns. They looked as though they were hunting for him—as though they knew Ron was somewhere around, and knew what he was doing, but didn't know exactly which plane he was on.

Soon enough, Luke thought, they'd find him. It couldn't take that long; there wasn't much of anywhere Ron could hide.

"I was almost free when I heard Herman bringing you in here," the evangelist said. "Climbing hand over hand toward that hook—kind of hard with my hands dead-cold for lack of circulation, but I almost had it anyway. Had to let go pretty suddenly when I heard Herman open the door. Think I might have yanked my wrist out of joint when I did—hard to be sure with everything so numb." He was looking around the room, his eyes scanning back and forth across the furniture and fixtures, as though he were searching for an idea. "Don't know if I can manage that trick again. You want to try it? You ought to be able to—you've probably still got the circulation in your hands."

Luke looked up at the rope, the hook. Looked over at the other man. "I've got a better idea," he said. "How bad are your wrists? Can you take a little extra weight for a few seconds?"

Luke saw George Stein wince at the suggestion for half an instant before he frowned and nodded. "Sure. Go ahead."

And quickly—quick enough to keep himself from thinking about what he was doing and feeling guilty about it—Luke kicked up with both legs. Wrapped his knees around George Stein's abdomen. Used the leverage that gave him to push his arms up to and over the hook that suspended him, freeing the rope—

And then momentum deserted him, and there was nothing left to suspend him, and he fell to the floor all but head first. His left shoulder ended up taking most of the impact of the fall, but all the same his head hit the carpet hard enough to leave him stunned and dizzy for a long moment.

He didn't let the dizziness stop him. He used his right hand to untie the rope from his left wrist. Let the rope hang from his right hand while he stood, wrapped his arms around George Stein's waist. Lifted him up and off of the hook; set him on his feet and unbound his wrists.

George Stein's hands were cold and wet to the touch; when Luke looked at them carefully he saw that there was a blue cast to them.

"You going to be okay? Think you'll be able to walk—or run, for that matter?"

George Stein rubbed his hands together clumsily, trying to bring the blood back into them. They didn't seem to move very well.

"I'll manage. Can you get us out of here? Do you know your way around?" He paused, looking thoughtful. "The people here think I'm dead. We'd better avoid them—if I know Herman he's told them to be wary of demons who come to them wearing my form."

Which sounded crazy to Luke. Didn't really change anything, since Luke planned to get away as discreetly as he could anyway. He was an intruder, and if George Stein was a prisoner here then it was best he didn't show his face either. He had to get both of them out of the building quietly, and then do what he could to help Ron.

And then? Luke felt more than a little hopeless. They had to do what they could to stop these people. And make sure that they didn't come back next week and start all over again. But for the life of him Luke didn't have a clue as to how three men might accomplish that.

Luke turned, walked toward the door. It wasn't locked—which, it seemed to him, showed an especially stupid arrogance on Herman Bonner's part.

Stupid or not, it was a blessing, and he wasn't about to complain.

There was no one in the next room; it was empty except for a couch and a few chairs—one of which faced the dead grey screen of Herman Bonner's terminal, staring out at Luke like a blind-cold eye. At the opposite side of the room the door still hung in pieces where Luke's shoulder had broken it.

"Come on," Luke said. "This way. There was no one watching the door by the loading bay when I came in. If we're lucky, there still won't be."

George Stein didn't say anything, but he followed Luke, limping a little, out through the broken door, toward the stairway.

Cheyenne County

Andy almost didn't notice when the monster turned away from the road.

He was way off ahead of the rest of them, chasing after the dog. Not doing a very good job of catching up with him, either. That dog was *fast*. Not that all dogs weren't fast, when you tried to run after them. But old Tom was fast and tricky, too. You could fool him, if you tried real hard. A couple of times he'd fooled Andy, too, and that'd left the boy more than a little impressed.

So, anyway, Andy and the dog were way off ahead of everybody else, when suddenly Andy looked back at the monster and the crowd of dead people who were following him. And what do you know: there they are, tromping off into somebody's cornfield like a parade that'd lost all its good sense.

Well.

Andy harrumphed.

You'd think, he told himself, that they'd at least call after me if they were going to change their minds about which way they were going.

That was exactly what they were doing, too. Up and changing course completely. Not just turning off at a different angle. Before they'd been heading down the dirt road, going west, more or less, as far as Andy could tell. And now they were turning northeast, heading right toward that big glowing thing on the horizon.

Andy didn't like the feel of that at all. He didn't know what could make a glow that bright and that big, but it wasn't anything he wanted to get close to, that was for sure.

"Hey!" he shouted. "Wait up! Where the heck are we going?"

No one answered and no one slowed down, not even for a second.

So Andy went running after them.

The dog followed him after just a little bit, as soon as he figured out that Andy wasn't chasing him any more.

The other creepy thing was one that Andy noticed when he got close enough to get a good look at everybody.

That Christine woman.

She wasn't anywhere in sight.

So he went up to the monster, who was walking zombie-like in front of everybody, looking like he was only halfway connected to the world. Tapped on his shoulder, and when that didn't work, slapped on his shoulder until he finally turned to look at Andy.

"So where we going, huh? And what happened to Christine?"

The monster shook his head. *We're going to the shore of the Lake of Fire. Christine will find us.*

And hard as Andy tried to get him to say anything else, the creature just kept walking.

Lake-of-Fire

There were half a dozen men guarding the loading bay doors when Luke Munsen and George Stein got in sight of them.

Luke saw them as soon as he poked his head out of the stairway door; he cursed under his breath and pulled himself back into the stairwell. Remembered that George Stein was a religious man, and apologized.

"The door is guarded, all right. And I heard voices in the hall too—coming from around the corner. We're going to have to find another way out of this place—another way completely. You know your way around here, don't you?"

George Stein nodded.

"Lots of other ways. Let me think for a second."

And stepped back for a moment, to rest his weight against the stairway rail. Which was a good thing, for that was when Luke looked up at the small eye-level window cut into the door, and saw three men with guns pass by outside in the corridor. He saw one of them turn and look into the stairwell; he only barely had time to move out of sight before it was too late.

"The basement," Stein said. "There's a passage downstairs that leads to the airfield, and as far as I know we haven't been using it. There's a lot of this base we haven't been using—not enough men."

That sounded pretty strange to Luke, especially when he thought of the crowds he'd seen storming the ABC building in New York.

"Really? I had the impression you had a large organization."

Stein shrugged. "Very large. But our paramilitaries are all out guarding the media network. *Were* guarding it. We couldn't afford to keep all of them here."

Stein was on the stairs again already, heading down; Luke followed him.

"Late yesterday," Stein said, "watching through the window up there, I saw a convoy of them coming in through the gate. And the convoy just kept coming, hour after hour. Through the gate, across the base, going to the empty barracks at the west end. It didn't take me long to realize Herman had lost the network and called everyone here."

"Here? Why here?"

"I don't know. Maybe Herman is expecting the Army to move in on us, after what he did to St. Louis."

"How many people do you think he has here?"

"Thousands." Stein stopped suddenly, went rigid. "Be quiet down here, and careful. I don't know my way around the basement, and God only knows what Herman's got them using it for."

Stepped down onto the basement landing. Opened the fire door like the ones on the floors above. Stepped out into a badly-lit corridor.

"We're going to have to explore a little," Stein said. "I'm not remembering my way around here very well at all. Only went down here a couple of times, and some things—some things are still a little fuzzy." Coughed. "You know what I mean? Herman . . . *did things* to me. After he killed me."

Luke didn't want to know. One of his own memories had come back to him as he listened to Stein—the memory of Herman and what he'd done to his creature, back at the institute. Of the day he'd walked in on Herman accidentally, and Herman had been stooped over his lab table, scalpel in hand, performing surgery. Could you call it surgery? No. Surgery was a sterile, careful, healing thing. Herman's lab was full of the air of the torture chamber. The creature was screaming when Luke opened the door, and all the while he stood in the doorway too shocked to move, it'd screamed and screamed, struggling against its straps to break free from Herman's knife.

A sign, taped to a door, misspelled and badly lettered in black marker:

REASTRICTED AREA—DO NOT ENTER WITHOUT AUTHORIZATION

And Stein walked right past it. Which seemed stupid to Luke; it had to be exactly the sort of place they ought to be looking. So he said "Shouldn't we look here?" and without waiting for an answer he turned, opened the door, began to step inside—

And Stein said, "No—! You don't want to see what's in there—"

By then Luke was already inside, and he *had* seen.

And George Stein was right: he wished that he hadn't.

Seen a man he'd only known as the President of the United States.

Lying naked and strapped to a bed. Staring at the ceiling like a congenital idiot, wide-eyed, not blinking. Drooling.

"God."

George Stein nodded.

"What's happened to him?"

Stein shook his head. "Wrong question." He looked away; the expression on his face looked like he felt ill. "You ought to ask: 'What is he?' or maybe 'What is it?'—what you're looking at isn't Paul Green. Never was Paul Green."

He was quiet for a good long while. The subject seemed to pain him.

"If that isn't President Green, who is he? Or what?"

George Stein shook his head.

"Paul had his appendix out—what, five years ago? A good while back, anyway. After the operation he had the doctors . . . save it for him. And put it in a jar full of alcohol (or maybe it was formaldehyde? don't ask me. I never wanted to know; too grisly for my taste by half) and kept it on his desk back home in Topeka. Used it for a paperweight." He stopped. Sighed. "When Paul died in that fire, Herman got it in his head that we could use the resurrection bacteria to bring him back. Somehow arranged for Paul's remains to be sent here. Might have worked, if the fire hadn't been so intense that it left no remains to find—just ash that no one could possibly sort from the ashes of the plane.

"Then Herman remembered the appendix. I thought it was—well, I thought it was too unnatural. Thought that from the start, in fact—from the time Herman first tried to get Paul's ashes sent to us. I *didn't* feel it strongly enough to start screaming at the top of my lungs. When Herman sent someone out to Topeka to get the jar off Paul's desk, I didn't try to stop him.

"An hour after Herman took the lid off that jar, something was *growing* inside the glass. If I'd known it was going to grow into this—" he nodded toward the bed, where the thing that looked like Paul Green was breathing slowly, but otherwise not moving at all "—if I'd known, maybe I would have raised hell and put a stop to it. Looking back, I can't really say that for sure. None of us was quite sure what was wrong with it. Maybe it didn't have any of Paul's memories? I don't know. The way I'd figure, if that was the case it'd act like a baby, maybe— screaming, crying. Carrying on. It's not like that at all. Won't eat—won't even swallow when you shove food down its mouth. I kind of tend to believe that there was something wrong with it in the first place—DNA stuff, you know? Like the part of it that tells how to grow the brain? You know what I mean?"

Luke had a vague memory of the idea behind DNA. A very vague idea. He remembered enough to know that he'd spent most of his adult life working with it, and that was about all. So he grunted, and nodded, and let George Stein go on, because he didn't want to think about the parts of himself that he didn't have any more.

George Stein shrugged. "There isn't much to be done

with—with him. Herman tried to kill him, but it didn't work; an hour after he died there he was again, staring at the ceiling. Drooling. Breathing slow, dead-steady. I had him put in this room—because this isn't a place where anyone ought to be in the first place."

Luke raised an eyebrow at that. A place where no one should go? Which led directly to: Why not?

And that was when he noticed the door at the back of the room.

A solid-looking, unpainted, unburnished, grey-steel door. Sealed with rubber around its edges. The sort of door he'd have expected . . . oh, in a military airplane. Guarding the passage of air into a room where someone worked with biological contaminants.

It wasn't a door to either of those things, of course. Luke remembered enough of his work to recognize a laboratory, and this place was nothing like a laboratory.

What it had, in fact, was the feel of a warehouse.

The door was the entrance to an institutional freezer.

Dear God.

Luke swallowed back bile; he was feeling sick with himself.

What has he got in deep freeze that no one should see?

And the answer to that was obvious, too.

Not what. Who.

The soldiers who are supposed *to be at this base.*

"We're going to open that freezer up, George." Luke was disgusted, and furious. *This man was a part of the murder . . . of how many men?* He thought of the number of buildings he'd seen as he'd walked toward the place. Thought of their size. *Thousands. Maybe he didn't kill them himself, and maybe he wasn't happy about it when it happened. He let it happen all the same.* "We're going to open up the freezer, and we're going to turn it off. And we're going to fix it so that it can't ever be turned on again."

George Stein was silent. His mouth hung agape. He looked terrified—and rattled and more than anything else his face was guilty.

"You understand me, don't you, George? Where are the controls to this thing? Nod if you know. Point to them."

He shook his head. So Luke stepped across the room.

And pulled the freezer door open.

It was an enormous freezer.

The kind of freezer you needed for a kitchen that had to feed several thousand men: a freezer the size of a banquet hall.

Bigger than that, maybe.

And big as it was, the freezer was crowded.

The corpses of soldiers were piled in rows like firewood, and stacked three and four deep. There was hardly room to pass through between the heaps of them.

None of the corpses looked as though it had come to death by violence. Well, maybe that one over there, the one covered with crystallized blood—there was a deep pit where the right side of its chest ought to have been. That one was an exception.

The rest of them, though—they looked as though they'd died in their sleep.

Which was ludicrous, of course: it just wasn't possible for several thousand young men to die peaceably and of natural causes all at once.

They were dressed as though they'd died in their sleep, too.

As though someone poisoned them, all at once. Poison in their food, maybe? It was possible, Luke thought. One big, industrial kitchen. Everyone eating more or less at once. A slow poison that would kill them all before they woke in the morning. He couldn't see that killing all of them, or even killing all of them but one. A few of them would have to have missed dinner, it seemed to Luke. And that would have made for an ugly scene.

No. It had to be poison, all right, but not something they'd eaten. Likely someone had gassed their barracks while they'd slept.

And Herman Bonner had piled their corpses here, in the freezer, where they'd be certain to stay dead.

There.

The box of circuit breakers was on the wall outside the freezer, right beside the door. Right where he'd have expected it if he'd thought to look. Luke pulled back the metal cover to the circuit box, pushed down each of the dozen switches inside it. By the time he was done it was black inside the freezer— God knew which one of the switches had been for the overhead lights inside it.

It wasn't enough, of course. Five minutes from now

someone could come through here and switch them all back on. And as soon as he stepped away the steel door would swing closed, and the freezer was cold enough and insulated enough that shut off it could stay frozen for days—maybe even weeks.

So Luke looked around the room and spotted the heavy wooden chair. Picked it up and used it to smash the circuit box, smash it again till the thing was beyond any hope of repair. When he was done he took what was left of the chair and jammed it into the hinge of the freezer door. It wouldn't be too hard for someone to yank it out and close the door, but it was the best Luke could manage—there was nothing in that room that could have been any use at all for destroying heavy-gauge steel doors.

"We should go," George Stein said. "Someone may have heard. And even if they haven't, it isn't *that* deserted down here. If we're here long enough, sooner or later someone will think to look for us down here."

Luke grunted. He was looking into the freezer—dark, now, except for what little light spilled into it from the open door. It would be a long time before anything in that room was thawed enough for the infection to take hold and bring them back to life. God knew what could happen between now and then. He wanted to do something . . . something more certain for the murdered soldiers. Hard as he tried to think of anything—anything at all—that would help to bring them back to life more quickly, everything he could think of he'd already done or sounded as though it could cause more harm than good.

So he turned back to face George Stein, and he said, "Yeah—you're right. We need to get out of here." And started out through the door. Into the corridor. There at the end of the hall was a glowing-red EXIT sign—Luke hadn't seen it when they'd been in the hall before, but he certainly should have. That sign was pointing toward the passage George Stein had told them about—the one that led to the airfield. He took off running toward it; he could hear Stein following a few feet behind him.

In a moment they'd be out of this place. They could give Ron Hawkins a hand, and then they could find a place to hide and figure out what it was they were supposed to be doing. They'd think of something. It'd all work out.

Luke told himself that, but he didn't have a whole lot of faith in it.

And when he turned the bend in the hall that the sign pointed toward, he saw Herman Bonner waiting for them, grinning. His arms crossed. Blocking their way.

He was alone.

"I thought I'd find you here," Bonner said. And he started toward Luke, bloodlust shining in his eyes—

Luke was still running. Right toward the man. And he didn't slow and he didn't stop—he threw up his arms like a football lineman. Slammed into Bonner, knocking him over.

And just kept going.

Cheyenne County

They were walking, now, along a bluff above the shore of hell.

That was what it seemed to Christine, at least. Out beyond the bluff was a pit of shattered glass and white-molten rock that seemed to stretch out to forever. Which was an exaggeration, maybe—maybe it was only the size and shape of a lake.

A lake of fire.

"Tell me now," Christine said. "There isn't much time. I can feel it. What do you expect of me?"

The old woman smiled. "I only want you to be yourself." It was a strange smile, unsettling. It made Christine feel as naked as she'd been the first time she'd met the woman. "Remember the pendant that I gave you. You still have it, don't you?"

Automatically, Christine's hand went to her breast. She drew the stone up out of her blouse, to look at it, to see it—

And when she looked up again, the old woman had disappeared.

Just as she had the first time Christine had met her.

Disappeared utterly, totally, and without leaving behind a trace of her passing.

And she'd left Christine alone at the gate of hell.

Lake-of-Fire

A dozen planes.

There were at least a dozen more planes to disable before Ron could get himself the hell away from here. Get the hell away from those half-dozen assholes with their machine guns who weren't positive he was on the airfield, weren't sure where he might be, but kept firing at shadows. Twice they'd come close to hitting him, but mostly they kept pounding holes in the planes.

And in the missiles.

That was the part that scared Ron. Scared him seriously. One of the bullets had hit squarely on the warhead of a missile while Ron was only a few feet away from it, and the shell of the thing had shattered in a thousand directions, and something *crack*ed inside the mechanism and for a moment Ron had seen himself devoured by a shell of fire hot and infinite as the sun—

Then the cracking sound was gone, and the bomb hadn't gone off, and after a moment Ron realized that he was still alive, and that he just might continue to be alive. It was enough of a relief that he almost lost his grip on the plane's fuselage. Breath leaked out of him in something that wasn't quite a sigh.

He managed to keep his grip. Barely. When he looked back up at the warhead he saw the bullet had torn lose the jury-rigged wiring for him.

Which left eleven planes. Or was it ten? He kept losing track of the count.

He eased himself down the cable that he'd used to climb up onto the plane. Let himself drop onto the runway. Stood still for a long moment, taking a good look around, spotting the fools with the machine guns so that he could avoid them.

Noticed that he wasn't hearing gunfire off in the woods any more. Which meant that the irregulars out there had either finally killed each other off, or figured out that Luke and Ron weren't out there any more. Or maybe it just meant that they'd run out of ammunition. It wasn't likely good news: as long as they kept themselves busy out there, there was no way for them to join up with the idiots here on the airfield. If enough of them showed up here, they just might be able to

find him—even in the dark, with so many planes to hide
among.

Shouting. At the far end of the runway. Up there by the
first plane he'd disabled. Whatever that meant, it wasn't good.
The last thing Ron needed was more trouble. Or was it bad?
Whatever it was, it'd got the attention of the irregulars. That
wasn't a thing Ron was going to complain about—it left him
free to run directly toward the next jet, instead of skulking
around carefully the way he'd had to since they'd first spotted
him.

Up. Hand over hand along the cable that ran toward the
next warhead. Both hands gripped around the wires where
they went into the missile. *Pull* and yank them back, toward
him. Out of the rocket's shell. Down again.

Ten left. (Nine? Eleven? *Those* planes, over there, and to
hell with how many of them there were.)

They were shouting at the other end of the runway.
Didn't he recognize one of those voices? Yes—he did. Of
course he did. That was Luke Munsen's voice. What in the
name of God was Luke doing here? Why was he making a
spectacle of himself? Even if they had lousy night vision, these
irregulars weren't the sort of people whose attention a sane
man would want to attract.

Christ. There wasn't *time* to worry about this now. Not
when he was so close to done. What was Luke doing? Ron stole
a glance down the runway. Saw the silhouettes of two men
down there by the first of the planes. Who was that with Luke?

No time. It didn't matter who it was—there wasn't time to
let it matter.

Back on the tarmac. Running toward the last of the
transport planes. Jumping up toward the cable, getting ahold
of it, climbing . . .

When he was near the top he stole another glance toward
Luke and his companion. What were they doing? Purposely
getting the attention of the irregulars, and now that they had
it—*running.* Not running sensibly in among the planes or out
toward the woods. They were running off across the open
landing field, toward the next runway over.

Where they'd make even better targets.

They were going to get themselves killed.

Very soon.

Ron pulled the cables out of the warhead. Let himself drop back to the runway.

Spotted Luke and the man with him, whoever he was. Damn it—here Ron was, trying to save the world, and they had to go and try to get themselves killed. There wasn't time for this kind of nonsense.

No time at all. The hell with them, he thought. If they wanted to get themselves killed, that was their business. Wasn't like there was a whole lot Ron could do about it, was there? . . . Well, maybe there was. It didn't matter. Saving the world had to come ahead of fishing a friend out of some boneheaded trouble he'd made for himself, didn't it?

Didn't it?

He thought about that for about ten seconds, cursing under his breath all the while. And realized that it didn't matter what ought to come first. Realized that it didn't matter what was at stake; he couldn't stand back and watch and do nothing as a friend was hunted down and shot.

Saving the world would just have to wait.

Ron took off after Luke and whoever that was and the irregulars running with everything he had. There weren't many times in his existence when Ron had run like he did then, and most of those times had been in the last few days.

Running for the love of life, in fact, was getting to be almost an ordinary occurrence. He'd certainly had enough practice to begin to get good at it. And he had an advantage over the irregulars, too: each of them was weighted down by a heavy machine gun, and by enough ammunition to blow up a bridge. A couple of them had other weapons, too—knives. Pistols. One of them looked as though he had a bayonet fixed to the muzzle of his gun, though it was hard to be sure of that in the moonlight.

Ron wasn't carrying anything heavier than the shirt on his back. Which was why he managed to catch up with the bastards, in spite of the fact that they had a couple hundred yards' lead on him when he started running.

They didn't even hear him coming. Partly that was because he was a quiet runner and they weren't expecting him. Probably just as much because they weren't all that bright. They had to be pretty stupid: this was the same crew that had been fueling the jets and shooting at him in the dark—what kind of an idiot, Luke asked himself, goes around fueling a plane with a loaded weapon in his hands? And then is stupid enough to start firing the thing indiscriminately?

The one Ron caught up with first never really knew what hit him. He had his hands wrapped around his gun, and he was firing it every now and then while he ran, and Ron grabbed the gun's shoulder strap right out of the crook of the man's neck, grabbed the gun right out of his hands. Which just happened to pull the fool right out from on top of his own feet, so that he went slamming back-of-the-skull-first right into the dirt. Ron didn't really mean for his foot to come down square in the center of the man's face—but when it happened it wasn't something he regretted especially, not when he thought about the way that atomic warhead's casing burst wide open only a couple of feet away from his head. Oh, maybe he did feel a little guilt—but not until he felt the man's nose, and then his whole face, give in and press up toward his brain. It wasn't the sort of thing you could feel good about.

It was about then that the man's three friends noticed what was going on. By the time they did, of course, Ron had his finger on the machine gun's trigger—

And the gun was out of ammunition.

Oh, there were plenty of rounds on the first man's corpse, of course. What good were they going to do Ron over there? What good could they do him at all, for that matter?—it wasn't like he knew how to load a machine gun.

The three irregulars who were still alive were turning toward Ron, now. Their guns were drawn, and Ron could see one of them beginning to pull his trigger.

And what was there for Ron to do? He hit the bastard with the butt of his rifle. Hit him good, too—right below the ear and a little forward, breaking the man's jaw right at the hinge as soon as he hit, and by the time Ron finished following through there were lots of teeth flying out of his mouth.

Not a pretty sight.

Especially not for the man standing next to him, who got two of those broken teeth right in the face. One of them actually stuck in the man's eye, and while he was howling mostly with disgust and a little from pain Ron jumped on the third man, grabbing his gun—

And a moment later Ron had shot both of those last two. One of them while he was all but unarmed, and Ron thought that maybe that was cold-blooded murder and he tried not to think about it.

Which wasn't all that hard, since there were a thousand headlights coming at them from every direction.

Ten thousand, maybe.

Luke and his friend were heading back toward Ron. Which was the last thing they ought to be doing right now. The fence was only a couple hundred yards away; if they could get over that the jeeps and trucks would have a hell of a time getting at them.

"No, damn it. *Run*. Go for the fence!"

Ron saw Luke look confused for a long moment before he turned back around and headed off. By the time he'd started Ron was running himself.

Not that it did any good.

Shooting. Off and on for most of an hour Graham Perkins had heard the sound of gunfire—and there it was again scratching through the softness of the summer night like the talons of a bird of prey.

Something was wrong.

No one had come to see him since late afternoon. Which meant that it had been hours since anyone had given him the medicine they used to ease his heart. For the first time since Herman Bonner had found him, Graham was feeling the worry and the tension that had followed him all through his life, and trailed beyond it.

It wasn't good. Graham was President now. He couldn't let himself sit back and do nothing but worry over things; it was a President's job—his duty!—to act on the things that worried him. And Graham knew that his heart wasn't ready for anything as precipitous as that.

Still. Still. A duty was a duty.

Herman was so good at taking care of these things. Herman ought to be here, Graham thought. If Herman were here, he'd know what to do about the sound of gunfire right outside his wall.

Herman wasn't here. He was . . . where? His office, maybe? Likely that was so. Herman spent most of his time in the suite of rooms he used as both office and living quarters.

Well then, the answer was obvious. What Graham had to

do was go up to Herman's office and tell him about the gunfire. Once Graham had done that, he was sure, Herman would get those guns taken care of.

It was so obvious, in fact, that Graham wondered why he hadn't thought of it before.

Graham began to wonder if it was such a wonderful idea when he saw how deserted the corridors were outside his room. It wasn't just as though there was no one in them— which there wasn't—but rather there was a cold emptiness in the halls, as though there wasn't another soul in the entire building.

By the time he got to Herman Bonner's office Graham Perkins was convinced that he was completely and utterly alone. And when he saw the broken door to Herman's office, and the blood all over everything in the adjoining room, Graham became certain that the worst had happened. He wasn't exactly certain what the worst might be—not even when he took a moment to reflect on the idea—but Graham Perkins was convinced of it all the same.

And if the worst had come to pass, then it was Graham's duty, as Commander-in-Chief, to take the situation into his own hands.

Graham's gut lurched when that realization came to him. The drugs might be fading, but they were still with him; he didn't have enough of his wits about him to be a Commander-in-Chief. Graham *knew* that. And he knew that even if his head had been clearer, he wouldn't have been ready for the Presidency: he still hadn't sorted himself out of the events and images of the week past.

The truth was that he didn't know if he'd ever get himself that sorted out. He didn't know if he'd be able to do that sorting. And he wasn't even sure that he wanted to do the sorting. In fact, when he thought of what he wanted to do what he thought of was a small cabin in the deep Vermont woods, not far from a stream. He owned that cabin—he'd owned it for most of ten years, since his grandfather had passed on and willed it to him.

The cabin held a lot of appeal.

But Graham had a duty, and there was no denying it. He was President. He'd taken responsibility for that job when he'd signed on to run for the Vice Presidency, and it wasn't the sort of responsibility you could deny once you'd taken it on yourself.

Out there—Graham saw tiny flashes of light through Herman's window. And again the sound of gunfire. Out on the landing field.

If that was where the trouble was, then Graham had to go to it. It wasn't a thing he wanted to do, but he had to go there even so.

And he did it, too. Graham was proud of that fact. Most of his life he'd shied away from the things he didn't have the heart to face. But a President was more than just a man, he was more than just a politician: a President had no right to be a coward, and even if he was afraid Graham Perkins didn't let that fear rule him.

It was a big step. A big enough step to change him, all by itself. It cleared his head, just to begin with, but it did more than that, too. By the time Graham Perkins got out to the runway and found it empty his heart was a stronger thing than it had ever been in all the years he'd been alive. And because it was strong, when he found the runway empty and void of whatever trouble he'd set out to pursue, he didn't skulk back to his room and hole up, the way he might have an hour or two before.

Instead he looked around until he found where the trouble had gone—to a field maybe a quarter of a mile away.

And he followed it.

Ron Hawkins wasn't the least bit inclined to give up a fight. Especially not a fight like this one—where not just his own future hung on the scale, or even the future of Luke Munsen and his friend, but—when you got right down to it—the future of the whole damned world.

He also knew that there are situations where a man has to surrender and bide his time. Not give up, exactly. Give in, and wait for an opportunity to present itself.

If this wasn't one of those, then nothing was.

They were surrounded, just the three of them. And not just surrounded by a dozen men, or even a couple dozen. Surrounded by hundreds of men—thousands. With odds like that, and only Ron among the three of them armed with a single gun, it wasn't even possible to go down fighting. (Oh, sure, he could take a few of them down. Maybe as many as a dozen—it was a machine gun, after all. But with that many

men, sooner or later they could just walk over him, and Ron
didn't have any trouble figuring that out.)

So when the trucks and the jeeps finally managed to sur-
round them—when they were still at least thirty yards from the
fence—Ron threw down the gun and put his hands in the air,
because if he could keep himself alive maybe he could figure a way
out of this. Luke and his friend did pretty much the same thing.
Maybe their reasoning was similar, and maybe it wasn't.

That was when Herman Bonner stepped out from between two jeeps, leering at them.

What in the hell was Herman Bonner doing here? Last
Ron had seen of him he was in Luke Munsen's lab, planting a
package that turned out to be a bomb.

That was what he was doing here—that package was
where all of this had started. And somehow Herman Bonner
was the source of all the events that'd happened since. He'd
started this long nightmare back then, and now here he was at
the core of things, putting an end to them.

Or an end to Ron, at least. And Luke. And Luke's friend,
whoever he was.

"Herman, let's put an end to this," Luke's friend was
saying, all but echoing the words inside Ron's head. "What do
you want from us? Why not let us be?"

And Herman Bonner's eyes got all righteous and bulging.
"Demon! Demons! You steal the form of my dearest friend—
our murdered shepherd—and now you ape his voice as well!
You will learn, now, demon. You will learn that a creature up
out of hell can die an excruciating, horrible, and eternal
death!"

And Bonner turned toward the man at his right, and for
just half a moment Ron saw surprise on his face, as though the
man were closer than he expected anyone to be, and perhaps
as though he wasn't the man Bonner had expected. Bonner hid
the surprise quickly, but once he recognized the man beside
him there was concern in his eyes that he didn't make any real
effort to mask.

When the man spoke to Bonner he spoke in a soft
voice—but not a voice too quiet for Ron to hear.

"They've disabled half the missiles, Dr. Bonner," the man
said. "Maybe more. I've only had a moment to look at them,
but from what I can see it'll take me days to get them wired
back together again. A couple look like they might not take too
much effort. Some of them—I don't know that they can be
fixed. The electronics are awfully delicate. There isn't much I

can do for a broken circuit board. Not with the equipment I've got here."

And Herman Bonner screamed with frustration.

"We need them all," he said. "*All* of them! Do you hear me?"

The soft-spoken man had stepped back at least half a dozen feet; he looked terrified. "Yes, Dr. Bonner. You know I do the best I can I—"

Bonner turned toward the man on his other side—a grizzled, bloody-eyed man with lieutenants' bars pinned to his Army-surplus camouflage coat. "There's no time. It will have to do. It must." Listening to the sound of the man's voice, Ron was sure he was about to lash out, hit somebody. "Get the missiles that we still have into the air immediately, Lieutenant. Direct them toward our highest priority targets. Don't waste a single moment."

Before the Lieutenant had taken three steps Ron heard another voice, somewhere out of sight but not far away at all.

"Herman?"

From out beyond the ring of jeeps and trucks.

"That was you I heard screaming, wasn't it, Herman? Hard to tell for sure, but it sounded like you. What's going on? Is everything all right?"

Ron recognized that voice. He'd heard it—on television? Yes. And on the radio, too. At election time.

It was the Vice President's voice.

Herman Bonner sighed. "Yes, Mr. President. Everything is fine now. We were attacked—by demons. We have them now. We've captured them, and momently we will execute them."

The Vice President—or was he President now? Herman Bonner was calling him President, but Ron wasn't the least bit sure that made it so—the Vice President stepped out through the circle of trucks, stood and looked Bonner in the eye.

"Execute them, Herman? How exactly do you go about executing a demon? Especially now, with God raising up the dead so fast that no one stays gone long enough to hold a funeral?"

Herman Bonner smiled.

"By casting them into the Lake of Fire," he said. "Come! As President, it is an execution you must witness!"

Over on the runway the first of the planes was taking off.

At the Edge
of the Lake of Fire

After she'd waited at the edge of the Lake of Fire for most of an hour, Leigh began to worry. Was it safe here? Wasn't nuclear radiation dangerous? Certainly the glow that came from the lake was radiation. And radiation was something that could kill you. Leigh knew that, even if she had been a lit major.

Maybe she had dreamed that phone call. Maybe she was going out of her mind. There wasn't anything here in the middle of radioactive nowhere that required her presence, was there? Seriously and genuinely *required* Leigh herself? There wasn't anything at all here, except the sound of the wind on scorched grass. And the glow. And the car. And Leigh.

She looked at the keys in the ignition. All she had to do was start the engine, pull away. . . . She could probably find a motel open down on I-70. Spend a quiet, easy night watching television.

Yeah. Anything was better than roasting herself slowly beside an atomic fire. Even television was appealing in comparison.

She looked at her watch. Thought about the phone call, the impossible phone call that had already sent her halfway around the world. How could she go that far, only to leave after an hour? Was the wait really that bad? No, not that bad. Tedious, maybe, but not terrible. She took a deep breath, looked at her own motives. Realized that the reason she wanted to go was because she was afraid. God knew what she was afraid of, but Leigh Doyle was afraid.

She sighed.

It wasn't right to leave. Not yet.

Another hour.

At least.

And maybe hours after that.

Lake-of-Fire, Kansas

The planes went up all at once, or nearly so. They took off one after the other on five separate runways, and inside of ten minutes there was only a single plane left on the airstrip. And that plane wasn't flying anyplace; even from this distance Ron could see the flaps on its left wing hanging shredded and useless. Bullet holes all over that wing, and the fuselage behind it. One of those fools had done a good job on it while he'd been trying to kill Ron.

The technician explained it to Bonner and the Vice President as Ron and Luke and George Stein stood waiting. It would take days to fix the plane, the tech said. He was sweating nervously. Fixing that kind of damage wasn't any small job, and besides they didn't have the parts. Or mechanics. Or tools. Well, maybe the right tools were somewhere on the base, but the tech hadn't been able to find them. Yes, the engines were working, working just fine. All the time he spoke he kept glancing nervously up at the departing planes, as though he didn't really want to help blow up the world—but couldn't find a way to avoid it.

Not that there *was* a way to avoid it; the last of the planes was in the air. There wasn't anybody in the world who could and would call them home.

If Bonner saw the technician's dis-ease, he made no sign of it. None Ron could see.

All through the explanation (planes rushing thunderous into the sky) the Vice President stood staring dumbly at Herman Bonner. Eyes kind of glazed, expression slack. Watching him, Ron almost thought that there might be something wrong with the man's brain.

Then the fireworks started. In the distance, at first. Roaring explosions and fiery clouds so bright that for half a moment Ron thought that the nuclear Apocalypse had begun at the edge of their horizon. Was that one of Bonner's planes? Yes. It had to be. Then that first fireball faded, and he knew that it wasn't any atom bomb going off. No atom bomb would burn that briefly. The explosion was the kerosene in the plane's fuel tanks, set afire by God only knew what—

All at once there were dozens of anti-aircraft rockets at the edge of the sky and planes were bursting into balls of heat and light all that filled the whole horizon.

And Herman Bonner screamed.

Ron almost started screaming himself, for fear that one of the exploding planes would ignite the nuclear missile that it carried.

None of them did.

Not a single one.

Then it was still beyond the far edge of the runway, and almost pretty, the way the warm summer dusk flickered with the light of kerosene burning in the distance.

Until Herman Bonner stopped screaming, and spoke. Shouted, actually.

"General Thompsen! General Bruce Thompsen!"

There wasn't any need to shout, of course. The general was right at Bonner's elbow.

"Here, Herman."

Bonner didn't say anything. He looked too choked on frustration and rage to speak.

"The Army, Herman. Whole divisions of it camped just over the hill. We knew this could happen."

Bonner tensed; for a moment Ron thought he was going to hit the man. But he didn't. Instead his eyes got cold and hard. "Then we need to get more missiles, don't we, General? And to get more missiles we need to move to another base. And to get there, we must first obliterate those who hem us in." He gestured off toward the hills where the rockets had exploded. "Take your army—take every man we have here—and destroy them."

"Yes sir." Thompsen said.

And then he glanced at Ron and Luke and George Stein.

"Tim and I will see to them. You have guns for us?"

"Of course." And the General nodded to an aide, who ran off on the errand.

That was when Ron realized that he was hearing the drone of a plane overhead. Had one of them gotten away? And if it had, what was it doing here, instead of heading off for points unknown? He glanced up, to get a look at it—

It was a serious mistake. Bonner and Thompsen both had their eyes on him just then; by looking up he drew their attention to the plane.

Bonner hissed. "Is it ours?"

Thompsen hesitated a moment, looking at it carefully. "No."

"Then shoot it down."

In Transit by Air
over Eastern Colorado

"I reckon that it isn't," Bill said. She looked at him kind of puzzled-like, which was understandable when you considered that the two of them had been there staring at each other for at least five minutes, and in all that time neither of them had said a word. "I mean, love isn't the kind of thing you ought to lie to yourself about. Not even when you don't understand it."

She nodded. "Ah. Yes."

After that they were both quiet again for a long time. And this time it was she who broke the silence. "What should we do?"

Bill stole a glance at the boy, who was watching the both of them with the kind of wrapped-up intensity most people reserve for campfires and lava lamps. "I don't know. Relax. See what happens. Seems to me we shouldn't push anything too hard."

She nodded again, looking a little impressed. A little reverent, even, which made Bill real uncomfortable. How could a woman like that, some kind of a superwoman, look at Bill like he was one of the three wise kings? Mind, now, Bill wasn't ashamed of what he was. Just the opposite, point of fact. He had his pride. He knew what he was, and wasn't. And if there was anything Bill wasn't, wise was it.

She was still looking at him like he was something he wasn't when the navigator came out of the cockpit.

"Heard some noise from back here a little while ago," he said. "Any trouble with the drop?"

Bill shook his head. Felt the whole world sway with the throbbing deep behind his nose. "Nah."

Was that the sound of thunder in the distance?

The navigator looked kind of skeptically at Bill and the blood still seeping out of his nose. Shrugged. "If you say so. We ought to be landing pretty soon. Pilot's got to find a highway or something to put this thing down—can't land at Eidner, under the circumstances. You heard the base was in the hands of a bunch of fundamentalist survival nuts? Well, it is. Landing's going to be someplace that ain't a runway, and it isn't likely to be smooth. I suggest all three of you get back into

your seats and get your seat belts on, if you don't want to end
up with any more broken bones."

Bill didn't especially appreciate the man's tone, but he got
into his seat anyway. Buckled his belt too. Which was a good
thing, since something went boom right about the time the
navigator closed the cockpit door. And the plane went into a
dive again.

And this time there was nothing to stop their fall.

Because the missile that hit them—a missile fired by
order of Herman Bonner, down at Lake-of-Fire née Eidner Air
Force Base—the missile that hit them took out one of the
plane's engines, and left the other all but useless.

As they dropped Bill stared through his window, watching
the molten Lake of Fire hurtling up to greet them.

At the Edge
of the Lake of Fire

Leigh had almost begun to lose heart again when the
fireworks started. First there were airplanes in the near
distance, bursting into shimmery clouds of fire as the missiles
struck them; then the final plane, out of sync with the rest
because it had come from another direction. Hit by another,
smaller rocket.

Hurtling down through the air like an eagle with a torn
wing.

Where it hurtled toward was Leigh herself.

After that it didn't matter much whether Leigh had the
heart for the mission that the President had set her to. She was
too busy being scared out of her mind, running away from the
rent-a-car because she couldn't get it started quickly enough
and it looked to be the exact target of the falling plane.

The way it turned out she was all wrong. Leigh misjudged
the trajectory of the plane about as thoroughly as was humanly
possible. It wasn't falling toward her car. It was falling into the
field, about a hundred yards away from her car.

And the direction in which Leigh had decided to run was
precisely the direction in which the plane was falling. As she
ran, her path and the plane's converged.

It seemed to Leigh as she ran for her life across that field
that the plane was chasing her, hunting her; trying to crush the

life from her body with the weight and momentum of its coming impact. The truth was, of course, that she was chasing it. The only luck she had to save her from her confusion was the fact that she wasn't able to run one whit faster than she did. If she had been, surely she would have made it to the spot where the falling plane hit ground. Even as it was she managed to get herself too close; when the plane dug itself into the dirt she wasn't more than half a dozen yards from the tip of its near wing. If it had hit as hard as she expected it to, Leigh would have been shredded by bursting wreckage and earth exploding under the impact.

The plane didn't fall like a stone, and its landing did surprisingly little damage. Either by the grace of God or through some device of the pilot, the plane met ground at a low, gentle grade, and instead of bursting like a bomb it dug a furrow into the soil like a plow sent down from heaven. Not to say it landed harmless like a feather: dirt went flying everywhere, so much of it that it knocked Leigh to the ground and covered her in three inches of soil and stone. Force broke against the plane, too; crushing the cockpit, reducing the three men inside to pulp and plasm. Further back, the fuselage cracked, tore, accordioned. By the time the plane finally came to a stop, hanging over the edge of the Lake of Fire, there were great rifts in the plane's hull, wide as doors.

Leigh sat up, shook away the dirt that covered her. Brushed as much of it as she could from her face. Her eyes especially. Her hands.

And looked at the fallen plane, poised as it was on a precipice over the Lake.

Is this why he sent me here? To save whoever I could from that plane?

There was no way to know. And what did it matter whether there was a plan behind it or not? It wasn't as though Leigh could ignore it all. If there were people in that plane who were still alive, she had to do what she could for them. There wasn't any way she could live with herself if she didn't.

Lake-of-Fire

A white heat of panic overtook Luke as he watched the army of irregulars roll out the gates of the base. He didn't understand that panic, and because he didn't understand it it scared him even more than it would have otherwise. There shouldn't have been any need for panic, after all. The story was over, wasn't it? The cavalry, out over the hill, had shot down the evil flying drones as they set out to destroy the world. There was still a horde of bad guys, here—the irregulars—but whatever threat they posed, it wasn't as immediate or ultimate as nuclear destruction.

Herman Bonner was smiling.

All by itself, that was a reason for panic: Herman Bonner wasn't a man for smiling. And when he did smile, it was the smile of a cat toying with its prey.

Was there something he knew—something that Luke hadn't yet noticed? Was he that confident of his army?

Bonner turned, spoke to the technician. "I've waited a hundred years, Tim," he said. "And I've planned very carefully. Do they really think they can stop me? How can they think this?" He laughed. The technician went white as a sheet. "They can give me pause, Tim. They truly can. But no man nor woman can stop me. *I* am inevitable."

When the technician spoke, there was a stutter in his voice. "Of course you are, Dr. Bonner."

"Thank you, Tim. That's very kind of you. Direct these . . . people into the plane that we still have. The President and I will join you momently."

"Plane, Dr. Bonner? I don't understand. That plane can't get off the ground with its wings such a mess. Nothing we can do with it but taxi around on the ground."

"Exactly, Tim. Direct them onto the plane. I will join you."

And Bonner put his arm around the Vice President, and he turned, and he walked away.

The technician gestured with his gun. "Go ahead," he said. He was looking at Luke. "You heard him. Get in the plane over there." The man was covered with his own sweat; he sounded more afraid than threatening. Afraid for his life, Luke thought.

Well, I can understand that.

Which didn't make Luke one bit more eager to get on that plane, or find whatever it was that Herman Bonner had planned for them at its destination.

He went where he was told anyway, because the man had a gun and he looked frightened enough to use it.

Ron and George Stein did the same.

It was only a moment after he went into the cabin that Luke had his revelation. Which was maybe a little too strong a word for it, since it was kind of obvious.

Even if he has a gun, there are three of us. And only one of him, until Bonner gets here.

Now, he thought. *We should jump him while we can.*

And he looked over at Ron, and saw the same idea rising up behind his eyes.

Then, before he could whisper to his friend, something came over Luke. Something strange, and wonderful, and frightening: that strange certainty that had guided him half-way across the continent.

No, it told him. *Not here, not now. It isn't time.*

And then it disappeared.

And because he had pure, blind faith, Luke Munsen looked into his friend's eyes. And ever so slightly, he shook his head.

At the Lake of Fire

The metal skin of the broken plane was burning hot to Leigh Doyle's touch; she found that out by bracing her hand on the fuselage as she climbed in through a fissure in the jet's hull. She felt the skin of her fingers begin to scorch, and yanked her hand away, almost immediately—but not soon enough to save her palm a wicked burn.

Maybe that was just as well; the pain distracted her for that long moment as she entered the plane. Because she was distracted she didn't notice the blood in the forward end of the plane. Blood so thick, so much of it that it covered the walls like wet red paint. When she saw it she might have mistaken it for paint—but couldn't, much as she wanted to make that mistake. Because of the gore straining out through the crushed, jammed door to the cockpit. There was no mistaking *that* for paint.

Leigh Doyle screamed.

She didn't even realize she was screaming, not at first.

She was too frightened to hear it; too unsettled by the sight of so much blood to feel the rawness it made of her throat.

The scream spent itself before she heard it.

After a while Leigh forced her eyes away from the sight, turned, looked toward the back of the plane, trying to find people she could help. And saw four who looked as though they might be alive: a boy, a woman, and two men. All of them dazed and bruised and bleeding.

A hospital. I've got to get them to a hospital.

Where was the nearest hospital? Leigh couldn't remember seeing one on her trip from Denver. Not that she'd been looking for one. She closed her eyes, tried to remember the map that the car-rental company had given her. The nearest good-sized town was . . . Kanorado. Yes, that was it. Kanorado. The town just over the Colorado border, down on I-70. She wasn't sure she'd be able to find it from here, especially after the way she'd got lost on the way in. Well, she'd have to find it anyway. There wasn't time for getting lost, or for worrying about it.

She went to the boy. Unbuckled his seat belt. Hesitated. Should she really be moving him? She wasn't an ambulance technician. She could end up hurting him, just by picking him up. Looked at him more carefully. He was unconscious, just as the others were. Bleeding from a deep gash just above his right eye. Big bruises all over his face. Swelling at his waist where the seat belt had dug into him during the crash. He didn't *look* like he had any bones broken. That was the biggest danger, she thought. If he had broken bones, they could grind against each other as she carried him back to her car. Which could do him a lot of harm, especially if the broken bones were in his spine.

Maybe she ought to go to St. Francis. Call an ambulance.

Maybe, heck. She shouldn't be here, shouldn't be trying to care for these people.

No, damn it. If there were ambulances in the area, wouldn't they be here already? Or be on their way, at least? Shouldn't she hear their sirens in the distance? Of course she should. The rescue people were in the same state of chaos as the rest of the country. If there were ambulances in this part of Kansas, they were busy. It could be hours before they got there. And by then it would be too late for these people.

Damn it. Screwed if I do, screwed if I don't.

And she lifted the boy into her arms, and carried him gentle as she could out to her car.

Approaching the Edge of the Lake of Fire

Bonner and the Vice President had only left them waiting for a couple of minutes.

Time enough, Luke thought, for them to have overpowered the technician. Sealed off the plane. Started their escape. For a while now, Luke had been wishing that they'd taken their chance while they'd had it. Wishing even harder since they'd crested that last rise, and the Lake of Fire had come into view, consuming the horizon all at once.

Out the other window, now, Luke could see the battle starting as the army of irregulars attacked the troops camped in the hills overlooking the base. For a moment he imagined that the battle *was* the battle of Armageddon, outside the gates of Jerusalem. The battle that meant they'd arrived at the end of the world. Hard as he tried to push that idea away from him, hard as he tried to deny it, it stayed with him. Weighed on him.

And the blood pressed against his temples, and he gritted his teeth. Something was coming, and Luke knew it. Something so crucial that it could well mean the end of the world. And Luke would be right there, right at the very heart of the events. And so would all of them who were here on this plane.

The plane lurched—had its landing wheels caught in a rut?—it wouldn't surprise him; certainly the ride so far had been smoother than it had any right to be—and as he caught his balance Luke got a new view out the plane's window. And he saw the wrecked plane up ahead at the edge of the Lake of Fire. Off to the left, maybe a quarter of a mile from the spot they were headed toward. A car in the distance beyond it.

The plane that Bonner had ordered destroyed; that had to be the one. Seeing it, Luke was certain that there were people alive inside it. And just as certain that they would be a part of the events to come.

Up ahead, in the cockpit, the technician was driving the plane through the field. The Vice President was in there with him, someplace. Herman Bonner stood not far from the cockpit door, watching Luke and Ron Hawkins and George Stein. He had a machine gun trained on them, but something in Luke's heart told him that it wasn't really necessary. Told him that Herman Bonner was more than a match for the three of them.

"I still don't get it, Dr. Bonner," the technician said. "Why are we using this plane? It isn't meant for this. It's a miracle that the landing gear have held up to it." A pause. "I could have found us a truck, or a jeep, or something. Wouldn't have taken long."

Bonner shook his head. "The missile, Tim. It's the only one I have at the moment. And I'm not letting it out of my sight."

And then they were slowing, coming to a stop. Right at the edge of the Lake of Fire.

And then they stopped.

Bonner opened the plane's forward door. Gestured toward it with his rifle.

"Come along, gentlemen," he said. "Your fate awaits you."

Luke started forward, wondering how in God's name they were going to get out when they'd left the landing stairs behind them, back at the runway on the base. He was still wondering when he got to the open door.

"Go ahead, Dr. Munsen. Jump. And don't think of running when you reach the ground—I'll have my gun trained on you. And Tim his."

What was it—ten feet? Fifteen? More than a hop and a skip, that was certain. A little higher than the top of the fence they'd climbed when he and Ron broke into the base. More distance than Luke wanted to drop.

It wasn't the moment to argue. Luke was certain of it.

So he jumped, and ended up landing too hard on the same damn leg he'd sprained coming down from the top of the fence. By the time he got done nursing it and opened his eyes Ron and George Stein were both on the ground with him, bruised and groaning from their own falls.

Luke looked up just in time to see Herman Bonner make the jump. And what he saw . . . unsettled him. Saw Bonner slide the distance gracefully, and land smoothly on his feet the same way most men step down from a curb. Not that there was anything impossible about the way he landed. Not exactly. It wasn't *right*, exactly, either.

Bonner looked up, into the plane. "Come along, Tim," he said. "Be sure to help the President before you see to yourself."

The technician was a lot more sensible about getting down: he took the Vice President's hand, bent low on his knees to lower him to within two feet of the ground before he let go. Then he slung his rifle over his shoulder, lowered himself from the doorway as though he were doing a chin-up in reverse. Let himself fall, and fell quick and rough.

Bonner looked at Luke. At Ron. At George Stein. Gestured with his machine gun toward the edge of the Lake of Fire. "Walk," he said. "All three of you. To the brink of the bluff."

He's going to push us off. As though we were walking a plank.

And Luke smiled at the image. If the three of them didn't make their break soon, there wouldn't be time for it. Now. . . ? No. Not yet. His gut still told him to be calm, to bide his time.

Ron Hawkins looked at him pointedly with wide, nervous eyes.

Luke shook his head. And walked to the edge of the Lake of Fire.

And looked down.

And saw the sea of molten stone glowing twenty-five feet below. A sheer drop between here and there, magma flowing along the base of the cliff. Looked right, and left, and saw that elsewhere the drop was less sheer—in places there was a shore at the base of the bluff that looked almost like a beach.

Behind him, Herman Bonner laughed like a creature up out of hell.

*Approaching the Edge
of the Lake of Fire*

Andy was beginning to wonder if they were *ever* going to get wherever it was they were going. All of this walking and walking—and now backtracking in almost the same direction they'd started out in! You'd think that monster wanted them to spend the whole night walking around in circles.

Well, Andy was getting tired of it. Damned tired. Even if

all of those dead people could just go walking around in circles all night, *he* couldn't.

Even the dog was beginning to look a little droopy around the ears.

Well, he thought, *if that old monster won't give us a rest break, then the thing to do is go ahead and take one for ourselves anyway*.

And he sat down, right there in the middle of nowhere with whatever that was out ahead of them glowing all over him, and the monster and all of those dead people tramping right by like he wasn't even there. The heck with them, then, if they weren't going to stop. Andy didn't care about them anyhow. At least the dog stopped to rest with him.

Then right away, of course, the dumb old dog starts whining at him. Like he'd sat himself right in the middle of an ant hill or something, and the dog knew it and Andy didn't, and he was trying to get Andy to get up and get himself the heck out of there.

Andy checked for an ant hill, of course, but there wasn't any. So he just ignored that old dog. He was a strange dog anyhow—who needed to pay attention to him?

Not Andy. Nuh-uh. He was *tired*.

Which was about when he saw the plane, and the people there at the edge of the glowy lake.

What the heck were people doing with an airplane in the middle of a wheatfield?

Well, at least things were beginning to get interesting. Not that Andy was any too sure that this was the kind of interesting that he wanted anything to do with. Two of those guys had guns, didn't they? Hard to be sure from this far, but it sure looked like it to Andy. People with guns were trouble, and Andy had got himself into quite enough trouble these last few days, thank you very much.

Old Tom the dog was still whining at him.

Well, go on and whine, you old dog, Andy told himself. *You see if I care*.

And that was when the dog attacked him.

Well, maybe not attacked him, exactly.

Darned near, though: dog lunged at Andy, real sudden-like. Set into Andy's right shoe like it was some cat he'd finally got his teeth into. Yanked back and forth with Andy wrestling to get it away from it and wondering what on earth it was that had finally drove the poor dog out of his mind.

"Hey, dog! You cut that out!" Andy hollered. Didn't slow that old dog down, not even for a second. In fact, it seemed to make him a little more desperate, if it did anything. And then all of the sudden Tom the dog managed to yank that shoe right off of him. And took off running like a dog bound for hell.

Which, of course, he more or less was.

And Andy thought: *Boy, is my momma going to be pissed at me if I don't get that shoe back.*

Boy was she.

And thinking about his momma when she was mad, Andy didn't give being tired or wary another moment's consideration. He took off running after that dog for all he was worth.

And then some.

Up ahead, by the plane, six people stood right at the edge of the fire lake. And that darned dog was heading right at them. Right at them!

It was trouble. Trouble.

Whatever kind of trouble it was, it just didn't compare to what his momma would have waiting for him if he didn't get that shoe back. Andy took a triple-E shoe, and sometimes they'd have to shop for two or three weeks before they could find a pair that wouldn't give him blisters.

One of those men was laughing now, laughing all crazy-like. Scary sounding. Andy definitely didn't want to follow wherever that dog had a mind to go. Not if it was going to take him toward that man.

Absolutely didn't.

He didn't figure his momma would take that for an excuse. She tended to get real annoyed when he outgrew a pair of shoes—and the one time he'd got those sneakers all ruined with tar she'd grounded him for a month. And spent the whole time scowling at him.

So Andy put the guns and the crazy man and the fiery lake out of his mind. Kept his eye on the dog, and kept running.

The Monster and the dead people were way back there, now. Stopped, and the Monster was pointing off in that direction where Andy could hear the soldiers fighting with each other. Were they going to go off and leave him behind? Andy didn't know what it was that old Monster had in mind. And he wasn't sure he wanted to.

And—

Damn! That dog!

There he was. Running right up to those people at the edge of the lake. And him being just a dog, he hardly drew any notice. And instead of running on, so that Andy could cut the six people a wide berth, the darned dog turns to face him. Stands there, right in the middle of trouble, looks Andy in the eye, and drops the shoe.

That dog was going to suffer for this.

Well—maybe not suffer. But he was definitely and absolutely going to get his. That was a true fact.

So Andy ducked low, trying to pretend like he was invisible, and darted after that dog. Ran quiet and close to the ground, hoping to go unnoticed the same way the dog had.

Almost worked, too.

Andy went up to the dog, sneaking around not ten feet from the legs of one of the two gunmen. Grabbed that shoe right from under the dog's face, and turned around to get the hell *out* of there.

And damned if that dog didn't pick that moment to start barking! Like he *wanted* to hand Andy over to those people!

Well, if that's what he wanted, then that's what he got.

It didn't take two seconds after the dog started making his racket for the nearer gunman to grab Andy by the collar. Like he was a kitten some cat was carrying around by the scruff of its neck.

Which was when Andy saw that two of the three people who had guns pointed at them were Luke Munsen and his friend Ron. There was another man who looked kind of familiar, too, and all three of them were perched on the edge of the bluff over the lake. Ron had this look in his eyes like he thought he was about to get pushed in. Damn that dog! What had he got Andy into?

And then this balding, pinched-faced guy, turned around and looked Andy up and down, smiling the way you smile at a roasted Thanksgiving turkey, only nastier than that. And after a little bit he started talking in low tones to the other guy who had a gun—Andy couldn't make out what he said, but he heard enough to know that the man had a *weird* accent.

And he turned back to Andy, and he smiled again, and started shouting.

"Behold!" he said, "Another demon, plunged into our

midst. And this time in the guise of a child! How foul! How vile! See the depths to which the minions of hell will sink!"

Aw, come *on*, Andy thought. You aren't really talking that way about me, are you?

But damned if he wasn't.

"It's time," the old woman said. "There isn't another moment to waste."

Christine looked at her. Frowned. Nodded.

"Is your heart certain, now? Have you freed yourself from fear? From doubt?"

Christine bit her lower lip. Sighed. "Yes," she said. That was all she said.

And the old woman began to lead her more quickly, more purposely along the shore of the Lake of Fire.

When Luke saw them hoist the boy up off his feet, he felt the bottom drop out of his own stomach. Christ on a crutch, couldn't that kid manage to steer himself clear of trouble even once? Just once?

Well, Luke thought, no. Of course he couldn't. It wasn't in Andy Harrison's nature to be clear of trouble; it drew to him and he to it like the opposing poles of magnets.

Damn, it, though: any moment now everything was going to fall into place, and Luke would have to *move*, and the last thing in the world Luke needed under the circumstances was to have to look after the boy. And he did have a responsibility to see after him, too. Luke had tried to deny it since Andy had first turned up stowed away in the trunk of his car, but denial hadn't changed even the first iota of his responsibility.

"Herman?" It was the Vice President's voice. Speaking the first he'd spoken since they'd left the airfield. Luke looked at him, saw him petting Ron Hawkins's dog, saw the dog licking the man's fingers. His eyes were clearer, now, weren't they? He looked, Luke thought, like a man coming out of a drug dream. "What are you planning to do to that child? What did you say about him?"

Bonner's lips pursed. "It isn't a child, Mr. President. Look carefully. Not a child, but a demon cloaked in a child's flesh."

"Set him down," the Vice President said. And he stooped

to look Andy Harrison in the eye. And kept looking, for a long, long while.

And then, finally, he spoke again.

"I don't know, Herman. I think maybe you're mistaken."

And Luke looked at Bonner when he saw the Vice President turn to face him. And saw Herman Bonner seething with anger.

"Mr. President!" he said, "how you can doubt me? Looking at this creature, how can you doubt its nature?"

"I don't know, Herman. I think I'd know a demon when I saw one. And he sure looks like a boy to me." Luke saw the man turn to look at himself. At Ron Hawkins. At George Stein. "Point of fact—I can't say that any of these people look like demons to me. If you say they are, then I'm inclined to give you the benefit of the doubt. But I won't have you killing little boys. Do you understand me, Herman? I'm talking to you as your President, now."

And quietly and suddenly and certainly, everything changed at once.

Changed as the Creature stepped into the light that came up from the Lake of Fire.

By his very presence the creature threw something that was almost his own light on everything around them.

Like a light—and something else, too. Here in the nuclear glow at the edge of the Lake of Fire the creature's presence seemed to bring out . . . Luke wasn't sure what it was. It was a thing that made Andy Harrison look elfin, impish. Made Ron Hawkins look deep and saintly and grim, like a knight set out to fight a crusade he didn't want but couldn't avoid. Made George Stein look like a fallen angel, struggling to repent.

Made the Vice President, Graham Perkins, look like a brave and noble man who'd been born to lead.

Made Herman Bonner—

None of them could compare to the way the light made Herman Bonner look.

The glow from the creature transformed Herman Bonner into the Beast from Revelation.

The image that surrounded Bonner looked, in fact, almost exactly as the creature had looked when Bonner had finished operating on him. Like a leopard in the general form of a man, but its feet like a bear's and its mouths were like a lion's.

And where the creature had been surgically transformed into a thing with three heads—and two of them dead—the thing that rose like a ghost above Herman Bonner had ten heads, each of them fully formed and alive.

The creature took a step toward Herman Bonner. And Bonner—Luke was sure of it—Herman Bonner cringed ever-so-slightly. Luke looked into his eyes, and what he saw in them was fear.

Leigh had just got the last of her charges into the car when she saw . . . there wasn't a word for it. Hundreds of people. Dozens, at least. Out away from the lake among the wheat-fields, only half visible in the moonlight. Like an army of the damned, they looked, risen up from hell.

She glanced back over her shoulder at the Lake of Fire. And shuddered. Who were they? Where were they going? With her eye she traced the line of their direction across the fields, toward its ultimate direction—and saw the armies, fighting on the plain and among the hills.

Were they going to join that battle? And why?

Someone groaned inside the car. Leigh didn't even hear it.

She was too caught up in watching the army out of hell. Trying to see how many of them there were, and where. She looked hard out into the dark, trying to see if there were more of them. And her eye caught on the scene quarter of a mile away. By the other airplane.

What she saw there, glowing in that strange light, drew her in even more surely than the sight of the army of the damned.

"There's nothing you can do to me," Bonner said. There wasn't an awful lot of conviction in his voice. "You're my creation! I *made* you, vile thing. And even if I made you a more powerful thing than I realized, I still hold the secret of your life in my hand."

The creature wasn't moving quickly, but he didn't slow down, either—didn't even hesitate. Out of the corner of his eye Luke saw the Vice President taking Andy in his arms, moving the boy away, out of the thick of things. The dog

followed just behind them, nipping at the man's heels as
though he thought he meant the boy some harm.

There was only a few feet left between the creature and
Herman Bonner. Both of them were caught up in the glow
from the lake, and Luke would have sworn there was some
other glow, too—a glow like the light the creature cast on those
around him. And more brilliant; bright enough to see even in
the light that shone up from the lake.

And the insubstantial thing above Herman Bonner began
to grow . . . solid-looking.

It was time to get the hell *out* of here.

The technician stood watching, terrified; his face was still
and slack as soft stone.

Luke frowned. Clenched his teeth.

Ron and George Stein looked nearly as terrified as the
technician did. Luke heard a noise, strange, small, like splinter-
ing bone; looked up at the creature, at Herman Bonner—

They were fighting, the creature and the beast that was
Herman Bonner.

It was the insubstantial part of Herman Bonner that
was doing the fighting. As Luke watched its claws like a
leopard's claws dug themselves into the muscular flesh of
the creature's belly, and the jaws on one leonine head dove for
the creature's neck.

Missed, and buried themselves in the creature's shoulder
instead.

And ghost jaws or not, the creature's blood was everywhere.

Not that the fight seeped out of him with his blood. The
creature wrapped his hands around that ghostly neck, and
strangled, and Luke saw the great muscles of his arms bulge as
he twisted and heaved—

—*and wrenched the head clear off its shoulders.*

The ghostlike thing sagged, and Luke saw Herman Bonner stumble. He thought for a moment that it was all over, that
whatever ectoplasmic substance a ghost had would flow from it
like blood until it died.

Until he saw the wound heal itself.

Saw a new head grow where the old one had been.

It only took an instant. And once that instant had passed,
and the wound had grown whole, the Ghost-Beast set into the

creature with an entirely new frenzy, claws ripping down into the creature's flesh again and again and blood everywhere and even when the creature's feet fell out from under him the Herman Bonner-thing didn't stop; it knelt and beat and tore and ripped—

And Luke thought *Oh dear God it's going to kill him, need to stop it need to do something*—but he knew he wasn't any match for Herman Bonner, let alone the Beast now visible that had been hidden inside him, and he thought he ought to run and get away with his life, at least, while he could—

Ron Hawkins didn't know any such thing. And, knowing Ron, wouldn't have paid it any mind, even if he had. He launched himself at the ghostlike Beast still savaging the creature—

And sailed right through it.

Into Herman Bonner himself.

Caught him in a flying tackle, which sent both of them tumbling into the grass. Got up so that he knelt astride Bonner's chest, and started pounding the man with his fists. The ghost-Beast was struggling, and Bonner was struggling, but Bonner was pinned and nothing the ghost did left a mark on Ron, and after a while Herman Bonner and the ghost-beast were both still as the dead.

Maybe they were dead.

The creature, over there on the grass, sure looked dead. When Bonner was still Luke saw Ron steal a glance over his shoulder, at the creature, and when he saw the damage that had been done him he screamed all fury and mourning—

And stood.

And lifted Herman Bonner up over his head.

And cast him, unconscious, over the bluff and into the Lake of Fire.

When he was gone Luke felt relief wash over him like a wave that very nearly took his legs out from under him. It was *over*, and they were safe, and soon enough the creature would recover from its wounds—

No, Leigh thought. *No, no, no.*

It was the wrong thing, throwing the Beast from Revelation into the Lake of Fire. Couldn't they know that? Couldn't they see? The Lake was an evil horror on the face of the earth, and the Beast was an evil horror on the face of the earth. And drowning in it couldn't possibly destroy him.

No.

The Lake of Fire would only make the Beast from Revelation stronger.

Without even thinking about it, she got into the car. Started the engine. And headed off toward the other plane as quickly as she could.

Or, at least, that was what Luke thought until he saw the Beast from Revelation crawl up out of the Lake of Fire.

"There is nothing you can do that will harm me," the Beast said. And Luke knew that it was so. There was nothing of Herman Bonner left in that voice. Nothing even remotely human.

Christine said, "It's true."

She was standing at the edge of the lake, not more than a dozen yards from them. The bag lady was beside her, calm, pensive. . . .

"There isn't anything any of them can do to you," she said. "But I gave birth to you, damn you. And there's something I can do."

The Beast lunged toward her.

Christine didn't move a muscle.

At first Luke thought that might mean the Beast couldn't harm her—that its claws and its fangs would be as insubstantial against her as they had been when Ron had attacked Herman Bonner. That Christine stood there, unmoving, because she knew there was no harm it could do her. If those were her reasons, she was mistaken; the first swipe of its massive foreclaw sent her flying through the air, and she landed at the edge of the bluff above the Lake of Fire.

The Beast walked to her. Stooped to look down into her eyes.

"And what is that?" the Beast asked. "What is it you can do to me?"

Christine smiled a little, in spite of the fact that she was clearly in pain. Smiled gently and genuinely, and sat up and wrapped her arms softly around the foremost of its massive heads.

Hugged the Beast.

"You're my child," she said. "I can love you."

And she kissed him a mother's kiss, kissed the forehead just above the eyes.

And the Beast from Revelation screamed.

And it grabbed its mother by the throat.

And threw her into the Lake of Fire.

The quarter of a mile between Leigh Doyle and the scene of carnage disappeared in slow motion. In spite of the fact that she had the gas pedal pressed to the floor.

A man's voice, from the back seat: "Who are you? Where is this? What are you doing?"

"I'm Leigh Doyle," she said. "And we're at the gates of hell. And I'm trying to save the world. Trying to save you, too."

And then suddenly they were only a dozen feet from the Beast from Revelation as he grabbed that woman by the throat, threw her out into the Lake of Fire—

She was going to run him down. Run him over. Without even thinking about it, Leigh knew that that was the only thing she *could* do, if she didn't want to go flying into the Lake of Fire, the same way that other woman was flying—

A man jumped into the inferno after her, like a lifeguard diving toward a rescue—

As Leigh braced for the thud of impact and the crush of soft flesh under the bumper of a car—

It wasn't like that at all when it happened. More like hitting a brick wall, hard and fast, and the front end of the rent-a-car crumpled under the force of the crash, and Leigh felt the steering wheel punch up into her abdomen, and in the seat beside her the boy she'd taken from the plane was screaming.

Things got a little grey for Leigh after that. The force of the steering wheel had broken or bruised or injured something up inside her, and most of what she knew while the Beast lifted the car and tore it open was a fog made of confusion and hysterical pain.

* * *

Luke's voice was the first thing Christine heard besides the sound of her own flesh cooking on her bones.

"Don't die, Christine," he said. He was sobbing. She thought of dying, thought of resurrection. And with half her heart she wished for the release that death would give her. With the other half she knew that dying here in a place so like the gate to hell meant dying forever. "I love you, Christine. Don't die."

He'd pulled her up out of the inferno, onto the thin shore of the Lake of Fire.

"I love you too," she said. The words hurt her throat, only partly because of the destruction that the fire had done her.

Above them was the sound of chaos, of violence.

Unconsciously, she reached for the pendant that hung from her neck. The pendant that the bag lady had given her. And she rubbed it between her fingers.

Leigh came to in time to hear the young man speak.

"That's enough, Dr. Bonner," he said. "Let them go. Put them down."

She opened her eyes, and saw all of them climbing on the Beast from Revelation, trying to subdue a creature out of hell with nothing but the force of their arms and legs. So foolish. They were only mortals, mortals like Leigh. There was nothing they could do to him, nothing but give him the joy of destroying them. Didn't they know that, just looking at him? No; they must not. All of them were there, climbing on his mighty frame—both of the men she'd rescued from the plane, and the boy and the woman. Another child, and two men— that was the Vice President, wasn't it? It was. She recognized him. Even that dog. And the strange, magical creature caked in its own blood. None of them knew.

"Put them down, Dr. Bonner. Let them go, or I'll shoot."

And the Beast spoke. "You Tim? You betray me, too?" His voice was almost sad, and that was a strange thing indeed. "Put the gun down, Tim. Cast it into the Lake of Fire, and run from this place. Do this now and I may forgive you."

When the man spoke his voice was shrill and frightened. "Put them down, damn it." And he fired a round into the air.

And the Beast lifted the boy—the dark-skinned one, not the one Leigh had pulled from the wreckage of the plane—lifted the boy perched on his fourth neck, pounding at that head. Lifted him by the scruff of his neck, and threw him at the young man with the gun.

Who ducked aside, only barely in time. And as the boy screamed at the agony of his broken, twisted arm, the man with the gun opened fire.

The first two bullets took out a pair of the Beast's eyes. Not that it mattered, especially. There were many others. Other bullets did more damage; two of its heads blew away at their necks, and great geysers of black blood shot up from the wreckage.

And the Beast screamed, in anguish and rage. And with his mighty legs he stamped his pain against the earth.

And the earth gave way under the force of those blows.

Not that the Beast was really hurt. He was healing even as the bluff slid away into the Lake of Fire, taking with it the car and the jet and the Beast and Leigh and the man with the gun and everyone else.

*On the Shore
of the Lake of Fire*

Yeah, Bill thought. This was why they were here. Why that dream had sent them halfway around the world.

What was it they were supposed to do, now that they'd got here? Oh, sure, they were supposed to fight with this . . . thing. Hadn't the President—the real, dead President, not this live, Vice-President-type President they had here—had the President called it Herman? Or had he called it *Beast? Beast* was what the thing looked like, if anybody was asking Bill. Beast as in Beast out of Revelation, as in something out of a fire-and-brimstone preacher's nightmare.

Even if they were supposed to put a stop to this Beast-thing, it didn't seem to Bill like fighting it head on was an especially intelligent thing to do. He was doing it, all right. Wasn't like there was anything else he could think of to do. But it wasn't making a damn bit of difference, and Bill knew it. Even if there were ten of them here, or twelve, or whatever it was, they weren't any match for a Beast that could tear cars apart with its bare hands, or shake the ground apart with its footsteps, or grow back heads that'd been blown off with a machine gun.

So what *were* they supposed to do? Hold hands in a circle that surrounded the thing, and sing pretty songs at it? Oh, right. That'd make a lot of difference. About as much difference as it did when that half-burned-to-death woman over there told it she was its mom and gave it a kiss.

Shit, Bill told himself. He wasn't ever going to think of a way for them to beat up this Beast-thing. He wasn't stupid, exactly, but Bill knew he didn't have the kind of special, extraordinary brain-power kind of thinking that the problem called for.

So Bill did the only thing he could think of: the same thing he done to that junior-high bully back in the fifth grade. Bill walked right up to that Beast from Revelation, who was in the middle of taking that machine gun out of the hands of that Tim guy. Bill walked up to the Beast from Revelation, and he kicked him in the balls.

Got his attention real good, too.

For a while.

Then he stood up again and started throwing everybody into the burning lake. And Bill got to go first.

Christine was the last to go. Partly because she lay on the shore, a dozen yards from the spot where the bluff had collapsed onto the Lake of Fire. Partly because the plane, which had fallen with the bluff, shielded them from the Beast's line of sight.

Most of all, though, Christine was last because when the Beast finally did turn his attention in her direction, Luke had shielded her. All while the others had fought the Beast, Luke had knelt beside her, holding her hand. And when it had come for them, Luke had attacked the Beast to protect her.

It was futile, of course. The Beast threw Luke into the inferno before he could even as much as land a blow.

And then it came for Christine. And threw her into the same spot where it had thrown everyone else. Where in an instant her flesh began to burn and fuse into the mass of the dying and near-dead.

That was when she remembered the pendant, and remembered what it was for. And she sat up as best she could, and took the pendant from her neck, and with what was left of her hand she held it out toward the Beast.

And something began to happen.

A light came from the stone that hung in the pendant. A light like the light that had come from the creature when it first reached the edge of the lake. And not like that light at all. Brighter, and more intense; and it drank in the glow of the glow that came from the burning lake, made it dim all around her.

When the Beast saw the pendant it screamed. Screamed unhumanly in rage and fear and in frustration. Christine half expected it to wade into the Lake of Fire and seize it from her.

It even started to come for her—it took three steps into the Lake—and stopped when it reached the edge of the bright shadow that the pendant cast. Cringed, as though it could not bear the touch of that dark light. And screamed again.

Something strange was happening; Christine could feel the burning soothe down in her legs.

"No!" it shouted. "Not now! Not here!"

And it reached back with its great arms, and seized the missile strapped to the top of the fallen plane. Tore it away. And, wielding it like some gargantuan club, the Beast swung it at Christine.

Reflexively, she raised the hand that held the pendant, trying to shield herself from the warhead's sharp tip.

Christine never really understood what happened next. Oh, she knew well enough that the warhead made contact with that strange pendant. And that making contact, the pendant ignited some potential at the missile's heart.

But the idea of an atomic implosion was alien to her; she didn't really understand how the force of the nuclear blast drank in through the strange gemstone. And through it, into Christine and the others whose flesh mingled and fused with hers in the molten rock.

And the force transformed them all.

Transformed them into something.

Into a single something that was all of them and none of them.

And more than the sum of them.

And not the sum of them at all.

* * *

Bill's mind rose up out of the cloud of the agony of the incineration of his body as the change began.

First came the fusion of his heart and his mind with the hearts of the others. The woman he loved who he didn't understand—the secret history she kept locked in her heart, amazed and astounded him. A man named Luke Munsen who Bill might have been if he'd lived a different life. Ron Hawkins—till now Bill hadn't even recognized him!—whose life more nearly was Bill's, and would have been if the world had been more harsh. A woman named Leigh Doyle, who burned with the need to be heard and be loved, and knew in her heart that the world would give her neither. Knew in Bill's heart, now, as all of them melded. A man named Graham Perkins, whom fate had made a leader of men in spite of the fact that it had taken from him the will to lead. Andy Harrison, Jerry Williams; both of them young and mostly innocent—though the first was impish where the second tended shy. A dog named Tom, whose heart was made of broad, simple strokes of the brush . . . but even so it was a noble heart, full of love and determination and loyalty. A woman named Christine, who'd spent most of a century moldering in a crypt. A man named Tim, full of fear. George Stein, full of guilt. A strange creature born in a laboratory, a creature whose sense of the world and the hearts of others went deep. . . .

And when their hearts had fused and together they were all of them and none, their bodies too transformed—into a single being. In the shape and proportion of a man, but far taller than a man, and stronger. When he—who was they—opened his eyes he saw that he was cloaked in the armor that Bill's lover had worn in his dream; impossibly sleek black steel that wore light as silk. Silver trim that shone like fire in the strange light. A helmet shaped like no helmet any of them had ever seen.

Most of all was the fiery sword, the sword made of the stone that the bag lady had given him as a pendant. And larger than that stone could ever have become. As the gem had drunk in the light and heat of the Lake of Fire, so did the sword. More: it drank so much, so hard, as to cool and congeal the magma that surrounded him. When he stepped toward the Beast, soft rock crumpled away from his feet.

The Beast's eyes were wild, fearful—but not cowed. There was still that hunger in them—the blood-hunger that excitement always brought to Herman Bonner's eyes. Looking at the Beast, he knew that that hunger ran so deep that the only satiation it could ever find was the destruction of every man, woman, and child on the earth. More than that, perhaps; perhaps the end of all life.

"Surrender, Herman," he said. "Surrender now. Your time will come. In its course. It isn't now."

"No," the Beast said. "*This* is my day. I won't allow you to steal it from me."

And the Beast lunged at him. Threw him off balance, and the Beast's weight took him down, onto the lake that now was stone.

And the great bright sword fell from his grip and went clattering away from him.

"I'll kill you," the Beast said. "Kill you, and destroy every trace that you ever existed." Hard, rough-strong hands around his throat, crushing his neck through the armor. "You don't frighten me."

For that long moment he thought that the Beast was right, thought that it would kill him. Destroy him beyond remaking.

That death didn't frighten him. Not for his own part.

But his own part was his least concern—he didn't exist to live, as most creatures do.

He existed for his world.

And the hands around his throat, crushing away his life, mattered only because of the Apocalypse they meant to create.

"No, Herman." Because he had so little breath the words were barely a whisper. "I can't allow that." And he set his hands on the Beast's forearms, and with all the strength he had he pressed them out and away.

And kept pushing, until he stood holding the Beast in the air over his head. It kicked at him; struggled to free itself. Which was pointless; the Beast's animal feet had little effect on the armor that covered him.

"You have to kill it now."

The voice came from behind him—from the direction of the broken bluff. The bag lady's voice? Yes, it was. He recognized it. Remembered it six times over.

"There isn't any other way. You cannot leave it alive."

Kill. . . ?

No. He did not want to kill. He didn't want that on his heart.

His hearts.

The Beast was struggling even more fiercely now. Screaming. Without thinking, he threw it away from him, turned to answer the woman.

Which was stupid; in a moment the Beast had leapt on him again, peeled back the visor of his helmet. Tried to claw out his eyes.

"Damn you," he said. And he leaned forward, grabbed the great clawlike hands by their wrists, pulled the Beast over his head, and slammed it into the ground in front of him.

Then for a long while the Beast lay still, and there was nothing he could do but stare down at it in horror.

By the time the old woman came to him, the Beast had begun to stir again.

She had the fiery sword in her hands, and she held it out to him.

"Through the heart," she said, "and into the ground beneath him."

He who was all of them who'd traveled to this place still hesitated.

"Look around you," the old woman said. "Look at the destruction. This is what he will make your world."

And he saw.

And he took the sword.

And just as the Beast from Revelation opened its eyes, he killed it.

It was a horrible, cold-blooded killing. A killing that shamed all of him for all of his days. As the Beast's blood welled up from the wound all black in the dim light, and the fiery blade bit into the once-molten ground, the glow that had filled the lake disappeared everywhere all at once, and the sword turned to light and dust in a great exploding instant.

And all that was left of the Beast was Herman Bonner, pale and dead in the moonlight.

Off in the distance, in the place that had been the center of the Lake of Fire, was a dim light even fainter from so far away.

"Yes," the old woman said. "You see it, don't you? You have to take him there. And then it's done."

He carried the corpse like a sick child in his arms across those miles. Until he found a circular hole in the air, exactly like the one he'd seen in his dream.

Inside that hole was the dead President who'd called him.

"Yes," the President said. He took the corpse from their arms, held it tenderly. "You've done well. *This* world is Herman's place, now. Not that one. His time will come—but not because he wants it to."

The old woman walked up from behind him, stepped through the portal, into that strange place. He had not even realized that she'd followed him.

And the hole in the air closed sudden as though it had never been, without even a good-bye.

He turned, walked back toward the edge of the hard Lake. As he went, he felt his strength waning; a few steps after he'd reached the shore it left him completely. And he blacked out, collapsing into the dry grass.

When he woke late in the afternoon of the next day, he was many again and not one.

A Year Later
Late in the Spring

Saturday
May Fifteenth

A year.

It has been nearly a year, now, since the explosion in the laboratory that changed the nature of human life everywhere on the planet. Most of the dead who ever lived now have risen from their graves—but not all of them. There are places in the world where bacteria do not easily permeate the soil. Even now, men and women return to life every day. It is likely that they will continue rising for a thousand years.

There was an awful scare late last August (as the world was calming, learning to cope with the newness of its circumstances) when someone realized that every man, woman, and child who'd ever lived would soon return to crowd the world. That man asked questions: How will we feed them? Where will they live? Who will find them work?

A week of awful panic followed. Riots. Burnings. Fear. People died, but they did not die for long.

Then someone realized that no one had been truly hungry in months. That for all that a meal was and is a great and wonderful thing, a body could no longer starve without one. Eventually, the panic ebbed; there was no need for it. People in the cities

*made room for one another. People in the fields are
glad of the company.*

*Other changes have been more terrible. And
sad. There is something in the nature of the bacteria
that maintains the world that will not abide a child in
its mother's womb—no more than it will abide a
cancer. In all the world these last six months, only
four dozen children have been born. Of those, only a
pair this month. The day is in sight when there will
be no children playing, laughing in the streets, and
that is a grim thing indeed.*

*Still other changes are frightening: the swine are
everywhere, hungry, devouring. All but unkillable.
Armies fight them daily, incinerate them with flame
throwers—if the pigs burn hard and hot and long
enough, they do not return. It is slow, uncertain
work; bloody and dangerous. More than one platoon
of soldiers has become a meal for swine.*

*Not to say there is no hope. The pigs reproduce
themselves no more than do the men and women—
the time will come when they are no more a threat.
Or are much less of one, at least.*

Northwest Georgia

When Luke finally finished getting Andy Harrison back to
his mother, he and Christine left New York behind. Left it on
foot, in spite of the fact that they'd come to the city by bus, and
Luke had money enough to get them anywhere they needed to
be. There was something *right* about walking, something that
Luke couldn't have explained for the life of him. The two of
them followed that rightness as far as it took them.

They wandered aimlessly, mostly south but west, too, for
most of the year, until one morning Luke woke in an abandoned summer cabin and knew that he'd found a perfect
place—cool enough, and warm enough, and always mild as an
island in a warm-current sea. It was in a hollow, near a roaring
stream somewhere in north Georgia not all that far from the
home he'd left in Tennessee before the world changed and
died and was reborn.

When they'd been there—Luke and Christine—for a time

that became vague as the soft edges of the seasons, Ron Hawkins found them. Showed up in the cabin's driveway very early one morning, driving a station wagon crammed with everything he'd ever owned. Or so it looked to Luke, at least. Luke was never too sure how Ron had done it—could they have left a trail, perhaps? Or did Ron have some sort of a homing instinct? Luke didn't think so. However Ron had found them, there was a rightness about it; it didn't surprise Luke at all that he had.

They invited Ron in, of course. How could they not invite him in? Ron was a friend, and he deserved their hospitality. Not that there was much in the way of hospitality to offer him. Neither of them felt much of a need to eat any more, and there was nothing to offer Ron. Luke always felt that there *ought* to be something to offer a guest; he felt like a poor host with an empty larder.

The three of them sat down at the kitchen table, in spite of the fact that it was empty, because it was a good place to talk.

"I wanted to stop by and see you," Ron said, "before I went north. Starting graduate school next month, up near Boston. Don't know when I'll get a chance to get down in the direction again."

Luke nodded, and smiled. Ron Hawkins in grad school. That was something, wasn't it?

"How did you find us?" Christine asked him. "You're welcome, of course. But I hadn't realized we'd left a trail. And we haven't seen anyone in the months we've been here."

Ron shook his head. "No—you didn't." Shrugged. "Damned if I know. It's spring and I'm here. I think the others will show up, too. Soon, now. Real soon."

Luke found himself looking absently out the window, wondering if the creature was somewhere out there in the woods, watching them. It was a strange idea, a little unsettling and a little comforting both at once.

He thought of the days just after the scene at the edge of the Lake of Fire. How they'd all waited there, the Vice President and George Stein and Ron and Andy and himself and all the others, waited for Christine and the creature to be well enough to leave. It hadn't taken that long—most of a day, maybe. And then they'd all traveled together for a while, but before they'd reached the first town George Stein had slipped away, and a while after that the creature and the dog had headed off in another direction while no one was looking. Bill and the dark-eyed woman did the same, as did the technician, Tim. By that time Tim had already taken the dead policeman under his wing. Looking in his eyes, just before they'd wandered off, Luke thought that he was helping the dead policeman to make some amends for the city of St. Louis, whose destruction Tim had largely caused.

In the town those of them still left had bought bus tickets to three different places. The Vice President, to Washington. Ron and Jerry Williams, back to Tennessee. And Luke and Christine and Andy had bought tickets to New York. Until Ron showed up, it'd been the last he'd seen of any of them.

"Has it changed much out there?" Luke asked. "Has the world changed?"

"Oof," Ron said—as though the question were bigger than he knew how to lift. "Yeah. It's changed a lot. An awful lot." He frowned, thinking. "People aren't dying any more. And they aren't starving when they don't eat. And when they're broke, it doesn't make a whole lot of difference. Hard to get anyone to do a job he doesn't want to do."

And they talked a long time after that, but nothing Ron said haunted Luke the way that idea did. Imagine that: a whole world where no one did anything against his will, or because he had to.

Would it even work? Ron wasn't all that clear on whether it *was* working or not. It was a thing Luke had to see, he decided. Real soon.

Later in the day the others arrived. Bill Wallace and his strange, dark-eyed wife; the creature and the dog who followed him everywhere. The preacher, George Stein. Graham Perkins, the man who'd been President (in the eyes of the law, at least) for the four weeks it took him to get to Washington and sign resignation papers. Andy Harrison and young Jerry Williams, each escorted by their parents. Last to arrive was Tim, the technician who'd worked for Herman Bonner. The vacant-eyed policeman, Jorge Rodriguez, came with him. Neither of the two had much to say, though Rodriguez looked as though something had begun to regrow inside him.

All of them sat in the hearth room of the cabin, and they broke the bread that the Harrisons had brought. Later they went out into the woods and walked for a long while. None of them said much of anything.

That night they made room for bedrolls near the fireplace, and those who felt a need for sleep rested.

Late that night, Luke sat awake at the kitchen table, counting how little he'd accomplished in the last year and thinking about whether people ought to *do* things or not. Or whether they should just *be*. After a long time he decided that there wasn't much point to life unless you did something with it.

Soon, he thought. *Soon*. Soon it'd be time to set himself back into the world and find things to accomplish—and accomplish them. And swore to himself that he'd set himself to the task in a day or three. Or a week. Or a month. Time wasn't a thing that could press on him now; soon was soon enough.

I will, he thought.

It was a promise, in a way. A promise to himself. And though there wasn't much urgency in it, it wasn't an empty pledge.

And now, here is a preview of Alan Rodgers' next novel

THE HAND OF GOD

Have you ever seen something, looked right at it, and not believed your eyes? Seen its shape, its form, and still could not bring yourself to believe that it was real? It's a feeling that makes you doubt the reality of everything around you. If you've ever had that feeling you know what Tim Fischer has lived with his entire life.

THE HAND OF GOD is Alan Rodgers' most thought-provoking novel to date. It's a story about an ancient mystery, an artifact born of the ultimate pain, which holds the promise of raising a paradise on earth or breeding an equally perfect hell. A story about a promise made long ago, a trust passed from generation to generation, and about the choices a young man has to make, choices that will forever change him, and the world.

It begins here. With Tim, on a late autumn afternoon in his childhood. . . .

Tim was five years old the first time.

He was five, and it was Christmas season, halfway between Thanksgiving and Christmas day, and his mom and his
dad went north to the mountains for the weekend.

And left him with his Grandpa.

Which was cool. Real cool, and more than cool; Grandpa
was just about Tim's favorite person in all the world. A whole
weekend alone with Grandpa was just about the neatest thing
a five-year-old Tim could ever think up. And he hadn't even
had to think it up! Mom and Dad had thought of it for him, and
they gave him barbecue and corn on the cob for dinner on
Friday night—like they were trying to make it up to him, if
you could believe that. Like they felt *guilty* for leaving him
with Grandpa for a weekend. Well, Tim wasn't about to tell
them otherwise. If they knew he was looking forward to it,
they might not give him barbecue and corn on the cob next
time. Or have ice cream for desert.

So after dinner while Mom was packing Dad drove him
out to Grandpa's enormous old place. And dropped him off,
and when he said he was sorry Tim sure didn't bother to tell
him that there wasn't anything to be sorry for. Not him.

When Dad was gone, Grandpa frowned at Tim and shook
his head. Not like he was *really* angry or anything, but like he
was kind of maybe a little bit disappointed only he was going
to get silly about it and tease Tim instead of letting on that he
was upset.

Well, that was Grandpa for you. Kind of like they always
say about Santa Claus—about knowing when you've been bad
and good and being good for goodness sake and all that.
Grandpa always knew what was going on. Whether you knew
it or not, whether you told him or not, whether you wanted
him to know or not. It didn't seem especially remarkable to
Tim; he'd known Grandpa as long as he'd been alive, and that
was what Grandpa was like.

"That wasn't too nice of you, was it, Tim?" Grandpa asked.
And of course it wasn't especially nice. But there were

ameliorating circumstances, to Tim's way of thinking. He had to protect his supply of barbecue and ice cream, after all. So he kind of cocked his head and didn't answer, and waited for Grandpa to go on.

"It wasn't, Tim. Your poor Dad is worried sick. You've never been away from your folks for a whole weekend before, and he's going to spend most of the next ten hours thinking about how you're getting on. All because you played your cards close to the chest."

Tim was beginning to feel just a little uncomfortable. Yeah, it was wrong, all right. And he'd known what he was doing, and known then that it wasn't right. But it wasn't *that* wrong, was it?

He shrugged, trying to act like it wasn't like it was. "Mom wouldn't have made barbecue if she'd known I was looking forward to coming to see you for a whole weekend. She never makes barbecue any more. And I never told them any lies. They just kind of made them up themselves."

Grandpa sighed.

"You. You're a rascal, all right. And cute as a button. But you're not the only person in the world, Timbo. Your mom and dad are people with feelings, just like you are. You wouldn't want to be left to feel like that, would you?"

And that hit home, all right. Hit a lot harder than it would have just a few weeks back, since lately Tim had been thinking about just exactly that idea: what it would be like to be somebody else, and standing in his shoes, and feeling his feelings, and how come they all felt like that anyway?

"Sorry, Grandpa." He couldn't think of anything else he was supposed to say. But he sure didn't feel any good.

Grandpa picked up his suitcase and started carrying it up to the guest room. "Don't take it that bad, Timmy. It isn't the worst thing any little boy ever did—not by a mile. Besides, your mom and dad won't be gone for another hour. Plenty of time to call before they go."

Well, that was Grandpa for you. Mom and Dad, when they found him up to something he ought not to be doing, would get stern and harsh and wag their fingers. And maybe they'd even slap his hand, mostly depending on what kind of a mood they were in and exactly how bad a thing he'd done. But Grandpa—he never got harsh. Not that Tim ever saw. Never got certain. Sure never raised his hand to hit you. And somehow he always found Tim exactly where he lived. It was enough to make Tim start considering ways to avoid getting Grandpa disappointed in him in the first place.

Anyway, after Grandpa unpacked his things he put on popcorn and they called Mom and Dad, and to help the feel better Tim acted like he was having a really good time, which he really was even if Grandpa had got upset at him, so it wasn't a lie. It wasn't good to tell a lie even if it was for a good reason—that was another thing Grandpa told him. (Grandpa did allow as how there were a goodly number of times when there wasn't any sense in coming out with the truth—lots of times people just weren't up to coping with it. It was the sort of thing, Grandpa said, that you had to use your judgment about. But all that was more in the category of keeping your mouth shut than it was about honesty.)

And they took the popcorn out to Grandpa's living room, and Grandpa turned on the TV to channel 44, and they spent a long time watching old Christmas movies and eating popcorn and playing Parcheesi. All in all, it wasn't the kind of night you had at home with Mom and Dad.

Sometime in the middle of the second movie they both sort of wandered away from the Parcheesi game and caught up with the picture. And a little while later Tim found himself losing interest again, because the movie was *A Miracle on Thirty-Fourth Street*, and he'd just seen it Wednesday afternoon on channel 10. And he got up off the couch and wandered off to explore Grandpa's house.

Which was another of his favorite things.

Grandpa's house was a really enormous place. *Really* enormous. Three storeys tall, at least, and more rooms than Tim could even begin to count at the age of five. And Tim had the run of it. Well, not the run of it, quite—Grandpa let him go anywhere he pleased on the first two floors. The upstairs upstairs was off limits. And that was just fine by Tim.

'Cause there was something up there on that third floor. Something that made him ache anytime he got near the stairs that led to it. Tim thought of that thing—whatever it was—as Grandpa's Secret. Deep in his heart someplace he knew that it had something to do with him. Which was maybe the reason why his desire to avoid it was more powerful than his curiosity. There was something about that thing, it seemed to Tim who'd never seen it, that made him think of cough medicine when he was sick: it tasted gross and it made him feel all pukey and even if Mom said it was needful Tim didn't see how it did anything but make him feel sicker.

So Tim got up off the couch, and headed off toward Grandpa's den, and as he did Grandpa called to him and reminded him not to get himself hurt.

The den was one of the neatest places of all. Grandpa's books were there, and so was his desk. Which was okay, when you wanted to play with things like that, Tim guessed. But the cool part was the models all over the place. Models of dinosaurs, and of sailing ships and cruising ships and warships. Models of the world, like that big globe beside the desk that stood in its frame taller that Tim could on tip-toe. And a globe of the moon, too. And other stuff that was even neater. Tim had spent lots of afternoons in that den of Grandpa's, and while he was there the evening spun by like a silent carousel, or the stars spinning round in the sky overhead. Till bedtime, when Grandpa came to get him, and carry him up to his room on the second floor.

Morning was almost as much fun as the evening before had been; Tim spent it playing cat and mouse with Grandpa's old tom, Duff. Sometimes Tim wasn't completely certain which of them was hunting and which the hunter—maybe they were taking turns. Or maybe the cat had a different game in mind than Tim did. Sometimes animals were like that. Minds of their own, and they'd get ideas in their heads and not bother trying to make themselves clear to you. And if a boy like Tim didn't get the point, well then that was his problem, so far as Duff was concerned.

Well, it didn't matter that much if they were playing different games. Tim had fun, and that was the point, wasn't it? It was.

He had so much fun playing with the old tom, in fact, that when Grandpa came in a little while before lunch and told Tim that he needed to go to the store, Tim barely even gave it any thought.

"So," Grandpa said, "are you going to tell me which one of you is the cat and which one's the mouse?"

Tim laughed. "I am!"

"You are, huh? You are what—the cat or the mouse?"

"I am the *cat!*" Tim said, and he ran to his grandpa and gave him *such* a hug. And Grandpa lifted him up and hugged him up in the air just the way Tim would've hugged his stuffed Teddy bear.

"I'm out of cigars, Timbo," Grandpa said after a while.

"Got to run up to the corner shop. You want to come along? Or are you and Duff too caught up in cat and mouse just now?"

Tim frowned. Rubbed his nose which was all itchy-tickly from breathing cat hair. He shrugged. "Play, I guess."

Grandpa nodded. "I thought so. You sure you're going to be okay by yourself for half an hour?"

"Uh-huh. 'Course I am, Grandpa."

Grandpa set Tim down, shaking his head. "All right, then. Just remember: don't play with anything sharp. Don't try to pick up anything heavy enough to hurt you if you drop it. And don't even think about going up to the third floor."

"I won't, Grandpa. Don't worry about me." And Tim honestly meant it: he had too much sense to try to make a toy out of something that could hurt him. And he sure wasn't going anywhere near the third floor.

Tim really and truly believed that when he said it. It wasn't a lie, and if it was a promise that he ended up breaking, it sure wasn't one that he broke on purpose.

"See you in a bit, kiddo," Grandpa said. And he patted Tim on the head. And he left.

In the front room, Grandpa's enormous old AM radio was playing Christmas carols.

The other part didn't start right away. For a good five minutes Tim stayed down there in the parlor, teasing old Duff and getting teased right back. Listening to the radio with half his mind as someone sang about the Baby Jesus having to be born in a barn and how it was kind of special anyway.

And then he began to hear it.

Not loud, at first. Not even so he noticed it, what with the cat and the music on the radio. But even if it wasn't loud enough to recognize, it had an effect on him right from the first. A peculiar effect, too; it got him thinking about church. And about how Grandpa was so mindful of church, and not mindful about it at all. Like for instance Grandpa said mean things about Father Thomas, and they always made Tim laugh because he could hear the truth in them, and Grandpa almost never went to Sunday Mass. But when he talked about church there was something awfully special in his voice. And there was a crucifix in Grandpa's bedroom, hung square on the wall above the head of his bed.

Crucifix.

Tim always hurt when he saw that crucifix. It wasn't like most of the crosses you saw here and there. It had Jesus right there on it, bronze long-haired Jesus with the nails through his hands and suffering. . . .

And that was when the sound got loud enough to hear.

Well, not a sound, exactly. Sound was the radio, where a chorus was singing: "*God rest ye merry, gentlemen—let nothing you dismay; remember Christ our Saviour was born on Christmas day—to save us all from Satan's power*. . . ."

There was something about that carol that always gave Tim the creeps. Mostly because whenever he thought about the word "rest" being used that way he thought about people resting in their graves—

There. That was it. Not a sound at all, but something like a sound. A sound like you hear it with your heart and feel it . . . kind of behind your stomach. Almost like a tickle, and almost like you touched an electric wire, and scary, too because what was there inside you that was like an electric wire?

At first Tim looked around for whatever made him feel that way. Glanced around the parlor, because he was curious and not really because it was pulling at him. Which it was. But gently. Gently, then, some kind of a pull but so soft it was hard to say which direction it meant to take him.

There was no sign of it, of course, in the parlor. Tim shrugged off the pull and the unease and tried to go back to playing with Duff—but the cat was gone, or maybe he was hiding, and Tim just didn't have it in him to hunt after the thing. . . .

Then the siren call grew loud enough to move him, whether he wanted to follow after it or not. And that was when Tim finally figured out that the feeling in his gut wasn't just trouble, it was something more than trouble. Much, much worse. Trouble, as far as Tim was concerned, was a thing that got you in bad with other people. The thing that drew him step by step across the parlor, into the front room, and up the stairs, had nothing to do with anyone but him.

He tried to stop in the second floor hallway. Focused every iota of his heart and his head, and paused, actually made himself come to a halt right outside Grandpa's room. Turned his head to look in, trying to think about anything else at all in the entire world but the thing that drew him up, up. . . . Looked at the sheets still rumpled where they lay on Grandpa's bed. The bureau, tall polished dark wood with its top still so high above his head. The tile floor, with the throw rug there on it pretty-pretty even now that it was threadbare—and looked up at the wall. Which was a horrible, horrible mistake. Saw the lord Jesus on his bronze-cast cross, dying—

And the sight of him sent the thing in Tim's gut sliding toward his heart easy as the blade of a razor cuts flesh. And his will went slack, and he was in the hall again, walking toward the far end where the stairway started.

The stairway that he'd never ever climbed before. The stair that he'd always avoided with every fibre of his self.

Downstairs, in the front room, a man with a deep voice was singing "We Three Kings of Orient Are."

And as Tim set foot on that ultimate stairway, the radio launched into the song's third stanza. Which, in Tim's book, was about the creepiest Christmas carol he could even imagine.

> *Myrrh is mine—its bitter perfume*
> *Breathes a life of gathering gloom.*
> *Sorrowing, sighing; bleeding, dying*
> *Sealed in the stone-cold tomb.*
> *Star of wonder, star of night. . . .*

was all he heard before he reached the head of the stair, and once he was there there was no way he could hear anything at all but the searing throb behind his gut.

Down a strange, dark hall with closed doors on every side. And at its far end, a final door, half open, and light coming from it that Tim knew wasn't daylight or the light of any lamp he'd ever seen.

He tried again to turn and run away, but it wasn't any use. He closed his eyes, to keep from seeing, but that didn't keep his feet from following one after the other after the other, slow and steady toward that room he didn't want to visit. Ahead of him he heard the door creak open and the light that came out was so blinding bright that he could see it red through the living blood of his pressed-closed eyes—

And the sound that he heard with his ears was a silence so big and powerful that it felt like the sound of the world shaking against its foundation. And the air that pressed on him like wind wasn't wind but the fevered air that rises up from an open oven. And the flavor in his mouth was the flavor of his own blood, or someone else's, and it had to be some one else's because he hadn't bit his tongue.

And the thing that he smelled was a thing he'd never

smelled before. And still a thing he knew for certain, recognized though he'd never been near it before.

It was the scent of a man about to die.

Tim gasped, and opened his eyes before he realized what he'd done.

And saw the Lord Christ Jesus dying on His Cross.

It was a great, tall, rough-wood Cross, made of crude-hewn beams. And here and there upon it the Lord's blood stained the splintered wood to a color that was neither brown nor red but darker than either, and slick.

There was pain on His face—pain like nothing Tim had ever seen before—and worse because it wasn't like watching someone else in agony. No. Looking at the Lord Christ writhing and suffering Tim could feel that pain in his own heart. . . .

There were nails through His wrists, pounded down into the great wide beam-arms. Nails almost the size of railroad spikes.

The Lord was strangling.

Strangling. Tim could see that, because he'd been born with a careful eye: There was no way the Lord could breathe when His body hung slack from His wrists. Hanging as He hung there pulled tight the muscles in His chest that drew air into His lungs.

As Tim watched Jesus pulled His shoulders tight and lifted Himself against the pain in His wrists to breathe. And as He eased down, and the life sagged out of Him again, Tim heard Him speak in a language he'd never heard and could not understand.

And somehow he knew what God had said, even though he had no way to know the words.

My father, Jesus said, *why have you abandoned me?*

Tim was crying. It wasn't a thing he meant to do. Or understood—not really. He was scared out of his mind, and he hurt for the God he couldn't help but love, and—

There. On His side. Just above the loincloth at His hip: a wound. Wide as a man's fist, and deep; looking at it Tim somehow knew that the gash went nearly to the Lord's heart. And knew that the wound would kill Him long before He grew too weak to lift Himself to breathe.

And he wondered if maybe—just maybe—that wound was someone's way of being kind. And shuddered because the idea chilled him down down into his deepest heart.

Tim took in a deep, self-conscious breath. Closed his

eyes. Swallowed. Forced himself to be brave enough to open them again.

And what he saw was different, now. Not that anything had changed, except inside Tim's heart. Christ's agony was everywhere in the air, like an impossible mist made of light or spirit. But it was quiet agony; suffering without bitterness or hate or blame. Almost as though divine purpose was behind it, tempering and intensifying it.

It only took him another moment to realize what that purpose was. *His agony holds our sins. Every sin ever committed, and every sin yet to be.*

And knowing that, Tim began to feel God's love. And he knew that Jesus loved him, and loved every man, woman and child ever born to the world—loved them powerful and true, in spite of and because of and completely without regard to everything they'd ever done. Would do. And were.

And everything changed. Sudden as though He'd never been, Christ dying on His Cross was gone, and where He'd been was a bloodstained ancient fragment of a wooden beam.

And he recognized it. Recognized and knew those bloodstains by their shape, because he'd seen them before.

Only a moment before.

Christ's Cross.

Christ's love for man, made whole and tangible in the world.

The three-foot shard of wood lying before him on the bare tile floor was all that remained of the True Cross. And trapped inside that shard, now and forever, was the agony of the death that He'd died so man could live.

And that scared Tim most of all. It broke the trance that held him and sent him running out of the room, back down the stairs, to the ground floor and he was going to run right out of Grandpa's house and never come back—

But he never got that far. Because down in the front room, standing beside the now silent radio, Grandpa stood waiting for him. And looking at his eyes, Tim knew that the old man knew what had happened. Had known that it would happen. And had intended it, just so.

THE HAND OF GOD by Alan Rodgers will be on sale in Spring 1991 wherever Bantam Books are sold.

John Saul is "a writer with the touch for raising gooseflesh."
—*Detroit News*

John Saul has produced one bestseller after another: masterful tales of terror and psychological suspense. Each of his works is as shocking, as intense and as stunningly real as those that preceded it.

DON'T MISS
THESE CURRENT
Bantam Bestsellers